2|05   8.36

Tom Holt was born in London in 1961. At Oxford he studied bar billiards, ancient Greek agriculture and the care and feeding of small, temperamental Japanese motor-cycle engines; interests which led him, perhaps inevitably, to qualify as a solicitor and emigrate to Somerset, where he specialised in death and taxes for seven years before going straight in 1995. Now a full-time writer, he lives in Chard, Somerset, with his wife, one daughter and the unmistakable scent of blood, wafting in on the breeze from the local meat-packing plant.

Find out more about Tom Holt and other Orbit authors by registering for the free monthly newsletter at:
www.orbitbooks.co.uk

By Tom Holt

TOM HOLT

For Two Nights Only

Contains
Overtime and
Grailblazers

www.orbitbooks.co.uk

An *Orbit* Book

First published in Great Britain by Orbit 2004
This omnibus edition © Tom and Kim Holt 2004

Overtime
First published in Great Britain in 1993 by Orbit
Copyright © by Tom Holt 1993

Grailblazers
First published in Great Britain in 1994 by Orbit
Copyright © Kim Holt 1994

A CIP catalogue record for this book
is available from the British Library.

ISBN 1 84149 267 1

Printed and bound in Great Britain
by Mackays of Chatham plc, Chatham, Kent

Orbit
An imprint of
Time Warner Book Group UK
Brettenham House
Lancaster Place
London WC2E 7EN

CONTENTS

OVERTIME

For Natalie

Caen.

If it's half past four, that *must* be Caen. From up here, it could be Lisieux for all he knew, or Pont L'Evêque, or perhaps just an unusually large railway shunting yard, because geography wasn't exactly his strong point; but for once the map and the radio beacons and the big sprawling thing directly underneath him seemed to tally exactly. Prepared to stake good money that that's Caen. Nearly home. Good thing, too, what with the lack of petrol and everything.

It hadn't been the most restful of nights, even by his standards. Flak he could cope with; he didn't take it personally, it was like rain or turbulence, something that came at you out of the sky, a natural occurrence that had no innate malevolence. Fighters, on the other hand, were different. They frightened him. They were doing it on purpose. Furthermore, since Guy had no great confidence in his own abilities and attributed his survival in these circumstances to random or religious factors, he felt quite strongly that one of these days they were going to get him. Tonight was a good

1

example. Tonight they nearly had. Well, they'd got Peter.

'Didn't they, Peter?' Guy said. Peter didn't reply; his navigator in the seat next to him was dead, and in no position to comment. Mind you, he'd never exactly been the most riveting company, even at the best of times.

Guy wasn't sure when Peter had died, or even what had killed him. A fair number of bullets had hit the Mosquito at various times – it hadn't helped that Peter, not the world's greatest authority on navigation, had taken them directly over the night-fighter base at Aachen – or it could have been flak, or perhaps Peter just had a weak heart. He was definitely dead, though, and that was another good reason for getting home sharpish. One doesn't like to seem intolerant or anything, but Guy preferred not to spend too much of his time in the company of dead people. For all he knew, it might be catching.

Behind him, Guy was aware that there was a pretty sensational sunrise going on, which ought to be having some beneficial effect on his morale. Apparently not. A warm bath might do the trick, or fermented liquor or even a smoke, but not a sunrise. Guy tried to whistle the tune he'd thought up last evening, but his lips were too cold. Better be getting home. Rosy-fingered Dawn. Nuts.

'You can drop me off here if you like.'

Guy blinked. If this was going to turn out to be a ghost story, he really wasn't in the mood. He waited for a moment, then looked round. Not that there was a great deal to see, even with the early light of a new day, but Peter still looked remarkably dead; head lolling forward, that sort of thing. Perhaps he was confusing the intercom with the radio.

'Sorry?' he said tentatively.

'Here will do fine.'

'Ah,' Guy frowned. If this was really happening, then he felt he would be entirely within his rights if he baled out now, took his chances with the Germans, and the hell with the cost of the plane. The Government had lots of others, and this one had several holes in it. 'Did you say something?' he asked.

'Yes. Here will do fine. Thanks for the lift.'

'Are you all right, Peter?' Guy asked.

'I'm fine. Actually, my name's not Peter.'

There was a long silence. Not long now till they were out of France and over the Channel. Not much fun baling out over the Channel if you can't swim.

'I think it's terribly clever the way you people work these things.'

'Sorry?' Guy asked.

'Of course,' Peter's body said, 'you'll get much better at it soon. In twenty years or so, for instance, they'll work out how to fit heaters in these things and then it'll be much more comfortable. Do you intend to carry on flying after the War?'

'No,' Guy replied. 'Look, Peter, are you all —'

'My name's John,' Peter's body said. 'John de Nesle. To be honest with you, there's not a lot about this century of yours that appeals to me, but these aircraft things are really pretty impressive. If my old father could see this, he'd have a fit.'

'Peter ...'

'You're lucky, though,' said Peter's body, 'that times have changed. I mean, when I was a lad they'd have

3

called this sort of thing witchcraft, and you'd have been tied to a stake and burnt so fast your feet wouldn't have touched. Very suspicious of technology they were, where I come from. Look, I hate to be a bore, but do you think you could just let me off here? I think we're getting pretty near the coast, and I don't want to be late.'

Guy could feel something uncomfortable happening to his insides. His mother had always declared that he had a nervous stomach. 'Peter,' he said sharply, 'will you please shut up? You're beginning to get on my nerves.'

'Sorry, sorry,' said Peter's body. 'I do chatter on, people tell me, but it's just my nature. Anywhere here will do.'

'Look ...'

'You do know how to land one of these things, don't you?'

Guy turned his head and scowled. 'Of course I know how to ... Look, who are you?'

The dead body didn't move. Thanks to the light of the spectacular sunrise, Guy could see that there was a large hole in Peter's head. Cannon-shell or something. The head was lolling forward. Extremely dead.

'John de Nesle,' said Peter's body. 'And will you please land this thing and let me out?'

'How can I let you out?' Guy said. 'You're dead.'

'Who's dead?' replied Peter's body huffily. 'If you can't do landings, just say and I'll do it. Which one of these things works the steering?'

I'll say this, Guy thought, going mad isn't nearly as bad as I thought it would be. I always imagined it hurt, but apparently not. I shall ignore the whole thing. I

4

shall switch the intercom off, and . . .

'Here,' Guy shouted as the Mosquito suddenly lurched in the air, 'what do you think you're —?'

'Sorry,' said the voice in his ear, 'I think I pulled the tiller the wrong way. Which way is down?'

'You leave the controls alone!' Guy said. 'You could get us both killed. Me killed,' he corrected.

After a moment he felt control of the plane pass back to him. 'Fair enough,' said Peter's body. 'Just so long as you take us down.'

So Guy took them down. He found what looked like a reasonably flat field with no trees and headed for it. This was silly.

'Sorry if I startled you,' Peter's body said. 'I'm not really used to these old-fashioned planes, to be honest with you. The sort I'm used to, you can do it all just by pressing a few buttons. Shouldn't you lower your undercarriage, by the way?'

'I'm trying to,' Guy said.

'Ah. You think it's got stuck?'

'Yes.'

'Damaged, probably. Hit by flak or bullets or something. Want me to try?'

'No.'

'Be like that.'

The undercarriage definitely wasn't having anything to do with it, and Guy could understand its point of view, in the circumstances. Ah well, he said to himself, never mind, I wouldn't have enjoyed Life being off my rocker anyway.

'Are you praying?' said Peter's body after a while.

'Yes,' Guy said. 'Seems sensible, don't you think?'

'Oh, I don't mind,' said Peter's body. 'A man's

5

beliefs are his own affair and all that sort of thing. No, I was just wondering whether you shouldn't be trying to do something about those dratted wheels. I mean, we could crash, you know.'

Guy frowned. 'Is Death usually like this?' he asked.

'Gracious me, what a question!' replied Peter's body. 'How should I know?'

'Well ...' Guy looked at the ground. It didn't seem to be getting all that much closer. An illusion of time slowing up, he reckoned, probably quite normal. 'You *should* know,' he added.

'Why?'

'Because you're the Angel of Death, or whatever it is you call yourself,' Guy said. 'I'm going to die, and so I'm imagining you've come to life, or something like that. Hallucinating.'

'Are you feeling all right?'

'No, of course I'm not, I'm just about to die!'

Peter's body tutted disapprovingly. 'Here,' it said, 'you just relax; I'll see to things. I had an idea all along you weren't very good at landings. You should have said earlier, instead of going all to pieces.'

About thirty seconds later, there was a terrible jolt, and for a moment Guy imagined that the safety harness would break and he would be catapulted out through the perspex. But he wasn't. The plane stopped moving and sat there. On the ground.

'Right,' said the voice in his ear, 'I think we ought to get out now. Sorry.'

'Sorry?'

'I'm afraid I've damaged your aeroplane,' said the voice. 'As I think I said, I'm not terribly well up on these old-fashioned models. I have an idea I've

6

ruptured the fuel-tanks. Shall we get out now?'

'Anything you say,' Guy replied. 'But I didn't think it mattered when you're dead.'

'It may well not,' said the voice. 'But I don't want to find out. Cheerio.'

The canopy was thrown back, and Guy saw someone jump out over the side. Interestingly enough, Peter's body was still there.

'Come *on!*' said a voice from outside the plane. Guy shrugged, took off his safety harness and clambered out. He was very stiff and his legs hurt. He nearly killed himself falling off the plane on to the ground, which was as hard as stone.

'Come *on!*' the voice said again. Guy picked himself up and ran clumsily in the direction of the voice. Not long afterwards, there was an explosion which landed him on his face.

He came round to find a tall young man standing over him. Odd chap. Dressed strangely.

'Are you all right?' said the odd chap. He sounded just like Peter's body.

'I think so.'

'Good. Here.' The odd chap reached out a hand and Guy pulled himself up to his feet. The odd chap smiled sheepishly.

'Very sorry about your aeroplane.'

Not far away, the Mosquito, or what was left of it, was burning merrily. Being made of wood it burnt well, and so there was plenty of light.

'That's all right,' Guy said. 'It wasn't actually mine. Belonged to His Majesty's Government.'

'Fair enough,' said the odd chap, 'but it's going to make it rather tricky for you to get home, isn't it?'

7

'How do you mean, home?' Guy replied, rubbing his eyes – odd; he could feel them itching. 'I'm dead, aren't I?'

'I wish you'd stop saying that,' said the odd chap. 'Makes me feel creepy, don't you know?' He looked around him, saw a church spire, and nodded. The sight of the spire had seemed to reassure him, Guy felt.

'We're about five miles from Banville,' the odd chap said. 'Can I offer you a drink?'

'A drink,' Guy repeated.

'Yes indeed,' said the odd chap. 'Don't know about you, but I feel a bit shaken. My place is only just round the corner.'

Guy thought about it. He thought very hard in a remarkably short space of time. It was probably the smell of burning flesh coming from the plane that decided him in the end. 'Thank you,' he said. 'I'm sorry,' he added, 'I don't think I caught your name.'

'John de Nesle,' said the odd chap. 'And you're ...?'

'Goodlet,' said Guy. 'Guy Goodlet.'

'Oh,' said John de Nesle. 'Where's Goodlet?'

'I'm sorry?'

John de Nesle shook his head. 'Tell me later,' he said. 'Come on. We need to find a town hall or something.'

'Here you are,' said the girl. 'I've brought you your tea.'

In the darkness of the cell the prisoner stirred and grunted. 'Don't want any tea,' he said in his characteristic muffled fashion. 'Go away.'

The girl frowned. 'Don't be silly,' she said. 'It's chicken broth. Your favourite,' she added.

The prisoner made an impatient gesture with one

manacled hand, startling a rat. 'Two points,' he said. 'First, it is *not* my favourite. Second, you put too much salt in it.'

'You should have said earlier.'

'When you put too much salt in it,' the prisoner continued, ignoring her, 'the drops that inevitably escape from the straw get in the fiddly bits of the mask and make it go all rusty. If there's one thing I can't be doing with, it's rust.'

'Sorry, I'm sure,' said the girl, nettled. The prisoner shook his head.

'It's me who should apologise,' he said. 'A bit grumpy, I'm afraid. What's the weather like outside?'

'Raining.'

'Really?' Although it was obviously impossible for the girl to see his face, she was sure the prisoner was smiling. 'I used to love rain,' he said.

'Did you?' The girl seemed surprised.

'Oh yes,' replied the prisoner. 'Everyone else in my family had this thing about sun, but I always preferred rain. What day is it today?'

'Thursday.'

'You don't say!' The prisoner sighed until the girl felt sure that his heart must break for pure nostalgia. 'Ah well. Chicken broth, you said? Yummy.'

She put the tray down. 'I'll put less salt in it next time,' she said.

'No, no,' said the prisoner, 'it's just fine the way it is. And what's for afters? Water? Oh good, I *do* like water.' Instinctively he reached for his belt; but there was nothing there. 'Sorry,' he said sheepishly and for about the ten thousandth time, 'I don't seem to have any money on me.'

9

The girl smiled. 'That's all right,' she said. 'Be seeing you.'

The prisoner nodded affably, and the door closed after her. With a soft moan, the prisoner sat down on the floor and stared at the wooden bowl, the earthenware cup and the straw. After a long time, he nerved himself to drink some of the broth, which was disgusting, as usual. Still, one had to keep one's strength up, apparently. Why, he was not quite sure; but it was a thing that one did, just as one always tried to be affable to the staff.

The rat scuttled up and sat on his knee, its sharp nose sniffing in the direction of the broth. The prisoner looked down.

'Hello, ratty,' he said, 'you want some? Well, help yourself, I disclaim all responsibility, mind.' He put the bowl on the floor and the rat scampered down his leg and hoisted its snout into the remaining broth. After a couple of sips, it looked up, shook its head and slunk away. From a far corner of the cell came the small, clear sound of a rat vomiting.

'Don't say I didn't warn you,' the prisoner said. Then he drank the water.

'It's all right,' said the odd chap. 'I've got a pass.'

Guy looked at him. By the full light of a summer's morning he had discovered that the odd chap was wearing: a pair of trousers with one red leg and one yellow leg; pointed red leather shoes with wiggly gold buckles; what looked suspiciously like a white silk long-sleeved vest; and a sort of cricket sweater made of tiny interlocking steel rings.

'Now hang on,' Guy whispered, but the odd chap

just smiled. He had an odd face too, very long, with a long, pointed nose, and his hair was cut strangely – all short at the sides and back, and thick and curly on top. It reminded Guy of something.

'You just leave this to me,' said the odd chap.

So saying, he walked round the corner, and Guy, to his amazement, found himself following. This was all extremely strange, but maybe being dead was like that.

The solid German soldier standing guard outside the Mairie of Benville looked up and started to unsling his rifle from his shoulder. Halfway through the operation, he stopped and appeared to relax.

'Morning,' said the odd chap. 'Let me show you my pass.' He reached inside the steel sweater and produced a scrap of folded parchment, which he opened up and showed to the guard. The guard read it, twice, thought about it, shrugged and saluted.

'Thanks awfully,' said the odd chap. 'The British airman is with me.'

The guard nodded. Guy followed the odd chap into the Mairie.

'Please don't get the wrong idea,' said the odd chap. 'I'm not German myself, if that's what you're thinking. It's a sort of all-purpose pass. Here, have a look.'

He handed Guy the scrap of parchment, on which was written:

THIS MAN IS A GERMAN GENERAL.

Guy thought about it. Then he started to reach for his revolver.

'No, no,' said the odd chap, stopping him. 'Sorry, I forgot you'd be convinced. Here, look again.'

Guy glanced down at the parchment in his hand, which now read:

THIS MAN IS *NOT* A GERMAN GENERAL.
HE IS JOHN DE NESLE.

'Sorry,' Guy said. 'It's just, you get suspicious, you know . . .'

'That's all right.' De Nesle put the parchment away, and looked round. 'This way, I think,' he said.

He led the way up a flight of stairs to a small landing, off which opened a number of offices. It looked very much like a town hall anywhere. There was nobody about, but then, it was still early. De Nesle was reading what was written on the doors.

'You spoke to that guard in English,' Guy said, 'but he understood you.'

De Nesle shrugged. 'It's a gift I have,' he said. 'Ah, this looks like it might do the trick.'

He stopped in front of a door, on which was written *Privée: défense d'entrer.* He tried the handle, but it was locked.

'Yes, this'll do,' he said. He rapped sharply on the door three times, muttered something under his breath, and turned the door knob again. The door opened. He walked through the doorway and vanished.

For reasons best known to himself, Guy followed.

It is well known that if you are fortunate enough to have a large amount of money and don't feel like paying more tax than you can help, there are skilled professional men and women who will gladly assist you. What is less well known is that fiscal advice comes on four levels: the ordinary, or High Street level; the superior or specialist level; the de luxe or international consultancy level; and the *ne plus ultra* or 32A Beaumont Street level.

12

32A Beaumont Street, London does not demean itself by trading under a name or logo. It does not advertise; in fact, it does its best to conceal its existence from the public, since, despite the murderously high fee scale it operates, if its existence were to become common knowledge it would soon become inundated with enquiries to such an extent that it would no longer be able to function.

The criteria for selection as a potential client of 32A Beaumont Street are almost prohibitively stringent. Wealth beyond the dreams of avarice is certainly not enough. Neither is discretion. Birth, rank, political standing and other such ephemeral factors are of no account. What 32A Beaumont Street looks for in a potential client is compatibility of outlook. Prospective clients of the practice must love acquiring money and hate parting with it more than anything else in time or space.

Once you have been selected, you are secretly vetted and then directly approached by a member of the practice. If, after a rigorous catechism, you are found to be of the right calibre, you are invited to number 32A to hear what the practice has to offer.

A prospective client, who need not be named, was sitting in the inner office. To be precise, he was sitting on an upturned orange box drinking instant coffee out of a chipped mug. The practice has never vulgarised itself by putting on a gaudy front merely to impress the punters.

The three members of the practice were grouped round him on the floor. They were all peculiarly dressed and strange-looking, but the anonymous client hadn't become as rich as he had through judging by appearances.

'You are familiar,' said the senior partner – he spoke English as fluently as he spoke all the other languages in the world, but with a curious accent that was probably nearer Italian than anything else – 'with the concept of the tax haven?'

The client nodded.

'Liberia,' said the senior partner, 'the Isle of Man, that sort of thing?'

'Yes indeed.'

'Well,' said the senior partner, 'our basic investment and fiscal management strategy is largely based on the tax haven concept, but with a unique additional factor that we alone can offer. That's why,' he added with a smile, 'our fees are so utterly outrageous.'

The client smiled bleakly. 'Go on,' he said.

'Traditional tax haven strategies,' said the senior partner, 'rely on transferring sums of money from one fiscally privileged state to another. We call this the *lateral* approach, and we find that it has a great many imperfections. We prefer what we term the *vertical* approach. In our experience, which is considerable, it has no drawbacks whatsoever.' The senior partner smiled. 'Except our fees, of course. They're diabolical.'

'When you say vertical ...'

'It's very simple, really,' said the senior partner. 'Whereas the traditional approach is to move money about from nation to nation, in other words to transfer money through *space*, we transfer money through *time*. Oh dear, you seem to have spilt your coffee.'

'Through —'

'Yes indeed,' said the senior partner, 'through time. Reflect. In Khazakstan in the third century BC, for example, there were no taxes whatsoever. On the other hand, there were no banks either, and nothing to invest in except yaks. We find that yaks offer a very low short-term yield. The Free World in the twentieth century, on the other hand, has a wealth of investment opportunities but insanely high levels of taxation. The obvious thing to do, therefore, is to find a time and a place which offers the golden mean between return on capital and fiscal intervention. We have found such a golden mean, and we can transfer your money there tomorrow, if you ask us to. For a fee, of course.' The senior partner chuckled. 'Oh yes.'

'Hang on a moment,' said the client warily. 'You mean you can actually send money back through time? Invest retrospectively or something?'

'Oh no,' said the senior partner, 'nothing as complicated as that. Let me put it this way.' He leaned forward and smiled pleasantly. 'You know what's meant by the Futures market, I expect. We trade in Pasts.'

'Pasts,' said the client. 'I see,' he lied.

'Because of – shall we say – a unique arrangement which we have with the central authorities,' the senior partner continued, 'we have access to time travel. We can take your money, travel back in time with it, deposit it in your name and arrange for the income to be mandated to you directly in whatever form – and at whatever time – you wish. We offer a return on capital of thirty-seven per cent.'

The client whistled. 'That's good,' he said.

'We can find better,' replied the senior partner airily. 'Much better. But,' he said, and leaned further forward still, 'we have chosen this particular location because of its unique fiscal advantages. The investment is entirely, one hundred per cent, tax-free.'

15

There was a silence – a complete, utter silence, born of reverence and awe. It was a bit like Sir Galahad's finding of the Holy Grail, except that, compared to the senior partner, Galahad exhibited a lack of due seriousness.

'Tax-free?' said the client at last.

'Absolutely,' said the senior partner. 'You see, the investment has charitable status.'

The client stared. 'You mean you've got hold of a charity that gives you money?'

'It isn't a charity,' the senior partner replied calmly. 'But it does have the status, as I just said. We invest all our clients' funds in the twelfth century AD, through the Knights Templar, for the purpose of financing the Second Crusade.'

A very long silence. 'I thought the Second Crusade was a war,' said the client.

'Strictly speaking,' replied the senior partner, 'yes. On the other hand, it's a very special war. God's war, and all that. As such, it qualifies as being for the purposes of the advancement of religion, which as you know is one of the fundamental heads of charity. At least,' said the senior partner, grinning, 'that's how they all regarded it at the time. And that, you'll agree, is all that matters.'

'Hold it just a moment,' said the client. 'I thought the Second Crusade was a gigantic flop.'

'Indeed it was,' the senior partner replied, and there might just have been a hint of sadness in his voice, 'indeed it was. A complete disaster. A shambles. A cock-up. The Crusader leaders Richard Coeur de Lion, Philip II of France and the Emperor Henry argued violently before they even got to the Near East, their

16

armies were ultimately defeated, and the result was a net loss of territory in the Holy Land to the forces of Islam. As for the investors, most of them were wiped out. So it's just as well that we always withdraw our clients' funds at the very height of the crusade fever in 1189. We then reinvest it back in 1186. And so on. For ever.'

'I see,' said the client. 'Well, that's ... that's very clever.'

The senior partner smiled. 'Coming from you,' he said, 'if I may say so, that's a compliment of the highest order.'

Thus it was that a substantial sum changed hands, and another client was added to the already magnificent client base of 32A Beaumont Street – a client base which includes, or included, such figures as all the Rothschilds, Louis the Fourteenth, Elvis Presley and (interestingly) Julius Caesar.

It is, however, a fact of life that the really canny broker never shares the very best investments with the customers; he reserves them for himself. 32A Beaumont Street was no exception.

32A Beaumont Street might have a finger in the financial services pie, but its heart and soul were in the music business.

'Well,' said de Nesle, 'here we are at last. Make yourself at home.'

Guy looked about him. It was quite unlike any town hall interior that he had ever seen.

The roof was high – Guy had to tilt his head right back to see it – and constructed of great oak beams which were obviously carved, but too far away for Guy to make out what the carvings were. On the walls were long, gorgeously coloured tapestries, depicting scenes of hunting, warfare and gallantry in what Guy imagined (although he was no art historian) to be the High Middle Ages. Where a few square feet of naked wall peeped through the gaps between the hangings, it was bare yellow rock.

The floor on which he was standing was paved with stone flags strewn with what Guy took to be rushes. The furniture was sparse but magnificent; a massive table at one end of the room – the room was circular, incidentally – with benches on either side of it and at the two ends, two huge, high-backed gilded chairs with coats of arms carved and painted on them. A roaring fire in the middle of the room provided just about enough light to see by, and Guy realised that what was obscuring his view of the carved beams was smoke, billowing about round the ceiling trying to get out of a rather small and badly thought-out hole in the roof. Hung above the tapestries on the wall were about fifteen or twenty pear-shaped shields with heraldic devices painted on them; the colours looked bright and fresh, and the workmanship was of the highest order, but the paintwork was scratched and gouged, as if someone had been using the shields recently for actual fighting. Beside the shields hung a selection of helmets, coats of mail and enormous swords, all polished until they sparkled in the red light of the fire. There were three stuffed stag's heads, on the antlers of which someone had (inevitably) hung a selection of hats. Even the hats were peculiar, however; not a single homburg or derby to be seen. The firelight was supplemented by about twenty or thirty small earthenware oil-lamps, which seemed to Guy to be producing twice as much smoke as light, and which smelt rather awful. In fact, to be brutally honest, the whole place was distinctly niffy; and this had apparently not escaped the notice of the proprietor, who had recently been burning some sort of sweet, pungent incense, in Guy's opinion rather counter-productively. Apart from de Nesle and himself and three huge dogs sleeping heavily and noisily in front of the fire, the place was deserted.

'Be it never so humble,' de Nesle said. He had opened the lid of what looked like a large oak steamer trunk and produced a jug, which looked for all the world as if it were made of solid gold. He put this on a similarly golden-looking tray with two golden cups, closed the lid of the trunk, and put the tray on it. Then he took the jug and filled it from a barrel standing on a trestle like a sawing-horse in a dark corner of the room. He turned off the spigot, smelt the meniscus of the jug's contents, shrugged, and poured out two cups. The liquid that came out of the jug was brown and opaque, like cold tea.

De Nesle handed Guy one of the cups, and Guy nearly dropped it. It was quite remarkably heavy. He began to wonder if it really was made of gold.

'Here's health,' said de Nesle, and took a long drink from his cup. He made a face, which didn't reassure Guy very much.

'Er,' he said.

'Mead,' replied de Nesle. 'Would you just excuse me for a moment? I'm expecting a call any minute now.'

He pulled back the edge of one of the tapestries, revealing a small low open doorway. He vanished through it, and the tapestry slid back into place.

Guy stayed where he was, looking round slowly and trying to come to some sort of conclusion; but all he came up with was the thought that he hadn't realised that the Kingdom of Heaven had been designed and fitted out by D.W. Griffith. That wasn't very helpful. He looked into his cup, saw a dead wasp floating slowly round with one wing pointing up at him, and looked about him for a flowerpot. There wasn't one.

This is all very well, Guy said to himself at last, but I think I'd better be pushing along now. I could go and find that nice-looking German guard and give myself up. He turned and headed for the door he had come in by. It wasn't there any more. In its place was a tapestry depicting a fair damsel with no clothes on looking at her reflection in a rather stylised pool. When he lifted a corner of the tapestry, there was nothing to be seen but wall.

Guy Goodlet was not a hasty man; he preferred to think carefully before acting, and was generally happy to let his intelligence talk him out of things. On this occasion, however, his intelligence very wisely kept its mouth shut and its head down.

Guy put down the cup, unbuttoned the flap of his holster, and took out his revolver. Then he headed for the door through which de Nesle had disappeared.

It was a favourite saying of Pope Wayne XXIII (AD 2567–78) that about ninety-five per cent of a man's life is like mashed potato; he doesn't have to have it if he doesn't want to.

This is, of course, a gross simplification of a complex field of theochronology; but Wayne, like most of the other Australian popes of the twenty-sixth century, was

20

selected more for his undoubted communication skills than for the clarity of his thinking.

What His Holiness was trying to encapsulate was one of the seminal arguments of theochronology, known since the twenty-third century as Bloomington's Effect. Bloomington observed that however much a man roams about in Time, it is inevitable, simply to maintain the continuity of history, for him sooner or later to return to the time and place from which he set out. Otherwise, people could simply disappear without trace and never come back; which would never do.

As a result of Bloomington's Effect, it follows that all time spent in time travel is Time Out — in other words, any period spent by an individual in wandering about in another century or centuries does not go towards filling up his allotted span of life. You can leave your own time on your twenty-fifth birthday, spend a hundred years in the past, the future, or both, and then come back to your own time, and you will still be exactly twenty-five years old. Your matter — the atoms and molecules making up your body — is thus preserved in the time and place where it rightly belongs, and you have not violated the fundamental laws of physics (because you have never been away). Your absence, in short, has about as much effect on the world about you as a dream.

It was very dark. There were more of those earthenware oil-lamps scattered about the place, but they gave out roughly as much light as the bedside lamp in a cheap boarding house, or a dying firefly. Guy bumped into at least three pillars before he found another doorway.

There was a thick, small door studded with large iron nails, very slightly ajar, and bright light was coming out from behind it in a long silver wedge. Guy pressed very gently on it and walked through. Contrary to his rather gloomy expectations, the hinges didn't creak.

He saw de Nesle, or rather his back, sitting at a long, low desk. There was a bright lamp beside him – a modern electric one – and on the desk were a collection of what appeared to be white boxes with glass windows in the front of them. Little green lights in the windows formed tiny letters, which changed as de Nesle touched what looked to Guy like a typewriter keyboard. It was all extremely odd and, Guy fervently hoped, nothing to do with him.

'Put your hands up,' he said.

He had hoped to say it rather more assertively; in fact, he squeaked the words rather than said them. But he did manage to cock the hammer of his revolver at the same time; and it was firepower rather than force of personality on which most of his hopes were pinned.

'Don't turn round,' he said.

'Why not?' said de Nesle to his glass window. Guy noticed that his hands were still on the keyboard.

'I told you, put your hands up,' Guy said. The voice was getting a bit better, but not much.

'What's the matter?' de Nesle said. 'Didn't you like the mead?' He raised his hands. 'Can I turn round now?' he asked.

'I suppose so,' Guy said. 'But remember, I'll shoot if I have to.' A thought struck him. 'I assume bullets can hurt you?' he added. He hoped, in vain, that it had sounded more like irony than a genuine request for information.

De Nesle was facing him now, still seated. 'That's a good question,' he said. 'Hurt, definitely yes, so I'd be awfully grateful if you were careful where you point that thing. I don't want to appear rude, but your hand is shaking rather a lot, and ...'

Guy tried looking stern. 'Never mind that,' he said. In retrospect, he felt, he could have done much better. Esprit d'escalier, and all that.

'As to whether bullets could actually kill me,' de Nesle went on, 'now there you have me, I'm afraid. Opinion, as they say, is divided. There's a school of thought that says that if I die, I come to life again immediately afterwards. There's another school of thought that agrees that I come to life again, but probably about five minutes before. They reckon five minutes because that gives me time to make sure that I stay well out of the way of whatever it was that killed me. The third school of thought, which includes my mother, feels that I probably stay dead. It's never actually been put to the test, thank goodness, and that's the way I like it. Was there something?'

'What?'

'The threat,' de Nesle explained. 'I generally find – don't you? – that when people wave weapons at you they want something. What can I do for you?'

'For a start,' said Guy, 'you can tell me how I get out of here.'

'Ah.' De Nesle made a sort of a sad face. 'That's tricky, I'm afraid. I'd have to come with you, and I *am* waiting for this *rather* important call. Do you think —'

'No.'

De Nesle considered for a moment. 'No, I imagine on balance that you probably don't. Sorry, that was very rude of me. But I do find being threatened puts me rather on edge, don't you know?'

Guy was beginning to feel bewildered. 'Look,' he said, 'exactly what is going on?'

De Nesle grinned. 'I must say,' he said, 'you do ask the most awkward questions. Might I suggest that you really wouldn't want to know?'

'All right,' Guy said. 'Just get me out of here and that's fine. I don't want you to come with me. Just show me the door.'

'I must advise —'

'The hell with your advice.'

De Nesle shrugged. 'Very well, then. To leave, go through that door behind you.'

Guy frowned, suspecting a ruse to make him turn his head. He felt that eye contact should be maintained at all times in these situations. He reached behind him with his free hand and found a door knob.

'This one?'

'That's the one. But really . . .'

Guy opened the door, backed through it, and vanished. The door, which was marked *Private – Staff Only – No Admittance*, closed behind him.

'Oh *bother*!' said de Nesle.

He looked at his watch, a Rolex Oyster which he wore under the sleeve of this steel hauberk, frowned, and picked up the microphone of his answering machine.

'Hello,' he said into the microphone, in the slightly strained voice that people always use for that purpose, 'this is Jean de Nesle here. Sorry I'm not available to take your call. Speaking *after* the tone, please state the time at which you called and on my return I'll arrange to be here then. Thank you.'

He switched on the answering machine, took a sword from under his desk, and went through the door.

Guy was at a party.

More like a reception, actually. In the split second before his appearance, walking backwards brandishing a revolver and causing the seventy-four people in the room all to stop speaking at once, Guy thought he heard several languages and the characteristic hyena-like yowl of diplomats' wives laughing at the jokes of trade attachés.

He froze.

The men, he observed, were all wearing dinner jackets, the women posh frocks. They were holding wine glasses. Women in waitress outfits were holding trays of bits of minced-up fish and tiny impaled sausages. There was no band.

A woman screamed, in isolation. Being English and of the social class brought up to believe that being conspicuous is the one crime which even God cannot forgive, Guy began to feel distinctly uncomfortable. He tried to smile, found that he was having problems with his facial motor functions, and looked down at the revolver, which was pointing at the third waistcoat button of a tall, stout gentleman who Guy felt sure was a chargé d'affaires.

'Er,' he said.

'M'sieur,' said the chargé d'affaires. It was the way he said it that made Guy's bowels cringe; also the fact that he said it in French. Guy was no linguist, and the thought of trying to apologise, or say, 'Sorry, I thought this was the Wilkinson's fancy-dress ball' in a foreign tongue, was too much for him. His tongue clove to the roof of his mouth so effectively that he might as well have forgotten not only Jerusalem but Damascus and Joppa as well.

He was just about to shoot himself, as being the civilised way out of it all, when a familiar figure appeared behind him. A figure in red and yellow trousers and chain mail, holding a sword, handing a piece of tattered parchment to the toastmaster.

'*Monsieur le Président de la République,*' announced the toastmaster.

There was a brief, thrilled murmur from the distinguished guests, and Guy realised that they'd forgotten all about him. They were forming an orderly queue.

De Nesle, smiling brightly, stepped forward to start shaking hands. As he passed Guy, he hissed, 'Go back through the door you came in by, quickly,' out of the corner of his smile and passed on.

Guy needed no second invitation. Despite the fact that the door was marked *Défense d'entrer*, he pushed through it and found himself back in de Nesle's peculiar study. He sat down heavily in the chair and began to shake.

'I warned you.'

De Nesle was standing over him, a comforting grin on his face. A small part of Guy's mind toyed with the idea of pointing the revolver at him, but was howled down by the majority. He put the gun on the table and made a small, whimpering noise in lieu of speech.

'Don't worry,' de Nesle went on, 'I said that you were a new and rather over-zealous security guard.'

Guy found some words. They wouldn't have been his first choice, but they were there.

'Are you the president of the republic?' he asked.

'Good Lord, no,' said de Nesle. 'I don't go in for politics much, I'm afraid. Not deliberately, anyway. I think you'd better have another drink, don't you?'

This time, Guy felt, it would be churlish to refuse; and besides, he needed a drink, dead wasps or no dead wasps. To his surprise, however, de Nesle produced a bottle of brandy from a drawer of the desk and poured out a stiff measure into two balloon-shaped glasses.

'You must excuse my offering you mead just now,' de Nesle was saying. 'I forgot that you don't drink mead any more, and it can be something of an acquired taste. Cheers.'

He drank and Guy followed suit. It was very good brandy.

'Now then.' De Nesle sat down on the edge of the desk and stroked his thin moustache with the rim of his glass. He was grinning. 'I'm terribly sorry if I've put you out at all.'

'Don't mention it,' Guy heard himself saying. Pure reflex.

'Nonsense,' said de Nesle. 'If you hadn't been kind enough to give me that lift – oh yes, let's see if my call came through.' He pressed a knob on the box attached to his telephone, and then continued; 'No, not yet, what a nuisance. If you hadn't been kind enough to give me that lift, you wouldn't have been put to all this trouble. Actually,' de Nesle said, in a confidential whisper, 'I think you'd have crashed in the sea, because you were almost out of fuel. Can you swim?'

'No.'

'Oh well,' de Nesle said, 'I needn't feel quite so bad about it after all. Still, it was a bit of a liberty when all's said and done, particularly since your friend was, well, dead. A bit tasteless in the circumstances. Still, needs must, as they say.'

'Er,' said Guy.

'The main thing now,' said de Nesle, 'is to get you back where you want to be. Now I'm not sure I'm supposed to do that – they get awfully cross Upstairs when I go interfering with things that aren't really any of my concern – but if you can't help someone out of a jam, what's the point of any of it, that's what I always say. Where would you like to go?'

Guy took a deep breath. 'Would London be out of the question?' he said.

'By no means,' de Nesle replied. 'Anywhere in particular in London, or can I just drop you off at Trafalgar Square?'

'Yes,' said Guy. 'I mean, Trafalgar Square will do fine.'

'Splendid. Now then, when?'

'Sorry?'

'When would you like me to drop you off?'

Guy frowned slightly. 'Well, now, if that's no ...'

De Nesle raised an eyebrow and pointed to the wall calendar. 'Are you sure?' he said.

Guy looked at the calendar. It was one of those mechanical perpetual-calendar things, and the little wheels with numbers on them to represent date, month and year were spinning like the tumblers of a fruit machine, turning so fast you couldn't read them.

'Now,' said de Nesle brightly, 'doesn't mean a lot here. We're in the Chastel des Temps Jadis, you see. Time here is very much what you make of it.'

A very silly thought made itself known in Guy's

28

mind, declaring to all who would listen that it might not be all that silly after all, if only it could get a fair hearing.

'Are you trying to tell me,' he said slowly, 'that this is a sort of, well, time machine?'

De Nesle grinned. 'Well,' he said, 'the strict answer to your question is No, but you're on the right lines. Now be honest; you'd really rather I didn't explain, right?'

Guy nodded.

'Good man.' De Nesle nodded approvingly. 'By *now*, I suppose you meant 6th July 1943?'

'Well, if that's all right . . .'

'Nothing simpler.' De Nesle stood up and pressed some keys on his typewriter keyboard. The green lights on the screen flashed and then went out. A moment later they read *6/7/43; #8765A7*.

De Nesle walked over to the door which, a few minutes earlier, had led to the diplomatic reception and pushed it open.

'Follow me,' he said.

Just then, the other door opened and a girl walked in. She put a cup of what looked like coffee down on the desk, picked up the two brandy glasses, smiled brightly at Guy, and walked out again.

'Er,' said Guy, 'just a moment.'

When Julian XXIII was installed as the hundred and ninth Anti-Pope, his unsuccessful rivals raised a number of objections, not least of which were the undisputed facts that he had previously been the Pope of Rome, and that he was now dead.

For his part, Julian treated these objections with the

29

contempt they deserved. Once established in his palace of the Chastel des Larmes Chaudes, he issued a bull pointing out that he wasn't dead at all, or else how come he could still do thirty lengths of the Anti-Papal swimming pool each morning, and that if he chose to travel to work each day from his home in the sixteenth century, how was that different, when you came right down to it, from the commonplace practice of millions of commuters all over the world? As to the other objection, the exact point in time he commuted from was a week before his election to the See of Rome, and thus he wasn't Pope yet, and it would be a fundamental breach of the rules of natural justice if the rules governing eligibility were to be applied retrospectively. He then had the bull pronounced by his Anti-Papal guard, who called on each of the disappointed candidates personally, usually at three o'clock in the morning and carrying big axes, and explained it carefully. As even his enemies had to admit, as a communicator Julian was hot stuff.

Once safely established in the Chastel des Larmes Chaudes, Julian set about the pressing task of clearing up the mess left over from the reign of his predecessor, the luckless Wayne XVII. Of the problems facing him, clearly the most urgent was that of Jean II de Nesle.

'I mean,' he observed to his chaplain, a timeless figure called Mountjoy King of Arms, 'the man's a menace. He's completely out of control. Zooming backwards and forwards between the centuries like the proverbial loose cannon. He just doesn't *think*.'

'Well,' said Mountjoy, 'it's not really his place to think, is it?'

'Be that as it may,' said Julian firmly. 'What gives

me sleepless nights is the thought that one of these days he might actually succeed. Find the wretched man. Then what? I don't suppose you've considered that.'

Mountjoy had the irritating habit of flickering at the edges when stuck for an answer. 'With all due respect,' he said, shimmering, 'that's not terribly likely, now is it?'

'Why not?' replied Julian gloomily. 'Stranger things have happened, you know that. I mean, by rights, none of us should be here at all.'

Mountjoy rematerialised completely. 'That,' he said stiffly, 'was an exceptional incident. Nothing like that could ever happen again.'

'You reckon?' Julian shook his head. 'Nothing like that could have happened in the first place, but it did. Now if I had my way, I'd go back and put a wet sponge down the back of his neck. That'd have woken the dozy so-and-so up right enough. Still, there we are. We're drifting away from the point. All this darting backwards and forwards has got to stop.'

'Well ...'

Julian tried giving his chaplain a hard stare, but instead found himself staring at the wall through a vague and insubstantial silhouette. 'Go on then,' he said wearily. 'Spit it out.'

'With *all* due respect,' said Mountjoy, 'I would ask you to consider whether it's really up to you whether de Nesle is allowed to continue or not. Isn't that a decision for ...?' Mountjoy made a gesture with his hands.

'Indeed it is,' said the Anti-Pope. 'And as his duly appointed agent, I take the view that I have full authority to ... Stop fading when I'm talking to you, it makes me lose my thread. Thank you.'

'*Full* authority?'

Julian frowned. 'Yes, dammit, why not?' he said. 'Why can't I rub out Jean de Nesle?'

'The Seventy-Fourth Lateran Council —'

'Stuff the Seventy-Fourth Lateran Council.'

'The Bull *Non tibi soli* —' said a patch of glittering mist.

'Is neither here nor there,' snapped the Anti-Pope. 'And if you don't want to do it, then I quite understand. There'll always be a job for you in the Pensions department.'

Mountjoy rematerialised with an almost audible snap. 'I see,' he said. 'Right.'

'Not,' said Julian pleasantly, 'that I'm threatening you or anything.'

'No.'

'I mean,' Julian went on, 'I hear they've brightened up the decor down there quite a lot recently. Someone even cleaned the window, I think.'

'Nevertheless ...'

'Good man,' said the Anti-Pope. 'Good Lord, is that the time? I must fly.'

'Um,' said Guy, as casually as he could. 'Who was that?'

'Sorry?' De Nesle was grinning.

'That, um, lady,' said Guy, 'who just came in.'

'Oh, *that*,' de Nesle replied. 'That was my sister, Isoud. Right, shall we be getting along?'

'Yes, yes, thank you,' said Guy, not moving. 'Your sister,' he repeated.

De Nesle sat down on the edge of the desk and picked up the coffee cup. He took a sip and grimaced. 'She's put sugar in it again,' he said. 'Yes, very much my sister. Makes a profoundly horrible cup of coffee, bless her, but otherwise she's better than having malaria. I take it you don't want to go home now.'

Guy lifted his head sharply, and saw that there was little point in lying. He nodded.

'You would prefer,' said de Nesle, with a certain degree of amusement in his voice, 'to spend the rest of your life as a knight of La Beale Isoud, doing deeds of note in her name and striving to be worthy of her?'

'Well,' said Guy, and then he nodded again. 'The

thought had crossed my mind, yes.'

De Nesle smiled. 'There's one born every minute,' he said, 'or at the outside, every ninety seconds. My sister has enough knights strewn across history to re-enact Agincourt. You may remember,' he added softly, 'what happened to the knights at Agincourt.'

'Oh.'

'Isoud,' de Nesle continued, 'is the plain one. My sister Mahaud, at the last count, had more admirers than there are Elks. Mahaud, by the way, isn't the pretty one. My sister Ysabel, *she's* the pretty one.'

'Um ...'

'Fortunately,' de Nesle went on, 'Mahaud and Ysabel are both happily married and living back in time. Furthermore, they're both putting on weight. They do that. Not that Isoud's a slouch when it comes to putting away the carbohydrates; she may look like she'd get blown away by the downdraught from a closing door, but put her in front of a dish of roast pullets and you'll begin to believe what they say about how thin the dividing line is between humanity and the lower animals. The sight of Isoud eating corn on the cob ... Sorry, I seem to have lost my thread.'

'I —'

De Nesle rested his chin on his hand and looked at Guy for a moment. 'When there's just one of them it's not so bad; it's when you've got three of them cluttering up the place that you've got problems. They gang up on you. They throw out shirts without telling you. They repaint bathrooms while you're out. Worse still, they repaint a third of the bathroom, get bored and leave the rest for you to do when you get back. They make funny remarks about you to visitors. They decide that they can't bear to live with the tapestries in the hall for another day, drag you round the fair looking at tapestries, moan at you for not taking an interest, and then sulk at you when you express an opinion. In my opinion, the idea of anyone wanting to fight knights and kill dragons just to prove themselves worthy of somebody's *sister* is so absurd as to be ludicrous.'

De Nesle finished his coffee and put the cup down. 'Anyway,' he said, 'that's all beside the point, isn't it? I take it that all my well-chosen words have been entirely wasted?'

Guy nearly said something but nodded instead. De Nesle shrugged.

'In that case,' he said, 'I suppose we'd better get down to business.'

Guy started. 'Business?' he said.

'Business.' De Nesle put a businesslike expression on his face. 'Terms and the like.'

'Terms?'

'Terms. I'd be only too glad for you to take La Beale Isoud off my hands – it wouldn't be losing a sister so much as gaining five hundred cubic metres of wardrobe space – but a man in my position has to make full use of all the resources at his disposal. So, terms.'

Guy swallowed. 'You mean,' he said, 'money?'

De Nesle scowled briefly, and then, as if remembering something, smiled again. 'Certainly not,' he said. 'My fault, should have made myself clear instead of trying to be delicate. Not money. Help.'

'Help?'

'Look,' de Nesle said, 'imitation may be the sincerest form of flattery and all that, but I wonder if you'd mind not repeating every single word I say? It makes one so self-conscious. Perhaps I'd better explain.'

'Yes,' said Guy.

'Right.' De Nesle stood up, walked round the room, and then sat down again. 'Yes,' he said. 'Cards on the table, and all that.'

Guy leaned forward slightly, to demonstrate attentiveness. This seemed to disconcert de Nesle somewhat, for he got up again and walked round the room the other way. Finally he sat down, scratched the back of his head and started making a chain out of paperclips.

'You see . . .' he said.

'Yes?'

'Oh never mind,' de Nesle exclaimed. 'It's like this . . .'

Once upon a time (said de Nesle) in a province of Greater France called England, there was a king; and his name was Richard. This king was so brave that people called him Richard the Lion-Heart; and at a time when most kings went down to posterity with names such as Charles the Bald and Louis the Fat, this must be taken as evidence that he was at least reasonably popular.

But then, King Richard wasn't like most of his fellow kings. For instance, when two peasants disagreed over who owned a particular pig and brought the matter to the King's court of justice for a ruling, Richard would usually end up giving the losing party a pig from the royal pigsties by way of a consolation prize. This was partly because Richard was not always fully capable of following the complexities of a fiercely contested legal argument, and so hedged his bets somewhat to avoid injustice. On the other hand, his royal cousin King Philip Augustus of France, who was rather better at law, tended to resolve all such disputes by finding technical irregularities in the pleadings of both parties, dismissing the case and eating the pig.

What King Richard was best at was fighting; in fact, he was the finest swordsman and horseman of his age. The trouble was that he didn't enjoy it. War bothered him. It was, he felt, morally questionable, and if he had his way he would quietly phase it out and replace it with something rather less destructive, such as tennis or community singing (for Richard was extremely musical). Unfortunately, the times he lived in were primitive, to say the least, and warfare was in fact one of the milder and least hazardous pastimes available; besides, as the greatest knight in Christendom, Richard had appearances to keep up. If he suddenly turned pacifist and went about the place sniffing flowers, his adoring people would in all probability change his name to Richard the Fairy and burn him at the stake.

It was then that King Richard came up with a quite brilliant solution. He would organise a Crusade.

There had already been a Crusade, about a hundred years earlier. It was basically a joint-stock, limited-liability Crusade, organised by two astute French noblemen, and after deductions it paid a twenty-seven per cent dividend on capital invested, and was accordingly a success. It also recaptured Jerusalem, but the overheads proved unrealistic after a couple of years, and following a period of restructuring the Crusaders rationalised Jerusalem to the Saracens. Jerusalem, when all was said and done, hadn't really been the point.

37

Nor was it the point as far as King Richard was concerned. What interested him was the idea that he might, with a little low cunning and a great deal of luck, be able to induce the King of France, the Emperor of Byzantium and the Holy Roman Emperor, the triple pillars of Christendom, to stop beating the pulp out of each other for a while and direct their royal energies towards a common purpose. It troubled him that the common purpose, at least initially, would have to be beating the pulp out of Saladin; but Richard was a realist as well as a dreamer, and knew that there always has to be a loser somewhere. Besides, he had it on excellent authority that Saladin and his subjects were incurably bellicose and warlike, and as such were a serious obstacle in the way of world peace.

It was what would happen after Jerusalem was recaptured that Richard was most concerned about; for it occurred to him that the triple pillars, flushed with success and self-satisfaction after liberating the Holy Land, would be in a very good mood, and might be persuaded to sit round a table and discuss freedom, justice, tolerance, the pursuit of happiness and other such matters – particularly if Richard threatened to smack them round the head if they refused.

If there was one thing that Richard Coeur de Lion had, it was personality, and one by one the potentates of Christendom agreed to take part in the great adventure. Money to finance the project started pouring in – where from, Richard wasn't exactly sure; but there seemed to be plenty of it, which was all that mattered – and soon the preparations were complete. Amid unparalleled scenes of jubilation, the great expedition set off for the long journey to the Holy Land;

and if the main cause of the jubilation was the relief of the peasants of Europe at having got so many incorrigibly warlike knights out from under their feet, then that was yet another beneficial side-effect of the great venture.

And then Richard disappeared.

He was last seen, according to most reliable accounts, sitting under an olive tree on a beach in Cyprus with a footstool, a jug of mead and a book – Aristotle, or some such frivolous holiday reading. His fellow crusaders searched high and low for him, but found nothing apart from a footstool, an empty jug and an odd sock.

Not long afterwards, ugly rumours began to circulate. The French said that King Richard had been abducted by the Germans and was being held to ransom in a castle in Bavaria. The Germans declared that he had been imprisoned by the French king, who was demanding Aquitaine and ten million gold livres for his safe return. The Byzantines, who were a frivolous nation, suggested that the book, which Richard had borrowed from the world-famous library of the Abbey of Cluny, was three months overdue and the Abbot was holding Richard's person as security for unpaid fines. At any rate, the Crusade broke up, France and Germany declared war on Byzantium and burnt the Great Library of Constantinople, presumably by way of revenge for the Byzantine's tasteless remarks, and life in Christendom gradually returned to normal. After King Richard had been missing for a number of years he was declared officially dead and his brother John acceded to his throne. History, in its impartial and eclectic way, made a selection from the leading rumours to account for what had happened, and the world snuggled down to wait for the Black Death.

'Yes,' said Guy, 'that's really very interesting. Are you sure all this is —?'

'Yes,' said de Nesle.

'Ah,' Guy replied.

As already noted, de Nesle continued, King Richard was intensely musical, and one of his closest friends had been a French duke, Jean II de Nesle, known as Blondel —

'Relative of yours?' Guy asked.

You could say that, de Nesle replied; or at least, relativity does come into it. This Blondel was, among other things, the finest poet and musician of his age, and it was for this reason that he was so welcome at Richard's court. Before the Crusade drove all other concerns from his mind, the King's favourite occupation had been to sing duets with the Duke (Richard had a voice remarkably like a dying pig, but one does not mention such things to a feudal magnate who can split an anvil with one stroke of his sword) and one evening, probably after rather too much mead, the King had confided to Blondel his fear of being kidnapped. Holding kings to ransom was, after all, a substantial industry in the twelfth century; and King Richard, though not a collector's item like the Holy Roman Emperor, knew his own worth. He made Blondel promise that if ever he was abducted, Blondel would find him and help him escape; he was damned if his subjects' hard-earned money would be wasted paying ransoms, said the King (hiccoughing, probably), when a little courage and determination and forty feet of rope ladder could get him out of any castle in Christendom.

To this Blondel replied that that was all very well, but what if whoever had kidnapped him locked him up in a remote castle and refused to say where he was? Richard (we assume) smiled, and said that he'd thought of that, and that was where Blondel came in. Blondel could go round all the castles in Christendom (at the time, there were at least fifteen thousand castles in Christendom, give or take a few, but perhaps Richard didn't know that) and in each one he should sing one verse of that song they'd been singing just now, the one with Tristan in it. *L'Amours Dont Sui Epris*? Yes, that's the one. Good song, that. Anyway, Blondel should sing the first verse; and when Richard heard him singing it, he'd sing the second verse – he had a good loud voice, so Blondel should have no trouble hearing him. No indeed, no trouble at all – and then Blondel could sing the third verse, which would be a secret sign between them that Blondel would be waiting under the postern gate forty-eight hours later with a good, stout rope ladder and two horses. Blondel agreed that that was a perfectly splendid idea, and if it was all the same to his Majesty, Blondel wouldn't mind going and getting some sleep now, as it had got rather late.

Blondel was as good as his word. For years he wandered through France and the Empire, singing under the walls of castles, until at last his money was all spent and he had nothing left to sell or mortgage. He was sitting in abject despair in a small inn in Lombardy when he happened to get into conversation with a small group of travelling merchants. Pardon their asking, they said, but were they right in thinking that he was the celebrated Blondel?

Tired though he was, Blondel knew an artist's duty to his public and forced a smile on to his face. The merchants bought him a drink and said that they had long been admirers of his work. They thought he had originality and flair and what do you call it, that thing, relevance. They all thought he had a lot of relevance, and did he have an agent?

'What's an agent?'

The eldest merchant broke the silence first. He leaned ever so slightly forward, smiled in that way people do when they're appalled but fascinated, and said, 'It's like this ...'

Blondel raised a polite eyebrow. He wasn't really all that interested, but it does no harm to listen.

'Look,' said the merchant, 'there's you, right, all creative, thinking high thoughts, goofing about humming and saying to yourself, Isn't the colour of my true love's hair just a dead ringer for a field of sun-ripened corn? That's great, absolutely. What you don't want to be bothered with is hiring a hall, getting your posters out, fiddling around with the popcorn concessions and getting the parking organised. That's where an agent comes in.'

Blondel thought for a moment. 'Like a steward or something?'

The merchant blinked. 'Well,' he said, 'yes. Sort of. Anyway, the main thing is, you'll be free to exercise your whatsit, artistic integrity, absolutely safe in the knowledge that the ticket office will be manned and the warm-up band'll be there on time.'

'How do you mean?' Blondel asked.

42

The merchants looked at each other.

'When you do your gigs,' one of them said. 'Concerts.'

'What's a concert?'

There was a long silence. It was as if God had said *Let there be light,* and the void had replied, *Sorry?*

'Um,' said the eldest merchant. 'It's like, lots of people gathered together in one place to listen to you singing.'

Blondel arched his brows. 'That sounds nice,' he said, uncertainly. 'Would they want to be paid, or do you think they'd make do with a cup of wine and something to eat?'

The youngest merchant said something very quietly under his breath, but the only word Blondel could catch was Idiot. 'I don't think so,' said the eldest, in a rather strained voice. 'In fact, they'd probably pay you …'

'A token fee, of course,' one of the others added. 'Just a sort of little thank you, really …'

'I don't know,' Blondel said. 'It sounds a bit, well, you know. Accepting money from strangers. Not quite the thing, really.'

'Covers expenses, though,' said the eldest merchant quickly. 'And a man as shrewd as you are, you'll see in a flash that that's got to be a good idea. I mean, you can get your message across to a wider audience, fulfil your destiny, all that sort of thing, and it won't cost you a penny. In fact, there might even be something in it at the end of the day, after expenses have been paid. You know, like ten per cent —'

'Five per cent,' said one of his brothers quickly.

'Five per cent of the net takings, all for you, to spend

43

on what you like. We'd take care of all the rest of it for you.'

'Really?'

'No worries,' said the eldest merchant. The middle partner, who had been writing something on the back of the wine list, nudged him and pointed at what he'd written. The merchant nodded. 'By the way,' he said, 'my partner here would like your, um, autograph. Not for himself, you understand, for his wife. She's a fan.'

Blondel frowned; it seemed a curious way to describe someone – flat, with crinkly edges, swaying backwards and forwards. Then the penny dropped and he realised that the man had meant a fan-*bearer*. One of those people who stood beside you and waved one of those big carpet-beater things. King Richard had had two of them in Cyprus, where it got very hot around midday.

'Certainly,' he said. 'Where shall I sign?' He squinted. 'Will underneath all this small writing do?'

The merchants assured him that that would do perfectly.

To his surprise, the Blondel Grand European Tour (as the merchants described it) was a tremendous success, and Blondel was able to carry on singing under the walls of all the castles in Christendom, frequently to audiences of well over ten thousand, without having to contribute a penny to expenses. For their part the merchants never seemed to grow tired of following him about and finding him castles to sing under, and if they insisted on him singing a lot of other songs as well as *L'Amours Dont Sui Epris*, Blondel didn't mind that in the least. He liked singing and was always making up new songs.

Eventually, however, Blondel found that he had sung under every castle in Christendom, and still he hadn't found the King. When he mentioned this to the merchants, they said that that was too bad, but they'd been thinking for some time now that the acoustics under castle walls didn't do him justice anyway, and what did he think to having a nice large arena built somewhere central with good parking facilities, proper acoustics and a seating capacity of, say, fifty to sixty thousand? It would, they said, take his mind off not being able to find King Richard.

And then, after Blondel had been singing to capacity crowds in the special arena for a month or so, a messenger came to see him. A great deal of detail can be omitted here; suffice to say that the messenger confirmed that Richard was alive and well, and was indeed being held captive in a castle. The problem was that the castle was very difficult to get to.

Blondel replied that he didn't care; he'd given his word to the King, and he wasn't going to give up now.

The messenger shrugged his shoulders and said that that was all laudable, but Richard hadn't been abducted by the King of France or the Holy Roman Emperor or any one of those small-time outfits. He was in the dungeons of the Chastel des Larmes Chaudes.

'So what?' Blondel asked. 'Where is the Chastel des Larmes Chaudes?'

'Good question,' said the messenger.

Blondel then requested the messenger to stop mucking about.

The Chastel des Larmes Chaudes, said the messenger, was hidden. Not only was it hidden in space, it was also hidden in time; it could be in the present, the past or even the future. Also, could Blondel please let go of his throat, as he was having difficulty breathing?

The messenger departed in search of witch hazel for his neck, leaving Blondel even more despondent than before. After all, time was time; nobody could travel to the past or the future. Nevertheless, he said to himself, he had come a long way and he wasn't going to let something like this stand in his way. The least he could do would be to put the problem to his agents (or rather his management company; they had incorporated under the name of the Beaumont Street Agency) and see if they could come up with anything.

'No problem,' they said . . .

'And that,' Blondel said, 'is how it happened. More or less.'

'More or less,' Guy repeated. 'Are you saying that you're . . .'

Blondel nodded. If his hand instinctively reached for something to sign his autograph on, his brain checked the impulse.

'You're telling me,' Guy went on, blundering through the words like a man in a darkened room, 'that you're nine hundred years old.'

To do him credit, Blondel simply nodded. Guy closed his eyes.

'Um,' he said. 'Mr . . . Monsieur . . .'

'Call me Blondel,' Blondel said.

'Thank you, yes,' Guy replied. 'Blondel, do you have a bathroom in this, er, castle?'

'Bathroom?'

'A privvy,' Guy said. 'A latrine. Er.'

Blondel raised an eyebrow. 'Not as such,' he said. 'After all, this is the twelfth century we're in now. Well, mostly. I get the electricity for the machines from the twenty-third century. By the time I reach there I'm going to have the most enormous bill. But the plumbing is, well, pretty medieval. Why do you ask?'

Guy thought hard, seeking to find the best possible form of words.

'I don't know about you,' he said at last, 'but I find physical discomfort is a great barrier to concentration, and just now I feel I ought to be concentrating on what you're saying.'

'Ah,' Blondel said, 'I see. Very sensible of you. We all use the channel that runs round the edge of the main hall. That's through the door immediately behind you.'

'Thank you.'

An empty bladder, Guy always felt, gives you a whole new perspective on things. Problems which had seemed insurmountable a few minutes before gradually begin to take on a new perspective. When he came back into the study a few minutes later, he was feeling much more able to cope.

'Well,' he said. 'Blondel, eh?'

'Yes indeed.'

'Pleased to, er, meet you.' Guy smiled weakly. 'Actually,' he said, 'I write songs too. That is, I, well, dabble a bit, you know.'

A very brief flicker of pain flashed across Blondel's eyes, and for a moment Guy wondered what he'd said; then he understood. It was the pain of a man who, for nine hundred years, probably more, has had strangers say to him, 'Let me just hum you a few bars, I expect it's the most awful rubbish really,' and has then had to

47

perjure his soul by disagreeing. Guy changed the subject quickly.

'So,' he said, 'how do you do it? The time travelling, I mean. Does it just come naturally, or . . .?'

'Good Lord, no,' Blondel said, smiling. 'Not a bit of it. My agents fixed it for me. You see,' he said, standing up and opening a drawer of his filing cabinet, 'they originally come from the twenty-fifth century.'

Guy swallowed. 'Oh yes?'

'They do indeed.' From the drawer, Blondel produced a bottle of port. 'Have some?' he asked. '2740. It's going to be one of the best years on record, so they say. Mind you, it all tastes the same to me.'

Guy shook his head. The thought of drinking something that hadn't been grown yet did something unpleasant to his stomach lining.

'In the twenty-fifth century,' Blondel said, 'time travel will be as familiar as, say, air travel is to you. It'll be so commonplace that they'll need to advertise it on posters to persuade people to use it instead of other, more convenient methods. "Let the clock take the strain. We've already got there." That sort of thing. You sure you won't join me?'

Guy, who didn't wish to appear rude, accepted a glass.

'Now,' Blondel went on, 'orthodox time travel operates on a system called Bluchner's Loop. It's very technical and I really don't understand how it works, but it's something about the law of conservation of reality. The Fourth Law of Thermodynamics,' Blondel frowned, then shrugged. 'Something like that,' he said. 'I read an article about it once in *Scientific Oceanian* but it was all Greek to me. Anyway, it means that when a person

48

travels in time, then time sort of heals up after him as soon as he's moved on; it means that whatever he does in the past, for example, the present and the future will be exactly the same as if he'd never been there. In other words, I couldn't stop the Napoleonic Wars by going back in time and poisoning Napoleon in his cot. No matter how many times I killed Napoleon in infancy, he'd still be there in 1799 overthrowing the Directorate. All right so far?'

'More or less,' said Guy. 'Very good port, this.'

'Like San Francisco,' Blondel agreed. 'That's orthodox time travel. My agents – the group of people who became my agents – found another way of travelling through time. It wasn't nearly as safe as the orthodox way, but it meant you could take things with you. The orthodox way, you see, only lets you take yourself; which can be awfully embarrassing, so they tell me. It means, for example, you run the risk of turning up at Queen Victoria's wedding with no clothes on. Another?'

'Thanks.'

'There's another bottle after we've finished this,' Blondel said. 'Plenty more where this is coming from. In fact, if you like, we can have the same bottle all over again.'

'No, really,' Guy said, 'a different bottle will do fine.'

'My agents,' Blondel said, 'saw at once that this new form of time travel had all sorts of possibilities. Commercial possibilities, I mean. The trouble was that if they told anybody about it, it'd be suppressed immediately; too dangerous. So they kept it to themselves. They used it for all sorts of clever financial

49

deals, apparently. I've never been much of a money man myself so I don't really understand it all, but it seems they move money about throughout the centuries.'

'Why?'

Blondel shrugged. 'Tax reasons.'

'Ah,' Guy said. That, he felt, would account for it.

'What they used to do,' Blondel said, 'and please excuse me if I get the tenses wrong, was to take money from the future and invest it in the Second Crusade; you know, King Richard's crusade. Well, don't you see?'

'No.'

'Oh. Well, I'm not a hundred per cent sure myself. But it occurs to me that if you start bringing lots of things – you know, gold coins, that sort of thing – back through time and depositing them in another century, then that's going to make the century they end up in rather – what's the word? – unstable. Volatile, even. You run the risk of upsetting the balance of nature, or physics, or whatever. I think that because they made rather a mess of time at about that point, they made the next bit of history go all wrong. It couldn't happen the way it was supposed to happen, because of all these influences from the future upsetting it. On the other hand, it had already happened – because, well, it did – and as a result of it happening, history's what it is today. Or then,' Blondel scratched his ear, and continued. 'Anyway, I think that because of this imbalance or instability or whatever you like to call it, the whole thing sort of blew a fuse. Since the Crusade could neither happen nor not happen, history just washed its hands of the whole thing and left a great big gap. A hole, if you like. And Richard fell into it.'

'My God.'

'Exactly,' Blondel finished his glass of port thoughtfully. 'Anyway,' he continued, 'that's beside the point. All I knew at the start was that my agents could take me about in time, so that's what I did. Instead of just going all round the world, I went all round time as well, looking for the King, like I'd promised I would. And that, basically, is what I'm still doing.'

'I see.'

Blondel lit a cigar and offered one to Guy. 'It's all right,' he said, 'we don't yet know how bad they are for you. After a while, I found out how to travel through time on my own, without any help from my agents, and it was about then that I started putting two and two together and wondering if perhaps Richard's disappearance might have been their fault. Once I'd come to that conclusion, of course, I didn't want anything more to do with them – well, you wouldn't, would you? – so I gave them the slip and set off on my own. I set up a sort of base here where I can slip back and keep a change of clothes and so on. A sort of *pied à temps.* Otherwise, I'm mostly on the move, I have to be,' Blondel added. 'You see, they're looking for me.'

Guy frowned. 'Who?'

'My agents,' Blondel replied. 'You see, they've got a contract. By the terms of it, I have to give two concerts a week for the rest of my life, and they get ninety-five per cent of the profits.'

Guy whistled.

'Not only that,' Blondel went on, grinning, 'but they've invested millions and millions of livres in setting up concerts – gigs, they call them – all through time and now I'm not there to sing at them. No wonder they're worried. It's not their money they're investing.'

Guy grinned too. 'Awkward,' he said.

'Exactly,' said Blondel, tipping a little ash into a saucer. 'But the last thing I want to do is get pinned down by them again. I've got to find the King.'

'Er,' Guy said. 'Has it occurred to you that he might be, well ...'

'Might be what?'

'Well,' said Guy, 'that when he disappeared, or fell through time or whatever, that he might not actually be anywhere? I mean ...'

Blondel's face became very cold; then he relaxed.

'Perhaps,' he said. 'But I've got to keep looking. After all, I did give my word. Now then, another bottle.'

Blondel filled both glasses and they sat in silence for a while.

Guy said, 'So, er, where do your sisters fit in?'

'Sorry?'

'Your sisters,' Guy repeated. 'Mahaud and Ysabel and, er ...'

'Oh yes,' Blondel said. 'I forgot, do forgive me. They very sweetly agreed to help out, at least to begin with. But you know what women are like. After a bit, you see, they lost interest, got the urge to settle down, that sort of thing. Mahaud and Ysabel met men they rather liked, got married, settled down. Can't blame them, of course. I find that women have this terrible urge to be normal.'

'And Isoud?'

'Isoud's still with me,' Blondel said, 'but probably not for much longer. She's been getting terribly restless

52

lately, I think she wants a change. I can recognise the symptoms. Once they start redecorating the place every five minutes, getting new curtains, you can be sure there's something in the air. Oh well, never mind.'

'So, er . . .' Guy said.

'By all means,' Blondel said. 'You look a respectable enough sort of chap to me. You are, aren't you?'

'Oh yes.'

'Well then, that's fine,' said Blondel. 'I only ask because as head of the family I have to choose husbands for them, give my consent, dowry, all that sort of nonsense. We're a bit old-fashioned in our family, you see. Or as least,' he added, frowning, 'we will be.'

'So . . .?'

'Absolutely,' Blondel said. 'Just so long as you do this one little thing for me.'

'Oh yes?' said Guy. 'And what's that?'

'Are you ready?'

'As I'll ever be.'

'Got everything?'

'Yes.'

'Right. If the horse gets restive, give him a lump of sugar.'

'Understood.'

'You're sure you checked the rope?'

'Positive.'

'Right then,' Blondel said. 'Here goes.'

A single shaft of moonlight cut through the thick clouds and, like a searchlight, picked out Blondel's hair and the silver mounts of his lute as he strolled up to the drawbridge of the castle. The drawbridge was raised, of course, but it was a narrow moat.

Guy looked round the trunk of the large oak tree he was standing behind and tried to work out how he had got there. There was something about the cold, the darkness and the rather ominous look of the castle that made him want to go away, but since he

hadn't the faintest idea of where – let alone when –
he was, he decided to stay and see what would
happen.

The horse, whose bridle he was holding, lifted its
head sharply and flicked its tail. Guy immediately
shovelled another sugar lump between its wet, smelly
lips. He disliked horses, and this one in particular.
He had an uneasy feeling that it was going to cause
trouble. It had been bad enough getting it here,
wherever and whenever that was; it had left mal-
odorous traces of its presence in the corridors and
had tried to pick a fight with the lift. He tried
thinking of the deep blue eyes of La Beale Isoud, but
somehow that didn't work.

The moon went behind a cloud, and Guy heard
Blondel clear his throat and touch the strings of his
lute. He was principally worried about dogs, but that
wasn't all, by a long way.

Then Blondel drew his hand across the lute
strings and began to sing:

'L'amours dont sui epris
Me semont de chanter;
Si fais con hons sopris
Qui ne puet endurer . . .'

A dog barked.

'Et s'ai je tant conquis
Que bien me puis venter . . .'

A light went on. Then another.

'Que j'ai piec' a apris
Leaument a amer . . .'

There was a flash of silver in the air, and a sound. A
sort of sploshing sound. Blondel stopped singing.

'And let that be a lesson to you,' came an angry

voice from the top of the wall. 'There's people up here trying to sleep.'

Blondel walked slowly back to the tree. He was very wet.

'Right,' he said, 'we can cross that one off the list. Well, don't just stand there. We've got a lot more to do tonight.'

Guy reached in the saddlebag and produced a towel. He'd wondered why Blondel had insisted on packing one; now he knew.

'Does that happen a lot?' he asked sympathetically.

'Quite a lot, yes,' said Blondel, drying vigorously. 'Some people, you see, have tin ears. However, that's beside the point. Ready?'

They walked in silence for a while. Guy, who wasn't used to walking about the countryside in the dark, was concentrating very hard on where he was going, while Blondel seemed to be wrapped up in his own thoughts.

'I liked the song,' Guy said at last.

'Sorry?'

'The song,' Guy repeated. 'I liked it.'

'Thank you.'

'Not at all.'

'Personally,' Blondel said, with a savagery that took Guy quite by surprise, 'I'm sick to the back teeth of it. If I never hear it again, I shall be extremely happy. After all,' he added, rather more calmly, 'I have been singing it now for longer than I can possibly hope to remember. No wonder I've had enough of it. In fact, all music makes me sick these days. If ever I do find the King, I'm going to spend the rest of my life not listening to music.'

That killed the conversation stone dead for the next ten minutes, during which they walked quietly along, Guy following Blondel and hoping that he knew where he was going. An owl hooted somewhere.

Guy was just starting to realise that he was feeling hungry when a large white shape appeared out of a bush beside the road, dashed across their path and disappeared into the darkness. As far as Guy was concerned it was one of those incidents which are best left shrouded in mystery, but Blondel suddenly seemed galvanised into action.

'Don't just stand there,' he said. 'After it.'

'After what?'

'The stag, silly. Quick, you get on the horse.'

Guy wanted to explain that he wasn't desperately efficient with horses, but by this stage Blondel was nowhere to be seen. With a despairing spurt of courage, Guy grabbed at one of the stirrups, put his foot in it and hauled himself up on to the horse. Thankfully, the horse took it quite well. He sorted out the reins, gave the horse a token kick, and was delighted to find that it seemed perfectly willing to accept that as a valid command to move. As he sped through the darkness, he tried to remember what his uncle in Norfolk had tried to teach him when he was ten about rising to the trot.

'Blondel,' he shouted, 'where are you?'

'Over here,' came a voice, a long way off. Blondel, it seemed, could run fast. Just as Guy had dragged out of his memory the recognised way of making a horse turn left, the horse pricked up its ears and set off towards the direction of its master's voice.

'He's in there,' Blondel hissed. Moonlight flashed on the blade of his sword, pointing (as far as Guy was concerned) in no particular direction at all.

'How do you stop this thing?' Guy asked.

'Pull on the reins,' Blondel replied. 'Get down and come and help.'

In the event, Guy found getting off the horse was quite simple, if not particularly dignified. He tied the reins to a handy bush and followed the sound of Blondel's voice. He longed for a torch.

'In the cave,' Blondel said.

'Which cave?'

'There is a cave,' Blondel explained, 'just over there. The white stag just went into it. You don't seem at home in the dark.'

'I'm not.'

'You should eat more carrots,' Blondel said absently. 'I think we should go in after it.'

Guy blinked. 'Do you?' he said.

'Absolutely,' Blondel replied. 'It had a gold collar round its neck, and the points of its antlers were gilded.'

'Escaped from a circus or something?' Guy hazarded.

'Something like that. Look, get the rope, we can use that as a halter. Then follow me.'

'Blondel . . .'

But Blondel had gone into the cave. As instructed, Guy fetched the rope. He took his time. No point in rushing these things.

'Hurry up with the damn rope,' came a voice from inside the cave. Against his better judgement, Guy followed. There was a silvery light coming from inside the cave. Perhaps someone in there had a torch.

As he entered, Guy saw that the light was coming from the antlers of the white stag; they were glowing, as if they were made of glass and had electric filaments inside them. The stag itself was milk-white, and it did indeed have a golden halter and some sort of gold leaf on the sharp bits of its antlers. It was eating sugar lumps from the palm of Blondel's hand.

'Tie the rope to its antlers,' Blondel whispered. 'Hurry up, man, we haven't got all night.'

Guy shrugged and edged forward, filled with the reckless courage of an elderly householder looking for burglars armed with his wife's umbrella. To his surprise and relief, the antlers were cold to the touch and the stag didn't try and stick them into him. He tied all the knots he could remember from his boy scout days and handed the other end of the rope to Blondel.

'Well,' Blondel said, 'this *is* a bit of luck, don't you think?'

Guy's eyebrows rose. 'Luck?' he said.

'Absolutely,' Blondel replied, patting the stag's muzzle. 'Not every day you run across an enchanted stag on Wandsworth Common, now is it?'

'Is that where we are?' Guy asked, stunned, 'Wandsworth Common?'

'We are indeed.'

'I've got an aunt who lives —'

'Will live,' Blondel interrupted. 'I make it the late fourteenth century, unless my calendar's stopped again.'

'Oh.' Guy felt suddenly wretched. 'I see.'

'Out there,' Blondel went on, 'they're having the Black Death and the Peasant's Revolt. Which makes having an enchanted stag a distinct advantage, don't you think?'

'Well yes,' Guy agreed. What he'd really like, he said to himself, in the circumstances stated, was a machine-gun and a gallon jar of penicillin, but he was prepared to accept any sort of edge he could get. 'Er, what do we do now?'

'Watch,' Blondel replied. 'Gee up there, boy,' he said to the stag. The stag turned its head and looked at him.

'My name,' said the stag, 'is Cerf le Blanc.' It said it coldly and without moving any part of its mouth. That, as far as Guy was concerned, put the tin lid on it.

'Where are you off to in such a hurry?' Blondel asked.

'Goodbye,' Guy explained. 'Thanks for everything.'

'Oh well,' Blondel called after him. 'Go carefully. Mind the wolves.'

Guy's head reappeared at the door of the cave. 'Wolves?' he enquired.

'Wolves,' Blondel replied, 'were still common in England in the fourteenth century, I think. I'm not sure, actually.'

'I think I'll come with you,' Guy said; then he whispered, 'Look, is that thing going to make a habit of talking?'

'I wouldn't worry about it,' Blondel said. 'I don't think it means to hurt us. Do you?'

'No.'

'There,' Blondel said, 'you see? Had it from its own lips.'

'I never *mean* to hurt anyone,' said Cerf le Blanc. 'Sometimes, though ... But it's always an accident. At least as far as I'm concerned, that is.'

Blondel gave the stag a reassuring pat. 'That's all right,' he said. 'Have some Turkish Delight and then let's be getting on.' He produced a pink cube from the purse at his belt. There were bits of fluff sticking to it, but the stag didn't seem to mind. When it had finished chewing, it lifted its head, and the light of its antlers dimmed to a discreet glow. It led the way.

Pursuivant rubbed his eyes and yawned.

At about this time, back at the Chastel des Larmes Chaudes, the lads would be opening a few cans, passing round the dry-roasted peanuts, getting on with the night shift. On Mondays, Wednesdays and Fridays they had a poker school. If the alarm rang, of course, they'd have to go and answer it, but somehow the alarm never seemed to ring any more. Not since Clarenceaux wedged a beer-mat between the bell and the clapper.

Although the regulation kagouls are supposed to be waterproof, it was Pursuivant's experience that there were a large number of vulnerable points through which rain could penetrate them, just as it had penetrated his sandwiches and his wellington boots. There was supposed to be an umbrella, but Mordaunt Dragon of Arms had snitched it for when he went fishing. The only waxed cotton jacket in the department belonged to White Herald; and given his personal habits, nobody in his right mind would want to wear it even if White Herald was inclined to offer, which he wasn't.

Pursuivant shivered and wiped the rain off his nose. They'd hired a video for tonight, too.

He peeled back his sleeve and looked at his watch, first wiping away the moisture that obscured the dial. He was due to be relieved at six, but there was a long way to go before then. Plenty long enough to catch pneumonia. There were few crimes he wouldn't commit for a nice hot mug of tea.

Out in the darkness, a long way off, a pale white light was glowing. Pursuivant rubbed his eyes again and stared. This was more like it, he thought. He reached for the night-glass, wiped the lenses and peered out. The light wasn't there any more. Seeing things.

No, he wasn't. Clear as anything, a pale white light. Fumbling with numb hands, Pursuivant adjusted the glass and saw two men, very wet, leading a horse and a white stag, whose antlers were producing the light. They were a long way off still, but heading this way. Pursuivant chuckled and wound the handle of the field telephone. It rang, and rang, and rang. Nobody answered it, and no wonder. Some clown had wedged a beer-mat between the bell and the clapper.

'Oh *shit*,' Pursuivant muttered under his breath.

Still, there it was. Nothing for it but to do it himself. Thinking very bitter thoughts about the rest of the department, he groped for his shield (a mitre argent on a sable field, a bend cross keys reversed gules, attired of the second) and his pickaxe handle with big rusty nails driven through it. Chivalry was a concept familiar to the staff of the Chastel des Larmes Chaudes, but they didn't make a big thing about it.

Feeling extremely foolish, Guy put his revolver away and came out from behind the horse.

'Is he all right?' he said.

Blondel looked at the body at his feet. 'Well,' he said, 'if he is then I've just been wasting my time. Thanks for your help, by the way. You meant well.' He stuck a finger through the bullet hole in his hat and spun the hat round a couple of times.

'Like I said,' Guy muttered defensively, 'I don't see terribly well in the —'

'Yes, well,' Blondel said, 'it's the thought that counts.' He put up his sword, gave the body a kick, and put his hat back on. 'Don't worry about him,' he said. 'He'll be right as rain in the morning.' He glanced up at the sky. 'Well, better, anyway.'

'Footpads?' Guy asked.

'Footpads be blowed,' Blondel replied. 'See that shield? Mitre argent on a sable field and bunches of upside-down keys? No, if it was footpads I'd be inclined to worry.' He turned round and stood in front of the stag, hands on hips.

'Now then,' Blondel said, 'I think you and I should have a little talk.'

The stag gave him a blank look, as if to say that deer are not capable of human speech. Their larynxes are the wrong shape, said the stag's eyes.

'Unless,' Blondel continued, 'you don't want to talk, of course, in which case it's venison rissoles for my friend here and myself. *Capisce?*'

The stag breathed heavily through its nose.

'I'll count,' said Blondel sweetly. 'Up to five. One.'

'All right,' said the stag, without moving its lips (the

larynxes of stags are totally incapable of forming human speech), 'there's no need to come over all unnecessary. I was only doing my job.'

Blondel smiled. 'And what might that be?' he said. In the background, Guy coughed.

'Excuse me,' he said.

Blondel turned his head. 'What?' he asked.

'Do you mind if I have a cigarette?' Guy said. 'All this excitement ...'

'Go ahead,' Blondel replied. He turned back to the stag. 'Your job,' he said.

'I serve His Excellency Julian XXIII,' mumbled the stag. 'All right?'

'Yes, I know that,' said Blondel. 'A mitre argent on a sable field and all that nonsense. You were told to come here?'

The stag nodded. The movement of its antlers jerked Guy's hand, sending his cigarette arcing through the air like a flying glow-worm. He said something under his breath and lit another.

'And when we turned up, you were to lead us towards where the idiot there was lying in wait?'

The stag nodded again but Guy was ready this time.

'Thought so,' Blondel said. 'Now then. Who said we'd be coming this way tonight?'

The stag gave him a blank look.

'Come on,' Blondel said. 'Someone must have said.'

The stag shrugged.

'Oh, be like that, then,' said Blondel. 'Now then, where did you come from?'

Silence. It wasn't (Guy felt) that the stag didn't want to say; more like it didn't actually know. Probably it didn't understand the question. Blondel rephrased it.

'Where,' he asked, 'do you live?'

Silence.

'You know what?' Blondel said to Guy. 'I think we're wasting our time. Just because the dratted thing can speak doesn't necessarily mean it's intelligent.'

'Here,' said the stag, affronted, 'just you mind what you're —'

'In fact,' Blondel went on, 'I think that if we look carefully ...' He went across and started to feel the fur between the stag's ears. 'Ah yes,' he said. 'Here we are.' He pulled, and something came away in his hands. The light went suddenly out.

'Blondel,' Guy complained, 'what are you doing?'

'See this?'

'No,' Guy replied. 'Somebody put the lights out.'

Blondel showed him a little grey box, with wires coming out of it. 'This,' he said, 'is a radio transmitter-cum-microphone-cum-hologram projector. It also sends electrical impulses into this poor mutt's brains to control its actions. Cerf le Blanc,' he said, patting the stag's nose, 'is just an ordinary white deer, aren't you, boy?'

'Oh,' Guy said. 'I see.' To a certain extent, he felt, he ought to be relieved. Somehow he wasn't.

'All those magical effects,' Blondel went on, 'were produced by this little box of tricks here. That's where the voice came from. I expect it's also transmitting what we say back to Head Office, wherever that is. Is that right, boys?' he said.

'Yes, that's ...' said the voice of Cerf le Blanc. Another voice said something rude and there was an audible click. Blondel chuckled softly and then put the box on the ground and jumped on it.

'All right,' he said, 'you can turn the deer loose now. We'd better be going.'

Cerf le Blanc, freed from the rope, picked up his hooves and ran for it. Blondel took back the rope, coiled it up neatly and stowed it in the saddlebag. 'Time we weren't here,' he said. 'Now, our best bet will be a corn exchange or something like that.'

Guy, who had just started to feel he could cope, on a purely superficial level at least, felt his jaw drop. 'A corn exchange,' he repeated.

'Or a yarn market will do,' Blondel replied. 'We can make do with a guildhall at a pinch, I suppose, but there may well be people about. Somehow I don't feel a church would be a good idea. They may be idiots, but they aren't fools. Coming?'

It was about two hours before dawn when they reached the town. Fourteenth-century Wandsworth was waking up, deciding it could have another ten minutes, and turning over in its warm straw. Blondel quickened his step.

'In the 1480s,' he whispered as they crept past a sleeping beggar, 'there was a corn exchange in the town square, but they may not have built it yet. Looked a bit perpendicular when I saw it. Hang on, this'll do.'

They were standing under a bell-tower. Blondel was looking at a small, low door, which Guy hadn't even noticed. It wasn't the sort of door that you do notice. Over its lintel were letters cut into the stone.

NOLI INTRARE, they said, AD VSVM CANONICORVM RESERVATA.

'That's the Latin,' Blondel explained, 'for No entry, staff only. This'll do fine. We'll have to leave the horse, but never mind.'

He knocked three times on the door and pushed. It opened.

'So?'

'He hit me,' Pursuivant explained.

'I gathered that. What else?'

Meanwhile the doctor's assistant was up a ladder in the stockroom, looking at the labels on the backs of what looked like shoe-boxes. 'We've only got a 36E,' he called out. 'Will that do?'

'Have to,' the doctor said. 'Means he'll get bronchitis from time to time, but so what?'

Pursuivant sat up on the operating table. 'Hold on, doc,' he said. The doctor pushed him down again.

'You never heard of the cuts?' he said. 'You're lucky we've got a 36E. There's been a run on lungs lately.'

'Yes, but ...'

'Don't be such an old woman,' said the doctor. 'We should have some 42s when you have your next thirty-year service. Until then, you'll have to make do.'

Mountjoy, who had been standing fiddling with his signet ring all this time, was getting impatient. 'He hit you,' he repeated. 'Then what?'

'Then I fell over,' Pursuivant replied. 'Look, boss, in the contract it plainly states that all damage will be made good, and —'

'Shut up,' said Mountjoy. 'You fell over. Go on.'

'But boss —'

'Look,' the chaplain snapped, 'I should be at an important meeting. Get on with it.'

In actual fact, Mountjoy was at the meeting – in fact, he'd been three minutes early – but there was no need to mention that. He flickered irritably.

'I fell over,' Pursuivant said. 'Then there was a bang and the bloke's hat came off.'

'What?'

'His hat,' Pursuivant explained. 'He was wearing a hat and it came off. Don't ask me why.'

'I see,' Mountjoy said. 'And what happened next?'

'I died.'

'I see,' Mountjoy said. 'And that was all you saw?'

'Well,' said Pursuivant, 'my whole life flashed in front of me, but I don't suppose you want to hear about that.'

'Not particularly, no. What was this other man like?'

Pursuivant furrowed his brows, thinking hard. 'Odd bloke,' he said. 'About my height, dark hair, wearing a sort of sheepskin coat, no sword. If you ask me, he didn't seem to have much idea of what was happening.'

'That,' said Mountjoy unkindly, 'would have made two of you.' He put away his notebook and turned to the doctor. 'Right,' he said, 'how long before this one's up and about again?'

'Let's see,' said the doctor. 'Neck partially severed, multiple wounds to lungs, stomach and shoulders, compound fracture of the left leg. I'll need to keep him in for observation, too. Say about twenty minutes.'

'Oh for pity's sake,' snapped Mountjoy petulantly. 'Doctor, you are aware of the staffing shortages?'

'Not my problem,' the doctor replied. 'All right, nurse, close him up.'

The staff nurse put down her visor and lit up the welding torch.

'Blondel,' said Guy, 'can I ask you something?'

The tunnel was damp and smelly. The ceiling was

low and the light from the torches in the wall-sconces wasn't quite bright enough. On a number of occasions, Guy had trodden in something. He was glad that he didn't know what it had been.

'Fire away.'

'How do you do that?'

'What?'

'Go through doors,' Guy said, 'that lead to ... well, this.'

Blondel laughed. 'This is how we travel through time,' he said. 'My agents taught me.'

'I see.' Guy walked along in silence for a while. He was getting a crick in the neck from keeping his head ducked. 'Er, how does it work?' he asked.

'On the principle of Bureauspace,' Blondel replied. 'Are you all right with the saddlebags or shall I carry them for a bit?'

'No, no, that's fine,' Guy said. 'What's Bureauspace?'

Blondel stopped under a torch and looked at a little book. He was actually rather shorter than he looked, Guy noticed, and didn't have to lower his head to avoid the ceiling. 'This way,' he said at last. 'I thought we'd taken a wrong turning back there, but it's all right. Now then, the proper name for it is the Bureaucratic Spatio-Temporal Effect, but we call it Bureauspace for short. It's really very simple, once you grasp the fundamental concept.'

'Oh good,' said Guy. He had the awful feeling that this was going to be one of those questions you regret asking.

'It's like this,' Blondel said. 'Oh, left here, by the way. Mind your head.'

'Ouch.'

'At the heart of all bureaucratic organisations,' Blondel said, 'there's a huge lesion in the fabric of space and time. It's like a sort of . . .' Blondel thought hard. 'It's like the gap between the sofa-cushions of time and space. Things fall into it, get lost and then get washed out again. In the meantime, they've been whirled round all through time and space until they end up more or less where they started. That's how the system works. They're all well aware of it in the public services, only they call it going through channels. However, it has its advantages.'

Guy stopped just in time to avoid walking into a pillar. 'Oh yes?' he said.

'Yes indeed.' Blondel had halted again and was screwing up his eyes to read small print by the light of a very dim torch. 'You see,' he said, 'all bureaucracies are one bureaucracy. The British Ministry of Works is in fact the same organisation as the Turkish Home Office, the Tresor Royale of Louis XIV and the Roman Senate's sub-committee on Drains and Sewers. They had different notepaper for each department, but they're all basically the same thing. And all bureaucracies are built over this lesion in the fabric of space and time, what Marcus Aurelius would have called the Great Chesterfield. This is why, sometimes, when the system breaks down, you get an income tax demand that should have been sent to the Shah of Persia, while the Archbishop of Verona gets your electricity bill.'

'I thought so.'

'Sorry?'

'Never mind,' Guy said. 'Go on, please.'

'Well then,' said Blondel, 'once you've realised that

fact, you can make use of it. We are presently in a duct in the bowels of the Civil Service. What they call the Usual Channels. Or, if you prefer, we've fallen down behind the back of God's filing cabinet. Right now we're directly underneath the Finance and General Purpose Committee of the Anglo-Saxon Folkmoot. Over there somewhere is the National Bank of the Soviet Union, and that corridor on your right leads under the commissariat division of the grand council of Genghis Khan. You soon find your way about down here. It's a bit like the Phantom of the Opera.'

'But how did we get here?' Guy asked.

'Easy.' Blondel stopped and rubbed his eyes. 'You'll have noticed how, in every public building ever constructed, from the Ziggurat of Ur to the Coliseum to Chichester Cathedral to Broadcasting House, there are always lots and lots of doors marked *Private, staff only, do not enter.* Yes?'

'Yes,' said Guy.

'Well then,' Blondel said, grinning, 'haven't you ever wondered where they lead to?'

'No,' Guy admitted.

'Of course not,' Blondel said. 'You're brought up not to. Nobody knows, that's the whole point. I mean, you've never actually seen anyone going in or out of them, have you?'

'Guy shook his head.

'Well,' said Blondel, 'now you know. They all lead down here. Which means,' he yawned, closing his little book and putting it away in his purse, 'that wherever there's a public building of any description – library, town hall, railway station, government ministry, kennel for the King's Wolfhounds –' Blondel sniffed and pointed upwards '– sewage farm, manhole cover, orbiting space station, anything like that – there's a gateway to the whole of time and space, and all you have to do is knock three times and enter. It's as simple as that. It certainly beats all that mucking about with transmat beams. Ah,' he said, 'I think we've arrived.'

In front of them was a door.

'For a while,' Blondel was saying, 'I thought they might have King Richard down here. You know, filed away in the archives, bound hand and foot with red tape. But they haven't, I've looked.'

'Where are we?' Guy asked.

'You'll see,' Blondel smiled. 'Ready?'

'Usher,' said Oliver Cromwell, 'take away that bauble.'

Behind the Speaker's chair, a door opened. Not many people had ever noticed it was there, probably because it had *staffe onlie* painted on it in gold leaf.

Slowly, and with infinite misgivings, the usher rose to his feet and walked towards the table on which the Great Mace lay. Cromwell's face remained implacable.

'It's his warts,' explained a colonel to the Member for Ashburton. 'When they're playing him up he can be that difficult ...'

On the back benches a solitary figure rose. The usher stopped dead in his tracks. He knew that history was being made; he was also acute enough to guess that the production of history, like coal-mining, is a highly hazardous occupation.

'Mr Protector,' said the solitary figure, 'by what right ...?'

Behind the Speaker's chair, Guy froze. He had a horrible feeling – not unlike the sensation of discovering that the large bowl of water one has just upset all over one's host's carpet had originally contained one's host's goldfish – that he knew exactly where he was, and when.

'Come on,' Blondel hissed, 'you're dawdling again.'

'Yes, but . . .'

But Blondel wasn't there. Instead he was standing in front of the Speaker, showing him a raggedly little scrap of paper. The Speaker, having read it, nodded and called upon Blondel to speak. Apparently he was under the impression that Blondel was the Member for Saffron Walden.

Actually, Blondel didn't so much speak as sing; he sang *L'Amours Dont Sui Epris,* and had got as far as *Remembrance dou vis* before the big spotty man who'd been talking when they came in shouted to a couple of guards to take this something-or-other and throw him in the river.

It was, Guy realised, a time for swift and positive action. He started trying to back through the door he'd just come through on his hands and knees.

Blondel had turned round and was glaring at Cromwell with a sort of paint-stripping fury in his eyes.

'Who are you calling a —' Then he noticed that a halberdier was trying to annex his collar, kicked the man neatly in the groin and jumped up on the table with the mace on it, his sword in his hand.

'Oh *hell . . .*' said Guy to himself.

If he'd had time to analyse his reluctance to get involved, he would have said to himself that this was a crucial moment in the development of English Parliamentary democracy, and that if he loused it up he would probably be responsible for a new Dark Age of

73

royal supremacy and baronial repression. As it was, time was short. Very tentatively, he stood up and drew his revolver.

'Excuse me,' he said.

The Lord Protector, the Long Parliament and an assortment of officials and soldiers turned and looked at him. In a brief instant of total perception, Guy realised that he hadn't shaved, his fingernails were dirty, his left sock had a hole in it, he was probably going to die very soon, his jacket was too big and his hair badly needed combing. He said 'Er.'

Blondel, meanwhile, had jumped down from the table, sheathed his sword, picked up the mace and clobbered two halberdiers with it. Then he swatted Black Rod across the kneecaps, stunned the Member for Kings Langley, caught the usher a savage blow on the funny bone and fell over. The guard who had felled him, rather unsportingly from behind, with a bound copy of Bracton, drew back his arm for another blow . . .

'Freeze!' shouted Guy.

Of all the peculiar situations he had found himself in recently, Guy felt, this had to be the loopiest. Here he was, Flight Lieutenant Guy Goodlet, bachelor, twenty-six, until the outbreak of war a respectable bank official, standing on the floor of the House of Commons pointing a loaded revolver at Oliver Cromwell. However, despite the ludicrous nature of what he was doing, it had to be admitted that he seemed to be having the desired effect. Nobody seemed terribly interested in doing anything just at that moment. The entire House was frozen, like a group of statues assembled by a dangerously eccentric collector.

What eventually happened was Blondel made a jump for it, a halberdier standing to his immediate right – not the one with the copy of Bracton, a different one – took a mighty slash at his head with a large sword, and Guy, more by way of a nervous twitch than with malice aforethought, pulled the trigger. There was a loud bang (the acoustics of the House are excellent) and everybody started yelling at once. Oddly enough, the only thought passing through Guy's mind was 'Oh fuck, I've shot Cromwell, Mr Ashton will never forgive me.' Mr Ashton had been Guy's history teacher, and was a great advocate of Cromwell and the seventeenth-century republican movement as a whole. In fact he had once lent Guy a copy of the collected works of John Lilburne, which Guy had always intended to read.

That was it, actionwise, as far as Guy was concerned, and the guard who had been stalking him for the last five minutes would have had no difficulty in grabbing and disarming him if he hadn't been hit over the head with the Great Mace of England first.

'Come *on*,' Blondel shouted in his ear. 'This way.'

A moment later the door marked *Staffe onlie* had closed behind them and three guards were unsuccessfully trying to lever it open with their halberds. Cromwell, meanwhile, picked up his hat and dusted it off. There was a hole in it. Pity. New hat, too.

'Order!' he shouted.

The halberdiers stood up, looked at their bent spearheads, shrugged and returned to their posts. The Long Parliament sat down. Cromwell resumed his seat.

'Well anyway,' he said, 'that's got rid of the mace.'

★

The negotiations had reached a critical stage.

With a practised hand the senior partner motioned a waiter to bring a fresh pot of coffee and five more pipes of tobacco.

'But if we withdraw all our clients' money from the South Sea Company,' the broker was saying, 'isn't that going to cause a crisis of confidence?'

'Maybe,' said the senior partner. 'So what?'

'But ...' The broker, lost for words, waved his hands about. His colleague took up the argument.

'If the public get the idea that there's something wrong with the South Sea Company,' he said, 'the effects could be catastrophic. There would be an immediate collapse. The economy of the nation – of Europe even – would —'

The senior partner cut him short with a wave of his hand. 'Listen,' he said, 'Mr, er ...'

'Smith,' said the broker's friend, 'Adam Smith.'

'Mr Smith,' the senior partner went on, 'you haven't answered my question. So what? All your funds will be safely invested in Second Crusade 67% Unsecured Loan Stock. What possible difference will it make to you if the whole British economy crumbles away into dust?'

Mr Smith's lower lip quivered slightly. 'But that's —' he started to say.

'In fact,' the senior partner went on, 'what could be better, from your point of view? Sell now, reinvest, buy back at the bottom of the market, make a double killing. The wonderful part of it is that, thanks to the unique facilities offered by our Simultaneous Equities Managed Fund, your money can be invested in both the Second Crusade and the slow but steady regrowth of the British economy at the same time. Well, concurrently, anyway. There is a technical difference, but I don't want to blind you with science.'

'I ...' Mr Smith stuttered, but his friend the broker stopped him.

'Actually,' he was saying, 'I rather like the sound of that.'

The senior partner smiled. 'That's the spirit,' he said. 'Now, if we can move on to the topic of life assurance, we offer a wide range of tailor-made retrospective endowment policies which —'

'Hold on,' Mr Smith interrupted, 'hold on just a moment.'

The partners turned and looked at him. 'Well?' they said.

'Gentlemen.' Mr Smith calmed himself down into an effort. 'You may not be aware of this,' he said, 'but I am by profession a student of economic theory; in fact, I pride myself on being on the verge of a breakthrough in monetary analysis which will, I sincerely believe, revolutionise the practice of economic planning in Europe, and my view is —'

'You mean,' said the senior partner slowly, '*The Wealth of Nations*?'

Smith's jaw dropped. 'You've heard of my book?'

'Naturally.'

'But that's impossible,' Smith replied. 'Why, I only completed the final draft today. In fact, I have it with me now. I'm taking it to my publisher.'

The senior partner smiled politely. 'You have the actual manuscript with you?' he said.

Smith, in spite of himself, could feel a glow of pride creeping over his face. It had been a long time since anyone had taken him seriously, since he'd been shown the proper respect his genius merited. 'I do indeed,' he said.

'Really!' The senior partner's manner changed; he became deferential. 'I have indeed heard of your work, Mr Smith,' he said. 'The word "seminal" would not be an overstatement.' Smith blushed. 'In fact, I would go further and say that your book brings the Dark Ages of economics to an end. May I see?'

After a very brief moment's hesitation, Smith dived into his battered brown bag and produced a manuscript. It was thick, dog-eared and bound up in red string. He handed it to the senior partner, who threw it on the fire.

'Now then,' he said, 'we offer a wide range of tailor-made retrospective endowment policies which ...'

'You really must learn,' Blondel said, 'to be more careful with that thing.'

'I wasn't —'

'I mean,' Blondel said, 'it's a nice trick if you can do it, but there are some people who have very pointy tops to their heads. You could injure somebody that way, you know.'

'It wasn't —'

'Anyway,' Blondel leaned against the wall and caught his breath. 'I don't think they're following us, do you?' he panted.

'No.'

'Splendid. Now, where are we, do you think?' He produced his little book and began to study it. Guy, who had got out of the habit of running shortly after leaving school, leaned with his hands on his knees and gasped for air.

'Blondel,' he said, 'I nearly killed Oliver Cromwell.'

'I know,' Blondel replied. 'Now, I make that the Un-American Activities archive over there, so if we head due south ...'

'I nearly changed the history of the world.'

'Then we can take a short cut through the New Deal, which ought to bring us out where we want to be. Sorry, you were saying?'

'History,' Guy repeated. 'I could have really messed it up, you know?'

'Exactly,' Blondel replied. 'Very volatile stuff, history. Give you an example. You tread on a fly. The fly is therefore not available to walk all over your great-great-great-great-grandfather's breakfast, and so he fails to die of food poisoning. Your family therefore does not sell up and move from Cheshire to Norfolk, with the result that your great-grandfather doesn't meet your great-grandmother at a whist drive, and you don't get born. That means you never existed, so you can't travel back through time and squash that fly in the first place. Result: your great-great-great-great-grandfather gets food poisoning, the family moves from Norfolk to Cheshire ...'

'Um.'

'And you,' Blondel went on, 'become a temporal anomaly, zipping in and out of existence like the picture on a television screen, thousands of times a second. Then you start to cause real problems, because of the knock-on effect and Ziegler's Mouse, and you end up with the Time Wardens after you.'

'Time Wardens.'

'Like game wardens,' Blondel explained, 'only with even more sweepingly wide powers. They won't be appointed for a hundred years or so yet, but when they are they'll travel back and start rounding up all the Loose Cannons.'

'Loose Canons,' Guy repeated. 'Is that some kind of religious order?'

'Not quite,' Blondel replied. 'You're thinking of the Giggling Friars, which is odd enough in its way, because they were all wiped out by the Time Wardens in about six hundred years' time. The Wardens have been looking for me since before I was born,' he added, 'or at least they will be. Actually, they're not a problem. It's the bounty hunters you've got to be wary of. Now, I think that if we go along this passage here, we'll come to a sharp left bend which should ... ah, here we are.'

As far as Guy was concerned it was just another tunnel, but Blondel seemed to recognise it at once. He said, 'Nearly there,' several times, and whistled a number of tunes, including *Stardust* and *The Girl I Left Behind Me.*

'History,' he was saying, 'is fluid: you've got to remember that. It's changing all the time, what with the Loose Cannons and the Time Wardens and the Editeurs Saunce Pitie. Now then, if I press this lever here ...'

A door opened, and Blondel walked through it.

Experience, the psychologists say, is like a man who walks into a lamppost, knocking himself out. When he comes round, the blow has caused a partial memory loss, which means that the victim forgets, inter alia, that colliding with lampposts causes injury. He therefore continues walking into lampposts for the rest of his unnaturally short life.

'Blondel,' said Guy, but Blondel wasn't there any more. He shrugged and followed.

*'L'amours dont sui epris
Me semont de chanter,'*
Blondel sang. A few passers-by threw small coins into

81

his hat, but otherwise nobody took a great deal of notice.

'Oh well,' he said at last, 'he doesn't seem to be here. Right, what about a drink?'

Guy had tried to explain to Blondel that there wasn't in fact a castle at the Elephant and Castle; that it was, to the best of his recollection, something to do with a mispronunciation of the Infanta of Castile; that even if there ever had been a castle here, there was highly unlikely to be one still here in 1987; and that even if there was one in 1987 they'd come up in the tube station instead. He'd done his best to convey all these things, and he didn't believe that 'That's what you think' was a satisfactory rejoinder. On the other hand, the idea of a drink sounded splendid, and he said as much.

'You're on, then,' Blondel said. 'Watch this.'

He laid his hat down beside him, produced his lute and sang some more songs, ones that Guy hadn't heard before and which he didn't like much. His view was not, however, shared by the passers-by, and they soon had a hatful of coins which Blondel judged to be adequate for the purpose in hand.

'There used to be a rather nice little Young's pub just round the corner from here,' he said. 'Nice beer, but the only way you could ever get on the pool table was to nip back through time and get your money down before the previous game started. Let's give it a try, shall we?'

'Used to be,' Guy repeated. 'When was that?'

'When I was last here.'

'1364?' Guy asked. '1570?'

Blondel grinned. '1997, actually. Like I always say, doesn't time fly when you're having fun?'

They wrapped Blondel's sword and Guy's revolver in a blanket to avoid being arrested and walked round the corner to the *Nine Bells*. As they sat down and tasted their beer, Blondel smiled.

'That's one of the advantages of my lifestyle,' he said. 'You get a better angle on progress.'

Guy wiped some froth from his lips. 'Come again?' he said.

'You know what I mean,' Blondel replied. 'You know how, as you get older, the beer never tastes as good, the policemen get younger every year, that sort of thing. Now I do my return visits in reverse chronological order whenever I can, so I get the opposite effect; yummy beer, geriatric policemen, and the last time I was here it was thirty pence a pint more expensive. Drink up.'

Guy drank up. It made him feel very slightly better.

'I suppose,' he said, 'I must be in my seventies by now. That's if I survive the War.'

'Quite so,' Blondel replied. 'There's an outside chance you might meet yourself, you never know. That's why it's so important not to get chatting about the War with old men in pubs.'

Guy nodded. 'Unless,' he said, 'I remember I was here before, of course. Then I'd know, I suppose.'

'Don't count on it,' Blondel said. 'I knew a chap once who met himself. Actually – he was a terribly clumsy sort of fellow, you see – he accidentally pushed himself under a train. It was his future self that got killed, of course, not his time-travelling self. Tragic.'

Guy looked up from his beer. 'What happened?'

'Poor chap,' Blondel said, 'went all to pieces. I said to him, Listen, George, it's no use living in the past.

But Jack, he said, I haven't really got any bloody choice in the matter, have I? In the end, the Editeurs came for him. It was the only thing to do.'

'Who are the —'

'Never you mind,' Blondel said. 'It'd only worry you. I think we have time for another.'

He went to the bar and returned with more beer.

'Blondel,' Guy asked, 'is that where ghosts come from?'

'Sorry?'

'Ghosts,' Guy said. 'Are they people who've got – well, lost in time? I mean, it sounds as if they could be people who've —'

'Nice idea,' said Blondel, 'but not really, no. Ghosts are something quite different. I'll tell you all about that some other time. Now then let's have a look at the schedule.'

He produced a tattered envelope, on the back of which was a long list written in minuscule handwriting. About a fifth of the entries were crossed off. Blondel deleted another three, and Guy noticed that three more added themselves automatically at the end. He asked about it.

'Automatic diary input,' Blondel explained. 'When I go to a place/time, it doesn't mean I've dealt with it once and for all. It just means that it goes to the back of the queue. However, I'm pleased to say we're more or less on —'

'Is this seat taken?'

A shadow had fallen across the table. Guy looked up and saw three men. They were dressed in smart charcoal grey suits and had dark grey hair. It was hard to tell them apart. They could easily have been brothers; triplets, even.

Blondel glanced up, smiled and said, 'Hello there, Giovanni, fancy meeting you here. Yes, by all means, take a pew. What'll you have?'

Guy stared. For some reason which he couldn't quite grasp, he could feel his hand walking along the seat on its fingertips towards the blanket.

'That's all right,' said Giovanni, 'Iachimo will get them. Same again?' He sat down, strategically placed between Guy and the blanket. Guy had the feeling that he'd done that on purpose.

'That'll be fine,' Blondel was saying. 'Guy, how about you?'

Guy said yes, that was very kind. One of the three went to the bar; the other one sat down next to Blondel and produced a cigar.

'We just missed you last time you were here,' Giovanni said. 'Marco, offer these gentlemen a cigar.'

'Your local, is it?' Blondel asked.

'Not really,' Giovanni replied. 'But we look in from time to time. Handy for the office, you know, meeting clients, that sort of thing.'

Blondel nodded. 'That's right,' he said, 'I forgot. Beaumont Street's just across the way, isn't it?'

Giovanni smiled. 'Well then,' he said, 'it's been a long time, hasn't it?'

'Quite,' Blondel replied. 'It must be —'

'Eight hundred years, exactly,' said Giovanni. 'To the day, in fact.'

'Is it really? Doesn't time —'

'Eight hundred years,' Giovanni went on, 'since you skipped out on us. Welched on your contract. Left us in a most unfortunate position.'

Blondel smiled. 'I don't think you've met my

colleague, Mr Goodlet,' he said. 'Guy Goodlet, the Galeazzo brothers; Giovanni, Iachimo, Marco. They're in the ...', Blondel considered for a moment, '... the timeshare business. And other things too, of course.'

The Galeazzo brothers turned and looked at Guy. Then they turned back and looked at Blondel, who was still smiling.

'Mr Goodlet,' he said, 'is a historian. In fact, he's with the History Warden's Office. Something to do with the fiscal division, aren't you, Guy?'

Some last vestige of native wit prompted Guy to sit still, say nothing and try and look very much indeed like a souvenir from Mount Rushmore.

'I see,' Giovanni said. 'No doubt he's got some means of identification.'

'Indeed I do,' Guy said. 'Would you like to see it?'

'If you don't mind.'

Guy nodded. 'I'll just get it,' he said. 'It's in that blanket over there, so if you'll just excuse me ...' He leaned across Marco, fumbled in the blanket, found his revolver and pressed it into Marco's side, discreetly below table level. Blondel thought for a moment, and then put his hat on Marco's head. Marco didn't move.

'Believe me,' Blondel said, 'you're much safer that way.'

After a long and slightly uncomfortable silence, Giovanni sighed and said, 'That's all very clever and impressive, but it doesn't really get us anywhere, does it?'

Blondel shrugged.

'I take it,' Giovanni went on, 'that your friend isn't actually a historian?'

'Correct,' Blondel smiled. 'Nor is he a top-notch marksman. At this range, however —'

'Yes, all right, I think you've made that point,' Giovanni scowled. 'Violence really isn't our way, you know,' he said. 'The last resort of the incompetent, and all that.'

'In which case, gentlemen,' Blondel replied, 'I think you probably qualify. Good Lord, is that the time?'

'All right,' Giovanni said, 'point taken. We have an offer.'

'I know all about your offers,' Blondel replied. 'Please don't try and stop us. I'm very fond of that hat, and another hole in it will leave it fit only for the dustbin. Thanks for the drink.'

He stood up and took hold of the blanket. Giovanni shook his head.

'We can help you find what you're looking for,' he said. 'That is, provided you're prepared to help us.'

Blondel raised one eyebrow. Then he sat down again, the blanket across his knees. To a certain limited extent, he looked like Whistler's Mother.

'The last time I listened to you gentlemen,' he said, 'I ended up with my face all over thirty thousand imitation satin surcoats.' He frowned. 'It's taken me eight hundred years to get over that,' he said.

Giovanni shrugged. 'So maybe we overdid the merchandising,' he said. 'You're an artist. Deep down, you need to perform. You need to communicate to vast audiences. You have a duty to your public.'

'I haven't got a public,' Blondel replied. 'And I am decidedly not an artist. Artists wear berets and smocks and cut their ears off. Messire Galeazzo, you are talking through your hat, and that is a very risky thing to do while Mr Goodlet's anywhere in the vicinity. Good day to you.'

Giovanni shrugged. 'It's up to you,' he said. 'But if you do actually want to find the King...'

Blondel closed his eyes for a moment and then sighed deeply.

'All right, then,' he said. 'Let's hear it.'

'Well —'

Before Giovanni was able to say anything else, however, the side door of the pub flew open and three men burst in. They were wearing dark green anoraks and holding big wooden clubs. Having entered, they stopped still and looked around them. Nobody seemed particularly bothered by their presence.

'Oh, how *tiresome*,' Blondel said. 'You just wait there.'

He got up, pulled his sword out from under the blankets, rushed at the three men and cut their heads off. A head rolled across the floor, was deflected off the leg of a chair, and ended up with its nose against Guy's foot. He looked down, feeling sick, terrified and, above all, horribly conspicuous. He needn't have worried, however; nobody was looking at him, particularly.

Someone behind the bar started to scream. Blondel frowned.

'Right,' he said, 'I think we ought to be getting along.'

There is a wide dichotomy between actual truth and perceived truth; and if the actual truth about the history of the world is that it was just one of those things, that is not necessarily important or even relevant to the people responsible for making sure that it doesn't happen again. Of this latter group, a considerable number have offices at the Chastel des Larmes

Chaudes; and one of them in particular, having just had a report from his senior operations manager, was not happy at all.

'Idiot,' he said.

Mountjoy King of Arms was far too spiritual, in the widest sense of the term, to be upset by vulgar abuse. He flickered for an instant, like a table lamp in a thunderstorm, and carried on with what he'd been saying.

'After that,' he said, 'they gathered up the bits and came back.'

Julian II snarled and stabbed the arm of his chair with a pencil, snapping it.

'Sack the lot of them,' he said. 'I ask you, what is this world coming to? You send out your top men – supposedly your top men – and what do you get? Unseemly brawls in public houses. I want them all back in the filing department by this time tomorrow, do you hear?'

Mountjoy nodded. His Unholiness' outbursts of temper rarely lasted long, and he never remembered what he'd said afterwards.

'And meanwhile?' he asked.

'Good question.' Julian's face calmed down slightly – the act of thinking always had that effect on him – and he stroked his beard gently. Small flashes of blue fire crackled away into the air.

'So where are they headed now, do you think?'

'We don't know,' Mountjoy replied. 'However, we have at last got some information on the men who were with him.'

Julian lifted his head and nodded approvingly. 'That's rather more like it,' he said. 'What have you got?'

Mountjoy took out his notebook. 'One of them,' he said, 'is a British citizen by the name of Guy Goodlet.'

'Yes?'

'From the mid-twentieth century,' Mountjoy went on. 'Some sort of professional warrior. His family held land in Norfolk at the time of the Domesday Book, but they've always been what you might call small to middling yeomen. No particular antecedents.'

'That doesn't sound very promising.'

'No indeed. The other three men are in fact the Beaumont Street Syndicate.'

Julian looked up. 'Are they indeed?'

Mountjoy nodded. He had decided that there was no point in trying to cover it up. After all, he really had nothing to hide. When he'd invested his small savings in the Beaumont Street Renaissance Income Fund, he'd had no idea that they were mixed up in anything untoward.

'The Beaumont Street Syndicate,' Julian repeated. 'Well, well. How deeply do you think they're involved?'

'Too early to say,' Mountjoy replied. 'It might be,' he added cautiously, 'that their involvement is entirely innocent.'

'Well quite,' Julian replied, nodding. 'In fact, I expect we'll find that that's it, entirely. I mean, everybody's got to have a financial adviser, even Jean de Nesle. No law against it.'

'No indeed.'

'Just common sense, really.'

'Quite so.'

'Well, there you are, then,' Julian said. 'Nevertheless,' he added, 'we'd better keep an eye on them. Discreetly, of course. Wouldn't want to start a scare on the Exchanges, would we?' He laughed brightly. 'Right, you get that in hand straight away. Put Pursuivant on to it, why don't you? He's got more brains than the others. I've even known him switch on a light without blowing all the fuses. Oh, and Mountjoy ...'

'Yes?'

'I wonder if you'd mind just sending a fax for me. To my broker, you know,' Julian said. 'Just a little bit of personal business.'

'Blondel.'

'Testing, testing, one, two, three,' said Blondel. 'Yes?'

Guy frowned. He didn't want to appear faint-hearted or anything like that, but he felt he had a right to know. 'Those people,' he said. 'You know, in that pub?'

Blondel thought for a moment. 'Oh,' he said, 'you mean in that pub in the Elephant and Castle?'

'That's right,' Guy said. 'After we'd been sorting things out with the Lombards; the men who came in and ...'

'Got you, yes,' Blondel said. He peered at the micro-phone and blew into it, giving rise to a sound like God coughing. 'What about them?'

'It's nothing, really,' Guy replied. 'It's just ... well, does that sort of thing happen very often? Because first there was the fight we had with the man when we followed the stag, and then that business in the Houses of Parliament, and now this ...'

'The Houses of Parliament thing was different,' Blondel said. He adjusted the microphone stand slightly and tightened up the little clips. 'They were just ordinary guards. Must be an awful job, I always think, being a guard. Complete strangers forever hitting you and so forth.'

'But the other ones,' Guy persisted. 'What about them?'

Blondel shrugged. 'I don't really know all that much about them myself. They just keep turning up and trying to attack me. They're not very good at it, as you'll have seen for yourself. Their arms and legs don't seem to ... well, to work properly, if you know what I mean. They've been doing it for as long as I can remember.'

'How can you tell?' Guy asked. 'That it's the same lot, I mean.'

'Easy,' Blondel replied. 'It's always the same people. They never seem to get a day older, you know. Been jumping out on me for years, some of them have.'

'Have you tried finding out who they are?'

'What, from them, you mean? No point.'

'Why not?' Guy asked. 'Do they refuse to talk, or something?'

Blondel scratched his ear. 'It's not that,' he said, 'far from it. It's just that when you try questioning them, they go all to pieces.'

'Perhaps if you tried, I don't know, being a bit less intimidating ...'

'No, you don't understand,' Blondel said. 'When I say they go all to pieces, I mean all to pieces. If you don't duck pretty sharpish, bits of them hit you. Legs, kidneys, that sort of thing.'

Guy stared. 'You mean they ...?'

'Blow up, yes. Now, where does this wire go?' He traced the course of the wire to the back of a huge amplifier and pulled it out. 'There,' he said, 'that's better. Never could be doing with all this gadgetry.' He picked up the microphone and tapped it. Silence. 'I always reckon that if you can't make them hear you at the back of the hall then you shouldn't call yourself a singer. Why they blow up, of course, I haven't the faintest idea, but they do. The odd thing is that it can't do them much harm, because a month or so later they come bouncing back, club in hand . . .'

'You're telling me,' Guy said, 'that the same men who blow up . . .'

'That's right,' Blondel said. 'Anyway, that's all I know about them. Except, of course, that they're something to do with the Chastel des Larmes Chaudes. They've got the Chastel livery, you see.'

'Fine,' Guy said. 'So what's the . . .?'

But Blondel had gone off to disconnect the boom mikes, and Guy thought it was best to leave it at that. The hell with La Beale Isoud, he had decided. If there was any way he could get back to his own time, he'd do it. If not, well, he'd have to settle down here (wherever here was) and get a job. But no more of this being jumped on by strange exploding assassins. Not his cup of tea at all.

'Now where's he gone?' said a voice behind him. It was Giovanni, the senior partner.

'He went off to look at something,' Guy replied. 'Something technical, after my time. Look, can I ask you something?'

Giovanni raised an eyebrow. 'What can I do for you?' he asked.

'It's like this,' Guy said. 'Have you known Blondel long?'

Giovanni grinned. 'Yes,' he said.

Guy nodded. 'All this stuff, about time travel and the civil service and Richard the Lion-Heart. It's not for real, is it?'

'I'm sorry?'

'I mean,' Guy said, 'it's not actually true, is it? None of this is actually happening, or about to happen or whatever; it's all just ...'

Giovanni had both eyebrows raised. 'Of course it's *true*,' he said. 'What a very peculiar thing to suggest. After all, here you are experiencing it; it must be true, don't you think?'

'I ...' Guy rallied his thoughts. 'I just find it hard to accept,' he said, looking out over the auditorium, 'that I'm here with the court poet of Richard the First, who's about to give a concert in a specially built auditorium somewhere in the middle of the Hundred Years War. With a public address system,' he added, 'which makes the sort of thing we have back in my own century look like two cocoa tins and a length of string. I mean, you'll understand my being a bit confused.'

'Indeed I do,' Giovanni said. 'And I think I can help.'

'You can?'

Giovanni smiled. 'I believe so,' he said. 'What you're really saying is that you're worried.'

'Extremely worried.'

'Perfectly understandable,' Giovanni said. 'After all, you can't be expected to know what's going to happen next. You've absolutely no way of knowing, from one moment to the next, what the future, immediate or long-term, has in store for you.'

'Exactly,' Guy said. 'So perhaps ...'

94

'What you need,' Giovanni said, 'is your own personal pension scheme. Now it so happens ...'

It had taken a long time.

Well, it would, wouldn't it, if all you had to dig with was the handle of a broken spoon, and the wall was thirteen feet thick and made of a particularly hard sort of toughened silicon.

And then there was the problem of disposing of the dust and the rubble; you can't just leave it there, or the guards will notice and get suspicious. You have to stash it somewhere out of sight. The prisoner had eventually hit on the idea of stuffing it into bags and hanging them from the roof, where it was so dark that nobody could see them. But the only materials he had for making bags from was spiders' webs – it takes literally hundreds of miles of spiders' web to weave three inches of reasonably strong thread – and the skins of rats. He had, over many years, found out that his cell produced only enough food for one spider and one rat to live on at any one time. But one thing that the prisoner had plenty of was time; and while he was waiting for the spiders to spin another few inches of gossamer and for the rats to die of old age, he could always get on with the digging.

And now he was almost through. Another half inch, no more, stood between him and whatever it was that lay on the other side of the wall. If he really got stuck in and put his back into it, he'd be through in five years, or six at the very latest. He was virtually free already ...

He was just about to set to work when he heard footsteps in the corridor outside. Hurriedly the prisoner dropped the spoon-handle back into the hole he'd gouged in the floor for a hiding-place, and sat on it. The door opened.

'Afternoon,' said the jailer.

'Afternoon,' replied the prisoner affably. He was always careful to be as pleasant as he could with the staff. After all, it couldn't be a wonderfully exciting and fulfilling job working in a place like this, and the prisoner was the sort of man who thought about such things.

'I've got some good news for you,' said the jailer. 'The bloke in the cell next to you's just died.'

The prisoner went as white as a sheet. Since he hadn't seen daylight for a very, very long time now, this wasn't immediately apparent to the jailer.

'Which side?' the prisoner asked.

'Sorry?'

'On which side was his cell?'

'That one,' the jailer replied, and pointed. The prisoner's heart started to beat again. Not the side he was digging on, thank goodness!

'Got to be that side,' the jailer continued, ''cos there isn't a cell the other side. The other side's the exterior wall of the castle. Anyway,' he went on, 'your neighbour's just snuffed it.'

'Ah,' said the prisoner. This was supposed to be good news, and the prisoner could see nothing pleasant in the news that a man had just died, even if it was a man he'd never even heard of before.

'And the good news,' the jailer went on, 'is that that means his cell's now empty. We can move you in there straight away.'

'But ...'

'You'll like it,' the jailer said. 'It's got a lovely south-facing aspect,' he went on. 'Bigger than this one, too; you'd have – oh, six inches at least more living area. Open plan. The door doesn't squeak, either, and it's ever so quiet and peaceful. It's even got a window.'

'I —'

'Well,' said the jailer, 'maybe that's a bit of an exaggeration. What I mean is, the door isn't exactly flush, and so when there's a lamp lit out in the corridor, that means that a little crack of light gets in under the door. Now isn't that something?'

'Yes, but I —'

'Kept it lovely, he did,' the jailer went on blithely. 'The bloke who's just died, I mean. He did this nice sort of mural thing all over the walls with chalk. Sort of pattern of bunches of six lines down and one line through them. Simple, if you know what I mean, but sort of striking.'

'Yes, but I can't —'

The jailer smiled. 'That's all right,' he said. 'I know what you're going to say, but really, no problem. You've never been any trouble, you haven't, not like some of them, and you've always had a cheerful word for me and the kids of a morning. We appreciate that sort of thing in the prison service, believe you me. So this is my way of saying thank you. I mean, if we can't help people out sometimes, what sort of a world is this, anyway?'

'But ...' The prisoner couldn't help turning and looking into the darkness at where his tunnel, which had occupied his waking and sleeping thoughts for so long now that he couldn't remember a time when ...

On the other hand, a voice said at the back of his

mind, this gentleman is being extremely kind and generous, doing his best to be helpful, and even when people do things for you and give you things that you don't actually want, you must always remember that it's the thought that counts. Anything else would be sheer ingratitude.

'Thank you,' said the prisoner. 'Thank you ever so much.' He looked round for the last time. 'I'll just say goodbye to my rat and I'll be right with you.'

The concert had been a success.

Nominally, it was a charity gig, with all the proceeds going to finance a last-ditch attempt to turn back the tide of Islam and recapture Jerusalem; hence the name of the organisation – CrusAid – and the stalls at the entrances to the auditorium selling a wide range of official souvenir missals, holy relics and I-Forcibly-Converted-The-World surcoats. In reality, CrusAid was a wholly-owned subsidiary of Clairvaux Holdings, the property arm of the United Lombard Group of Companies, which in turn was a satellite corporation of the Second Crusade Investment Trust (established 1187) into which the Beaumont Street Syndicate funnelled the accumulated capital of the centuries. By the time the proceeds reached SCIT, however, the money had been not so much laundered as washed in the blood of the Lamb.

In spite of all that, however, they came in their thousands from all over Christendom, and when Blondel sang *O Fortuna Velut Luna, Imperator Rex Graecorum, Aestuans Intrinsecus* and other numbers from his 1186 hit missal *Carmina Burana*, they had to be forcibly restrained by the Templar security guards from ripping up the seats and setting fire to them.

Afterwards, Giovanni came backstage. He looked exhausted and his hands were black with silver oxide from helping his brothers count the takings. They had had to hire fifteen mules and three hundred Knights Templar to transport the money to Paris to be banked.

'Blondel,' he said wearily, 'that was great. I mean really great. Stupendous.' He sat down heavily on a chest and massaged his wrists.

'Good,' said Blondel absently, towelling his damp hair. 'Can we be getting on now, please?'

'I'm sorry?' Giovanni said.

'Well,' Blondel replied, 'there's no point in hanging about here, is there? I thought you said you wanted me to do several concerts.'

'Yes,' said Giovanni, 'but not now, surely. I mean ...'

'No time like the present,' Blondel said, 'if you'll pardon the expression. When to?'

'Now hang on a minute ...'

Blondel shook his head. 'We had a deal,' he said. 'I was to do a certain number of concerts, and then you'd tell me what you know about the Chastel des Larmes Chaudes. You didn't say anything about intervals between the concerts. I just want to get all this fooling about over and done with and then get back to work.'

Giovanni shuddered. 'Fair enough,' he said, 'but –'

'But nothing,' Blondel replied firmly. 'Where's the next venue?'

Just then the door of the dressing room burst open, and in tumbled three large men in armour, all with that air of complete discomfort that comes from charging a door with their shoulders without first ascertaining whether or not it's actually locked. They grabbed at a table to try and stop themselves, succeeded only in turning it over, skidded across the flagstones, collided with the wall and fell over, stunned. On their surcoats they bore a coat of arms comprising a mitre argent on a sable field, a bend cross keys reversed gules, attired of the second. Blondel blinked, stood motionless for a second as if rapt in thought, and then grabbed a fire extinguisher and hosed them down until they were all thoroughly drenched in white foam.

'Now try it,' he said. 'Go on.'

The three men made various gestures. Their reactions suggested that what they'd expected would happen hadn't.

'Thought so,' Blondel said. 'I thought you wouldn't be able to blow up if you were all wet. Now, I think it's time we had a chat, don't you?'

'We're saying nothing.'

'All right, then,' Blondel replied grimly. 'Guy, shoot their hats off.'

'But they aren't wearing ...'

Blondel scowled, and then grabbed the headgear from the Lombard brothers and rammed it down over the ears of the prisoners. 'They are now,' he said.

Guy reached, rather hesitantly, for his revolver. One of the prisoners let out a howl of anguish and asked Blondel rather urgently what it was that he wanted to know.

'You could start,' Blondel said, 'by telling me where the Chastel des Larmes Chaudes is.'

The prisoner thought for a moment and then said 'Pursuivant, Sergeant at Arms, 87658765.'

'Come again?' said Blondel. 'Was that supposed to

be a map reference or something?'

'Name, rank and number,' Guy interrupted. 'It's all a prisoner of war has to tell you, under the Geneva Convention.'

'Which hasn't been signed yet,' Blondel replied. 'Mr Pursuivant, if you will insist on talking through your hat, perhaps you'll find it easier with a hole to talk through.'

'Pursuivant, Sergeant at Arms, 8765 —'

'Oh for pity's sake,' Blondel said. 'Go and make some custard, somebody.'

There was a baffled silence for a moment. 'Custard?' Giovanni eventually enquired.

'That's right,' Blondel said, 'custard.' He folded his arms, smiled, and leaned against the table.

'What's going on?' Pursuivant demanded querulously. 'What are you playing at?'

'You'll see,' Blondel replied. 'Now then, while we're waiting for the custard, would either of you two gentlemen care to tell me anything?'

'Clarenceaux, Sergeant at Arms, 987665723,' mumbled the shorter of the other two prisoners. His companion said nothing.

'Fine,' Blondel sighed. 'We'll do it the hard way if you wish. Anybody got any peanuts out there?'

'Here,' said Clarenceaux, but his companion told him to shut up. Blondel's smile widened into a wicked grin.

Giovanni came back with a large pudding-basin. 'You're in luck,' he said. 'Just by chance I found some in the kitchens of the Burger Knight stall. It's cold, I'm afraid, but ...'

'Oh that's all right,' Blondel said. 'Cold's fine. Now

101

then, one last chance. Any offers?'

Clarenceaux would have said something if his companion hadn't stamped viciously on his foot. Blondel made a sort of tutting sound and lifted Clarenceaux up by the collar of his kagoul.

'Sorry about this,' he said, 'but that's how it is. To a certain extent, of course, I admire your courage.'

'Courage?' Clarenceaux whimpered.

'Sorry,' Blondel replied. 'I should have said heroism. You see,' he went on, as he lifted the borrowed hat off the prisoner's head, 'when you're dealing with people who, every time they get beaten up, mutilated or killed, are somehow magically restored to life and health by their bosses, there's clearly not much mileage in conventional torture. But,' he said, tipping a copious amount of custard out on to the top of Clarenceaux's head, 'pain and death aren't the only things we're afraid of in this life. Oh no. There's also,' he said, flexing his fingers and massaging the custard into Clarenceaux's scalp, 'humiliation, embarrassment and being made to look a right nana. I mean – anybody got any jam? – I expect your comrades in arms are a right little bunch of humorists, aren't they? Once they get hold of something they can be funny about, you'll never – blackcurrant'll do fine, thanks – hear the last of it. And correct me if I'm wrong, but since you're effectively immortal, and stuck doing the same job with the same bunch of people for effectively the rest of time – that ought to do it; now, I'll need some flour, some eggs, some feathers and, of course, the peanuts and a razor – the very worst thing I could do to you would be send you back to Headquarters all covered in horrible sticky mess with half your beard shaved off and a

102

packet of peanuts down the back of your neck. Oh, I forgot the shoe polish.'

'All right,' Clarenceaux squeaked, 'all right, I give up.' His companion tried to jump at him but Guy hit him with the fire extinguisher and he sat down again. 'Just let me wash all this off and I'll talk.'

'After you've talked,' Blondel said. 'And any mucking about and it's the honey and feathers treatment for you. No, not honey,' he added. 'Treacle.'

Clarenceaux made a sort of rattling noise in the back of his throat. 'You wouldn't do that,' he gargled. 'That's ... that's not *fair*.'

Blondel grinned and shook his head. 'Let's have it,' he said. 'Where's the Chastel des Larmes Chaudes?'

'I —'

'Yes?'

Clarenceaux gagged, spat out a mouthful of custard which had dripped down his nose into his mouth and said, 'I don't know.'

'You don't know?'

'Really I don't.'

Blondel paused for a moment, while the prisoner watched him with big, round eyes.

'Have you thought,' Blondel said at last, 'what your so-called mates are going to do to you when you turn up later on this evening all covered in rice pudding and with a banana shoved right up your —'

'I don't *know*,' Clarenceaux screamed. 'We aren't allowed to know, just in case we're caught, see? There's this sort of bus thing picks us up and takes us to where we got to go, and then takes us back when we finish. They put paper bags over our heads while it's moving. Honest, I'm telling the truth.'

103

Blondel stroked his chin with the custard-free back of his hand. 'I don't believe you,' he said. 'Guy, see if you can find some rice pudding. Lots of rice pudding, there's a good chap.'

'Look, mister ...'

'And a banana, of course. Mustn't forget the banana.'

Clarenceaux started to sob, but Blondel's face remained unchanged. 'The Chastel,' he said. 'Where is it?'

'I don't ...'

'Got that rice pudding yet, Guy?' Blondel asked. Guy stood up. Where, he asked himself, was he expected to get rice pudding from at this ...?

'Leave him alone,' Pursuivant interrupted suddenly. 'Can't you see he's telling the truth?'

Blondel turned slowly round and looked Pursuivant in the eye. '*Lots* of rice pudding,' he said.

'It's the truth, I tell you,' Pursuivant whined. 'We don't know nothing, any of us. The bus just comes, and then it takes us away again after. It's a big grey thing,' he added desperately, 'with a duff exhaust.'

Blondel nodded and folded his arms, inadvertently getting custard on himself. 'Go on,' he said.

'What do you want to know?' Pursuivant asked.

'Well,' said Blondel, 'you could start with the number plate.'

'That's easy,' Pursuivant said. 'It's Z —'

Then something happened which Guy didn't expect. Giovanni, who'd been standing behind Blondel holding the pudding-basin full of custard, suddenly lifted it up, turned it over, and shoved it down on top of Blondel's head. As Guy moved to strike him, one of the others —

Iachimo, probably – threw the flour in his face and squirted an aerosol of whipped cream, which he apparently happened to have by him, in his eyes, leaving him momentarily blinded. The third brother, meanwhile, bundled the three prisoners to their feet and towards the door. Guy wiped cream furiously out of his eyes, gave Iachimo a shove that sent him reeling, pulled out his revolver and fired a shot at the retreating prisoners. There was a crash of splintering china, and the pudding-basin over Blondel's head split exactly in two and slid down over his shoulders to the floor. Giovanni was hit on the ear by a fragment of ceramic shrapnel, yelped and sat down heavily on a plate of mince pies. Iachimo had fallen into a laundry basket. The third brother, Marco, had jumped out of his skin when Guy fired his revolver, slipped on a patch of custard and collided with a standard-lamp, the shade of which fell down over his shoulders like a jousting-helm. The door closed with a bang, and from the corridor outside came the sound of hurried squelching, fading away into silence.

Blondel found a towel and wiped the custard out of his eyes and ears. 'Right,' he said, 'that's quite enough of that for one evening. Now then.'

He turned towards Giovanni, who cringed slightly, and Guy instinctively realised that, for all his dexterity with a pudding basin, the eldest Lombard was not primarily a man of action.

'It's all right,' said Blondel wearily. 'But what the devil possessed you to do that? The so-and-so was just about to ...' He checked himself, flicked a fragment of custard-skin irritably out of the corner of his eye, and sighed. 'I think I see. It's because that ... he was just

105

about to tell me the bit of information you lot know. And if he'd told me, you lot wouldn't have had any way of making me do those other confounded concerts.'

Giovanni had the grace not to meet Blondel's eye. He nodded. 'After all,' he said, 'it's not our money we put up to arrange those gigs. We've got a duty to . . .'

Blondel held up his hand. 'Please,' he said, 'spare me all that. The important thing now is to get on with it. You lot get all this mess cleared up and ready to go. I think I'd better wash my hair.'

He shook his head once more and started to walk towards the bathroom. Then he turned to Guy, who was standing holding his revolver as if it was a dead fish and gave him a very significant look.

'Practise a lot, do you?' he said, and left the room.

'Are you *sure* we're going the right way?' Giovanni asked.

'Positive,' Blondel replied. 'If you'd rather navigate ...'

Giovanni shrugged. Ever since the slight misunderstanding in the dressing room at the auditorium, there had been a slight coolness between Blondel and his agents, which the perennial map-reading debate wasn't helping. 'Not at all,' he said. 'Leave it entirely up to you. That way, if we end up in the Second Ice Age and get frozen to death, it won't be my fault.'

After that they went on in silence for a while, until they came to a quite indisputably dead end. The tunnel stopped leading anywhere, and there was just a wall.

'Well?' Giovanni said.

'Yes,' Blondel replied. 'Yes, on balance, I think you may have a point. Pity about that.'

They sat down and Giovanni produced a cigarette-lighter, by whose light Blondel studied his little book.

'I see,' he said after a while. 'What I thought was the Quattrocento was in fact the Enlightenment. One's marked blue on the map, you see, and the other's a sort of dark mauve. Easy to get them muddled up.'

Giovanni made a faintly contemptuous noise. 'So where are we, then?' he said.

'Well,' Blondel replied, 'if I'm right about where we went astray before, that wall is the Fall of Constantinople, so really we want to go back the way we came, turn left at the next interchange and keep on till we come out into the European Monetary System. How does that sound?'

There was a little muted grumbling, and Iachimo said something about next time it being easier just to go the long way round. They picked up their luggage and set off back down the tunnel. They had gone no more than a quarter of a mile when they came to another dead end.

'Oh, that's marvellous,' Giovanni said. 'Now what's happened?'

Blondel walked forwards and examined the obstruction. 'There's been a timeslip,' he said. 'We'll have to go back and find a way round.'

Guy asked what a timeslip was.

'Like a landslip,' Blondel explained, 'only more awkward if you're in a hurry. All that's happened is that the roof of the tunnel's caved in, and a slice of some other period has fallen through and is blocking the way. Someone from the Work of the Clerks' office'll be along sooner or later to patch it all up. Meanwhile —'

'Don't you mean Clerk of the Works?' Guy asked.

'I mean what I said,' Blondel replied, nettled. 'This whole network, you'll recall, is the work of generations and generations of government clerks. They have an unofficial agreement that when something goes wrong with the fabric, they take it in turns to fix it. Just as well, really. If nobody looked after it and it all started falling to pieces, you'd have massive timeslips all over the shop – it'd be chaos. Luckily they keep it all in quite good order. Now ...'

He broke off and stared at the obstruction in front of him. 'Hello,' he said, 'I don't like the sound of that.' He turned to Giovanni. 'What do you think?' he said.

'What?'

'Listen,' Blondel replied. 'Oh, how aggravating!'

Guy pushed his way past Iachimo and asked what was going on.

'I don't want to alarm you,' Blondel said, 'but I think this lot may be unstable. Listen.'

Guy listened. It was just as well, he told himself, that he had a firm grip on reality, because otherwise he might have believed that he was hearing little faint voices coming out of the wall of rubble in front of him.

'Hear them?' Blondel asked. Guy nodded. 'That's that, then,' he said firmly. 'Back the way we came, quick.'

They started to walk fast down the tunnel. The voices followed them, gradually getting louder; then, not so gradually, getting louder still. It was rather disturbing, in fact.

'Run!'

As he ran, Guy tried to hear what the voices were saying. Most of them were talking languages he couldn't understand – there was French, and a lot of Latin, and probably Spanish; just occasionally, though, someone said something in English. None of it sounded particularly cheerful, whatever it was. Guy ran faster.

'Come on,' Blondel was shouting, 'for pity's sake get a move on.' Guy looked up, but in the darkness of the tunnel he couldn't see where the others had gone. Meanwhile the voices were getting louder all the time. They seemed to fill up space behind him. He stumbled over something and nearly lost his footing, and as he staggered along he distinctly felt something fly over his head, shrieking in French as it went. After it came some Italian, and some Latin, and what sounded like Turkish. Guy kept his head bent low and tried to run faster, but there was a limit to what his muscles could achieve.

'*Dear Sir*,' something was yapping behind him, '*Dear Sir, Dear Sir.*' He could almost feel it, close on his heels. There were others with it, all saying the same thing, but in many different voices, high and low, old and young, male and female, friendly, unfriendly and very, very hostile.

'*G. Goodlet Esquire*,' they screamed, '*37 Mayflower Avenue Sutton Surrey Our reference Jay Oblique Three Seven Nine Dee Four Six Thirteenth October Nineteen Seventy One Dear Sir ...*' Guy put his hands over his ears but it didn't seem to make any difference. Some of it was coming from over his head anyway. Something inside him told him that if they once managed to get in front of him, that would be it. He somehow managed to run faster.

'*It has come to our attention*,' they screamed, '*that you have failed to complete an annual return for any fiscal year since Nineteen Forty Two.*' Guy started to howl, but he couldn't hear himself, only a lot of voices, very cold voices, saying '*You are reminded that interest at the statutory rate runs on all tax due and unpaid*

110

*within thirty days of the date of the respective assess-
ments.*' Something was holding on to the lobe of his ear
now, bending it back, and shouting directly at him,
'*Unless the prescribed forms are completed and returned
to this office within the next seven working days, we shall
have no alternative but to* ...' Then he lost his balance,
crashed into the wall of the tunnel, lurched hopelessly
and fell. A great wave of sound rolled over him, in
every language ever heard or read, physically crushing
him. He tried to move ...

Further up the tunnel, Blondel stopped and collapsed,
gasping, against the bulkhead door he had just managed
to slam shut. It was beautifully quiet here ...

'That was close,' he said.

Giovanni, huddled on the ground at his feet, interrupted his panting to make an indeterminate noise and
then rolled over onto his back. Iachimo and Marco had
fainted.

'Never mind,' Blondel said, 'all's that well that ...
Hello, where's Guy got to?'

Giovanni looked up. 'Who?'

'Guy Goodlet,' Blondel replied. 'You know, English-
man, doesn't like hats.'

'Oh,' Giovanni said, 'him. Lord knows. Fell over his
feet, I think.'

Blondel sighed deeply and slid down the door to the
ground. 'Oh *bother*,' he said. 'What a confounded
nuisance.'

'Well,' Giovanni replied, 'there's no point getting all
emotional about it. These things happen in time, you
know that.' He shrugged his shoulders. 'Just as well he
didn't take out any life cover after all,' he added.

111

Blondel gave him a disapproving look. 'What's that supposed to mean?' he asked.

Giovanni shrugged again. 'Look,' he said, 'the man's popped it. Got drowned in a timeburst. All very sad but there it is. There's absolutely nothing any of us can do about it.'

'You reckon?'

'Yes,' Giovanni said, 'I do. It's just one of those things. Look, shouldn't we be ...?'

But Blondel wasn't listening. He was very gingerly lifting the bar on the bulkhead door. Before Giovanni could stop him, he'd opened it. There was a sudden deafening roar of voices, and then the door slammed again, with Blondel on the other side of it.

'Hey ...' Iachimo had come round just in time to see. He tried to get to the door before it shut, but he was too late.

'Forget it,' Giovanni said. He was very white in the face, and shaking slightly.

'Giovanni,' Iachimo said, 'did you just see that? He deliberately —'

'I said,' Giovanni interrupted, 'forget about it.'

'Yes, but —'

Giovanni slapped his brother across the face. It worked; Iachimo calmed down a little. 'He's had it, too,' Giovanni said. 'Pity, after all that trouble we've been to, but there it is. Gone. That's it. No more Blondel.'

The three brothers sat there for some time, not saying a word, until at last Giovanni got to his feet and pulled the others to theirs.

'Come on,' he said, 'we've got work to do.'

'Work?' Iachimo looked at him with empty eyes.

'Giovanni, it was horrible, he just —'

'Work,' Giovanni repeated. 'Now.' His mouth quivered slightly. 'Or had you forgotten?'

'Forgotten what?'

Giovanni was grinning now. 'Forgotten that we've insured the bastard's life for fifty billion livres. Come on, let's find a notary.'

They got up and walked slowly down the tunnel. After a while, they all started whistling.

La Beale Isoud, having washed her hair and done her nails, wandered down into the Great Hall of the Chastel de Nesle and plugged in the hyperfax.

There have been many inventions that might have revolutionised the world if only someone had had the vision to invest in them at the crucial moment; one thinks automatically of the frictionless wheel, the solar-powered night storage heater (stores up warm summer evenings for winter use) and the Wilkinson-Geary hingeless door. The hyperfax was no less remarkable, technologically speaking, than any of these; but it differed from them in never having had a chance to be neglected. The prototype and all the blueprints and design specifications had vanished mysteriously from an office in the Central Technology Department of the Oceanian Ministry of Science back in 2987, and the design team were so dispirited by this setback that they forgot all about the project and went back to designing sentient sleeping policemen for the Road Traffic Department. The only working hyperfaxes now in existence are the original prototype, installed in the Chastel de Nesle, and the Mark IIb. Nobody has ever been able to find out what happened to the Mark IIb.

113

La Beale Isoud sat down and pressed the necessary keys. The screen flickered for a few moments and bleeped. The word

READY?

appeared. La Beale Isoud rubbed her palms together and nodded.

CAN WE START NOW?

La Beale Isoud shook her head. 'Let me just have a think, will you?' she said. 'I'm not sure what I want to send yet.'

YOU SHOULD HAVE THOUGHT OF THAT BEFORE

'Oh, nuts to you,' replied La Beale Isoud. 'Don't fluster me, or I'll never be ready. If you want something to keep you busy, you can print me out all the towns in Europe with a population of over ten thousand.'

There was a high-pitched screaming noise, and a stream of paper flew out of the side of the machine. It took about three seconds.

FINISHED

It is impossible for eight illuminated green letters to look smug, but somehow the word FINISHED managed it. The hyperfax was, after all, very good at faffing about with the laws of possibility.

'In alphabetical order?' Isoud asked sweetly.

NATURALLY

'Oh.' Isoud frowned slightly. 'Well done. Now do me

the same for every year between 1066 and 2065.

The machine beeped, and then started screaming again. Meanwhile, Isoud scratched her nose and tried to think of something that would be fun to do, but which wouldn't irritate the machine, which was inclined to be touchy.

FINISHED AGAIN

'Well aren't you clever!' Isoud said. 'Right, I'm all ready to start. Receive mode, please. Bring me ...' She made a random sweep of her subconscious mind '... a tail-feather from the Golden Phoenix of the Caucasus Moun —'

A bell rang, and a silver plate popped out of a door in the front of the machine. On it was a single green feather.

'Oh,' said Isoud. 'You might let me finish my sentence.'

SORRY, I'M SURE

Isoud picked up the feather, looked at it closely, sniffed it, sneezed and asked, 'Are you sure this is from —' The machine beeped at her. 'Sorry,' she said, 'sorry. It's just it's not, well, very special looking, is it?'

TOUGH

'I didn't mean to imply —'

DIDN'T YOU, THOUGH?

'No,' Isoud said patiently, 'I didn't. I just thought —'

READY?

'Oh don't sulk!'

'Now I've offended you,' Isoud said. 'I'm really very sorry and it's a lovely feather, really. Look, it just goes nicely with my scarf!'

YOU'RE JUST SAYING THAT

'No I'm not,' said Isoud, through gritted teeth. 'Now, why don't we forget all about it and you bring me something nice.'

SUCH AS?

'Oh,' said Isoud, 'I don't know. Strawberries. An ice cream. Violets. Anything. Use your bloody imagination.'

TOGETHER OR SEPARATELY

Isoud's fingernails dug into her fine lawn handkerchief. 'Separately, please.'

WRAPPED?

'If you like, yes.'

The bell rang, the door opened, and a little spring began firing strawberries, individually wrapped in silver foil and ribbon, straight at Isoud, who ducked. Then came the ice cream, which fortunately she was able to avoid, followed by a bombardment of violets, which burst on hitting the opposite wall and went everywhere.

'Thanks,' Isoud said grimly when it was all over. 'Now can I have a vacuum cleaner, please?'

The bell rang, and a beautiful chrome-plated Electrolux rolled out and sat at her feet. It too was festooned in ribbon, which managed to get tangled up with the lead.

Isoud sighed. The hyperfax was all very well in its way, but she could see now why they'd said it needed working on before it was ready for mass market release. 'All right,' she said. 'Switch from receive mode to transmit mode, please. I want to send all this lot back.'

SUIT YOURSELF

The door opened, and a great wind blew through the hall. A few moments later, the feather, the strawberries, the ice cream, the violets and the hoover had all gone. So had two cushions and the heel of one of Isoud's shoes, but she knew better than to try and make something of it. She thanked the machine, decided that she would far rather get on with her embroidery instead, and stood up to switch it off at the mains.

Then the little bell rang again, and a man fell out of the door, rolled round on the carpet a couple of times and came to rest under the sideboard. He lay there very still. The screen read:

STILL RECEIVING

'Really!' Isoud said, irritably. 'Please prepare to transmit immediately!'

The screen flickered – a sort of digital shrug – and the man was dragged slowly back the way he had come. As his head collided with the leg of the table he let out a pitiful howl and Isoud, on impulse, pressed the Pause button. The screen went insufferably blank.

'Ouch,' said the man.

Isoud looked down at him. 'Mr Goodlet, isn't it?' she said. 'Would you care for some tea?'

117

Blondel woke up, hauled himself painfully to his feet, and looked at the notice. It said:

THIS WAY

That didn't seem to make a great deal of sense. From what little he could see of his surroundings, he was in the middle of a huge empty space, and the only light was a sort of pale glow around the notice; there was no sign of any roof, sky, walls or anything helpful like that, and there was nothing in the notice itself to suggest which way was the way referred to. On the other hand, he instinctively felt, this wasn't the time to start making difficulties. He had just, as far as he could judge, drowned in time, and the best thing to do was probably keep a low profile, just in case he was really supposed to be dead.

The scabbard by his side was empty, and a quick survey revealed that he had lost all the cherished little artefacts which he had collected over a very long life of time-travel: the map of the tunnel network, for example; the mirror which showed demons in their true shape; his all-purpose combined season ticket, identity card, passport, museum pass and phonecard; even his calculator watch and his comb. On the other hand, apart from a number of bruises and a nagging pain in his left wrist, he was reasonably undamaged, so the odds were still on his side. *Dum spiro spero*, and all that.

He decided to walk; in which direction he neither knew nor cared, now that he'd lost his matchbox with the compass in the lid. He set out brightly, on past the notice, into pitch darkness. He started to whistle; then it occurred to him that, since he had never been this way before he might just as well give it a shot, and he sang *L'Amours Dont Sui Epris.*

Another notice loomed up at him out of the darkness. It too seemed to be self-lit, and it said:

MAXIMUM HEADROOM 4′ 7″

Since it was at least ten feet high, it was obviously lying, and Blondel ignored it. If any of this was supposed to impress him, it wasn't going to work. He'd been in places that made this seem boringly normal.

A noise behind him – a sort of soft creaking – made him look round, and he saw a ship sailing past, about a hundred yards or so away. He had no reason to suppose that there was any water over there, or certainly not enough water to float a fifteenth-century Flemish merchantman, and so he put it out of his mind. Sure enough, the ship veered slowly away and vanished. Kids' stuff. If someone was doing this deliberately, they hadn't got beyond Grade II yet.

The gradient changed to a fairly steep descent, and Blondel realised that what he was walking on was waves; invisible, bone-dry, rock-solid waves. If he stood still, he could feel them rising and falling very slowly. An English privateer bobbed through the shadows at extreme range, but too far away for him to be able to pick out any identifying marks. He could, however, just make out what they were singing.

'*Por li maintaindrai l'us*
D'Eneas et Paris
Tristan et Pyramus
Qui amerent jadis.'

With an effort, Blondel closed his mouth, which had

119

fallen open, and then picked up his feet and started to run. The crew were singing:

'*Or serai ses amis*
Or pri Deu de la sus
Qu'a lor fin soie pris . . .'

. . . a bit he'd never been particularly fond of. He could make out the ship properly now; a heavy twin-castled long-distance flying the pennant of the Cinque Ports and the arms of Winchelsea. And they were singing:

'*L'amours dont sui epris*
Me semont de chanter.'

Blondel filled his lungs and shouted, 'Ahoy!' Well, why not? He waited. The ship was still going. Then it changed tack, slewing around slightly. There was a sort of flat-bottomed thud and he looked up to see that they had launched a boat. He stood up and waited.

'Are you all right?' The man in the boat was talking to him.

'Fine,' he shouted back. 'Why were you singing that particular song?'

'I'll throw you a line,' said the man. 'Tread water till I get to you.'

Blondel was about to comment but he thought No, why bother? He yelled back his thanks and stayed where he was. After a while, the boat came close enough for the man to throw him a length of rope, which he caught. Then he walked across to the boat and climbed in.

'Ahoy,' he said affably.

The man in the boat looked at him for a moment. He seemed very worried. 'Where are we?' he said.

Blondel smiled. The man didn't look like he was ready for this; but then, people who can't handle heavy answers shouldn't ask heavy questions. He decided to put it as gently as he possibly could.

'I can't say for sure,' he said, 'but I have a feeling that we're in the Archives.'

'The Archives,' the man repeated.

'That's right,' Blondel replied.

'You don't mean the Maldives?'

'No, not the Maldives,' Blondel answered. 'The Archives are quite different. Not that I'm sure, like I said. Did you sail off the edge of the world?'

The man nodded.

'I thought so,' Blondel said. 'Somebody told you the world was round, and that if you kept sailing due west you'd end up in India. A man in a pub, right?'

The man nodded again.

'And you thought about it, and you reckoned Yes, it must be, else the sea would all fall off the edge, and so you set out and you got to the edge and you fell off. Yes.'

'Yes.'

Blondel sighed. 'And all these other ships must have done the same, I suppose. That settles it. We're definitely in the Archives.' He thought about it for a moment. 'Pity, that,' he added.

The man gave him a long, deliberate stare. 'So where are we? I mean, is there any chance of getting back?'

'Your guess,' Blondel replied, 'is as good as mine. I got here another way, so maybe there is. On the other hand maybe there isn't, that's the trouble with this lot here. Nobody knows anything about it. Except that it exists, of course. Everyone's pretty definite about that.'

The man's two friends who had been rowing the

boat were beginning to get restless. 'I'm sorry,' Blondel said, 'maybe you'd prefer it if I left.'

'For God's sake, man,' said the man, 'tell me where the hell we are and stop fooling about.'

'You may not like it.'

'For God's sake . . .'

'Oh,' said Blondel. 'All right, then.'

History, as has been observed before, is constantly changing. This is partly due to the activities of irresponsible time-travellers; but mostly the changes are quite natural.

Consider leaves. For a while they hang about on trees; then they die, fall off and lie about on the ground. If nobody happens along to sweep them up, they rot down into a compacted mass and stay there until geological forces put heavy weights on top of them and turn them into coal. Later still, they become diamonds.

Just as the strata of the earth have faults in them, so does history; chunks of it get pushed out of shape, deformed or misplaced. In the same way that some leaves become coal and some become diamonds, so not all events decay in the same way. Some of them, in fact, go wrong. Badly wrong. In due course, they can become extremely unstable and accordingly hazardous.

The Archives are where events are stored which shouldn't have happened but did. It is impossible to be exact, but recent estimates suggest that they now occupy a much larger area of SpaceTime than the Orthodox or Correct course of history, and the number of reported leaks of excluded matter from the Archives into the Topside (as the Orthodoxy is called in theo-chronological jargon) increases alarmingly each year. To a certain extent this is due to the irresponsible and highly illegal exploitation of the mineral resources of the Archives by pirate chemical companies – most areas of Archive time predate the commercial use of fossil fuels, and so there are enormous untapped reserves of oil, coal and natural gas down there, but of course it is incredibly hazardous to bring it back – and the Time Wardens have recently been awarded Draconian powers to prevent the traffic. Unfortunately, their efforts so far have been less than successful, and the conclusion of their latest report – 'Whether it is possible to eradicate this menace, time alone can tell' – has been widely criticised as extremely unhelpful.

'You're having me on,' the man said.

'I didn't think you'd like it,' Blondel replied. 'Why were your crew singing that song?'

'Which song?'

'*L'Amours Dont Sui Epris,*' Blondel said.

'Is that what it's called?' the man said. 'Because it's a good song, I suppose; everybody knows the words and when you've got a ship full of men all on the point of complete and utter panic, I always find the best thing to do is sing something, terribly loudly. Look, does it matter?'

'You haven't,' Blondel persevered, 'seen Richard the Lion-Heart anywhere, by any chance?'

'Who?'

'Never mind,' Blondel said. 'It was only a thought. Look, I mustn't keep you. Thanks for everything.' He stood up and climbed out of the boat.

'Look . . .'

'Cheers, then!' Blondel waved, and started to walk.

'Come back!' the man yelled. 'Look, how do we get out of here?'

Blondel turned round and looked at him sadly. 'You don't,' he said. 'You never happened. Ciao.'

He walked on for a while, thinking deeply. It was logical, after all, that by stepping out into a timeslip as he had done, he would be swept into the Archives; presumably Guy was down here too somewhere, although quite possibly not in the same Archive. For all he knew, the poor chap was swanning around somewhere in the Trojan War, shooting the hats off Greek heroes. Blondel groaned; the last thing he needed was somebody else to look for. How, Blondel now asked himself, am I going to get out of here?

For a while he gave that some serious thought, but nothing brilliant occurred to him, and he decided not to let it worry him. At least he knew where he was, and he always found that that was the main thing. Once you'd got that sussed, in his experience, everything else fell into place somehow or another. He remembered the time he'd accidentally come up on the wrong side of the Day of Judgement. That had been a bit hairy, for a while, but he'd got away without any difficulty in the end, with the aid of a sheepskin rug and a great deal of charm. Whatever else he was, Blondel wasn't a worrier.

Far away in the distance he saw a light, and he started to walk towards it. As he approached it, the non-existent waves under his feet became clammy and smelt unpleasantly of chemicals. Strange.

He walked on, squelching now, and quite soon came to another notice. Whoever set up this Archive had been pretty conscientious about keeping people informed.

EXTREME DANGER

it said, and a little bit further down, in tiny little letters:

MEN AT WORK

Well indeed. Blondel stopped and scratched his head. Logic told him that it was highly unlikely that anyone could be bothered to do anything in an Archive; once you were here you were here, and either you found a way out or you got used to it. Anything in the way of industrial activity was counter-intuitive, to say the least. However, in the circumstances EXTREME DANGER probably wasn't to be taken at face value. When you have just been edited out of history and thus caused to cease to have existed, it's hard to think of anything that could actually make things worse.

About a hundred yards further on, he came to another notice. This one said:

HARD HAT AREA: NO ADMITTANCE

Blondel grinned; then he took off his belt and wrapped it round his right hand. When people didn't want you to go in somewhere, it usually meant there was something worth taking a look at.

He stepped forward, stopped suddenly, and rubbed his nose. He'd bumped into an invisible brick wall. More promising still.

Very cautiously, he felt his way along the wall until his sense of touch suggested that he'd come to a gateway; then he crouched down and waited. About a quarter of an hour later, a door opened and a man in a boiler-suit and a yellow hard hat came out and started to light a cigarette. Whatever it was they did in there, they weren't allowed to smoke while they were doing it.

Something dropped into place in Blondel's mind. He edged forward, tapped the smoker gently on the shoulder, and punched him.

Fortunately, the man's clothes fitted Blondel pretty well. He carefully stubbed out the cigarette, opened the door and walked in.

Inside, things were very different. There was light, for one thing; lots of it, coming from a battery of big white arc-lamps on a scaffolding tower, which loomed over a collection of huts and big machines. There was also a tall flame, rather like the flare from an oil well, rising up from a hole in what one could probably call the ground, although Flaubert would have found a more apt word for it. An illicit drilling station, of the sort that was causing all those headaches in the Time Warden's department. How very convenient.

There were a lot of men in boiler-suits and yellow hats scurrying about, and Blondel found no difficulty in blending in. He found a clipboard and wandered around for a while pretending to be bored. After the first half-hour, he didn't have to pretend very hard.

It was the tannoy that put the idea into his head; and once it was there it made quite a nuisance of itself. Left to himself, Blondel would have bided his time, slipped aboard the bus or whatever it was that took the workers back Topside when their shift was over, and gone on his way singing. As it was, the Idea insisted that he locate the site office, find the man with the microphone who worked the tannoy, stun him with the fire extinguisher and start singing *L'Amours Dont Sui Epris*

126

into the PA system. And, under normal circumstances, he'd probably have found a way of getting away with it. He'd been in worse scrapes than this before now and still been back home in time for *Cagney and Lacey*.

As it was, something happened which he hadn't bargained for.

Someone began to sing the second verse.

'Thank you,' Guy said.

'Milk?'

Guy nodded. La Beale Isoud picked up a little bone-china jug and fiddled about with it.

'Sugar?'

'Thanks, yes. Look ...'

'How many?'

'I'm sorry?'

'How many lumps? One? Two?'

Guy wrenched his mind back to where it should be. 'Two,' he said, 'thanks. Look, I hate to be a nuisance, but ...'

Isoud looked at him, and he realised that she was going to offer him something to eat. If he refused the biscuits she would offer him cake. Best not to fight it, said his discretion, just get it over with.

'Would you like a biscuit?' said La Beale Isoud. Guy nodded, and was issued with a rather hard ginger-nut. That seemed to be that.

'The weather,' La Beale Isoud said, 'continues to improve.'

'Good,' said Guy. He noticed that he was sitting in a low, straight-backed chair and wondered how the hell he'd got there. Instinct, probably.

'Are you interested in gardens, Mr Goodlet?'

enquired La Beale Isoud. Guy shook his head. 'A pity,' La Beale Isoud went on. 'We have rather a nice show of chrysanthemums this year.'

'What's happening?' Guy asked.

'We're having tea,' Isoud replied. 'Please do not make any sudden movements.'

'Oh, quite,' Guy said quickly, 'certainly not. My mother likes chrysanthemums,' he added. It was a lie, of course, but with luck she wouldn't notice.

'Another biscuit?'

'Yes, thank you.' Guy leaned slowly forward, picked up a ginger-nut and put it on his knee with the other one. He hadn't eaten anything for a very long time, he remembered. He fiddled with his teacup.

'I don't know how long my brother is likely to be,' said La Beale Isoud. 'He's terribly unpunctual, I'm afraid. Still, he's usually back around this time, if you'd care to wait a little longer.'

'If you don't mind,' Guy said. 'How did I get here?'

'I don't know,' said La Beale Isoud politely. 'I thought you might be able to tell me that.'

'Ah.' Guy stirred his tea for a moment and then raised the cup to his lips, without actually going so far as to drink anything. 'I fell over,' he said.

'Did you really, Mr Goodlet? How intriguing.'

'In a tunnel,' Guy went on. 'I was running away from a lot of voices which kept trying to ask me things about income tax, and I must have tripped over my feet and fallen over. And the next thing I knew, I was here. Something seemed to pick me up and . . .'

'I see,' Isoud said. 'In that case, the fax must have brought you. What a curious coincidence, don't you think?'

'Er,' said Guy. He looked up over his teacup and smiled. La Beale Isoud pursed her lips, as if trying to reach a decision, and then smiled back.

'Would you care to see some photographs?' she said.

Drink generally made Iachimo rather maudlin. Usually that was no bad thing; he was, Giovanni had long since realised, one of Nature's accountants, and anything which let his long-repressed emotions out of their cage and let them walk around and stretch their legs was to be encouraged, in moderation, so long as he didn't actually start to sing.

'I mean,' Iachimo said, 'we shouldn't just have left him like that. Really nice bloke, he was. Do anything for you. Lovely voice. Generous.'

'Gullible,' Giovanni said. 'Very, very gullible.'

'The most gullible bloke,' Iachimo agreed, 'you could ever hope to meet. Could have sold him anything. Anything.' He sighed. 'And now it's too late. Poor Blondel.' He reached for his drink and drank it.

'Never mind,' Giovanni said firmly. 'We've got to think of the future. I'm sure that's what he'd have wanted.'

Iachimo looked up unsteadily. 'You think so?'

'Absolutely,' Giovanni said. 'Blondel,' he went on, fixing his brother with a businesslike look, 'was an artist ...'

'Can you say that again?'

'An artist,' Giovanni repeated, 'and what do artists really want? They want —'

'Twenty-five per cent guaranteed return on capital,' said Marco. He was the dozy one, and they had had to teach him little set phrases, of which *twenty-five per cent guaranteed return on capital* was the longest by some way.

'No,' Giovanni said, 'that's where artists are different from you and me. Artists don't care about things like that, or at least,' Giovanni added, thinking of Andrew Lloyd Webber, 'most artists don't. What they care about is posterity, the opinion of future generations, their place in the gallery of fame.'

'Go on!'

'They do,' Giovanni said, 'and Blondel was an artist to his fingertips. Absolutely zilch use as a businessman, but give him a rebec and a mass audience, and there was nobody to touch him.'

'Too right,' Iachimo said. 'Bloody genius, that's what he was.'

'Exactly,' Giovanni replied, 'a genius, which is why we have a duty to continue marketing his material just exactly the way we did while he was alive. In fact,' he added, thinking of Blondel's lapsed five per cent share of royalties, 'even more so. With a genius, you see, the real appreciation comes after they die.'

'Really?'

'You bet.' Giovanni rubbed his hands together involuntarily. 'It's only when they die that you can be absolutely sure there isn't going to be any more. When you get to that point, you're in a controlled supply marketing environment, and if you've been clever enough to get sole distribution rights —'

'Have we got sole distribution rights?'

'Yes, Iachimo, we have indeed.' Giovanni grinned. 'Go and get another jug of this stuff, will you, Marco? I think a modest celebration is in order.'

The Beaumont Street Partnership had long ago

sorted out the problem of management role coordination. Giovanni did the thinking, Iachimo kept the books, Marco went to the bar. Usually, too, Marco paid.

'What it boils down to,' Giovanni said, when his cup was once more full, 'is that the only thing better than a sucker, from an investment management point of view, is a dead sucker. Cheers.'

'Pity he's dead, though,' said Iachimo with a sigh. 'Wrote some lovely songs, he did.'

'He did indeed,' Giovanni replied. 'And there's no reason why he shouldn't write plenty more.'

'But he's ...'

'I know, Marco,' Giovanni said patiently. 'But he wasn't dead this morning, was he? All we have to do is go back to when he wasn't dead, get him to hum something, and there we go. No reason why we can't go on indefinitely. And no royalties, either.'

Marco looked up from his drink, most of which he'd managed to spill on his tie. 'No,' he said, 'you're wrong there.'

His brothers looked at him. 'Come again?' Iachimo said.

'He fell into a timeslip, right?' Marco said. The other two nodded. 'Well then,' he continued, 'stands to reason, doesn't it?'

'Ignore him,' Giovanni said. 'He still hasn't worked out what a Thursday is.'

'No, listen,' Marco protested. 'Look, if he fell into a timeslip, right, then it stands to reason he'll have drowned in time. Loose Cannons. Time Wardens.' Marco made an effort and marshalled his thoughts, which was a bit like trying to produce *Die Frau Ohne*

Schatten with a cast of five-year-olds. 'What's a time-slip made of?' he asked.

Giovanni was about to interrupt, but he didn't. 'Unstable time,' he said. 'Like lava from a volcano, you might say. What of it?'

'Anything that gets trapped in a timeslip,' Marco ground on, 'gets taken away to the Archives, right?' He looked up, waiting for someone to interrupt him, but for once they were both listening. He smiled happily. This was good fun. 'And anything that gets taken to the Archives, right, it's like it never existed. So if Blondel's gone there, it's like he never existed.'

'Jesus Christ,' Giovanni said quietly.

'And if he never existed,' Marco continued – it was like watching a woodlouse climbing a wall, listening to Marco doing joined-up speaking – 'then he couldn't have made up any of those songs. Which means his songs don't exist any more. Which means they never existed to start with. Which means – where are you going, Giovanni?'

'Get your coat.'

'But Giovanni ...'

'I said get your coat.'

Marco pulled a face, but it was no good; they weren't listening to him any more. He got his coat.

'And this one,' said La Beale Isoud, 'is Blondel, my sister Mahaud and me at Deauville.' She squinted at the picture. 'Summer, 1438,' she added. 'It's changed a lot since then, of course.'

'Yes,' said Guy. He was beginning to have second thoughts about being in love with La Beale Isoud. She seemed to have enough photograph albums to fill up at

132

least seventy years of matrimony. 'Er ...'

'And this one,' she continued, 'is Blondel, my sister Mahaud, my sister Ysabel and me in Venice. You can't see Ysabel terribly well, I'm afraid, because she moved just before the picture was taken. That's her, look, behind the prow of the gondola.'

'Ah yes. Would you mind terribly if —'

'And this one ...' La Beale Isoud stared at the album for a moment. 'No,' she said, 'that one hasn't been taken yet. It's too bad of Blondel, he keeps getting them muddled up and out of order. Oh look,' she said, 'it's got you in it.'

Guy blinked. 'Me?'

'That is you, isn't it?' Isoud said. 'Standing there on the steps of the church with a bouquet of flowers in your hand. And who's that beside you?'

Guy examined the photograph. 'That's my friend George,' he said. 'Who's that?'

'That's my aunt Gunhilde,' Isoud replied. 'She's dead now, of course, but she comes back occasionally for visits. Christmas, you know, and weddings. That's the good thing about having all this time travel in the family, it means one can keep in touch.'

Guy was still examining the photograph. 'Whose wedding is this?' he asked.

'No idea,' Isoud replied. 'Oh look, I think that's Mahaud there, in the blue. She never did suit blue, but you couldn't tell her.'

Guy could feel his hand shaking. 'It looks,' he said, 'rather like I'm meant to be the bridegroom.'

'Yes,' Isoud replied, nodding, 'it does rather, doesn't it? Now this one here ...'

'So who,' Guy said, 'is the bride?'

'You can't see,' Isoud replied. 'She doesn't seem to be in the photo. Oh look, there's Mummy. What a big hat she's wearing.'

Guy stood up. 'Well,' he said, 'thank you ever so much for the tea. I don't think I'll wait for Blondel if you don't mind.' He could feel the sweat running off his forehead. 'So if you'll just tell me where the time tunnel is ...'

'Are you leaving?' Isoud said.

'Better had,' Guy said firmly. He had always previously believed that he was too young to die, but now he was absolutely positive that he was too young to get married. 'This door here, isn't it?' He opened it and walked through. A moment later he came back again, immediately followed by three raincoats, a hat and an umbrella.

'No,' said Isoud, 'that's the coat cupboard.'

'I rather thought so,' Guy said. 'Which door leads to the time tunnel, then?'

Isoud looked at him. '*I* don't know,' she said. 'Blondel deals with all that sort of thing.'

'But you must know ...'

Isoud smiled grimly. 'It keeps changing,' she explained. 'One day it's one door and the next day it's a different one. Terribly difficult to know where to put your coat sometimes.'

'Ah,' said Guy.

'Not to mention,' Isoud went on, 'the empty milk bottles. I expect there's a doorstep in the future or the past somewhere with hundreds and hundreds of our milk bottles on it. The milkman must wonder what we do with them all.'

'Quite probably.' Guy could feel the hairs on the

back of his neck rising. 'You don't mind if I just, sort of, investigate, do you? Only ...'

'Oh look,' Isoud said, 'here's another one of the same wedding. Oh *look*!' She lifted her head and stared at him. 'Mr *Goodlet*!' she said.

'Goodbye,' Guy said firmly. He opened a door, saw with great relief that there was nothing on the other side of it, and stepped through.

'Mr Goodlet,' Isoud said, a few moments later. 'You seem to have fallen into the coal cellar.'

'Yes,' Giovanni said, 'but can you do it?'

The man scratched the back of his head doubtfully, and then made a few rough sketches on the back of an envelope, ending up with something that looked perilously like the Albert Memorial. Then he played with a calculator for a while, looked some things up in a price list which seemed to have an awful lot of noughts to each digit, and spat on the floor.

'Dunno,' he said. 'It's the stresses, see. Could tear the wings off, the stresses we're talking here. Then there's your frame. Got to be titanium.'

'Is that expensive?' Iachimo interrupted. He was making a parallel set of notes on the back of another envelope. In fact, the place was beginning to look like a sorting office.

'Ignore him,' Giovanni said. 'Look, I don't care what it costs. Can you do it?'

'And then there's your PCVs,' the man said. 'I can put you in Bergsons, no difficulty there, mind, Bergsons, but what's that going to do to your lateral stability? You put too much stress on your laterals, you're going to be really stuffed up. Mind you ...'

The man seemed to pass into a sort of coma or trance, from which it would probably be dangerous to arouse him. Any minute now, Giovanni said to himself, he'll be asking if there's anybody here called Vera.

'Mind you,' said the man, recovering, 'if you use titanium alloy *throughout*' – he made the word throughout sound so expensive that Iachimo winced, as if something had bitten him – 'then you might get away with it. Hard to say. Wouldn't want to be responsible, really, I mean titanium alloy B-joints could pack up on you just like that. Real dodgy.'

Giovanni breathed out heavily through his nose. 'Look ...' he said.

'All right,' replied the man severely, 'all right, hold your water a minute. Let the dog see the rabbit.' He bent down and started to leaf through a huge pile of dusty, cobwebby magazines on the floor. 'Saw something like what you're after in one of these once,' he said, 'twenty, twenty-five years ago now, mind. One of them big mining companies did it, only they used carbon fibre. Can't use carbon fibre now, of course.'

Giovanni asked why not but the question was obviously beneath contempt. 'Now then,' the man said. The three brothers leaned forward to look. 'See that?' the man said, pointing to a picture of something or other, 'that was one of mine, that was. Nothing to do with what you're after,' he added. He threw the magazine to one side and went on looking.

'Look,' Giovanni said, 'all we need to know is —'

'Magnesium,' the man said suddenly. 'You just wouldn't believe what some people do with magnesium. No,' he added.

'No what?'

'No, I can't do it. Impossible,' he explained. 'Bloody silly idea to start with.'

'Thank you so much,' Giovanni replied through gritted teeth.

'I mean,' the man went on, 'drill a probe through the Archive walls, absolutely out of the question. What do you want to do that for, anyway?'

'Pleasure to have met you,' Giovanni said, putting on his hat and pocketing the card he had put on the table at the beginning of the interview. 'Send us your invoice.'

'What invoice?'

'Any bloody invoice,' Giovanni said, and closed the door quickly.

'Overtime,' said White Herald, suddenly.

The others looked at him as if he'd just gone mad. The bus went over a patch of turbulence, jolting them about. The sort of turbulence you get in time travel makes a little bit of rogue cumulonimbus over the Alps seem like a feather bed.

'We could all claim overtime,' White Herald continued. 'Dunno why I didn't think of it before.'

Nobody said anything. Pursuivant looked at Clarenceaux and then nudged Mordaunt, who giggled. Clarenceaux glared at them both, as if challenging them to make something of it. They beamed at him. Just when he thought he was safe, Mordaunt turned to Pursuivant and said, 'If we went around asking for overtime, we'd end up with egg on our faces all right, eh?'

'Look ...' Clarenceaux said angrily. They smiled at him.

'Sorry?' Pursuivant enquired sweetly.

'Just watch it,' Clarenceaux replied. 'That's all.'

'Sure thing,' Mordaunt replied, and turned back to his companion. 'No, the yolk would be on us then, wouldn't it?'

'Did you say something?'

Mordaunt shook his head innocently. Clarenceaux dragged a sigh up from his socks and let it go. Blondel's horrible prophecy had come horribly true, starting with the moment of their return to the Chastel, when Mountjoy King of Arms had seen him squelching up the drive covered all over in custard, jam and cream and had observed, somewhat inevitably, that Clarenceaux was clearly not a man to be trifled with. Since then, if anything, it had got worse.

'Other people get overtime,' White Herald continued, 'so why not us? Time and a half, even.'

'Do you mind?' Clarenceaux said irritably. 'We got enough trouble travelling through it without claiming it as well. Where are we going this time, anyway? Anybody know?'

Silence. Three blank faces. At least nobody said anything about eggs, or custard, or bananas. If ever he saw that sodding Blondel again, he'd give him bananas all right ...

The bus slowed down, jolted violently, and stopped. After a moment the automatic doors opened, and the crew climbed out. White Herald, whose turn it was to be Sergeant, took out the sealed envelope and opened it.

'Orders of the day,' he said. 'Er ...'

'Give it here,' said Clarenceaux testily. 'You got it upside down,' he pointed out.

'Reading isn't everything,' White Herald replied.

'Cretin.' Clarenceaux ran his finger along the lines. '*You have arrived at the South-Western Main Archive,*' he read. 'Here, what's an Archive?' he asked. Nobody knew. '*Proceed to the oil well which you will find approximately half a mile due east of your arrival point and arrest Jean de Nesle, also known as Blondel. You are authorised to use maximum force if necessary.* Then there's a big blob of red wax with a picture on it. Ouch!' The paper had burst into flames, and soon Clarenceaux was holding only the corner. '*PS,*' he read, '*this message will self-destruct in thirty (30) seconds.*'

'Nice of him to tell you,' Mordaunt commented. 'Anybody got a compass?'

It isn't all fun and games commanding an illicit oil rig in the middle of an insubstantial sea, and unauthorised visitors don't help. To make matters worse, Commander Moorhen was only too aware that he was running about a fortnight behind schedule, as a result of the Mistral Chronologique arriving a month earlier than forecast and the diamond-molybdenum drill-bit breaking, and that there were reports of Warden patrols not a million years away. He was not a happy man.

'Music while you work,' he said, 'I can handle. But aliens breaking in and coshing the staff just so's they can sing to them is another matter. Take him away and chuck him off the derrick.'

Sergeant Peewit looked at him and didn't move. The prisoner, for his part, smiled.

'Come on,' Moorhen shouted. 'Jump to it.'

'No sir,' said Peewit, back straight as the proverbial ramrod.

'You what?'

'With respect, sir.'

Moorhen stared. 'And why the hell not, sergeant?'

'Because, sir,' Peewit replied, 'with respect, sir, this here is Blondel de Nesle, and the lads won't stand for it.'

The biro in Moorhen's hands snapped, apparently of its own accord. 'What did you say?'

'No, sir.'

Moorhen hesitated for a split second. They'd done mutinies at training school, naturally, but it had clashed with his violin lessons and so he'd pretended to have a cold. To the best of his recollection, you had people shot, but he couldn't swear to it. Besides, there weren't any guns on the rig.

'Do you know,' he said quietly, 'what happens to NCOs who disobey a direct order?'

'Yes, sir,' Peewit replied. 'Regulation 46, subsection (b), sir.'

'Oh. Yes, thank you. Here, stand back, I'll do it myself.'

Peewit placed a piano-sized fist on Moorhen's chest. 'With respect, sir,' he said, 'Blondel de Nesle is the greatest all-round entertainer the world has ever known, and the lads said to tell you that if you hurt one hair of his head, like, they'll chuck you down the main shaft, sir.'

Moorhen was about to say something extremely pertinent and germane when the alarms went off. A second bombardier, very much out of breath, came clattering up the stairs to report that four armed intruders had broken in via the main gateway. Then a grenade exploded somewhere below them, and life began to get extremely complicated.

★

'Are you trying to say,' said the Chief Warden, 'that you're attempting to bribe me to let you into the Archives?'

'Yes,' Giovanni said.

The Chief Warden stroked his beard. 'How much?' he asked.

'How much do you want?'

'No.' The Chief Warden smiled. 'I admit I was tempted, but no. And now I think we'd better have a word with Security.'

Giovanni was about to simper appealingly when he noticed the CD player and the stack of discs in the corner of the office. 'Of course,' he said, 'the bribe wouldn't necessarily have to be money, would it?'

The Chief Warden paused, his hand over the buzzer. 'I beg your pardon?' he said.

Giovanni walked over to the CD player. 'You're a Blondel fan, I see,' he said.

'What's that got to —'

'Very impressive collection you've got here.'

'Complete,' the Chief Warden said involuntarily. 'Look —'

'I could get you tickets,' Giovanni said.

The Chief Warden's hand moved away from the buzzer. 'Tickets?' he asked.

'Tickets,' Giovanni repeated. 'St Peter's Square, 1173.'

'Out of the question. I —'

'Constantinople, 1201.'

'You don't seem to realise that —'

Giovanni shrugged his shoulders. 'Whatever you say,' he replied. 'Of course, if two tickets for the Piazza

141

San Marco gig of '98 made any difference . . .'

There was a very long pause.

'Near the band?'

'You could reach out,' Giovanni said, 'and pinch the second flautist.'

'If anybody found out . . .'

Giovanni shrugged again. 'You're right,' he said. 'If I were you I'd call Security and have us thrown in jail.' He picked up a framed photograph of a very pretty girl in an official Blondel European Tour wimple from the Warden's desk. 'Your wife?' he asked.

'No,' said the Chief Warden. 'My, er, niece.' He leaned forward conspiratorially. 'There wouldn't be any chance,' he whispered, 'of, well, going backstage after the show . . .?'

Having been blown to smithereens by the explosion of the oil storage tanks (caused by one of their own ineptly-placed grenades) the identifiable fragments of Clarenceaux, Mordaunt, Pursuivant and White Herald were collected by a relief team sent from the Chastel des Larmes Chaudes, packed in dry ice and taken directly to the central works depot, where a team of highly qualified and extremely resentful mechanics were ready to begin work.

'I mean,' said the Chief Footwright, taking a handful of toes from a cardboard box and sorting through them for a reasonable match, 'what the hell is the point of it all? You spend half an hour getting the right and left legs all nicely balanced, the cornering and the foot wear all sorted out, and then a few days later back it comes, all mangled to cock and fit for nothing but the breakers.'

'Hoy!' said Pursuivant. The Lead Vocalist, who had just reconnected his vocal chords, disconnected them again.

The Master Armerer frowned savagely. 'You think

you got problems,' he replied, 'you want to try it from this end.' He looked at the mess on the bench in front of him and shook his head sadly. 'The really daft thing about it is the way they try and patch 'em up themselves in the field units.' He placed a spatula under a limp forearm and pointed to it with disgust. 'Just look at that, will you?' he said. 'Talk about a Friday afternoon job. Dunno who fitted that, but he didn't know his elbow from —'

'You can talk,' broke in the Head Technician. 'All you've got to do is get the bits out of a box and bolt them on. Me, I've got to wire the whole lot in. Look at *that*, for Christ's sake.' He pointed at Clarenceaux's trepanned skull, which lifted its eyes and scowled at him. 'You don't want a nerve specialist for that lot, you want a bleeding plumber. I ask you! Great big lumps of loose solder everywhere, bits held on with crocodile clips, contacts twisted round rusty old nails – it's a wonder the whole lot didn't short out. And they expect the perishing things to be able to read.' He sighed, adjusted his torque wrench, and went to work on the cervical joint.

'Right,' he continued after a while, 'that'll have to do for now. So long as they don't use it for competition stuff or expect it to win any Nobel prizes, should be OK for another fifty thousand. Expect it'll get blown up before then, anyway. Close it up, George.'

Fully restored and operational, Clarenceaux had his permitted cup of tea – more to test the hydraulic lines than to restore him after his ordeal; at any rate, they never put sugar in it – donned his regulation fatigues and went to report to his superior.

'Well?' Mountjoy said.

'Well ...' Clarenceaux reported. Mountjoy invited him to expand on that. 'Well, sir,' Clarenceaux continued, choosing his words with care, and (bearing in mind that the portion of his brain that handled such matters had been in a cardboard box in the stockroom half an hour ago) doing better than he expected, 'you could say it was a qualified success. On balance, like.'

'Oh yes?' replied Mountjoy ominously. 'Go on.'

'Well,' Clarenceaux said – his new sweat glands were working fine, he noticed – 'we got there all right —'

'Hardly surprising, considering you had nothing to do with it.'

Since his self-respect had not been replaced (shortage at the supply depot), Clarenceaux ignored that. 'And then,' he went on, 'we found the oil rig, no trouble at all. There was a guard on the gate so we had to use all reasonable and necessary force to get in, and then some other guards came up and tried to grab us, so we, er ...'

'Yes?'

'White Herald,' said Clarenceaux – peer-group loyalty is an optional extra on the Popular range – 'had got hold of this hand grenade thing from somewhere, and he chucked it at them.'

'Really.'

'Oh yes,' Clarenceaux confirmed. 'Worked a treat so far as reasonable and necessary force was concerned. Trouble was, it blew the rig up. And that's where we, sort of ...'

'Yes,' said Mountjoy, 'I think I get the picture. Do you think there were any survivors?'

Clarenceaux thought for a moment. 'Well, not us,

for a start,' he said firmly. 'We copped it. Hell of a bang, it was.'

'So I gathered,' Mountjoy replied. 'But do you think it likely that de Nesle could have survived the explosion? If he was on the rig, I mean?'

Clarenceaux shook his head, an unwise move considering that the bearings were still stiff. 'Can't see how he could have, sir,' he said. 'Like, we'd heard him singing, right, over the tannoy, when we were approaching the rig?'

'So?'

'So,' Clarenceaux continued, 'stands to reason that if he was singing into the tannoy, he must have been in the office building, or near it. And the office building was next to the storage tank. In fact, I seem to remember it was a bloody great chunk of the office building took my head off. Don't see how anyone could have survived in there when the tank went up.'

'I see.' Mountjoy nodded. 'That's pretty good deduction, Clarenceaux. You thought that up all by yourself, did you?'

Praise was something that Clarenceaux had heard about, even vaguely believed in, like telepathy, but had never previously experienced in the flesh. He glowed slightly. 'Yes, sir,' he replied.

'Thought so,' said Mountjoy. 'That fool of an engineer's gone and fitted you with a Mark IVB instead of a Mark III. Go back to the sick bay and tell him to take it out again at once. Hasn't he heard about the cut-backs?'

As Clarenceaux wandered sadly away, Mountjoy turned himself back up to full illumination and considered the position. If Blondel really had been blown to bits ... But that was a very big if. The wretched man seemed to have the knack of getting out of certain death, the way a really dedicated twelve-year-old always gets out of Sports Day. Personally, he wasn't going to believe it until they brought him Blondel's head on a dish; and even then he'd want indemnity insurance. In short, he wasn't sure, and would institute further enquiries. He reached across and switched on the intercom.

'Get me Intelligence,' he said.

A luminous white Land Rover was bumping across the insubstantial waves of the Great North Archive. The passengers were not enjoying the experience much.

'If,' grumbled the Chief Warden, 'after all this, he doesn't sing *Ma Joie Me Semont*, I'll have your guts for braces.'

'He'll sing it,' Giovanni assured him, taking his hand briefly away from in front of his mouth. 'I was there, I know.'

'He'd better, that's all,' the Warden snarled. 'All right, we're here. Now, what exactly are you looking for?'

'Well,' Giovanni said. 'Actually, we aren't quite sure.'

The Warden stared at him. 'You commit the biggest crime in the Universe, corrupting a Time Warden, and you aren't sure what you're looking for. What are you, tourists?'

'We're looking for someone,' Marco started to say, but Giovanni trod on his foot. Too late.

'Oh yes?' asked the Warden suspiciously. 'Who?'

'Oh, nobody you know,' Giovanni said. 'What's that over there?'

The Warden raised his field glasses. 'Looks like a column of smoke,' he said. 'That's odd, this is all water.'

'Water?' Marco looked out of the window nervously. 'Then why aren't we ...?'

'Deactivated water,' the Warden told him. 'It's got all the hydrogen and oxygen taken out. Keeps better,' he explained. 'If you gentlemen wouldn't mind, I think I'd better take a look.'

'That's fine,' Giovanni said.

They drove on until they came to the ruins of a stockade. The surface of the immaterial sea was littered with mangled scraps of iron; the place looked like a battlefield, or the Hayward Gallery. Here and there lay yellow plastic helmets, boots, fragments of office furniture. No corpses, needless to say; anyone who dies in the Archives was never born in the first place.

'It's one of those pirate rigs I was telling you about,' the Warden said. 'Looks like someone got careless.'

'There's somebody over there, look,' Iachimo said, pointing. 'In that rowing boat.'

They drove over, climbed out and stopped the boat with their hands. Inside was a very frightened-looking man in the remains of a pair of overalls. After a while, they were able to get some sense out of him.

'These men,' he said, 'soldiers, guards, something like that. I was on sentry duty. They hit me.'

'Were they Wardens' officers?' the Warden asked.

'No idea,' the sentry replied.

The Chief Warden turned to the Galeazzo brothers. 'My men have orders to destroy these places on sight, no questions asked,' he explained. 'I know it seems hard, but you've got no idea the damage they can do.'

148

He turned back to the sentry. 'They knocked you out, did they?'

The sentry nodded. 'Bloody lucky they did, I guess,' he went on. 'I'd just come round when the whole lot blew up. No survivors, except me. I was lucky; a bit of the fence fell on me and shielded me from the blast, I suppose. About half an hour later a van turned up, more like an ambulance; they took the bodies of the soldiers away. Our blokes just sort of —'

'Yes,' said the Warden, who wasn't a cruel man. 'Yes, I wouldn't worry about that. No survivors, then?'

The sentry shook his head. 'None of our lot,' he said. 'No sign of the other one, either.'

The Warden raised an eyebrow. 'What other one?' he said.

'Blondel,' said the sentry.

There was a silence. It probably seemed longer than it actually was.

'Did you say Blondel?' the Chief Warden asked. 'Blondel the singer?'

The sentry nodded. 'That's right,' he said. 'I recognised the face when he thumped me.'

'He thumped you ...'

'When he broke into the rig,' the sentry explained. 'That was, oh, fifteen minutes before your blokes.'

Giovanni pushed his way past the Chief Warden. 'You can't be sure it was him,' he said. 'Just a quick glance ...'

'But I heard him,' replied the sentry. 'He sang, over the tannoy. I'd know that voice anywhere. He sang that big number from the 1189 White Album. You know, goes like —' He hummed a few bars.

'*L'Amours Dont Sui Epris?*' the Chief Warden

whispered. He had gone very pale all of a sudden.

'That's it,' the sentry said. 'Dead good, that, especially that bit where ...'

Nobody was listening. The Chief Warden turned to the Galeazzo brothers.

'Did you know,' he said softly, 'that Blondel was in the Archives?'

By a feat of great dexterity, Giovanni stood on the toes of both his brothers at once. 'I had no idea,' he said. 'That's awful.'

The Warden gave him an extremely unpleasant look. 'You're sure, are you?' he said. 'Well, what a coincidence. Because if you'd known he was here, and there had been a chance of saving him ... You realise that now none of his songs were ever written?'

'Really?' Giovanni raised both eyebrows. 'What a tragedy.'

'Well ...' The Warden shrugged his shoulders. 'You'd better help me get this man in the car. We'll need him for questioning.'

Together they lifted the sentry into the Land Rover. It wasn't till he was safely installed on the back seat and propped up on two cushions that the Chief Warden produced a gun and ordered the brothers out of the car. Once they were out of it, but while they were still reacting strongly and making a variety of protests and appeals to his better nature, he slammed the door and told the driver to drive on.

The choice between being forcibly married to a beautiful but incompatible girl and remaining indefinitely in a coal cellar is not one that many people have to confront. Even Aristotle, whose works cover a wide range of possible moral dilemmas, glosses over it in a very perfunctory manner; and Guy wasn't exactly one of Aristotle's greatest fans in any event. He decided to rely on instinct.

'If it's all the same to you,' he shouted through the door, 'I'll stay where I am, thanks.'

'Mr Goodlet . . .'

'Thank you,' Guy repeated, politely but firmly. To reinforce the point, he piled coal against the door.

'You're being rather childish, Mr Goodlet.'

Maybe, Guy thought. So what's wrong with children all of a sudden? Clever people, children. Don't have to go to work.

'I'm sure that if we discussed this in a sensible manner,' said La Beale Isoud, 'we could easily sort matters out.'

'No, really,' Guy said, 'I like it here. So, if it's all the same to you . . .'

'It is *not* all the same to me,' retorted La Beale Isoud, and there was something in her tone of voice when suggested that her previously inexhaustible-seeming reservoir of ladylike behaviour might be running a trifle low. 'Mr Goodlet,' she went on, 'whether you like it or not – whether either of us likes it or not, come to that – it would seem that at some time in the future we are to become man and wife. I really think that we should be trying to establish the ground-work for a mature and meaningful relationship, and I don't really see how that can be achieved with you in the coal cellar.'

Guy said nothing. Something or other ran lightly over his foot and up his leg as far as his knee. He shuddered slightly.

151

'Mr Goodlet. Guy,' said La Beale Isoud, 'I'm not going to plead with you indefinitely, you know. What will be, will be, and if you want to start off our relationship on this sort of note, then I for one will not be answerable for the consequences.'

Guy considered this for a moment; then, having reflected maturely on what Isoud had said, and also the way in which she had said it, scrabbled around for some more coal to pile against the door. The woman sounded exactly like his cousin Flora.

There was a long silence, but Guy wasn't going to be fooled. She might have gone away; on the other hand, she might be waiting outside the door, holding her breath and with an attendant clergyman and two bridesmaids standing behind her fingering sacrificial implements.

'Are you there, Mr Goodlet?'

'Yes.'

'It may interest you to know,' said La Beale Isoud, 'that I am none too happy about this idea myself. However, instead of shouting at each other through the door, perhaps we should be considering how we can prevent this thing happening?' A long pause. 'Mr Goodlet?'

'Still here.'

'Mr Goodlet, I'm rapidly running out of patience. Would you at least have the good manners to answer me when I speak to you?'

'Look,' Guy said, 'I really don't want to seem rude, but if there's a photograph of us on our wedding day, then I'm afraid I'm just going to stay put. The way I see it, we can't get married if I stay here. If you want to get on and do something else, please don't mind me.'

'Oh, for heaven's sake . . .'

Guy heard the sound of bad-tempered heels clacking away across flagstones, and relaxed slightly. It might be that she'd gone to fetch a crowbar, but as far as he could remember it had seemed like a good, solid door, opening inwards. He lay back on the heap of coal and considered his situation in some detail.

He tried to puzzle out, from what Blondel had told him, how time worked. On the one hand, it seemed, you could whizz back and forwards through time as easily as catching a train. On the other hand, it stood to reason that if a photograph of him on his wedding day had been taken, then he'd had a wedding day at some time or other – some time in the *future*, of course – and in that case, the thing had already happened and there was absolutely nothing he could do about it. Except, of course, that it was in the future, so it couldn't already have happened. He could stop it happening by taking his revolver and shooting himself here and now – assuming he didn't miss, which seemed on recent experience to be quite a large assumption – but since he wasn't seriously proposing to put it to the test, that one could be shelved for the time being.

Meanwhile, what he needed most of all, he decided, was a smoke; and to this end he produced from his pockets his last remaining cigarette, his last two matches and the remains of his matchbox, which had not been improved structurally by having been fallen on several times recently. He struck a match.

No Entry. Authorised Personnel Only.

The match went out and he struck another, which flared up, managed to find a gust of wind in the entirely draught-free environment of the cellar and blew out. Guy stretched out a hand and felt for the door he'd just seen.

As Aristotle said, when caught between a ravening tiger and a process-server bearing a legal document, it's always worth looking for the fire escape.

The Chief Warden returned to his office tired, worried and upset. In the space of a single day he had broken all the laws and regulations of his vocation, only to discover that his aiders and abettors were responsible for the annihilation of (in his opinion) the greatest musical genius who had ever lived, who had perished in one of his own Archives. As if that wasn't bad enough, he remembered, his wife had told him they had people coming to dinner and he was on no account to be late. As he unlocked the office door, he toyed briefly with the idea of nipping back through time to half past six and thus at least saving himself a degree of aggravation. It would be a flagrant breach, of course, but compared with what he'd done, it was a mere parking ticket on the windscreen of his honour. Still, perhaps not. Now, all he had to do was open the safe, put the key back in it for the night, and think of a reasonable excuse on the way home ...

There were people in his office. They had been sitting in the dark, because the light was off when he walked in; almost as if they were waiting to catch him unawares.

'Good evening, Chief Warden.'

Even if he'd contemplated turning and trying to make a run for it, there wouldn't have been any point; a very substantial security officer had filled up the doorway. The Chief Warden relaxed. After all, since it

154

was all such a foregone conclusion, there was no point in getting all tense about it.

'Come in and take a seat, please.' Although it was – what, two hundred years? About that – since the selection committee meeting when he'd received his appointment, he recognised the voice instantly; and when the speaker swivelled round in the chair and faced him, he was ready for it. But he still couldn't help making a sort of mouse-in-a-blender noise and turning his head away. The Chief Warden was, after all, human, and no human being, however cool or laid back, can hope to face a man split down the middle with equanimity.

'That's all right,' said the half-man, pre-empting the apology. 'I'm used to it by now, Lord knows. I won't be offended if you look the other way.'

'Thank you, sir,' the Chief Warden said, to the opposite wall. He sat down.

'Now then,' the half-man continued, 'you can't see them, but sitting on my right is His Holiness Anti-Pope Julian II, whom I believe you've met. Yes? And on my left,' the half-man continued, with a chuckle, 'is His Holiness Pope Julian XXIII. Before you say anything, yes, they are one and the same person; as you know, Julian was Pope of Rome, died, and now commutes from the sixteenth century to be Anti-Pope. Well, he's kindly agreed to make two simultaneous trips, one in each capacity. Apparently it's the first time it's been done, so he asks you to make allowances. For a start, it means he can't speak.'

The Chief Warden's curiosity got the better of him. 'May I ask …?'

'For fear,' replied the half-man, 'of contradicting

himself. Since he is speaking *ex cathedra* in both capacities, the results might be extremely unfortunate. He will therefore communicate with me by means of sign language, which does not qualify as a medium for Infallible statements, and I will relay his points to you myself. Since you cannot, understandably enough, bear to look at me, you'll have to trust me to interpret accurately. Are you agreeable to that?'

'Perfectly,' said the Chief Warden.

'Splendid,' said the half-man. 'Finally, as these are judicial proceedings, we have a shorthand writer present who will take a transcript for the record. You have no objection?'

'None whatsoever.'

The half-man nodded to Pursuivant, who was sitting at the end of the desk. Pursuivant sharpened his pencil, opened his notebook, and wrote down the date. He spelt it wrong.

'Right,' said the half-man. 'Here goes, then. You are John Athanasius, Chief Time Warden, of "Hourglasses", Newlands Road, Bleak City, Atlantis?'

The Chief Warden nodded. 'Yes,' he said.

'John Athanasius, you are – can't read my own writing, dammit; Julian, what does that ...? Oh yes, thank you – you are charged with contraventions of the Chronological Order, in that you did knowingly and for purposes of private gain admit unauthorised persons into one of the Time Archives, contrary to Sections 3 and 67 of the said Order. How do you plead, guilty or not guilty?'

'Guilty,' said the Chief Warden.

'Oh,' said the half-man. 'How tremendously unimaginative of you. We've been to a great deal of

156

trouble to track you down, you know. I've got a whole corridor full of witnesses all hauled back from temporal oblivion just to say they saw you at it. Are you sure you won't change your plea?'

'I'm sure.'

The half-man shrugged – difficult to do, with only one shoulder – and reached into his bag for half a black cap. 'Is there – where *is* the dratted thing? – anything you wish to say before sentence is pronounced upon you?'

'No.'

'Ah, here we are. Are you sure?'

'Yes, sir.'

'Be like that. Now, which way round does it go? You'll have to take my word that I've got it on, of course. Just as well you aren't looking, you'd probably get a fit of the giggles, which'd be Contempt, and you're in enough trouble as it is. John Athanasius, you have been found guilty of a wholly unforgivable breach of the sacred truss – confound it, that's a T – *trust* which has been reposed in you. You try reading this with only one eye and see how you like it. I have listened with patience to your attempts at mitigation ... No, scrub round that. Pity. You have made no attempt to mitigate your crime, and I am therefore obliged to sentence you to filing in the Main Archive. *Now* have you anything to say as to why such sentence should not be imposed upon you?'

'No, sir.'

'Nothing at all? Not even *It's a fair cop, bang to rights, guv*? Nothing at all?'

'No, sir.'

The half-man sighed. 'Fine,' he said. 'The whole

evening has been a complete frost. Had we known, we could have entered judgement by default, Julian could have stayed at home, I could have gone out to dinner, Mr ... whatever his name is here could have gone to the greyhound races, or whatever it is his sort of person does in the evenings, but there it is. Sentence accordingly.'

The Chief Warden hung his head, waiting for the feel of the guard's hand on his shoulder. Instead, he heard the half-man's voice again.

'I told the driver to come back in five hours' time,' he said, 'so we're stuck here till then. How about a game of something?'

'Thank you,' said the Chief Warden, 'but I don't really feel in the mood for ...'

'I wasn't talking to you,' the half-man said. 'Julian, what about a rubber of bridge? You and you against me and Mr ... Oh, sorry, I forgot. Can't bid when you're being Infallible, might go two no trumps and get doubled, and what would that do to the Ninth Lateran Council? Oh well, this *is* going to be a jolly evening, isn't it?'

There was a long silence, during which the Chief Warden stared at the wall. By now, his wife would have given up waiting and served the cold beetroot soup with sour cream and chives. Where he was going, he reflected, not only would he never taste his wife's cooking ever again; he would also never have eaten it in the first place. The corners of his lips rose involuntarily.

'I spy,' said the half-man, 'with my little eye ... Literally, in my case, of course. Let's see. Something beginning with ... Chief Warden, is this a *complete* set of Blondel recordings?'

The Chief Warden nodded.

'Including the 1196 White Album?'

Without wanting to, the Chief Warden smirked. 'Yes, sir,' he said.

'The pirate edition, naturally?'

'No sir,' the Chief Warden replied – O grave, thy victory – 'the official recording, sir. With,' he added vindictively, 'Gace Brulé on drums.'

'I see,' said the half-man. 'Chief Warden, have you, er, made a will?'

The Chief Warden nodded.

'Yes,' said the half-man, 'I expect you probably have. Invalid, of course. If you never existed, you can't have made a will, which means that all your property will be forfeit to the —'

'If I never existed, sir,' replied the Chief Warden, with relish, 'then I could never have bought the very last copy of the *official* recording of the 1196 White Album. Which means,' he added happily, 'that somebody else must have bought it, sir. Don't you think?'

'I . . .'

'Which is a pity, sir, wouldn't you say, since I left it to you in my will.'

'I . . .'

'Specifically. And there's the Chastelain de Coucy,' said the Chief Warden, as if to himself, 'on tenor crumhorn. Blow that thing!' he added.

'Chief Warden!' The half-man's voice was suddenly as hard as diamonds. Black diamonds, industrial grade. 'Look at me when I'm talking to you.'

The Chief Warden turned smartly and smiled. No worries about looking that half-skull in the eye; not in the circumstances. For it had occurred to the Chief

159

Warden that, if his collection of Blondel records still existed, then Blondel too must have existed; and if he had existed, then he must, somehow or other, have got out of the Archive. In which case, sang the Chief Warden's heart within him, I'm going to get out of this mess somehow or other, quit this bloody awful job, find another copy of the 1196 White Album and retire.

'Have you any idea,' said the half-man, 'how serious an offence it is to attempt to pervert the course of *my* justice?'

'No, sir.'

'Well,' said the half-man, 'it's very serious. So don't do it, d'you hear? Leave it out completely. Understood?'

'Sir.'

'Splendid. You, whatever your name is.'

Pursuivant lifted his head from his notebook and clicked his heels smartly under the table. 'Yes, Your Highness?' he said.

'Is that the court record you've got there?' the half-man enquired.

'Yes, Your Highness.'

'Hand it to me.'

Pursuivant closed the notebook and passed it over. The half-man took it, flipped it open, and took hold of several pages between his teeth. Then he leaned his head back and pulled. The pages ripped away from the spiral binding, and the half-man stuffed them into his half-mouth, chewed vigorously with his half-set of teeth, and swallowed.

'Yuk!' he said.

'Sir!' Pursuivant shouted. His eyes were so far out of his head that he looked like a startled grasshopper.

'You can't do that!'

The half-man looked at him. Of that look there is nothing to say, except that a few hours later Pursuivant showed up at the sick bay waving a studded club and demanding to have his memory wiped.

'Next time,' the half-man said, 'don't use pencil, it tastes horrible. Shut up, Julian, you'll sprain your hands. Now then, Chief Warden. John,' he corrected. 'Or rather, Jack, my old son. Why didn't you tell me you were a Blondel man?'

'Well, sir ...'

'Tony,' said the half-man. 'Call me Tony.'

'Well, Tony,' said the Chief Warden, 'I wouldn't have thought ... In the circumstances, I mean —'

'Nonsense,' said the half-man. 'Just because I don't hold with the feller personally doesn't mean I can't admire his music. And I may only have one ear, but it isn't made of tin. Is it really Gace Brulé on drums?'

The Chief Warden nodded. 'There's this incredible riff,' he said, 'in the bridge section in *Quand flours et glais* ...'

'Cadenet on vocals?'

'They do this duet,' replied the Chief Warden, 'in *San'c fuy belha* ...'

There was silence for a while, broken only by two — one and a half — men humming. Julian looked at each other and shook his heads sadly.

'Anyway,' said the half-man, with an effort, 'this court finds insufficient evidence of the charges alleged and rules that these proceedings be adjourned *sine die* with liberty to restore.' He tried to wink but, naturally, failed. 'And let that be a lesson to you, Chief Warden.'

'Sir.'

The half-man rose to his foot. For the record, he moved in a strange – you might say mysterious – way; the half of his body which was there moved as if the other half was there too. 'All rise,' he said. 'Come on, Julian on your feet. Go and make a cup of coffee or something. You too, whatever your name is. Go and see if you can raise that blasted driver on the radiophone. Now then, Jack ...'

The Anti-Pope and his previous life shrugged and went to look for a kettle. Pursuivant, mentally exhausted, found a cupboard under some stairs and went to sleep in it. From the Chief Warden's office came the sound, in perfect Dolby stereo and highly amplified, of Blondel singing *L'Amours Dont Sui Epris*.

If anybody – apart, of course, from the man and a half in the office – joined in the second verse, nobody heard.

The waiter who brought him his iced coffee and a glass of water looked familiar, and Blondel asked him his name.

'Spiro,' the waiter said.

'Yes,' Blondel replied, 'but Spiro what?'

'Maniakis,' the waiter replied. 'Is it important?'

Blondel shrugged. 'Did your family use to farm down near Mistras, a while back?' he asked. The waiter looked at him. 'Do excuse my asking, but you remind me of someone I used to know.'

'Really?' The waiter gave him an even stranger look. 'A hundred, maybe a hundred and fifty years ago, my mother's family lived in a village near Mistras. What of it?'

Blondel suddenly remembered who the waiter reminded him of. 'Sorry,' he said, 'my mistake. Sorry to have bothered you.'

The waiter shrugged and walked away, whistling. The tune, incidentally, was a very garbled recollection of *L'Amours Dont Sui Epris*, which the waiter had learned from his great-grandmother. Blondel finished his coffee quickly and left.

A tiresome sort of day, so far, he said to himself as he wandered back towards the Town Hall; and it had been just as well that he'd noticed the door marked *Staff Only, No Admittance* in that split second before the oil rig blew up. It was good to be out of the Archives again, but disturbing that he'd heard someone singing the second verse of the song. It could just have been a coincidence, of course; but he had the feeling, although he had no scientific data to back it up with, that coincidences didn't happen in the Archives. Something to do with the climate, perhaps. Another missing person to look for, too. Just one damn thing after another.

He looked at his watch. In twenty minutes or so he planned to sing the song under the ruined Crusader castle on the promontory; then (assuming no response) he ought to be getting along to the 1750s, where he'd pencilled in a couple of Rhine schlosses to round the day off with. Then, with any luck, bed, with the prospect of looking for two characters lost in history instead of just one to look forward to. Well, it doubled his chance of finding something, if you cared to look at it that way, although it could be argued that twice times sod all is still sod all.

He decided to walk down to the promontory by way of the market, just for the hell of it. It was nine months and seven hundred years since he'd been here last – the

163

time before that had been fifty years in the future, but that had been years ago now – and he liked to see what changes had been, or were to be, made in the places he visited. Had they filled in the enormous pothole in the road just opposite the Church?

He had stopped to buy a packet of nuts in the market and was just walking up the hill towards the steps when somebody waved at him – just waved, as if to say hello to a not particularly close acquaintance – and walked on. This was, of course, an extremely rare occurrence. He looked round and tried to find the face in the crowd by the motorcycle spares stalls, and was just about to write if off as another very distant cousin when the wave came again, causing Blondel to drop his packet of nuts.

Oh *bother*, Blondel thought.

'Hello?' Guy said.

In the darkness, something moved; something small and four-legged. Guy, who was not the sort of person who readily backed down from positions of principle, nevertheless began to wonder whether he'd done the right thing. La Beale Isoud wasn't his cup of tea, but at least she wasn't four-legged and didn't scuttle about in pitch darkness. Not so far as he knew.

'Hello?' said a voice in the darkness. 'Is there somebody there?'

'Yes,' Guy replied, feeling that his line had been stolen. 'Er ...' he continued.

'Make yourself at home,' said the voice, and something in its tone implied that it really meant it. 'Don't mind the rat,' the voice went on. 'It doesn't bite. It's a cousin of a rat I used to know quite well, actually.'

'Oh yes?'

'Yes indeed,' the voice went on. 'The rats here are all related, you see. Generations of them. It doesn't seem to have had any adverse effect on them. If anything, it seems to have made them unusually docile and friendly.'

'Right,' Guy said. 'Good. Is there any light in here?'

'I'm afraid not, no,' said the voice. 'Are you from the cell next door?'

Guy quivered slightly. 'Excuse me,' he said, 'but did you say cell?'

'Well,' said the voice, 'yes I did, actually.'

'You mean,' Guy continued, 'that this is a, well, prison?'

There was a brief silence. 'So I've been led to believe,' said the voice. 'It's always seemed fairly prison-like to me, at any rate.'

'Oh.' Guy paused for a moment and reflected. 'You've been here a long time, then?'

'Quite a long time, yes.'

'How long?'

'Now,' the voice said, 'there's a good question. Let me see now; five, ten, twenty, twenty-five ... I make it about a thousand years, give or take a bit.'

Guy made a sort of noise. This was not his intention; he had been trying to say, 'But it's impossible for anyone to be still alive after a thousand years, let alone a thousand years in a place like this,' but it came out wrong. The owner of the voice, however, seemed to get the gist of it.

'It does seem rather a long time, doesn't it?' he said, as if he was mildly surprised himself. 'It's amazing, though, how quickly you fall into a sort of a routine, and then the time just flies by. Of course, I haven't been *here* for all of the time.'

'I was just about to say —'

'For about – oh, nine hundred and ninety-nine years

and eleven months, I was in the cell next door,' the voice said. 'Then they moved me in here. I must say, it is an improvement.'

'Improvement,' Guy repeated. Although it was pitch dark, his senses were sending him a series of reports of their initial findings, which were generally rather negative. Probably just as well, they were saying, that it *is* pitch dark in here. So much less depressing.

'Roomier,' said the voice. 'There's a bit over there, where the draught comes in, where you can almost stand upright. Talk about luxury.' Guy realised, with a feeling of intense horror, that the voice wasn't being ironic. Far from it.

'Well,' he said, 'it's been terribly nice meeting you, but, oh *gosh*, is that the time? I really ought to be getting along.'

He edged back towards the door, which wasn't there. He made a swift but thorough search for it, using his sense of touch, and arrived at the conclusion that the door had slung its hook, good and proper. He started to howl.

'Now then,' said the voice, and two hands grabbed him firmly by the shoulders. 'You'll upset yourself,' the voice said. 'It really doesn't help, you know, and you'll disturb the guard. He likes to have his afternoon nap about this time of day, and the poor fellow has a hard enough time of it as it is ...'

Guy stopped in mid-shriek. Whoever this lunatic was, he was actually concerned about the guard's wellbeing. You could hear it in his voice.

'I mean,' the voice went on, 'I don't suppose he gets paid very much, and it's not much of a life for a chap, sitting around in dark corridors all day making sure

167

people don't escape. I think he bears up terribly well, in the circumstances. Nice chap, too. Collects butterflies, so he told me once. Or was that his great-great-grandfather? One tends to lose track, you know.'

Guy found that he no longer wanted to shriek; a succession of low whimpers seemed much more appropriate. He could tell that the owner of the voice approved.

'Good man,' he said. 'If I may ask, and please don't think I'm prying, but, er, how did you get here?'

'Um,' Guy said. This wasn't going to be easy. 'You're not going to believe this,' he said, 'but ...'

'Don't tell me,' said the voice. 'You found my tunnel.'

'I'm sorry?'

'You came from the other cell,' replied the voice. 'Did you find the tunnel I'd been digging?'

Guy decided to take the line of least resistance. After all, there was relatively little of value that he could learn from a man who'd been in prison for the last ten centuries. 'Yes,' he said, 'that's right.'

'I think I see,' said the voice. 'You came through my tunnel, thinking it led to the ... the ... whatsitsname, outside, and then when you found it just came here you were disappointed – naturally enough – and then, well, went off your head a bit. Is that it, more or less?'

'Yes,' Guy said. 'That's it exactly. Where did I just come in by, do you think? It's hard to get your bearings in the dark.'

'Do you think so?' the voice said. 'I find it hard to imagine it not being dark, to be honest with you, but perhaps that's just me getting set in my ways. I think you'd most likely have come in through there, over where the draught comes from. Nice draught, that, don't you think? Did you have a draught in your cell, may I ask?'

'I beg your pardon?'

'Your cell,' the voice repeated, 'the one you've just come from.'

'Oh yes,' Guy said. 'Yes, it had a draught. Lovely draught. Like this one, only better.'

'Really?' There was just a tiny spark of envy in the voice. 'Well, that must be nice. But I mustn't complain. This draught is perfectly adequate for my needs, perfectly adequate.'

That seemed to conclude the conversation for a while, and Guy began to feel uncomfortable. He edged towards the draught, found the wall, and began pawing at it again. It was smooth and continuous; no sign of any door. He felt another series of howls germinating in his stomach.

'Did you have a rat in your cell?' the voice asked.

'A rat?' Guy said. 'No, I can't say I did.'

'Oh dear,' the voice said, 'I am sorry. I do find they're such a comfort, rats. I've always had rats, for as long as I can remember. Mind you,' the voice continued, 'it might be nearer the mark to say the rats have had me; it's sometimes hard to know which of us is the master and which is the pet!' There was a mild little laugh. 'Terribly independent-minded creatures, bless them. Ah well!'

The voice seemed to have subsided into a sort of reverie – doubtless contemplating the infinite variety of rats, or something of the sort – and Guy could feel the panic creeping back into the silence. He wasn't having that; on the other hand, he didn't want to start talking

169

about rats again, or draughts, or anything else of the kind. He decided to sing something.

'Do you mind if I sing?' he said.

'Sing?' replied the voice. 'No, please, be my guest. I haven't heard singing since – oh, what was that chap's name? He was a relief warder here about, oh, six hundred and thirty years ago now, it must be, or more like six hundred and fifty. He used to sing sometimes when he brought the food ...'

'Really,' Guy said. He didn't want to know about six hundred and fifty years ago; it sounded rather depressing. 'Well then,' he said, 'I'll sing something then, shall I?'

'Thank you,' said the voice, politely.

So Guy cleared his throat, and wondered what on earth he could sing. He had just decided on *They Say There's a Wimpey Just Leaving Cologne* when a sound came from outside. A distinctly familiar sound; a voice singing. It sang:

*L'amours dont suit epris
Me semont de chanter;
Si fais con hons sopris
Qui ne puet endurer ...'*

Guy's mouth fell open. Blondel! The voice was unmistakable, and the song – well, he'd heard it rather a lot lately. It had to be Blondel.

'I say!' said the voice, quietly.

'*A li sont mi penser
Et seront a touz dis;
Ja nes en quier oster ...'*

For a split second, Guy wasn't sure whether or not he could remember how it went on. Then he started to sing himself; loud, hoarse and flat.

170

'*Remembrance dou vis*
Qu'il a vermoil et clair
A mon cuer a ce mis
Que ne l'en puis oster ...'
'Excuse me,' said the voice. 'May I just ...'

Guy hurled the last words of the second verse out of his lungs and waited for a breathless, desperate instant; and then Blondel's voice came back, closer now and loud, clear and joyful.

'*Plus bele ne vit nuls*
De le nors ne de vis;
Nature ne mist plus
De beaute en nul pris ...'

The voice cleared its throat, with a sort of different urgency, and said something, but Guy wasn't listening. He was singing, very badly:

'*Or serai ses amis*
Or pri Deu de la sus
Qu'a lor fin soie pris,'

and scrambling on to his hands and knees as the door flew open, letting a dim, pale light – starlight, perhaps, or a very thin moonlight – into the cell. 'Blondel!' he shouted, 'Is that you?'

'Oh,' said Blondel, outside. 'Is that you in there, Guy? Come on, then, we haven't got all day.'

Guy hurled himself at the door, which had already started to close, all of its own accord. He just managed to get through before it closed, with a very assertive click, and faded away, as suddenly as it had appeared.

In the cell, there was a very long silence. You could plainly hear the sound of a rat, snuffling about, scratching its ear plaintively and making a little, high-pitched whining noise, as if demanding to be fed.

'Oh,' said the voice. 'Oh well, never mind. Here, ratty, nice crusts! Who's a *good* ratty, then?'

It was a cold morning, that fateful day beside the banks of the Rubicon, the little river which divides the province of Gaul from Italy, and Julius Caesar wrapped his cloak tightly round his neck. He didn't want anybody to see him shivering and think he was afraid.

'Everything ready?' he said to his commander of cavalry. The soldier nodded in reply; he didn't feel like talking. The whole army was unnaturally quiet, as if they somehow knew that the history of the world was about to be changed.

To be absolutely accurate, they did know that the history of the world was about to be changed; it was only the nature of the change that was going to come as a complete shock to the whole lot of them, Julius Caesar included.

Just before noon, Caesar summoned his most intimate and trusted friends and supporters to meet him. Rain had set in; the cold, wet, malicious rain of Gaul which Caesar was only too familiar with. He pointed to a stunted oak tree that offered some vestige of shelter from the elements, and it was there that the historic council of war was held.

Caesar was, of course, bald; although, as his one concession to vanity, he took great pains to comb his remaining hair forward over the top of his head. The rain, however, threatened to wash his coiffure down over his ears in a long, soggy tress; he borrowed a leather travelling-hat from a trusted freedman and crammed it down over his wide temples. The rain fell off the brim in a steady drip.

'Friends,' Caesar said, 'we've come a long way these last ten years. First, we had to sort out Ariovistus; the man was a menace, more a wild animal than anything else, and it was our duty to deal with him once and for all. That led to a confrontation with the Bellovaci; and no sooner had we put them in their place but the Nervii rebelled; that involved us with the Veneti, and that meant taking on the Germans, and then the Britons. No sooner had we smashed one lot of them than another mob of the brutes appeared out of nowhere, just when we thought it was safe to go home. Yes, it's been a long haul.'

Caesar paused and wiped the rain out of his eyes with the back of his hand. His face was tired, they noticed; as if ten years' strain was suddenly taking its toll. They leaned forward to catch his words against the dull whistle of the wind and rain.

'But now it's over, thank the Gods; and let me tell you, I've had enough. Now there are a lot of irresponsible idiots in Rome who'll tell you that all along I've been planning to make myself Emperor, and all this fighting and conquering in Gaul has simply been a preparation for a military coup. They say that as soon as Gaul is quiet, I'm going to lead my army across the Rubicon and into Italy, on to Rome itself.'

Caesar grinned. This was the moment he'd been waiting for.

'Well, the reason I've called you all here today is to make it absolutely plain that I have no intention – no intention whatsoever – of making myself Emperor. You know as well as I do that if a single one of my men were to cross that river, it would mean a civil war; and all my life has been devoted to preventing that. I'm going

173

back now, lads; I'm crossing the river, but I'm going alone. You're all to stay here and wait for the Senate to send you a new Governor. That's it. Dismiss.'

Caesar's staff stared at each other, unable to believe what they were hearing. For as long as any of them could remember, they had all been convinced that it was only a matter of time before Caesar made his move; and now here he was, throwing it all away. The hardest part of it was that they all knew, in their heart of hearts, that it was the right decision. If Caesar's army crossed the river, the world would never be the same again. Now that the moment had come, however, they were all so thunderstruck that none of them could move. They stood, rooted to the spot, waiting for something to happen.

And happen it did. A tent-flap in the quarter-master's tent was thrown back, and two men walked out. They looked different from all the Roman soldiers milling about in the camp; one of them wore a brown sheepskin jacket, and the other a rather travel-worn scarlet doublet and hose. A number of legionaries turned and stared at them dubiously.

'God, I'm glad you showed up,' Guy said. 'I was beginning to get worried. Thanks.'

'Think nothing of it,' Blondel replied. 'At least that's one of you found. Pure luck, really.'

'Was it?'

Blondel frowned. 'I don't know,' he said. 'There I was on Aegina, having a rest before pressing on and getting back to my schedule – we're terribly behind, by the way; as soon as we can get back on to the main line we're going to have to put in a bit of overtime, I can tell you – when I saw this bloke I know.'

'How do you mean?' Guy said.

'A bloke I used to know,' Blondel repeated, 'at Richard's court. He was dressed as a Greek traffic policeman, but I'd know his face anywhere. Used to be something or other in the kitchens. He just sort of waved at me – you know, the way you acknowledge someone you see in the street – and went on. Well, I followed him, naturally, and the next thing I knew I was standing under this – well, post office. So I started to sing. And then you sang back, and this ...'

'Door?'

'... Pillar-box opened, and I went in and found you. And here we are. Where are we, do you know? I just followed the arrows up the tunnel. Looks like an army camp of some sort to me.'

'Could well be,' Guy replied. 'How do we get out of it?'

Blondel looked round. 'Don't be in such a hurry,' he said, 'I don't think I've been here before, not in a long time. In fact,' he added, smiling at a legionary who was giving him a very suspicious look, 'not ever.' The legionary shrugged and went back to polishing his shield with olive oil.

'The odd thing,' Blondel continued, strolling towards the enclosure where the siege engines were parked, 'was that I'd heard someone singing the song before that.'

'Did you?' Guy asked. 'Where —?'

'In the Archives,' Blondel replied. 'Now that *was* peculiar. I must have ended up there when I went back after you into the timequake; all the escaped time from the quake – what you might call the lava – got swept

175

up and dumped in the Archives, and I sort of got swept along with it. I wandered about for a bit until I found an oil rig —'

'Oil rig?'

'They have them in the Archives sometimes,' Blondel explained. 'It's strictly forbidden, of course. I was lucky enough to find a door just before some idiot blew the whole lot sky high. But there was definitely someone down there singing the second verse of the song — you know, *L'Amours Dont* ... Pity I couldn't stay and find out, really. May have to go back.' He stopped and looked at Guy. 'By the way,' he said, 'you haven't told me how you —'

Just then, a centurion and two troopers came up behind them and shouted at them. They turned and were about to ask politely if there was anything they could do for anyone when they were accused, in rather intemperate language, of being spies in the pay of Pompey and the Senate, and ordered not to move. Naturally, they ran for it.

'I said,' Caesar repeated, 'dismiss.'

Nobody moved. They had all turned their heads to watch something directly behind Caesar's right shoulder.

'Hey,' Caesar protested, 'so what's so bloody interesting all of a sudden that —' He looked round too, and saw a large group of angry soldiers chasing two eccentrically dressed men through the camp. They were heading directly for the oak tree.

'Don't just stand there, you morons,' Caesar snapped. 'Grab hold of them and find out what —'

He got no further. The more brightly coloured of the two intruders had come dashing up, exhibiting a quite remarkable turn of speed, and collided with the military tribune Titus Labienus, sending him reeling back. Labienus lost his footing on the damp grass, wobbled violently, and fell over. The intruder recovered his balance with an effort and was about to continue running when Caesar himself reached out a long thin arm and attached it to the intruder's ear.

'Ouch,' the intruder said. He froze.

'Now then,' Caesar said, 'just what the hell do you think you're doing, barging in here when I'm having a —'

'Let go!'

The words came from the second intruder, who was standing about ten yards away from the tree, with a mob of soldiers gaining on him fast. The second intruder didn't seem to be paying any attention to them; he was pointing at Caesar with a small black metallic object in his hand.

'Let go!' he repeated.

'Hoy!' Caesar replied angrily. 'Who do you think you're talking to?'

The brightly dressed intruder squirmed in Caesar's grip. 'For crying out loud, Guy,' he yelled, 'put that confounded thing away! You know what happened the last —'

'If you don't let go,' said the other intruder, 'it'll be the worse for you.'

Caesar gave him a blank stare; then threw back his head and burst out laughing, at the same time giving the ear in his grip a savage tweak. The second intruder swore, and then there was a loud crack, like a thunderclap. Caesar's hat jumped about a foot into the air, was caught by a gust of wind, and floated away towards the river.

'My hat!' Caesar shrieked, and clapped his hands to his bald head, too late to stop a great long lock of damp grey hair from slithering off his bald dome and flopping down over his ear. He directed a murderous look at the two intruders and set off in furious pursuit of his floating hat.

'Guy, you pillock,' Blondel panted, 'now look what you've done.'

They watched as Caesar, intent only on the recovery of his hat, dived into the waters of the river and started to swim. The current was almost too strong for him but he struck out vigorously, reached the other side and flung himself with a cry of exultant triumph on the hat, which had come to roost in the branches of a stunted thorn bush.

The army, meanwhile, was watching with fascinated attention. As soon as Caesar set foot on the far bank, a great whoop of joy rose from the ranks, as thirty thousand men shouted, all at once;

'The die is cast! Caesar has crossed the Rubicon! To Rome! Rome!'

Caesar looked up, the hat wedged once more over his slightly protruding ears. A look of supreme disgust crossed his face.

'Oh *shit*,' he said.

The army had started to cross the river. Someone had hoisted up the sacred Eagle standards. They were singing the battle song of the Fifteenth Legion.

'I told you,' Blondel said. 'Didn't I tell you?'

They were alone now in the abandoned camp. On the other side of the river Caesar was being carried on the shoulders of his bodyguard, on inexorably towards Rome and Empire.

'But I thought that was what was supposed to happen,' Guy whimpered.

Blondel shook his head. 'In a sense, yes,' he replied. 'But ... oh, never mind. Let's get out of here and go and have a drink.'

Giovanni smiled.

'What I always say to people in your situation,' he said, 'people who've fallen off the edge of the world and are sailing aimlessly about, is that one of these days you're bound to find your way back again, and in the meantime, don't you think your money should be working for you as hard as it possibly can, so that when you *do* finally get out of here ...'

The Genoese merchant gave him a blank, empty-eye-socket stare. Giovanni kept going. In his youth, when he was just another Florentine wide boy hawking scarlet hose and fragments of the True Cross door to door through Gascony, he'd come up against harder nuts than this.

'Think how long you've been down here,' he said. 'A hundred years? Two hundred? Would five hundred be nearer the mark, maybe?'

The Genoese made a little muffled noise, somewhere between a moan and a shriek. Giovanni nodded.

'Okay,' he said, 'call it four hundred and fifty years, give or take fifty on either side. Now, a modest stake of say one thousand bezants, invested at twenty-five per cent compound interest, tax-free for four hundred and fifty years ...'

The Genoese suddenly howled and tried to bite Giovanni in the neck. Being a man of action as well as a man of intellect, Giovanni sidestepped, picked up an

179

oar and clubbed him savagely on the head. Being an insurance broker he mentioned to him the benefits of proper accident insurance and private health cover. Before he could get any forms out or unscrew the top of his fountain pen, however, the Genoese stopped twitching and lay still. Giovanni sighed; an opportunity lost, he couldn't help feeling.

'Is he . . .?' Marco asked.

Giovanni nodded. 'Fool to himself,' he said. 'I suppose we could retrospectively insure his life for a couple of grand, but it hardly seems worth the bother. Come on, let's try over there.'

They walked on over the insubstantial sea, keeping their spirits up by offering passing ships the opportunity to take advantage of low-start endowment mortgages. After about an hour, they came to what looked remarkably like a bank.

'Don't look at it,' Giovanni said, 'it's probably just a mirage or something.'

Iachimo shook his head. 'Look,' he said, 'they're members of FIMBRA, it says so in the window. It must be a bank.'

'Iachimo . . .'

'But Giovanni,' Iachimo said, 'they aren't *allowed* to display the FIMBRA logo unless they're . . .'

Giovanni shrugged. If he was going to start hallucinating, a bank was a nice thing to hallucinate. Especially a bank which, in the circumstances, must count as definitively offshore.

'We might just wander in,' he said tentatively. 'Just on the off chance, you know . . .'

It was a very nice bank, and before he knew what he was doing Giovanni had filled his pockets with leaflets.

Then he noticed something.

'Iachimo,' he said, 'Marco, there's nobody here.'

Iachimo sniffed like a dog. 'You're right,' he said. 'Completely deserted. How can they be members of FIMBRA if there's nobody . . .?'

Giovanni rang the bell; nobody came. Mind you, that didn't mean very much. Next he tried the door that led to the area behind the bulletproof screen. It opened.

'Coming?' he asked.

Marco looked nervously at the security cameras. 'Do you think we should?' he said. 'I mean, we are in the Archives, and —'

'There's nobody here,' Giovanni replied. 'Come on.'

They walked through. At once, all the computer screens, which had been blank, sprang into life. They started displaying stock market results from all over the Universe. There were one or two that Giovanni had never heard of before.

'Here, Iachimo,' he said, 'you know about these things. What's the $\psi\gamma\uparrow\gamma\beta\leftarrow\leftrightarrow\downarrow\phi$ 600 Share Index when it's at home?'

Iachimo frowned and shook his head; clearly, it worried him that he hadn't heard of it. Giovanni, meanwhile, had sat down in front of one of the consoles and was tapping keys. After a while, he looked round.

'Lads,' he said, 'I think I've sorted it out.'

The others looked at him.

'It's pathetically simple, really,' Giovanni said, with a grin. He tapped a key, and a dazzling display of little twinkling figures appeared on the screen in front of him. He paused for a moment and read them. 'Getting us out of here is going to be no

181

trouble at all. Iachimo, what's the sort code for our bank in Geneva?'

'7865443,' Iachimo said promptly. 'Why?'

'Because,' Giovanni replied, 'I'm going to pay us into our deposit account there. By telegraphic transfer. A doddle, really. Hold tight.'

He typed in 7865443, then a couple of codes, and then their names. A moment later, they had vanished.

They stayed vanished.

'Giovanni!' Iachimo screamed. It was dark and cold and he had the sensation of falling and he couldn't feel anything – anything – with any of his limbs or senses. 'What's happening? Giovanni?'

'Sod it,' came Giovanni's voice, drifting in nothingness. 'We must be after business hours. The bastards have put us on hold.'

'What does that mean?'

'Means we've got to stay here till the bank opens for the next day's trading,' Giovanni yelled back. 'Means we'll lose a whole day's interest. When I get out of this, somebody's going to get sued.'

As if in response, there was a deafening crackle and the three brothers felt as if they were being squeezed, like toothpaste, through some sort of nozzle. Then there was a crash, and they fell, head-first, through a computer screen.

'Giovanni,' Marco said, 'you've got a bar code printed all over your forehead.'

'So have you,' Giovanni replied. He picked himself up, dusted splinters of broken cathode ray tube out of his hair, and smiled at the terrified computer operator in whose lap he had landed. She stared at him and then, without removing her eyes from his face, started to fill in an Input chit.

'Right then,' Giovanni said. 'Come on, you two. Mademoiselle,' he asked the girl, 'je vous prie, où sommes-nous, exactement?'

The girl replied that they were in Geneva, and did he want to be taken off deposit? Giovanni confirmed that he did, and the three brothers walked out of the bank into the open air.

'Quick thinking, that, on my part,' Giovanni said, 'wouldn't you say?'

'We should have offered to pay for the broken machines,' Marco replied. 'They aren't cheap, you know.'

They found a café and had a drink. They could afford it, after all; Marco's lucky silver threepenny bit, which he kept on his key ring, had just accumulated 10,000 Swiss francs interest. Accordingly, it was adjudged to be his shout. He paid.

'The next thing on the agenda,' Giovanni said, 'is to find Blondel.'

Iachimo shook his head. 'Can't do that,' he said. 'That man said he'd been destroyed, right? Blown up in a Time Archive. Means he never existed.'

Giovanni put down his glass, wiped his lips on his tie and sighed. 'Don't be a prawn, Iachimo,' he said. 'If he never existed, how come we both know who I'm talking about?'

'Who are you talking about?' Marco asked. They ignored him.

'Stands to reason,' Giovanni went on. 'If we both remember him, it follows that he must have existed. Thus he can't have been killed in the Archives. Furthermore, if

183

we can remember him here, Topside, then he must have got out of the Archives somehow. In which case he's still here somewhere. *Capisce?*'

Iachimo wrinkled his brows, thought about it and then nodded enthusiastically. 'That's brilliant,' he said. 'How do we find him?'

Giovanni shrugged. 'There,' he said, 'you have me. That's a difficult one. I mean, we had enough trouble finding him last time.'

'You could try the phone book,' Marco said.

'I suppose,' Giovanni went on, 'we could try going back to all the gigs we set up for him which he never actually did and see if he's done any of them yet. Then we could sort of work backwards, and ...'

'There's a phone book here,' Marco said. 'Look.'

'Alternatively,' Giovanni continued, 'we could hire an enquiry agent. There's Ennio Sforza, only he's semi-retired. Or maybe we could try Annibale Tedesci; I know he really only does cross-temporal divorce work, but he might be prepared to stretch a point ...'

'Here we are,' said Marco. 'Blondel. Blondelle Cash & Carry, Blondella Hydraulic Systems, Blond Elephant Night club ...'

'Do you know how much Annibale Tedesci charges per hour?' Iachimo replied. 'We'd have to do extra gigs just to cover the fees. How about if we did a credit search? We could go back in time, issue him with a credit card, and then ...'

'Blondel,' Marco said, '32 Munchenstrasse.'

His brothers turned and stared at him.

'32 Munchenstrasse,' he repeated. 'Here, look for yourselves if you don't —'

His brothers examined the entry. They read it again.

Giovanni said something profane under his breath, and grinned.

'Now that,' he said, 'is what I call landing on your feet. Marco.'

Marco smiled, preparatory to preening himself. 'Yes?'

'Get them in, there's a good lad,' Giovanni said, indicating the empty glasses. 'And while you're at it, see if anybody's got a street map.'

La Beale Isoud tapped her foot.

'Mr Goodlet,' she said, 'enough is enough. I can take a joke as well as anyone, but this is getting silly. Either you open that door this minute, or —'

The door opened, and Blondel crawled through. 'Hello, Sis,' he said. 'Is supper ready? I'm starving. You've met Guy, haven't you?'

'Mr *Goodlet*!' said La Beale Isoud. 'Come back here at once.'

Guy, halfway back down the coal-cellar steps, froze. Like an exhausted stag turning at bay, he knew when he'd had enough. He smiled weakly.

'We have met, yes,' he said. 'Blondel . . .'

But Blondel wasn't listening; either to Guy, who was trying to explain in a loud and urgent whisper, or to La Beale Isoud, who was providing a different version of the same basic facts in a much louder voice. He waved a hand placidly and walked through into his study, leaving Guy and La Beale Isoud together. He probably thought he was being tactful.

'Mademoiselle, er de Nesle,' Guy said, 'I think we really ought to . . .'

La Beale Isoud swept past him and locked the coal-

185

cellar door with a little silver key, which she then dropped down the front of her dress. It must have been cold, because she winced slightly. 'Now then, Mr Goodlet,' she said grimly, 'I think we most certainly ought to get a few things straight, here and now. First, if you think for one moment that I want to marry you, you couldn't be more wrong.'

'Oh,' Guy said. He felt like a boxer whose opponent has just punched himself forcefully on the nose. 'Well, I . . .'

'If you were the last man in the entire world,' La Beale Isoud went on, 'and they were giving away free alarm clock radios with every wedding bouquet, I still wouldn't marry you, if it was up to me.'

'It is, surely.'

La Beale Isoud looked at him. 'What?' she asked.

'Up to you,' Guy said. 'I mean, I'm with you a hundred per cent there. Who you marry – who you don't marry, more to the point – surely that's your business and nobody else's. You stick to your guns.'

'Mr Goodlet,' said La Beale Isoud dangerously, 'the fact remains that we are married – or we will be, which is roughly the same thing, I suppose. The question is, what can we do about it?'

'We could get a divorce,' Guy said. 'If we book one now, perhaps it could be ready by the time we —'

'Divorce,' said La Beale Isoud, 'is out of the question. The scandal would be unthinkable.'

'Surely not.'

'Kindly,' said La Beale Isoud, 'do not interrupt. As far as I'm concerned, divorce is entirely out of the question. If you have any *sensible* suggestions, I should be pleased to hear them.'

186

Guy thought, but all he could come up with was suicide. He stared at his feet uncomfortably.

'I take it,' Isoud went on, 'that you have nothing constructive to suggest. Very well, then. I take it that we'll just have to find some – how can I put it? – some form of civilised compromise.'

Guy nodded. 'That suits me,' he said. 'I'm all for civilisation. What had you in mind?'

La Beale Isoud glowered at him. 'Frankly, Mr Goodlet,' she said, 'I feel that only one form of compromise is likely to be acceptable; namely that, after we are married, we see as little of each other as possible.'

'Fair enough,' Guy said. 'Separate beds, you mean?'

'I mean,' Isoud replied, 'separate centuries.'

Guy raised an eyebrow. 'Don't get me wrong,' he said, 'I think it's a perfectly splendid idea. But you said a minute ago that you didn't want a divorce because of how it would look. Wouldn't having a husband hundreds of years in the future look almost as bad? Or doesn't it work like that?'

'If you intend to make difficulties —'

'No, no,' Guy said quickly, 'perish the thought. Besides,' he added, 'if we're hundreds of years apart, then really the whole thing becomes pretty well academic anyway, doesn't it? I mean, you could marry someone else, I could marry someone else, nobody would ever know ...'

'Mr *Goodlet*!'

'Oh come on, now,' Guy said, 'be reasonable. Anyway, doesn't it say somewhere in the book of rules that if your wife hasn't been heard of for seven years she's assumed to be dead? Think it's seven years, though I'd have to ask my lawyer. I mean, that way we'd have all the advantages of a divorce without the . . .'

Something about La Beale Isoud's expression – perhaps it was the ferocious look in her limpid blue eyes – gave Guy to understand that he wasn't really doing himself much good. He decided to change the subject.

'Anyway,' he said, 'we can sort something out, between us, you know, later. Plenty of time for that. Um.'

That seemed to be that. La Beale Isoud, perhaps not able to trust herself to speak further, stomped out of the hall, and shortly afterwards Guy heard the sound of large copper pans being banged about.

Then Blondel came back into the hall. He had changed out of his usual outfit into another, exactly the same but cleaner, and had combed his hair. Guy had the feeling that La Beale Isoud was rather strict about such things. He shuddered; and Blondel, observing him, grinned weakly.

'Isoud told me the good news,' he said, 'I ought to congratulate you, but I'm a realist. Never mind, it may never happen.'

'Thanks,' Guy replied, 'but it already has. Or it already will have. How do you cope with all these future tenses, by the way?'

'I don't,' Blondel replied. 'When you whizz about in time like I do, you tend to get the sense of what people say rather better if you don't actually listen to the words. Just stick with the general sort of tune and you won't go far wrong. Fancy a drink?'

Guy nodded. A drink, he felt, would be almost as good an idea as something to eat. It was a very long time since he'd had anything to eat, and he didn't want to get out of practice. He mentioned this; and the words were no sooner past the gate of his teeth when there came from the far room the sound of somebody hitting a piece of quick-fry steak with a wooden mallet, very hard.

'It sounds to me,' Blondel said, 'as if Isoud's fixing something for us right now. You're welcome to stay.'

'Thank you,' Guy replied. 'But I'd hate to impose, I mean ...'

Blondel nodded. 'So would I,' he replied, 'but I'm stuck with her. Look, Guy, my dear fellow, are you *sure* you wouldn't like to marry her? Permanently, I mean. Sort of, take her a long way away? I'm sure she'd make you a wonderful wife, and then I could just get a hamburger or a couple of pancakes on my way home in the evenings, instead of having to gnaw my way through scale models of the Krak Des Chevaliers in mashed potato.'

'Mashed potato?'

'Exactly,' Blondel replied, shaking his head. 'My sister has this problem with mashed potato. She gets it confused with food. Mind you, all the women in my family believe in substantial meals. You take,' he added, with a slight grimace, 'my sister Ysabel. Give her five loaves and two fishes, and you could invite both Houses of Parliament.'

'Er ...'

'Thought not,' Blondel said. 'Don't blame you. I'm told it's worse once you've actually married them, but mercifully I'm not in a position to speak authoritatively on that point.'

'I ...'

'Pretending to have toothache doesn't help, either,'

Blondel continued, with the air of a man settling down to a cherished topic, 'because then they've got an excuse to make soup. Do you have any idea of the number of saucepans an active, able-bodied woman can use making soup? They aren't allowed to wash up, by the way, because of their fingernails. Cracks them, or something similarly absurd. On that basis, I should be walking around with half a pound of shrapnel on the ends of my arms. It's a conspiracy, that's what it is. They learn it from their mothers.'

Guy nodded. 'In the meantime,' he asked, 'have you got any biscuits, or anything like that? Sorry to be a nuisance, but ...'

'My dear fellow, I was forgetting.' Blondel looked round at the door behind which La Beale Isoud was, to judge by the sound effects, lacerating carrots, checked that it was firmly shut, and then jumped for one of the lamp-brackets. He caught it, swung himself up into one of the window mullions, picked something out of a crack in the stonework, and threw it down to Guy. It was a leather satchel containing three and a half rolls of chocolate digestives.

'It's my secret supply,' he called down in a loud whisper. 'Got to keep them hidden, or she'll pound them up for cheesecake base. She makes a cheesecake that'd stop crossbow bolts. Help yourself.'

Guy tipped some biscuits into his pockets and threw the bag back quickly. Blondel, having restored his treasure, lowered himself back down again, his jaws moving furtively.

'It's not as if she doesn't make biscuits too,' he said, through a mouthful of crumbs. 'But they're those brick-hard ones with almonds and no chocolate. I mean, brilliant for lining a fireplace, but not much use for constructive eating. Now then, we were thinking about having a drink.'

But before they could get to the decanters, there was a hammering at the coal-cellar door. Blondel raised both eyebrows in astonishment.

'Expecting anybody?' he asked.

Guy shook his head.

'Well,' Blondel said, 'I'm not, and unless it's double glazing then someone would appear to have followed us. And we don't get many offers of double glazing in the eleventh century. Be different if this was Chartres or Saint Denis. I think I'd better see who it is.'

With a swift movement of his hand, he drew a sword down from the wall and hid it behind his back. With the other hand he undid the bolts on the door and pulled it open. Through the door came Giovanni, Iachimo and Marco.

'I wasn't far wrong,' he said, 'at that. What on earth do you gentlemen want?' He produced the sword and smiled. 'You'd better come in,' he said. 'And take your hats off quick.'

The Galeazzo brothers uncovered their heads immediately. Blondel grinned and put up his sword.

'Drink, anybody?' he said. 'I hope you all like mashed potato. Now, how did you get here, and what do you want?' He poured out five glasses of mead with a flourish and handed them round.

'We were telexed,' Marco said, and would undoubtedly have explained further had not Giovanni trodden on his foot. He had to get up and walk across the hall to do it; but Marco was trained to obey certain signals, and if one didn't use them it only confused him.

'We were just passing,' Giovanni said, 'on our way back from the Archives; stopped off for a drink, happened to notice your name in the phone book, thought we'd drop in on the off chance you were in.' He looked about him. 'Nice place you have here,' he said. 'I wonder if you've ever considered whether you've got it adequately insured. We can offer you ...'

Blondel shook his head. 'No point,' he said. 'In five days' time it gets burnt down. Not a stone left standing.'

'Ah.'

'Mind you,' Blondel went on, 'every four days I move it back in time. That means I get to pay reduced rates, too. Handy.'

Giovanni looked at his brothers and shrugged. 'Anyway,' he said, 'this isn't entirely a social call.'

Blondel grinned. 'You amaze me,' he said.

'In fact,' Giovanni went on, 'we have some very serious business to discuss. You realise that you are in breach of your contract?'

'Oh yes?'

Giovanni nodded gravely. 'Clauses 1, 2, 3, 4, 5, 6, 7, 8, 9, 10, 11, 12, 13, 14, 15, 16, 17, 18 and 20.'

'Really?' Blondel said. 'What's Clause 19 about, then?'

'There isn't one,' Giovanni replied. 'Originally it was your right to receive a duly audited account every financial year, but it got deleted.'

'Did it?'

'Yes.'

'I see.' Blondel poured himself another glass of mead, picked some beeswax out of it with his fingernail, and smiled. 'But I'm in breach of the rest of it, am I?'

192

'I'm afraid so,' Giovanni said. 'However —'

'That's very serious, isn't it?'

'It could be,' Giovanni replied, 'potentially. That's why —'

'If I was you,' Blondel purred, 'I'd sue.'

Giovanni blinked. 'You would?'

Blondel nodded vigorously. 'Too right,' he replied. 'Can't have people going about the place playing fast and loose with binding agreements, can we? No, bash on, that's what I'd do, and stand up for your rights.'

'Um ...'

'In fact,' Blondel said, 'there's no time like the present, is there? Now it so happens,' he said, standing up and taking down a sword and a shield from the wall, 'that this castle is within the jurisdiction' – he swung the sword in his hand to check the balance; it passed – 'of the Supreme Court of the Barony of Nesle, of which I' – he tested the point, swore, and licked his finger – 'am hereditary Chief Justiciar. Normally, there's quite a backlog of cases, but just at present I think we could fit you in. Trial by combat, naturally.'

Giovanni swallowed hard. 'Combat,' he repeated.

'Absolutely,' Blondel replied. 'We tried the other way, but we kept on coming back to combat. Quicker, cheaper, and above all, fairer; not to mention a damn sight less traumatic for the participants. Would you like me to lend you a shield? You seem to have come out without one.'

'Actually,' Giovanni said, 'perhaps we ought to try a little without prejudice negotiation. I find litigation positively counter-productive sometimes, don't you?'

'Ah yes,' Blondel replied, making his choice from a rack of double-bladed battle-axes, 'but that's because you've never had the advantage of the Nesle judicial system. No, I think a couple of bouts ought to' – he weighed two maces, picked the heavier one and put the other back – 'get this business knocked on the head – if you'll pardon the expression – in two shakes of a lamb's tail. Here, catch!' He tossed a helmet to Giovanni, who dropped it with a clang. 'Up to you,' Blondel said, putting on his own helmet and feeling the edge of his axe. 'Helmets are optional, and I can understand your feeling nervous, what with Mr Goodlet being in the same room. Shall we make it best of three, do you think? Or would you prefer sudden death?'

Giovanni made a small, whimpering noise and looked round at his brothers for support. They weren't there. They were right behind him, hiding.

'Alternatively,' Blondel said, removing his helmet and putting down his axe on a handy coffee table, 'we could forget all about the contract. I mean, we all trust each other, don't we? Nod if you agree.'

The Galeazzo brothers nodded in perfect unison, like a miniature Cerberus in the back window of a Vauxhall Cavalier.

'Glad you think so, too,' said Blondel. 'You wouldn't happen to have it with you, by any chance?'

Marco put his feet carefully out of Giovanni's way and said 'Yes.' He went on to explain that it was in Giovanni's briefcase, inside an envelope marked *Tax Returns 1232/3*, and would have enlarged on the theme had not his brothers put a helmet on his head, the wrong way round, so that the neckguard obstructed his mouth. By then, however, the contract was on the fire.

'Now then,' Blondel said, 'I think it's time for some food.'

Giovanni was looking at the contract curling up on the fire. It was possible that he might have felt similar sensations of loss and sadness for the death of his grandmother; but the theory would be hard to prove, given that he'd sold her to Barbary slavers hundreds of years earlier, and since then they'd lost touch. He moistened his lips with the tip of his tongue.

'Right,' he said. 'Well, I think we've now established a forum for negotiations leading to a new contract ...'

Blondel turned round slowly and looked at him. 'You think so,' he said.

'Absolutely,' Giovanni replied. 'I mean,' he added, and his will to profit battled briefly with his instincts of self-preservation; the will to profit won. 'Perhaps a little fine-tuning of some of the clauses might be called for, what with the passage of time and changes in circumstances; but what the hell, Blondel, you're still an artist, and artists need agents. Now then ...'

'Just for that,' Blondel said, 'you get a double helping of mashed potato.'

Giovanni looked wounded. 'You disappoint me,' he said. 'I think we can do business together. After all,' he said, 'you'd be interested in finding the Chastel des Larmes Chaudes, now wouldn't you?'

Blondel gave him a long look. 'You're bluffing,' he said.

'Maybe.'

'You don't know where the Chastel des Larmes Chaudes is, any more than I do.'

Giovanni smiled. 'True,' he said. 'But I know where they bank.'

There was a long silence, broken only by the sound of Guy eating a few stale peanuts he'd found in a deserted finger-bowl. Finally Blondel stood up and walked about the room for a while.

'Where they *bank*...' he said.

'Absolutely,' Giovanni said. 'After all, it's a fundamental rule of nature. Everybody banks somewhere.'

'Oh yes?' Blondel replied. 'What about ...' He tailed off.

'What about?' Giovanni repeated.

Blondel suddenly grinned. 'I was trying to think of an example,' he said, 'and I couldn't. All right, then, tell me how you know where the Chastel des Larmes Chaudes banks.'

Giovanni shook his head. 'I wasn't born yesterday,' he said. 'We've got to have a contract first.'

Blondel sighed. 'Have it your own way, then. Even when I've found out where their bank is, how does that help me find them?'

'That's up to you,' Giovanni replied. 'You're a very resourceful man. Now then, we were discussing terms.'

'Were we?'

'Yes.'

'Oh,' Blondel shrugged. 'Go on, then.'

'Just one gig,' Giovanni said. 'One very big concert. We'll network it, naturally; every country, every century, every dimension.'

Blondel frowned. 'How?' he said.

'Simple.' Giovanni spread his hands in a gesture of extreme simplicity. 'We'll do it in every country, in every century, simultaneously.'

'Hang on,' Blondel said. 'Nobody's ever done that before.'

Giovanni's smile widened until it came close to being a geographical feature. 'They soon will have,' he replied. 'Just one gig, Blondel. How about it?'

As he spoke the kitchen door opened, and Isoud trotted angrily out, plonked down a huge dish of mashed potato on the table, and trotted back again. The door slammed behind her.

'All right,' Blondel said. He looked at the mashed potato and shuddered. 'Just this once.'

FAX
From: Galeazzo, Galeazzo and Galeazzo, Beaumont Street, Londinium
To: The Chastel des Larmes Chaudes
Your reference: AC
Message follows

'If it's one of those junk faxes,' Mountjoy's secretary said, 'I'll get him to write to the company. I've got enough to do without running up and down stairs delivering mailshots.'

Congratulations! the message continued. *You have been selected as this month's lucky winner in the Galeazzo Brothers Financial Services Draw. This month's fabulous prize is two tickets for the greatest ever Blondel concert.*

'Thought so,' said Mountjoy's secretary, and she went to pull the paper out of the machine. An arm stopped her.

'Leave it,' said a voice harshly behind her. 'I want to see what it says.'

'Yes, *sir*,' squeaked the secretary. She retreated.

All you have to do to receive your fabulous prize, went on the message, slowly ballooning out of the printer, *is to invest ST50,000 or more in a Galeazzo Brothers*

Managed Fund of your *choice before the end of the month; but hurry! If you don't claim your fabulous prize within the specified time, then Galeazzo Brothers Financial Services reserve the right to offer your fabulous prize to another lucky winner. All enquiries about Galeazzo Brothers Managed Funds should be addressed to . . .*

And then the paper got wedged and the toner ran out and the rollers jammed and the printer got stuck, and a few moments later the whole thing seized up and started beeping hysterically. An arm reached out and tweaked the paper free. Someone opened a door for the distinguished visitor, and he left. Gradually, life in Reception returned to normal.

'Who was that?' Mountjoy's secretary asked. Everybody looked at her.

'Funny,' said the office junior. 'Dead comical.'

'Straight up,' she replied. 'Who was it? I've never seen him before.'

'That,' said the postboy, 'was Mr A.'

'Who's —'

'So next time,' the postboy went on, 'if I was you, I'd mind your manners, right? It doesn't do to get on the wrong side of Mr A.' The postboy frowned. 'So to speak,' he added.

'I still don't know . . .'

But everyone was wandering off; some to make coffee, others to file memoranda, others to stand around waiting for the man to come and fix the photocopier. Mountjoy's secretary was just scratching her head, wondering if she'd missed something somewhere, when the phone rang. She hurried back to her place, sat down and put on the headphones.

'Chastel des Larmes Chaudes, can I help you?' she warbled.

'I want to speak to the proprietor,' said the voice at the other end. A nice voice, Mountjoy's secretary thought; not the sort to bite your head off.

'Thank you,' she replied. 'Who shall I say is calling, please?'

'My name's de Nesle,' the voice said. 'Jean de Nesle. I think he'll take my call.'

The atmosphere at a Blondel concert is not easy to describe. When the concert in question has been billed as the Very Last Ever Farewell Charity Concert, the atmosphere is heightened to such an extent that barometers are brought into the auditorium entirely at their owners' risk.

For the occasion the Galeazzo Brothers had built – over the course of centuries, naturally, and entirely funded by retrospective borrowing (which meant that the bank ended up paying *them* interest) – the biggest, grandest, most garish neo-Gothic auditorium ever. Every inch of the surface area of the huge massed banks of speakers was carved with intricate scroll-and-acanthus work, and the leads entered them through the mouths of grinning gargoyles. The stage itself was supported on slender pinnacles of stone at a dizzying height above the ground, and was roofed over with a breathtaking canopy of stained glass, providing an unrivalled light show without the expense of electric power.

Up in his dressing room, Blondel wasn't feeling the

slightest bit nervous. As far as he was concerned, he was going to sing. He quite liked singing, although he found it got a bit tiresome if you did it day in, day out, and since he'd written all the songs himself he wasn't worried about forgetting the words. Even if he did, he could make up some more. They'd like that, probably.

'I do wish you'd stop walking up and down like that,' he said to Giovanni, who had worn a little freeway in the pile of the carpet. 'You know I like to get forty winks before I go on, and you're keeping me awake.'

Giovanni spat out a mouthful of fingernail and scowled at him. 'The biggest gig in the history of the world,' he snarled. 'If they suddenly ask for their money back, it'll wipe out the financial structures of the entire civilised world. For God's sake, most of the money we've been paid for seats hasn't even been made yet. I've got a right to be nervous.'

Blondel shrugged. 'Fair enough,' he said, 'if it makes you feel any better, by all means be nervous. But it'd be awfully sweet of you if you'd just go and do it somewhere else.'

Giovanni shook his head furiously, until it became a blur of movement. 'Oh no,' he said. 'I'm not letting you out of my sight till this is all safely over. Not after Wurtemburg.'

'Come on, Giovanni,' Blondel sighed. 'Not Wurtemburg *again*.'

Giovanni ignored him. 'A sell-out,' he said. 'Not a seat to be had for any money. Crown Prince of Denmark sitting in the front row, eating popcorn. And you take it into your head to slope off and sing under some castle instead, just because —'

'It was seeing the Crown Prince put it into my head,

201

actually,' Blondel commented. 'I thought, Elsinore, haven't been there for ages, worth a try. A complete washout, actually. I nearly got spitted by a nervous guard with a halberd, but that was all.'

Giovanni growled at him. 'That was not bloody well all,' he snapped. 'I had to pay out ninety million groschen in returned admittance. The Crown Prince nearly did his nut. Tried to stab me through the safety curtain. And that's why I'm not letting you set foot outside this room until ...'

Blondel shrugged. 'All right,' he said amicably, 'entirely up to you. I just thought you might be more comfortable sitting down. Have an aspirin or something.'

'I don't want an aspirin,' Giovanni replied. 'For two pins I'd take a short cut through a couple of hours and only come back when it's all over. Only then I wouldn't be able to keep an eye on you ...'

The door opened and Guy came in with a tray. It contained a glass of water, a dry biscuit and a handful of seedless currants.

'There's a man outside,' he said, 'claims he's from the *Anglo-Saxon Chronicle*, wants an interview. I told him to get lost.'

Blondel drank half the water and nibbled the edge of the biscuit. 'He was probably telling the truth, actually,' he said. 'Still, I don't much care for reporters. Silly of me, I know, and they're only doing their job, but —'

'Job nothing,' Giovanni interrupted. 'We've done an exclusive deal with the *FT*.'

'Never mind,' Blondel said. 'Now, if it'll take your mind off worrying, we can run through the programme.

Will that make you feel any better?'

Giovanni nodded. He'd grown his fingernails for two years just to be ready for tonight, and he'd finished them already.

'Well,' Blondel said, 'we'll start off with *Purgator Criminum*, something with a bit of go to it; then we'll have *Ma Joie*, follow that up with a couple of numbers from the CB —'

'Which ones?'

'I thought *Estuans Intrinsecus*, followed by *Imperator Rex Grecorum*. Or do you think that's wise, after what happened at Antioch?'

'Don't worry about that,' Giovanni reassured him, 'I've brought in the whole of the Knights Templar to cover security. First sign of any trouble, they'll be out, dead *and* excommunicated.'

Blondel shrugged again. 'Nothing to do with me,' he said. 'Then I thought we'd do the rest of the White Album stuff, finish off with *Mihi Est Propositum*, and have the break there. That sound OK?'

Giovanni nodded. 'That's good,' he said. 'That way we'll sell a hell of a lot of peanuts in the interval. So what about the second half?'

'Pretty straightforward,' Blondel said. 'We'll do all the new material there.'

'New material?' Guy interrupted. 'You mean you've written more songs since you ...'

Blondel grinned. 'I like to keep my hand in,' he said, 'just for fun. So I reckon we might as well do *Greensleeves*, *Molly Malone*, *Shenandoah*, *Au Près De Ma Blonde*, *Liliburlero* and *The Bonnie Banks of*—'

'Hang on,' Guy said.

Blondel wrinkled his nose. 'Maybe you're right,' he

said, 'not *Loch Lomond.* Don't know what I was thinking of. How about *Swing Low Sweet Chariot?*'

'Ever since Blondel ... retired,' Giovanni explained, 'he's written under a nom de plume.'

'What's that?'

'Anonymous.'

Guy closed his eyes and then opened them again. 'What, all of them?' he asked.

Blondel made a tiny movement with his shoulders. It might have been wincing. 'Pretty well,' he said.

'Did you write *Kiss Me Goodnight, Sergeant Major?*'

Blondel nodded. He did not speak.

'And *Frankie and Johnny?*'

Blondel's head dipped, just perceptibly.

'Really?'

Blondel nodded again and smiled; or at least he lifted the curtain of his lips on a set of clenched teeth.

'Gosh,' Guy said. He seemed to experience an inner struggle, as perhaps between hero-worship and extreme embarrassment. 'Er, can I have your auto —'

Blondel gave him a cold look. 'I also,' he said, 'wrote —'

'It's not for me,' Guy went on, 'it's for my —'

'*Western Wind, When Wilt Thou Blow, Silent Night* and *The Vicar of Bray,*' Blondel went on. He signed the envelope-back that Guy had thrust at him without comment. 'Anyway,' he added, after a while, 'that ought to do for tonight. And of course we can finish up with *L'Amours Dont Sui Epris.* End up with something they can hum on the way home, you know.'

'You didn't write —'

'No,' Blondel snapped, 'certainly not. Look, unless anyone's got anything important they want to talk

204

about, I really am going to try and get a nap now. All right?'

'Anything you say,' Guy said. He folded the envelope carefully and put it away. Even then, he felt he had to add something. You don't meet a seminal genius every day, after all.

'Mr Blondel,' he said, 'I take my hat off to you.'

'So long as it's your own hat,' Blondel replied sleepily, 'that's fine by me. Shut the door behind you when you go.'

Guy did so. By this time, Giovanni had disappeared to have another tearing row with the electricians. The man from the *Anglo-Saxon Chronicle* had retired to the bar, and was probably trying to coax a story out of the PR people in an attempt to scoop the *Tres Riches Heures Du Duc De Berri*. There was nothing, Guy decided, that he could usefully do; which meant he had time to go and find something to eat. Now that was a good idea.

A section of the audience was having trouble finding its seat.

'This,' it said, 'is Row 8765, right?'

'Yes,' said the usher, 'but —'

'And this is a ticket, right?'

'Looks like one,' the usher admitted, 'but —'

'Read me,' said the section of the audience, 'what it says on the ticket.'

'Row 8765 Seat 3654,' said the usher, 'but —'

'Thank you,' said the section of the audience. 'Now, if you'll kindly throw out the man who's sitting in my seat, I can take the weight off my foot and sit down, and you can go and do something else.'

But he's got a ticket too, the usher would have said, if he hadn't met the full force of the section of the audience's eye. As it was, he said, 'Yes, sir,' and shortly afterwards, 'You, out of it.' This remark was addressed, as it happened, to the music critic of the *Oceanian*, whose great-great-great-great-great-grandfather had booked the seat five hundred years in advance and left it in his will, together with strict instructions to his descendants to devote themselves solely to preparing themselves for this event.

'Thank you,' said the section of the audience, as the music critic of the *Oceanian* was carried away on an improvised stretcher. 'You can go now.'

'Yes, sir.'

The section of the audience turned to the two men sitting beside him. They looked identical; not surprisingly.

'Pity,' he continued, 'we could only get two tickets. I don't like having to pull rank like that, let alone use a forged ticket. Bad form. Still, I didn't want you two to miss the fun.'

His two companions nodded. Simultaneously. With one voice they said, 'Thanks.'

The section of the audience waved a deprecating hand. 'That's all right,' he said. 'Now then, let's have a look at the programme. Oh *good*, he's doing *Mihi Est Propositum*. I remember at the Orleans gig of '88 ...'

Guy wasn't having the best of luck. The bar was packed, the hot dog stall had been stripped down to bare wood within thirty seconds of opening, and he found when he reached the front of the queue that the candy-floss, at ST125 a go, was beyond his means. He was beginning to feel decidedly peckish.

He walked along the front of the stage, trying not to trip over the various serpentine bunches of wires, heading for the electricians' staff canteen. With luck there might be a cheese roll or so over there. Electricians of this particular type were outside his immediate knowledge, but the rules of their guild never change; if these electricians were anything like the ones they'd had in the 1940s, they never moved a step without an adequate supply of cheese rolls. Stale, usually, and with bits of translucent yellow rind on the exposed edges of the cheese; but edible, within the broad meaning of the term.

He stopped. In the middle of one of the middle rows there was a man who was only half there.

Guy's mother had taught him three guiding rules of civilised behaviour, and his ability to forget them was a pretty effective gauge of his efficient functioning as a human being in the real world. They were:

(1) Don't push in queues.

(2) Don't talk with your mouth full.

(3) Don't stare.

As to the first; if he'd ever paid any heed to it, he'd still be standing in line in the sub-post office at the end of Garner Street waiting to buy ten first-class stamps for the cards for Christmas 1931. As to the second; as matters stood at present, chance would be a fine thing. And as to the third; well, the possibility of men who were only half there had obviously not been within his mother's contemplation when she formulated the rule. He stared.

The man – he could see him very clearly indeed, although he was quite some way off – didn't seem at all put out about being only fifty per cent present. He was laughing at a joke or something similar, and his hand was extracting peanuts from a packet balanced precariously on his one knee. Peanuts!

Guy wrenched his mind away from thoughts of peanuts. There were plenty of odd-looking people in the audience – the party sitting in the front row were not the sort of thing Guy had ever come across outside the Saturday morning Buck Rogers serial – but none as odd as ... The man was split neatly and precisely down the middle. The dividing line ran down across his forehead, followed his nose down through his lips and chin, bisected his neck and continued down his shirt front. Guy felt a strong urge not to find out what the man looked like viewed in right profile.

'I'd better tell Blondel,' he said to himself.

He turned and walked up the stage towards the small door in the back, which led to the dressing rooms; and would undoubtedly have reached his destination, woken Blondel, told him what he'd seen and so changed the course of past and future history, if only he hadn't caught sight of an unfamiliar figure holding a heaped plate of individual pork pies flitting like a shadow through the wings. He changed course abruptly and followed.

It goes without saying that the pork pie carrier was Pursuivant, and that he wasn't wearing a hat.

Guy made a muffled grunting noise and tried to move his feet. Pointless.

Out of either irony or compassion, they had stopped his mouth with a ham and watercress club sandwich of phenomenal proportions; too thick to bite through

208

without the use of one's hands, at any rate. His tongue could sense the presence of tomato, cucumber and (he felt sure) green peppers and English mustard. He gave up grunting and tried growling instead.

No chance of being heard, of course; not with that noise going on out there. To be sure, it wasn't an unpleasant noise – it was Blondel singing the big numbers from the White Album, and on a number of occasions Guy would have stopped struggling and sat open-mouthed with admiration if it hadn't been for the club sandwich – but what with the amplification and the acoustics and Blondel's natural power of voice projection, the likelihood of anybody hearing his frantic oinking noises, or wishing to leave the music and come and investigate if they did, were pretty well minimal. He was stuck.

Being a realist, therefore, he stopped making a noise and tried thinking instead. The only conclusion which ensued, however, was the feeling that contemplation was probably overrated as against, for example, escaping from tight knots or eating. The thinking made his head hurt, especially on the lower left back where whoever it was had hit him, and he packed it in. The only thing left to do was to sit still and stare at the heaped plate of sausage rolls which some sadist had left on the straight-backed chair opposite.

In the auditorium, Blondel was launching into yet another popular favourite. Guy stretched out his hands, which were tied firmly behind his back, and groped to see if his fingers could encounter anything sharp and useful. No such luck; only what felt, to Guy at least, like a plateful of cheese sandwiches.

Then the door opened and a man came tiptoeing in.

Guy froze (not that that made a vast amount of difference in the circumstances, but he was always one to show willing) and watched.

The man's eyes clearly hadn't got used to the nearly complete darkness in the room (whatever sort of room it was) and quite soon he barked his shin on something, swore quietly and stopped to rub himself. Then he lit a cigarette lighter, and found himself staring straight at Guy.

'Mnnnnnnnn,' Guy said, tersely.

'Who are you?' the man replied, thereby demonstrating a complete absence of all the qualities that Guy had hoped to find in him.

'Mnnn,' he explained. 'Mnnnn mnnnn mnn mnn mn.'

'What?'

By the light of his cigarette lighter, the man appeared to be of medium height, thirtyish, with scruffy long hair, dressed in a sports jacket, an open-necked shirt, light blue baggy trousers and white canvas shoes. He wore spectacles and had the kind of face you'd expect to register bewildered surprise no matter what you said to it. Guy shook his head, causing the club sandwich to oscillate wildly.

'Has someone tied you up?' the man said.

'Mnn,' Guy replied with studied irony. 'Mnnn mnn mnnnn.'

'Here,' the man said, 'this is my card, I'm with BBC television. My name's Danny Bennett.'

'Mnn.'

The man thought for a moment, and then said, 'Would it help if I took that sandwich out of your ...? Right, fine, hold on.'

'Thank you,' Guy replied. 'Now get these ropes off me, for crying out loud.'

'Ropes?'

'The ropes with which my hands are tied behind my back,' Guy said. He remembered something his mother had told him, many years ago. 'Please,' he added.

'Sure, sure,' the man said. He picked up a bread-knife – someone has been using that to make *sandwiches*, Guy reflected – and started to saw at the ropes.

'I'm covering this concert,' the man said, 'for the North Bank Show. Perhaps you could explain something for me. When is this?'

'Ouch,' Guy replied, 'that was my —'

'Sorry,' the man said. 'Only my producer said I was to get in the car and not ask daft questions, and when I got here my calendar watch was reading 35th March 2727, I reckoned – sorry – that it must have gone funny so I reset it, and now it says 43rd August 1364. And not only that, but —'

'What's a calendar watch?' Guy asked.

'Um . . .'

'Don't worry about it,' Guy added quickly. 'Look, if you could just hurry up with these ropes . . .'

The man leaned forward and whispered. 'It's OK,' he said, 'you can tell me, I'm a reporter. Is something going on around here?'

'Yes,' Guy replied.

The man stared – at least, he stared even more. 'You mean —'

'It's a . . . a plot of some kind,' Guy said. 'And I've got to go and tell someone something terribly important, so if you'd just —'

'Can I come?'

211

Guy turned his head and stared. 'You *want* to come?' he said.

'Sounds to me like there's a story in it,' the man replied. 'You know, like a scoop or something.'

Guy narrowed his eyes for a moment. 'Are you from the *Anglo-Saxon Chronicle*?' he asked.

'You what? I'm from the BBC.'

'The BBC?' Guy repeated. 'You mean the British Broadcasting Corporation?'

'Yes, of course I mean the —'

'What date was it when you left home this morning?'

The man gave him a look of almost liquid bewilderment. '5th April 1994,' he replied. 'Look, what *is* —'

'Thank you,' Guy said. 'Have you nearly finished with that rope?'

'There,' the man answered, 'try that.'

Guy flexed his arms and felt his hands come free. He dived forward, snatched up the club sandwich from where it had fallen, and ate it, very quickly.

'That's *better*', he said. 'You have no idea how much better I feel now.' He grabbed the breadknife and started sawing through the ropes that constrained his ankles.

'Don't mention it,' the man said. He had reached into his pocket and taken out a notebook. 'Now, then,' he said, 'what's happening?'

Guy cut the last strand of rope, put down the knife, and levered himself gingerly to his feet. 'Don't worry about it,' he said, 'it's nothing, really. Just a little —' he searched for the right word – 'temporary problem. Soon get it sorted out. Have a sausage roll, they're really good. Really good.'

'No thanks. Look —'

'Suit yourself,' Guy replied, and he tipped the rest of the plateful into his pocket, shoved a jam tart into his mouth, and started to run. The man tried to follow him, but fell over a packing-case, banged his head and passed out.

This was a pity, because if he hadn't he would have been the only reporter to have witnessed one of the most crucial events in history – in all history, past, present and future. As it was, he came round to find himself fast asleep on a bench in Central Park, with a sore head and a calf-bound copy of *Silas Marner* in his left hand, where his reporter's notebook had been when he fell over.

Some people are just plain unlucky.

Guy ran out of the room into what turned out to be a corridor, stopped and looked both ways. Nothing. Nor any indication of which way he should go. He could hear the music, which seemed to be coming from directly above his head. A great deal of help that was.

Being one of those people who automatically turns left unless firmly directed to do otherwise, Guy ran down the left branch of the corridor, and so arrived at a glass fire door, which was locked.

Oh *good*, he thought, I've always wanted to do this.

He picked up a nearby fire extinguisher, ate a sausage roll, and attacked. The glass was much tougher than it looked, but not nearly tough enough, and when Guy had quite finished, he reached through, found the bolt on the other side, drew it back and opened the door. Easy.

Standing on the other side of the door, hands on hips and looking decidedly unfriendly, was La Beale Isoud.

'There you are,' she said. 'I've been looking for you everywhere.'

Guy noticed that he was still holding the fire extinguisher, and that he had slightly grazed his hand on the glass. He put the extinguisher down slowly and found a weak smile from somewhere.

'You have?' he said.

'Yes,' replied La Beale Isoud. 'You've got to warn Blondel.'

'Why can't you do it?'

'What?'

'You've got the message,' Guy replied. 'You probably know what's going on. You tell him.'

'Don't be *stupid*,' La Beale Isoud replied. 'You're supposed to be a man, aren't you?'

'What's that got to do with —'

'It's probably dangerous,' said La Beale Isoud, fiercely. 'Are you saying you'd just stand there and leave a defenceless woman to —'

'All right, all right,' Guy said. 'You tell me how to find Blondel and I'll give him the message.'

'He's up there,' said La Beale Isoud, pointing to where the sound of someone singing *Floret Silva Nobilis*, rather well, was coming from, 'on the stage.'

'Yes,' Guy replied, 'thank you, I had actually worked that one out for myself. How exactly am I supposed to —'

'Go back down the corridor,' La Beale Isoud replied coldly, 'the way you came. It leads straight out into the wings. I suggest you wait for him to come off stage at the end of the first half.'

'What a truly brilliant plan,' Guy said. 'All right, what's the message?'

'Come on,' said Isoud. 'Follow me, and I'll tell you as we walk. But for heaven's sake don't *dawdle*.'

She turned and trotted briskly away. After a moment's instinctive thought, Guy ran after her and caught her up.

'I was sitting at home,' said La Beale Isoud, 'looking at the hyperfax —'

'What's a —'

'When the message came through which I couldn't make out. It said, *Beware the one-armed man*. Now even you'll agree that that's a very unusual message to get out of the blue like that.'

Guy ignored the even-you bit. 'Odd,' he agreed politely. 'Perhaps it was an advertisement for something.'

'Please, Mr Goodlet,' Isoud said, 'don't interrupt. Your untimely flippancy is quite probably your most disagreeable characteristic. I was wondering what on earth this message could possibly mean when — Mr Goodlet, is that gentleman a friend of yours?'

Guy looked up, blinked twice and reached for where his revolver ought to be. Of course, it wasn't there any more.

'Looking for this?' Pursuivant said. He waggled the revolver tauntingly. Probably out of sheer spite, it went off.

'Eeek!' said La Beale Isoud, and for the first time Guy noticed that she was wearing — had been wearing — one of those tall and picturesque pointed female headdresses that one sees in illuminated manuscripts. He suppressed a snigger, jumped on Pursuivant, and banged his head hard on the ground.

'Here we go again,' Pursuivant sighed, and died.

Guy looked down. 'Damn,' he said, 'I've killed him. Oh well, can't be helped.' He prised his revolver out of Pursuivant's fingers and slipped it back in its holster. 'Sorry,' he said, 'you were saying?'

But La Beale Isoud didn't reply. She was staring at him; no, not so much staring as *looking*.

'Mr *Goodlet*!' she said.

Guy frowned in puzzlement for a moment, and then a light bulb went on inside his head. He got up, retrieved Isoud's perforated headdress and handed it to her.

'All in a day's work,' he said, smiling.

'That was very —' Isoud said.

'Brave?'

'Yes,' replied La Beale Isoud, with just a touch of irritation. 'That was very brave of you, Mr Goodlet. You saw that I was in danger and you unhesitatingly . . .'

'Yes,' Guy replied, 'I know. It's not every chap who'd do that, you know. Anyway, there you were, pondering this message.'

'Oh yes. I was just wondering what on earth it could mean when another message came over the hyperfax. And do you know what it said?'

'No.'

'It said, *Beware the one-legged man*, Mr Goodlet. Well of course, that started me thinking, as you can imagine.'

'Did it?'

'And I was just beginning to get an inkling of an idea when a third message came through. *Beware the one-eyed man*. So of course I came here as fast as I could.'

'You did?'

216

'Naturally.'

'Have a sausage roll?'

'No, thank you, I had tea before I came out. The question is, Mr Goodlet, will we be in time?'

'Who can say?' Guy replied. 'In time for what?'

He got the feeling that under normal circumstances, La Beale Isoud would have said something less than complimentary. She didn't, however. How nice.

In front of them was a door marked *Stage Door; No Entry*. On the other side of it, Blondel's voice stopped singing, there was a moment of complete silence, and then a deafening outburst of applause.

'It's the interval,' Isoud cried. 'Come on, quickly!'

She pushed the door and, before Guy could stop her, walked through.

'Isoud!' Guy shouted, but it was too late. Too late to point out what was written on the door.

He hesitated, just for a moment. It wasn't, he told himself, just the fact that he would be delighted to be rid of her; there was also the question of this cryptic message and the mysterious man who, despite his apparently overwhelming disabilities, was perceived to be so dangerous. On the other hand ...

'Sod it,' he said, and followed.

It wasn't a big apple; but to a man with a bad head, brought on by drinking slightly too much mulled ale in the *Three Pilgrims* the night before, it was plenty big enough.

'Ouch!' said Sir Isaac Newton. He stood up, winced, and looked round for the gardener.

'George!' he yelled. 'Come here this instant.'

The gardener, an elderly man with a face that

217

seemed to indicate feeble-minded dishonesty, waddled across from the asparagus bed. He was hiding something behind his back, as usual.

'Look, George,' said Sir Isaac, 'didn't I tell you to get those damned apples picked last week, before they fell off the tree and spoiled?'

George looked blank. Everyone, after all, is good at something.

'Why haven't you picked the apples, George?'

'Dunno, Master Isaac.'

'Well,' said Sir Isaac, 'bloody well pick them now, all right? Before they do somebody a serious injury.'

'Yes, Master Isaac.'

'And if anybody wants me, I'll be in my study.'

'Yes, Master Isaac.'

As soon as Sir Isaac was safely out of sight, George took the bundle out from behind his back, unwrapped it carefully, and looked at it with pleasure.

It was a pigeon. Very dead. Dead for some time. Still, a poor man has to eat, and on the wages Master Newton paid, a pigeon was a pigeon and to hell with minor decomposition. George grinned.

Then the small gate in the wall opened and a young lady came bursting through. She was wearing funny, old-fashioned clothes, like someone out of one of those old stained-glass windows George had helped smash up during the Civil Wars, and she wore a sort of white witch's hat with a hole in it. George frowned, puzzled.

The lady came to a sudden halt and stared at him.

'Excuse me,' she said. George nodded vigorously. It was just possible that she hadn't noticed the pigeon.

'Excuse me,' the lady repeated. 'Where —'

'In the study, miss,' George replied. 'That way.' He pointed with his left hand.

'I beg your pardon?'

'In the study, miss,' George said. 'Just this minute gone in, miss.'

The door flew open again, and this time it was a man.

'Come on,' the man said to the lady, 'we'd better get back.'

The lady turned. 'Mr Goodlet,' she said, 'what's going on?'

'The door,' said the man. 'It had *No Entry* on it. Didn't you see?'

The lady looked puzzled. 'What do you mean? Oh,' she added. 'It was one of those doors, was it?'

George coughed deferentially. 'He's in the study, sir,' he said.

'Exactly,' said the man to the lady, ignoring George. 'So here we are. We'd better find a town hall or something quick. With luck, we might just be able to find our way back to precisely the right moment. Have you got one of those maps?'

'What maps?'

'Ah,' the man said, 'that means you probably haven't. Never mind.' He turned and faced George. 'Excuse me,' he said.

'He's in the —'

'Which way to the town hall?' the man asked.

George frowned. 'What town hall, sir?' he asked.

'All right then,' said the man, 'what about a police station. Army barracks. Magistrate's court. Something like that.'

George couldn't help shuddering. In court, at his

age, and all for one lousy pigeon. He started to whimper.

The noise had obviously reached the study, because Sir Isaac came out. He was holding a cold towel to his head, and he wasn't looking happy.

'Will you please,' he said, 'keep the noise down?'

'Sorry,' the man said. 'I wonder if you could help us. We're looking for a public building.'

Sir Isaac gave them a look, as if trying to work out what on earth they were on about. A thought occurred to him, painfully. 'If you're desperate,' he said, 'you can use the one at the bottom of the kitchen garden.'

'No, thank you,' the man replied, 'a public *building*. Like a corn exchange or a guildhall or something like that. Something with *No Entry* on the door.'

'I ...' Sir Isaac said. 'Look, I don't want to seem inhospitable, but if this is some sort of a joke ...'

'Really,' the man replied, 'this is an emergency, so if you could just ...'

Sir Isaac closed his eyes. He had known it help sometimes. 'George,' he said, 'escort these people to the Municipal Hall.'

'Yes, Sir Isaac.'

The man was staring; looking at Sir Isaac's clothes and his periwig, apparently making some connection in his mind.

'Sir Isaac?' he said.

'Yes,' said Sir Isaac, 'that's right. Now if you'll just —'

'Sir Isaac *Newton*?'

'That's right. Do I know you?'

The man was looking at him with something resembling awe. '*The* Sir Isaac Newton? The Sir Isaac

220

Newton who discovered gravity?'

'I beg your ...' Sir Isaac stopped suddenly. In his ale-clogged mind, something suddenly clicked into place. '*Gravity!*' he exclaimed. 'Yes, of course, that's it! Gravity!'

The man was looking sheepish. 'Whoops,' he said, 'there I go again, putting my foot in it.'

Sir Isaac's face was alight with joy. 'My dear sir,' he said, 'how can I ever ...?'

But the man and the woman had gone.

In the beginning, God created the heaven and the earth.

And the earth was without form and void, and darkness was upon the face of the deep. And God saw that it had potential, if it was handled properly.

Originally, he had in mind a three-tiered development programme, with a residential area of high-quality executive starter-homes, a business and light industrial park and a spacious, purpose-built shopping precinct, all centred round a general amenity area and linked with a grid-pattern road layout. It was good; and maybe it wouldn't have won any design awards, but it would have done the job and returned something like 400 per cent on the initial outlay.

The problem was the Eden (Phase II) Area Plan, and it was the same old story all over again. You hire an architect, he draws the plans, the quantity surveyor does the costings, the contractor does the schedules, everything's ready to roll and some shiny-trousered bureaucrat refuses to grant planning permission. And there you are, with a thousand billion acre site, eighty billion supernatural brickies, forty million miles of

221

scaffolding, nine hundred thousand JCBs (all balanced on the head of a pin) and terminal planning blight.

God, however, has patience. With a shrug of his shoulders, he walked away from the whole mess and occupied himself with a forty billion acre office development on Alpha Centauri. By the time he'd finished that, plus a little infilling in Orion's Belt and a couple of nice barn conversions in the Pleiades, there had been a number of changes in the political makeup of Eden County Hall. At long last, there were people in charge there whom he could do business with.

Of course, there had to be a public enquiry; there always is. But the problem was that, since the earth was still without form and void, there were no human beings, therefore no public, therefore there could be no enquiry and the previous decision would have to stand. Deadlock.

It was then that the venture capital consortium funding the project, Beaumont Street Retrospective Developments Inc., took a hand. The three members of the consortium were admittedly domiciled millions of years in the future, but they were all bona fide human beings, and they would be delighted to hold an enquiry. No problem.

The result of their deliberation was that the whole purpose of planning controls is to preserve the environment; but no development can actually damage the environment in the long term, because eventually, in the fullness of time, the physical laws of entropy will have effect, the world will come to an end, the Void will creep back, matter will implode into nothingness, and everything will be exactly the same as it originally was. The proposed development was, therefore, strictly temporary, and planning consent was not required for temporary structures.

In the end, they did a deal: God was granted a ten billion year lease, the paperwork was tidied up, bulldozers rolled, and the rest is theology. Almost.

It was, of course, the lawyers who cocked it up. When they sublet the development to the human race, there was some sort of snarl-up in the small print, and when the Antichrist turned up in AD 1000 to serve notice to quit, the human race grinned smugly, pointed to the appropriate page and refused to budge.

The various flies on the wall of God's office that afternoon of 31st December AD 1000 all agree that the ensuing meeting was stormy. There was a free and frank exchange of views, which resulted in the Antichrist being turned into a skeleton and split down the middle (or as we would say nowadays, promoted sideways); the upshot was that the Antichrist was sent off to find a loophole in the lease, which he did.

One of the conditions of the lease was that Mankind was obliged to worship the Landlord regularly and according to the forms prescribed by Mother Church. The Antichrist therefore immediately founded a rival church, presided over by Anti-Popes, with the aim of subverting religion, destroying faith, and nipping in to get the locks changed and the suitcases out on the street before 1690. It worked well to begin with, and eviction proceedings were actually under way when a minor human potentate called Richard Coeur de Lion started in motion a chain of events which would inevitably lead to universal peace, a return to the True Faith, and the building of the New Jerusalem. And there was absolutely nothing that anybody could do about it.

Until, that is, the Antichrist overheard a minor Chastel des Larmes Chaudes functionary by the name of Pursuivant remarking that it would have been better all round if Richard had never been born. Something fell into place in the Antichrist's mind, and the result was the concept of time revision, editing and the archives. All they had to do was edit Richard out of history, and they could have Mankind out of there in a hundred years flat, with a massive bill for dilapidations thrown in.

It would have worked, if it hadn't been for one Blondel, a courtier, who inconveniently refused to accept that Richard had never existed, and started looking for him everywhere. As long as Blondel knew Richard had existed, Richard would have to continue to exist. The man was, to put it mildly, a menace.

Somehow, all the efforts of the Chastel staff to find Blondel failed – remarkable enough in itself, since he spent a material amount of his time appearing at well-publicised concerts – until the day when the Antichrist received two tickets for the biggest Blondel gig of all; according to the pre-concert hype, the very last Blondel gig of all.

Well yes, the Antichrist said to himself, the very last. The very last ever.

'Do come in,' Blondel said. 'Would you like a drink? Do please sit down.'

The Antichrist found no difficulty in walking, despite the lack of one leg; he walked perfectly naturally, as if he refused to believe that the other leg wasn't there. He could even stroll, trot and run if he saw fit. Just now, he was swaggering.

'Thanks,' he said. 'I'll have a dry martini.'

Blondel nodded and fiddled with the bottles on the drinks tray. 'What about you, Your Excellencies?'

The two Popes Julian – or, to be exact, Pope and Anti-Pope – shook their heads. 'Not while they're on duty,' the Antichrist explained.

'I thought that was only policemen.'

'And Popes,' he replied, 'but only when they're being simultaneous.'

'Ah yes,' Blondel said, handing the Antichrist his drink. 'I meant to ask you about that. They don't mind being discussed like this, do they?'

'Not at all,' the Antichrist said. 'Since they can't speak, I do the talking for them. Not that they matter a damn, anyway, since I'm here. I only brought them in case they wanted to see the show.'

'Thank you,' Blondel said, accepting the compliment. 'I gather that you're a fan, too.'

'Absolutely,' the Antichrist replied. 'I've got a complete set. In fact, quite soon I shall have the only complete set in existence. It'll be a nuisance having to go down to the Archives every time I want to hear it, but never mind.'

Blondel raised an eyebrow. 'The Archives?' he said. 'How do you mean?'

'Now then,' the Antichrist said, 'don't be obtuse. You're coming with me, Blondel, whether you like it or not. You've had your bit of fun, but it's all over. You do understand that, don't you?'

'Have an olive,' Blondel replied. 'They're quite good, actually.'

'Thank you.'

'Enjoying the show?'

'Yes. Very much.'

Blondel sat down and put his hands behind his head. 'Pity you won't hear the second half, then.'

The Antichrist shrugged. 'That's how it is,' he said. 'Why did you do it, Blondel? Have you just got tired of running? Or have you finally seen how much damage you've been doing all these years?'

'You mean,' Blondel replied, 'why did I invite you to my concert?'

'That's right.'

Blondel leaned forward and rested his chin on his hands. 'Simple,' he said. 'I'd have invited you to all my concerts, but I've only just found out your address. Or at least your telephone and fax numbers. I've wanted to get in touch with you for a *very* long time.'

The Antichrist grinned. 'I'll bet,' he said. 'But why didn't you just go along with Pursuivant and Claren-ceaux? I sent them to fetch you, hundreds of times.'

'And it was very kind of you,' Blondel said. 'To be absolutely frank – another olive? – I don't feel entirely comfortable with Clarenceaux and Pursuivant and that lot. If I'd gone with them when you so kindly sent them to fetch me, I'd have felt – how shall I put it?'

'Captured?'

'Yes, that'll do. Captured. How is Richard, by the way?'

The Antichrist smiled. 'I don't know,' he said. 'I gather he's still down there, somewhere. Can't be very comfortable for him, what with the rats and the complete isolation and the darkness and the damp and everything, but until you've been sorted out, we can't send him on to his Archive. Pity, really; it's a nice Archive. He'll like it. And so will you.'

'No doubt.' Blondel sat on the arm of the sofa and looked at his watch. 'Look, I hate to rush you, but I've got to be back on stage in five minutes, and I want to have a word with the idiot in charge of the lights. Don't you think it's time we did a deal?'

The Antichrist laughed. It wasn't a pleasant sound.

'Listen, mortal,' he said. 'You're in no position to make a deal. You're coming with me, and that's that.'

'Actually,' Blondel said, 'you're wrong there. I took the liberty of putting something in your drink. Apart from vermouth and gin, that is. In a very short time you'll be sleeping like a baby.'

The Antichrist tried to get up, but his knee refused to operate. His mouth opened but nothing came out of it except an olive stone.

'Oh good,' Blondel went on, 'it's starting to work. I will be brief, for a change. What I propose is a simple exchange of hostages. You for Richard.'

'But I'm not a ...' The words came very slowly out of his mouth, which was scarcely surprising, since his jaw was setting like concrete.

'Very soon,' Blondel said gently, 'you will be in the dungeons of the Chastel de Nesle. I'll try and make things as comfortable for you as I can. Clean straw once a year, all that sort of thing. Honestly, I'm surprised at you; and you, Julian and Julian. Didn't you realise this was likely to be a trap?'

The two Popes tried to get to their feet; unfortunately, the effort of manifesting themselves simultaneously without cocking up the balance of history was too great, and they flopped back against the cushions. Blondel pressed a buzzer and the door opened.

'Be a good chap, Giovanni, and fetch that laundry

basket,' he said. Giovanni nodded and left.

'You won't get away with this,' the Antichrist managed to say; but by the time he'd finished the last word he was fast asleep. Blondel removed the glass from his hand, smiled gently and put a pillow behind his head. They might be mortal enemies, but there was no point in letting the fellow get a crick in his neck for no reason.

'Here we are,' Giovanni said. 'You two, give me a hand.'

The Galeazzo brothers gently transferred the Antichrist and the two Julians into the basket, secured the lid and sat on it. Blondel nodded his approval.

'Right then,' he said. 'Let's be getting on with it. You take the basket back to the Chastel and we'll meet there after the show.'

'Will do,' Giovanni replied. 'And I can be getting on with the ransom note.'

Blondel shrugged. 'If you like,' he said. 'I don't think that's entirely necessary, though, do you?'

'Maybe not,' Giovanni said with a grin, 'but it'll be fun.'

'We're lost, aren't we?' Isoud said.

Guy sat down on the step and nodded. They'd been down here for a very long time, and there were no more sausage rolls left. This was a silly game.

'It's not your fault,' said La Beale Isoud reassuringly, and while Guy was still recovering from that one, she added, 'I think you're coping very well, in the circumstances.'

'You do?' Guy asked, bewildered.

'Oh yes.'

'Oh.'

They sat together for a while in silence. If it wasn't so dark, Guy would have been able to see that Isoud was looking at him with something approaching affection. It was probably just as well that it was so dark.

'Mr Goodlet.'

'Call me Guy,' Guy said wearily. 'If it's all the same to you, I mean.'

'Thank you, Guy,' Isoud replied. 'And you can call me Isoud, if you like.'

'Thank you, Isoud, that's a great weight off my mind.'

Isoud either didn't hear that or else she ignored it. 'Guy,' she went on, 'I've been thinking.'

'Oh yes?'

'Would it help,' said Isoud, 'if we had a map?'

Women, thought Guy darkly. 'Probably,' he said. 'But we don't.'

'No,' Isoud agreed. 'But perhaps we could get hold of one.'

'Oh yes? How do we manage that?'

Isoud was fumbling in her handbag. It was the first time that Guy had noticed she'd got one with her; but women's handbags aren't things one tends to notice, not consciously at any rate. One assumes that they have them without looking, just as one assumes that they have feet.

'We could try the hyperfax,' she said.

'You mean,' Guy said, as sweetly as he could manage, 'that you've had that ... that thing with you all this time and you haven't seen fit to —'

'Sorry,' Isoud said, girlishly. 'Have I been very silly?'

On balance, Guy said to himself, I think I preferred her when she was being unpleasant. 'No,' he said, 'not at all. You *have* got the wretched thing?'

'Here,' Isoud replied. She took a tiny metal cube from her bag and handed it to him.

'This is it, is it?'

'It folds away,' La Beale Isoud replied. 'I'd forgotten all about it until —'

'That's fine,' Guy said. 'Now, just show me how it works, and we can be getting on.'

Isoud reached across and pressed a tiny little knob

on one side of the cube. At once it opened up into a miniature replica of itself. 'Now all we have to do is plug it in,' Isoud said.

'Plug it in?'

'Yes.'

'Plug it into what?'

'Oh.'

Guy made a tiny, thin noise like linen tearing. 'Oh, for crying out —'

'Sorry,' Isoud said, and snuffled indistinctly.

Very much against his better nature, Guy reached out a tentative hand and patted Isoud on the shoulder. Under normal circumstances it was the very last thing he would have done, but if the bloody woman started crying on him he doubted whether he'd be able to cope. There are limits.

'There there,' he said stiffly, like a bank manager addressing a small, overdrawn child, 'it doesn't matter. And it was a very clever idea, really. Just a shame there isn't —'

To his horror, Guy felt a small, warm hand slip into his. His mouth went dry and he felt like a fish who has realised, too late, that if earthworms suddenly appear out of thin water and hover invitingly above one's head, there is probably a catch in it somewhere. Numbly, he gave the hand a little squeeze. One must, after all, be civil.

'Anyway,' he said in a strained voice, 'we mustn't sit about here all day, must we? Let's be getting along.'

'Yes, Guy,' said Isoud, meekly. 'Shall I put the hyperfax away again?'

'Yes,' Guy replied. 'Or rather, no. I've just had an idea.'

Which was actually true.

231

★

The President of Oceania was sweating.

What he wanted to do most of all was get out his handkerchief and wipe his forehead; but if he did that, the Chairman of the Eurasian People's Republic would see him do it on her Visiphone monitor, and might take it as a sign of weakness. And that would never do.

'Is that your last word, Madam Chairman?' he said.

'It is.'

Despite the flickering screen he could see that her face was set in an expression of monolithic determination. Bloody woman.

'In that case,' he said 'I fear that the United States of Oceania has no alternative but to consider itself at war with the Eurasian People's Republic. Madam Chairman, we have switched out a light that shall not be relit within our ...'

Hold on, thought the President, somebody *has* switched out the light. 'Are you still there, Madam Chairman?' he asked. But the screen had gone blank.

'Hey,' said the President angrily, 'what the hell is going on around here?'

From a corner of the darkened room a voice said, 'Sorry.'

The President wheeled round in his swivel chair. 'Who is that?' he demanded.

'It's all right,' said the voice, 'won't keep you a minute. Just borrowing your plug.'

The President groped for the security buzzer under his desk, and then realised that that wouldn't work either. All the electrics in the room were fed off just the one plug. Damn fool of an electrician had said it would be cheaper that way.

232

'Who are you?' said the President. 'And what do you want?'

'We're just using your plug,' said the voice. 'Sorry if we're disturbing you. Is that something coming through, Isoud?'

'Put that plug back on *immediately.*'

'Certainly, certainly,' replied the voice. 'Won't be two ticks.'

The President leapt to his feet, tripped over the leg of his desk, and fell over. 'Ouch,' he said.

'Careful.'

'How did you get in here?'

'Through that door over there,' replied the voice. 'It's probably got *No Entry* written on it, all the others do. I assure you it's nothing personal,' the voice added. 'It's just that yours was the first door we came to that didn't lead to somewhere in the Middle Ages.'

'I ...'

'Yup, it's the map all right,' said the voice, 'just the ticket. All right, then, Isoud, you can switch the thing off and let the gentleman have his electricity back. Sorry for any inconvenience,' the voice added.

A few seconds later, the lights went on, just in time for the President to catch a glimpse of the door marked *Maintenance Staff Only* closing. The Visiphone screen crackled and lit up. He dived for his chair and tried to look nonchalant.

'All right,' said the voice of the Chairman, 'you win.'

'You what?'

'You win,' replied the Chairman bitterly. 'You have – how you say? – called our bluff. We withdraw our missiles from Sector Three.'

'Oh,' said the President. 'Thank you.'

'Mr President.'

The screen went blank. Gasping slightly, the President found his handkerchief and wielded it vigorously. Obviously, the screen had been switched off *before* he'd made his declaration of war. Lucky.

He switched on the intercom. 'Frank,' he said, 'get me the briefing room. And,' he added, 'get me that god-damn electrician.'

'This way.'

Guy folded the map, put it away and pointed. Absolutely no doubt in his mind this time. The map had said *Stage Door of Blondel's Concert* on it in big bold letters. He turned the handle and pushed.

And fell forward.

A split second later, Isoud followed him, landing on the small of his back. He complained.

'Sorry,' Isoud said. 'Are you all ...?'

Guy raised his head and groaned. It wasn't just because Isoud had nearly broken his spine; it was more because he had a very strong feeling that he knew exactly where he was.

'Guy, are you all right?' Isoud repeated. Then, sensibly, she moved off his back and let him breathe.

Guy rolled over on to his side and groped for the map. Not that there was any light to read it by, of course. Something small and furry brushed past his hand.

'Hello,' said a sleepy voice in the depths of the gloom, 'who's there?'

'Oh, hellfire,' Guy moaned. He was right.

'Hello?' said the voice again. 'Why, my dear fellow, you've come back again.'

Guy moved his hand – slowly, so as not to startle the rat – and buried his face in it. A trap. The faxed map hadn't been sent from the Chastel de Nesle at all. It had come from ... Well, it didn't take a genius to work it out. From here.

'Guy?' Isoud said.

'Yes, all right,' Guy replied testily. 'Excuse me,' he said, projecting his voice into the darkness, 'but I wonder if you can tell me, is this the Chastel des Larmes Chaudes?'

'Certainly, my dear fellow,' replied the voice. 'Didn't they tell you at Reception when they brought you in?'

'I ...' Guy shook his head; for his own satisfaction more than anything else. He wanted to see if anything rattled about in it.

'Isoud,' he said, 'I'm afraid we've come the wrong way.'

Pursuivant woke up, opened his eyes, and wiggled his toes. They still weren't right. Typical. If he'd mentioned the duff bearing in the offside right joint once, he'd mentioned it a hundred times, but nobody listened. Next time he was brought in to the Service Bay, he'd damn well insist.

'I don't know why I bother.'

It was the voice of the Head Technician, and now he came to think of it, Pursuivant could see his face glowering down at him. He shrugged his shoulders, only to find they weren't there. Probably off having the rubbers changed.

'I mean,' the Head Technician was saying, 'why don't I just scoop the whole lot out and fill in the hole with wet newspaper or something? Then, next time you

235

get them all bashed out, it won't take me an hour and a half with the small scalpel to put them back together again.'

'Bad, was it?' Pursuivant asked.

The Head Technician pulled a face. 'For two pins,' he said, 'I'd have binned the lot and put in a brand new unit. Only then I'd have the bloody Quartermaster down on me like a ton of bricks. First thing in the morning, I'm going to ask my brother-in-law if there's any jobs going down the canning factory.'

He waved to the orderlies, who switched on the conveyor, transporting Pursuivant to the Armery section.

'What the hell did you do to it this time?' the Armerer demanded. 'Roll about on it? Try and use it to lever open a safe? These are precision instruments, you know.'

'Sorry,' Pursuivant said. 'Can I have a new one?'

'No,' replied the Armerer. 'Instead, you can have arthritis. I've fitted it,' he added with a malicious grin, 'personally.'

'Hey, doc, that isn't —'

'Nobody said it had to be,' replied the Armerer, swinging his ratchet spanner like a football rattle. 'Next.'

Three quarters of an hour later, Pursuivant was standing outside Mountjoy's office, waiting to be told he could come in.

'Let's just go through this one step at a time,' Mountjoy said. 'You and your colleagues captured the renegade Goodlet backstage and tied him up. Then you left him.'

'Yes, sir.'

'Then,' Mountjoy went on, glimmering unpleasantly, 'a quarter of an hour later you meet him sauntering down a corridor with a girl.'

'Yes, sir.'

'Whereupon he kills you.'

'Sir.'

'Pursuivant,' Mountjoy said, glowing like a constipated firefly, 'you excel yourself. Thanks to you, they've disappeared. Completely. Without trace.'

'They, sir?'

'The Pope, you idiot. And the Anti-Pope, And ...' Mountjoy mimed a one-armed, partially-sighted man. 'Vanished into thin air. What were you playing at?'

'I was being killed, sir.'

'When I've finished with you,' Mountjoy roared, 'you'll wish you were dead ...' He tailed off, and a few desultory sparks crackled from his nose, singeing the hairs. Pursuivant stayed rigidly at attention. He knew from long experience that having your arms drawn tightly in towards your body made you a smaller target.

'Anyway,' said Mountjoy, 'the question now is, what are you going to do about it?'

'Me, sir?' Pursuivant said, realising as he did so that he'd gone and cocked it up again. 'I mean, sir —'

'Yes, soldier, you.' Mountjoy stood silently for a moment, looking for all the world like a pensive table lamp. He turned as the door opened and White Herald came in. He was limping, probably because they'd run out of offside tibias in 63E again. He held a sheet of paper.

'Fax just come through, sir,' he said. 'Marked *F.A.O. Acting General Manager*. Brought it straight here.'

Mountjoy frowned and grabbed at the paper. A

moment later he made an unpleasant noise in the back of his throat, grating and ominous, like the sound of hubcap on kerb.

'Now look what you've done,' he said. 'This is from de Nesle.'

'Sir.'

'Stop saying sir like that. He claims to have overpowered them and locked them up in his dungeons.' Mountjoy sighed. 'Well now, this is a bit of a problem, isn't it? Well?'

'Yes, sir.'

'Yes, sir. And there's not really much point in sending you to get them out again, is there?'

'No, sir.'

'No, sir. Because you don't know where to look. And even if you did, you're too incompetent to do even the simplest ... What is it?'

Pursuivant knew better than to look round. In the arcane and convoluted code of regulations by which the Chastel guard was governed, looking round in the presence of a superior officer was punishable in a number of cleverly devised ways, most of which included swapping components around between the individual offenders. When the newcomer spoke, however, he recognised the voice of the chief warder of the dungeons.

'Sorry to interrupt, chief,' said the warder, 'but I thought you ought to know. I was just doing my rounds when I noticed, there's two new prisoners in Cell Fifty-Nine.'

Mountjoy dimmed incredulously. 'Two *new* prisoners?'

'Yes, chief.'

'You mean somebody's broken *into* the prison?'

'Looks like it, chief.'

The Chaplain furrowed his brows, producing interesting kaleidoscopic effects on the ceiling. 'Cell Fifty-Nine? You're sure?'

'Sure, chief.'

'Well, now,' Mountjoy said, 'I think we'd better have a look at this.'

Musicology records that the concert was a success.

'His lambent woodnotes,' wrote the critic of the *New Theosociologist,* 'blended pellucid *leitmotiven* with an extravaganza of polychromatic detail, often resulting in a vibrant antagonism between line and length which found its ultimate apotheosis in the semi-cathartic culmination of *Nellie Dean.* De Nesle continues to build on the firm foundations of his earlier flirtation with the neo-structural; and if he manages to resist the meretricious temptations of the merely beautiful, may yet prove that his pan contains further and more transcendent flashes.'

As far as Blondel was concerned, though, it had been a good sing-song, it was nice when the audience all joined in the final verse of *L'Amours Dont Sui Epris,* and what he really needd now was a shower and a cup of warm milk.

He was annoyed, therefore, to find his dressing room deserted and in rather a mess. In fact, ransacked would be a better word. It looked like a haystack in which someone has eventually managed to find a needle.

'Mmmmmmmm,' said a voice from inside the wardrobe.

Blondel raised an eyebrow. One of the wardrobes in

this room led directly to the past, the future and a tasteful selection of presents. The problem was, there was no way at any given time of knowing which.

'Hello?' he enquired

'Mmmmmm.'

'Giovanni? Is that you?'

'Mmm.'

'What on earth are you doing in there?'

It's remarkable how quickly you can pick up a new language. Quite soon, Blondel was fluent enough in gagged noises to understand that Giovanni was trying to tell him that he'd explain much better if only somebody took this sock out of his mouth.

'Coming,' Blondel said.

He tracked the noise to the smaller of the two wardrobes and opened it. A quick glance revealed three bound and muffled investment consultants.

'My dear fellow,' Blondel said, gently removing the sock from Giovanni's mouth, 'whatever's been going on?'

Giovanni gurgled, made a noise like a rasp on formica, and said, 'Revenue.'

'I beg your pardon?'

'I think,' Giovanni muttered, 'they were from the Revenue. Looking for receipts or something.'

'Who?'

'The men,' Giovanni replied. 'The men who searched the place. We tried to stop them but . . .'

Blondel looked round. Come to think of it, the place did have a distinctly frisked look. 'What makes you think they were tax men?' he asked.

'Just look at the place, for God's sake.'

Blondel scratched his head. 'Good point,' he said;

then he thought of something. 'My dear chap,' he said, 'what must you think of me? Do let me help you out of those ropes. They look awfully uncomfortable.'

Once freed from his bonds, Giovanni immediately ran across the room, upended a tubular metal chair and fished around for something inside one of the legs. After a short, frantic burst of activity he produced a tight roll of papers and waved it round his head in relief.

'It's all right,' he said, 'they didn't find it.'

'Oh yes?' Blondel said. 'What's that?'

'Er . . .'

'Do you know,' Blondel went on, 'I don't think they were from the Revenue at all.'

'No?' Giovanni paused, balanced on one leg, in the act of stuffing the papers inside his sock. 'Customs and Excise, you reckon?'

'Maybe,' Blondel replied. 'Or perhaps they were some of the Antichrist's people.'

'You think so?'

Blondel picked up something from the floor and displayed it on the palm of his hand. 'Look at this,' he said. 'It's a button off a tunic. See there, that's the arms of the Chastel des Larmes Chaudes. I think they're on to us already.'

'Phew!' Giovanni said. 'Thank God for that. I thought we were in trouble there for a minute.' He sat down and pulled his shoe back on.

'How long since they left?' Blondel asked. He threw the button up in the air and caught it. 'Not long, I don't imagine.'

'Dunno,' Giovanni replied. 'Five minutes, maybe, perhaps ten.'

'And it wasn't Pursuivant a̶ d̶ Clarenceaux or any of that lot.'

Giovanni shook his head. 'I'd have recognized them,' he said. 'Like I said, this lot were *frightening*.' He reached out for his briefcase and started riffling through papers.

'Ten minutes,' Blondel repeated, 'and not Pursuivant and Clarenceaux. So it must be the other squad.' He turned to the Galeazzo brothers. 'If I were you,' he said, 'I'd head for the wardrobe. The other wardrobe. Now.'

'But you said . . .'

'Now. If it'll help create an illusion of urgency, pretend there's a party of Department of Trade investigators coming up the stairs.'

Very shortly afterwards, the wardrobe door slammed, hard. Blondel started to count to ten. Give them a head start, he reckoned, and then follow. Because if he was right, the gentlemen who would very shortly be coming back were not the sort of people he wanted to meet.

Every military and paramilitary outfit has an elite force of some kind, a hand-picked bunch of utterly ruthless and determined professionals who think nothing of dyeing perfectly good balaclava helmets jet black and cutting holes in them. The Chastel des Larmes Chaudes is no exception. It has the Time and Motion department.

Some special units are trained to operate in specific conditions, such as mountains or the arctic. The TAM is designed to operate in time.

They know how to live off the land, snaring lost

opportunities and roasting them on spits; how to blend imperceptibly into the temporal landscape, disguised as fleeting moments; how to ambush unsuspecting hostile forces by attacking them before they've even been born. Intensive training has taught them to withstand the devastating metabolic effects of rapid time travel, which can only too easily lead to a meal being digested before it is eaten. And they can follow a trail through history better than the combined postgraduate resources of all the universities in the world.

The TAM is recruited exclusively from temporal misfits – men who have somehow or other fallen out of their own time, anachronisms; as can readily be deduced from the narrow lapels and flared trousers of their battledress uniforms. As might be expected, therefore, they are pitiless, determined and incorrigibly unpunctual.

It stands to reason, then, that when the Chastel des Larmes Chaudes sees fit to turn the TAM loose, it's probably had enough of messing about.

Once Zeitsturmbahnfuhrer Uhrwerk had satisfied himself that Blondel wasn't hiding under the floorboards or inside the sofa cushions, he started to search for the time door. He was equipped with the latest in Chronological Anomaly Detectors and it didn't take him long to find the right wardrobe door. The fact that it was open and palpably led nowhere helped, of course.

'Right, men, follow me,' he snapped. 'Synchronise your watches.'

The platoon laughed dutifully. Zeitsturmbahnfuhrer Uhrwerk was essentially a one-joke man.

It was dark in the tunnel, but TAM soldiers are equipped with both foresight and hindsight, and can if necessary navigate by sound alone, listening out for their own future muffled curses as they stub their toes on concealed obstacles. It was not long before they picked up the trail. The litter of bent and distorted historical potentials, imperceptible to the naked eye, were easily detected by the CADs. The squad broke into a run.

For the first time in a very long time, Blondel wasn't sure where to go next. His basic instincts told him to head for the Chastel de Nesle, bolt the doors behind him and get Isoud to heat up a huge cauldron of boiling mashed potato for pouring on the heads of would-be besiegers. The thing to remember about basic instincts, however, is that they don't always work. If beavers and rabbits used their brains instead of following their natural instincts, fur coats would be rather more expensive.

The alternative, of course, was to try and lose them somewhere in time; but that was rather like trying to drown a fish. The third alternative, standing his guard and fighting it out with cold steel, made his basic instincts look quite intelligent by comparison.

Standing at a fork in the tunnel, Blondel hesitated and tried to reach a decision. The right hand fork led, via the Icelandic Foreign Office and the Cultural Revolution pension scheme, to the Chastel de Nesle. The left hand fork led to DVLC. He had no idea what lay beyond. To the best of his knowledge, nobody did.

Behind him, he heard the sound of heavy boots and the distant muffled swearing noises of men learning by mistakes they never got around to making. He turned left. Robert Frost would have been proud of him.

244

To get to DVLC you have to pass through some undeniably hairy situations, as anyone who has ever tried to get hold of a replacement logbook for a 1978 Cavalier will confirm. First you have to go past the Arts and Heritage secretariat of the Long Parliament (watch out for splinters of broken stained glass underfoot), then turn left at the Irish Postmaster General's office, circa 1916 (a terrible beauty is born, so be ready to duck) and left again through the Spanish Feudal System. It's at this point that it's all too easy to get lost. The through route across the Customs and Excise of the later Byzantine empire is, well, byzantine in its complexity, and if you aren't careful you can easily find yourself in the Ottoman Ministry of Works; which is remarkably like being dead, only not as restful. You'll know you're on the right road if you come to a long corridor which you try running down only to find that you're either staying exactly where you are or moving slightly backwards. That means you're in driving licence application territory.

The main thing to remember, once you're there, is *not to go through any of the doors.*

Blondel stopped, selected a door at random, opened it and fell through. These guys, he told himself, know the score. They'll never follow me in through here.

The true nature of Time has puzzled the best brains in the human race throughout history; but only because nobody has ever grasped the fact that the stuff comes in two quite different isotopes.

There is Time; and there is Overtime.

Time is the shortest distance between two events. Overtime is the scenic route. In Overtime, things happen in the same order as they do in Time, but temporal units have different values of magnitude. To put it another way, an egg boiled for three minutes in Overtime would penetrate steel plate.

The trick is to be able to tell which system is in force on any given occasion. There are no hard and fast rules, but here are a couple of examples of situations where you can expect to find Overtime:

(a) Public transport; for instance, someone who arrives at an airport two hours early will have to wait another two hours because his plane is late getting in, whereas someone who turns up three minutes before takeoff will invariably find that the plane left three minutes early.

(b) Government departments; consider how entirely different temporal concepts apply when you want them to do something, and when they want you to do something. It's a little-known but revealing fact that the supertemporal forces inside the IRS Headquarters in Washington are so strong all the clocks in the building had to be specially designed by Salvador Dali.

The effects of mixing Time and Overtime were harnessed by a pioneer firm of time-travel agents, who used them to make it possible for their clients to take relaxing and indefinite holidays in the past or the future. In order to travel, holidaymakers booked an ordinary holiday with an ordinary package tour company. Three weeks before the holiday, they sent their passports off for renewal. Two days before the departure date, they cancelled the holiday.

The result of sending the passports off was the creation of a massive Overtime field which would ensure that the passports would take at least four months to process. Cancelling the holiday broke the field, bringing the most tremendous pressure to bear on the Time/Overtime interface and tearing holes in it large enough for human beings to pass through. The time-holiday was spent in Overtime, which meant that you could spend six weeks in Renaissance Florence and still be home in time to go to work the morning after you'd left.

In other words, the earth's temporal system, which was installed on the afternoon of the fifth day by a team of contractors found by God in the Golden Pages under the trading name of Cheap 'n' Cheerful Chronological Engineers, is a classic example of a Friday afternoon job, and fundamentally unstable. If Man had stayed put in the Garden of Eden, where the chronostat is jammed stuck at half past six on a summer afternoon, it wouldn't have mattered. Once Adam cut loose, however, it was inevitable that any sudden violent dislocation – a successful Crusade, for example – could knock the entire thing into the middle of next week. Or possibly worse.

Accordingly, on the eighth day, God telephoned his lawyers and began asking all sorts of questions about product liability.

Blondel stared, and grabbed at the doorframe to stop himself falling. The problem was that the doorframe wasn't there any more.

Which was reasonable enough; you don't need a doorframe on a cave, and a cave was quite definitely what Blondel had just come out of. A cave opening directly on to the sheer side of a cliff. Oh well.

Four seconds later he was relieved to find himself in

water. It could just as easily have been rock, or sun-baked earth, or a thick brown bush, but it wasn't. Having thrashed his way to the surface again and spat out a newt, Blondel trod water for a moment and tried to work out what was going on.

He was still, he gathered, in a cave; a cave inside a cave; a cavern. High above him he could see the roof, with a tasteful display of stalactites. The entrance he had fallen out of was one of several. There were crudely-made ladders tied to the walls, which led down to the narrow strip of beach, or whatever you liked to call it, that ran round the edge of the pool he was currently bobbing about in.

It was perishing cold, too.

With slow strokes he swam to the edge and pulled himself out. As he did so, he noticed a pair of feet directly in front of him. He stayed where he was.

It was hard for feet to look menacing, but these ones seemed to have the knack. It wasn't so much the size of them or the inordinately bizarre cut of the toenails. It wasn't even the context. The feeling of being in deep trouble was a purely intuitive one, but Blondel had always had an excellent working relationship with intuition. He looked up.

The owner of the feet stood about five foot four and was distinctly hairy. What little of his face was visible through the undergrowth had a simian look, mostly to do with the jaw, which looked as if it had been care-lessly left out in the sun and had melted. As if that wasn't offputting enough, there was a heavy-looking rock in the stranger's hands, and he probably wasn't lifting it over his head like that simply to exercise his pectoral muscles. For one thing, they didn't look like they needed it. Blondel ducked, and a moment later the rock hit the patch of beach he'd just been using.

'Steady on,' Blondel said, resurfacing a few feet out into the pond. The stranger grunted irritably and picked the rock up. It looked unpleasantly as if what he lacked in intellectual stature he made up for in dogged persistence.

Out of the corner of his eye, Blondel saw another, similar figure approaching. This one was carrying a stone axe, and gave every indication of having been woken up from a badly needed sleep. There were others following. Bad news.

'Excuse me,' Blondel said, in the most nonchalant voice he could find, 'but could any of you gentlemen direct me to the nearest —'

There was a loud and disconcerting splash in the water about a foot from where he was standing, and a wave hit him in the face. The rock, probably. That one or one just like it. Blondel dived down again and resurfaced some way further out.

It was difficult to know what to do for the best. If these were, as Blondel suspected, cavemen, there was a fair chance that if he stayed there long enough they would probably catch some disease or other from him to which they had not yet had a chance to build up an immunity, and die. On the other hand, that might well take some time, and the water was quite distressingly cold. So Blondel decided to try his other option. He sang *L'Amours Dont Sui Epris*.

With hindsight, Blondel realised, he'd been expecting a bit much there. The romance tradition of chansons and trouveres, though considerably more accessible than many other musical genres, isn't entirely suited for absolute novices. He might have done better, he felt, with something a bit more basic, such as *Baa Baa Black Sheep*. That might have had them standing in the aisles. As it is, they threw rocks.

Having resurfaced ten yards further out, Blondel decided to try a little lateral thinking. On the one hand, there were rather a lot more of them now, and some of them seemed to have grasped the principle of the slingshot. If one chose to look on the bright side, though, one couldn't help noticing that they weren't terribly good marksmen. It might be worth giving it another ten minutes to see if there was any chance of them wiping themselves out with stray missiles.

A feeling of acute numbness in his toes argued against that, and Blondel came to the conclusion that getting cramp and drowning wasn't exactly the most positive step he could think of at this juncture; so he chose the least inhabited part of the beach and started to swim towards it. He was just about to come within easy boulder range and was wondering if this was the best he could do when an idea struck him, with a number of small, fast-moving stones.

It might justifiably be said that leaving it until now to reveal that Blondel had had a small, high-volume, waterproof personal stereo in his jacket pocket from the outset smacks of rather meretricious storytelling; however, since Blondel had only just remembered it himself, the omission is probably justifiable. He hadn't given the thing a second thought since he'd acquired it, as his introductory free gift on taking out a Galeazzo Brothers With Profits Ten Year Endowment Policy, just before the concert. Now he realised that even the things you get given for free can sometimes come in very handy. He trod water, fished the thing out, removed the headphones, turned the volume to maximum and switched it on.

It was an added bonus that the machine contained a tape of the massed bands of the Royal Marines playing *The Ride of the Valkyries*, although since all tapes for which one does not have to pay money have exactly the same thing on them, it probably was only to be expected. At any rate, it worked. The cavemen dropped their improvised weapons and fled. All except one, who reacted rather like a rabbit caught in the headlights of a fleet of oncoming lorries. The noise seemed to paralyse him, his knees gave way and he sat down heavily on a short, thick log. Perhaps, Blondel said to himself, the poor chap isn't a music lover. Or perhaps, rather more likely, he *is* a music lover.

He clambered out of the water, shook himself and started to squelch up the beach, trying not to startle the dazed caveman, who was sitting with his head between his knees, whimpering. Unfortunately the band chose that moment to launch into the Soldier's Chorus from *Faust*, and that seemed to do it for the caveman. He lurched violently and disturbed the log, which started to roll slowly towards the water.

Feeling slightly ashamed of himself, Blondel switched the music off and helped the caveman to his feet. He tried to apologise in sign language, but he didn't seem to be getting through, somehow.

'Come on, old chap,' he said. 'You run along and we'll say no more about it ...'

The log rolled to the edge of the water and fell in. Blondel realised that the caveman, far from being

251

paralysed with fear, was concentrating single-mindedly on the log and what it was doing.

'We'll,' the caveman repeated. '*We'll*!'

He scampered to the water, fished the log out, lugged it back up the beach and set it rolling again. 'We'll!' he yelled.

'Oh *bother*!' said Blondel to himself, 'I've done it again.' Then he trudged off to find the tunnel.

Back in the tunnel, Blondel felt simultaneously relieved, dry and very, very lost. The last feeling was the worst, and it wasn't helped by the discovery that the water in the cave pool had turned his map to sticky and illegible porridge. It would have to be intuition again. He turned left and ran down the tunnel.

Fifty yards or so further on, he discovered the flaw in his basic strategy. A squad of heavily armed men were coming down the tunnel towards him. They seemed pleased to see him, a feeling he found it hard to reciprocate. He skidded to a halt, turned athletically, and ran back the way he'd come. Mistake number two.

If he hadn't been so preoccupied he'd have seen himself coming; as it was, he collided with such tremendous terminal velocity that both of him were thrown backwards. For a moment, he was both stunned.

'You clumsy idiot!' he panted, simultaneously.

'Look who's talking.'

'Why don't you look where you're going?'

'I like that, coming from you.'

'Look,' said his later self, 'I'm being chased by a platoon of Time and Motion, I haven't got time ...'

'So am I,' replied his earlier self.

'But they're not behind you,' replied the later self, 'they're behind me. You're heading straight for them.'

'I am?'

'Yes.'

The earlier Blondel gave his later self a funny look. 'How do you know?' he said.

'Because I nearly ran straight into them, idiot,' replied the later Blondel, 'that's how. Now, if you don't mind ...'

'Before or after you ran into me?'

'Before. No, after. Look, does it matter?'

'But that's crazy,' replied Mark I. 'It's impossible.'

'Is it?'

'Must be,' said Mark I, backing away slightly. 'Because I – we – can't be just about to run into them, because you've just warned me they're coming.'

Mark II tried, very briefly, to think about this, and then came to the conclusion that now wasn't the time. So to speak.

'Look,' he said, 'will you just ...?'

Mark I shook his head. 'Oh no you don't,' he said. 'If one of us is going to turn round and carry on running in the safe direction it might as well be me.'

Mark II stared. 'How do you make that out?' he said.

'Well,' Mark I replied, 'I'm not the one who went blundering into them in the first place letting them know where I was, am I? No, I reckon the best thing would be for them to catch you, so's I can get away.'

'Look ...' Mark II said angrily, and then tailed off. 'Why don't we both ...'

Mark I gave him a look. 'Don't be silly,' he said.

Down the tunnel came the sound of heavy boots

running. 'But if they catch you,' said Mark II frantically, 'they'll catch me too.'

'And vice versa.'

'Toss you for it?'

'Do I look like I was born yesterday?'

'Right now,' Mark II replied, 'I wouldn't like to bet on it. For all I know you probably were. And tomorrow. Now can we adjourn this and do some running away, because —'

'If we toss for it,' Mark I went on, ignoring him(self), 'you'll know which side the coin came down, because you're later than me and . . .'

This is crazy, said Mark II to himself; a third self, presumably. Perhaps that's what's meant by a multi-faceted personality. Or terminal schizophrenia. 'All right,' he said, 'you can call.'

'Ah yes,' Mark I replied smugly, 'it's all right for you to say that, because you know I called wrong and so . . .'

Blondel took a deep breath, shouted 'Behind you!' and, while his head was turned, kicked himself in the reproductive organs. Then, while he was lying on the ground groaning weakly, he jumped over himself and ran.

Straight into an oncoming TAM patrol.

He turned and fled. It wasn't exactly easy running, not with this awful pain in his lower abdomen, but somehow he managed. Fear probably had something to do with it. Also a very great desire to find himself again and kick his head in.

About fifty yards down the tunnel, he collided again.

'Right, you,' he chorused, and let fly a powerful right hook. His two right hands landed in his two left eyes at exactly the same moment. He fell over and went to sleep.

'Straw.'

'No.'

'Shadows.'

'No.'

'Spiders' webs.'

'That's two words.'

Guy snarled quietly. 'Very true,' he said, 'but are they the right two words?'

'No.'

'That sounds like a very interesting game,' said the voice pleasantly, from his corner of the cell. 'Would you mind explaining the rules to me?'

Guy turned his head. He prided himself on his adaptability, but the prospect of this state of affairs continuing much longer wasn't exactly cheering him up. 'It's a very boring game, actually,' he said. 'Sand,' he added.

'There isn't any sand,' Isoud replied.

'How do you know?'

'She's right, actually,' the voice broke in diffidently. 'Or at least I haven't come across any. Not yet, that is. I may be wrong, of course.'

'What we do,' Isoud said to the voice, 'is I think of a word and then I say I Spy With My Little Eye Something Beginning With S. That's a clue.'

'Oh yes?' said the voice.

'That lets you know the word begins with S.'

'Excuse me if I'm being a bit slow,' said the voice, 'but what if the word begins with something else? G, for example, or T. Or can you only choose a word beginning with S?'

'No,' said Isoud, 'if the word began with G, I would

say I Spy With My Little Eye Something Beginning With G.'

'Oh I *see*,' said the voice. 'Can I have a go?'

'I haven't finished yet,' Guy said irritably. 'Stones,' he suggested.

'No.'

'It must be stones,' he protested. 'There isn't anything else beginning with S.' He looked around sadly. 'There's not a hell of a lot beginning with anything, really.'

'Well that's where you're wrong, Mr Clever,' Isoud replied smugly. 'There's sandstone, frinstance.'

'Is it sandstone?'

'No.'

Sotto voce, Guy asked God to give him strength. 'All right,' he said, 'I give in, now tell me what it is before I go completely round the bend.'

'Shank,' said Isoud proudly.

'*Shank*?'

'The shank,' Isoud explained, 'of the lock. I told you it was a clever one.'

'Very clever indeed,' said the voice, 'if I may make so bold.'

'*Shank*?'

'There is such a word,' Isoud said defensively.

'Yes,' Guy replied, 'but you can't see it.'

'Yes I can.'

'Then you must have bloody good eyesight,' Guy snapped, 'because the shank is part of the works, ergo it's inside the lock, ergo you couldn't see it from here even if it wasn't as dark as a bag in here, which it is. I win.'

'Be like that, then.'

'Actually ...' said the voice, and then became aware, no doubt by some form of low-level telepathy, that he was being glowered at by both parties. 'Sorry,' he said, and went back to plaiting spiders' webs.

'My go,' said Guy firmly.

'It's not,' Isoud said, 'you cheated.'

'I did not cheat,' Guy said. 'A shank is part of the works of a lock, ask anybody. If you like, I'll call the warder. He should know about locks if anybody does.'

'I'm not playing with you any more.'

'Good.'

A rat nuzzled affectionately up to Guy's hand and was both shocked and profoundly disillusioned when the hand tried to swat him. He retreated into a distant part of the cell and, since rodents can't cry, started to gnaw at a splinter of wood.

'Of course,' Guy said suddenly, 'it could be that we've been missing something important here.'

'Oh yes?' said the voice eagerly. 'Do tell.'

Guy reached inside his jacket and felt for something. To his great relief it was still there. 'All we have to do in order to get out of here,' he said, 'is to open the door, right?'

'That would help, certainly,' the voice agreed. 'But, and far be it from me to play devil's advocate or anything, isn't that going to be —'

'Not,' Guy said, 'if I shoot the lock off.'

'Gosh!' The voice sounded impressed. 'Can you do that?' it asked.

Guy drew his revolver and screwed up his eyes. There was just enough light to see that it was loaded. 'Don't see why not,' he said. 'Stay well back, everyone.'

He advanced to the door, felt for the lock, placed the

muzzle next to it, and fired. The noise, which was ear-splitting in the confines of the cell, slowly died away. From the other side of the door came the sound of someone saying, 'Look, do you mind?' in a querulous tone. Guy tried the door. It was solid. There was a bullet-hole clean through the wood about an inch above the lockplate.

The peephole in the door slid back, filling the cell (or so it seemed) with a beam of blinding light.

'See that?' said the warder.

'Pardon?'

'That's a brand new hat, that is,' the warder went on. 'And now look at it.'

Guy blushed. 'Sorry,' he said.

'Bloke can't pull up a chair and take forty winks in this place without getting holes in his hat,' the warder grumbled. 'What's the world coming to, that's what I want to know.'

'It was an accident,' Guy said. 'Honest.'

'Oh yes?' The warder didn't sound impressed.

'It was,' Guy insisted. 'I was trying to, er, shoot off the lock, and I must have ...' He closed his eyes and tried to swallow the shame. 'Missed.'

There was a long silence.

'Missed.'

'Must have.'

'I see.'

'Good.'

'I was,' the warder went on, 'going to come in there and take that thing off you as an offensive weapon. Still, seeing as how you can't even hit a lock, I don't think I'll bother.' The peephole cover slid back, flooding the cell with darkness, and Guy put his

258

revolver back in its holster. More than anything else in the world, he realised, he hated hats.

Blondel opened his eyes and looked round. To his relief, he found that he wasn't there any more.

Lying next to him, however, were a large number of recumbent bodies; about thirty of them. They looked as if they'd been in a fight.

One of them groaned and lifted its head slightly. The effort proved too great, however, and it sagged back.

'Hello,' Blondel said, 'what happened to you?'

The soldier looked up and instinctively reached for something at his side. Blondel put his foot on it and smiled.

'Not now,' he said. 'What happened?'

'It was those other blokes,' the soldier said.

'What other blokes?'

'The ones who came down the corridor a few minutes after we got here,' the soldier replied. 'We were just about to take you into custody when they got here and started arguing the toss. Said it was their collar and why didn't we back off. Well, we weren't standing for that. There's a reward.'

'Oh yes?'

'Too right.' The soldier grinned. 'We showed them all right,' he said, and fainted.

Blondel sighed. It was at times like this that he wondered why he bothered. He had this strong suspicion that all he really had to do was wait quietly and everybody would beat the springs out of everybody else without him having to lift a finger.

He stood up and counted the bodies. It came to an odd number. Not so good.

In the distance, he could hear the sound of running feet.

'Listen,' he said out loud, and pointed towards the direction the sound was coming from. 'You go that way, right?' Then he picked up his feet and ran the other way.

He hadn't gone far when he stopped. Not voluntarily; there was this door in the way.

Blondel picked himself up off the ground, rubbed his nose and looked at the door warily. Something told him that whatever there was on the other side wasn't going to be friendly. It had that sort of look about it.

Behind him he could hear footsteps, getting closer. They sounded like the footsteps of heavily armed men who have just had a fight with themselves and are dying to vent their embarrassment on an unarmed and vulnerable third party.

On the other hand, it was perhaps the least prepossessing door he'd ever seen, in quite possibly a uniquely wide experience of the subject. Not only did it have the words *No Entry* written on it, but also the word *Honestly*.

Behind him, Blondel could hear voices. They seemed to be discussing, in a breathless but enthusiastic way, who was going to have the privilege of mutilating which part of him.

When is a door not a door?

When it's a jar.

Obviously.

'... Which, together with a balanced portfolio of Beaumont Street Gilt and Fixed Income Trust units and a modest cash balance in, say, the Beaumont

Equitable Building Society, provides for maximum income potential without undue prejudice to long-term capital growth. What do you say?'

'No.'

Giovanni sighed. It was cold down here in the cellars and he was getting cramp. On the other hand, he enjoyed a challenge. 'Fair enough,' he said. 'How about putting the bulk of the capital sum into Carribeanis $9\frac{1}{2}$% Convertible Treasury Stock, and investing the balance in something like, oh, I don't know, Second Crusade $3\frac{1}{2}$% Loan Stock 1192? Now you can't say fairer than that. Safe as the Bank of England, that is.' He remembered the investment package he'd worked out for the Chancellor of the Exchequer back in 2343. 'Safer,' he added firmly.

'No.'

'It so happens,' he said, 'I know of this horse running in the 2.15 at Doncaster. When I say running, what I really mean is ran, of course ...'

'No.'

There are times when even the most persistent financial adviser has to call it a day. 'Ah well,' he said, 'it's entirely up to you, naturally. If you don't want to provide for your old age ...'

'Talk sense,' the Antichrist replied.

It was raining. It was coming down in bucketfuls and nobody had invented the umbrella yet. Mountjoy, who generally insisted on dressing in period ('When in the Renaissance, do as the Renaissancers do') looked out from under the soggy top edge of his cowl and blew a raindrop off the end of his nose.

'He's late,' he said,

'With respect, sir.'

Slowly, the Anti-Chaplain turned his head and scowled at his chief henchman. Acting Chief Henchman; he'd asked for White Herald, but apparently Maintenance were all out of 63B knee joints.

'You said something?'

'Yes, sir,' Clarenceaux replied. 'With respect, sir, given that we are presently in a temporal anomaly, with respect, um, how *can* he be late, sir? I mean ...'

Mountjoy let him tail off without interrupting. He felt it would be more humiliating. 'Have you quite finished?'

'Sir.'

'Then shut up.'

Clarenceaux mouthed the word *Sir* and continued to stand to attention. After all, he said to himself, I may be the lowest form of life and completely unintelligent and little better than a robot, but at least I've got the sense to wear oilskins.

Mountjoy was just beginning to suspect that this was some sort of practical joke when a small figure appeared on the opposite side of the bridge. He was carrying an umbrella. Typical.

'Sorry to have kept you,' Blondel sang out as he approached, splashing through the puddles in his green wellington boots. 'I got held up on the way here.' He turned his head and nodded to the castle on the other side of the river. 'Not there, of course, but the castellan turned out to be a fan and they insisted I stay for a glass of mead. One does like to be polite, you know.'

Mountjoy glowed peevishly, evaporating a pint or so of rain out of his cowl. 'It doesn't matter,' he replied, 'you're here now.'

'So I am, yes,' Blondel said. 'Look, do you think we could just step in out of the wet somewhere? This is my sister's umbrella, and it's a bit small for me.'

They found a degree of shelter under a small tree, and Blondel put the umbrella down. It was a sort of beige-fawn colour with rather restrained black patterns, Mountjoy noticed. So that was what women went in for. One of these days, it might be quite intriguing to meet one. Or maybe not. He flickered in the cold, and cleared his throat.

'Right,' he said, 'let's get down to business, shall we?'

'With pleasure,' Blondel opened the flap of the small leather satchel he was carrying round his neck and produced a tape recorder. 'You don't mind if I take notes, do you?' he said. 'I find my memory isn't what it was these days.'

'Please yourself,' Mountjoy replied frostily. 'I had assumed that we could trust one another, but —'

'I know,' Blondel replied. 'Wretched, isn't it? Actually, it wasn't my idea, it was my agent's. There's a born negotiator for you. Spent the last few days trying to sell your boss life insurance.'

Mountjoy looked down his nose. 'Unsuccessfully, I assume.'

Blondel grinned. 'Not entirely,' he replied. 'Didn't manage to kid him into taking out any life cover, but he did manage to interest him in an accident policy. He's now fully covered in the event of loss of limb.'

That, Mountjoy decided, was enough small talk. It was time to show his hand.

'It might interest you to know,' he said, wiping rain out of his eyes with the heel of his hand, 'that we have some guests staying at the Chastel at the moment.'

'Oh yes.'

'Friends of yours,' Mountjoy said. 'Or rather, one friend and one relative.' He smiled stroboscopically (a neat trick, if you manage it. Being two-faced, like Mountjoy, does of course help).

If Blondel was disconcerted for a moment, he recovered quickly. Someone who can teach themselves tightrope walking at the first attempt shouldn't have any problem with mere mental agility.

'Oh,' he said, 'you mean that Goodlet chap and my sister Isoud. Perhaps I ought to warn you that unless Isoud has a cup of tea first thing after waking up she's about as sociable as a puma. Or have you found that out already?'

'La Beale Isoud,' Mountjoy replied, 'has the sense to realise that she has more pressing things to worry about than where her next cup of tea is coming from.'

'Are you sure we're talking about the same person?' Blondel said. 'About this height, sort of mousy blond, keen on carbohydrate-rich foodstuffs?'

Mountjoy ignored him. 'I am told,' he went on, 'that they have already made one fumbling attempt at escape, which naturally ended in failure. You may be sure that they won't be in a hurry to try again.'

A gentleman, Blondel's mother had always insisted, is unfailingly polite at all times, even when being lowered into a pit full of scorpions by black-hearted and incorrectly dressed Infidels. He shrugged slightly.

'Clever old you, then,' he said. 'I take it you're going to suggest an exchange of hostages.'

'That was my idea, yes.'

'Fair enough,' Blondel replied. 'Swap me King Richard for the Antichrist, and I'll let you have the two Julians for Guy and Isoud.'

'Certainly not,' Mountjoy replied with an unpleasant little snicker. 'That would be grossly unfair to us, given that the Pope and the Anti-Pope are one and the same person.'

'But wearing different hats,' Blondel replied quickly. 'Hats make an awful lot of difference. You ask my friend Guy about hats.'

'Nevertheless,' Mountjoy replied, 'the terms are unacceptable.'

'How about if I get my agent to throw in a free radio alarm clock?'

Mountjoy scowled, making the world momentarily dark. 'If I were you,' he said, 'I would advise your friend Galeazzo to stay off the topic of free radio alarm clocks, particularly when he's in the presence of My Lord.'

A terrible thought struck Blondel, and he struggled with his muscle control in a desperate attempt not to giggle.

'You don't mean . . .' he said.

'Shortly before the date scheduled for the Day of Judgement,' Mountjoy intoned, 'My Lord, on the advice of his legal advisers, took out a public liability policy. Part of the package offered by the insurance broker, it appears, was a free radio alarm clock, which subsequently failed to go off on a rather important occasion. As soon as My Lord has finished with you, Master de Nesle, I rather fancy he means to take the matter up with the broker in question.'

Blondel, who had closed his eyes in the interests of mirth suppression, opened them again and nodded. 'Fair enough,' he said, 'we'll scrub round the alarm clock. But don't you think a deal whereby you give me two relatively unimportant civilians in return for two high-ranking clerics and the Antichrist is a bit, well, one-sided. If you'll forgive the pun,' he added.

'It depends,' Mountjoy replied luminously. 'Unimportant to us. Unimportant, indeed, to history. But unimportant to you . . .'

Blondel frowned, and noticed something out of the corner of his eye. 'Hello,' he said, 'is that my old friend Clarenceaux under all that oilcloth? How's things, Clarenceaux?'

Clarenceaux, who had set in a position that was half standing to attention and half frozen rigid by the cold, stared straight in front and replied, 'Sir.'

266

'Bad as that, are they?'

'Sir.'

'Oh well,' said Blondel sympathetically. 'Stiff upper lip and all that.'

'Sir. Ran out of my size again, sir,' Clarenceaux explained. 'Quartermaster said it'd soon bed down, sir.'

'I see.' Blondel shrugged and turned back to Mountjoy. 'Tell you what I'll do,' he said, 'and I'm cutting my own throat, I really am. I'll let you have the two Popes and the Antichrist, you give me the King and Guy, and you can keep La Beale Isoud. Now I can't say fairer than that, can I?'

Mountjoy, for all his phosphorescent detachment, was shocked. 'You'd sacrifice your own sister?' he said.

Blondel tried to look innocent. 'Absolutely,' he said. 'A man's first duty is to his king, and next to that, to his fellow knights. Sisters just do the washing.'

Mountjoy's brain turned like the dials of a fruit machine. He remembered what the warder had told him the woman had said when he brought her her rations. They had enough trouble filling the existing staff vacancies without looking for another warder. 'I wouldn't dream of it,' he said.

'Pity.' Blondel sighed. 'Right, then, this is my very last offer, take it or leave it. You release Richard, Guy and Isoud, and you can have your lot back plus me.'

'You?'

'Certainly. You can ship me off to the Archive of your choice, and I promise you faithfully that you won't know I'm there.'

Mountjoy shook his head, diffusing second-hand rain. 'That would be, Messire, because you weren't there. You've been in one Archive already and escaped.

We wouldn't be able to sleep at night. No, our terms are quite straightforward. Goodlet and La Beale Isoud in return for My Lord and Their Excellencies. Otherwise . . .'

'Otherwise what?' Blondel asked innocently.

'Otherwise,' Mountjoy replied, 'your sister and your friend won't even be fond and fragrant memories. They will never have existed. Do I make myself plain?'

'Absolutely, my dear fellow,' Blondel replied. 'After all,' he added, 'it'll just mean we're back to where we started.'

'Not quite,' Mountjoy said. 'If we were back where we started, none of this would be necessary.'

'Sorry?'

'I said,' Mountjoy repeated, 'if we were back where we started, none of this —'

'No,' Blondel interrupted, 'you're wrong there. If *you* were back where *you* started, then I wouldn't be here. We'd all be in the future, surely.'

'That's not the point,' Mountjoy retorted. 'If *we* were back where *we* started, then *you* wouldn't be here, but *we* would.'

Blondel shook his head. 'But surely in that case we wouldn't be we, we'd just be you.'

'That's what I said.'

'No, what you said was —'

'Hold on,' Clarenceaux interrupted. 'I think I see what's gone wrong. Mountjoy is taking a view of events as they would have occurred in Basic Time, while Blondel is looking at it all from an Overtime-based perspective which would naturally lead him to interpret . . .'

He stopped. He had this feeling that everybody in the world was looking at him.

'Sorry,' he said, and died of embarrassment.

'Anyway,' Blondel said, 'I suppose it's a deal, then. Shake on it?'

'No thank you.'

'Suit yourself.' He stepped out from under the tree and opened his umbrella. 'I'll meet you back here, same time, same place, this week. All right?'

'Agreed.'

'Ciao, then,' Blondel said, and walked away over the bridge.

Half an hour later, a battered red pick-up came and collected Clarenceaux and took him back to the depot. Because of an acute shortage of embarrassment neurons at Central Dispatching they had to close off the circuits and double-bank the guilt centres to make up; with the result that, in the six weeks until he next died and they had a chance to take him to bits and do the job properly, he had a distressing tendency to burp in mixed company and then feel awful about it for days afterwards.

Blondel was driving the cart. It was difficult, because the cart was about seven inches wider than the tunnel, and it was only because of strange distortions caused by anomalies in the temporal field that he was able to get the blasted thing through at all. The key thing was, at all costs, not to meet himself coming the other way.

'Hold tight, everybody,' he said, 'this is our turning.'

Giovanni looked up to see a low, narrow doorway the size of a coal chute, with a picture of a cart in a red circle with a diagonal line through it stencilled on its central panel. Although he was used to this sort of thing, he closed his eyes and ducked.

It was already dark when they reached the bridge. It was also raining. Of course.

Under a tree by the side of the road at the other end, Blondel could see Mountjoy, Clarenceaux and, of course, himself, working out the terms of the exchange. At least there would be reliable witnesses in the event of any dispute about the terms. He made a chuck-chuck noise to the horse, pulled his hood down over his face and asked Marco if the lanterns were ready.

Two carts waiting at opposite ends of the bridge, in the pouring rain. For a while they just sat there. Then, on one cart, a lantern flashes three times. Then a lantern flashes three times on the other cart. The first cart flashes back four times. The signal is reciprocated.

There is no known reason for this performance, which is believed to be compulsory on these sorts of occasions. Presumably it's just tradition.

He had kept calm up till now; but the other cart hadn't moved, and Blondel began to worry. In keeping with the rest of his character, on the rare occasions when Blondel went to pieces, he went to very small, very numerous, very fast-moving pieces. In fact, you could use him to shoot clay pigeons with.

'For God's sake,' he muttered, 'what do they think they're playing at? Marco, you stupid idiot, don't just sit there, flash 'em some more. Come *on*, for God's sake.'

The other cart remained still. It flashed back; five flashes and then one more for luck. Blondel demanded angrily of the world in general what the hell that was supposed to mean.

Marco coughed politely. 'Maybe they're trying to remind you it's a one-way street, boss,' he said.

Blondel looked down at him. 'What do you mean, one-way street?'

'Well,' Marco said, marshalling his thoughts and hoping he was remembering this right, 'it means that if it's a north-south-only street, you can go from north to south but not south to north. If it's a south-north-only street, it means you can go from south to north but not north to south. If it's ...'

Marco suddenly found that his cap had somehow left his head and got wedged in his mouth. He took it out again.

'*Is* it a one-way street, Marco?' Blondel asked.

'Yes,' Marco replied, 'didn't you see the signs? It's a west-east-only street, that means you can go —'

'Yes, thank you,' Blondel replied, 'eat your nice hat now, there's a good lad. Silly of me not to have noticed, wasn't it?'

It made sense, after all. There was a serious risk that going through a No Entry sign in this particular context might result in something rather worse than a fine and two penalty points. He pulled himself together, chirruped softly to the horse, and moved the cart forwards.

'You're late again,' said Mountjoy. 'What kept you?'

'Got held up in traffic,' Blondel improvised. 'Anyway, I'm here now.'

Mountjoy flickered like a portable television in a thunderstorm. He hated getting wet; the last thing he needed to do at his time of life was to fuse. 'Can we get on with it, then?'

'You've come alone, then, like we agreed?'

'Of course I have,' Mountjoy replied wearily. 'For a start, nobody else'd be crazy enough to come out in this weather. Are they in the back?'

Blondel nodded. 'Want to check the merchandise?' he asked. This too was traditional.

'I trust you,' Mountjoy replied. 'I mean,' he added, 'if you can't trust slippery, devious little bastards, who can you trust?'

'Very true,' Blondel replied. 'But, since you're none of those things, I'd be grateful if you'd just lift that tarpaulin there.'

Muttering, Mountjoy did so. There was a loud protest in a distinctive female voice as rain came into the back of Mountjoy's cart. They were there all right.

'Any problems getting here?' Blondel asked.

'No,' Mountjoy replied suspiciously. 'Why?'

'Because every time I drive her anywhere,' Blondel replied, 'it's *Shouldn't you be in third gear?* and *I'm sure that was the turning back there on the left* all the bloody way. You must tell me how you managed it some time. Ready?'

'Ready.'

Mountjoy waved his hand. Pursuivant and Mordaunt jumped down and pulled two anthropomorphic bundles out of the cart. There was a bump as they hit the ground.

'That's fine,' Blondel said quietly. 'Giovanni, Marco, Iachimo, give me a hand, will you?'

The Galeazzos unloaded their cargo, plus a free simulated calf attaché case and solar calculator each, and laid them on the damp roadway. The two carts moved forward a few paces and took on their new respective cargoes.

'Right,' Blondel said. 'That's that, then. Pleasure doing business with —'

'*Seize them!*'

Blondel gave Mountjoy a very brief look of utter contempt, and then cracked the reins sharply. A moment later, his cart was surrounded by dark shapes; looming, ominous shapes, all the more disturbing because their visors were down over their . . .

'Look, Guy!' Blondel shouted. 'Hats! Iron hats! Lots and lots of them!'

There was a loud crack, and the sound of a bullet ricocheting off the crest of a helmet. A dark shape swore loudly and ran for its life. Or at least its five-hundred-year parts and labour warranty. The cart lurched forward and trundled off.

'After them!' Mountjoy yelled. The dark shapes stayed exactly where they were, all apart from one, who was wandering around bumping into things. Later they explained that you can't hear a damn thing inside those bleeding steel helmets.

From the back of Mountjoy's cart came a loud and authoritative protest. You'd have had no problem hearing it through six inches of plate steel.

'Good,' it added. 'Now don't just stand there, get after them.'

'Do you know,' Blondel said, as the cart thundered down the road, 'I'm getting just the teeniest bit sick and tired of all this running about and being chased by people, aren't you?'

Guy nodded. He was more than the teeniest bit sick at the way the cart was lurching about, too, but it seemed so long since he'd eaten anything that that was probably academic. He found what seemed to be a handrail and clung on to it fiercely.

'Ouch,' said Marco.

'Sorry,' Guy said, letting go of his ear. 'What are you doing down there?'

'I'm looking for my cap,' Marco replied. 'It fell off when we —'

'Forget it.'

'But it's nearly new,' Marco said. 'It's got a feather on it and —'

'I said,' Guy repeated, 'forget it.'

The cart went over a pothole rather too fast, sending everyone up in the air about six inches. There was a cracking sound and a great deal of turbulence. Then the cart stopped.

'The axle's snapped,' Giovanni said. 'Now I bet you're glad you decided to have the Fully Comprehensive.'

'Shut up, Giovanni,' Blondel said, 'and you, Isoud.'

'I didn't say a —'

'Then don't.' Blondel jumped down from the box. The lanterns of Mountjoy's cart weren't far behind. 'Come on,' he shouted, 'this way.'

'Why this way?' Isoud said.

'Look —'

'I think we should turn right.'

'*Look* —'

'It says on the map —'

'*This way*!'

They set off at a run, and made the cover of a small thicket just as Mountjoy's cart, heavily laden with dark shapes, failed to notice the obstruction in the road in time to stop. There was a pleasant crunching noise.

'I think,' Blondel observed, 'something just ran over Someone's foot.'

Dark shapes spilled out of the cart. Lanterns were

waved about, Mordaunt slipped in the mud, fell, impaled himself on a broken spear, died, and was accused by Mountjoy of skiving. Then the lanterns began to head towards the thicket.

'Oh bother,' Blondel said. 'Come on, everyone, all except you, of course, Isoud. I expect you want to go that way. The rest of you follow me.'

'Where the hell are we going?' Guy demanded.

'Back to the road, of course,' Blondel replied. 'Use your head.'

'But —'

'And when we get there,' Blondel continued, 'we're going to go up it. That's east-west to you, Marco. It's a one-way street, remember?'

'When are we?' Guy asked.

'At least it isn't raining,' Blondel replied. 'Come on, you two, I'll buy you each an ice cream.'

They walked towards the source of the noise and then, subconsciously adjusting their pace to the context, strolled. It is impossible to do anything other than stroll at a church fête, especially if it isn't raining.

'What happened?' Guy said. 'I mean, one minute we were running directly at those ... And then, bang! Or rather,' he added, puzzled again, 'not bang.'

'Oh look,' Blondel said, 'they've got a band. Salvation Army, probably. I like silver bands, don't you?'

'I suppose,' Guy continued, 'it was because it was a one-way street, and therefore, by implication, there was a no entry sign, and that meant it was somehow linked into the time tunnel network. Does that always happen when you go the wrong way up a —'

'Probably,' Blondel replied. 'Personally, I've never tried it before. Have you?'

'Well, no,' Guy admitted. 'When do you think this is?'

Blondel looked round with the eye of experience. 'Twentieth century,' he said, 'second half, definitely. Of course, the twentieth is a right little tinker to get your bearings in, because you can't go by the clothes. They were always having nostalgia. You could be strolling along looking at the hemlines and the shoulder-pads and thinking, Yes, I know when this is, perhaps there's a new Elvis Presley picture on at the cinema, and the next thing you know you're nearly knocked down by a Datsun. Cars, though, are a dead giveaway. You can date things by cars to within six months, usually.' He stopped, looked round and nodded. '1986,' he said. 'Funny sort of place to end up, 1986.'

'Is it?'

Blondel nodded. 'Nothing happened,' he explained. 'You may not have noticed, but there's a strong tendency when you leave the time tunnels at random to come out at a turning point of history.'

'You mean like Caesar crossing the —'

'Yes,' Blondel replied sternly, 'and keep your voice down. I don't want anybody finding out that was us. I don't know why it is,' he went on, 'this forever popping up at crucial moments. Maybe they've just got a stronger temporal field than your average wet Thursday in Dusseldorf. Anyway, as far as I can see, nothing of any significance whatsoever is happening here.'

'Good,' said Guy, and added, 'you mentioned something about an ice cream . . .'

Blondel nodded, borrowed five pounds from Giovanni – or rather, borrowed the use of his Beaumont Express Card – and wandered off in search of the refreshments tent. The Galeazzo brothers found a hoopla stall, which they proceeded to strip bare. Guy and Isoud sat down under a chestnut tree.

'Well,' Guy said awkwardly, 'here we are.'

'Yes,' Isoud replied.

'Um,' Guy continued, feeling it would probably be easier as well as nicer to try wading through waist-high custard, 'about this future of ours. The getting married and everything.'

'Yes,' Isoud said. Expressing oneself in unhelpful monosyllables in the course of extremely embarrassing conversations is a woman's prerogative, Guy remembered, and the thought struck him that his father had probably had a conversation like this, or else he wouldn't be here. And his father, and his father before him, right back to the period of human history when it was socially acceptable to crack girls over the head with clubs and drag them off by their hair. It was a wonder the world was populated at all.

'Don't get me wrong,' Guy went on, 'but, well, in a sense . . .'

He realised that he hadn't the faintest idea what he was going to say next, and was just about to change the subject and point out a perfectly ordinary tree on the other side of the green when Isoud turned to him and said 'Oh, Guy!'

There you go, monosyllables again. I think all the bride's lines in the wedding service are made up of monosyllables. Follows.

277

'Yes, well,' he said, 'like I was saying, we really ought to consider —'

'Kiss me, Guy.'

'Sorry?'

'I said,' said Isoud, with just a touch of residual personality showing through, 'kiss me.'

Guy wanted to say, Hold on a minute there, I think you've got hold of the wrong end of the stick, because what I was going to say was that now that we've found out how flexible and adjustable time is, perhaps we won't have to get married after all, and since neither of us is desperately keen on the idea ... But since he'd been taught not to speak with his mouth full, he didn't.

'Hello, you two,' Blondel said, grinning at them over a mobile barricade of white froth. 'Thought so.'

Isoud detached herself, leaving Guy realising what a rock must feel like when there are limpets about. She blushed prettily, said something about having a look at the white elephant stall, and skipped away, for all the world, Guy reckoned, like a radiantly happy electro-magnet.

'Have an ice cream,' Blondel was saying. 'So Isoud showed you the family photograph album, did she?'

'Gug,' Guy replied.

Blondel shrugged his shoulders. 'Took me a long time to find you,' he went on. 'Well, to be honest, I wasn't looking all that hard, what with searching for the King and everything. Still, better late than never, I suppose.'

'Hold on a minute,' Guy said. There was ice cream all over his nose, but he didn't care. 'You mean you ... you *chose* me specially? I thought it was just a coincidence or something.'

'Hardly,' Blondel replied. 'I don't want to sound rude, but if I'd had a free and unrestricted choice of assistants, I think I'd probably have chosen someone who's a rather better shot. Not that you've done badly,' he added. 'Just the reverse. But you see what I mean.'

'Yes, I see,' Guy lied. 'You mean, Isoud and me, it's been sort of, fated ...'

'If you like,' Blondel replied. 'That is, we knew the ending, all we had to do was reconstruct the plot a bit. Your ice cream's melting all down your sleeve, by the way.'

'How long has it been –' Guy winced; the word was so bloody *fey*, '– fated, then?'

'Ever since we got the photographs back from the developer,' Blondel replied. 'That's one of the weird things about living in a timewarp. You get the photos back centuries before they're taken and sent off, rather than the other way round, which I believe is the usual way. So we knew it was going to be you Isoud would fall for, it was just a case of finding you. And while you were handy, of course, you might as well make yourself useful in the quest.'

'I see.'

'Honestly,' Blondel continued, chuckling quietly, 'you should have seen Isoud's face when she first saw the picture. Talk about horrified disbelief! Still, I think she's just about come round to the idea.'

'Thank you very much.'

'Don't mention it.'

'Yes,' Guy said, 'that's all very well, but it still doesn't explain why you dragged me out of my century —'

'You were just about to be killed,' Blondel interrupted. 'Remember?'

'Was I?'

'Didn't I mention it? Oh yes, you wouldn't have stood a chance if I hadn't ... well, there we are. Couldn't have you getting killed before the wedding, it would have messed things up terribly. Not,' he added, 'that anyone wants you to get killed after the wedding, needless to say.'

Guy frowned. 'Not even Isoud?' he said. 'I still don't think she's likely to have changed her mind that much. She doesn't have a terribly high opinion of me, I reckon.'

'And that,' Blondel replied, 'is a prerequisite of a successful marriage, as far as I can tell.'

Guy thought about it for a moment, considering all the examples in his experience of happily married couples. Yes, he definitely had something there.

'Even so,' he persisted, 'if it was fated, why did you have to go to all the trouble finding me? Wouldn't I have just turned up anyway?'

'Probably,' Blondel replied, 'but it might have taken ages, and I've always been particularly keen to get the wedding over and done with. Partly,' he said, grinning, 'because I have this rooted aversion to mashed potato, but mostly because, in the wedding photograph you haven't seen, the man giving the bride away at the wedding is Richard Coeur de Lion.'

Guy choked on his ice cream. Blondel patted him on the back.

'So you see,' he went on, 'I've been quite shamelessly fiddling about with your destiny for my own purposes, just like you were going to say yourself. Hope you don't mind. Anyway, you'll understand what I'm getting at when I say that I'm not a believer in long engagements. Ah, here she is.'

280

Isoud was walking back, holding a lampshade, a sink tidy and a colander. It's started already, Guy said to himself. A door marked *No Entry* would go down very well at this juncture.

'Come on,' Blondel said, 'let's go and have a look round the sideshows. I think we can all afford an afternoon off, in the circumstances. No, Guy, I'd stay clear of the rifle range if I were you, there's a man in a cap just over there and I don't think he'd be too ...'

'Blondel? What's the matter?'

Blondel was staring, so hard that his eyes were almost circular. His mouth had fallen open and his face was wet with sweat.

'What is it?' Guy said.

'Look,' Blondel croaked, and pointed.

Guy followed the line of his finger, and saw one of those rubber inflatable castles designed for children to bounce up and down on. It was doing good business, as far as Guy could tell, and the proprietor was throwing two little cherubs off it for trying to puncture the inflatable bit with a penknife. 'So?' he said.

'Look,' Blondel repeated. 'Are you blind or something?'

Guy looked; and noticed that there was a pattern of little teardrops painted all down the side. And he began to wonder.

Blondel had broken into a run. The proprietor, seeing him coming, let go of the two little cherubs and stared at him. A policeman on duty in the beer tent came out, wiping his mouth. Guy looked across at Isoud, and ran after him.

'Here,' said the proprietor, 'you can't go on it, it's just for the kids. Here ...'

Blondel was standing in front of the moulded rubber gate. The musical attachment stopped in the middle of the tune it had been playing and then started to play something else. Guy recognised the tune at once. He'd heard it a lot lately.

Blondel waited for a moment, counting the bars for the start of the vocals. Then he sang:

'*L'amours dont sui epris*
Me semont de chanter;
Si fais con hons sopris
Qui ne puet endurer . . .'

The policeman stopped dead in his tracks and let his hands fall to his sides. Everything was quiet, except for Blondel's voice, soaring away into the clouds and ranging outwards in every direction, until it seemed to fill the entire world.

'*A li sont mi penser*
Et seront a touz dis;
Ja nes en quier oster . . .'

Guy felt like a diver who has miscalculated and can no longer hold his breath and is still a long way from the surface. The air seemed to tighten unbearably round him, crushing him until he could feel his ribs and the sides of his skull being driven inwards. And then, from somewhere a long way down inside the inflatable rubber castle, a voice sang:

'*Remembrance dou vis*
Qu'il a vermoil et clair
A mon cuer a ce mis
Que ne l'en puis oster . . .'

The voice sounded like an air-raid siren with bronchial trouble. It was the most beautiful sound that Blondel, or Guy, or Isoud, or even the Galeazzo brothers (who had been on the point of interesting the vicar in their exclusive range of tax-free clerical pension schemes when the music started) had ever heard in their entire lives.

The voice fell silent, and Blondel sang again. He sang like the first green shoot of spring, the first snow-drop, the first drop of rain in a dry season. He sang:

'*Plus bele ne vit nuls*
Ne cors ne de vis;
Nature ne mist plus
De beaute en nul pris
Por li maintaindrai l'us
D'Eneas et Paris,
Tristan et Pyramus
Qui ameraient jadis,'

and it seemed like the whole world, the entire human race, eight centuries of it suddenly realising their mistake and being glad that things were right now, joined in and sang:

'*Or serai ses amis*
Or pri Deu de la sus.
Qu'a lor fin soie pris.'

Giovanni blinked and reached for his handkerchief. He was crying for pure joy. He was thinking of the royalties.

Talking of royalties; the castle suddenly deflated and fell to the ground, and out of nowhere stepped a man. A tall man, dazzled by light he hadn't seen for eight hundred years, a man stooping and stiff, nursing his pet rat. A man who had been wronged, and who was going to set things right.

'Blondel, my dear chap,' he said, 'this really is most awfully decent of you, you really shouldn't have

283

bothered, you know, I was getting on splendidly, digging tunnels and so forth. But ...' He stopped, and breathed in the pure, wild air, and soaked up the light until he seemed to glow with it. 'Thank you, my dear fellow,' he said.

'Your Majesty,' Blondel replied. He was kneeling. There were tears streaming down his face, just like the teardrops painted on the side of the rubber castle. 'Your Majesty,' he repeated. 'It was nothing.'

The King reached out a stiff hand and raised him up. The light didn't seem to be troubling him now; indeed, he looked like a man who would never be troubled by anything ever again.

'Right,' he said. 'Now, then.'

Timestorms are, of course, much rarer these days than they used to be in five hundred years' time, thanks to the tireless efforts of the Time Wardens, and as the threat they will pose receded, humanity will forget the almost indescribable chaos they will cause and will have neglected to be about to take even the most elementary precautions, such as having their names and dates of birth tattooed indelibly on their foreheads.

In a timestorm, events which in the usual course of things will have happened or will happen consecutively suddenly happen concurrently. In other words, people are born, live long and purposeful lives, select a pension scheme which will grow with them, marry, spend small fortunes on carpets, have children, age gracefully and die all at the same time. Trees are simultaneously acorns, oaks and HB pencils. All the days of the week take place at once. Endowment policies mature on payment of the first premium, and vintage wines suddenly fall drastically in price. Such concepts as relativity, the laws of thermodynamics and early closing cease to have any meaning. Giving up smoking becomes easy but pointless.

One kind of timestorm has effects that are so devastating as to be almost without exception terminal; and it was with some relief that the Caernarvon Commission was able to report that none of the reported instances of such a catastrophe having taken place could be factually substantiated.

Once someone has become caught up in one, he can never get out again; and nobody undergoes the phenomenon without incurring material ruin, irreversible psychological damage and a free digital stereo alarm clock radio.

'Where are we?' Guy shouted.

He didn't want to, but it seemed that his role in life, over the last however-long-it-was-now, was to ask that sort of question; as if some sort of unseen Narrator needed him to establish the mise en scène.

'I don't know,' Giovanni yelled back. 'Do you honestly think it matters?'

Well, no, Guy conceded, probably not. Not particularly likely that anything matters, or will ever do so again. I mean, this is it, isn't it?

A tiny voice in the back of his mind agreed that yes, it probably was.

Time and space are, of course, connected at a fundamental level. To give a basic example: because of tectonic shift, the various land masses are no longer where they used to be, and the people who invested in valuable building plots on the strip of land joining England and France have long since given up trying to get hold of the representatives of Beaumont Street

Realty who sold them to them, and died.

In other words, where you are depends to a great extent on when you are. However, when you are in the middle of a timestorm so massive in scale that eight centuries of history are being rolled back like the duvet on the bed of Causality, the whole thing becomes academic, and the only really important question to consider is whether or not it's ever going to stop.

'What was that?' Guy screamed dutifully.

'1789,' Giovanni replied, emerging from under a log. 'Didn't you see its markings?'

The huge shadow that had momentarily blotted out the sun receded into the distance, became a small, vividly bright spot on the sun's disc, and exploded like a firework. About fifteen seconds later there was a soft, distant plop.

'Pity,' Giovanni said. 'We did good business in 1789. The French Revolution, you know.'

'Ah,' Guy replied. He listened, and noticed the absence of a sound. It had been going on for some time, getting louder and louder and worrying him very much. If it was worth trying to find something inside his own experience which came within long rifle shot of resembling it, he would suggest that it sounded like enormous reels of film ticking through the gate of a projector backwards.

He lifted his head and looked around. Something very strange had happened to the surface of the earth.

It had happened quite quickly. One moment, there had been King Richard and Blondel and, in the background, the sagging rubber castle and a crowd of bemused villagers. The next moment; well, moments had been pretty plentiful after that. The trick had been

287

not to be hit by them as they ricocheted off each other and sang screaming through the air. As for the landscape, it had sort of faded away. It was as if (and the librarian of Guy's meagre archive of imagery started to giggle hysterically when the request came through for this one) the world was a huge watercolour painting which had just been put under the cold tap. First it had run, and then it had been washed away.

'Giovanni,' Guy asked quietly, 'are you still there?'

'Depends,' Giovanni replied. 'It's all down to criteria really, isn't it?'

'You what?'

By way of illustration, Giovanni stuck his fingers into Guy's eyes.

'Look,' Guy said, 'just stop clowning about and answer me. Are you there or ...?'

'You didn't feel that, then?'

'What?'

'Or this?'

'*What*?'

'Or,' Giovanni said, grunting with the effort, 'this?'

'Look,' Guy said, 'will you stop it and ...?'

Giovanni put the knife down. 'Part of me's here,' he said. 'Part of you, too. The rest ...'

They both ducked. There were three large bangs as the main factors leading to the Industrial Revolution were torn up by the roots and flung into the air, or at least flung. Snippets of speech floated down and settled round them, still gibbering faintly. Fortunately for Guy's sanity, they weren't in languages he knew.

'Stuff it,' he said, 'would it make it any easier if I didn't want to know what was happening?'

Giovanni shrugged. 'No,' he said. 'What's happening

is that the historical part of you, and me, has been vaporised. All that's left is what ...' Giovanni considered for a moment, during which time a splinter of the American War of Independence floated down like a sycamore seed and lodged in his hair. 'What you're really made up of, I suppose,' he concluded lamely. 'In your case, inquisitiveness, fear and a certain amount of angry disbelief. In my case a strong will to self-preservation coloured by a strong dash of financial acumen. Have you any idea,' he added, 'what this lot's doing to the exchange rate?'

'But ...'

'Exactly,' Giovanni replied smugly. 'The first time I met you, I put you down as a but-and-three-dots sort of person. Me, I'm more of a therefore.'

But Guy wasn't listening. He was looking up at what he stubbornly persisted in thinking of as the sky. The greatest motion picture of all time was about to start.

It started far off in the future, and it employed a range of split-screen techniques beyond the wildest dreams of any mortal director. There were billions of them, tiny little images, each showing a tiny segment of an overall image which, taken together, Guy supposed was The World. And each individual film crew was using that rather arty style whereby the camera is supposed to be looking through the hero's eyes. To make it that bit more baffling (although Guy knew several people, most of whom wore scruffy old tweed jackets and smoked pipes, who'd undoubtedly have approved) the whole thing was being shown *backwards*.

He looked round for Giovanni, but he'd gone. In the darkness, Guy could make out a tiny figure walking across the blurred and naked foreground, not looking at the sky. He had a torch in one hand and a tray round his neck. He was, Guy realised with grudging admiration, selling popcorn.

The film show moved with considerable pace; and although the voices were all so faint that he couldn't hear any of them, he found that he was able to follow what was going on. This was the Sixth World War; then the foundation of the United States of Oceania and the Eurasian People's Republic; the 2120 World Cup; the Macclesfield Missiles Crisis; the restoration of the Jacobites; the Fifth, Fourth and Third World Wars; the Berlin wall; the Second World War ...

'Hey,' Guy shouted, 'that's me ...' Then the screen he'd been looking at suddenly went blank, and he suddenly didn't want to watch any more.

The film show went on, however, gaining momentum as one spool grew bigger than the other, so that the discovery of America and the reconquest of Spain seemed to merge into one another, and the Apaches merged seemlessly with the Moors. The Moors became Turks under the walls of Constantinople, then Mongols streaming across the steppes of Russia, and then Saracens laying siege to Antioch ...

Then the film stuck, as if a huge hair had got itself jammed in the gate of Time; and, as always seems to happen, the film seems to crackle, and little wisps of smoke ...

'Satisfied?'

'All right,' said a muffled voice from inside the rubber castle, 'there's no need to make a bloody great performance about it.'

'Come out, then.'

The rubber castle stirred uneasily. One of the small children who had been bouncing about on it a few minutes before dropped its ice cream and started to yell.

'Can't we talk about this like sensible adults?'

'No.'

'How about arbitration?'

'No.'

'Toss you for it?'

'No.'

The castle writhed a little, like a dyspeptic python. 'Best of three?' it said hopefully. 'Use your own coin?'

'No.'

'Look, there really isn't anything personal, it's just ...'

King Richard raised his sword again and pointed at the ground in front of him. He was smiling, but his smile had about as much to do with joviality and bonhommie as a cap pistol with a Howitzer.

'You wouldn't,' said the castle, shaking like a crenellated jelly.

'Watch.'

'But opening the Archives ... You haven't got the faintest idea ... Thousands of years ... They just won't *fit* ...'

King Richard raised the sword in both hands, whirled it round his head, and brought it down in a flashing circle of light that seemed to cut a section out of the sky. A fraction of a second before it hit the ground, he checked the stroke and wobbled furiously. The castle unhuddled itself.

'Very funny,' it said, and its voice was on the thin edge of hysteria. 'Knew you wouldn't have the ... No!'

The sword rose.

'*All right*!'

And where the rubber castle had been, there stood a gateway, and behind it, mile upon mile of winding battlements and cloud-topped watchtowers and sun-spearing keeps and mottes and baileys and ...

And the gate was open.

Something fell from nowhere and landed at Richard's feet. It was a small, brass Yale key, attached to a scruffy rectangle of cardboard by a broken rubber band. On the cardboard someone had written, Chastel des Larmes Chaudes. If nobody in, leave with Number 47.

Guy stood up and looked around.

About forty yards behind him lay the burnt-out wreckage of his plane. Somehow, he realised, he had got out of that thing before it blew up. Pretty impressive; shame he hadn't the faintest idea how he'd done it.

Nor, he realised, had he very much idea where he was. France, presumably; which meant his troubles weren't over yet. It would probably be a good idea to run somewhere.

'M'sieur!'

He looked round, feeling more foolish than anything else. 'Hello?' he said.

'M'sieur!' the voice hissed again. 'Allez! Allez vite!'

Ah yes, you (plural) go fast. Just what I was thinking, miss. Where, though?

The owner of the voice appeared out of the darkness, and Guy allowed himself to relax slightly. Not likely that the Germans were recruiting seventeen-year-old

French girls into the SS. More likely, this was a friendly native.

'Hello?' he said. 'I think ... I think I've banged my head.'

The girl scuttled forward, grabbed him by the arm and dragged him behind a bush. Ambiguous, Guy said to himself; but she's probably hiding me from a German patrol. Ah yes, there they go. Let's not say anything for a minute or so, until they go away.

When they had gone, the girl hauled him to his feet again – just when he was getting comfortable, but that's women for you – and bundled him off into a sort of small wood. He followed her, trying to trip over as little as possible, until they came to a little cottage. There was a light in the window. The girl stooped down, picked up a small stone, and threw it against the pane.

'Here,' Guy said, 'don't do that, you could break something —'

'Tais-toi, idiot,' the girl hissed (a high-class hisser, this one; of course, French is a much more sibillant language than ...). The light went out, and the door opened. Probably the householder, come to give us a piece of his mind.

'Isoud,' came a low voice from the darkness, 'c'est toi?'

'Si. On arrive.'

Guy felt himself being dragged towards the cottage. A young man appeared and grabbed his other arm. Tall chap, light blond hair, moustache.

The young man closed the cottage door and the girl pulled down the blinds. 'Etes-vous blessé, m'sieur?' the young man said – are you (plural) wounded, sir? Oh I *see*, am I all right?

293

'I'm fine,' Guy replied. 'I think I may have banged my head ...' Then he fell asleep.

When he woke up, he discovered that the girl's name was Isoud and her brother was Jean, and they were with the Resistance. Nice girl, too. Reminded him of someone, too, but for the life of him he couldn't remember ...

Out of the gate had ridden an army.

There were knights, and squires, and men at arms, landschnechts, halberdiers, bombardiers, longbowmen, crossbowmen, arquebusiers and, somewhere near the back, Pursuivant, Clarenceaux, Mordaunt and White Herald, with their eyes tightly shut. In any military force, there are always a select of body of men whose job it is in the event of an ambush to clutch their sides, scream convincingly and fall off their horses. It's a lousy job, but somebody's got to do it. Poor bloody henchmen.

At the head of the army rode a figure in half a suit of shining, night-black armour. The way in which he stayed on the horse is best left to the imagination.

The procession halted, and two trumpeters cantered ahead to blow the parley. A rather bemused sun glinted off ten thousand jet-black spearpoints. Behind the Antichrist's shoulder, two identical figures sat impassively in their saddles and looked down. By this stage, the only way they could stay materialised simultaneously was to sit absolutely still and breathe once every ten minutes.

'Well now,' said the Antichrist, 'here we all are, then.'

Richard (who had acquired some pretty impressive

294

armour of his own from somewhere; probably a while-you-wait armourer caught up in the gales of time) lifted his visor and smiled.

'Yes indeed,' the Antichrist went on, 'you with your victorious hordes.' He counted on his fingers; he had enough. 'Me with my ten thousand defeated but still quite highly motivated spectral warriors. Bit of a turn-up, don't you think?'

Richard continued smiling and saying nothing.

'Nice firework display,' the Antichrist continued. 'Looks like you rolled back – what – eight, nine hundred years there. Neat trick. And now you've won.'

Richard nodded. 'Apparently,' he said.

'So?'

'So what?'

The Antichrist leaned forward in his saddle. Cautiously.

There was a long, significant silence. Nature waited. Time listened.

'Um,' said Richard.

The Antichrist leaned forward in his saddle. Cautiously.

'Sorry,' he said, 'didn't quite catch that. Bit deaf on this side, to tell you the truth. What was it again?'

King Richard suddenly found the toe of his chain-mail socks very interesting. The Antichrist raised an eyebrow.

'I mean,' he went on, 'you must have had a bloody good reason, mustn't you? Winding back eight hundred years, threatening to open up the Archives, bringing the Chastel des Larmes Chaudes to its knees. Or rather knee. So, just give us the word and we'll get on with it.' He paused. 'Whatever it is.'

Something complicated seemed to be going on in the King's mind.

'If you'll bear with me a tick,' he said, apparently to his sock, 'I just want to, um, talk things through with my advisers. Get things straight in my own mind, you know.'

'That's fine,' the Antichrist replied. 'All the time in the world.'

Richard took two steps back and pulled Blondel and Guy into a huddle. The Galeazzos drifted up, like iron filings to a magnet.

'Quick,' Richard hissed sideways under the nose-guard of his helmet. 'Think of something.'

'Sorry?'

'Something to ask for,' Richard whispered. 'Demands. That sort of thing. Quickly.'

There was a deathly hush.

'How about,' Guy started to say. 'No, that'd be . . .'

Five anxious voices assured him that it was fine. They really wanted to hear from him. This administration accorded the very highest value to the voice of public opinion.

A moment later, Richard stepped forward.

'Ready?' said the Antichrist.

'Yes,' Richard said, looking round over his shoulder. 'In just a . . . Yes. Ready.'

'Well?'

'We demand – and we won't take no for an answer.'

'Yes?'

'Sorry?'

'You were demanding something.'

'Oh yes, that's right. We insist that you, er . . .'

'Yes?'

'Do something about the way it gets dark so early in December,' Richard said. His visor had fallen down over his nose, muffling his voice. He didn't see in a hurry to do anything about it.

The Antichrist blinked. 'Granted,' he said.

'I mean,' Richard mumbled, 'it's a disgrace.'

'Agreed,' the Antichrist said. 'So what shall we do?'

'Sorry?'

'About the long winter evenings,' the Antichrist said patiently, and with malice. 'I mean, do you want more sun in winter, which will bugger up the crop cycles but never mind, or less daylight in summer, which'll —'

'Surely that's your problem,' Richard muttered quickly. 'Just do something about it, all right?'

'Fine.'

'Right, then.'

The Antichrist leaned further forward still, until his ribs were almost on his horse's ears. 'That's it, then, is it?' he said. 'Shorter winter evenings. All this was about shorter winter evenings?'

Giovanni pushed his way forward. 'Go on,' he said, nudging Richard hard in the ribs, 'tell him. Tell him about the calendar reforms.'

'Ah yes,' Richard said, with a strange edge to his voice. 'I was, um, forgetting. You tell him,' he said desperately.

'We demand,' Giovanni said, doing his best to speak with a palate apparently composed of leather, 'that something is done about the calendar. I mean, it's a disgrace.'

'Absolutely,' Richard boomed through his visor. 'A scandal.'

'Infamous,' said Blondel.

'Outrageous.'

'And we won't stand for it.'

'You can say that again.'

'We won't —'

'Shut up.'

'Sorry.'

'Is it now?' the Antichrist said. 'Do tell me all about it.'

'I mean,' Giovanni went on, giving the impression that somebody had wound his tongue up with a large metal key, 'you've got some of your months thirty days long, some of them twenty-eight, some of them thirty-one. Just think of the havoc it plays with watches.'

'Watches?'

'You heard me,' Giovanni snapped. 'Calendar watches. How the hell is a poor dumb machine supposed to know which months have twenty-eight days and which ones have —'

'And there's leap years,' Blondel added loyally. 'Somebody's bright idea, I suppose.' He tried to find a bitter twang in his vocal repertoire, and failed.

'Right, then,' said the Antichrist. 'Winter evenings shorter, reform the calendar. No problem there, I mean, they might have a bit of trouble fiddling the moon's orbit, but let nobody say we're not ready to give it a go. Are you sure there wasn't something else? Something,' he hissed viciously, 'almost equally important?'

'Um,' Richard said.

'I mean,' the Antichrist rasped unpleasantly, 'otherwise I think that when you come to explain all this' – and he waved his hand at the horizon – 'to the Boss and say it was all to get the calendar sorted out and

298

tack an extra hour on before lighting up time in December, He might get just a bit aereated, don't you?'

As if on cue, the sky darkened. Clouds knitted together like huge eyebrows. The Antichrist's grin widened, until it stretched from ear to ... to ...

'I mean,' he said, 'Somebody Up There might take a less than tolerant view. Words like irresponsible and troublemaker might be used, don't you —'

SHUT UP

'Who said that?' Guy asked. Nobody could accuse him, he felt, of taking his duties lightly.

I DID, YOU CLOWN.

'How did you all manage to say that without moving your —'

AND AS FOR YOU, YOU CAN TAKE THAT GRIN OFF YOUR FACE.

The Antichrist looked straight up at the sky and wilted. Then he slid down the side of his horse like an oily raindrop.

THROWING YOUR WEIGHT ABOUT LIKE THAT, YOU OUGHT TO BE ASHAMED OF YOURSELF. NOW, IF YOU'VE ALL QUITE FINISHED MUCKING ABOUT, LET'S GET THIS MESS CLEARED UP AND WE'LL SAY NO MORE ABOUT IT.

'But,' the Antichrist said, and then clung frantically to the patch of air his horse had occupied before the lightning hit it. That, it occurred to him, was a hint. Bloody good hint, too.

Guy leaned over and whispered in Giovanni's ear. 'Is this what they call a *deus ex machina*?' he said.

'I wouldn't,' Giovanni whispered back, 'not if I were you.'

299

'All right, don't tell me, then,' Guy said. 'And you can all work it out for yourselves for all I care.'

The clouds swirled. A patch of cumulonimbus raised itself.

'And that,' Guy shouted, 'goes for you too.'

Suddenly he was alone. It wasn't another temporal shift or anything like that; it was just that everybody had suddenly realised how sensible it would be to be somewhere else.

WHAT DID YOU SAY?

'I'm fed up,' Guy yelled, 'and I want to go home. Nobody ever tells me *anything*.'

There was a long silence. A small thorn bush a few yards to Guy's left started to smoulder quietly.

DON'T THEY?

'No,' Guy said, 'and I'm not standing for it any longer, understood?' He raised his fist in a gesture of defiance, realised how silly he looked, and lowered it. 'If you were wearing a hat ...' he wailed.

ALL RIGHT.

'Sorry?'

I SAID ALL RIGHT. YOU WANT TO KNOW WHAT'S GOING ON AND I'M GOING TO TELL YOU, READY?

'Well, yes,' Guy said. 'Um ...'

IN THE BEGINNING ...

'He's asleep,' said Blondel.

'Good,' Isoud replied, pounding the boiled potatoes with a wooden spoon and a great deal of force. 'Did you really have to hit him like that?'

'If he thinks he's got concussion —'

'He has got concussion.'

300

'Let me rephrase that,' Blondel poured himself a drink and held it up to the light. 'If he thinks he got concussion getting out of the plane, he won't be surprised at not being able to remember anything. Best way,' he added. 'Santé.'

Isoud added a drop of milk to the potatoes. 'You know,' she said, 'he seems much nicer than he did.'

'That's just because he's incoherent with concussion,' Blondel replied. 'I've noticed, you women tend to go for the concussed type. Brings out the nursing instincts, I suppose. Can I get you one, sir?' he said, turning to the man sitting in the shadows in the corner of the room.

'Thanks awfully,' said the man, 'but not for me. Well then, that just about wraps it up for now, then, don't you think?'

'More or less,' Blondel replied. 'Thanks ever so much for dropping us off here, by the way. It'll make things much easier for Isoud and Guy.'

'Don't mention it,' Richard replied. 'They've got their own lives to lead, after all.' Richard shrugged and grinned. 'Not like us.'

'Right,' said Guy. 'Thanks.'

YOU GET THE GENERAL IDEA, ANYWAY?

Guy rubbed his eyes. 'More or less,' he said. 'Only ...'

MMM?

'That bit with the whale,' Guy said doubtfully. 'I mean, I've often wondered about that. You see, I always understood that whales couldn't swallow people, because of all this sort of mesh stuff they've got in their throats, so how come ...?'

301

IT'S A . . . THING.

'Thing?'

BEGINS WITH M. METRONOME, NO, META-PHOR. IT'S A METAPHOR.

'Oh,' Guy reflected for a moment. 'And that's allowed, is it?'

OH YES. PERFECTLY LEGITIMATE DEVICE, METAPHOR.

'Great,' Guy said. 'I didn't mean to imply . . .'

WHICH WOULD YOU RATHER LISTEN TO, ANYWAY, A NICE STORY WITH A HAPPY ENDING AND A STRONG WILDLIFE ELEMENT, OR THREE HOURS OF TECHNICAL METAPHYSICAL JARGON FULL OF WORDS LIKE COUNTER-INTUITIVE AND NEO-TRANSUBSTANTIATION? SOME PEOPLE DON'T KNOW THEY'RE BORN.

'Thank you,' Guy said. If in doubt, his mother had told him, just say thank you. People will understand. 'Er . . .'

NOW WHAT?

'Sorry,' Guy said, 'and really, I don't mean any disrespect or anything like that, it's just . . .'

BEFORE YOU ASK, IT'S ANOTHER META-PHOR.

'What is?'

STANDS TO REASON, REALLY. EVEN IF YOU COULD HAVE A TOWER THAT HIGH, THEY MUST HAVE HAD SOME WAY OF TALKING TO EACH OTHER, OR ELSE HOW DID IT GET BUILT IN THE FIRST PLACE? JUST THINK ABOUT IT, WILL YOU? YOU'D HAVE HAD ONE LOT DIGGING OUT THE FOOTINGS ON ONE SIDE AND ANOTHER LOT —

'No,' said Guy, 'actually it wasn't that so much as ...'

OH. LOT'S WIFE, MAYBE?

'No,' said Guy, 'not Lot's wife.'

Silence. SO YOU ACTUALLY BELIEVE ALL THAT STUFF ABOUT —

'Yes. What I was going to ask was ... um ...' Guy nerved himself. It wasn't nearly as hard as he'd imagined. 'You're not Him, are you?'

There was a slight rustling sound as something shuffled about in the burning bush. 'How did you guess?' it said.

It turned out to be a little white gnome with no hair and singed eyebrows, which clambered out, dusted itself off and extended a sooty hand.

'Melroth the Pole-Star,' it said. 'Pleased to meet you. Now you know,' it added, 'why angels always wear white. Asbestos.' It coughed.

'I hope you aren't offended,' Guy said.

'Not a bit,' Melroth replied, 'only too glad to get out of that thing.' The thorn bush collapsed in a cloud of white ash. 'Now then, where were we?'

'Um,' said Guy, 'you do have ... I mean, I can take it you're fully authorised to ...'

Melroth stared at him for a moment and then winced slightly. 'Sorry,' he said, 'memory like a sieve. My identification.' He showed a small plastic square with a blurred photograph half obscured by a red inkstamp. That alone was enough to convince Guy that it was genuine.

'He couldn't come himself, you see,' Melroth was saying. 'I know He's supposed to, but it just doesn't work like that. I mean, He can't be everywhere, can

303

He? Well, He can, of course, but —'

'Thanks,' Guy said. 'Now, about this time thing.'

'Yes?'

'Don't you think we should —'

'Hold on a tick,' said Melroth. He looked at his watch and made a few notes on a clipboard. It was a clipboard of burning gold and it had appeared out of nowhere, but it was palpably a clipboard. Suddenly Guy found himself understanding something very fundamental about the nature of Time.

'Right,' Melroth said, 'fire away.'

'Time,' Guy said, and he took a deep breath. 'It's a bit of a mess, isn't it?'

'Well,' said Melroth indistinctly, 'yes, it is. A bit.'

'Wouldn't it be easier if there was just the one sort of time,' Guy went on, slowly so as to let Melroth take notes, 'the sort that people could understand? You know, hours and minutes and seconds, and things happening one after the other, and then not happening ever again. None of these Archives and editing and all that. No time travel. No timestorms. Just time.' He paused, and added, 'I'm sure it'd make things much easier for your lot, as well as us.'

A very long silence. Eventually, Melroth scratched his nose.

'Interesting idea,' he said. 'But no. Wouldn't work. Administrative inertia. Unions'd never stand for it. Manifesto commitments. Cost too much to implement. Limited budget resources for new capital projects. Um.'

'Are you sure?'

'No call for it. Weight of public opinion against it at this juncture. Tried in the past and found to be impractical. Careful studies carried out by highly qualified

304

specialist research groups have shown. Constitutional reasons why not. Other unspecified reasons.'

'Sure?'

'Look.' Melroth diminished visibly, and the sleeves of his robe came down even further over his knuckles. 'It's not as if you're the first one to suggest it, right? It's just —'

'It's just,' Guy said, 'somebody made a cock-up a long time ago and nobody wants to admit it. Right?'

Melroth nodded.

'That's fine,' Guy said. 'Nobody minds. Nobody knows. Nobody need ever know. Just ... sort it out, and that'll be that. Do you see what I mean?'

Melroth looked at him. 'You reckon?' he said.

'Yes.'

'Um.'

Guy squeezed the last drop of determination out of the spongy mess he was keeping his brains in these days. 'You'll never get a better opportunity than this, you know,' he said. 'Think about it.'

'All right.'

'I know, that's easy to say, but ...' He stared. 'What did you say?'

'I said all right,' Melroth replied. 'Satisfied.'

'Yes,' said Guy, startled. 'That's fine, thank you.'

'I mean to say,' Melroth continued irritably, 'we do actually listen to what residents, I mean mere mortals, tell us, you know. It doesn't just all go in a great big shoe-box somewhere, or if it does we have to empty it out every month or so and things sometimes fall out and we pick them up and sometimes we read them and ... I mean, there is feedback. Definitely.'

'That's very reassuring,' Guy said. 'Really.'

'Good,' said Melroth. 'I think we understand each other.'

'Absolutely.'

'Well, then ...' Melroth hesitated. It's very rare these days for an angel to have to do something he's never done before, and he was nervous. He closed his eyes and took a deep breath. 'Thank you,' he said.

'Don't mention it,' Guy replied. 'Any time.'

Melroth turned and gave him a look. 'Any what?'

'Time.'

'Oh,' said Melroth slowly. 'That old thing.'

A wheelbarrow moving slowly across an infinite, blank landscape.

Behind it, doing the best he can with limited resources, a one-legged, one-armed, half-headed humanoid.

In the wheelbarrow, a large rubber sack with brightly coloured designs painted on it. Behind, a small knot of men carrying tea chests.

The servants of the Central Authority cannot, for fairly obvious reasons, be made redundant. But they can be redeployed, rationalised, reassigned and, in extreme cases, promoted sideways.

Of the Chastel des Larmes Chaudes staff, about ninety per cent had been seconded to the Parks and Amenities Department, where they were set to work whitewashing the stars and cleaning out black holes after interstellar conferences. They had been the lucky ones.

'Boss.'

The Antichrist looked round and noticed Pursuivant under three hundredweight of files and a typewriter.

'Well?' he said.

'What exactly are we going to do when we get there?'

'Shut up.'

'Yes, boss.'

Nobody spoke for the next ten minutes or so, during which time Mordaunt dropped the packing-case that contained the fax machine (probably on purpose) and Mountjoy tripped over the flex of the electric fan. Then they saw it, stretched out in front of them like a magnified sky.

'Oh *shit*,' said Pursuivant.

'All right,' snapped the Antichrist furiously, dropping the handles of the wheelbarrow and discovering that it was directly above his big toe, 'you can pack that in from the start. I mean,' he added hopelessly, 'it's not as bad as all that.'

'It isn't?'

'No.'

'Oh.'

Pope Julian, of course, had had it easy. Since he was by definition an incurable temporal paradox he had simply ceased to exist. Jammy little toad.

They had been standing there for a while when the caretaker came out. He was carrying three huge tins of blue paint, six moulting brushes, and he was grinning like a cracked wall.

'Here they are,' he said, 'the boys from the blue stuff.'

They ignored him. He chuckled unpleasantly, like a blocked drain.

'There you go,' he said, plonking the equipment down in front of them. 'And watch the bits round the edges. Gone a bit mouldy there, it has. You'll probably need to rub it right down and fill it before you can start.'

The Antichrist didn't answer. Somewhere on the other side of this lot the rest of his erstwhile subordinates were toddling about in a leisurely fashion, daubing a bit of glitter on a star here, polishing a.red dwarf there. If ever he got his hand on that bloody de Nesle ... Well, there'd be trouble.

The caretaker handed over the keys to the tiny shed which was to be their home for the next ... for a very long time, and pottered away into the vast white distance, sniggering. The Chastel men stood for a while, staring; just as stout Cortez would have gazed on the Pacific if he'd just been told that he was going to have to walk home.

‘Oh well,’ the Antichrist said. He took a handkerchief from the top of the wheelbarrow and gripped it in his teeth while he tied knots in the corners of it with his hand. Then he put it on his head. ‘The sooner we make a start ...’ he said, and his voice seemed to drain away into the immensity in front of him. ‘Anyway,’ he said.

Then he and the others began to paint the sky.

The jury room of the United Global Criminal Court.

‘Whose is the giblets?’ called out the foreman of the jury. Eleven hundred and ninety-eight people shook their heads in turn; and then somebody nudged the eleven hundred and ninety-ninth juror, who had been staring out of the window, and who turned, shook himself, and said, ‘Sorry, I was miles away.’

‘Right,’ said the foreman. ‘Eat it while it's hot.’

The culture that had evolved in the jury room over the last eighty years was distinctive, to say the least. Only Mr Troon and Mrs Cartagena were left from the original panel; the rest were second, third or even fourth generation. When Mr Troon died – and he'd been in a coma for six weeks now, the poor old sod – nobody would be left who had heard the original evidence (Mrs Cartagena had, by her own admission, slept through the whole trial), but that was largely irrelevant. Opinion as to the guilt or innocence of the accused was now a matter of clan belief; and ever since the last outbreak of inter-tribal warfare, positions had become utterly entrenched. The politics of it all defied simple explanation; however, basically it came down to the fact that so long as the Macdonalds refused to give up their nine of the original twelve chairs and the Battistas clung on to their right to first choice of the bread rolls, further negotiation was a waste of everybody's time.

Stephen Ogilvy III (the foremanship had been hereditary in the Ogilvy family for as long as anyone could remember) banged on the table with the handle of his knife, and was rewarded with the usual silence.

'Right,' he said – as his father had said, and his father before him – 'have we reached a decision yet?'

Eleven hundred and ninety-nine voices answered him, and so it was time to start eating. At the far end of the table the Court Midwife announced that a new juror had just been enrolled.

Meanwhile, in their cell in the basement, the Galeazzo brothers lay motionless on their mattresses and reflected bitterly on the fact that, if they'd been found guilty in the first place and awarded the maximum sentence, they'd have done their time and been back on the street seventy-two years ago. But, as Someone had remarked at the outset, when the charge is one of mucking about with the very fabric of time itself, the interests of justice could only be served by ensuring that the lack of punishment really did fit the crime.

'Well,' said Blondel.

King Richard grinned at him and brushed confetti out of his hair. 'Got her off your hands at last, then,' he replied.

Blondel nodded. 'Took some doing,' he said. 'Have you decided yet?'

'Decided what?'

'What you're going to do,' Blondel said, looking away.

'I think so,' the King said. He sat down at one of the tables and watched as the wedding car bumped its way down the one cobbled street of the village. 'I saw an advertisement in the paper for a little pet shop in Poitiers, and I made enquiries. I reckon it's time to settle down and breed rats.' He leaned his head over his top pocket, made a cooing noise, and added, 'Isn't it, George?' A pair of small brown eyes gave him a look in return.

Blondel shrugged. 'Money in rats, is there?' he said.

'No,' Richard replied. 'But so what?'

'True. Anyway,' Blondel added, 'that's over at last. Now I can get out of this bloody collar.' He did so, and smiled.

'What about you?' asked the King, pouring the last of the champagne into a tumbler. 'Any plans?'

Blondel shook his head. 'The thing about life ...' he said.

'Yes?'

'Is,' Blondel went on after a moment, 'that there's

310

an awful lot of it, and the last thing I want to do is get involved. I mean, why break the habits of a lifetime?'

Richard sighed. 'I don't really think you can say you were never involved, Jack,' he said. 'You of all people.'

'Ah,' Blondel replied, 'but that's all over and done with, isn't it? I mean, all that history I mucked about with has been scrubbed. Clean slate. That means I'm a whatsisname, anathema. So long as I'm still around, can things really get back to how they should be? I'm not sure.'

'How come?' Richard said.

Under the canopy stretched across the village square, under the shade of the twisted old mulberry tree, a small, over-excited child was sick. 'Think about it,' Blondel said, lying back on the table and contemplating his fingernails. 'You were just the victim. I was the one who caused all the trouble. I was the one who went around singing *L'Amours Dont ... L'Amours ...* thingy all the time.'

'*L'Amours Dont Sui Epris*,' said Richard softly.

'That's the one,' Blondel said. 'Do you know, I've forgotten how it goes now. *L'Amours Dont ...* Ah well, never mind. I never liked it much anyway.'

'Didn't you?'

'No,' Blondel said, frowning. 'That bit in the third verse. Tum tum tumpty ... How *does* that bit go, can you remember?'

Richard shook his head. 'Sorry,' he said.

Blondel grinned. 'The hell with it,' he said, 'it's only a song, that's all. Some day somebody'll write another one, I expect. Anyway, I always reckoned it wasn't a patch on *Ma Joie Me ... Me ...* the other one.'

'Which one was that, Jack?'

'Can't remember.'

They sat quietly for a while, Richard remembering, Blondel just staring, while the last few friends and relations wandered away. A wedding guest hurried up, explained that some damn fool of an ecology canvasser had kept him talking for hours with some rigmarole about endangered seabirds, was told that he'd missed the ceremony and the reception, and clumped off in a huff. The sun went down.

'Anyway,' said Blondel.

'Anyway,' said Richard. 'Have you paused to consider that, if you put in a claim for overtime, you'd be the richest man in history?'

'No,' Blondel replied.

'Good,' Richard said, and fell asleep.

Blondel lay still for a few minutes more, gazing up at the battlements of the Chateau de Nesle in the far distance. Although he couldn't remember details, he had an idea he'd lived there once, a very long time ago. And, as the thought crossed his mind, he had the feeling he could hear somebody in one of the turrets singing a song which once he might have recognised.

'*L'amours dont sui epris*,' it sang,

'*Me semont de chanter;*
Si fais con hons sopris
Qui ne puet endurer.
Et s'ai je tant conquis ...'

Blondel sighed, and grinned, and stood up. At the foot of the tower, a low door materialised and opened.

And Blondel strolled through it, hands in pockets, singing.

GRAILBLAZERS

For GLH
Thanks

1

It is quite some storm.

It had started out with a perfectly ordinary squall on the strings, but then the brass had joined in, followed shortly afterwards by the entire woodwind section, and now the tubas and the double-basses are in full cry, with the trombones in the background doing the lightning effects. It is also slashing down with rain.

A flash of brilliant electric whiteness cleaves the darkness and reflects, painfully bright, off a man in armour staggering up the steep escarpment of the fell. His visor is up, and his face is lined with agony. He is an idiot. You can tell, just by looking at him. It's not so much his tall, youthful, athletic build or the sopping wet golden hair plastered like seaweed down his forehead that gives him away; it's just that nobody with anything substantial between his ears would climb up a steep mountain in full armour in a thunderstorm.

True, there is supposed to be a sleeping princess at

the top of this mountain, whom a kiss will awaken from a century of enchanted sleep. True, this princess is alleged to be beautiful, wise and extremely rich, and quite likely to be well-disposed towards the man who wakes her up. But common sense, even if it can handle the concept of sleeping princesses on mountain-tops, must surely insist that if she's been up there for a hundred years she's probably still going to be there in the morning, when it'll have stopped raining and a chap can see where he's putting his feet.

The knight stumbles on, and something – fool's luck, probably – guides his footsteps clear of the anthills, tussocks of heather and other natural obstacles which would send him and his fifty pounds of sheet steel slithering back down the hillside like a heavy-duty toboggan. The lightning forks from the sky again, and instead of electrocuting him chooses to illuminate the mountain-top. In fact it goes further, setting a wind-twisted thorn tree nicely on fire, so that the knight can make out the figure of a sleeping human under the lee of a rocky outcrop. Short of providing an illuminated sign saying YOU ARE HERE, there's not much more anybody could do to make things easy.

'Ha!' says the knight.

He lays down his shield and his spear and kneels for a moment, lost in wonder and awe. A sheep, huddling under a nearby gorse bush and chewing a ling root, gives him a look of utter contempt.

The sleeper remains motionless. The funny thing is that, for somebody who's been asleep on a mountain-top for a hundred years, she's in a pretty good state of preservation. When one thinks what happens to a perfectly ordinary pair of corduroy trousers when they inadvertently get left outside on the washing line overnight, one is amazed at how tidy she is. But of course, the idiot doesn't notice this. In fact, he's praying. He doesn't half choose some funny moments.

And now it has stopped raining, and the dawn pokes its rosy toe outside the duvet of the clouds and shudders. A single exquisite sunbeam picks out the scene. The knight's armour rusts quietly. Somebody is going to have to go over it later with a wire brush and a tin of metal polish, but you can guess, can't you, that it isn't going to be the knight.

Finally, having said quite a few paternosters and the odd Te Deum, the knight rises to his feet and approaches the sleeping figure. Dawn is now in full swing, and as he lifts the veil off her face – please note that some unseen force has protected the veil from mildew and mould for over a century – the sun lets fly with enormous quantities of atmospheric pink light. Creaking slightly, the knight bends down and plants a chaste, dry little kiss on the sleeper's cheek.

She stirs. Languidly, she opens her eyes. Consider how you feel first thing in the morning, and multiply that thirty-six thousand, five hundred times. Correct; you'd feel like death, wouldn't you? And the first thing you'd say would be, 'Nnnggrh,' surely. Not a bit of it.

'Hail, oh sun,' she says, 'hail, oh light, hail, oh daw . . .'

Then she checks herself. She blinks.

'Hang on,' she says.

The knight remains kneeling. He has that utterly idiotic expression on his face that you only see in Pre-Raphaelite paintings.

'Who are you?' says the princess.

The knight clears his throat. 'I,' he says, 'am Prince Boamund, eldest son of King Ipsimar of Northgales, and I have come—'

'Who?'

The knight raises both eyebrows, like someone by Burne-Jones who's just trodden on something sharp. 'I am Prince Boamund, eldest son of King—'

'Boamund?'

'That's right,' says the knight, 'Boamund, eldest son of—'

'How do you spell that?'

The knight looks worried. Where he comes from you can take advanced falconry, or you can take spelling; not both. Guess which one he opted for.

'Bee,' he says, and hesitates. 'Oh. Ee . . .'

The princess has a curious expression on her face (which is, of course, divinely beautiful). 'Are you being funny or something?' she says.

'Funny?'

'Kidding about,' she replies. 'Practical joke, that sort of thing.' She considers the situation for a moment. 'You're not, are you?'

'No,' says Boamund. He thinks hard. 'Look,' he says, 'I am Boamund, eldest son of King Ipsimar of Northgales, and you are Kriemhild the Fair, and you have been sleeping an enchanted sleep on top of this mountain ever since the foul magician Dunthor cast a spell on you, and I've just woken you up with a kiss. Agreed?'

The princess nods.

'Right, then,' says Boamund.

'So?'

'What do you mean, so?' says Boamund, flushing

318

pink. 'I mean, it's supposed to be . . . well . . .'

'Well what?'

'Well . . .'

Kriemhild gives him another peculiar look and reaches under a nearby stone for her cardy. It is, of course, pristinely clean.

'I mean,' she says, 'yes, you qualify, yes, you're a prince and all that, but . . . well, there seems to have been some mistake, that's all.'

'Mistake?'

'Mistake. Look,' she says, 'who told you? About me being here and everything?'

Boamund thinks hard. 'Well,' he says, 'there was this man in a tavern, if you must know.'

'A knight?'

Boamund scratches his head. Imagine a knight by Alma-Tadema who's somehow managed to fall off the picture and is wondering how to get back in without breaking the glass. 'I suppose he might have been a knight, yes. We were playing cards, and I won.'

Kriemhild's roseate lips have set in a firm line. 'Oh yes?' she says.

'Yes,' replies Boamund, 'and when I asked him to pay up he said he was terribly sorry but he didn't have any money. And I was just about to get pretty angry with him when he said that he could put me on to a pretty good thing instead, if I was interested. Well, I reckoned that I didn't have much choice, so . . .'

'I see,' says Kriemhild icily. 'Tell me, this knight, was he sort of dark, good-looking in a blah sort of way, long nose, hair fluffed up at the back . . .?'

'Yes,' says Boamund, surprised. 'Do you know him? I mean, how can you, you've been asleep . . .'

'Just wait till I get my hands on him, the treacherous little rat,' says Kriemhild, vigorously. 'I should have guessed, I really should.'

'You *do* know him, then?'

Kriemhild laughs bitterly. 'Oh yes,' she says, 'I know Tancred de la Grange all right. The little weasel,' she adds. 'I shall have a thing or two to say to Messire de la Grange when he finally condescends to get here.'

Something sinks into Boamund's slowly grinding brain. 'Oh,' he says. 'So you're going to, er . . .'

'Yes.'

'And you're, um, not going to . . .'

'No.' Kriemhild takes off her cardy, rolls it into a ball and puts her head on it. 'Please replace my veil before you go,' she says firmly. 'Good night.'

'Oh,' says Boamund. 'Right you are, then.' He stoops awkwardly down and picks up the veil, not noticing that he's standing on one corner of it. There is a tearing sound. 'Sorry,' he says, and drapes it as best he can over the face of the princess, who is now fast asleep once more. She grunts.

'Damn,' says Boamund, faintly; then, with a shrug which makes his vamplates crunch rustily, he sets off slowly down the mountain.

He's about a third of the way down when it starts raining again.

Fortunately there is a small cave nearby, its entrance half hidden by a wind-twisted thorn tree, and he squelches heavily towards it. Just inside he sees a dwarf, sitting cross-legged and munching a drumstick.

Promising.

'Hello, dwarf,' says Boamund.

'Wotcher, tosh,' replies the dwarf, not looking up.

'Still pissing down out there, is it?'

'Um,' says Boamund. 'Yes.'

'Rotten bloody climate, isn't it?' says the dwarf. 'I suppose you're coming in.'

'If you don't mind.'

'Suit yourself,' says the dwarf. 'I suppose you want a drink, an' all.'

Boamund's face lights up under his sodden fringe. 'Have you got any milk?' he asks.

The dwarf favours him with a look of distilled scorn and indicates a big leather bottle. 'Help yourself,' he says, with his mouth full.

It's a strange drink. Boamund thinks there are probably herbs in it; cold herbal tea or something. Then he suddenly feels terribly, terribly sleepy.

When he's fast asleep the dwarf jettisons his chicken leg, grins unpleasantly, makes a cabalistic sign and gets up to leave. A thought crosses his mind and he turns back. Having stolen Boamund's purse, penknife with corkscrew attachment and handkerchief, he leaves, and soon he has vanished completely.

Boamund sleeps.

Quite some time later he woke up.

Localised heavy rain, perhaps; or else someone had just emptied a bucket of water over him. He tried to move, but couldn't. Something creaked.

'It's all right,' said a voice somewhere overhead. That was probably God, Boamund thought; in which case, what he'd always suspected was true. God did indeed come from the West Riding of Yorkshire.

'You're not paralysed or anything like that,' the voice went on, 'it's just that your armour's rusted solid.

Really solid,' the voice added, with just a touch of awe. 'We're going to need more than just tinsnips to get you out of there.'

Boamund tried to see who was talking – probably not God after all – but the best he could do was crane his eyes. Result, a close-up of the bottom edge of his visor. 'Where am I?' he asked.

'In a cave,' replied the voice, and then continued, 'You've been here for some time, actually, sorry about that.'

Boamund cast his mind back. A fiery mountain. A maiden. A dwarf. Milk that tasted funny. Something his mother had told him, many, many years ago, about not accepting milk from strange dwarves.

'What's going on?' he asked.

'Ah,' replied the voice. 'You're the perceptive type, I can see that. Maybe all it needs is a dab of penetrating oil. Hold still.'

This injunction was, of course, somewhat redundant, but at least Boamund caught a very brief glimpse of someone small, in a purple hood, darting across his restricted line of vision. 'Here,' he said, 'you're the dwarf, aren't you? The one who . . .'

'Close,' said the dwarf, 'but not quite.'

'Hang on,' Boamund remonstrated. 'Either you are or you . . .'

'I'm not the dwarf you're thinking of,' replied the dwarf, 'but I'm a relative of his.'

'A relative . . .'

'Yes.' A small, ugly, wide grin floated across Boamund's sight-plane for an instant and then vanished again. 'A relative. In fact . . .'

'Yes?'

'Um.' A scuttling noise. 'A direct relative.' There was a curious swooshing sound near Boamund's left knee. 'Try that.'

Boamund made an attempt to flex his leg, without results.

'Give it another go,' said the dwarf. 'Brilliant stuff, this WD-40, but you've got to let it have time to seep through.'

Something began to tick inside Boamund's head. 'How long *have* I been here, exactly?' he asked. 'If my armour's really rusted solid, I must have been here . . .' He considered. 'Weeks,' he said.

'Try that.'

'Nothing.'

'Sure?'

'Of course I'm . . .'

Sound of intake of dwarfish breath. As well as being notorious for their alliance with enchanters, sorcerers and other malign agencies, dwarves are celebrated blacksmiths and metalworkers. This means that they have that profoundly irritating knack, familiar to anyone who's ever taken a car to a garage to have an inexplicable squeak sorted out, of drawing their breath in through a gap in their teeth instead of answering questions. The gap in the teeth, so current research would indicate, is usually the result of getting a smack in the mouth from telling a short-tempered customer that you can't get the parts.

'You're stuck solid there, chum,' said the dwarf. 'Absolutely solid. Never seen anything like it.'

Boamund felt a tiny twinge of panic, deep down inside his digestive apparatus. 'What do you mean,' he said, 'solid?'

The dwarf seemed not to have heard him. 'Not really surprising, though, amount of time you've been here. Suppose we could give it a try with the old cold chisel, but I'm not promising anything.'

'Hey!' said Boamund; and the next moment the entire universe began to vibrate loudly.

'Thought not,' said the dwarf, after a while. 'Helmet's rusted solid on to your vambrace. Looks like a hacksaw job to me. Stay there a minute, will you?'

In an ideal world Boamund would have pointed out, very wittily, that he didn't have much choice in the matter; however, since the world he was in fact inhabiting was still badly polluted with the after-effects of the dwarf attacking his helmet with hammer and chisel, Boamund didn't bother. What he in fact said was, 'Aaaagh.'

'Right then,' said the dwarf at his side. 'I've got the hacksaw, the big hammer, crowbar and the oxyacetylene cutter. Hold still a minute while I just . . .'

'What's an oxy-whatever you said?'

'Oh yes.' The dwarf was silent for a moment. 'You know I said I was a relative of that other dwarf?'

'Yes?'

'Well,' the dwarf replied, 'the fact is, I'm his . . . Just a tick.' The dwarf muttered under his breath. He was counting.

'You're his what?'

'I'm his great-grandson,' said the dwarf, 'approximately. I'm basing that on, say, fifteen hundred years, thirty-five-odd years per generation. You get the idea.'

There was, for the space of several minutes, a very profound silence in the cave, broken only by the sound of the dwarf having a go at the hinge-bolt of Boamund's visor with a triangular-section rasp.

'What did you just say?' Boamund asked.

'I'm the great-grandson of the other dwarf,' said the dwarf, 'the one you mentioned just now. And my name is Toenail. Ah, that's better, I think we're getting somewhere.'

Boamund made a gurgling noise, like a blocked hotel drain. 'What was that you said,' he asked, 'about fifteen hundred years?'

Toenail looked up from his raspwork. 'Say fifteen hundred years,' he replied, 'give or take a year or so. That's your actual oral tradition for you, you see, handed down by word of mouth across forty generations. Approximately forty generations, anyway. Hold on a second.'

There was a crash, and something gave. A moment later, Toenail proudly displayed a corroded brown lump. 'Your visor,' he explained. 'Now for the tricky bit.'

'I've been here for fifteen hundred years?'

'We'll call it that,' said the dwarf, 'for ready money, so to speak. You got enchanted.'

'I'd guessed that.'

'It was the milk,' Toenail continued. 'Big tradition in our family, how Toenail the First put the Foolish Knight to sleep with a drugged posset. About the only exciting thing that's ever happened to us, in fact. Fifteen hundred years of unbroken linear descent we've got – there's just the three of us, actually, now that Mum's passed on, rest her soul, that's me, our Chilblain and our Hangnail – fifteen hundred years and what've we got to show for it? One drugged knight, and a couple of hundred thousand kettles mended and lawnmower blades sharpened. Continuity, they call it.'

'I . . .'

'Hold still.'

There was a terrific creak, and then something hit Boamund very hard on the point of his chin. When he next came to, his head was mobile again and there was something looking like a big brown coal-scuttle lying beside him.

'Your helmet,' said Toenail, proudly. 'Welcome to the twentieth century, by the way.'

'The what?'

'Oh yes,' Toenail replied, 'I forgot, back in your day they hadn't started counting them yet. I wouldn't worry,' he added, 'you haven't missed anything much.'

'Haven't I?'

Toenail considered. 'Nah,' he said. 'Right, it's the torch for that breastplate, I reckon.'

In spite of what Toenail had said, Boamund felt he'd definitely missed out on the development of the oxy-acetylene cutter.

'What the hell,' he said, when his voice was functional once more, 'was that?'

'I'll explain it all later,' Toenail replied. 'Just think of it as a portable dragon, okay?' He lifted off a section of breastplate and tossed it aside. It clanged and disintegrated in a cloud of brown snowflakes.

'Basically,' Toenail went on, 'you've had your Dark Ages, your Middle Ages, your Renaissance, your Age of Enlightenment, your Industrial Revolution and your World Wars. Apart from that, it's been business pretty much as usual. Only,' he added, 'they don't call it Albion any more, they call it Great Britain.'

Boamund gurgled again. 'Great . . .?'

'Britain. Or the United Kingdom. Or UK. You know, like in Kawaguchi Industries (UK) plc. But it's basically the same thing; they've changed the names a bit, that's all. We'll sort it all out later. Hold tight.'

Boamund would have enquired further, but Toenail turned the oxy-acetylene back on and so he was rather too tied up with blind fear to pursue the matter. At one stage he felt sure that the terrible white-blue flame had gone clean through his arm.

'Try that,' Toenail said.

'Grr.'

'Sorry?'

Boamund made a further noise, rather harder to reproduce in syllabic form but indicative of terror. 'Don't worry about it,' said the dwarf. 'Just count yourself lucky I didn't think to bring the laser.'

'What's a . . .?'

'Forget it. You can move your arms now, if you like.'

For a moment, Boamund felt that this was a black lie; and then he found he could. Then one and a half millenniums' worth of pins and needles began to catch up with him, and he screamed.

'Good sign, that,' Toenail shouted above the noise, 'shows the old blood's beginning to circulate again. You'll be up and about in no time, mark my words.'

'And the first thing I'll do,' Boamund yelled at him, 'I'll take that oxy thing and . . .'

Toenail grinned and went to work with the torch on Boamund's leg-armour. Wisely, Boamund decided not to watch.

'Anyway,' Toenail said as he guided the terrible flame, 'I bet that what you're dying to ask me is, *Why* was I put to sleep for fifteen hundred years in a cave with all my armour on? I'm right, aren't I?'

'Aagh.'

'Well,' said the dwarf, 'oops, sorry, lost my concentration there for a minute. The armour was a mistake, I reckon, personally. Bit slapdash by old Toenail the First, if you ask me.' The dwarf grinned pleasantly. 'The actual going-to-sleep bit, though, that was your destiny.'

'AAGH!'

'Butterfingers,' muttered the dwarf. 'Sorry. The way I heard it, anyway, you're destined to be this, like, great hero or something. Like the old legends, you know, Alfred the Great, Sir Francis Drake—'

'Who?'

'After your time, I suppose. Like the great national hero who is not dead but only sleeping and will come again when his country needs him, that sort of thing.'

'Like Anbilant de Ganes?' Boamund suggested. 'Or Sir Persiflant the—'

'Who?'

'Sir Persiflant the Grey,' said Boamund wretchedly.

'You must have heard of him, he was supposed to be asleep under Suilven Crag, and if ever the King of Benwick sets foot on Albion soil, he'll come again and . . .'

Toenail grinned and shook his head. 'Sorry, old son,' he said. 'Guess he forgot to set the alarm. Anyway, you get the idea. That's you.'

'Me?'

'You. Not,' Toenail admitted, 'that there's much going on just at the moment. I mean, they say on the telly that unless someone does something about interest rates pretty soon it's going to mean curtains for small businesses up and down the country, but that's not really your line of work, I wouldn't have thought. Maybe you're going to do something about standards in primary school education. That it, you reckon?'

'What's a school?'

'Maybe not,' said Toenail. 'What else could it be?' He paused. 'You're not a fast left-arm bowler, by any chance?'

'What's a . . .?'

'Pity, we could really do with one of those. Anyway, whatever it is we need, apparently you're it. Try your feet.'

'Ouch.'

'Champion,' Toenail said. 'We'll give it a minute, and then you can try getting up.'

Boamund shifted slightly and discovered that he'd spent the last fifteen hundred years lying on a small but jagged stone. 'Ow,' he said.

Toenail was packing tools away in a small canvas bag. 'I'll say this,' he said, 'they made stuff to last in those days. Fifteen-hundred-year-old steel, eh?' He

329

picked up a massive armguard and poked his finger through it. 'Should be in a museum or something, by rights. There's probably people who'd pay good money . . .'

Boamund gave up the effort and lay back, wondering if you could die of pins and needles. Outside there was a noise; it had been there a while but he now perceived it for the first time. A low, ominous growling, like an animal – no, like a huge swarm of bees. Only these bees would have to be eight feet long to make a noise like that.

Toenail grinned at him.

'What you can hear,' he said, 'is the M62. Don't worry about it.'

'Is it safe?'

Toenail considered. 'Depends,' he said. 'But as far as you're concerned right now, yes. Try standing up.'

He reached out a hand and Boamund grabbed it. A moment later he was putting his weight on his fifteen-hundred-year-old shoes. Oddly enough, they were fine. A spot of polish wouldn't hurt, mind.

'My clothes,' said Boamund. 'Why aren't they . . .?'

'Enchanted,' Toenail replied. 'Keeps them all nice and fresh. Come on, we're running late as it is.'

Boamund followed Toenail to the door of the cave, looked out, and screamed.

A year or so back, a television producer, one Danny Bennett, made a documentary which implied that the poet T.S. Eliot was murdered by the CIA.

According to Bennett's hypothesis, Eliot was killed because he had, quite by accident, stumbled upon highly secret metaphysical data which the Pentagon

330

was in the process of developing for military use. Not aware of what he had done, Eliot published his findings in the *Four Quartets*; twenty-nine years later, he was dead, yet another victim of the Men in Grey Suits.

According to Bennett, the fatal lines were:

Time present and time past
Are both perhaps present in time future

and Bennett's argument was that this was taken by the nasty men to be an exposé of the strange things that people seem to get up to in the parts of ancient monuments and historic houses which are never open to the public.

Take, Bennett said, Hampton Court Palace, or Anne Hathaway's cottage. More than half of the rooms in these jewels of England's heritage are permanently shut. Why? Is it, as the Government would have us believe, simply because there isn't the money to maintain them and pay attendants? Or is there a more sinister explanation? Could it be that top secret experimental research into the nature of time itself is being carried out behind the nail-studded doors – research that, the nasty men hope, will lead to the perfection of a super-weapon that will allow NATO forces to zap back across the centuries, assassinate Lenin, and so prevent the storming of the Winter Palace? And was it his unfortunately ambiguous statement in the opening lines of 'Burnt Norton' that signed Thomas Stearns Eliot's death warrant?

Shortly after completing the filming of the documentary, Bennett was promoted sideways and appointed to be the new head of BBC local radio on

Martinmas Island, a small coral reef three thousand miles due east of Sydney. Interpretations of this outcome differ; Bennett, on his mid-morning phone-in *Good Morning, Martinmas*, has proposed the view that he has been muzzled, and this only goes to prove that he was absolutely right. The BBC, on the other hand, say that he was posted there because he had finally, irrevocably, fallen out of his tree, and although the next three years were likely to be tough going for the two marine biologists and six thousand penguins who inhabit Martinmas, short of having the wretched fellow put down there wasn't much else they could do.

Oddly enough, and by the purest coincidence, there is something extremely fishy about the back rooms of ancient monuments. These areas are used, as one would expect, for administration, storage and similar purposes; but nobody as yet has come up with a satisfactory (or at least comfortable) explanation for the fact that, when the staff come in every morning, they tend to find that someone's been using the typewriters and the kettles are warm.

'That's it?' Boamund said.

'Basically, yes,' the hermit replied.* 'I've left out Helmut von Moltke and the Peace of Nikolsburg, and maybe I skated over the Benelux customs union a bit, but I think you've got the essentials there. Anything you're not sure about, you can look up in the book.'

Boamund shrugged. He had learnt that, in the one

---

*He was short, round, fiftyish; and Boamund had an uncanny feeling that his beard was stuck on with spirit gum.

and a half thousand years he'd been asleep, Albion had indeed changed its name and they'd invented a few labour-saving gadgets, but basically things were very much the same. In fact, to be absolutely honest, they were worse. He was disappointed.

'My dad used to tell me,' he said, 'that by the time I was grown up, mankind would have grown a third arm it could use to scratch the small of its back.'

The hermit smiled, a tight-lipped, well-there-it-is-and-it's-too-late-now sort of smile, shrugged, and examined the crumpet on the end of his toasting fork. Outside in the street, small children rode up and down on bicycles and smacked the heads off flowers with plastic swords.

'I know,' agreed the hermit sadly. 'We've tried, God only knows, but people just won't listen. You try and guide them in the right direction, and what do you get? Apathy. You drop heavy hints to them about harnessing the power of the sun, the wind and the lightning and they go and invent the vacuum cleaner. Nobody's the slightest bit interested in mainstream technology any more.'

Boamund looked sympathetic. 'It must be hard for you,' he said.

'Not really,' said the hermit. 'I get by more or less. It's not like the old times, but as far as I'm concerned, the main thing is to try and blend into the landscape, as it were, and bide my time.'

'Bide your time until when?'

'I'm coming to that,' said the hermit. The insubstantial red glow had burnt the crumpet, and the hermit impatiently dismissed them both and opened a packet of biscuits instead. 'Have one?' he asked. 'You

333

must be starving after all this time.'

'Thank you,' Boamund said, and took a mouthful of Rich Tea. A moment later, he made a face, spat out a mouthful of crumbs and coughed.

The hermit apologised. 'I should have warned you,' he said. 'It's organic, I'm afraid. Made from ground-up grass seeds and processed sugar-beet, would you believe. The art of synthesising food was lost centuries ago. You get used to it after a while, but it still tastes like eating your way through somebody's compost heap. Here, have a doughnut.'

A doughnut appeared on the arm of Boamund's chair and he ate it thankfully. With his mouth full, he asked, 'So how do you manage it? Blending into the landscape, I mean?'

'Simple,' replied the hermit, 'I pretend to repair televisions. You won't credit it, but this country is full of little old men with their elbows showing through the sleeves of their cardigans who make a living mending televisions.'

Boamund considered. 'Those are the little box things with pictures in them?'

The hermit nodded. 'I've been here forty years now,' said the hermit, 'and nobody's taken the slightest notice of what I do. If anyone hears strange noises or sees flashing green lights late at night, the neighbours say, 'Oh *him*, he mends televisions,' and that seems to satisfy them. I imagine that, since they expect you to work miracles, they aren't too bothered if you do. In fact, I do it so well that some of them bring them back afterwards and complain that they still aren't right, even when I've hexed the dratted things so hard they'd withstand a nuclear attack.'

'That sounds like a really good cover,' Boamund said. 'Actually, while I'm here, I'll get you just to have a quick look at my astrolabe. I think it's the bearings.'

The hermit ignored him. 'I'm fortunate, of course,' he continued, 'in still having a dwarf.'

'You mean Toenail?'

'That's right. They're getting a bit thin on the ground, dwarves, though it's not as bad as it was. I think it was the free milk they used to give out to schoolchildren. Plays havoc with calcium deficiency, milk.' The hermit frowned. 'I'm drifting off the point a bit, aren't I? You and your destiny, all that sort of thing. I expect you want to know what your destiny actually is. Well . . .'

'Atishoo!' Boamund said.

'I beg your pardon?'

Boamund explained that he'd just spent the last fifteen hundred years in a draught. 'Sorry,' he said, 'you were saying . . .'

'What you've got to do,' said the hermit, 'is go to Ventcaster-on-Ouse and discover the Holy Grail.'

Boamund thought for a moment.

The curriculum of chivalry is selective. It consists of, in modern terms, A-level heraldry, genealogy, religious instruction and falconry, horsemanship and weapon-handling to degree level, and the option of post-graduate studies in either mysticism or dalliance. Essential as all these disciplines are to the profession of arms, none of them tends to stimulate the rational faculties. If you can't kill it, hit people with it or worship it, then as far as chivalry is concerned it clearly can't be all that important. To set a knight thinking, therefore, a proposition has to be fairly startling.

'If you know it's in Ventcaster-on-Ouse,' said Boamund carefully, 'how come you need me to go and look for it? Couldn't you just send a dwarf to fetch it or something?'

The hermit smiled kindly. 'Sorry,' he said, 'perhaps I could have put that better. I'm not saying the Grail is in Ventcaster. In fact, it's a pretty safe bet that that's one place on earth that the Grail isn't. But if you're going to look for it, going to Ventcaster is an essential preliminary step, because that's where the rest of the Grail Knights are. They need a new Grand Master. That's you.' He paused. 'Better?' he asked.

Boamund nodded. He was still thinking. 'Yes,' he said, 'that's fine. But why me, what's a Grail and why?'

Maybe the hermit smiled again, or maybe it was the original smile winched up another eighth of an inch.

'When the powers that be decided that Albion was finally going into Europe and we had to start changing over to continental ways,' said the hermit with obvious distaste, 'a few of the more far-sighted of us reckoned that it would be a good idea to ... how shall I put it? We salted away a few essential personnel – knights and hermits and sages and the like – just in case. They had to be fairly low status, or else they'd have been missed, but with potential nevertheless. You were one of them.'

'Oh,' Boamund said.

'What you might call low-flying high-flyers,' the hermit explained. 'Bright lights under heavy bushels. Anyway, from time to time, when we need you, we wake you up. The Grail Knights have just lost their leader, and so ...'

'Killed?'

'Not exactly,' said the hermit, sourly. 'He left the Order to start a window-cleaning round in Leamington Spa. So, of course, we need a replacement. It's a good posting,' the hermit added, as Boamund gave him a look you could have broken up with a hammer and put in a gin and tonic. 'Grade C status, company horse, makes you eligible for the pension scheme.'

'That reminds me,' Boamund started to say, but the hermit frowned at him.

'Also,' he went on, 'actually finding the Grail immediately qualifies you for a place in Avalon, remission of sins and a legend. If I was a bright, ambitious young knight wanting to make my mark, I'd jump at it.'

Boamund looked at him.

'And,' the hermit continued, 'if you don't I'll send you back to sleep until you do. Right?'

'Right,' said Boamund.

'Splendid,' said the hermit. 'Toenail!'

The dwarf-flap in the living-room door pushed open and Toenail appeared. His arms were oily to the elbow and he was holding a spanner.

'What?' he said.

The hermit frowned. 'Are you fiddling about with that motorbike again?' he asked.

Toenail looked shiftily up over the footstool. 'What if I am?' he said.

The hermit gave him a despairing look. 'Why, that's what I want to know,' he said. 'If the wretched thing doesn't work, then I'll hex it for you, and then perhaps we won't have so many oily fingerprints on the tea-towels.'

The dwarf scowled. 'You leave my bike alone,' he

replied. 'I'm a dwarf, fixing things is in our blood.'

'Putting new washers on taps isn't,' replied the hermit pointedly. 'I was soaked to the skin, that time you—'

'That's plumbing,' replied the dwarf. 'If you want plumbing done, call a plumber. Anyway, what can I do you for?'

The hermit sighed, and stared the oily footprints out of the carpet. 'Sir Boamund will be needing some new armour,' he said, 'and a sword and a shield and all that sort of thing. Have a look in the cupboard under the stairs, see what we've got.'

'Ah,' said the dwarf. 'Now you're talking.' He bowed and hurried away.

'He's a good sort, really,' said the hermit. 'I just wish he wouldn't keep trying to put a saddle on the cat and ride it round the house. It doesn't like it, you know.' The hermit got up, shook Boamund by the hand and clapped him on the shoulder. 'Anyway,' he said, 'best of luck, pop in after you've found the Grail, tell me how you've got on.'

Boamund nodded. Chivalry is like that; one minute you're sitting under a tree, chewing a blade of grass and dreaming of nothing in particular, and the next you're in the middle of some peculiar chain of adventures, which may end up with you marrying the king's eldest daughter but is just as likely to end up with you getting knocked off your horse and breaking your neck. You learn to go with the flow in chivalry. In that respect at least, it's a bit like selling door to door.

'Bye, then,' Boamund said. 'I'll leave the astrolabe with you, just in case you've got a moment to look at it.'

'Yes indeed,' said the hermit. He was gradually sinking into a pool of blue light, drifting away into the heart of the great Glass Mountain. A pair of carpet slippers crackled suddenly into flame, and then there was nothing left but an empty chair. Boamund turned to go.

'Oh yes, I forgot to mention,' whispered a faint voice. 'Whatever else you do, make absolutely sure you don't go near the . . .'

'Sorry?' Boamund asked. He waited for three minutes, but all he heard were the chimes of an ice-cream van, far away in the distance.

'What's this?' Boamund asked, puzzled.

Toenail sighed. He had this feeling that Boamund was going to turn out to be a difficult bugger, and resolved to do his best to be patient. Unfortunately, patience isn't one of the Three Dwarfish Virtues*.

'It's a zip,' Toenail replied. 'Look, it does up.'

'Does up what?'

'Does up like this.'

'Ow!'

Toenail sighed. 'It's sort of instead of a codpiece,' he explained. 'You'll get used to it.'

Boamund rubbed himself painfully, and muttered words to the effect that he thought it was a bloody silly way of going about things. Toenail smiled brightly and handed him the helmet.

---

*Honesty, manual dexterity and, would you believe it, dental hygiene.

'What's this?' Boamund asked. Toenail was getting sick of this.

'It's a helmet,' he replied.

Boamund stared at it. 'Look,' he said, 'I know I'm new to most of this, but don't try being funny with me. A helmet is heavy and shiny and made of the finest steel. This is made of that stuff ... what did you say it was called?'

'Plastic,' Toenail replied, 'or rather, fibre-glass. It's a crash helmet. They're different from the ones you know about.'

'But ...'

Toenail decided to be firm, otherwise they'd never get anywhere. 'Look,' he said, 'in your day, you had jousting helms and fighting helms and parade helms, and they were all different, right? Well, this is a helm for riding on a motorbike. That's why it's different.'

Boamund started to sulk. He'd already sulked twice; once when Toenail had handed him a bike jacket and Boamund had tried to make out that only peasants and archers wore leather body armour, and once when he'd been told that he was going to be riding pillion. He'd started to say that the knight always rode the horse and the dwarf went on the pillion, but Toenail had managed to shut him up by dropping a toolkit on his foot. He anticipated big trouble very shortly.

'And here's your sword,' he said, 'and your shield. Grab hold, while I just ...'

'Here,' Boamund said, 'why're they in a canvas bag? It's not honourable to go around with your sword cased.'

Toenail decided it wouldn't be sensible right now to try and explain why it would be injudicious for

Boamund to wear his sword. Terms like 'arrested' and 'offensive weapon' probably didn't form part of his vocabulary. Instead, he made out that the quest demanded that he travel incognito, to save having to fight lots of tiresome jousts on the way. Oddly enough, Boamund swallowed that without a murmur.

'Right,' Boamund said. 'Where's the horse?'

'It's not a horse,' Toenail replied tentatively. 'Not as such. Look, follow me.'

He led the way out the back. There, under the washing line, stood his treasured Triumph Bonneville, the only thing in the whole world that he really and unreservedly loved.

'What's that?' Boamund asked.

Toenail clenched his fists tightly and replied, 'It's a motorcycle. It's like . . .' He closed his eyes and ransacked his mind, pulling out the drawers and throwing their contents on to the floor. 'It's like a magic horse that doesn't need shoeing,' was the best he could come up with.

'Does it fly?' Boamund asked.

'No,' said Toenail, taken aback. 'It goes along the ground. Downhill, with the wind behind her, she'll do a hundred and fifteen, no worries.'

'A hundred and fifteen what?'

'Miles.'

'Oh.' Boamund frowned. 'And then what do you do?' he asked.

'How do you mean?'

'After you've gone a hundred and fifteen miles,' Boamund replied. 'Do you get another one, or . . .?'

'No, no,' Toenail said, screwing up his eyes and resisting the temptation to take a chunk out of

Boamund's kneecap. 'A hundred and fifteen miles an hour.'

'Hang on,' Boamund said. 'I thought you said it didn't fly.'

'She doesn't.'

But Boamund didn't seem convinced. 'All the magic horses I ever heard about could fly,' he said. 'There was Altamont, the winged steed of Sir Grevis de Bohun. She could do three hundred and forty-two, nought to a hundred and six in four point four three—'

'Yes, well,' Toenail said. 'Now—'

'My uncle had a magic horse,' Boamund went on, 'he did from Caerleon to Tintagel once in an hour and seven minutes. You could really give it some welly on that horse, he used to tell me.'

'Um . . .'

'Had all the gear, too,' Boamund continued dreamily. 'Monoshock stirrups, power-assisted reins, three-into-one hydraulically damped underneck martingale, customised sharkskin girths with three-position auto-adjusted main buckles . . .'

Toenail stumped across to the bike and unscrewed the filler-cap. 'Come on,' he said, 'we haven't got all day, you know.'

Boamund shrugged. 'All right,' he said. 'Where do I sit?'

'Behind me,' Toenail said. 'Up you get. Got the bag?'

Boamund nodded and pulled on his helmet. Muttering something or other under his breath, Toenail opened the choke, flicked down the kickstart, and stood on it and jumped.

Needless to say, the bloody thing wouldn't start.

342

Boamund tapped him on the shoulder. 'What are you doing?' he said.

'I'm trying to get her to start,' Toenail replied.

'What, by pulling out its whatsit and jumping on it?' Boamund replied. 'What good's that supposed to do? You'll just make it cross, and then it'll bite you or something.'

I could try and explain, Toenail thought, but why bother? He located the kickstart under the ball of his foot, lifted himself in the saddle and jumped again. As usually happened, the kickstart slipped from under his foot and came up sharply against his shin. Toenail swore.

'Told you so,' said Boamund. 'Why don't you just say the magic word?'

'There isn't a magic word, you pig-brained idiot!'

Boamund sighed and said something incomprehensible. At once the engine fired, revved briefly and then fell back into a soft, dreamy purring. Of the usual wittering of maladjusted tappets there was no sign. Toenail sat, open-mouthed, listening. Even the camchain sounded good.

'Can we go now, please?' Boamund said. 'It'll take us at least an hour, if all this thing does is—'

'How did you do that?' Toenail demanded. 'She *never* starts first time. Never.' He felt betrayed, somehow.

'Simple,' Boamund replied, 'I said the magic word. I'm not a complete ignoramus, you know.'

Right, Toenail thought, enough is enough. You've asked for it. He flipped up the sidestand, trod the gearlever into first and opened the throttle. The front wheel hoisted itself gratifyingly skyward and, with a

343

squeal of maltreated rubber, the bike careered down the drive and out into Cairngorm Avenue. By the end of the road, Toenail was doing nearly fifty, and as they went round the corner he slewed the bike down so hard that the right-hand side footrest touched down with a shower of sparks.

Magic horses be buggered, he thought. I'll give him magic horses, the cocky little sod.

They were doing a cool seventy down Sunderland Crescent, weaving in and out round the parked cars like a demented bee, when Boamund leant forward and tapped Toenail on the shoulder.

'All right?' he shouted back. 'You want me to slow down?'

'Certainly not,' Boamund replied. 'Can't you get this thing to go any faster?'

Toenail was about to say something very apposite when Boamund muttered another incomprehensible phrase and the road suddenly blurred in front of Toenail's eyes. He screamed, but the wind tore the sound away from him. There was this furniture van, right in front of them, and ...

And then they were flying. It had been a near thing; the front tyre had skimmed the roof of the van, and quite probably he was going to have to go the round of the breakers' yards to get another rear mudguard (you try getting a rear mudguard for a '74 Bonneville and see how you like it), but they were still alive. And airborne.

'Put me down!' Toenail shrieked. 'How dare you! This is a classic bike, I've spent hours getting it up to concourse standard. You crash it and I'll kill you!'

'But it's so slow,' Boamund replied. 'You hang on tight, we'll soon be there.'

Toenail was beginning to feel sick. 'Please,' he said.

The laws of chivalry, which are as comprehensible and practical as the VAT regulations, ordain that a true knight shall have pity on the weak and the feeble. Boamund sighed and mumbled the correct formula, and a moment later the bike touched down on the southbound carriageway of the M18, doing approximately two hundred and forty.

Jesus Christ, thought Toenail to himself, I could write to *SuperBike* about this, only they'd never believe me. He exerted the full strength of his right hand on the brake lever, and slowly the bike decelerated. He made his way across to the hard shoulder, cut the engine and sat there, quivering.

'Now what is it?' said Boamund testily.

Toenail turned slowly round in the saddle and leant towards Boamund until their visors touched.

'Look,' he said, 'I know you're a knight and I'm only a dwarf, and you've got a Destiny and know all about the old technology and your uncle had some sort of drag-racer that could do the ton in four seconds flat, but if you pull a stunt like that ever again, I'm going to take that sword of yours and shove it right up where the sun never shines, all right?'

Three foot seven of shattered dreams and injured pride can be very persuasive sometimes, and Boamund shrugged. 'Please yourself,' he said. 'I was just trying to help.'

'Then don't.' Toenail jumped on the kickstart, swore, tried again and eased the bike out into the slow lane.

In the course of the next fifty miles he was overtaken by three lorries, two T-registration Mini Clubmen, a scooter and a Long Vehicle with a police escort transporting what looked like a pre-fab bridge; but he didn't mind.

'If,' as he explained to Boamund when the latter implored him to try going a bit faster, 'God had intended us to travel quickly and effortlessly from one place to another, He wouldn't have given us the internal combustion engine.'

As far as Boamund could see, there was no answer to that.

'Where are we going?' Boamund asked.

Toenail took his left hand off the bars and pointed.

'Yes,' Boamund said, 'I can read. But what does it mean?'

This puzzled Toenail; to him, the words 'Service Station' were self-explanatory. He made no effort to explain, and drove into the car park.

'I mean,' Boamund said, taking off his helmet and shaking his head, 'service is what you owe to your liege lord, and a station is a military outpost. Is this where knights come to bow down before their lords and beg favours of them?'

Toenail thought of the palaver he'd been through the last time he tried to order sausage, fried bread, baked beans and toast without the fried egg, and replied, 'Yes, sort of. You hungry?'

'Now you mention it,' Boamund replied, 'yes. All I've had in the last fifteen hundred-odd years is a cup of poisoned milk and a biscuit.'

'Not poisoned,' Toenail pointed out, 'drugged. If it'd been poisoned you wouldn't be here.'

'Must just have been wishful thinking, then.'

Toenail took great pains to explain the system. 'You get your tray,' he said, 'and you stand in line while they serve the people in front of you, and then you ask the girl behind the counter for what you want. Food-wise,' he added. 'And then she puts it on your tray and you take it up to the cash desk. Got that?'

Boamund nodded. 'And then what?' he asked.

'Then we sit down and eat,' Toenail said.

'Where?'

Toenail looked up at him. 'You what?'

'Where do we sit?' Boamund repeated. 'I mean, I don't want to make a fool of myself by sitting in a dishonourable seat.'

Jesus flaming Christ, thought Toenail to himself, why didn't I just bring sandwiches? 'You sit wherever you like,' he said. 'It's a service station, not the Lord Mayor's Banquet.'

'What's a—?'

'Shut up.'

To do him credit, Boamund waited very patiently in the queue. He didn't push or shove or challenge any of the lorry drivers to a duel if they trod on his foot. Toenail's stomach began to unclench slightly.

'Next,' said the woman on the Hot Specials counter. Toenail asked for steak and kidney pudding and was about to move on when he heard Boamund's voice saying:

'I'll have roast swan stuffed with quails, boar's chine in honey, venison black pudding, three partridges done rare and a quart of Rhenish. Please,' he added.

The girl looked at him.

'I said,' Boamund repeated, 'I'll have roast swan stuffed with . . .'

One of the few advantages of being a dwarf is that you can walk away from situations like these without anybody noticing, if necessary by ducking down between people's legs. Very carefully, so as not to spill his gravy, Toenail started to walk . . .

'Toenail!'

He stopped and sighed. Behind Boamund, quite a few people were beginning to get impatient.

'Toenail,' Boamund was saying, 'you told me to ask the girl behind the counter for what I wanted to eat, and she's saying all I can have is something called *lassania*.'

'You'll like it,' Toenail croaked. 'They do a very good lasagna here.'

Boamund shook his head. 'Listen,' he said to the girl, whose face was doing what concrete does, only quicker, 'I don't want this yellow muck, right, I want roast swan stuffed with quails . . .'

The girl said something to Boamund, and the dwarf, whose genes were full of useful information about the habits of insulted knights, instinctively dropped his tray and curled up into a ball on the floor.

But Boamund just said, 'Suit yourself then, I'll get it myself,' muttered something or other under his breath, and started to walk away. Against his better judgement, Toenail opened an eye and looked up.

Boamund was still holding his tray. It contained a roast swan, a boar's chine in honey, some peculiar-looking slices of black pudding, three small roast fowl and a large pewter jug.

'Here,' said the girl, 'that's not allowed.'

Boamund stood very still for a moment. 'Sorry?' he said.

'Eating your own food's not allowed,' said the girl.

Toenail felt a boot digging into his ribs. He tried ignoring it.

'Toenail, I don't understand this at all. First they don't have any proper food, only *lassania*, and now she says I'm not allowed to eat my food. Does that mean we all have to swap trays or something?'

Toenail stood up. 'Come on,' he said, 'we're leaving. Quick.'

'But . . .'

'Come on!'

Toenail grabbed Boamund by the sleeve and started to drag him doorwards. Behind them somebody shouted, 'Hey! Those two haven't paid!'

Boamund stopped dead, and try as he might Toenail couldn't induce him to move. 'What did you say?' Boamund enquired.

'You haven't paid for that.'

'But I didn't get it from you,' Boamund was saying, very patiently, very reasonably. 'Your people didn't have anything I wanted so I got something for myself.'

Toenail betted himself that he knew what was coming next. 'You're not allowed,' said the voice, 'to eat your own food in here.' Oh good, said Toenail to his feet, I won.

'Look.'

'No,' said the voice, 'you look.'

Honour, its cultivation and preservation, are at the very root of chivalry. It is thus highly unwise to say something like, 'No, you look,' to a knight, especially if he's hungry and confused. Although Toenail had deliberately averted his head, on the slightly irrational grounds that anything he didn't see he couldn't be

349

blamed for, he didn't need eyes to work out what happened next. The sound of an assistant cafeteria manager being hit with a trayful of roast swan is eloquently self-explanatory.

From under his table, Toenail had a very good view of one section of the fight – roughly from the feet of the participants as far as their knees – and as far as he was concerned that was quite enough for him, thank you very much. You had to say this for the lad, fifteen hundred years asleep on a mountain, you'd think he'd be out of practice, but not a bit of it.

After a while, Toenail could only see one pair of feet, and they were wearing the pair of motorcycle boots he'd bought specially, after measuring the sleeping knight's feet about a week ago. How long ago that seemed!

'Toenail!'

'Yes?' said the dwarf.

'You're not particularly hungry, are you?'

Toenail put his head out. 'Not really,' he said. 'Let's have something when we get there, shall we?'

'Good idea,' Boamund replied. He wiped gravy off his face and grinned sheepishly.

They got to the bike and got it started about four seconds before the police arrived. Fortunately, the police had omitted to bring helicopters with them, so when the bike suddenly lifted off the ground and roared away in the direction of Birmingham there wasn't very much they could do about it, except take its number and arrest a couple of students on a Honda 125 for having a defective brake light.

2

'Yes,' Toenail replied.

'Are you sure?' Boamund said. 'Give me that street map a second.'

Toenail did so, and Boamund studied it for a while. 'Looks like you're right,' he said. 'It just doesn't look like any castle I've ever seen before, that's all.'

Toenail was with him there a hundred per cent. It looked far more like a small, rather unsavoury travel agent's office. Closed, too.

'Maybe it's round the back,' he suggested.

Boamund looked at him, 'I think you're missing the point rather,' he said. 'The thing about castles is ...' He paused, trying to choose the right words. 'Well,' he said, 'you just don't get castles round the backs of things. It's not the way things are.'

'Maybe it is in Brownhills,' replied the dwarf. 'Have you ever been here before?'

'I don't know,' Boamund confessed. 'Things have

changed a bit since my day.'

'Well,' said the dwarf, 'there you are, then. Maybe the fashions in castle architecture have changed too. The unobtrusive look, you know?'

Boamund frowned and got off the bike. It occurred to Toenail that this was probably one of the best opportunities he was going to get for quite some time to jump on the bike, gun the engine and get the hell out of here before something really horrible happened to him; but he didn't, somehow. What he told himself was that the bike wouldn't start, and that knights took a dim view of attempted desertion. The truth of the matter was that his dwarfish genes wouldn't let him. Stand By Your Knight, the old dwarf song goes.

Boamund was knocking on the door. 'Anybody home?' he called.

Silence. Boamund tried again, with the air of a man who knows that the proper way to do this would be to sound a slug-horn, if only he had such a thing about his person. Still nothing.

'It must be the wrong place,' Toenail said. 'Look, let's just go away somewhere and think it over, shall we?'

Boamund shook his head. 'No,' he said. 'I think this is the right place after all. Look.'

He pointed at something, and Toenail stood on tiptoe and looked. He could see nothing. He said so.

'There,' Boamund said, 'can't you see, on the doorframe, very faint but it's there, definitely.'

Toenail squinted. There was, he had to admit, the faintest possible pattern or design, crudely scratched on the paintwork. He stared at it for a while, until his imagination got him thinking that it could be mistaken for a bunch of roses, their petals intertwined. 'Oh yes,' he said. 'What's that, then?'

'It's a waymark,' Boamund replied. 'Part of the Old High Symbolism. Must mean that there are knights here.'

'Is that what it means, then?' Toenail demanded.

'Strictly speaking, no,' Boamund replied. 'What it actually means is, "No insurance salesmen or Jehovah's Witnesses; beware of the dog." But reading between the lines . . . Here, what's this?'

'Another one?'

'Maybe,' Boamund muttered. 'Let's have a look.' He rubbed away a dried-on pigeon dropping, scrutinised the doorpost carefully and then chuckled to himself. 'It's definitely a waymark,' he said. 'Look.'

'This time,' Toenail said, 'I'm going to have to take your word for it.'

'It's the ancient character designed to let bailiffs know that you've moved,' Boamund observed. 'We call it the Great Self-Defeating Pentagram. This is the right place, I reckon.' He thumped on the door so hard that Toenail reckoned he could feel it wince, and then called out very loudly in what Toenail would ordinarily have guessed was Bulgarian.

Several seconds of complete silence; and then a window above their heads ground open.

'We're closed,' said the voice. 'Go away.'

Boamund was staring, open-mouthed. 'Bedders!' he yelled out joyfully, and waved. 'Bedders, it's me.'

Toenail looked up at the man in the window; a round-faced, bald head with a big red nose. 'Bo?' it replied, and its tone of voice implied that this was better than pink elephants or spiders climbing the wallpaper, but still uncalled for. 'It can't be.'

'Bedders!' Boamund repeated rapturously. 'Come and open this door before I kick it in!'

This, Toenail surmised, was entirely consistent with what he knew of the way knights talked to each other. Apparently, under the laws of chivalry, the way you expressed warm sentiments of friendship and goodwill to another knight was to challenge him to put on all his armour, be knocked off his horse, and get his head bashed in with a fifteen-pound mace.

'You touch that door,' the head replied, 'and I'll break both your legs.' An expert on courtly repartee would immediately have recognised this as being roughly equivalent to our, 'George, you old bastard, how the devil are you!', but Toenail decided to hide behind the bike, just in case.

'You and whose army, you drunken ponce?' Boamund replied tenderly. The head grinned.

'Stay right there,' he said, and the window slammed. Boamund turned round.

'What are you doing down there?' he asked.

'Hiding,' said a voice from behind the bike's rear wheel. 'What does it look like I'm—?'

'You don't want to take any notice of old Bedders – that's Sir Bedevere to you,' Boamund replied. 'Soft as porridge, old Bedders. Here, quick, where's that sword?'

He rummaged around in the luggage, and when the door opened (to reveal a huge-looking figure completely covered in steel, Toenail couldn't help noticing) he had found the sword and the shield and had put his crash helmet back on. For his part, Toenail, having assessed the various options available to him, jumped into the bike's left-hand pannier and pulled the lid

354

down over his head. There are times when it feels good to be small.

'Ha,' he heard someone saying. 'Abide, false knight, for I will have ado with you.' Toenail shuddered and closed his eyes.

'I will well,' said the other idiot. 'Keep thee then from me.'

Then there was a noise like a multiple pile-up, followed by the inevitable sound of something metal, as if it might be a hub-cap, wheeling along the ground, spinning and then falling over with a clang. And then shouts of boisterous laughter.

And then someone pulled open the lid of the pannier and extracted Toenail by the collar of his jacket.

'Toenail,' Boamund was saying, 'meet Sir Bedevere. Bedders, this is my dwarf, Toenail.'

'Pleased to meet you, Toenail,' said the armoured lunatic. By the looks of it, the thing that had come off and rolled about on the floor must have been his helmet, since he was bareheaded and bleeding from a cut over his left eye. 'Well, then,' said Sir Bedevere, 'you'd better come in. The others,' he added, 'are all out, and it's muggins' turn to do the kitchen floor again.' A thought occurred to him. 'Hang on,' he said, brightening, 'your dwarf can do it, can't he?'

Toenail was just about to protest violently when Boamund said, 'Good idea,' and clapped Toenail heartily on the back. Much more of this, the dwarf muttered to himself, and I'm going to be sick. However, as it transpired, things could have been worse. Bedevere did show him where the mop and the Flash were kept, and it was a smaller kitchen than, say, the one at Versailles.

'Anyway,' said Bedevere, showing his guest to the comfortable chair, 'sit down, make yourself at home, tell me all about it.'

'About what?' Boamund replied, helping himself to peanuts. 'That reminds me,' he added. 'I'm starving. I haven't had any food – *proper* food, that is – in ages.'

'Help yourself,' said Bedevere politely, and Boamund, having recited the necessary formula, set about eating his way through a side of venison which obligingly materialised in front of him. In fact, thought Toenail to himself as he crouched on his hands and knees trying to shift a particularly stubborn stain, if all knights can do this, what do they need a kitchen for, let alone a kitchen floor?

'You were saying,' said Bedevere.

'Was I?'

'Yes,' Bedevere replied. 'About what you've been doing and, er . . .'

'Yes?'

'How come you're still alive. I mean,' Bedevere assured his friend, 'wonderful that you are. Spiffing. But it's rather a turn-up, don't you think?'

Boamund put down a pheasant's wing and looked at him. For all that they'd been through basic training, Knight School and the Benwick campaign together, that still didn't entitle young Fatty to go asking him personal questions. 'What about you, then?' he demanded. 'You're the one who was always stuffing himself with honey-cakes and second helpings of frumenty. If anyone should have pegged out . . .'

Bedevere winced. 'It's a long story,' he said.

Boamund gazed at him defiantly over a roast quail. 'Go on, then,' he said, 'I'm in no hurry.'

'All right, then.'

The gist of what Bedevere said was this:

Boamund no doubt remembered how sticky things were getting towards the end of Arthur's reign, what with the Saxons and everything . . .

Well, no. Boamund was asleep at the time, but he'll take your word for it. Do go on, please.

. . . what with the Saxons and everything, and the last thing the King wanted was for his knights to offer any resistance to the vastly superior Saxon forces. This could only make things worse, and was fundamentally a bad idea. On the other hand, chivalry would undoubtedly forbid the knights to do nothing while a lot of Danish bacon entrepreneurs took over the country and drove small shopkeepers out of business.

Arthur therefore decided on a diversion; and since chivalry was about to end, he felt it only right and proper that it should go out with a bang. He therefore summoned his knights to Camelot, told them a little white lie about the Saxons all having gone home, leaving money to pay for all the broken doors and windows, and suggested that they might all like to go and look for the Holy Grail.

The knights accepted the challenge with enthusiasm, for all that none of them had the faintest idea what a Grail looked like, and agreed to reassemble at Camelot a year and a day later and bring the Grail with them.

The idea succeeded beyond Arthur's wildest dreams. When the court reassembled it turned out that of the hundred knights who had set out on the quest, fifty were dead, fourteen had been arrested, twenty-two had defected to the court of the king of Benwick, and eight

357

had given up chivalry and gone into personnel management. The remaining six, King Arthur reckoned, were unlikely to bother anyone. He therefore provided them with a chapter house and a pension scheme, named them the Order of Chevaliers of the Sangrail, and left by the fire escape while they were all in the bar.

The Chevaliers of the Sangrail continued with the quest for a while; but it should be obvious from the fact that they alone had survived out of the original hundred that they were all knights who held quite firmly to the rule that discretion – or, even better, naked fear – is the better part of valour, and besides, none of them knew what a Grail was. For three years they toured Albion on the off-chance that the Grail was to be found either in an inn or a greyhound track, and then decided by a majority of five to one to abandon the quest. Their reasoning was that Albion was a small place and in their travels the chances were that they'd probably come across it; find it, His Majesty had told them, there was nothing in the fine print about recognising it once found. They then put the chapter house on the market and went to draw their pensions. All would probably have been well, had not the chairman of the trustees of the pension fund been a diehard magician and reactionary Albionese nationalist by the name of Merlin. He insisted that the Grail had to be brought to Camelot in order that the quest be fulfilled; and until it was they could whistle for their pensions.

The Chavaliers decided to make the best of a bad job. Instead of actively searching for the Grail, they resolved in future to look for it passively; that is to say, to do something else, hopefully something more interesting and profitable, while waiting for the thing to turn up. After investing all their spare capital in a scheme to dig a tunnel connecting Albion with Benwick, which was frustrated by the fact that Benwick disappeared into the sea when they were five miles short of it, they moved into the chapter house, let the ground-floor premises to a man who arranged bucket-shop pilgrimages, and got jobs in the local woad factory.

The woad factory is, of course, long gone. The knights are still there.

'Except,' Bedevere said sadly, 'for Nentres, of course.'

Boamund surreptitiously wiped a tear from his eye and murmured, 'Dead?'

'Not quite,' replied Bedevere. 'About six months ago he announced that he'd had enough and was going south. Apparently he'd met this chap who was starting up a video shop somewhere. The blighter,' said Bedevere savagely, 'he buggered off with our outings fund. Seventy-four pounds, thirty-five pence. We were planning to go to Weymouth this year.'

'Where's Weymouth?'

Bedevere explained. 'So,' he went on, 'here we all are, and here you are too. It's a small . . .'

Then the penny dropped. Bedevere had been in the process of raising a glass containing gin and tonic to his lips. He spilt it.

'I see,' Boamund was saying. 'That would account for it, I suppose.'

Bedevere picked a slice of lemon out of his collar. 'Always delighted to see you,' he gabbled, 'and it would have been nice if you could have stayed for a while, but if you're really busy and in a hurry to get on with whatever it is you're here to do, which must be really important, then please don't let us . . .'

'Actually,' Boamund said.

'. . . stop you. After all,' he wittered frantically, 'we're just here, minding our own business, or rather businesses – Turquine delivers pizzas, you know, and Pertelope's got a really nice little window-cleaning round, shops and offices as well as houses, and Galahaut's an actor, though he's resting just now, and Lamorak buys things and sells them in street markets and I . . .' He broke off and, unexpectedly, blushed.

'Go on,' said Boamund, intrigued. 'What do you do?'

'I . . . I'm an insurance salesman,' Bedevere muttered into his beard. 'It's a really interesting job,' he said hurriedly. 'You've no idea what a wide cross-section of society . . .'

'An insurance salesman,' said Boamund.

'Um,' Bedevere mumbled. 'You wouldn't by any chance be interested in a . . .?'

'I see.' Boamund was frowning. On his broad, plain, straightforward, honest and, well yes, stupid face a cold look of displeasure was settling, like ice on the points of a busy commuter line. 'You know what we used to call you back at the old Coll, Bedders?'

'Er, no,' said Bedevere. Actually he had had a fair idea and he'd always resented it. The way he saw it, a chap can't help it if he's born with big ears.

'Li chevalier li plus prest a succeder,'* replied

---

*Since Bedevere's father was the Duke of Achaia and ninety-seven years old, the term 'most likely to succeed' might be interpreted rather more literally than Boamund thought.

Boamund, severely. 'Double first in tilting, I seem to remember. Honours in falcony. Dalliance blue. Captain of courtesy three years running. And now,' he sighed, 'you're an insurance salesman. I see.'

'It's not like that,' Bedevere growled unhappily. 'Times change, and—'

'I remember,' Boamund went on obliviously, 'I remember when your father, rest his soul, came to Sports Day one year, and you were jousting for the Deschamps-Mornay Memorial Salver. He was so proud of you.'

Bedevere snuffled. 'Look,' he said, 'they don't have jousts any more. It's all your televised snooker, your American football—'

'And when he heard you'd been selected for the Old Boys match,' Boamund continued cruelly, 'well, I've never told you this before, Bedders, but—'

'Look!' Bedevere was close to tears. 'It's not as simple as that. We tried our best, honest we did. We looked all over for the wretched thing. We even went to,' and the knight winced, 'Wales. But we just didn't have the faintest idea of what it was we were looking for. Chivalry doesn't prepare you for things like that, Bo. Chivalry is all about finding someone who's big and strong and mean sitting on a ruddy great black horse and clouting him around the head till he passes out. In chivalry, you leave all the planning and the thinking to someone else. You're just there to do the important bit, the bashing people up side of things. We couldn't manage it on our own, Bo, with nobody to tell us what to do. There's no place for knights in the modern world, you see. We're . . .' He searched for the exact term. 'I suppose you could say we're over-

361

qualified. Too highly trained. Over-specialised. You know what I mean.'

'Useless, you mean.'

'Yes,' Bedevere agreed. 'It's just that there aren't any dragons left any more. And no damosels to rescue, either. Young Turquine tried to rescue a damosel the other day. It was some sort of a party, and he was delivering pizzas. He walks in through the door and there's this terrible barbaric music and all these men pulling girls about by the arms and . . . Well, he jumped right in, like a true knight, sorted a few of them out, I can tell you. And then this damosel kneed him in the—'

'I see, yes.'

'Then they called the police,' Bedevere said. 'Luckily, Galahaut and I happened to be passing, so we were able to pull him off before he did any of them a serious injury, but . . .'

'Nevertheless,' said Boamund. His face looked like something rejected by Mount Rushmore for excessive gravity. 'I think it's probably just as well I've come to take charge here, don't you? Delivering pizzas! Selling insurance! Old Sagramor would turn in his grave if he knew.'

Bedevere, remembering their old venery tutor, secretly agreed, and hoped that this would involve his brushing up against something sharp. 'But . . .' he said.

'What I was about to say,' Boamund went on, 'is that I've been woken up from a fifteen-hundred-year sleep to take charge of this Order, and by God, take charge of it I jolly well will!'

Just then, the door of the Common Room flew open and a large, round man with a red face bustled in, holding a portable telephone in one hand and a huge stack of thin styrofoam boxes in the other.

'Bedders,' he called out, 'there's a dwarf in our kitchen. I went in there to heat up the pizzas and the nasty little thing was making the floor all wet. I chucked him in the bin, naturally, but the damage was done. How many times have I told you about leaving the back door open in the . . .'

He froze, and stared. The pizzas fell from his hand and started to roll around the room like slow, anchovy-garnished hoops.

'Bloody hell,' he said at last. 'It's Snotty Boamund!'

'Hello, Turkey,' replied Boamund coldly.

Sir Turquine went, if anything, redder than before. 'Hell fire, Bedders, a joke's a joke, but what the hell do you think you're playing at? I was only saying the other day, things may be a bit smelly these days, but at least we don't have to put up with that sanctimonious little toad and his incessant wittering on about ideals any more. And you agreed with me, I remember. You said—'

'Er, Turkey,' said Sir Bedevere. 'I—'

'And now,' Sir Turquine protested, 'you get some-one all dressed up with a mask on or something, just to give me the fright of my life! Look at my pizzas, you stupid idiot, they've got fluff all over them . . .'

'It's me, Turkey,' Boamund whispered, in a tone of voice that would have frozen helium. 'How are you keeping?'

Turquine now dropped the portable telephone as well. 'My God,' he said, 'it is you! What in the name of . . .?'

Bedevere swallowed hard, stood up and, as briefly as

he could, explained. The other two knights exchanged looks that would have had a sabre-tooth tiger yelping for joy and growing an extra thick winter coat.

'Bollocks,' said Sir Turquine at last. 'He's got no authority. If he'd got any authority, he'd have a commission or something, sealed by that bastard Merlin. He's just having us on.'

Without speaking, Boamund reached inside his jacket and produced a thick, folded parchment, from which hung a seal. The odd thing about the seal was the way it glowed with a strong blue light.

Sir Turquine, whose mouth had suddenly become extremely dry, took the parchment and opened it. He stared at it for a moment and then said, in a kind of quavering roar, 'Nuts. It's in gibberish. He's just written it himself.'

'Tell Sir Turquine,' said Boamund quietly, 'that he's holding it the wrong way up.'

Sir Turquine glowered at him helplessly and turned the parchment round, so that the seal hung from the bottom. Boamund sniffed; Turquine could remember that damned supercilious sniff as though it were yesterday. He glanced down at the writing.

'Although,' Boamund went on, 'as I seem to remember, Sir Turquine was never exactly adept at reading. One seems to recall that when the rest of the class were halfway through the *Roman de la Rose*, Sir Turquine was still sitting at the back of the room saying "Pierre has a cat. The cat is fat. The fat cat sits on the—"'

'All right,' shouted Sir Turquine, 'commission or no commission, I'm going to kill him.'

Sir Bedevere hastily placed a hand on Turquine's

chest while Boamund said 'mat', very deliberately, sat down and ate an olive. Turquine gave a last infuriated snarl, threw the commission on the ground and jumped on it. Since it was, of course, enchanted parchment, all that happened was that his shoelaces broke.

Boamund smiled, that same smug, teeth-grindingly infuriating smile he'd had when he was Helm Monitor back in the sixth form, and made a little gesture with his left hand. Turquine, bright red in the face, snorted like a horse, knelt down, and extended his hands, their palms pressed together. Boamund, looking down his nose like an archbishop, stepped forward and pressed his palms to the backs of Turquine's hands, as lightly as possible; thus signifying that he had accepted Turquine's fealty. It didn't help to soothe Turquine's feelings to find that he'd knelt in one of his own pizzas.

'Arise, Sir Turquine, good and faithful knight,' said Boamund, obviously enjoying every moment of it. Turquine gave him a look you could have roasted a chicken on, made an obscure noise in the back of his throat, stood up and made a great show of brushing mozzarella off his right knee. Boamund turned to Sir Bedevere and made the same gesture.

Sir Bedevere hesitated, muttered, 'Oh, all right then,' and performed the same simple ceremony.

'And now, Sir Turquine,' said Boamund, 'you will kindly oblige me by retrieving my dwarf from wherever it was you put him.'

'I might have guessed it was your dwarf,' Turquine grumbled as he plodded to the kitchen. 'Funny the way that even when we were at school, some of us always seemed to have dwarves when the rest of us had to polish their own armour. 'Course, that came of some of us having great soft-hearted sissy mothers who wouldn't have their dear little boys hurting their hands with nasty rough . . .'

The kitchen door slammed behind him, and Boamund sighed. 'He always was inclined to whine a bit,' he observed, and Bedevere, never a man given to nostalgia, found himself harking back to the happy days of boyhood, when he'd gladly have given a whole week's pocket money for the chance of doing something unpleasant to young Snotty.

And then it occurred to him that, although young Snotty was exactly the sort of pompous little swot that Authority invariably made a prefect, nevertheless there was a sort of malign justice that had always ended up by landing him in the smelly, right up to the vambrace, even when (as was generally the case) it wasn't actually his fault.

Bedevere, having checked that Boamund wasn't looking, smirked. The way he saw it, the mills of the Gods may grind slow, but they don't half make a mess of you when the time comes.

Dwarfish society is well ordered and stable to the point of inflexibility, and the average dwarf generally knows his place* to within 0.06 of a micron. As a result, sudden promotion is something that dwarves are ill-equipped to deal with.

---

*Which is either in the kitchen or the armoury, depending on status, and, in either case, set behind a very big jar of metal polish.

Toenail was no exception. From being a lowly hermit's gopher, he had, at a stroke, risen to being Chief Factotum to a whole order of chivalry. The only other dwarf in the oral tradition of the race who'd ever achieved that distinction was Lord Whitlow King of Arms, who superintended the household of King Lot of Orkney in King Uther's time. It was an honour.

On the other hand, Toenail couldn't help feeling, Lord Whitlow probably had a few lesser dwarves to help him out, or at the very least a vacuum cleaner. And he couldn't be positive about this, because oral tradition can be a right little tease when it comes to matters of detail, but he had a feeling that Lord Whitlow probably got paid.

Boamund was all right, of course, as knights go – and Toenail was rapidly becoming an authority on knights. Not only had the new Grand Master paid him back for the petrol and the damage to the rear mudguard of the bike as soon as Toenail had found him the old teapot which served the Order as its exchequer, but he'd expressly forbidden Sir Turquine and Sir Pertelope (who was nearly as bad) to put him in the dustbin without authority, on pain of dishonour. Toenail wasn't sure what dishonour now meant in the context of the Order, but he guessed it was something to do with not being allowed to use the van at weekends. Given the trades which Turquine and Pertelope now followed, this was clearly a sanction of the utmost weight.

Of course, it was now Toenail's job to clean out the van every morning (which meant scrubbing caked-on tomato purée off the back seat and occasionally unloading cartons of Hungarian training shoes which

Lamorak had bought cheap and somehow forgotten to disembark himself), but that in itself was an honour, if one translated it into the terms of the Old Days. You'd had to be a pretty high-ranking dwarf to be Chief Groom and Lord High Equerry.

On balance, the first fortnight of the new state of affairs had gone off all right, so far as Toenail could judge. There had been a few tricky moments; Turquine, Lamorak and Galahaut the Haut Prince had mutinied and tried to ambush Boamund on his way back from the newsagent's, with a view to loading him with chains and casting him in the toolshed, but Bedevere (rather, Toenail had felt, against his better judgement) had betrayed the conspiracy, with the result that Boamund had foiled the plot by getting the number 6 bus instead of the number 15a. He had given them all a very stern talking-to in the Common Room after tea, following which Turquine had stalked out of the room and been very ostentatiously sick in the kitchen sink. Apart from that, however, a routine was developing. Basically, it consisted of the other five going out to work as usual, while Boamund sat in the Common Room with his feet up on the sofa and watched the snooker on the television. Boamund had taken to snooker very quickly, Toenail had noticed, and was talking freely of having a table installed in the garage, which would mean Lamorak finding a home for seven hundred pairs of flood-damaged Far Eastern jeans, fifty one-handed alarm clocks and all the rest of his stock-in-trade.

Toenail sighed and dipped his cloth in the metal polish. So far, Boamund's main effort in the direction of starting the quest up again had been ordering him to get all the armour and weapons from the cellar and polished up to tiltyard standard. That seemed to suit the other five, who he knew had no intention of giving up their settled if unprofitable lives just to go looking for that damned Grail thing; but Toenail, with a degree of perception that is not uncommon among dwarves, had a shrewd suspicion that things might change once the Embassy World Snooker Championship was over. Call it, Toenail said to himself, astrology.

He breathed a fine mist on to the surface of a shining gauntlet, polished it off on his trouser-leg, and added it to the pile. There was enough armour there to equip an army, and he hadn't even started on the horse-furniture yet. Mind you, he couldn't really see how there was going to be much call for that. A couple of sheets of corrugated iron welded on to the sides of the van was probably all that would be needed.

From the direction of the Common Room he could hear raised voices, and his genes told him that the Lords were holding a High Council.

Racial memory is very powerful among dwarves. Putting down his cloth, he tiptoed to the linen basket, raised the lid and jumped in.

'No,' said Turquine.

Boamund glowered at him and struck the table with his mace of office. Lamorak, who had forty-two others just like it in the lock-up, sighed. As he'd suspected at the time, they weren't solid teak at all.

'This,' Boamund said grimly, 'is mutiny.'

Turquine grinned. 'Well done, young Snotty,' he said. 'You're learning.'

'Mutiny,' Boamund went on, 'and treason. Unless

Sir Turquine immediately repents of his words, I shall have no alternative but to declare him dishonoured.'

'You try it,' Turquine replied, 'and see how far it'll get you. Because,' he added, with the confidence of strength, 'I don't need that clapped-out old scrapheap of a van any more. Look at this!' And, with a magnificent gesture, he threw a set of keys on the table. 'They're so pleased with me,' he said, 'they've let me drive the company van. And,' he added conclusively, 'it's a Renault. So you can take your honour and you can . . .'

Boamund's expression did not change. He simply leant forward, took the keys from the table, and put them in his pocket.

Turquine nearly fell over.

'Here,' he said, 'you can't do that, it's not my—'

'Agreed,' replied Boamund. 'It has now become the property of the Order. And you, Sir Turquine, are dishonoured. Now, then . . .'

There was uproar for a moment, what with Sir Turquine trying to explain that it didn't work like that, and Sir Lamorak and Sir Pertelope both simultaneously asking if they could have it for the weekend. Boamund silenced them all with a blow from the mace, the top of which came off and rolled under the sofa.

'Since Sir Turquine is no longer entitled to speak,' Boamund said, 'is there anyone else who wishes to express an opinion?'

There was a long silence, and then Galahaut the Haut Prince got up, rather sheepishly, and looked around.

'Look, Bo,' he said, 'you know, in principle I'm with you all the way about finding the Grail. One hundred per cent. I think finding the Grail is right for us, so let's do it,

370

yes, fine. Only,' and he drew a deep breath, 'timing-wise, perhaps we could, you know, readjust our schedules a bit, because my agent says there's this bit in a dog-food commercial coming up . . .'

Boamund's face became ominous, but Galahaut seemed not to have noticed. 'It's a real opportunity for me,' he went on, 'to get myself established in dog-food work generally. They say they want me for the tall, good-looking man of mature years in a chunky Arran sweater who says that top breeders recommend it. Play your cards right, they said, this could be a second Captain Birds Eye.'

'No,' said Boamund. 'We leave in a week.'

Galahaut looked round the room reproachfully; but everyone happened to be looking the other way, apart from Turquine, who was sulking. 'Come on, Bo,' he said, 'this could be the break I've been waiting for. One really good commercial, it's better than a West End hit these days. Look at the Oxo woman,' he added.

'Who's Oxo?' Boamund asked.

The flame in Galahaut's eyes kindled for a moment, and then died away, to be replaced by an unmistakable flicker of guile. 'All right, then,' he said meekly, 'you're the boss. You can count on me.'

Very true, Boamund thought; I could count up to two on your faces alone, you devious little toad. I know what you're thinking, and we'll see about that. 'Anyone else?' he said.

Lamorak was getting to his feet, and Boamund narrowed his eyes. He'd been practising it in front of the mirror for days.

'And before Sir Lamorak addresses us,' he said, 'I should like to make it plain that I don't think we're

371

going to find the Grail down the Portobello Road. So Sir Lamorak can jolly well unload all those boxes and things he put into the van when he thought my back was turned.'

Lamorak groaned. 'Oh, come on,' he said. 'It's got to be worth a try, Bo. You go to a street market these days, there's all sorts of old junk . . .'

'The Grail,' Boamund replied icily, 'is not old junk. It's—'

'Yes,' said Pertelope suddenly. 'What *is* it exactly? I'm sure we'd all be fascinated to hear.'

'Ah yes,' said Boamund, drawing the tip of his tongue around lips suddenly dry as sandpaper, 'I was hoping someone would ask me that.' He paused; and as he did so, a tiny snowflake of inspiration drifted into his mind.

He could lie.

'The Holy Grail,' he said, smoothly and confidently, 'is the cup, or rather chalice, from which Our Lord drank at the Last Supper. No doubt you remember the relevant passage in scripture, Pertelope? Or did you spend that lesson drawing little dragons in the margins of your breviary?'

The Grail Knights were sitting with their mouths open, staring at him. It was easy, this lying business. Gosh, yes . . .

'Anyway,' Boamund went on, 'the Grail is a fluted, double-handed cup wrought of the purest gold. Its body is inlaid with the richest gems, amethyst and chrysophrase, diamonds and rubies, and across the rim is engraved in letters that shine like fire . . . er . . .'

Five stunned faces watched him move his lips desperately, as he ransacked his brain for something

372

appropriate. He closed his eyes, and the words came. In fact, they came so easily that you could almost believe . . .

'In letters,' he repeated briskly, 'that shine like fire:

IE SUI LE VRAY SANC GREAL

. . . if memory serves me correctly,' he added smugly. 'Any questions?'

There was a long, long silence. Finally, Pertelope stood up again. He was trying to look sceptical but his heart wasn't in it, you could tell.

'What was that again?' he asked.

Boamund repeated the text of the inscription. It sounded better and better. Maybe this was a what-you-call-it, miracle.

'Why's it in French?' Pertelope demanded. Something wobbled inside Boamund's stomach. He was about to say 'Er' when Pertelope continued.

'I mean,' he said, 'it ought to be in Latin, shouldn't it? All your religious stuff's always in Latin, so . . .'

Boamund smiled. He'd had time to think, and the words came smoothly from him.

'You forget, Sir Pertelope,' he said, 'that at Our Lord's passion the Grail was taken by Joseph of Arimathea and borne away by him to Albion, where,' he added cheerfully, 'as everyone knows, we speak French. Satisfied?'

Pertelope growled unhappily and sat down. In his place, Turquine got up. Although he was dishonoured and not allowed to speak, Boamund felt that a magnanimous Grand Master could allow himself to be flexible, especially if he could make old Turkey look a prize ass in front of the others. He nodded, therefore, and smiled.

'So this whacking great gold cup thing,' said Sir Turquine slowly, 'with all these jewels and what have you stuck in it, is the cup from the Last Supper, is it?'

Boamund's smile remained fixed, and he nodded. Much more of this, he thought, I could get a job hanging from someone's rear-view mirror.

'I see,' said Turquine. 'Times must have been good in the carpentry business back in Our Lord's time, if they could afford huge great gold cups with jewels and—'

'Thank you,' said Boamund, 'I think you've made your point. Naturally,' he said, 'at the moment of Christ's transmutation of the wine, the chalice too underwent a similar metamorphosis. Hence its present nature.'

Turquine sat down again, red-faced as a traffic light, while someone at the back sniggered. This time, however, Galahaut was on his feet.

'Great,' he said, 'that's clarified that one for us, no problem. But,' he added, nastily, 'you don't happen to have any idea where the thing is, do you? I mean, yes, it was brought to Albion by Joseph of – wherever it was you said – we're all agreed on that, but that was all rather a long time ago, don't you think? I mean, it could be anywhere by now.'

Boamund's smile became, if anything, a little bit wider. He really had hoped someone would ask him that.

'Sir Galahaut,' he said, with the air of a man who's just about to find his way into the dictionary of quotations, 'if it were not lost, we should not have to find it.'

There was silence again, and then a buzz of Yes-buts from the assembled knights. Boamund silenced them with a bang of the mace.

'Brothers,' he said, and ignored the voice at the back who asked who'd appointed him shop steward, 'when the ancient hermit gave me my commission, he also entrusted me with a parchment of great antiquity, which will surely guide us to the resting place of the Holy Grail. I have this same parchment . . .' He patted his inside pocket, frowned and started to rummage. Just then the kitchen door opened, and Toenail trotted through.

'Here it is,' he whispered. 'You left it in the back pocket of your brown cords. Just as well I looked through them before I put them in the washing-machine, because otherwise—'

'Yes, thank you,' Boamund said, 'you may go now. This parchment,' and he held it up for them all to see, 'will surely guide us to the spot.'

Pertelope was up yet again. 'Hold on,' he said. 'If that thing's so old, and says where the bloody thing is, then how come . . .?'

But the mood of the assembly had changed. Bede-vere kicked him on the shins, while someone behind him told him to stop being such a clever little devil and sit down. With an appropriate flourish, Boamund broke the seal, opened the parchment and read it.

'Oh,' he said.

The Order of the Knights of the Holy Grail were not the first adventurers to seek out this fabulous and evocative item. Far from it.

To give only one example: in the seventeenth year of

the reign of King Ban of Benwick – Benwick, it should be explained, was a kingdom lying between Albion and Europe which to a large extent shared Albion's isolation from the rest of humanity and her devotion to magic and chivalry; it vanished into the sea shortly after Arthur's abdication, and tradition has it that this was a deliberate decision on the Benicians' part, to save their nation from ever becoming a mere federal part of the united states of mediocrity that made up the World. Since all known Benicians vanished with their kingdom it would be interesting to learn where this attractive little tale is supposed to have originated – a young Benician knight by the name of Sir Prime de Ganys was riding forth upon errantry one day when he came across a castle in the middle of a desolate land.

Since night was rapidly closing in and the young chevalier had strayed far from his path, he knocked at the gate of the castle and was admitted by the duty dwarf.

It turned out that the castellan of the castle was a beautiful damosel without a lord, who lived there all alone apart from twenty-seven tall, well-built young esquires and a small colony of dwarves, who had spacious and well-appointed quarters of their own at the bottom of a disused wellshaft. Sir Prime was ushered in to a splendid banquet, feasted on broiled duck with lapwing, and entertained by a quartet of dwarfish minstrels playing all the bits they could remember out of *Ma Beale Dame*.

Happening to fall into conversation with the castellan, Sir Prime discovered that the castle, which was large and rather a nuisance to keep up, was supposed to be the repository of the Holy Grail, left there hundreds of years previously by Joseph of Arimathea as security for a substantial Snakes and Ladders debt. The only problem was that, what with the castle being so big and so many of its rooms having to be shut up for most of the year, nobody could remember where the dratted thing had last been seen. Naturally, periodic attempts were made to find it; but since these searches tended to reveal nothing more cheerful than further outbreaks of dry rot and death-watch beetle, they were usually abandoned at an early stage. What was needed, the castellan continued, was a fearless young hero who wasn't easily cowed by the sight of huge patches of purple fungus growing out of the walls, who would make a thorough search of the place, find the Grail and thus provide the damosel with a nice capital sum with which to finance her dream of turning the old place into either an eventide home or a sports complex.

Sir Prime's imagination was fired by this entrancing tale, and he pressed the castellan for further details. She obligingly produced a complete set of plans and elevations, builders' estimates, grants of outline planning permission, detailed budgets, profit-and-loss projections prepared by her accountants, and a joint-venture agreement by which, for the investment of a paltry seventy thousand marks, the knight would be entitled to a forty-per-cent share in the equity, together with interest on capital and fifty per cent of net profits. Delighted, Sir Prime produced his cheque book, wrote out a draft for seventy thousand marks, signed the contract and at once fell into a deep slumber.

When he awoke, he found himself lying on the cold

fells. All trace of the castle, the castellan and his signed part of the contract had vanished. Furthermore, he seemed to have misplaced his gold crucifix and a number of other trifles of personal adornment.

As he rode homewards, he encountered an ancient hermit, to whom he related his strange and terrifying adventure. The hermit, controlling his laughter by stuffing the sleeve of his robe into his mouth, mumbled that Sir Prime would have appeared to have had the ill fortune to wander into the fabulous castle of Lyonesse. If that was the case, then the damosel was none other than La Beale Dame de Lyonesse, and the knight should count himself lucky to have got away with just being ripped off for seventy grand. Some poor fools, he explained, had fared far worse than that. Really stupid knights, for example, had been known to buy two weeks in July and August at Lyonesse for the rest of time; fortunately really classic suckers like that were as rare as virgins in a . . .

Predictably, Sir Turquine was the first to break the silence.

'What,' he asked, 'does it say?'

'Um,' Boamund replied.

'It says Um, does it?' replied Turquine. 'Gosh, how helpful.'

Boamund stared at the paper in his hands, oblivious even to Turquine. At last he cleared his throat and spoke, albeit in a rather high voice.

'I think it's probably a riddle of some sort,' he said. 'You know, like My first is in—'

'What,' said a voice from the back, 'does it say?'

Blushing fit to shame Aurora, Boamund replied, 'It's

a ... I don't know. It's like a sort of list. Or a recipe.' He thought for a moment. 'Or a receipt, maybe.' He scratched his head.

Turquine grinned. 'Give it here,' he demanded, and Boamund made no effort to resist when he grabbed at the paper. It was almost as if he wanted someone else to have the job of reading the thing out.

'Now,' said Turquine, 'what have we ...? Good Lord.'

Various knights urged him to get on with it. He bit his lip, and then read out:

'LE SANC GREAL: INSTRUCTIONS
The Apron of Invincibility
The Personal Organiser of Wisdom
The Socks of Inevitability

The first may be found where children are carried in pockets, and came with the *first* First Fleet.

The second may be found in the safe haven where time is money, where money goes but never returns, and in the great office under and beyond the sea.

The third, God's gift to the Grail Knights, may be found where one evening can last forever, in the domain of the best-loved psychopath under the arch of the sky, in the kingdom of the flying deer.

Armed with these, let the Grail Knight reclaim what is his, release Albion from her yellow fetters, and enjoy his tea without fear of the washing-up.'

At the back somebody coughed. At moments like this, somebody always does. 'I think young Snotty is right,' said Turquine at last. 'It's some sort of riddle.'

Bedevere closed his mouth with an effort, blinked and said, 'That bit about the safe haven. Rings a bell, don't you know.'

Five knights looked at him and he swallowed.

'Well,' he went on, 'reminds me of something I read once. Or perhaps I heard it on something. It's on the tip of my . . .'

'It's a tricky one, isn't it?' Lamorak ventured. 'Maybe there's someone we could ask, you know, a hermit or something. Anybody know a good hermit?'

'Read it again.'

Turquine obliged and this time there was a hail of suggestions, all made simultaneously. Eventually, Boamund restored order by hammering on the table with the mace.

'Gentlemen,' he said, stretching a point, 'we obviously can't decipher this. It's not our job. The cardinal rule is, knights don't think. So the next step is to find someone who can make sense of it all. Now then, in the old days, you'd ask a hermit, or an anchorite, or else you'd be riding along through the woods one morning, minding your own business, looking for a stray falcon maybe, and there'd be this old crone sitting beside the road. "Prithee master," she'd say, "carry me across yon river to my cottage." And you'd say . . .'

Somebody at the back urged him to get to the point. He pulled himself together.

'Anyway,' he continued, 'the point I'm trying to make is, that's what we'd have done *then*, but that was *then* and this is *now*. Right?'

Five heads nodded cautiously. This was either wisdom or the bleeding obvious, the problem is always to tell the two apart.

'So,' said Boamund, 'you lot know all about now. Who do you go to nowadays when you've got something you don't understand that needs explaining?'

'Yes?' said Miss Cartwright, briskly. 'Can I help you?' She smiled that toothpaste smile of hers, which any of the seasoned timewasters of Ventcaster would recognise as an invitation not to try her too high this morning. 'Something about a form you'd like me to explain to you?'

'That's right,' said Boamund, blushing slightly. Apart from the girl in the service station, who was clearly a person of no status, feudally speaking, and so didn't count, this was the first woman he'd spoken to in fifteen hundred years. 'Actually,' he said, 'before we get down to that part of it, there's just one thing . . .?'

It's one of them, Miss Cartwright's inner voice said to her, I can feel it in my water. 'Yes?' she said.

'Um,' Boamund replied. 'Only, do you have to be a citizen to get advice, or . . .?' He bit his lip, obviously embarrassed. 'You see, I'm not sure I qualify, because if a citizen's the same thing as what we call a burgher or a *burgoys de roy*, I'm not really one, being more your sort of knightly . . .'

One of the maxims that had always guided Miss Cartwright in her job was that the good adviser always answers the correct question, which may not necessarily have been the question the enquirer originally asked. Focusing on the word 'citizen', therefore, she reassured Boamund that the services of the Bureau were available to all, regardless of race, creed, nationality or colour, and it followed that you didn't have to be a British subject to use it.

'Ah,' said Boamund after a while, 'I think that's all right, then. Mind you,' he went on, 'I don't think I am a, what you said, British subject, because I'm not British, I'm Albionese, and as for the other part I don't really think I'm a subject, more a sort of—'

'What exactly was your enquiry?' asked Miss Cartwright. 'Something to do with a form, was it?'

'Oh yes,' Boamund said, 'that's right.'

Miss Cartwright looked at him. Sometimes you just have to guess. 'Housing Benefit?' she asked, basing the assumption on the leather jacket. 'Income Support?'

'What's Income Support?'

Now, said Miss Cartwright to herself, we're getting somewhere. She explained. She was used to explaining, and she did it quickly, clearly and concisely. When she had finished, there was no doubt that Boamund understood; but his reaction was – well, odd. It was as if he was surprised. Shocked even.

'Really?' he said at last.

'Yes,' said Miss Cartwright, breathing through her nose. 'Do you wish to claim Income Support, Mr . . .?'

Boamund's eyes showed that he was sorely tempted, but that his mother or someone like that had warned him about accepting money from strange women. He shook his head. 'It's this paper we've got,' he said. 'We'd like someone to—'

'A summons, maybe? A writ?'

Boamund nodded. He knew all about summonses and writs. Summonses and writs were the only way things got done in Albion. If, for example, King Arthur wanted the windows cleaned, he issued a summons by the Herald of Arms challenging all the window-cleaners of Albion to meet under the town cross at Caerleon on midsummer day and elect a champion. Or if he wanted an extra pint of gold top instead of silver top, he'd leave a writ for the milk-knight.

'Probably,' he said. 'Have a look and see what you think.'

From the inside pocket of his jacket he produced a thick parchment with what looked like a seal hanging off it. Miss Cartwright stared at it as if it were alive.

'Um,' she said, and opened it.

Some time later, she put it down and looked Boamund in the eye. She hated to admit it, even to herself, but there was something about this lunatic that gave her the horrible, creeping feeling that he was for real. You couldn't *pretend* to be as weird as that and still be convincing; it would be like trying to pretend you were dead.

In circumstances like these, there is a well-established procedure. One finds the most junior member of staff and leaves him to get on with it. Miss Cartwright rose, smiled, asked Boamund if he'd mind waiting, and walked hurriedly into the inner office.

'George,' she said, 'be a love and see to that man in the leather jacket for me.'

Oddly enough, George was grinning from ear to ear. 'Sure,' he said. 'Thanks.'

As he jumped down from his chair and scampered across to the door, Miss Cartwright scratched her head and wondered. It was all very well, she said to herself, making a conscious effort to recruit handicapped and disabled people, but she still couldn't get used to working with someone who was only three foot four. You were always worried about, well, treading on him.

383

Boamund was just starting to wonder what was going on when he caught sight of a dwarf coming out of the back office. He smiled. It had been the right place to come to after all.

'Hello,' said the dwarf, 'You're a knight, aren't you?'

'Yes,' said Boamund.

'It's not hard to tell,' replied the dwarf, 'if you know what to look for. My name is Harelip, but you'd better call me George while there are people about. People can be very funny about names, Mr . . .'

'Boamund,' said Boamund. 'Look, we've got this document thing and we can't understand it.'

'By we,' said George, 'you mean . . .?'

'Me and my Order,' Boamund said, 'Knights of the Holy Grail.'

George raised an eyebrow. 'You don't say?' he said. 'My great-uncle-to-the-power-of-thirty-seven was dwarf to a Sir Pertelope who was a Grail Knight.'

'Still going strong,' Boamund assured him. 'Fancy that.'

'It's a small world,' George agreed. 'Well,' he added, looking down at the gap between himself and the floor, 'not as far as I'm concerned, obviously, but you know what I'm driving at. Can I see the document?'

Boamund nodded and handed it over. George read it carefully, occasionally making notes on his scratch-pad. Finally he handed it back and smiled.

'Fine,' he said. 'Congratulations. So what's the problem?'

Boamund blinked a couple of times. 'Well, what does it mean, for a start?' he said.

'Oh, I see,' said George, 'I was forgetting, yes. I can

384

see that to a knight it might present problems.'*

'So?'

'So,' said George, 'basically, it's a list of three things which you and your knights have got to find before you can hope to recover the Grail. They are an apron, a personal organiser – like a sort of notebook – and a pair of socks. They're hidden in remote and inaccessible places. Okay so far?'

Boamund nodded. He had the glorious feeling that at last things were getting back to normal.

'There are cryptic clues as to where these things are to be found,' George went on, wiping his nose with the back of his wrist. 'Now I'm not really allowed to help you too much . . .'

'Why not?'

'King's Regulations,' explained the dwarf. 'However, I can drop hints.'

'Such as?'

'Such as . . .' replied the dwarf, and he went on to drop several very large hints. In fact, compared to the dwarf Harelip's hints, the Speaking Clock is a paragon of obscurity.

'I see,' said Boamund. 'Right. Thanks.'

---

*Dwarves are, of course, naturally gifted at solving riddles, explaining conundrums, cracking codes and doing crossword puzzles. Partly, this is because they are, by their very nature, fey and uncanny creatures, much more at home inside the Glass Mountain than outside. The other reason is that, being too short to reach the pool table and too weak to be able to throw a dart, there's nothing else for them to do in the pub on their night off.

'Don't mention it,' said the dwarf. 'A pleasure. Remember me to Sir Pertelope. Tell him he owes my great-uncle-to-the-power-of-thirty-seven three farthings.'

'How is your great-uncle-to-the-power-of-thirty-seven?'

'Dead.'

'I'm sorry to hear that.'

'These things happen,' replied the dwarf. 'Anyway, never mind. Could you just sign here?'

From his inside pocket he produced an official-looking form.

'What's that?' Boamund asked.

'My discharge,' the dwarf replied happily. 'You see, my family's been indentured to the Grail Knights for generations. We're obliged to do so many hours of service before the indenture is up. My great-uncle-to-the-power-of-thirty-seven had done all his time except for ten minutes when King Arthur abdicated and the Orders of Chivalry came to an end. We've been ...' The dwarf shuddered slightly. '... hanging about ever since, waiting for an opportunity to get all square. And now, thanks to you, we can call it a day and retire. Lucky you came along, really.'

'Very,' Boamund agreed, signing the form with a big X.

'Or rather,' George said, 'Destiny. Yours and mine. Ciao. Good hunting.'

He folded the form, reclaimed his pen (which Boamund had absent-mindedly put in his pocket), bowed thrice to the Four Quarters and jumped off his chair. In the middle of the room, where just a moment ago there had been a display of Family Credit leaflets, the Glass Mountain appeared, blue and sparkling. A door slid open and the dwarf stepped in, waving.

'Fancy that,' Boamund said, and smiled. The way he saw it, the world he was in now was a huge, muddled heap of inexplicable things with just the occasional glimpse of normality showing through. Still, it was nice to know it was still there really; important things, like Destiny and the Unseen. He was, deep down, a rational man and it would take a damn sight more than the odd microwave oven and radio alarm clock to get him really worried.

He picked up the Instructions, smiled at a bucket-mouthed, gibbering Miss Cartwright, and left.

'Right,' said Boamund.

Leadership is a volatile, almost chimerical quality. The same aspects of a man's character that tend to make him a natural leader of men usually also conspire to make him an unmitigated pain. Cortes, for example, who overthrew the fabulously powerful empire of Mexico with four hundred and fifty men, fifteen horses and four cannons, was an inspirational general, but that didn't prevent his devoted followers from wincing in anticipation every time he rubbed his hands to-gether, smiled broadly, and said, 'All right, lads, this is going to be easier than it looks.' In Boamund's case, all his undoubted drive and energy couldn't make up for the fact that he prefaced virtually every statement he made by hitting the palm of one hand with the knuckles of the other and saying, 'Right.' That, in the eyes of many of his men, was calculated to raise their morale to lynching-point.

'The plan,' Boamund went on, 'is this. We split up into three parties of two, we find these three bits of tackle, we bring them back, we find the Grail. Easy as that. Any questions?'

'Yes,' said Lamorak. 'Who's having the van?'

'Which van?' interrupted Pertelope. 'We've got two now, remember?'

'No we haven't, you clown,' shouted Turquine. 'I keep telling you—'

'Shut up, you, you're dishonoured.'

'Don't you tell me . . .'

Boamund frowned. 'Quiet!' he shouted, and banged the top of the orange box which had been brought in to replace the table. 'If you'd been listening,' he went on, 'it'd have sunk in that it's really academic who gets the van, since we're all of us going thousands of miles beyond the shores of Albion. The van is neither here nor—'

'All right,' Lamorak replied, 'except it's my turn, *I* haven't been dishonoured, so I think it's only fair . . .'

Boamund sighed. 'Nobody's getting the van,' he said. 'All right?'

There was a ripple of murmuring, the general sense of which was that so long as nobody had it, that would have to do. Boamund banged the orange box again.

'Now then,' he said, 'the next thing to do,' and he turned up the radiance of his smile to full volume, masking the disquiet in his heart, 'is to decide who's going to go with who. Shut up!' he added, pre-emptively.

The knights stared at him.

'The pairings I've got in mind,' he said, 'are: Lamorak and Pertelope; Turquine and Bedevere; me and Galahaut. Any objections?'

He braced himself for the inevitable squall of discontent. It would, he reckoned, be school all over again. I'm not playing with *him*. We don't want *him* on *our* team. Wait for it . . .

Nobody said anything. Boamund blinked, and went on.

'Deployment as follows: Lammo and Perty, the apron; Turkey and Bedders, the personal organiser thing; Gally and me, the socks. Any objections?'

They're up to something, Boamund thought. They've never agreed to anything without a fight in their lives. They must be up to something.

His mind wandered back to the Old Boys Joust of '6, when he'd been Vice-Captain of tilting, and the Captain, old Soppy Agravaine, had twisted his ankle in a friendly poleaxe fight with the Escole des Chevaliers seconds, leaving him, for the first and only time, to pick the teams. As his memory swooped back on that day like a homing pigeon, he could almost feel the hot tears of shame and humiliation on his cheeks once more as he'd watched them going out, in deliberate defiance of his Team Orders, wearing their summer haubergeons with rebated zweyhanders and Second XI surcoats. They'd pretended to agree with him, he remembered, and then when the moment came, they'd just gone and done as they jolly well chose. Well, not this time. He was ready for them.

'Well,' he said, 'that's fine. Now, here are your sealed orders,' he went on, handing out the envelopes, 'and you're all to promise on your words of honour not to open them until after you've left the chapter house. And,' he added, 'the three parties will leave at fifteen-minute intervals, just to make sure.'

389

'Make sure of what, Snotty?' asked Turquine innocently. Boamund let his lip curl just a millimetre or so, and smiled.

'Just to make sure, that's all,' he said. 'Any questions?'

No questions.

'Splendid,' he said. 'All right, dismiss.' He sat down and started to go over the packing list one last time.

The other knights filed out, leaving him alone. He was halfway through his list when Toenail came in. He looked furtive.

'Psst,' he whispered.

There are people who simply can't resist conspiratorial noises, and Boamund was one of them. 'What?' he whispered back.

Toenail looked round to see if any of the knights were listening, and then hissed, 'You know those envelopes you gave them?'

Boamund nodded.

'You know,' the dwarf went on, 'they weren't supposed to open them until after they'd left here?'

Boamund nodded again.

'Well,' said Toenail, 'they're all out there now, reading them. I, er, thought you ought to know.'

Boamund smiled. 'I thought they'd do that,' he said. 'That's why I didn't give them the *real* envelopes.'

'Oh.' Toenail raised an eyebrow. 'They looked like real envelopes to . . .'

Boamund frowned. 'Yes, of course they're real *envelopes*,' he said impatiently. 'Only the message in them isn't the real message.'

'It isn't?'

Boamund allowed himself a sly chuckle. 'Oh no,' he

390

said. 'All it says is, *Shame on you, you're dishonoured.*
That'll teach them.'

Oh God, thought Toenail to himself, and I've got to
go on a quest with these lunatics. 'Then why,' he asked,
as nicely as he could, 'did you give them the envelopes
now?'

'Because I knew they'd open them.'

'But,' replied the dwarf cautiously, 'if you knew
that...'

'And,' Boamund went on, 'this way, they'll know that
I knew they'd open them, and that way, they'll know
they're all rotters, and then we'll all know where we are,
do you see?' And Boamund grinned triumphantly. 'I
think they call that man management,' he added.

Not where I come from they don't, sunshine, Toenail said to himself. 'Ah,' he replied. 'Man management. Right, sorry to have bothered you.'

He bowed slightly and went back into the kitchen,
where the other knights were sitting on the worktops
waiting for him.

'You're right,' he said. 'He has gone stark raving
bonkers.'

'Told you so,' said Turquine. 'Right, the way I see it,
there's nothing in the book of rules says that you've got
to obey a Grand Master who's gone round the twist. I
vote we tie him up, chuck him in the cellar and get back
to normal.'

Bedevere held up his hand.

'Okay,' he said, 'point taken, he's acting a bit funny.
But—'

'A bit funny!' Turquine snorted. 'Come on, Bedders, face facts. Young Snotty's finally broken his
spring. Had to happen, sooner or later. Trouble with

391

Snotty is, his head's too small for his brain. Leads to an intolerable build-up of pressure, that does, and you end up going potty. I'll just go and get some rope, and . . .'

Bedevere remained firm. 'Hold on, Turkey,' he said quietly. 'Just because Bo's behaving a bit oddly, that doesn't mean we should abandon the quest, does it, chaps?'

Four pairs of eyebrows lifted as one. Having got their attention, Bedevere slid down off the worktop, helped himself to a biscuit from the jar, and went on.

'What I'm getting at,' he said, 'is, sooner or later we've got to find the ruddy thing, or we're all going to be here for ever and ever. Right?'

Silence. Bowed heads. Bedevere cleared his mouth of crumbs and continued.

'Precisely,' he said. 'So, just when we're all getting a bit slack and not really with it any more, what with Nentres going off like that and taking the . . . Anyway, who should turn up but young Bo, with this really quite exciting clue thing, and actually knowing what a Grail *is*, for Heaven's sake. You've got to admit, it gets you wondering. Well, it does me, anyway. Can't be co-incidence.'

From the unwonted silence, Sir Bedevere deduced that his colleagues conceded he had a point. He continued briskly.

'What I'm trying to get at, chaps, is that, all right, Bo's as potty as they come, but so what? We've got the clue, we know what a Grail is, let's all jolly well go out and look for the blessed thing. And,' he added force-fully, 'I for one think the best way to go about it is the way Bo says, splitting up and getting all these socks and things. Must be right,' he said. 'That clue thing said so. Well?'

The knights looked at him shame-faced.

'But Bedders,' said Pertelope, almost pleading, 'he's barmy.'

'So was Napoleon,' Bedevere replied.

'No he wasn't.'

'Well, then,' Bedevere answered, 'Alexander the Great, then. Lots of great leaders are a bit funny in the head, well-known fact. That's what makes them great. Not,' he added, 'that I'm saying Bo's great. All I'm saying is, we don't want to make asses of ourselves just because he's an ass. That'd be silly, don't you think?'

Turquine growled. 'So he's let you have the van, has he?' he snarled contemptuously. 'Typical.'

Bedevere ignored him. 'Come on, chaps,' he said, 'let's vote on it. All those in favour.' Four hands, including his own. 'Against.' One hand. 'That's settled, then. Go on, Turkey, be a sport.'

'All right, then,' Turquine grumbled. 'Just don't blame me, that's all.'

Bedevere grinned. 'Certainly not,' he said, 'we can blame Bo. That,' he said, sagely, 'is what leaders are for.'

It was a ship.

Oh *good*, said Danny Bennett to himself, now I won't have to die after all. What a relief that is.

For the last six days, ever since the pirate-radio ship *Imelda Marcos* hit an iceberg and sank, Danny had been wondering whether, career-wise, his sideways move from BBC television into commercial radio had been entirely sensible. On the one hand, he told himself, as he lay on his back in the inflatable dinghy and stared at the sun, I had my own show, complete editorial freedom, unlimited expense account and the chance to develop a whole new approach to radio drama; on the other hand, Bush House didn't start shipping water the moment anything hit it.

In the last few panic-stricken minutes of the ship's life, Danny had been so busy choosing his eight gramophone records that the rest of the crew got fed up waiting for him and shoved off with the lifeboat. To make things worse, there was no portable record player. They don't make them any more, apparently.

And now, just as he was reproaching himself for neglecting to pack any food and water, here was a ship sailing directly towards him. How reassuring, Danny muttered to himself, as he propped his emaciated body up on one elbow and waved feebly. Somebody up there must like me.

The ship drew closer, and a head appeared over the side. 'Ahoy!' it shouted. 'Excuse me, but am I all right for the International Date Line? There hasn't been a signpost or anything for simply ages.'

'Help,' Danny replied.

'Sorry?'

'I said help.'

The head was female, thirtyish, blonde, nice eyes. 'Fair enough,' it said. 'Would you like to buy some unit trusts?'

Danny made a peculiar noise at the back of his throat; imagine the sound of a bathful of mercury emptying away down the plughole, and you might get some idea.

'Unit trusts,' the head repeated. 'It's a very simple

394

idea, really. You pay a capital sum to the fund managers, and they invest your money in a wide range of quoted equities, which . . .'

'Yes,' Danny croaked, 'I do know what unit trusts are, thank you very much. Have you got any water?'

The head looked round at the infinite vastness of the sea. 'I think there's plenty for everyone,' it said. 'Why?'

'Fresh water,' Danny said. 'Drinking water.'

'Oh, *that* sort. Perrier, stuff like that?'

'It'd do.'

'Sorry, we're right out, all we have is gin. If you're not interested in unit trusts, how about a personal equity plan? There are several really excellent products available at the moment which I would unhesitatingly recommend. For instance . . .'

'All right,' Danny said, dragging breath into his lungs, 'food. I haven't eaten for three days.'

'Oh.' The head frowned. 'Does that mean you haven't got any money? Because if you don't, I can't see that there's a great deal of point in continuing with this discussion, do you?'

Danny cackled wildly. 'I've got plenty of money,' he said. 'I've got two years' back pay from Radio Imelda, for a start. What I haven't got is—'

'A flexible pension scheme tailored to *your* needs and aspirations, I'll be bound,' interrupted the head, nodding. 'Now I think I can help you there, because it so happens that I'm an agent for Lyonesse Equitable Life, and there's one particular package . . .'

'Can you eat it?'

The head emitted a silvery laugh. 'Alternatively,' it went on, 'I could do you a very nice index-linked Lyonesse Provident Flexible Annuity Bond, which would provide access to capital as well as a guaranteed rate of income, paid monthly, with a very competitive tax position. Interested?'

Danny shook his head. 'Maybe you're missing the point here,' he said. 'Here I am, cast adrift in an open boat, dying of hunger and thirst . . .'

'Ah,' said the head, 'got you. What you're really concerned about here is some really constructive inheritance tax planning, possibly involving the creation of an offshore trust. Silly of me not to have realised that before.'

'But I don't *want* to die,' Danny screamed. I—'

'Well,' said the head patiently, 'in that case we can adapt the package to allow maximum flexibility by making the fullest possible use of the annual exempt giftable sum. I wish you'd said, by the way. I hate to rush you, but time is money, you know. Now . . .'

Danny sank back into the dinghy and groaned. The head peered back over the rail at him.

'Hello?' it said. 'Is that a deal, then?'

'Go away.'

'Pardon?'

'I said go away. Bog off. Sink.'

'I don't think I quite heard you. You do want the pension policy, don't you?'

'No.'

The head looked shocked. 'You *don't*?'

'No.'

'Really?'

'Really.'

'Well!' The head wrinkled its brows. 'Suit yourself, then. Look, if you change your mind, you can always fax us on 0553 . . .'

Danny rolled over on his face and started to scream; he was still screaming nine hours later, when he was picked up by the captain of an oil tanker. When he told the captain of the tanker about his experiences with the strange ship, the captain nodded grimly.

'I know,' he said, and shuddered. 'I've seen it myself. *The Flying Channel-Islander*, we call it.'

Danny was half-dead from dehydration and exposure, but he was still a journalist, and a story is a story. 'Tell me about it,' he said.

'It's horrible,' the captain replied, crossing himself. 'Really terrible things happen to people who sight her.' He paused, his eyes closed. 'Terrible things,' he repeated.

'Such as?'

'Well,' the captain replied, 'some of them die, some of them go mad, some of them live perfectly normally for five or six years and then run amok with machetes. Some simply vanish. Some of them . . .'

'Yes?'

'Some of them,' said the captain grimly, 'even go and buy the insurance.'

3

Between the town of Giles, to the north of the Tomkinson Range, and Forrest in the Nullarbor Plain, lies the Great Victoria Desert. It is hot, arid, desolate and merciless; and whatever the Creator had in mind when He made it that way, it most certainly wasn't human beings.

It's a really awful place to be if you've got toothache.

'I've got some oil of cloves in my rucksack,' said Sir Pertelope. 'Supposed to be very good, oil of cloves. Never seemed to do me any good, mind you, but maybe I'm just over-sensitive to pain.'

'Mmmm,' replied his companion.

'There's some aspirin in the first-aid kit, of course,' Pertelope went on, 'but I wouldn't recommend that, because it's water-soluble, and since we've run out of water...'

'Mmmm.'

'Needless to say,' Pertelope continued helpfully, 'if

398

we found some water it'd be a different matter altogether. But somehow...' He looked up briefly into the steel-blue sky and then turned his head quickly away. 'Now my aunt Beatrice used to say that sucking a pebble—'

'Shut up,' said Sir Lamorak.

Offended, Pertelope shifted his rucksack on his shoulders and pointedly walked a few yards to the east. Then he stopped.

'If that's north,' he said, pointing due south, 'then England is seventeen thousand miles away over that big jutting rock over there. Fancy that,' he added. He stood for a moment in contemplation; then he shrugged and started to walk; for the record, due west.

They were trying to get to Sydney.

For two men who had alighted from an airliner in Brisbane several months before, this shouldn't have been too great a problem. True, neither of them had been to Australia before, but they had taken the precaution of buying railway tickets, advance-booking their hotels and securing copies of *What's On In Sydney* before leaving England. Their problems had started at Brisbane Airport, when Pertelope had left the little bag containing all the paperwork behind on the airport bus.

No problem, Pertelope had explained. All we have to do is hitch a lift. The Australians are a notoriously friendly, hospitable people who take pleasure in helping travellers in distress.

Sixteen hours along the road, they had indeed managed to hitch a ride on a truckful of newly slaughtered carcases as far as St George, where the lorry driver had finally thrown them forcibly from the cab after Pertelope had insisted on singing *Vos Quid Admiramini* in his usual nasal drone. After a short pause to regroup and eat the last of the bag of mint imperials that Lamorak had bought at Heathrow, they had set out to walk as far as Dirranbandi. It's hard to explain concisely how they came to be thirteen hundred miles off course; the best that can be done without embarking on a whole new book is to explain that in the back of Sir Pertelope's National Trust Diary was a map of the world; and that although Pertelope had heard about Columbus and the curvature of the earth, he had never been entirely convinced. The central premise of his navigational theory, therefore, was that the centre of the world lay at Jerusalem, and that maps had to be interpreted accordingly.

Pertelope looked at his watch. 'What do you say to stopping here for lunch?' he asked. 'We could sit under that rock over there. It's got a lovely view out over the, er, desert.'

Although Death had been trailing them pretty closely every step of the way, in the manner of a large fat pigeon outside a pavement cafe, the nearest he had come to cutting two more notches in his scythe handle had been fifty miles west of the Macgregor Range, where Pertelope had inadvertently knocked over the rusty beer-can containing the last of their water while doing his morning exercises. They had wandered round in circles for two days and collapsed; but they were found by a party of wandering aborigines, whom Lamorak was able to persuade that his library ticket was in fact an American Express card, and who had sold them a gallon of water and six dried lizards in return, as it turned out, for the right to borrow three fiction and three non-fiction titles every week from the Stirchley Public Library in perpetuity. From then on, it had simply been a matter of lurching from one last-minute borehole to another, and sneaking up very quietly indeed on unsuspecting snakes.

Pertelope had, however, refused to harm the Paramatta horned python they'd finally caught after a six-hour scramble among the rocks of Mount Woodroffe, pointing out that it was an endangered species. It was shortly afterwards that Lamorak's upper left molar started to hurt.

'Now then, let's see,' said Pertelope. 'There's ...' He unslung his rucksack and started to go through its contents (three clean shirts, three changes of underwear, a copy of *What's On In Sydney* with a bookmark stuck in to mark the details of the New Orleans Jazz Festival, a Swiss Army knife with six broken blades, an electric razor, a pair of trousers, a tennis racket, a mouth organ, two flannels, a towel, Germolene, oil of cloves, a packet of plasters, a bottle of dandruff shampoo, entero-vioform tablets, nail scissors, a quantity of ladies clothing ...).

'What have you got in your pack, Lammo?' Pertelope enquired. 'I seem to be fresh out.'

Lamorak unshipped his head from his hands, said, 'Nothing,' and put it back.

'Oh.' Pertelope frowned and scratched his head. 'That's awkward,' he added. 'I suppose we'll have to look for roots and berries and things.' He looked round at the baked, sterile earth. It had been a very long time since anything had been so foolhardy as to entrust its roots to so hostile an environment.

'Pertelope.'

Sir Pertelope looked up. 'Yes?' he asked.

'There's always cannibalism, you know.'

Pertelope blinked. 'Cannibalism?' he repeated.

'That's right,' said his companion calmly. 'You know, eating human flesh. It used to be quite popular at one time.'

Pertelope thought for a moment, and then shook his head.

'I wouldn't dream of it,' he replied firmly. 'Not after all we've been through together. You'd stick in my throat, so to speak.'

Lamorak stood up. 'That's all right,' he said quietly. 'I quite understand. Now then, if you keep absolutely still it won't hurt a bit.'

A small cog dropped into place in Pertelope's brain. 'Hold on,' he said. 'A joke's a joke, but let's not get silly. I mean, people can get hurt larking about, and . . .'

Lamorak smiled, and lunged at him with a small stone. Hunger, thirst and toothache had taken quite a lot out of him, but he only missed by inches. He landed in the dust, swore and raised himself painfully from the ground.

'Lizards,' Pertelope was saying. 'I'm sure there're plenty of lizards about, if only we knew what we were supposed to be looking for. Trouble is, the little so-and-sos are masters of camouflage. Would you believe it, there's one species of lizard in the New Hebrides . . .'

He leant sideways, and the haymaking blow Lamorak had aimed at him wasted its force in the dry air.

'Shut up about sodding lizards and help me up,' Lamorak growled. 'I think I've twisted my ankle.'

'It's your own fault,' Pertelope replied, 'lashing out at people with whopping great rocks like that. Anyone would think...'

Lamorak jumped to his feet, thereby giving the lie to his own earlier statement, and tried a full-length tackle. As his full length was only a little more than five feet, he failed.

'Lamorak,' said Pertelope sternly, 'you do realise you're making a most frightful exhibition of yourself. What would a passing stranger think if he saw you now?'

'Depends,' Lamorak panted in reply. 'If he knew what I'd had to put up with from you ever since we left Birmingham, *Bloody good luck to you*, probably.' He hurled the rock, which landed about two feet away, and then sat heavily down.

'Really!' said Pertelope, offended.

Lamorak drew in a deep breath, looked for a moment at his scuffed and bleeding palms, and sighed. 'Tell you what,' he said. 'We'll make a deal. You take the compass, the map, your rucksack, my rucksack, the whole lot, and I'll stay here and die in peace. How does that sound?'

Pertelope shook his head. 'Don't you worry,' he said cheerfully. 'I'm not just going to up and leave you, you can count on that?'

'Really?'

'Really.'

Lamorak nodded, and then stretched out his trembling hand for the rock once more. Pertelope kicked it away, and then went and sulked under a sand dune.

It didn't last, though; Pertelope's sulks never did. Thus, when Lamorak had just fallen asleep and was already dreaming rapturously of a swimming pool full of frosted beer surrounded by club sandwiches, Pertelope sat down a few judicious feet away, extended his right leg and prodded his companion in the ribs.

'Never mind,' he said. 'Something'll turn up, you'll see.'

Lamorak groaned feebly and turned on his side. Pertelope shuffled a little nearer.

'Apart from lizards,' he said, 'there's snakes, and a sort of small bird. Actually they're quite rare these days, because of the erosion of their natural environment by toxic industrial waste; so we'll only eat those as a *very* last resort. But like I said, there's lizards and . . .'

'Mnnn.'

'Or perhaps,' Pertelope continued, 'we'll be rescued by a party of wandering aborigines, although really you shouldn't call them that, because really they're a very ancient and noble culture, with a very sophisticated neo-mystical sort of religion that makes them in tune with the earth and things. Apparently . . .'

'Pertelope,' Lamorak said, 'I'm lying on a packing case.'

'Well then, move a bit. I read somewhere that they can walk for days at a time, just singing, and come out precisely where they intended to go, just by harmonising their brainwave patterns to the latent geothermal energies of . . .'

'It says Tinned Peaches, Pertelope.'

'Sorry?'

'On the lid,' Lamorak replied. 'There's a label saying Tinned Peaches.'

There was a momentary pause.

'What did you say?' Pertelope enquired.

'Oh for Christ's sake,' Lamorak shouted. 'Come over here and look for yourself.'

Between them they scrabbled the half-buried case out of the ground, and broke the screwdriver blade of Pertelope's Swiss Army knife levering off the lid.

The crate was full of tins of peaches.

'Quick,' Lamorak hissed, 'Give me the bloody penknife.' He grabbed it and feverishly flicked at the tin-opener attachment with his brittle thumbnail.

'Hang on,' said Pertelope, turning a tin round in his hands. 'I'm sorry, Lammo, but we can't eat these. It's a pity, but . . .'

Lamorak froze. 'What the hell do you mean, we can't eat them?' he said. 'Okay they're a bit rusty, but . . .'

Pertelope shook his head. 'It's not that,' he said firmly. 'Look, see what's written here on the label. Produce of South Africa. I'm afraid . . .'

Lamorak gave him a very long look, and then put the penknife down.

'That's it,' Pertelope said. 'I know it's hard luck, but what I always say is, principles are principles, and it's no good only sticking to them in the good times, because . . .'

He was still talking when Lamorak hit him with the tin.

The Fruit Monks of Western Australia are one of the few surviving branches of the great wave of crusading monasticism that originated shortly after the fall of Constantinople in 1205. The Templars, Hospitallers and Knights of St John have largely disappeared, or been subsumed into other organisations and lost their identity; but the *Monachi Fructuarii* still cling to their ancient way of life, and their Order remains basically the same as it did in the days of its founder, St Anastasius of Joppa.

Legend has it that St Anastasius, inspired by the example of the soldier who gave Christ the vinegar-soaked sponge on the cross, set up his first fruit-juice stall beside the main pilgrimage route from Antioch to Jerusalem in 1219. By the middle of the thirteenth century, the brightly coloured booths of the Order were a familiar sight the length and breadth of the Holy Land; and after the Fall of Acre ended the Crusader presence in the Middle East, the monks turned their attention to the other desert places of the earth. Dwindling manpower has, of course, severely limited their operations, so that nowadays they have to be content with depositing cases of canned fruit at random points, relying on Providence to guide wandering travellers to them.

In 1979, the Order was taken over by an Australian-based multinational food chain, and coin-operated dispenser machines are gradually replacing the simple wooden packing cases; but the process of rationalisation is far from complete, even now.

It was a suitable moment for reconciliation.

'Have a tinned peach,' Lamorak said. 'If it helps at all, it doesn't *taste* South African.'

Pertelope raised his head, and lowered it again almost immediately.

'What hit me?' he enquired.

Lamorak shrugged. 'You're not going to believe this,'

he said through fruit-crammed cheeks, 'but it was a tin of peaches.'

'It was?'

Lamorak nodded. 'Probably fell out of a passing aeroplane. Or maybe they've got a serious peach glut problem here, something to do with the Common Agricultural Policy. Anyway, it fell on you, and out you went like a light. Pity,' he added, 'that Sir Isaac Newton's already scooped you on gravity, otherwise you could be quids in. Never mind,' he concluded, and burped.

'Lammo,' Pertelope whispered, 'I'm hungry.'

'I can believe that,' his companion replied. 'Pity you can't eat these peaches, really, because . . .'

There was a silence, broken only by the sound of Lamorak's jaws. For a man with serious toothache, he seemed to be able to cope perfectly well with the chewing process.

'I've heard it said,' Pertelope ventured cautiously, 'that a lot of tinned stuff that's supposed to come from South Africa is only tinned there. It's actually grown in the Front Line states, apparently.'

Lamorak nodded. 'Well-known fact,' he replied. 'I read it somewhere,' he added confidently. 'Dirty trick, if you ask me.'

'Absolutely,' Pertelope agreed; and then said, 'How do you mean?'

'Economic sabotage,' replied his companion, shaking his head. 'The Pretoria regime puts their fruit in South African tins so's nobody'll buy it, thus undermining their economic development. It's time people did something about it.'

'Yes. Um. Like what?'

'Like eating the fruit,' said Lamorak, handing him the tin. 'That'll teach them, eh?'

About half an hour later the two knights collapsed, surrounded by empty tins, and lay still.

'We'd better bury them, you know,' Pertelope murmured.

'Sorry?'

'The tins. Can't just leave them lying about. Pollution.'

Lamorak thought about it. 'In theory,' he replied.

'I mean,' Pertelope continued, 'this is one of the few completely unspoilt natural environments left. We owe it to the next generation . . .'

'Yes,' Lamorak muttered, casting an eye across the desert landscape, 'right. Unspoilt.' He shuddered slightly. 'You get on with it, then. I'm just going to get a few minutes' sleep.'

He rolled on to his back and closed his eyes. Then he sat bolt upright and grabbed Pertelope's arm.

'Bloody hell fire,' he hissed, and pointed. 'Look, Per, over there.'

Pertelope narrowed his eyes. 'Where, Lammo?'

'There.'

'Oh, yes, right. What am I supposed to be looking for?'

Lamorak ignored him. 'We've found one, Per. We've found a bloody unicorn.'

Pertelope's jaw dropped. 'Where?' he whispered.

'Oh for crying out loud.'

On the edge of a small escarpment, about five hundred yards away, the unicorn stopped, lifted its head and sniffed. For a minute or so it stood like a statue, its ears and nostrils straining; then its head dropped once again, and its tail swished rhythmically to and fro, although there were no flies for it to dispel. Its lips brushed the sand at just the level grass would have been growing at, had any grass been so ill-advised as to try and survive in a totally dehydrated environment.

'Oh, I see,' Pertelope gasped. 'Lammo, it *is* a unicorn. That's the most incredible—'

'Yes, right, fine,' Lamorak muttered. He was trying to get his binoculars out of his rucksack while at the same time remaining perfectly still, and the strap had caught in something. 'Just keep quiet, will you, while I . . .'

'It has a golden horn,' Pertelope crooned, 'growing out of the middle of its forehead.'

'Really,' Lamorak mouthed darkly. 'How unusual. Maybe it's an experimental model or something. Look, can you just free the strap of these glasses? It seems to have got wound round the . . .'

'Its coat is milk-white,' Pertelope drivelled on. 'Look, Lamorak, it's got gold hooves as well, isn't that just—?'

'*QUIET*!' It's amazing how loud you can shout when you're whispering. The unicorn's head jumped up like the handle of a low-flying rake, and the animal stood poised for a moment, a paradigm of nervous grace, before bounding away out of sight.

There was an ominous silence.

'Oh dear,' Pertelope said. 'We must have frightened it off.'

Lamorak made a gravelly noise deep in his throat and rubbed the vicinity of his protesting molar. 'You think so?' he growled. 'You're sure it hadn't just

409

remembered an appointment somewhere?'

'It was your fault,' Pertelope retorted, 'yelling at it like that. That's the trouble with you, Lammo, you're out of tune with Nature.'

From his pack, Lamorak had fished out a length of rope, a bundle of cloth, a small bottle and a box of sugar-lumps. 'Come on,' he said. 'It should be easy enough to follow its hoofprints in the sand.'

Pertelope nodded and stood up. They filled their bags with tins of peaches, scraped sand over the empties ('Though really we should take them with us, you know, until we can find a proper litter-bin. This sort of can is fully recyclable.') and trudged off towards where the unicorn had put in its brief, perfectly staged appearance.

Once upon a time, unicorns were extremely scarce.

So elusive were they that there was only one way to catch a unicorn ... Well, in fact there were two. The simple way was to collect a bag of leftover scraps, soak them in cherry brandy, put them in a perfectly ordinary dustbin bag and leave it outside the back door overnight. The unicorn would then rip open the dustbin bag, gorge itself silly and fall asleep. That only worked for the urban unicorn, however; and since urban unicorns were scruffy, tallow-caked, marlinspike-nosed killing machines standing about twelve hands high and entirely devoid of fear or compassion, it was more a case of not catching them if it could possibly be avoided. An urban unicorn with a hangover was capable of doing more damage to life and property than most bombs.

When it came to the white unicorn, however, only

one method stood any chance of success. It required a maiden of unspotted virtue, and six foot of stout hemp rope. The rope was usually no problem.

As time went on, and for various reasons connected with the decline of moral standards and the spread of Humanism, the annual unicorn cull became harder and harder to achieve, so the unicorns grew more and more plentiful. In fact, they became a pest. Their natural habitat could no longer support the huge herds of migratory unicorns sweeping down from the Steppes each spring, and as the cities grew, more and more unicorns drifted into them, gradually evolving into the urban mutation noted above. Fortunately for the human race, they were entirely wiped out by a form of myxomatosis in the early twelfth century; but the disease never took hold among the white unicorns of the plains, which continued to devastate crops and strip the bark off young trees at an alarming rate. Finally, the Holy Roman Emperor reached an agreement with the Great Khan and Prester John, whereby the unicorns were herded across Europe into Asia, down through China and across into Australia, which at that time was still connected to the mainland by a narrow isthmus. Once the last unicorn had crossed over, the land bridge was immediately destroyed, and the very memory of Australia was deliberately erased from the memory of the human race.

It didn't take long for the unicorns to devastate their new environment, and now they are once again a comparatively rare and elusive species. To get an idea of what would have happened to Europe if this step hadn't been taken, one only has to look at the arid deserts of central Australia and consider that, before

411

the coming of the unicorns, they were the most fertile and productive grasslands on the face of the earth.

As time passed, however, times also changed; and although unicorns are by no means common, there are other species rarer and more elusive still. Thus there is only one sure-fire way of catching a maiden of un-spotted virtue. It requires a unicorn and six feet of rope.

'You know,' muttered Pertelope, as they limped to the top of yet another escarpment and looked down across a thousand acres of emptiness, 'I'm still not sure we're going about this the right way.'

'Shut up,' replied Lamorak.

'It's all right for you,' Pertelope protested. 'You've got sensible heels on.' He sat down, removed his left shoe and shook sand out of it.

'Don't start,' Lamorak sighed. 'We tossed a coin, remember, and—'

'Yes,' said Pertelope, 'and I've been thinking about that.' He put the shoe back on his foot. It was a patent navy court shoe with a two-inch heel and a rather smart brass buckle, and it rubbed like hell. Still, as Lamorak had pointed out, it did go very nicely with the plain halter-neck navy dress, pill-box hat and matching handbag that now made up the rest of Pertelope's outfit. 'You remember,' Pertelope added, 'you said call, and I called heads?'

Lamorak looked away and nodded. 'Quite right,' he said.

'I recall wondering at the time why you insisted on using a Portuguese coin,' Pertelope went on, 'and it's just occurred to me that, what with Portugal being a republic . . .'

'Time we were on our way, Per.'

'. . . there isn't a head on a Portuguese coin,' Pertelope continued, 'only a sort of coat of arms thing on one side and a number on the other. *I* think . . .'

He broke off. In the far distance there was a tiny speck. They froze, and Lamorak raised his binoculars.

'That's it,' he hissed. 'We're in business. Now then, stay absolutely still and do what I told you. And for God's sake put your veil down.'

'I still think—' Pertelope whispered, but Lamorak cut him short.

'Actually,' he said, 'I didn't want to have to say this, but I wouldn't be, er, suitable anyway, so . . .'

Pertelope frowned. 'Well, I'm hardly suitable either, Lammo,' he replied. 'I mean, I'm not a woman, am I?'

Lamorak bit his lip. This was embarrassing. 'It doesn't actually specify a woman,' he said, 'not as such. Just a . . . Hold on, it's coming this way. Right then, action stations.'

'I still think . . .' Pertelope said, and he was still speaking as Lamorak crawled away over the sand and hid himself behind a large boulder.

Forty-five minutes can be a long time.

It wasn't, of course, a unicorn that they had been sent to get. If all they'd needed was a unicorn, they could simply have strolled into Harrods' or Bloomingdales' pet department and ordered one.

In other words, this was the easy bit.

'Stone the flaming crows,' exclaimed the unicorn, 'it

isn't a bloody sheila after all.'

But by then it was too late; the noose, cast by Lamorak's well-practised hand, was already flying through the air. There was a brief struggle, some extremely colourful language from the unicorn, and it was all over.

'Quick,' Lamorak grunted, 'grab the rope while I get the chloroform. And watch out for that horn.'

'Pommy bastards,' snarled the unicorn, hurling its weight vainly against the rope. Pertelope dug his heels into the sand and strained backwards, while Lamorak emptied the bottle on to his handkerchief.

'You didn't tell me they could talk, Lammo,' he gasped. 'Just imagine that, a talking animal.'

As if to confirm his statement, the unicorn said something else. It was largely to do with how this particular unicorn's father had been right in his warnings about the extreme effeminacy of the English; and for all his naturalist's curiosity, Pertelope was quite relieved when Lamorak managed to stuff the handkerchief up its nose. Slowly, and still muttering imprecations under its breath, the unicorn sagged to the ground and passed out.

'Well,' Lamorak said, 'we did it. Next time, though, we use a tranquilliser gun and the hell with tradition.' He knelt down and set to work with the rope.

'Can I get out of these clothes now?' Pertelope said. He was bright red in the face, only partly as a result of his exertions.

'In a minute,' Lamorak snapped. 'Give me a hand over here first, quickly, before the blasted thing wakes up.'

Pertelope sighed and grabbed a length of rope. He

wasn't sure that what they were doing wasn't a gross interference with a majestic wild animal in its natural habitat. He firmly disapproved of such things, along with zoos, circuses and leaving dogs in cars with the windows done up. 'Don't tie it so tight, Lammo,' he said at intervals, 'you'll hurt the poor thing.'

'Right,' said Lamorak at last, standing up and breathing heavily, 'we've done that. Now I suggest we have five minutes' sit-down and a rest.'

Pertelope brushed the dust off his skirts. 'After,' he said firmly, 'I've got out of these dreadful clothes.'

'Go ahead,' Lamorak replied. 'I'm just going to sit here and . . .'

Pertelope blushed furiously. 'I need you to unzip me,' he snarled.

'Sorry.' Lamorak hoisted himself to his feet again. 'This time, for pity's sake hold still. You nearly put my eye out with your hairclips last time, remember.'

But before he could make any further movement, a bullet hissed through the air, just missed his eyebrows and lifted Pertelope's hat off his head. The two knights remained where they were, standing very still indeed.

'Thtick 'em up,' said a voice somewhere behind their backs, 'or I'll blow your headth off.'

The Australian wilderness is a place of many strange and terrible noises. There's the unmistakable yap of the dingo, the screech of the kookaburra, the soft bark of the kangaroo, the rasping growl of the mezzo-soprano gargling with eggs beaten in stout – all these can be disconcerting, and to begin with, even terrifying. But there's one sound guaranteed to fill even the hardiest heart with fear and turn the brownest knees to water;

415

and that's the sound of a hearty contralto voice singing:

> *Onthe a jolly thwagman camped bethide a billabong*
> *Under the thade of a tumpty-tum tree . . .*

over and over again, apparently through a megaphone.
The repetition is attributable to the fact that the singer
doesn't know the rest of the words. The amplification
effect, on the other hand, is due to the large metal
drum that covers the singer's head.

'Can we put our hands down now, please?'

'Thorry?'

Lamorak closed his eyes, and then opened them
again. 'I said,' he reiterated, 'can we put our hands
down now, please?'

'Oh. Yeth. Only nithe and eathy doth it, right?'

'Yeth. Yes. Sorry.' Lamorak lowered his arms experimentally, and ran quick checks over himself to discover
whether he'd been shot yet. All clear. 'How about
turning round?' he suggested.

There was a pause. 'Go on, then,' said the voice. It
sounded like a cow at the bottom of a deep, steel-lined
pit.

The proprietor of the voice looked at first sight like
the after-effects of the sorceror's apprentice run riot
in a breaker's yard. Starting from the top, there was
a big round drum, with two tiny holes. Under that,
unmistakably, what had once been the bonnet of a
Volkswagen Beetle, before someone with a degree in
design flair and enormous biceps had beaten it into
a vaguely anthropomorphic shape with a big hammer.

Two steel tubes stuck out from the sides at right angles, and there was a rust-mottled revolver at the end of one of them. Finally, two more tubes projected out from the underside and linked up with a pair of old-fashioned diver's boots.

'Ith either of you laughth, I thall be theriouthly angry,' it said.

Pertelope blinked. 'Excuse me,' he said, 'but why are you wearing those funny clothes?'

The ironmongery quivered slightly. 'Look who'th talking,' it replied.

'Please,' Lamorak said hastily, 'you mustn't mind my friend. It's just that he's an idiot, that's all.'

There was a dubious, rusty sound from inside the drum. 'You're *thure* that'th all?' it said. 'I mean, that ith a *throck* he'th wearing.'

Pertelope winced. 'There's a perfectly good reason—' he started to say, but a sudden pain in his foot, the result of Lamorak inadvertently stamping on it hard, cut him short.

'Anyway,' Lamorak said brightly, 'it's been very nice meeting you, and the very best of luck with whatever it is you're doing, but I'm afraid we've got to be getting along. Cheerio.' He started to walk purposefully towards the unicorn, but the muzzle of the revolver followed him.

'Not tho fatht,' said the ironclad. 'What're you two doing with that 'roo, anyway?'

The two knights looked at each other. 'That *what*?' Lamorak enquired.

'The kangaroo,' replied the voice from inside the drum. 'Come on, thpit it out.'

'Excuse me,' Lamorak said, in the very recherché

417

tone of voice one uses when pointing out the blindingly obvious to a heavily armed idiot, 'but strictly speaking, that's not a kangaroo.'

'It ithn't?'

There was something in the modulations of the voice that gave Lamorak the clue he'd been looking for. 'You're not from these parts, are you?' he said.

The ironmongery didn't reply; but it shuffled and clinked in such a way as to confirm Lamorak in his belief. 'Or this time, come to that,' he added slowly. 'You're from the future, aren't you?'

'Oh thit,' mumbled the ironclad. 'How did you know?'

Had Lamorak been truthful, he'd have replied that it was the logical conclusion when you came across someone who'd heard of kangaroos but didn't know what they looked like, and had the idea that in the Outback, the way to dress inconspicuously was to make up as Ned Kelly. Instead, he said, 'Lucky guess.'

Pertelope, meanwhile, had been doing a very good impersonation of a man swallowing a live fish. 'How do you mean, from the future?' he finally managed to say. Lamorak smiled.

'Allow me to introduce you,' he said. 'Sir Pertelope, this is the Timekeeper. Timekeeper, Sir Pertelope.'

For his part, Pertelope looked like someone who has just been told that the sun rises in the east because of horticulture. He furrowed his brows.

'Excuse me,' he said, 'but could somebody please explain what's going on?'

The Timekeeper shrugged – a gesture which would have been rather more elegant if it hadn't involved the movement of quite so much rusty sheet metal – and removed the iron drum to reveal a young, freckled and quite unmistakably female face; fourteen going on fifteen, at a guess, and with braces on her teeth.

'It'th all right,' she said, 'I'll ecthplain. I'm uthed to it,' she added. 'But thirtht, can I get out of all thith bloody armour?'

There was a confusing interval while she peeled off the metalwork. It was like watching a destroyer getting undressed.

'That'th better,' sighed the Timekeeper. She was now dressed in a scarlet boiler suit and silver trainers, and stood about five feet two in them. The revolver was still in her hand, but probably only because there wasn't anywhere to put it down that wasn't covered in sheet steel. 'I'm throm a thpathethip,' she said.

'I see,' commented Pertelope unconvincingly.

'It'th very thimple,' the Timekeeper went on, standing on one foot and massaging the other vigorously. 'There'th ten of uth, and we were put into orbit in a time capthule travelling at just over the thpeed of light.'

'The Relativity Marketing Board,' Lamorak interrupted. 'It was the biggest scientific experiment ever attempted. Years ahead of its time,' he added.

'Yeth,' said the Timekeeper, bitterly, 'ecthept the thools went and thent uth off in the wrong direction. Inthtead of going into the Thuture, we went into the Patht.'

'Sheer carelessness,' said Lamorak sadly. 'Somebody forgot to read the instruction manual, apparently.'

'And they thorgot to pack any thood,' the Timekeeper added, 'which meanth every tho ofen one of uth hath to take the ethcape capthule down to thome detherted thpot on the Thurthathe and forage for provithionth. Gueth whothe turn it wath thith time.'

Pertelope gave Lamorak a bewildered look. 'How do you know all that, Lammo?' he asked.

'Simple,' the knight replied. 'I met one of them – oh, two hundred and fifty years ago now, maybe more. Not you,' he added to the Timekeeper, 'one of your, er, colleagues. He was about nine years old, with sort of carroty red hair.'

The Timekeeper nodded. 'That thoundth like Thimon,' she said. 'I'll warn him to ecthpect you.'

Pertelope was about to say 'But—' again, but Lamorak forestalled him.

'Our past is their future, you see,' he explained, 'so although I've already met – Simon, was it? Yes, I remember now – he won't meet me for another two and a half centuries, or whatever it is in his timescale. And of course, where we get older as time passes, they get younger.'

The Timekeeper nodded. 'I wath thorty-thicth onthe,' she said savagely, 'and now look at me. And having thethe thodding thingth on my teeth doethn't help.'

'It must be awful,' agreed Lamorak. 'Why don't you take them off and the hell with it?'

'Becauthe,' the Timekeeper replied sadly, 'when I wath thorty-thicth I had really thraight even teeth and no thillingth. Which meanth I've got to wear thucking bratheth and bruth three timeth a day, otherwithe it'll cauthe a temporal paradocth. It'th a real bummer.' She paused for a moment, as something jammed in her mind. 'Hold on,' she said. 'How can you have met Thimon two hundred and thithty yearth ago? You'd be dead by now.'

It was Lamorak's turn to sigh.

'Let me explain,' he said.

Not far away, a real kangaroo – one without golden hooves or a horn in the middle of its forehead – was bounding happily along, its mind occupied with the one great mystery which obsesses the consciousness of the species; to the extent that it has stopped them dead in their evolutionary tracks and prevented them from developing into the hyper-intelligent super-lifeforms they would otherwise have become.

Namely; how come, no matter how careful you are about what you put in your pockets, in the end you always find two paperclips, a fluff-covered boiled sweet and a small, worthless copper coin at the bottom of them?

It had just come to the conclusion that the Devil creeps up and puts them there while you're asleep, when a terrifying apparition shot up out of a hollow in the rocks, waved its arms and grinned fearfully. The kangaroo stopped dead in mid-hop, landed awkwardly, and twisted its ankle. The force of the landing jerked a shirt button and a scrap of peppermint wrapper out of its pouch, and the wind bore them away.

The monster advanced, slowly and with infinite menace. Behind it, a man with a camera and another with a big tape-recorder put their heads up above the escarpment. The monster was talking, apparently to itself.

'These spectacular creatures,' it was saying, 'the world's largest true marsupials, hounded by mankind to the verge of extinction in some parts of the Outback . . .'

The kangaroo cowered back on to its hind paws and raised its forepaws feebly; whether to make a show of aggression or to hide behind them was far from clear. The monster continued to advance.

'And now,' it was saying. 'I'm going to try and get in close to the kangaroo, and if we're really lucky we might for the first time ever be able to show you . . .'

The kangaroo tried to move; but completely without success. It fought the urge to grin feebly and wave into the camera with every fibre of its being. It failed.

'The largest species – Barry, can you zoom in on the little bugger's head please – the largest species of kangaroo, the Red, can leap twenty-five feet at a single bound and clear objects six feet high,' said the monster. 'I'm going to see if I can get close enough for you to see in detail . . .'

The spell broke. With a shrill bark of terror, the kangaroo launched itself into the air, twisted frantically round and bounded away, pursued by strange and distinctly unfriendly cries from the monster. Only after half an hour's high-speed bounding did it stop, crouch down and drag breath into its heaving lungs.

And then stiffen in cold despair; for just behind its shoulder it could hear the sound of human breathing, and that terrible voice, saying:

'And if we're extremely quiet, we might just be able – Kieron, if you scare the bugger this time I'll make you swallow your polariser – we might just be able to get a glimpse of its . . .'

A single massive jump might just reach the edge of that rock over there, but why bother? There was clearly no point.

With a soft, despairing cough, the kangaroo turned,

faced the camera and waggled its forepaws, hating itself almost to death.

'Let'th get thith thtraight, thall we?' said the Timekeeper, after a long, long pause. 'You're really ecthpecting me to believe that you're a pair of Arthurian knighth on a quetht to find an *apron*?'

'Yes.'

'Fine.' A sharper than usual pair of eyes would have seen her suspended disbelief bobbing for a moment above her head before drifting away on the breeze. 'And that'th what you need the tied-up horthe for?'

'The horthe?'

'*Horthe*, yeth.'

'Oh I see, the horse.' Lamorak scratched his head. He was hot, tired, confused, overdosed to the eyebrows with tinned peaches and dying of toothache. He didn't really want to do any more explaining just at the moment. 'It's not a horse,' he said, 'not as such.'

Just then the unicorn woke up, struggled ineffectually in its bonds, and embarked on a stream of invective.

'Hey,' said the Timekeeper, 'the horthe jutht thaid thomething.'

'Yes, only it isn't a—'

'Listen, you bastards,' screamed the unicorn. 'Tell that flamin' sheila that if she calls me a bloody horse just one more time, then so help me—'

Pertelope, showing more intelligence than anyone would have given him credit for, grabbed a sugar-lump and slapped it into the unicorn's mouth. The tirade broke off abruptly, and was replaced by a crunching sound.

423

'If it'th not a horthe,' whispered the Timekeeper, 'then what ith it?'

Lamorak sighed. 'It's a unicorn,' he said. 'Satisfied?'

'Oh.'

'And now, we've got to get on with what we were doing, and I'm sure your colleagues are getting very hungry up there in orbit, so . . .'

'What do you need a unicorn for?'

It took Lamorak just over six seconds to count to ten slowly under his breath. 'If you must know,' he said, 'we want it as bait to catch a maiden of unspotted virtue.'

The Timekeeper looked at him. 'You'th got that the wrong way round, you know.'

Lamorak prised his lips apart into a smile. 'Have we? Oh *damn*. That *is* a nuisance, isn't it, Per? Oh well, it's back to the drawing board for us, then. Thanks for the tip, anyway. And now we really must be getting along.'

'And bethideth,' continued the Timekeeper, 'you thaid you were questhting for an apron, not a maiden of unthpotted . . .'

'It's her apron,' said Sir Pertelope.

'Ith it?'

'Yes.'

After the unicorns came the convicts.

There were two waves of them. The second wave arrived with the First Fleet in 1788, seven hundred years after the first wave.

The aborigines, whose permission nobody bothered to ask, had a phrase for it. One damned thing after another, they said.

★ ★ ★

424

The first man in the first wave to set eyes on Australia had been the overseer. His first reaction was to shudder slightly. Then he jumped down from the observation platform and told the drummer to stop marking time.

'Right,' he shouted, 'everybody out.'

Nobody moved. Two thousand dragon-headed prows bobbed silently up and down in the still waters of Botany Bay.

The overseer blinked. 'Did you lot hear what I said?' he yelled. 'Everybody off the ships, now.'

'We're not going.'

The voice came from behind an oar in the third row back. It was backed up by a mumbled chorus of That's Rights and You Tell Hims. The overseer started to perspire.

'What did you just say?' he demanded. The faint blur of grey smoke behind the oar coruscated in the sunlight. If it had had shoulders, it might well have been shrugging them.

'I said we're not bloody going,' it replied evenly. 'We can see into the future. It sucks. We stay here.'

In the back of the overseer's mind, a little voice nervously started asking around to see if anyone had any ideas about what should be done next. The overseer's hands were more positive. They reached for the big knotted whip hanging from his belt.

'We'll soon see about that,' he said, and he aimed a ferocious blow at the cloud of smoke.

'Idiot.'

With aggravating slowness, the wisps of smoke coalesced into a cloud once more. There was an expectant silence.

'There's no way you can force us to get off the ship, you know,' went on the voice, calmly. 'So you might as well accept the situation, turn this thing round and head for home. Yes?'

'No,' said the overseer.

He was sweating heavily now.

He hadn't wanted to come in the first place. When he'd joined the company, all those years ago, he'd seen his future career developing in an entirely different direction. After five years or so loading sides of bacon on to the ships and sailing them from Copenhagen to Dover, he reckoned, he'd have proved himself the sort of man they could use in marketing. There would follow an orderly progression, from sales representative to assistant sales manager, then regional sales manager, then sales director, and so on until he was given overall responsibility for the whole Danish operation in Albion. And here he was, ten years later, trying to cajole a boatful of deported supernatural entities into colonising New South Cambria. Something, somewhere, had gone wrong.

'Please?' he said.

There was a swirling of mists and fogs the length of the ship that left him feeling dizzy. He could feel the roof of his mouth getting dry.

Two thousand longships; each one crammed to overflowing with minor divinities. There were river-gods, wood-nymphs, fire-spirits, elves, wills o' the wisp, pixies, chthonic deities, earth-mothers, thunder-demons, even a few metaphysical abstractions huddled wretchedly at the back and insisting on soft lavatory paper. As part of the dismantling of the magical culture of Albion, her entire population of supernatural bit-

426

players had been rounded up and sent to Van Demon's Land.

The overseer dug his fingernails into the palms of his hands and took a deep breath. 'Come along now, people,' he wheedled, 'you'll like it once you get there, promise.'

'Nuts.'

'But there's rivers,' whined the overseer. 'Majestic, awe-inspiring torrents, crashing over dizzying waterfalls, winding lugubriously through ancestral forests. There's deserts. There's rock formations any red-quartzed troll'd give his right arm to live in. There's bush fires that make Hell look like a camping stove. What in God's name are you complaining about? It's a bloody spook's paradise out there.'

'There are also,' said the spokeswraith, 'spiders.'

There was a soft thunk as the overseer's jaw dropped on to the studded collar round his neck. 'What was that?' he gasped.

'And snakes.'

'And mosquitoes.'

'And,' added the spokeswraith meaningfully, 'it's not as if it's exactly got vacant possession, you know. The whole place is absolutely crawling with . . .'

With a massive effort, the overseer hoisted his jaw back into place. 'Yes?'

'You know,' replied the smoke-cloud diffidently. 'Things. It's really *creepy* out there, you know?'

'They go around singing all the time,' ventured a voice from the last bench but one. 'It's enough to give you the willies.'

'Bloody unsocial hours, too,' added a scratching, grinding sound from somewhere near the middle of the

427

ship. 'Dream-time-and-a-half, that sort of thing.'

'Let's get this straight,' said the overseer, with an ever so slightly unbalanced lilt in his voice. 'All you ghouls and ghosts and things that go bump in the night are refusing to get off the ship because you think the place is *haunted*?'

'Yes.'

'Be reasonable,' added the scratching sound – a fever-wraith from the Plumstead Marshes – 'they're natives, they're used to living here, we're not. They'd have us for breakfast. If you turn us off the ship, it'd be mass murder. Exorcism. Whatever.'

The overseer lowered his head, stuck his hands in his pockets – where, inevitably, he found a small piece of string, a half-eaten apple and two small bronze coins of purely nominal value – and thought about it for a while; then he retired into the helmsman's cabin and banged his head against the ship's wheel for a while. Oddly enough, it helped, because when he emerged he knew exactly what he was going to do.

And it worked. It was, of course, bitterly unfair on the indigenous paranormals; and it has to go down as one of the biggest stains on the superhuman rights record of the English nation. Now, however, it's far too late to do anything about it, because within five years of the arrival of the deported spirits from Albion, the native deities had been completely wiped out, leaving the entire continent empty to receive the newcomers. In due course, they settled in, adapted themselves to their new environment and evolved an entirely original lifestyle of their own which bore no resemblance whatsoever to the culture they had left behind them, and which survived for seven hundred years before being completely destroyed by the coming of the First Fleet.

Which, so the aborigines say, served the buggers bloody well right.

'Tho what did they actually *do* to the native thpiritth?' the Timekeeper demanded. Lamorak winced. He hated this part of the story. It was, he had always felt, enough to make one ashamed of being Albionese.

'They methylated them,' he replied quietly. 'Well, it's been really nice meeting you,' he said, 'and I look forward very much to having met you before, but unless we make a start immediately we're going to be very, very late. Ciao.' He picked up his rucksack, slung it on his back and advanced purposefully towards the unicorn.

'That'th horrible,' said the Timekeeper, and shuddered. 'But it thtill doethn't ecthplain about the apron and the unicorn.'

'Very true,' replied Lamorak over his shoulder. 'Right then, Per, you grab hold of the rope while I push.'

'The apron,' said Pertelope, 'was a talisman belonging to one of the deported spirits. It has magical powers of its own. We managed to track it down, through newspaper reports of unexplained happenings which could only have been caused by the apron, and it turns out to be owned by a maiden of unspotted virtue living in Sydney. Hence the unicorn.'

'I thee,' murmured the Timekeeper. 'At leatht I think I thee. What thort of unecthplained happeningth?'

Lamorak smiled unpleasantly. 'It's kind of hard to explain,' he said.

The Timekeeper was not amused. 'Try me,' she said.

'Football results,' said Pertelope. 'The apron plays merry hell with the results of Australian Rules football matches. All we had to do once we knew that was to plot all the results on a big graph and wait until a significant mutation in the sine curve became apparent.'

'And?'

'Paramatta Under-Twelves 22, Sydney 0,' Lamorak growled. 'Which was as good as putting up a big neon sign saying OVER HERE.' He paused and scowled. 'I can explain the mathematics of it in very great detail if you want me to,' he added.

'No thankth,' said the Timekeeper, and Lamorak noticed that her eyes looked as if someone had accidentally slapped three coats of weatherproof varnish over them. 'Actually,' she went on, 'it'th time I wath getting along, tho . . .'

'Of course. We quite understand. Right, Per, when I say heave . . . Per? What the hell are you staring at?'

Pertelope was standing bolt upright, his face contorted into an expression of terminal sheepishness. He swallowed once or twice, raised his left arm and waggled his fingers.

'Smile, Lammo,' he hissed out of the side of his mouth. 'I think we're on television.'

Faster than the speed of light is very fast. And, it goes without saying, dark.

'Ouch.'

'Sorry.'

'That was my foot.'

'Yes, all right, I said I'm sorry.'

'Well, mind where you're going next time.'

Sleek, streamlined, virtually frictionless and as devoid of light as six feet up a drainpipe, the mighty starcruiser pounced like a giant cat across the vastness of space. Far below – so far that distance became just another deceptive illusion – the earth spun on its languorous axis, while Time found itself dragged inexorably up the down escalator.

'For crying out loud, George, watch what you're doing with that bloody kettle.'

'Sorry.'

'You'd have thought the dozy cow would've been back by now. I'm *starving*.'

'So are the rest of us, Simon. The difference is, *we* don't make such a great big performance out of it.'

'Oh yes? And who asked for your opinion, Priscilla?'

'I'm not Priscilla, I'm Annabel.'

'And I'm Priscilla. You just put your teacup down on my head.'

'God, sorry, Priscilla.'

'I'm not Priscilla, I'm George.'

Aboard the starship *Timekeeper*, there are three levels of Time: earth time; relative time; and the time they'd all been cooped up on this small, cramped and above all *dark* spaceship. The third variety had the weirdest properties of all. It seemed to last for ever.

'Look, this is hopeless. I'm going out for a pizza. Anybody else fancy coming?'

'Listen, George . . .'

'Trevor. I'm George.'

'Listen, Trevor, you just can't do that. This is a scientific experiment, right? We're playing sillybuggers with the fabric of causality as it is; I mean, God only knows what damage we're doing just by being here. If you suddenly touch down in the middle of the twentieth century and start stuffing yourself with a deep-pan quattro stagione, there's no limit to what could happen. So just sit down and shut up, okay?'

There was complete silence.

'I said *okay*, Trevor?'

'I'm not Trevor, I'm Nick.'

'Where's Trevor, then?'

'How the hell am I supposed to know that, Louise? There's no light in here.'

'Actually, I'm not Louise, I'm Angela. Who the hell is Louise, anyway?'

Meanwhile, the second escape capsule roared away across the indescribable magnitude of Nothing, piloted by a ninety-seven-year-old child, straight as an arrow towards where he remembered the best pizza restaurant in the world used to be. The problem was that it wasn't open yet; it wouldn't be open for seventy years.

There was complete silence, except for the unicorn. It raised its head, saw the maiden of unspotted virtue, blushed, and said 'G'day' awkwardly, and started chewing the cud ferociously.

Then, very slowly, Lamorak reached out for Pertelope's pack, took out the sponge bag and found the oil of cloves; then he drank it, wiped his mouth on his sleeve, and smiled.

'Hello there,' he said.

'Actually, Lammo,' Pertelope hissed, 'you're not supposed to drink it, you're supposed to—'

432

'Shut up, Per, I know what I'm doing.' Lamorak stood up, brushed dust off his trouser-knees and walked up to the maiden of unspotted virtue.

'Swap,' he said. 'My unicorn for your apron. How about it?'

The maiden of unspotted virtue stared at him. 'Have you gone out of your tiny mind?' she said.

Lamorak raised an eyebrow. 'I'm sorry,' he said, 'I don't quite follow. Straight swap. You get your award for best nature programme, I get the apron, everybody's happy. Where's the problem in that?'

There are many cold places on earth, but few of them are as cold as two feet away from the maiden's eyes. 'Listen, whoever you are,' she said. 'I'm trying to make a serious film here. If I go home and tell my producer I've got ten minutes' footage of live unicorns in the can, I'm going to spend the rest of my career filming the weather forecast. Now will you please both go away? You're frightening the kangaroos.'

For perhaps the first time ever, Lamorak was at a slight loss for words. After considerable effort, he managed to say, 'But it's a *unicorn*.' The maiden of unspotted virtue sighed.

'Buster,' she said, 'I don't care if it's a performing woolly mammoth. I have my credibility as a serious wildlife presenter to think of. Understood?'

'But it's a—'

'Quite.' The maiden pursed her lips. 'That's fine. You take it along to the satellite boys, they'll probably give it its own chat show. Meanwhile, some of us have work to do, so if you wouldn't mind . . .'

Lamorak said nothing. Even if he could have found any words appropriate for the situation, he'd have had

433

difficulty saying them with his lower jaw hanging loose like a second-hand drawbridge. He shook his head in disbelief, turned away and sat down under a rock.

'Excuse me,' Pertelope said.

'Well?'

'I think,' Pertelope said, 'there may have been a slight misunderstanding here. You do have the apron, don't you?'

'What apron?'

'Ah. So you're not a maiden of unspotted virtue?'

A moment or so later, Pertelope picked himself up off the ground, rubbed his jaw and joined his colleague under the rock.

'Something must have gone wrong,' he said.

Lamorak nodded. 'Wrong bloody maiden,' he replied. 'I mean, how the devil was I supposed to know there were *two* of . . .?' He broke off. A horrible thought had just occurred to him.

'Oh *shit*,' he said. 'Of course. Why didn't I realise?'

Pertelope looked up at him. 'What do you mean?'

'The football results. We must have misinterpreted them. Here, hand me your rucksack, quick.'

Pertelope did as he was told; and, while the maiden of unspotted virtue and her camera crew raced off into the distance, with a doomed kangaroo a mere ten yards in front of them, he thumbed through the Sports section of *What's On In Sydney.*

'Per,' he said at last, closing the book, 'you might have told me that Lightning Darren O'Shea had signed for the Paramatta Under-Twelves.'

Pertelope registered dismay. 'Oh drat,' he said. 'Yes, that does put rather a different complexion on it, I suppose. What do we do now?'

434

The Timekeeper leant over the rock and cleared her throat. 'We could eat,' she suggested.

'Not peaches, please,' Lamorak sighed. 'Not right now, I couldn't face it.'

The Timekeeper grinned. 'All right,' she said, 'how doeth thcallop chowder, chicken with bathil and oregano and apricotth in brandy thtrike you?' By way of explanation, she opened her shopping bag and produced three large tins. 'I'll just thet up the tholar-powered microwathe and we're in buthineth.'

Lamorak smiled wryly. 'Why not?' he replied. 'And afterwards, could you give us a lift in this spaceship of yours? Otherwise it's going to be a long walk.'

'Thure thing.' The Timekeeper took a small tin cube from her pocket, pressed a knob on the back, and held it at arm's length. It grew into a microwave oven.

'Only don't tell anyone you'the theen one of thethe, becauthe they haven't been invented yet,' she added. 'You could thet off a complete Dark Age with one of thethe thingth.'

'No problem,' Lamorak replied. 'You keep stumm about the unicorn, we'll forget about the technology.'

The Timekeeper laughed and set to work with a tin-opener. It was some time since she'd used it last, and she nearly burnt a hole the size of a large geological fault in the landscape before she got the atomiser beam properly adjusted, but there was no harm done.

'That still doesn't explain things, Lammo,' Pertelope was saying, and his voice sounded remarkably like the buzzing of a fly against a windscreen.

Lamorak shook his head and said, 'Not now, Per. Later, perhaps.'

Pertelope scowled at him. 'But Lammo,' he said, 'it

435

doesn't matter about Lightning Darren O'Shea, because it says here his brother Norman is now playing for the Melbourne Werewolves, and that means the x-coefficient no longer reciprocates the reflected tangent of pi—'

'Later, Per.' Lamorak closed his eyes, settled his head against his rucksack and lay back. You know, he said to himself, I could get to like failure after a while. It's so much more relaxing . . .

And then he sat bolt upright again, and grabbed for the book.

'Told you,' Pertelope was saying. 'And of course we'd have to recalculate the differential shift in the y-axis.'

Lamorak wasn't listening. He was staring at the Timekeeper; who had opened the tins and emptied their contents into little plastic bowls, which she was loading into the machine.

'Nearly ready,' she said.

'Great,' Lamorak replied, trying to sound calm. 'Tell me, when it was your turn to go shopping, why did you come here?'

'It'th where my tholks came throm, originally,' she replied. 'Of courthe, I don't thuppothe it'th anything like it'll be in their day, but . . .'

'I see,' Lamorak said. 'Um, that's a nice pinny you've got on, if I may say so.'

The Timekeeper smiled. 'You think tho? Actually, it'th been in my thamily for yearth. Nithe embroidery round the edgeth, look. Thlowerth and thingth.'

The two knights exchanged glances. Then Lamorak drew Pertelope to one side.

'All right,' he said, 'you're obviously thinking the same as me.'

'It'd explain the distortion in the base coefficient, certainly,' Pertelope replied. 'It's a very interesting effect, actually, because—'

'Yes, all right, I believe you.' Lamorak drew in a deep breath, then let it go. 'Look,' he said, 'one of us is going to have to ask her, and I think it's probably your turn. Okay?'

'Ask her what, Lammo?'

'Never mind,' Lamorak replied. 'Forget I spoke.'

The Timekeeper shut the oven door and twiddled the dial a couple of times. 'It'll be about three min-uteth,' she said. 'Tho that'th a unicorn, ith it? I've alwayth wanted to thee a real unicorn.'

'Bingo,' muttered Lamorak under his breath. At her age, *and* with those braces on her teeth, I don't need to ask, I just *know*. 'Can I just have a closer look at that apron thing for a moment?' he asked.

There are two ways of landing a spaceship escape capsule on the surface.

The first way is to ease your way down through the upper atmosphere and sidle back into gravity with the aid of your stabiliser rockets. The alternative method is to keep on going until you hit the ground. This technique should on no account be confused with crashing, although the net result is more or less the same.

Fortunately, anything that happens to the landscape of the Great Victoria Desert is almost certain to improve it, and Trevor would no doubt have been only too pleased had he known that in years to come (long after he was born, in fact) the enormous crater brought into being by his textbook Method II landing would be flooded with water and turned into Australia's first inland surfing park, with tides automatically stimulated by a huge solar-powered turbine.

As he dragged himself out of the remains of the cockpit, however, all he could think of was the rather depressing fact that his spacecraft had had its chips, which meant that unless he could find the foraging party, he was going to have to stay here for the rest of his life. Quite apart from the fact that he seemed to have landed in a distinctly unprepossessing spot, he faced the horrible prospect of reverting to the normal life-pattern of a surface-dweller, with all the morale-sapping repetition that would entail. It's bad enough turning thirty once in one's lifetime. Having to do it twice is enough to make anybody very depressed indeed.

And even that unattractive prospect, he realised, was going to be pretty remote unless he found something to eat. Quickly.

He had been trudging generally eastwards for about half an hour when the smell of something edible floated past him on the sluggish desert breeze. He stopped in his tracks and concentrated. About thirty seconds of intense inhaling satisfied him that it wasn't some sort of olfactory mirage. If the smell was simply a product of his imagination, then his imagination wouldn't have put so much garlic in it. He walked quickly in the direction he guessed the scent was coming from, later breaking into a run.

'It's not for me, you understand,' Lamorak said hastily. 'It's for a friend of mine.'

The Timekeeper continued to stare at him. 'A friend

of yourth,' she repeated. 'A friend of yourth who liketh drething up in women'th clotheth.' She shot a glance at Pertelope, and then added, '*Another* friend of yourth who liketh drething up in women'th clotheth. I *thee*.'

'Now hang on a minute,' Pertelope started to say, but Lamorak ignored him. 'It's not like that,' he said. 'Look, we're on this quest, right, and we've got to recover the Holy Grail, okay, which means that—'

The Timekeeper raised her ladle threateningly. 'I'd thtay right there ith I wath you,' she hissed. Or rather hithed.

'Now look . . .' Lamorak began to say; then he broke off, bent double and clutched his jaw. 'Now look what you've done,' he mumbled.

'He's got toothache,' Pertelope explained. He was like that, of course; he was also perfectly capable of explaining that you were getting wet because it was raining, and that you'd just broken your leg because you'd fallen off your ladder.

'Nethertheleth,' replied the Timekeeper grimly, and swung the ladle demonstratively. You don't get to stay a maiden of unspotted virtue for long on a pitch dark spaceship without knowing how to handle heavy kitchen implements. She backed away, didn't look where she was going, and tripped over the unicorn.

Startled out of its narcotic dreams (in which, behind a bush with a gang of other unicorns, it lay in wait for a maiden of tarnished virtue to be attracted by a tethered kangaroo), the unicorn started, kicked against the ropes restraining its legs, and succeeded in loosening them.

'Right, you bunch of Pommy woofters,' it started to say; and then the Timekeeper fell on it, knocking it out cold. It subsided into a heap, taking up its dream where it had left off.

'Don't just stand there, you pillock,' Lamorak shouted. 'Grab the bloody apron.'

Pertelope hesitated. On the one hand, he was a Knight of the Table Round, and he distinctly remembered the bit in the rule book about succouring damsels in distress. He mentioned this.

'So?'

'So I should be succouring, shouldn't I?'

'Right,' Lamorak snarled. 'And the thing to remember about succouring is never to give them an even break. Now move!'

'Oh,' Pertelope replied. 'That's what it means. I always thought it meant—' He got no further than this, because the Timekeeper belted him across the head with her ladle.

Lamorak said something under his breath – it rhymed with *pit* – and made a half-hearted sort of lunge. He was hampered by the fact that he was trying to shield his jaw with his body, and only succeeded in putting his foot in the Timekeeper's discarded armour. There was a crash, and he landed heavily.

'Thcumbag,' the Timekeeper yelled, and raised the ladle above her head. Then she froze.

'If it's any consolation,' Lamorak said after a while, 'I really don't feel good about doing this.' He waggled the Timekeeper's revolver, which had somehow found its way into his hand when he landed. 'One, it's unchivalrous. Two, it's an anachronism. Three, these things terrify the life out of me. On the other hand . . .'

The Timekeeper wasn't listening. She was looking at something over Lamorak's left shoulder, while trying to do high-level semaphore with her eyebrows.

'Don't give me that,' Lamorak sighed. 'Oldest trick in the book, that is, pretending to see something so's I turn round, and then you hit me with—'

Then he too fell silent, as Trevor thumped him hard on the side of the jaw with a rock.

The true origin of the Apron of Invincibility will probably never be known.

One school would have it that the apron was worn by the head chef at Belshazzar's feast, and the distinctive red marks down the front are all the remains of the venison casserole, spilt there by the chef when he saw a huge hand materialise out of thin air and start writing graffiti on the walls of his newly decorated taverna.

Others claim that the red marks are the stains left by the particularly virulent Algerian beaujolais served to the guests at the wedding at Cana just before the wine finally ran out. This view is substantiated to a certain extent by the fact that generations of owners have done their best to bleach them out, but without success.

Still others say that the red marks are just red marks, and that the Apron is a seventh-century Byzantine forgery; although what it's a forgery of, nobody even pretends to know.

Whatever the truth of the matter is, the fact remains that the Apron has curious properties which cannot be explained in rational terms. For example; the touch of its hem cures certain extremely rare varieties of scrofula (not a particularly useful property, this, since the bacteria in question are so rare that they count as protected species, and anyone harming them is liable to a substantial fine); it mucks up Aussie Rules football like nothing else on earth; and a sponge cake baked by a person wearing it will invariably turn out as hard as millstone.

After a while, Lamorak came round. He shook his head and gathered together the splinters of his memory.

He realised that he was feeling a lot better.

Something sharp was digging into his neck. He fished around inside his shirt, and found a dislodged tooth. He seemed to recognise it from somewhere.

'Ah,' he said. 'Good.'

He looked up, and saw the barrel of the revolver. Behind it stood the Timekeeper and another figure, similarly dressed, male, its jaw moving steadily.

'Threethe,' rasped the Timekeeper. 'Or Trethor here'll drill you full of holeth.'

It'th okay,' Lamorak replied, 'don't thoot. Oh thit,' he added, rubbing his swollen jaw. 'You'the got me at it now.'

'What the hell's going on here, anyway?' Trevor enquired, with his mouth full. 'The fight. The unconscious guy in the frock. The horse with a flagpole up its nose. I mean, what is this?'

Lamorak grinned painfully. 'Let me ecthplain,' he said.

'I'the got a better ...' The Timekeeper growled impatiently, opened her mouth, and pulled out two little strips of shiny metal. 'That's better,' she said, stuffing them in her pocket. 'The hell with dental consistency. I've got a better idea, Trevor. Let's tie these two idiots up and get back to the ship, okay?'

Trevor shrugged. 'Please yourself,' he said. 'What'll we tie them up with?'

Lamorak coughed politely. 'Ith I may make a thug-gethtion,' he said.

The Apron of Invincibility, torn into thin strips, produced enough material to keep the knights securely bound for six hours; at the end of which they were released by a party of wandering Fruit Monks on their way to replenish the cache of tinned lychees at Ayers Rock.

On their return to Albion, the knights entrusted the job of restoring the Apron to the Sisters of Incongruity, an even smaller and more secretive order who devote themselves to prayer, meditation, needlework and spot-the-ball competitions (from which source is de-rived the fabulous wealth of the community). Three months of round-the-clock work resulted in an Apron that was almost, but not quite, as good as new. True, it no longer affected the outcome of football matches; on the other hand, it developed a quite staggering knack of turning anything left overnight in its pockets into small balls of disintegrating paper, discarded fruit-gum wrappings, delaminated metro tickets and de-monetised fifty-lire coins.

4

'Admit it, Turkey,' said Bedevere, 'we're lost.'

You can tell of the Hanging Gardens of Babylon, or the Colossus of Rhodes; if you're looking for the world's great wonders, try a knight of an ancient order of chivalry coping with a statement of the painfully obvious.

'I know we're lost,' Turquine replied cheerfully, folding the road map and shoving it under the seat of the van. 'We're supposed to be lost. If we weren't lost, we'd be going the wrong way.'

Bedevere looked at him.

'After all,' Turquine went on, 'we're looking for a lost city. *The* lost city. Therefore . . .'

'Yes,' said Bedevere patiently, 'point taken. But right now, we aren't looking for Atlantis, we're looking for the M6.'

Turquine grinned. 'Not necessarily,' he replied.

When Bedevere made an uncharacteristically impatient gesture, Turquine went on: 'You don't seem to have tumbled to it yet, young Bedders. We're talking mysticism here.' He broke off to avoid and swear at a T-registration Allegro which had churlishly insisted on its right of way on the roundabout.* 'You remember what old Beaky Maledisant used to say about mysticism.'

Bedevere confessed that he'd forgotten. Turquine nodded.

'Thought you had,' he said. 'I seem to remember you spending the Wisdom lessons looking out of the window at the girls from the—'

'Anyway,' said Bedevere.

Turquine changed gear noisily. 'The point is,' he said, 'if you're looking for a lost city, or a lost priory, or a hermit's cell under an enchantment of oblivion, anything like that, it's no good going through the index at the back of the *A–Z*; you've got to get lost yourself. Then it sort of finds you. That's,' he added proudly, 'logic.'

Bedevere raised an eyebrow. 'Logic?' he asked.

---

*By right of his position as Seigneur de Montcalm and Earl-Banneret of Belfort, Turquine had a hereditary right of precedence over traffic feeding in from the right on roundabouts; and, being Turquine, insisted on exercising it even against articulated lorries and bulk tankers. His ambition was to cause an accident and get charged with reckless driving, so that he could stand up in court and produce the original charter, bearing the seal of Uther Pendragon. Unfortunately, all the drivers he pulled out in front of without warning either had hair-trigger reflexes or ABS brakes.

'Well,' Turquine replied, shrugging, 'theology, then. All those that are lost shall be found, or words to that effect. Hell fire and buggery,' he added, staring at a road sign, 'that's the Stirchley turn-off. How the devil did we get here?'

Bedevere smiled wanly. 'Theology, probably,' he said. 'That and taking the wrong exit back at Brownhills. You want the A37.'

'Give me the map a minute,' Turquine said. 'I know a short-cut that should . . .'

Bedevere was about to protest, from long experience of Turquine's short-cuts, when it occurred to him that all that stuff about being lost on purpose sounded uncomfortably reasonable. 'Great,' he said, therefore, and even added, 'Good idea.'

Turquine's short-cut, predictably, took them up a single-lane cul-de-sac terminating in a deserted farmyard. They always did. In fact, Bedevere had often felt, if only one took the trouble to get out of the car and have a look, it would probably turn out to be the same farmyard each time. Which made sense, somehow . . .

'Right,' he said, releasing his seat-belt and opening the door, 'we're here.'

Turquine looked at him.

'What on earth are you doing?' he asked.

'Following your premise to its logical conclusion,' Bedevere replied, grabbing his haversack from the back of the van and putting on his hat. 'Coming?'

'But . . .'

Bedevere smiled nicely, slammed the door and set off towards the farmhouse. After a moment's therapeutic blaspheming, Turquine followed him.

'You see,' Bedevere explained, as they squelched

446

through the slurry, 'if you've got to be lost in order to find a lost city, it follows that you've got to be as lost as humanly possible. I think a farmyard up a five-mile lane with grass growing up the middle of it is about as lost as we can get without actually poking our eyes out with a stick, don't you?'

He smiled and knocked at the door. Surprisingly quickly, the door opened.

'Good afternoon,' Bedevere said. 'We're looking for Atlantis. Can you put us on the right road?'

The woman who had answered the door looked as if she probably could, in a sense. She struck Bedevere as the sort of woman who has a son called Oak and two daughters called Skychild and Mistletoe, and she was wearing rather a lot of that peculiar silver jewellery that nobody ever buys at craft fairs.

'Sorry?' she said.

'Atlantis,' Bedevere repeated. 'You know . . .'

'Oh,' said the woman, 'yes, right. You don't look the type, that's all. You'd better follow me.'

She led the way into the house, and Turquine and Bedevere exchanged looks.

'That's probably the nicest thing anyone's ever said about me,' whispered Turquine under his breath. 'God, this place smells a bit.' He sniffed distastefully. 'Looks like they go in for the old wacky baccy around here.'

The woman opened a door and stepped aside.

'In here,' she said. 'You know what to do.'

It was an odd room, in context. It was, Bedevere decided, exactly like the more fashionable sort of building society, except that there were no girls in uniform sitting behind the computer screens. Not a pentangle or a cabalistic sign in sight.

'If you need anything,' the woman said, 'we're all in the scullery, meditating.' She closed the door, and the knights could hear the plopping of her bare feet in the corridor.

For about a minute, neither of them spoke. Then Bedevere shrugged.

'All right,' he said, 'maybe we should have gone left at the Shard End underpass.'

Turquine sat down behind one of the screens. 'Not at all,' he said. 'I think I'm getting the hang of this. Neat,' he added, with a hint of admiration. He closed his eyes, flexed his fingers like a concert pianist, and dabbed the keyboard at random.

'After all,' he said, as the screen went blank and the machine beeped a couple of times, 'there's lost, and there's lost. Now, then.'

'Do you know how to work one of those things?' Bedevere asked.

'Previous experience is not essential,' Turquine replied. 'Think of a number.'

'Seven.'

'And why not?' Turquine tapped a key. 'For example,' he went on, 'when was the last time you had any dealings with the Inland Revenue?'

Bedevere blushed. 'I . . .' he said.

'All right,' said Turquine, 'the telephone people, DVLC, British Gas, any of that mob. People who use computers a lot.'

'They all have screens at the office,' said Bedevere, the insurance salesman.

'And,' Turquine went on, 'what's the commonest explanation for things getting cocked up?'

'Lost in the computer, of course,' Bedevere said automatically, and then bit his lip. 'Oh,' he said, 'yes. I think I see what you're getting at.'

Turquine smirked. 'Took your time, didn't you?' he said. 'How to lose something while still permitting it to exist. Feed it into the computer. Easy. I mean, it'll be in there somewhere; it's just lost, that's all, along with half a million renewal notices, paid parking tickets, standing orders, estimated meter readings and revised assessments. And all you need to do to get it back again is type in the magic word.'

Bedevere smiled, full of admiration. 'Which is?'

'Ah,' Turquine wheeled round on the swivel chair. 'There you have me. Still, we're almost there.'

Bedevere slumped a little; then he perked up. 'Absolutely,' he said. 'Allow me.'

He pushed Turquine gently out of the chair, sat down and rubbed his hands. 'They do this at the office,' he explained, 'whenever the wretched thing has a bit of a paddy and nobody can get anything out of it. You're not meant to, of course . . . Ah, here we are.'

He found the button he was looking for and pressed it. The screen went blank and a floppy disk popped out of a slot. He pressed it back in, pressed the button again and smacked the side of the console with the flat of his hand.

There was an interval while the machine swore at him in morse code; then the screen went completely blank. Bedevere was just about to start feeling a complete idiot when letters appeared on the screen.

ALL RIGHT, YOU WIN

'Bingo!' Bedevere exclaimed. 'Right, let's see.'

He typed in a message, one-fingered, and the screen went blank again.

'What was that you just—?' Turquine started to ask, but Bedevere shushed him.

READY TO TRANSMIT

'Brace yourself,' Bedevere whispered. 'This could be a bit disconcerting.'

'How do you mean, brace myself? Brace myself against what?'

'Ssh!'

TRANSMITTING

The world vanished . . .

The question, 'How did people manage before there were fax machines?' is fortunately academic.

There have always been fax machines, but they have gone under other names, and some of the experimental models bear as much relation to the modern versions as, say, a pair of cocoa tins connected by a piece of string bears to a cellular carphone.

For example; the Pyrolex IV Turbo, which had a passing vogue in the Near East around the time of the Pharaoh Rameses II of Egypt, operated by a primitive form of fibre-optics, whereby concentrated beams of light were conducted through the upper air in the form of radio waves, collected by a rough and ready transducer – the leaves of a rare variety of palm tree, now long since extinct – and then focused on to the receiving medium through an organic lens formed by the tree's blossom.

The fax was, of course, known to the Romans, who used it to communicate with the gods. The Lector Lucius model favoured for this purpose was reliable but slow; the message was relayed into the DNA of a flock of sacred chickens, and was read by cutting open a chicken chosen at random and having a look at its entrails.

Albion used a form of fax technology very similar to our own; but after the fall of the Albionese kingdom we enter a period known to information-technology historians as 'the long dark winter of the postcard', during which only a vestigial form of fax was available.

The exception, of course, was Atlantis, where the fax machine has been known since the very earliest times; so much so that the seminal text of the Atlantean Apostolic Church, *The Gospel According to St Neville*, begins:

> 'In the beginning was the Word, and the Word was with God, and by the time it reached the other end of the line the Word was Gnzd.'

which suggests that at the time the Gospel was first reduced to writing, the Atlanteans were still using the Mark IVc.

Where the Atlanteans outstrip all other fax-using nations, of course, is in their ability to transmit more than mere facsimiles of the written word . . .

'Bedders?'

The word hung for a moment in the empty air,

glowed like embers, and died away. Then there was nothing but the faint howling of the wind that blows round the stars.

'Is that you, Turkey?'

The same, except that these letters flickered with a pale blue fire, and crackled in the thin air like sparklers.

'Where are you?'

'Over here.'

'Where's here, for God's sake?'

'I don't know, do I? Turkey, what's going on?'

And then they both felt the message; felt, not heard or saw. The message was:

There is no here or there. There is only information.

Two disembodied voices started speaking at the same time. It was a bit like Guy Fawkes Night.

Shut up and listen, then, came the message. *There is no here or there, up or down, you, me, they, he, she, now, then, right, wrong, fat, thin, black, white, yellow, green, alive, dead. There is only information. Transmitting.*

'All right,' the blue fire traced irritably. 'Transmitting what?'

You.

There were a few spurts of inchoate orange fire, and then a blaze of virtually illegible pyrotechnics. From the fact that most of the words spelt out were extremely vulgar, one can hypothesise the presence of some part of Sir Turquine.

Look at it this way, suggested the message. *You know how heavy gold is, right? And all money, broadly speaking, is gold. And you can send money by telegraphic transfer, right? Well, then.*

The orange flames flickered testily but got no further

452

than a bad-tempered incandescence. Then everything went black.

Two enormous rollers grinding out a roll of paper; except that it isn't paper. It has one dimension too many for that.

Sir Turquine and Sir Bedevere emerged from between the rollers as two-dimensional silhouettes, flopped out and gradually began to take shape, like balloons being blown up. Not until they were fully inflated did they animate; but as soon as that part of the process was over, Turquine at least was profoundly animated.

'Right,' he said, grimly. 'Nobody shoves me head first through a wireless set and gets away with it.' He rolled up his sleeves and looked round for somebody to take the matter up with.

'Turkey,' whispered Bedevere urgently beside him.

'What?' said Turquine, not looking back. 'Don't try and talk me out of this, Bedders. Somebody is going to get their heads punched for this, and—'

'Turkey.'

'What?'

'Look down, will you?'

Reluctantly, Turquine obeyed. He noticed that they seemed to be standing in a ploughed field. The earth was a pale reddish sort of colour, like clay. Very pale. Almost pink.

'Turkey,' said Bedevere, 'we're standing on somebody's finger.'

It's very hard to get yourself accustomed to truly enormous scales. The eye can only take in a certain amount of information, and the brain can only process a certain amount of the eye's input. You need to be able to eke these resources out with a lot of imagination if you want, for example, to identify a twenty-five-foot-wide strip of ground as a finger.

'Oh yes,' said Turquine quietly, 'so we are.'

Welcome, purred the message, *to Atlantis. Do you want to be enlarged?*

'I think so,' said Bedevere, 'don't you, Turkey? I think that'd be a jolly good idea, if it's all the same to—'

Then we'll have a bit less of it from both of you, and particularly him. Understood?

'Understood.'

The finger shrank, until it became a hand, and it shrank and it shrank and it shrank until the hand closed over Bedevere's fingers and shook them warmly. It was attached to an arm which connected it to a round, bright-eyed, middle-aged man in a dark grey suit.

'Let's get one thing straight, sir, shall we?' he said, smiling. 'Here, we do things the civilised way. No heavy stuff. All sanctions strictly economic. Got that?' And he gave Turquine a look. Turquine growled and nodded.

'Splendid,' said the round man. 'In that case, sir, let me introduce myself. I'm Iophon, and this' – and the two knights noticed another, identical man standing beside him – 'is Pallas. We're from Exchange Control.'

'I'm sorry?' said Bedevere.

Iophon smiled. 'We're here to make sure that only permitted amounts of authorised currency come in or out,' he said. 'You can't be too careful, you know.'

'Excuse me,' said Bedevere. He pulled Turquine aside by the sleeve and whispered to him for a moment, and then turned back to Iophon, who was writing something on a clipboard. 'I think perhaps there's been a slight misunderstanding here.'

'I hope not,' said Iophon cheerfully. 'Now then, if you'll just let me have your amounts, denominations, account numbers and sort codes, I can pay you straight in. You're expected, you see.'

'Yes,' said Bedevere, 'like I was saying, a misunderstanding. You see, we're not money, we're people.'

Iophon grinned a little. 'That's all right, sir,' he said. 'People are accepted at more than two billion outlets galaxy-wide. People, if you'll pardon the phrase, sir, will do nicely. Just sign here, and we'll have you debited in no time.' He held out the clipboard. Bedevere backed away slightly.

'I don't think you quite understand,' he said. 'We don't want to . . . to be cashed. I think we'd probably bounce. We just want to see someone about . . .'

The other man, the one referred to as Pallas, stepped forward. There was something extremely unsettling about him. Bedevere explained it later as his having the air of someone who'd grab you by the scruff of the neck, shove your head under a spring-clip and slam the till shut on you without a second thought.

'Look, sir,' he said, 'you can either be paid in or' – and he made an unpleasant little gesture – 'paid out. Which is it to be?'

Turquine, meanwhile, had had enough. He was not, to put it mildly, as sensitive as Bedevere, and as far as he could see, here they were being threatened by two middle-aged men, the taller of whom came up to his breast pocket. He pushed past Bedevere and reached for a handful of lapels.

When he came round he was lying on his face. Whatever had happened to him, he hadn't enjoyed it. Bedevere, he noticed, was still on his feet, and his face had that Never-seen-him-before-in-my-life expression he remembered so well from their mutual schooldays. He groaned.

'Right,' Pallas was saying, 'that does it. Take them away and put them on deposit.'

Turquine groaned and loosened his belt.

'I mean,' he said 'it's inhuman. There's something about this in the Geneva Convention, isn't there – unusual or degrading punishment?'

'I think that's the American constitution,' Bedevere replied. Somewhere at the back of the cell there was a dripping noise. There always is in prisons. They have worse plumbing than hotels.

'Four stone in two days!' Turquine burst out, and pointed to his stomach, which had slopped over his waistband and was threatening to run down his legs. 'For God's sake,' he said bitterly, 'if this goes on any longer, even my socks won't fit. And,' he added desperately, 'they haven't even given us anything to eat.'

Bedevere nodded sadly. He'd never been exactly slender himself – he was one of those people who only have to look at a chocolate biscuit to start thickening up around the tummy – so it wasn't quite so bad for him; but Turkey, he knew, had always been quite fanatical about keeping his figure. Even, he remembered, at school; not that there'd been any danger of running to fat on half a loaf and a mug of stale mead a day. He smiled wanly – and, since it was pitch dark in the cell, pointlessly – and tried to think of something cheerful to say. He couldn't.

It's no fun being put on deposit. You ask a five-pound note.

Bedevere stirred about in the straw, finding to his distress that there was rather more of him than he was used to, and that it took quite a lot of effort just to move it about. 'You never know, there might be something clever we could do. Let's just stop a minute and think, shall we?'

'Fine.' Turquine glowered at him, or at least where he remembered seeing him last. It was very dark in the cell. 'Let's take stock of the situation, okay? We're in a cell in the depths of some sort of castle . . .'

'Vault,' said Bedevere.

'All right then, it's a bloody vault, so what? We're chained to the wall, in a vault, and . . .'

'In a bank,' Bedevere went on, talking more or less to himself. He'd found over the course of a long acquaintance that when one has nobody but Sir Turquine for company, quite often talking to oneself is the only way to get an intelligent conversation. 'In a bank,' he repeated.

'Fine,' Turquine growled, 'in a bank, if it makes you any happier. Chained to a wall, fat as pigs and getting fatter by the second . . .'

'And heavier.'

'Thank you, Mr Tactful. And, as you so perceptively say, heavier. And . . .'

Bedevere opened his eyes. 'Yes,' he said quietly. 'Heavier, and in a bank vault. On deposit. Yes, I think we're on to something here.'

'My God,' Turquine went on, ignoring him, 'I hate to think what this is doing to my arteries. They must be

457

so hard by now you could use them for gun barrels. Ten years of eating high-polyunsaturated marge gone for nothing.'

'Turkey,' said Bedevere, 'shut up whingeing for a moment, and listen to me.'

Turquine stopped in mid-complaint. There was something about the boy Bedevere – he'd half-noticed it a few times over the years – that made you listen to him when he sounded like that. Not that he ever said anything remotely sensible, of course; usually he'd come up with some remark like, 'I think we're lost,' or, 'It's late, perhaps we should be heading for home now,' or even, 'Hitting people doesn't really solve things, you know.' The trouble with young Bedders, if the truth were known, was that there was a lot of good ware-house space standing idle between his ears.

'Right,' Bedevere said calmly, 'I want you to stand up.'

Ah well, thought Sir Turquine, why not? Nothing else to do. He stood up.

'You standing up, Turkey?'

'Yes.'

'Thank you. Now walk forward until you reach the end of the chain.'

'Is this some sort of aerobics, Bedders? Because if it is, I've tried all that, and ...'

Bedevere shook his head. 'Just do what I say, old man, all right? Thanks. You there yet?'

'Yes.'

'Great. Now, then,' said Bedevere, 'I want you to fall forwards.'

There was a faint clink in the darkness. 'What did you say?'

'Fall forwards, there's a good fellow,' said Bedevere. 'As if you were trying to fall flat on your face. Just try it, would you, please?'

'Are you feeling all right, Bedders?' Turquine enquired cautiously. 'Starvation isn't getting to you, is it? Because I've heard stories, not eating makes you go all light-headed. You aren't seeing things, or anything?'

'No, thanks all the same,' Bedevere replied calmly. 'Now then, I'll count to three. One. Two.'

On the count of three, there was a grinding noise, and the sound of unhappy stone.

'Ah,' said Turquine, catching his breath, 'I think I see what you're getting at. You think my increased weight will mean I can pull the chain out of the wall. Good thinking.'

Bedevere, masked by the kindly darkness, made an exasperated face and counted quietly up to five. 'That's it, Turkey. Give it another go, why don't you?'

It took seven goes before finally there was a loud crash and a vulgar expression, muffled by having Sir Turquine's bulk on top of it. Then a small whoop of joy.

'Right,' said Bedevere, 'how are you doing?'

'Fine,' Turquine replied. 'Chain came out of the wall like a cork out of a bottle. My God, Bedders, I must have put on a hell of a lot of weight to manage that!'

Bedevere sighed. 'Splendid,' he said. 'Stout fellow, if you'll pardon the expression. Now, come over here and help me with my chain.'

With two extremely tubby knights yanking away at it, the staple holding Bedevere's chain to the wall didn't stand a chance. Bedevere would have preferred it if his comrade-in-arms hadn't landed on top of him when the staple gave way, but you can't make an omelette, as they say. He struggled out, stood up and dusted himself off.

'Now,' he said, 'we're getting somewhere.' He reached out with his foot and felt something cold, small and heavy. A pile of them. He nudged, and there was a heavy clunk, like a lead brick falling.

'Like I said,' he muttered to himself, 'a bank vault. Hey, Turkey, did you know that we were in a bank vault?'

'You may have mentioned it, yes.'

'And do you know what we're going to do next, Turkey? Well,' said Bedevere, smiling to himself, 'we're going to rob it.'

There was a silence broken only by that blasted drip. If ever I get out of here, Turquine thought to himself, I'm going to beat the pudding out of the first plumber I meet.

'What did you say?' he asked.

'We're going to rob the bank, Turkey,' Bedevere said cheerfully. 'What's up, got wax in your ears or something?'

Time, Turquine said to himself, to get a few things sorted out; such as priorities. 'Look,' he said, 'a place for everything and everything in it's place, that's what my old mother used to say. Let's get out of here first, and then we can think about—'

'You're an idiot, Turkey, do you know that?' said Bedevere, highly pleased about something. 'Listen. This is what we're going to do.'

Deputy Cashier Callistes woke from his doze and pulled on his helmet. Bells were ringing all over his office. Either the world was coming to an end or someone was robbing the vault; which, in the circumstances, was six of one and half a dozen of the other.

With his five deputy clerks at his back and a big wooden club with nails in it clutched in his right hand, he tiptoed down the corridor, opened the safe door and went in. The deputy clerks, who were also brave men, followed him.

Once they were all inside, somebody with no sense of fair play hit them over the head with gold bars, took the keys, locked them in the safe and ran away. By the time they were rescued by a SWAT team of trained auditors, they were all so fat that it took hydraulic lifts to move them.

Because they were native Atlanteans, with their biorhythms linked by the central computer to their current accounts, their short spell on deposit meant that each of them came out of the vault not only many stones heavier but many millions of dollars richer; and they were therefore taken directly from the vault to the courthouse, tried and found guilty of embezzlement. Under Atlantean law there is only one possible penalty for such a terrible crime. They were loaded on to a lorry, taken to the Till and cashiered.

'I knew a bit of exercise would get the fat off,' gasped Turquine, leaning on a doorframe and wiping the sweat from his eyes. 'Look!' He pointed to the waistband of his trousers.

'Good job too,' Bedevere panted in reply. 'Only I don't think it's the exercise, somehow.'

He was, of course, right. By leaving deposit without filling out the necessary withdrawal slips, both the

461

knights had become hopelessly overdrawn, which accounted for the fact that they could barely stand up. It was probably just as well they didn't know what was happening to them; or that if they hadn't been picked up by a patrol fifteen minutes later, they would have been hit by massive bank charges and killed outright.

'Where the hell are we?' Turquine asked.

And that's bloody typical of the man, Bedevere thought, as he leant on the doorpost and tried to coax some air into his traumatised lungs. I mean, Turkey, how am I supposed to know where the hell we are? You think I nip over here on my days off for a spot of being hunted or something?

'Lord knows,' he replied. 'Look, is this actually getting us anywhere?'

Turquine stared at him. 'Say that again,' he said.

Bedevere put his back against the wall and slid down until he was crouching on his haunches. 'Running away,' he said. 'I mean where's the bloody point? It's not as if we know where the door is. Why don't we just . . .?'

'Well?'

Bedevere shrugged. 'Forget it,' he said. 'Don't mind me, I'm out of condition. Leave it to you.'

Turquine made no reply, and Bedevere suddenly realised that he – Turkey, of all people – was more or less at the end of his rope. Probably as a result of his habit of absent-mindedly eating the leftover pizzas.

'Stuff it,' said Turquine. 'I vote we stand and fight. Or stand, at any rate. Better still, let's sit down and fight.'

He sat down, let his head fall forward, and fell asleep.

About ten minutes later, the men from the Chief Clerk's department arrived. They were clearly intended to be the heavies. You could tell this by the way the pencils in their top pockets all had rubbers on the ends.

'Okay,' said Bedevere, 'it's a fair cop. I'm easy, but I think my friend here wants to hold out for a better exchange rate.'

The clerks looked at each other, and Bedevere noticed that they were, in a curious way, all trying to stand behind each other. Then one of them was propelled forward, politely but firmly, and cleared his throat.

'Resistance is useless,' he said.

'I know,' said Bedevere.

'Well, all right, then,' said the clerk, nervously. 'Try anything, buster, and you're history. You got that?'

'Absolutely.'

'Good.'

Nobody moved. It was all rather embarrassing, and Bedevere found he had this very strong urge to offer them all a cup of tea or something.

The spokesman made another soft, throat-clearing noise. He was standing on one foot now.

'We can do this the hard way,' he whispered. Or—?

'Sorry,' said Bedevere. 'Do you think you could speak up a bit?'

'Yes, certainly. We can do this the hard way, or we can do it the easy way. If that's all right with you,' he added. One of his colleagues gave him a shove. He turned round.

463

'All right,' he said, 'I've had enough, you hear? And I don't give a monkeys what they said at the office party.' He threw his clipboard to the ground, trod on it, slowly and rather majestically walked to the very back of the small knot of clerks and stood there with his arms folded.

Bedevere had had enough, too. 'Excuse me,' he said. 'I don't want to be a pest or anything, but perhaps you could see your way clear to taking me to your leader.'

'Right,' squeaked a voice from the middle of the posse. 'And no tricks, okay?'

'No tricks,' Bedevere sighed.

One of the clerks pointed to Turquine. 'What about him?' he said to his comrades.

'He looks so peaceful just sitting there.'

'It seems a pity to wake him, doesn't it?'

'No law against sleeping.'

'Doesn't look dangerous to me. Does he look dangerous to you, George?'

Oh for crying out loud, Bedevere thought. 'Please,' he said abruptly, 'can we make a start, if it's all the same to you? Only—'

'Cool it, all right?' snapped a small clerk, and then ducked behind the shoulder of the man next to him. Bedevere came to a decision.

'Actually,' he said, 'I expect you're all quite busy, really. Perhaps it'd be easier all round if you just showed me the way – draw a map or something – and then you lot could get on with whatever it is you're supposed to be doing. I mean, there's no point all of us trooping around, is there?'

The clerks looked at each other.

'Sounds all right to me,' one of them said.

464

'Great.'

'Fine.'

'Thank you.' Bedevere reached down and pulled Turquine by the ear.

'Go 'way,' Turquine growled. ''Nother ten minutes.' He lolled forward and began to snore.

'Turkey!' Bedevere shouted. 'Wake up!' He turned round. 'Sorry about this,' he said.

'Quite all right.'

'Don't mention it.'

Bedevere nodded amiably and kicked Turquine hard on the knee.

Ten minutes or so later, they were sitting in an office.

Quite a nice office, if you like them tidy, with matching matt-black in-tray, out-tray, anglepoise lamp and desk tidy. The chairs were comfortable, at any rate.

'Pleased to meet you,' Bedevere said.

'Likewise.'

The Atlantean was different, somehow. He was tall, young, with short hair and big ears. He looked at home in his surroundings; in fact, you could well believe that he was chosen to go with the decor.

'Allow me to introduce myself,' he said. 'Diomedes, Chief Assistant Technical Officer, at your service.'

'Thank you,' Bedevere replied, and gave Turquine a savage nudge in the ribs. Turquine simply nodded and went back to sleep. Diomedes smiled.

'Don't worry about it,' he said. 'It takes some people like that, being put on deposit. Especially if you're not used to it.'

'Um . . .'

'Exactly. And now,' Diomedes went on, 'I expect you'd like to know what Atlantis is all about, wouldn't you?'

'Yes,' Bedevere lied. 'Absolutely.'

'Right.' Diomedes nodded, and pulled a jar of paperclips towards him. As he spoke, he linked them up to form a chain.

'In a sense,' he said, 'Atlantis is a bank.'

He stopped speaking, and gave Bedevere a keen look. Oh hell, thought the knight, he wants me to say something intelligent. 'In a sense,' he hazarded.

'Spot on,' Diomedes replied, nodding vigorously. 'That is, in the same way Mussolini did his bit for the Italian railways, and Jesus Christ had his City and Guilds in carpentry, Atlantis is a bank. It's also something else, something rather special.' Diomedes smiled, catlike, and folded his fingers, by way of saying, Wow, this is going to curdle your brains.

Bedevere was uncomfortably aware that his right leg had gone to sleep.

'Atlantis,' Diomedes said, 'is a repository for money.'

'Right.'

'Precisely.' The smile widened, until it was in danger of losing itself behind Diomedes' ears. 'You're starting to get the point now, aren't you?'

At this point, Turquine woke up.

He blinked, rubbed his eyes, and then leant forward.

'Hello, Trev,' he said. 'What are you doing here?'

Diplomats must feel this way, Bedevere thought. You spend hours in airplanes, hotel rooms, bloody uncomfortable conference rooms with hard seats and nowhere to stretch your legs out; and just when you think you've got something lashed together that might just possibly work, some idiot of a basketball player defects and you might as well have stayed in bed.

Leave them to it, he said to himself.

'It *is* Trev, isn't it?' Turquine was saying. 'Trev Hastings, used to be behind the counter at the Global Equitable in Perry Bar? You remember me, I used to deliver pizzas. Yours was always ... Hold it, I never forget a pizza. Double pepperoni and—'

'That,' said Diomedes coldly, 'was a long time ago.'

In retrospect, Bedevere couldn't remember actually moving from his seat, but he would have sworn blind he jumped about a mile in the air.

'Perry Bar?' he said.

'We have many offices,' Diomedes said. 'It's a big organisation.' Something about the juxtaposition of his eyebrows and the bridge of his nose passed messages to Turquine's brain.

'Anyway,' said Turquine, 'long time no see. Sorry, you were saying?'

Diomedes relaxed his eyebrows. 'Money,' he said. 'What *is* money?'

Before Turquine could reply, Bedevere gave him a smart tap on the shins with his toe. Then he lifted an eyebrow and said, 'Ah!'

It was the right thing to do. 'I mean,' Diomedes went on, 'we all know what it does. Great. So the Son of Man was quite capable of knocking you up a perfectly decent Welsh dresser. But that's not what he was all about, is it?'

Turquine, to Bedevere's great relief, seemed to have got into the swing of it, because he scratched his ear, nodded and said, 'Precisely.' He spoilt it rather by winking at Bedevere immediately afterwards; luckily, though, Diomedes didn't notice.

'Gold 337,' Diomedes said. He reached across the desk and caught hold of one of those Newton's cradle things. 'This continent is built on it. It's anti-magnetic. Anti-magnetism makes the world turn. Okay so far?'

Bedevere nodded. 'Sure,' he said. He shrugged nonchalantly. 'Everyone knows that. Tell me something I couldn't get from the Sunday supplements.'

'Right,' said Diomedes, and just then, Bedevere realised that yes, this man *could* be called Trevor. In fact, he probably was. 'So gold is money, okay?'

'Okay.'

'And money is magic.'

In another part of the building, the bell rang for the afternoon history lesson.

Two junior Atlanteans took their place at the back of the class. One of them had a mouse in his pocket. Just as some flowers did manage to grow between the trenches in Flanders, so the schoolchildren in Atlantis do have mice.

They catch them. They build little hutches for them out of shoe-boxes. They feed them on breadcrumbs and bits of apple-core. Then they sell them.

By the time they reach the sixth form, some Atlanteans have already made their first million just from dealing in mouse futures.

The teacher, a tall lady with deceptively thin arms, rapped on her desk.

'Good morning, children,' she said.

'Good morning, teacher.'

'Open your history books,' said the teacher, 'and turn to page 58.'

She took a deep breath, and hesitated for a moment. She'd been teaching for twenty years, and this bit still gave her the willies.

'Now then,' she said. 'Which of you can tell me what money is?'

The usual bewildered silence. The usual rustle at the back of the class as a mouse changed hands under the desk. The usual blank faces.

'Well?'

'Please, miss.'

Isocrates Minor, the teacher noticed. Ten and a half years old, and already he's got a cellular phone strapped to the handlebars of his bike. The teacher nodded approvingly and made a mental note to ask him about moving heavily into short-dated gilts after the lesson.

'Please, miss,' said Isocrates Minor, 'money is magic, miss.'

'Well done, Isocrates Minor. Now then . . .'

'Miss.'

The teacher frowned. There is such a thing as showing off. 'All right,' she said. 'Questions later.'

'Yes, but miss . . .'

'Later! Now then, money is magic. What does magic do, anyone?'

'Miss!'

'No, someone else this time. Diogenes, let's hear from you for a change.'

A small face crumpled at the back of the room, as a daydream of a nationwide chain of mousebroking offices faded away and was replaced by panic.

'Don't know, miss.'

'Anyone else? Laodicea?'

A small girl stood up and smirked. 'Magic,' she recited, 'is the name commonly given to the technology based on the exploitation of the remarkable properties of the gold isotope Gold 337. Gold 337 was discovered by Simon Magus ...'

'Yes, thank you, dear.'

'... in the year 4000 BC,' continued Laodicea, 'when he was hoeing his turnip field. He quickly grasped the immense potential of—'

'Thank you, dear,' said the teacher. 'Now, as soon as the early Atlanteans realised how special gold was, they started digging it up and making magical things out of it. Now, can anyone give me an example of the sort of things ... yes, Lycophron?'

The small boy blushed under his freckles. 'Buttons, miss?' he suggested.

The teacher sighed. 'No, not buttons.'

'Waste-paper baskets.'

'Catapults.'

'Space rockets.'

'My uncle's got gold buttons, miss, on his blazer. He showed me ...'

'The ancient Atlanteans,' said the teacher magisterially, 'made *coins* out of the gold they found in the earth. When they'd got lots of these coins, they put them in a bank ...'

A hand shot up. 'Please, miss.'

'Yes, Nicomedes?'

'Why, miss?'

The teacher braced herself. 'To keep them safe, of course. Now...'

'Why didn't they put them under the bed, miss?'

'That's not terribly safe, is it, dear? Now . . .'

'My dad keeps all his money under the bed, miss.'

The teacher felt her knuckles tightening up. 'Well, I don't think that's a very sensible thing to do, dear. Now . . .'

'My dad says he doesn't trust banks. He says if he put his money in the bank, Mummy would see the statements and know how much money he's got. What's a statement, miss?'

'A bank,' said the teacher firmly. 'And then the bank would lend money to people so that they could start up businesses, and so the money was all put to work, and the country prospered. But then something very peculiar started to happen. Now, does anyone know what that was?'

Silence again. This time, the teacher decided, just tell them. Then we'll all be home in time for tea.

'What happened,' she said, therefore, 'was that all the magic in the coins in the bank started *leaking out* – ' She said it well. Several of the more nervous and imaginative children went quite pale. '– leaking all over the place. It got so bad that the rooms in the bank where they kept all the coins stopped being square and became round.'

Several hands shot up, but she ignored them. She didn't want to explain; it wasn't very nice to think about. When she'd been a student, she'd had to read the description of it by a clerk who'd got trapped in the vault overnight. The bit where he described what the gold ingots did to each other when they thought nobody was looking still made her feel ill to this day.

'Quite round,' she said. 'And that wasn't all, not by a long way. So the wise elders of Atlantis decided that they'd have to do something about it. Now, does anyone . . .?'

A mistake. But it was too late by then.

'Please, miss.'

'Yes, Hippolyta.'

Hippolyta cleared her throat. 'The Atlanteans founded the Central Research Institute (AD 477), whose principal objects were research into the relationship between the gold's powerful anti-magnetic field and the rest of the world, which is of course attuned to positive magnetism, miss. Their researches revealed that if too much anti-magnetic material was released into the outside world, it would have drastic effects on the stability of the planet, miss. They . . .'

My God, thought the teacher, that girl will probably be Chief Cashier one day. She shuddered.

'Very good, Hippolyta,' she said. 'In other words, if any more gold left Atlantis, it would be very bad indeed. So the gold had to stay where it was, buried underground, and all the gold they'd dug up and made into coins had to be put back. *Alcibiades, what are you doing with that mouse, bring it here immediately!*'

The mouse safely locked in her desk, the teacher pulled herself together and hurried through the rest of the lesson . . .

How the Atlanteans realised that the unique relationship between their gold deposit and the similar deposit on the moon would be jeopardised by further gold exports . . .

How this was a problem, because the entire civilization of Atlantis was now based on the exploitation of

472

money. How the Atlanteans thought about it, and came up with a way of trading in money which didn't actually involve the money ever leaving the earth's crust; a way of getting lots of money in but never paying any money out . . .

How they renamed the gold 'capital' and invented financial services . . .

'Now then,' said the teacher, and looked at her watch. In exactly five seconds, the bell would go, the children would run out into the playground to play football, swing on the swings and form mouse-holding syndicates, and she would retreat to the Common Room for a cigarette and a large sherry.

'Any questions?' she said.

For maybe twenty seconds, which is a long time, nobody said anything. Eventually, Turquine closed his eyes, shook his head and laughed.

'Come on,' he said, 'this is a wind-up, isn't it? You always were a bloody comedian, Trev, like the time you got that girl on your reception to swear blind you'd ordered a deep pan Cheese Banquet with double pepperoni and . . .'

It was Diomedes' turn to look bewildered. He frowned, as if someone had just suggested to him that the sun was a huge practical joke.

'Are you saying you think I've made all that up?' he asked.

'Well,' said Turquine, still smiling jovially, 'you have, haven't you? All that cod about the moon being made out of gold . . .'

'It is not,' said Diomedes coldly, 'cod.'

'I mean,' Turquine went on, oblivious to the danger

473

signals, 'if you'd said made of *silver*, or maybe if you'd said it was the *sun* that's made of gold, yes, you might have had me going there for a minute. But . . .'

Turquine's voice did roughly the same thing as a pint of water might do if spilt in the middle of the Kalahari Desert. 'Trev?' he asked.

'I must ask you,' said Diomedes, 'not to call me Trev.'

Turquine bristled. 'Why not?' he demanded. 'It's your name, isn't it?'

'Was.'

'Bloody good name, too,' Turquine went on. 'If ever I saw a born Trev, that's you. All young men with big noses and ties like road accidents who work in building societies are called Trev; it's a well-known fact. Like all dogs are called Rover,' he added sagely.

'Please . . .' said Diomedes. Tiny red spots appeared behind the lines of his mouth, and Bedevere came to the conclusion that it was time he intervened. Idiots are all very well in their place, but one mustn't let things get out of hand.

'We're just a little – well, taken aback,' he therefore said. 'I mean, it's a bit of a shock, finding out all of a sudden that the world revolves because of money on the moon, and . . .' Something occurred to him. 'Mind you, it explains things, though, doesn't it? Are interest rates linked to the tides, or something? And what about inflation?'

Diomedes sighed. 'Look . . .' he said.

He got no further; because Bedevere, having drawn him off guard with his questions, now chose what was, after all, the perfect moment to hit him very hard with the base of the anglepoise lamp. Diomedes made a little gurgling noise, and fell forward across the desk.

'You see,' Bedevere said calmly, standing up and reaching across the table for a bunch of keys he'd spotted some time earlier, 'it's all a matter of finesse. Sure, we thump the bastards. But we use our heads, too.'

Turquine grunted. 'Speak for yourself,' he replied. 'Tried it a couple of times, had a headache for weeks, cut my forehead. Look, you can still see the scar.' He pointed. 'Mind you,' he conceded, 'one of the little perishers was wearing a helmet at the time.' He pushed the stunned Atlantean away from the desk, rolling his swivel chair aside, and started to go through the desk drawers.

'Calculator,' he said, 'another calculator, *another* calculator . . . Hey, what's this?'

'What?' Bedevere was looking through Diomedes' briefcase. 'Oh, that. It's a small solar-powered calculator that looks like a credit card.' He frowned. 'Hold on, you don't even know what we're looking for yet.'

'Yes I do,' replied Turquine. 'We're looking for the Personal Organiser of—'

'It's not going to be here, is it?' said Bedevere impatiently.

Turquine scowled at him. 'And why not?' he said. 'It's in Atlantis, young Snotty said as much. This is Atlantis. Ergo . . .'

Bedevere was surprised. 'Where d'you learn expressions like ergo, Turkey?' he asked.

'There was a radio in the van,' Turquine replied. 'What are we looking for, then?'

'Food,' Bedevere replied. 'I'm starving.'

★ ★ ★

475

When they got out into the corridor, unfed and disguised as dangerous fugitive knights, they heard the PA yelling, 'Warning! Warning! Unauthorised intruders! Accept no cheques without a banker's card!' This worried them until they found that the noise stopped if you ripped the speakers off the wall and jumped on them.

Actually, that was Turquine's idea. One of his better efforts.

'We're not really making ourselves popular around here, are we?' Bedevere muttered, as they ran along yet another identical passageway.

'Bloody touchy, this lot,' Turquine agreed. 'You were right saying we should try the softly-softly approach.'

He paused to bang together the heads of two passing actuaries, and then added, 'Mind you, it doesn't seem to be working.'

'True,' Bedevere replied, and he kicked a third actuary in the groin. 'You know, I have this feeling we're going about this in the wrong way.'

Turquine nodded. 'I vote we—'

But he was interrupted. A hidden door opened in the wall, and a face materialised and grinned at them.

'This way,' it said. 'Quick.'

Turquine hesitated for a split second. 'Why?' he said.

'Why not?' the face replied. 'Come on.'

The two knights looked at each other.

'That's the best reason I've heard for anything since we got here,' said Bedevere. 'After you.'

It was dark, and cold. The walls were bare stone. In the

shadows, water dripped and a rat scuttled.

'This is more like it,' said Turquine enthusiastically. 'You know, that place was starting to give me the creeps. All that carpet . . .'

The owner of the face beckoned, and they followed.

'Really bad for the nerves,' Turquine went on, 'all that carpet. You get to thinking, My God, if all the sheep that got sheared just to make this lot were lined up nose to tail, they'd probably reach from' – he made a wide gesture with his arms – 'Paddington to Euston. But this, it's more like, well, homely.' He stopped to admire a skeleton hanging from chains on the wall. 'My dad had one of those,' he said. 'Bought it at a wagon boot sale. Said it made him feel all baronial.'

Bedevere quickened his step and drew alongside their guide.

'Where is this?' he asked. The guide chuckled, and the sound echoed away into the darkness, where something probably ate it. 'We're just passing under the main bourse complex,' he said, 'midway between the Old Exchange and the Rialto. We're about five hundred feet beneath cash level. Are you having trouble breathing?'

'No,' Bedevere replied.

The guide shrugged. 'Well,' he said, 'it takes all sorts. This way.'

He disappeared through a low archway; the sort of opening Jerry the mouse might have built if he'd had access to explosives. Turquine, who was too busy looking about him and sighing happily to look where he was going, banged his head and swore.

'Along here,' the guide was saying, 'we're going directly under the registered office itself, so watch

477

where you're going. Reality can be a bit iffy . . .'

As he spoke, the floor and ceiling vanished. When it came back again a few seconds later, Bedevere had the distinct impression that everything had moved about a yard to the right.

'It does that,' the guide explained. 'It's because of the registered office's main relocation matrix.'

'Ah,' said Bedevere, 'of course.'

The guide grinned at him. 'Which works like this,' he said. 'Because, you see, Atlantis is what you might call an offshore tax haven. In fact, *the* offshore tax haven.'

'Gosh.'

'Quite true. Now,' said the guide, 'I expect you've often thought that one day, what with one thing and another, all the money in the world is gradually going to get sifted and slipped offshore, till there's nothing actually left to spend. Right? Thought so. Well, that already happened. A long time ago.'

'Um.'

'In fact,' the guide was saying, 'that's what Atlantis is all about. You see, Atlantis is where money started . . .'

'Um, yes,' Bedevere said. 'Someone just told us.'

'I wouldn't be at all surprised,' said the guide. 'They love telling you all about it, don't they? Mind your head, it's off again.'

In the two or three seconds when all the dimensions were up for grabs, Turquine yelled and said something very vulgar. This was because he hadn't ducked, but the world had. They were now four and a half metres lower than they had been.

'The registered office,' the guide was saying, 'is not

478

only offshore, it keeps dodging about. Brilliant, really. How can they ever assess you to tax if you never stay still for more than thirty seconds running?'

'Absolutely,' Bedevere agreed. 'Look, are we nearly out of that bit, because . . .'

The guide laughed. 'Depends, doesn't it?' he said. 'You never know. I've known days when the registered office just sort of follows you about. Ah, that's better, we're clear of it now.'

They had come out under a broad dome; the sort of thing Justinian would have put on Saint Sophia if he'd had peculiar dreams and lots of money. Far above them was a tiny point of light.

'That's the blowhole,' the guide explained. 'What with all the magical money directly underneath us, and the registered office darting about like a mouse in a maze, there's got to be some way the excess pressure can find its way out. It's the only point where Atlantis is open to the sky. We tend to like it in here.'

'Pardon me asking,' Bedevere asked, 'but who's we?'

The guide smirked at him. 'Thought you'd never ask,' he said. 'We're the hackers. The Atlantis underground, so to speak.'

'Right,' said Turquine. 'So you hate the little bastards too, do you?'

'Right on,' said the hacker. 'That's why we're helping you.'

Turquine extended a massive paw. 'Put it there,' he said. 'Right, let's get the little . . .'

The hacker smiled sadly. 'Good idea,' he said, 'but not practical. Instead, we just try and get as far up their noses as we possibly can.'

Turquine shrugged. 'So why are you called hackers?' he asked.

'Partly,' the hacker replied, 'because we live by tapping into the natural energy discharges of the money reserves and turning them into food. Partly because if ever we catch any of the Topsiders down here, we hack their—'

'Fine,' Bedevere interrupted, 'point taken. You were explaining.'

'Was I?'

Bedevere glanced quickly at Turquine, on whom all this talk of hacking was probably having a bad effect. 'Yes,' he said firmly. 'So how does it all work?' he went on. 'How come Atlantis can't be found from the outside?'

The hacker beckoned. 'This way,' he said. 'It's very simple, really. Atlantis is a corporation, right? And the address of a corporation is its registered office. That's where all its official letters and faxes are sent to, that's where its books of record are kept, and the place where the registered office is decides which tax jurisdiction it falls under. Follow?'

'I think so.'

'Well,' said the hacker, 'the registered office of Atlantis moves every thirty seconds, so it follows that Atlantis isn't anywhere, or at least not anywhere in particular. It's mobile. It's flicking backwards and forwards all over the place. It therefore has no geographical reality; just a fax number. That's how you got here, isn't it?'

They were looking at a huge steel column which ran up from the ground into the roof. It was humming slightly, and when Turquine tried touching it he pulled his hand away quickly, yelped and sucked his fingers.

'That,' said the hacker, 'is the main matrix coil. It controls the movement of the registered office; sort of generates the field which bobs it around. If we could only cut through that . . .'

'Yes?' said Turquine, enthusiastically.

'But we can't,' continued the guide. 'Nobody can. That thing's driven down into a five-kilometre-thick layer of molten Gold 337, and it sort of pipes magic up into a network of conductors that runs through the whole structure. We've tried dynamite, we've tried diamond-tipped drills, we've tried walloping it with big hammers, but all we manage to do is have a really good time and break a few tools. It's magic, you see. Can't touch it without magic of your own.'

'I see,' said Bedevere, thoughtfully. 'And what would happen if you did manage to . . .?'

The hacker grinned. 'God only knows,' he said. 'Probably the world would come to an end. Who cares? Come and have a coffee.'

He led the way to a little lean-to propped up on the side of the pillar, where a small group of people – more hackers, presumably – were boiling a kettle over a fire of what Bedevere recognised as thousand-dollar bills. The hackers grinned at them and waved.

'Hiya,' said one of them. 'Grab a mug, sit down, help us blow up the world.'

Over a mug of truly awful coffee – Bedevere learnt later that it wasn't coffee at all but an *ersatz* made out of deutschmarks steeped in radiator oil – Bedevere tried to find out a bit more about their new hosts.

The hackers, it turned out, had been here almost since the beginning. They were, in fact, dissenting

481

shareholders, who had refused to accept the recommended offer when Atlanticorp was taken over by the present holding company Lyonesse (Atlantis) plc . . .

'Lyonesse?' Bedevere asked suddenly.

'Who else?' replied a friendly, red-faced hackeress. 'Been in charge around here for – what, getting on for eighteen hundred years since the big takeover bid. We were all on the wrong side, of course. We held out for the rescue package offered by the White Knight—'

'Thought we had 'em, too,' interrupted a large, hairy hacker with a lot of scars on his neck. 'Got it referred to Monopolies, full investigation, the works. Then they mounted a dawn raid.' He shuddered.

'We're the ones who got away,' went on the hackeress. 'Most of us didn't, though.'

Bedevere tried to look sympathetic. 'Killed?' he asked. The hackers started to laugh.

'God, no,' said their guide. 'Atlanteans don't die. We're all companies, see, and you can't kill a company. You can only wind it up.' He made a horribly expressive gesture with his hands. 'They're all up there somewhere,' he said, 'in the Receiver's Department. Being wound up.'

The hairy hacker nodded. 'We calculated the other day,' he said, 'that if you attached a propeller to one of them and let him go suddenly, he'd probably fly from here to Jupiter before he ran out of —'

'Ah,' said Bedevere. 'So, er, what is it exactly that you're hoping to, well, achieve?'

The hackers gave him a funny look.

'We don't want to achieve anything,' said their guide, after an uncomfortable pause. 'Bugger achievement. We want to get our own back on the bastards. Pity, really,' he added.

'We're into impotent resentment, mostly,' explained a thin hackeress. 'We harbour grudges, too, but mostly we resent. That and a bit of conspiracy.'

Bedevere was thinking. 'This White Knight,' he said. 'Anybody I'm likely to have heard of?'

The hackers looked at each other. 'Come to think of it,' said the guide, 'that's a very good question. Anybody here know who . . .?'

'It was a consortium,' said the red-faced hackeress. 'An international consortium negotiating a management buy-out.'

'No it wasn't,' replied the hairy hacker. 'It was the original shareholders on a rights issue. They issued a Declaration of Rights. I've got a copy of it.' He patted his pockets. 'Somewhere,' he added.

'You're both wrong,' broke in a tall, freckled hacker, 'it was a market-led refinancing programme backed by the Bank of Saturn.'

'It was the Martians. They were trying to break into the oxygen-based lifeform market, and they wanted a way round the tariff barriers . . .'

'I always thought it was us,' said a small, dumpy hacker. The others stared at him, and he went bright red.

'Anyway,' said the guide, 'it was them. Have some more coffee?'

'No thanks,' said Bedevere. 'Anyway, there was this takeover, and these people – the Topsiders, you called them – they took over?'

'Absolutely,' said the guide. 'They had new sorts of magic, you see. New ways of making the gold do what

483

they wanted. We were decimalised.'

'You mean decimated.'

'I meant,' said the guide grimly, 'what I said. Anyway, that's enough about us. What can we do for you?'

Bedevere kicked Turquine quickly on the shin and then smiled.

'Actually,' he said.

484

5

Midnight.

The last tourist had long since gone, the bookstall was closed, the curator had locked up. The place was empty.

Well, almost.

In the back room – in his day it had been a sort of secondary scullery – the immortal remains of William Shakespeare sharpened a pencil, licked his lips and turned over a handbill about guided tours of Warwickshire.

Amazing, he said to himself, the cavalier attitude they have towards paper these days. The nerds. They only use one side of it, and then as often as not they screw it into a ball and chuck it on the floor. He sighed as his insubstantial fingers smoothed the paper out. Don't know they're born, the lot of them. In my day, he muttered under his breath, you wanted to write something, first you had to get a sheep, then you knocked it on the head, peeled off the wool, scraped the thing down with a whacking great knife ... Made you choose your words that bit more carefully. But now ...

Uncharacteristically, he hesitated for a moment before getting down to work and looked around him. This had always been a good room for writing in, he remembered; which was just as well, seeing as how it was the only one he could ever get any peace in. Then, of course, the fact that it was only just big enough for a man to sit down in and close the door had been a problem. Now, it didn't matter very much.

He shook his head. Youth, he said to himself, ah, youth! You can stuff it.

A quick glance at the clock reminded him that time was getting on. Not that he'd ever had difficulties in meeting deadlines; far from it. Still, they'd been most insistent, and he had been in the game too long not to know that you're only as good as your word. He lowered his head and, his lips moving rhythmically, he began to write.

Scene Four, he wrote. *The Rovers Return. Bet is checking the mixers while Alec puts the float in the till.*

Well, yes. Structurally speaking, the situation demanded it, and these days, of course, you didn't have to bother about giving them time to change the set. You could have any scene you liked. Have a scene at the North Pole next, if you wanted to. Long live progress!

Bet: Jacko's late again.

Alec:

He scratched his head and thought hard. There was something about Alec; perhaps he hadn't yet got the voice properly fixed in his mind. It just wasn't coming; the true Alec hadn't yet come to life. He rubbed his chin thoughtfully and tried to think about the motivation behind the character. Here we have a man, he thought, apparently successful, in the prime of life, happily married, popular in the community. But something is lacking; and that which should accompany old age (honour, love, obedience, troops of friends) he cannot look for . . .

Ah! Gotcha.

Alec: (snorts) Typical! If he spent less time supping ale down the Legion and . . .

Just then, there was a faint but distinct noise from the old back parlour, as of somebody walking stealthily in the dark and barking his shins on the firedogs.

Burglars!

It had to be burglars. Nobody else was likely to be about at this time of night. He bit his lip, screwed his courage to the sticking point and reached for the poker.

If you're hunting burglars through a deserted and darkened house, it helps to have been born there and to have spent the last four hundred years haunting it. You tend to know the more important facts about the place, like where the chairs are. You aren't liable to walk straight into a . . .

'Sod it!' he howled, rubbing his toe and hopping up and down. 'What bloody fool put that there?'

There were sounds of hurried movement from the back parlour, and a sliver of light appeared under the door. Voices, speaking urgently and low. More than one of them.

In situations like these, one has a choice. One can seek the bubble reputation, even in the cannon's mouth. Or one can hide in the grandfather clock.

There was a faint oath as something insubstantial but fragile collided with the pendulum, and then the door of the clock swung shut, just as the back parlour door flew open. They have their exits and their entrances, you might say.

A woman was silhouetted against the light; a tall, slim woman. Light flashed on a loose coil of golden hair. Behind her, the shape of a man loomed ominously. Inside the clock-case a mouse, searching for a light supper for herself and her nest, bumped into something she didn't recognise, squeaked in terror, and started to climb for all she was worth, until she banged her head against the escapement, staggered, and darted back.

For the record, the clock struck one. Life is full of these little coincidences.

'Hell's bells,' said the woman testily, 'is it that late already? Come on, we'll leave it for now. Time we weren't here.'

It was difficult to tell from inside the clock what was going on; there was a series of bleeps, a whirring sort of noise, and then a sort of peculiar ringing. Then the sound of tiny rollers feeding something. Then another bleep. Then silence.

After about five minutes of the silence, the door of the grandfather clock swung open and nothing emerged carefully from it. This time he was properly dematerialised. Like the man said, discretion was the better part of valour.

A brief investigation showed that the funny noises had indeed come from the back parlour, which the tourist people used as a sort of office. The room was empty, but the strange white machine that sat by the telephone was

488

winking its little red light at him. He sat down on the desk and looked at it. It was the thing he always thought of as the paper-wasting machine, in that during the day, whenever it was used, the tourist people were always complaining about bits of paper not feeding in properly and getting screwed up. A crying waste.

Just then, it bleeped once more and started to churn out a little slip with some numbers on it. He waited until the rollers had quite finished, shook his head sadly and pulled the little slip clear. You could get ten or twelve lines on that, if you wrote small. He folded it neatly, switched out the light, and went back to the scullery.

Transmitting . . .

The Queen of Atlantis, Managing Director of the Lyonesse group of companies, stepped out of the fax and walked briskly towards her office. Behind her came her seven personal assistants, carrying the luggage.

The Queen sat at her desk, kicked off her shoes and looked through the sheaf of While-you-were-out notes that had gathered like a drift of wind-blown leaves in her absence. Some she put to one side, the rest she distributed like a sort of Royal Maundy among her PAs.

'What's this?' she demanded. 'Unidentified transmission from – where? I'll swear that woman's hand-writing is getting worse.'

'Stirchley, Your Majesty.'

'Stirchley . . .' The Queen bit her lip and pondered for a moment. 'What's at Stirchley, somebody?'

The PAs looked at each other for a while, until the faint tapping of long nails on the leather of the desktop goaded one of them into action.

'Nothing, Your Majesty,' he said. 'Or at least, nothing much. We maintain a small transmitting station there as part of the network, but it's never used.'

The Queen swivelled round in her chair and smiled at the unfortunate spokesman. 'Well,' she said brightly, 'somebody's been using it recently, haven't they? Perhaps you'd be awfully sweet and find out what's been going on.'

The PA blanched, bowed swiftly and hurried backwards out of the room, and his colleagues heard the sound of hurried footsteps climbing the stairs. The Queen, meanwhile, was looking at a security report and frowning.

'Listen to this,' she said. 'Apparently, someone's been duffing up the cashiers while we've been away. Fancy! And what's more, two intruders were put on deposit but escaped. I didn't know it was possible to escape from deposit. One of you' – she swept the remaining PAs with a smile like a prison-camp searchlight – 'be a dear and look into that for me, will you?'

The smile stopped at the second PA from the left, who set his jaw, swallowed hard and dashed away. That just left five of them.

'Honestly,' the Queen was saying, 'one pops out of the office for five minutes and everything gets into such a tangle! Who was duty officer, someone?'

A PA consulted the register. A name was mentioned. The PA was ordered to be an angel and have a quiet word with him. Trembling slightly, the PA hurried off. It's a filthy job, he said to himself as he went, but somebody's got to do it.

'Otherwise,' the Queen said at last, 'everything seems to be in order and running nicely. Good. Perhaps now we can get down to some work. My briefcase please, someone.'

She had just started dictating a long memo about unit costings when the door flew open and the PAs reappeared. In defiance of some of the leading laws of physics, they all seemed to be trying to stand behind each other. The Queen looked up.

'Well, boys?' she said, smiling at them over the top of her reading glasses. 'Any luck?'

'Um.' The PAs had had an informal ballot, and the loser had been elected spokesman. 'Not as such,' he said. 'At least, we do seem to have found out who the intruders are, but not where they are. Not,' he said, and his voice withered like a daffodil in a furnace, 'strictly speaking, that is. Or at least, we think there's a chance they may be . . .' He gulped and pointed at the floor.

The Queen took off her glasses and nibbled one earpiece thoughtfully. 'Go on,' she said. 'You were saying who these people might be.'

'Um.' A small globe of sweat bounced down the PA's nose. 'We, um, did a credit search on them while they were on deposit, and they seem to be a couple of, ah, knights.'

'Knights?'

'Um.'

'Knights,' enquired the Queen, 'as in Arabian, or knights as in shining armour?'

'Knights as in shining armour, ma'am. Bedevere and Turquine, Your Ma—'

There was a tiny brittle sound, caused by the

491

snapping of the earpiece of a pair of dainty gold-framed spectacles. 'Dear me,' said the Queen, 'how extremely tiresome.'

'Yes, Your M—'

'Drat.'

'Yes, Your—'

'And in the . . . in Thing, you say?'

'Yes, um . . .'

The smile, bright as the oncoming headlights to a dazzled rabbit, flicked from one pale, drawn face to another and finally came to rest.

'Be an absolute sweetheart, one of you,' said the Queen, 'and go and fetch them.'

'It's not fair.'

By way of emphasis, the lantern swayed violently, revealing a narrow spiral stone staircase. A worn brown chain running up the central column provided the only handgrip. It was spooky.

'Shut up.'

'Yes,' replied Iphicrates, senior assistant Assistant to the Queen of Atlantis, but why's it always us, for crying out loud? It's not as if she hasn't got about fifty thousand other bloody gophers who could—'

'Shut up.'

The lantern wobbled violently. 'Don't you tell me to shut up, you crawler,' Iphicrates snapped. Above his head, something whirred, and if this was a hotel rather than the bowels of Atlantis City, you'd have sworn someone had just had a bath. 'Oh hell. Freeze, everybody.'

The staircase disappeared, only to rematerialise a moment or so later three feet to the right. The lantern,

492

which had gone out, lit up again as several million confused photons groped their way through the stonework towards it.

'And that,' said Iphicrates firmly, 'doesn't help matters, does it? I mean, how the hell are you supposed to keep a sense of direction around here when the whole place keeps going walkabout? I mean, how do we know this staircase still goes anywhere, for a start? We could spend the rest of our lives—'

'Look.' A hand tightened on Iphicrates' ear. 'For the last time, be quiet.'

Iphicrates shook himself free. 'No,' he said angrily. 'The hell with you, Androcles. This is a lousy, dangerous job and I'm damned if I'm going to go chasing around in the basement among the hackers for a bunch of lunatic burglars, just because Madam's got her knickers in a twist again. Bloody good luck to them, I say.'

'Shut—'

'No,' said Iphicrates, firmly, and there was a grating sound as he put the lantern down. 'Go on, you tell me, why should I?'

'Because,' hissed a voice in his ear, 'Her Majesty is just behind us on the stairs. All right?'

'But don't mind me,' sang the proverbial silvery voice from the darkness. 'You boys just carry on with what you were doing and pretend I'm not here.'

There was a profound silence; then the sound of a lantern being picked up and somebody nervously humming the national anthem. The procession continued on its way.

It was a very long staircase.

'Er, chaps . . .'

The lantern stopped. 'What's up?'

'Have you, sort of, noticed something?'

'Like what?'

Pause.

'Like,' said the voice from the back – and if there had been any light it would have been possible to see the speaker looking extremely self-conscious – 'put me straight if I'm not on the right lines, but we are going *down* the stairs, aren't we?'

'So?'

'So, why are the stairs going *upwards*?'

Pause.

'Not that I'm the slightest bit bothered myself, one way or the other,' the voice continued. 'All the same to me, really. Just thought I'd . . .'

Grating sound of grounded lantern. A distant scraping sound, which could be a man scratching his head.

'You know,' said Iphicrates, 'he's got a point there, hasn't he?'

Shuffling of footsteps, and the sound of seven people waiting for somebody else to be the first one to say something. Eventually—

'Excuse me.'

'Yes, Your Majesty?'

'Someone be terribly sweet and pass me the lantern. Ah yes, got it, thanks ever so much. Now then, let's just have a quick look, shall we?'

The lantern flickered and then started to blaze out light like a beacon. It showed up seven very nervous men, a composed but frowning woman with golden hair, and a spiral staircase. Going up.

'Perhaps,' suggested Iphicrates, 'it would help if we all turned round. Then surely . . .'

Then the world disappeared. As the perceptible

494

parameters of reality faded away, there was an audible sigh of relief. The lantern went out.

'Has anybody got a match or something?'

Fumbling in pockets noise. Scraping sound. The hiss of flaring sulphur.

'Oh look,' said the Queen, 'we would appear to be in a corridor. Now, anyone, how did that happen?'

Before the light died, it had a chance to explore a patch of what looked like a straight, flat passageway with tiled sides. Perfectly normal looking for, say, a walkway in an Underground station; but a bit counter-intuitive for a staircase, unless you're very heavily into lateral thinking.

Pause.

'Oh well, everybody, looks like we're here. Anybody mind if I lead the way?'

There was a muffled chorus of Fines and Greats and, rather more accurately, Right behind you, Your Majestys, and then a sparkling flash of yellow light as the Queen of Atlantis lit the end of her sceptre and walked purposefully down the corridor.

Transmitting . . .

There was a grinding noise, rather like a crate of milk bottles being run over by a road roller, and then a bleep. Turquine, Bedevere and ten hackers fell out of the fax machine and on to a plain rough plank floor.

The fax machine whirred on for a moment, gave its customary hiccup, and wound out its little slip of paper. Then it realised what it had done, and whimpered.

'Well,' said Bedevere, picking himself up and brushing a fair quantity of dust off his knees. 'It worked, then.'

Nobody seemed to be listening. The hackers were staring with open mouths and eyes like compact discs at this small, unfurnished, bare-walled, scruffy room. Turquine was feeling in his pocket for something.

'Got it,' he said, producing a rather grubby peppermint. 'Knew I'd lost one in there a while back.' He popped it in his mouth and crunched it.

'So this is it,' Bedevere was saying. He was aware that, for all intents and purposes, he was talking to himself; but what else could you do if you wanted an intelligent conversation around here? 'Pretty smart thinking on my part, that, I thought. Yes,' he agreed, 'a neat piece of detection, though I say it myself as shouldn't. Now then.'

He looked around. Apart from the fax machine, himself, eleven men, an empty styrofoam milkshake carton and a small cardboard box, the room was empty.

'The way I saw it,' Bedevere went on, 'it was all down to relativity. Relativity? Yes, relativity. Because although you could say that the world stays still and the registered office moves about, you could also say that it's the registered office that stays still and . . .'

Turquine had picked up the milkshake carton. He looked into it, turned green and dropped it.

'And then you said,' Bedevere went on, turning to one of the hackers, who wasn't listening, 'that nobody had ever found the door to the registered office. They'd looked hard enough, you said, but never actually *found* it. Almost, you reckoned, as if it only existed on the outside, not the inside. And it was that, you see, that set me thinking.'

Turquine drew a finger along a wall until the build-up of dust grew too thick to be ploughed any further. 'This place could do with a good clean,' he observed. 'Not like any office I've ever been in before, really. No phones, for a start.'

'And what I thought was,' Bedevere continued, staring hard at the cardboard box, 'if nobody's ever seen the door, maybe there isn't a door. And what do you know,' he concluded triumphantly, 'there isn't a door.'

Nobody was listening; but that didn't mean to say he wasn't right. There was no door. No window, no ventilation shaft, no cat-flap, nothing. Just four walls of immaculate integrity.

Bedevere knelt down and felt in his pocket for a penknife to cut the string which held down the lid of the cardboard box. 'Like the man said,' he muttered, 'eliminate the impossible and you're left with the truth. I wonder where the light's coming from, in that case.'

The room went suddenly dark.

'The map, somebody.'

In the corridor, it went very quiet.

'One of you,' said the Queen, sweetly, 'did remember to bring a map, didn't you?'

'Did you say something, Bedders?'

Bedevere, who couldn't find his penknife, grunted. It was that strong nylon string that burns your hands if you try and break it.

'Something,' Turquine went on, 'about the light.'

Around him, Turquine could hear strange, soft noises coming from the hackers. At the back of his mind, he could understand why; after all, they were in the registered office, the holy of holies of all Atlanteans. And they'd just found out that it didn't have a door. And it was dark.

'Odd,' Turquine went on, thinking aloud as much as anything, 'the way there's no way in or out of here, just walls. Makes you think, really.' He passed his tongue round his mouth, searching for a tiny residual taste of peppermint. Nothing. 'Not surprising nobody's dusted it in yonks, I mean, how'd they get in, let alone get a hoover up here as well. In fact,' he added, 'makes you wonder how the air gets in. I mean, those walls look pretty airtight to me . . .'

In the darkness, a hacker choked.

'Well, then, a compass maybe. Any of you boys got such a thing as a compass on you?'

No answer. The Queen tutted briskly.

'Well really,' she said, 'no offence, but isn't that a bit feeble on somebody's part?'

In a dead straight, level, tiled corridor that stretches away for miles in either direction, there is only one place to hide; behind somebody. Without apparent movement, the rest of the PAs formed an orderly queue behind Iphicrates.

'Sorry,' he said. The Queen looked at him and smiled until he could feel the skin start to peel on his cheeks.

'That's all right,' she said. 'We all make mistakes. Well, anybody, what do we do now? Any bright ideas?'

The Queen waited for a moment, tapping her nails very gently against the tiled wall of the corridor, until you could find yourself believing that the whole place was vibrating like a drumskin.

'Nobody? Pity.' she licked her lips. 'Well,' she said, 'it's just as well I'm here, then, isn't it?'

The PAs relaxed slightly. Terrifying she undoubtedly was, and nobody much liked the idea of having her along – why was she here, by the way? – but there was no question that Madam would get them out of the tunnel somehow. The dodgy bit was what would happen afterwards.

You can get to like it down a tunnel.

'How would it be,' the Queen said, 'if we all had a cup of tea?'

Bedevere's teeth were in remarkably good shape, considering.

At school, of course, they'd made fun of him. Hidden his toothbrush. Put chalk in his dental floss. But he'd stuck to it – he'd promised his mother – and now he understood why she'd been so insistent.

'Gotcha!' he said, and spat out a few strands of nylon thread. A moment later, he found the lid of the box, and opened it.

This is not going to be easy to describe.

At the root of the problem are the lingering effects of the catastrophic outbreak of Adjective Blight which hit the Albionese-speaking world shortly after King Arthur was deposed. Remarkably little known, the blight (later found to be transmitted by fleas carried on the back of the Lesser or Journalistic Cliché) did to descriptive prose what phylloxera did to the French vineyards. Whole classes of similes were wiped out. Generations of authors have been left poking awkwardly at raw wounds in the collective subconscious where extinct metaphors once grew.

Anyway, here goes. As the lid folded back, something like light in that it was bright and insubstantial and assisted vision, but unlike light in that it jumped out and rushed around the room banging into people, hopped out and whirred through the air like a released balloon. Wherever it made contact with anything it left a big orange phosphorescent glow. It smelt awful.

Air swelled up out of the box like the biggest extrusion of bubble-gum you could possibly visualise, and whacked the hackers and Turquine smack up against the wall. Oddly enough, it didn't seem to affect Bedevere. Perhaps that was because he was still holding on to the box.

Time ... You want to know what Time looks like? Time that's been trapped inside a one-time baked-bean carton ever since prehistory, and which is then suddenly released into an atmosphere rich in carbon dioxide, looks rather like a very expensive Roman candle. Having burnt out, it leaves behind a floating, sparkling yellowy-red ash, rather like gold dust.

Time is money.

Time is, of course, also of the essence. It is the first, the only pure element. Everything else is made up of Time, in one form or another. When Time burns in carbon dioxide, however, it precipitates deposits of that extremely rare and highly volatile element known as Gold 337. Which is why the fax machine suddenly started to glow, steamed, melted and changed shape. It became a jar.

Bedevere, kneeling beside the box and wondering what on earth was going on, slowly began to understand. Gosh, he said to himself, as simple as that ...

He turned back to the box, which contained a heavy

metal seal, a sheaf of share certificates and some old-fashioned ledgers. He picked out a ledger at random, opened it, and began to read. From time to time he smiled knowingly.

'Excuse me,' Turquine said, 'but when you've quite finished, some of us are being squashed to death over here.'

Bedevere looked up. 'Sorry,' he said, 'I was miles away. It's not here.'

'What isn't here?'

'That personal organiser thing,' Bedevere replied. 'All we've got here is the statutory books of Lyonesse Ltd. Tremendously interesting stuff, all of this, but not what we're actually after. Shall we be getting along?' He stopped talking and lifted his head, with an expression on his face like Archimedes seeing the pattern of the universe in a damp bath-mat. 'Oh,' he muttered to himself, 'I think I see.'

Turquine tried to reach out a leg and kick Bedevere, but a lot of air got in the way. 'Look,' he said.

'All right,' replied Bedevere, engaged in the ledgers once more, 'you lot go on ahead and I'll catch you up.'

Exercising more self-control than he ever imagined he possessed, Turquine replied, 'How?'

'Sorry?' said Bedevere. 'Oh, yes. Why not try going out of the door and turning left? If I've got my bearings right, that should bring us out—'

'What door?'

Bedevere pointed to where the fax machine had been.

'Excuse me,' Turquine answered, 'but that is not a door.'

Bedevere grinned. 'Bit slow today, aren't we, Turkey

501

old man? Correct, that is not a door. When is a door not a door?'

'Oh I *see* . . .'

As if by magic; or rather, by magic, the air pressure dropped away to normal, and Turquine slid himself off the wall, squared his shoulders, took a brief run-up and gave the jar one hell of a kick.

'Happy?'

'Yes,' replied Turquine from the corridor. 'Coming?'

Bedevere smiled. 'In a minute,' he said.

The main thing to remember if you are ever offered tea by the Queen of Atlantis is that you should accept, without question or hesitation. Never mind if you can't take the tannin or if you'd rather have coffee; when the Queen offers you tea, you have tea.

Six of the seven PAs knew this. The seventh had no objection to tea, but didn't quite understand where it was going to come from, seeing as how they were standing in a bare, deserted corridor that extended as far as the eye could see. In the grip of what, with hindsight, he identified as a subconscious urge to self-annihilation, he pointed this out.

The Queen smiled.

'Gosh,' she said, 'aren't you the clever one. You're quite right, we'll have to improvise.' She closed her eyes, clenched her elegant white hands and said:

'Let there be tea.'

And tea there was, in Snoopy mugs, with a matching milk jug, sugar bowl and biscuit jar.

'There,' said the Queen, 'it's surprisingly easy so long as you aren't too ambitious to start with.'

Closer inspection revealed that there were seven mugs for eight people. That, as even the PA could recognise, was a Hint.

When they had finished their tea, the Queen beamed at them, vanished the mugs ('Saves washing up,' she explained) and rapped hard on the biscuit jar with her sceptre. There was the necessary quantity of blue light and burning sulphur, and the jar turned into a door in the wall.

'Explanations wanted, anyone?' she said sweetly. Silence. 'Fine,' she said, nodding in approval, and loosed off a small but powerful burst of personality at the doubting PA. 'After you,' she said.

Some are born brave, others achieve bravery and some are forced into acts of great courage by the unimaginable terror of what might happen to them if they refuse. The PA closed his eyes, reached for the door handle, turned it and pushed.

Nothing. Wouldn't budge.

'I think you'll find it opens better if you pull,' said the Queen.

The number of native-born Atlanteans who have been inside the registered office is small, but not nearly as minute as the number who've ever wanted to be inside it. As to the number of those who have ever got out again, there are no reliable statistics. The PA smiled sheepishly at the Queen, mumbled something about a far, far better thing and preferring to be in Philadelphia, and stumbled in.

'Name.'
 'John Wilkinson.'
 'Occupation.'

'Tax inspector.'

'Thank you, please take a seat over there, we'll get back to you in just a moment. Right then, next, please. Name.'

'Stanislaw Sobieski.'

'Occupation.'

'Revenue official.'

'Thank you, please take a seat over there, we'll get back to you in just a moment. Right then, next, please. Name.'

'Li Chang-Tseng.'

'Occupation.'

'Customs officer.'

'Thank you, please take a seat over there, we'll get back to you in just a moment. Right then, next, please. Name.'

'François Dubois.'

'Occupation.'

'Revenue official.'

'Thank you, please take a seat over there, we'll get back to you in just a moment. Right then, next, please. Name.'

The fourth man smirked.

'Guess,' he said.

The desk clerk didn't look up. She had another twelve thousand, five hundred and seventeen more management trainees to deal with, and already she could feel a headache coming on. 'I don't guess,' she said. 'People tell me. Name.'

'Weinacht,' said the fourth man. 'My name is Klaus von Weinacht.'

'Occupation.'

Von Weinacht laughed. He laughed so loud you

could hear him all over the reception area, and twelve thousand, nine hundred and ninety-nine revenue officials looked up and stared. What they saw took them back an average of thirty years . . .

. . . To a child, half-delighted, half-terrified, peeping out from under the blanket at the knife-blade of light under the door. To the sound of silence audible, darkness visible, stillness palpable; and a half-imagined clattering of hooves and clashing of bells in the unspeakable enigma of the night.

'Well now,' von Weinacht said, throwing back his hood, 'how about delivery man?'

The Queen stood in the doorway and stared.

'You!' she said.

Bedevere looked up and smiled vaguely. 'Yes,' he said. 'Long time no see.'

For a moment, the Queen hesitated; then she turned and yelled for the guard. Bedevere shook his head.

'Sorry,' he said, 'but it isn't going to work. You know your trouble? Bloody awful management relations.' He indicated the stunned PA curled up by the door. 'All the rest have scarpered,' he said, 'and I don't think *he's* in a fit state to be of much use to you. I hit him,' he added, 'with the door.'

The Queen looked down and saw a few shards of smashed porcelain. Then she smiled.

'Never mind,' she said, 'plenty more where that came from.'

'Doors or heavies?'

'Both,' replied the Queen, 'although I was thinking more of the jar. Actually, I was rather fond of that one. Been in the family for ages and . . .'

Bedevere was impressed. 'That old, huh?' he said. 'Oh well, never mind. You can't make an omelette, as they say.'

The Queen laughed lightly. 'Very true,' she said, and sat down on the cardboard box. 'Now then,' she went on, 'what can I do for you?'

Bedevere looked at her, and his face seemed to have undergone something of a transformation. Gone was the slightly sheepish look that always reminded Turquine of the last thing but one he saw in his mind's eye before going to sleep; in its place was an expression of gentle but hard determination, such as you might find on the face of someone who will break both your arms if necessary, but with a fitting sense of gravity and decorum.

'I want my money back,' he said.

The Queen's mouth fell open, and for the first time since the groat was demonetised she couldn't think what to say. 'I'm sorry?' was the best she could do.

'So you should be,' replied Bedevere sternly. He was silent for a moment, and then added, 'You don't remember, do you?'

The Queen shook her head. 'Frankly,' she replied, 'no.'

Bedevere frowned. 'A castle,' he said, 'in the middle of a waste and desolate plain, somewhere in the middle of Benwick. A dark and stormy night, with the rain lashing down and lightning playing about the battlements. A young and innocent knight, hopelessly lost on his quest to pay the month's takings from the family dye works into the bank in Rhydychen. The knight sees the castle, murmurs "Thank God!" and craves the right of hospitality. The chatelaine of the castle invites

506

him in, makes him welcome. There is light, and warmth, and food. And then . . .'

A brief spasm of pain shot across Bedevere's face and then his jaw set, as firm as a join in a superglue advertisement.

'In the morning,' he said, 'the castle has gone. So has the money. The knight awakes on the cold fell, with nothing but his armour and a share certificate for twenty thousand Lyonesse Goldfields plc three-mark ordinary shares. He returns home. He explains as best he can. Stunned silence; then the reproaches, the recriminations, how could you *do* such a thing . . .?'

Bedevere shook his head and sighed. There were tears in the corners of his eyes, but his face remained as grim as death.

'The young knight was me, of course,' he said. 'Of course, you don't remember, how could you? Another day, another sucker. But we were different. We couldn't afford it. Dammit, it was hard enough being in trade as it was. God, when I think how they scrimped and saved just so that I could go to the Ecole des Chevaliers! It ruined us, you realise, completely ruined. My father had to get a job as a fencing master. My mother had to go out posing for illuminated manuscripts. *And kindly have the courtesy not to powder your nose when I'm talking to you!*'

The Queen closed her compact with a firm click and looked up. 'Sorry,' she said, 'I was miles away. Did you say something about wanting some money back?'

Unable to trust himself to speak, Bedevere reached inside his jacket and pulled out a folded paper, which he tossed contemptuously on the ground. The Queen leant forward and picked it up.

'Gosh,' she said, 'haven't seen one of these for years. Twenty thousand shares!' She giggled, then composed herself rapidly. 'At the time,' she said, 'a greatly fancied investment. I believe they tried to put together a rescue package.'

'Be that as it may,' Bedevere growled. 'My money back, please. Now.'

The Queen raised an eyebrow. 'Terribly sorry,' she said, 'no can do. It's this thing – terrible bore, but a fact of life nevertheless – called limited liability. It means that—'

'I know what it means, thank you very much,' said Bedevere, his voice ominously soft. 'It means you can do something and get away with it scot free.'

The Queen nodded brightly. 'Exactly,' she said. 'Keystone of the enterprise economy, that is.'

'Because the company has ceased to exist.'

'That's right.'

'Fine.' Bedevere stood up. 'Now then,' he said quietly, 'on the same principle, how would it be if this company of yours ceased to exist? For the sake of argument,' he added, picking up the ledgers he'd been sitting on. 'Unlikely, but possible. If, for example, all the statutory books went missing? No, that wouldn't work. How about if the company secretary and majority shareholder took it into her head to wind the whole thing up, just like that?'

The Queen laughed shrilly. 'Now, then,' she said, 'why on earth would I want to—'

'And if she did,' Bedevere went on, 'I wonder what would happen to all this?' He made a sweeping gesture with his free hand. 'This ... this *remarkable* set-up you've got here? The registered office that nobody can

508

find, and which keeps dodging about, so that it's never in any one jurisdiction long enough for the courts to dissolve the company. Or the strong magical field that keeps the whole enterprise hidden, so that the only way to get into it is by fax? All it would take is one special resolution of the shareholders, with a straight seventy-five per cent majority vote.' He held the register of shareholders open. 'I notice,' he said, 'that you hold ninety-nine per cent of the shares, so all you need to do is vote yes, and that's that.'

'Quite true,' said the Queen, very calmly. 'I hold ninety-nine per cent.'

Bedevere reached inside his jacket again. 'And I,' he said, 'hold this very sharp knife.' He grinned. 'Ready?'

The Queen started to back away towards the jar of pickled onions that had appeared out of nowhere in the corner of the room, but Bedevere simply laughed and threw the register at it. It smashed into a thousand pieces, and no door came.

'Ready?' he repeated. 'In the Articles of Association, which I've just been reading, it says that only a director can move a special resolution.' He advanced slowly, holding the knife very steady in his right hand. 'I think,' he said, 'there's just been a vacancy on the board.'

The Queen's eyes were glued to the knife. 'Surely not,' she said. 'I'd have been the first to know.'

'Not in this case,' Bedevere replied. 'Your friend there,' and he nodded at the recumbent PA, 'resigned just before he passed out. I heard him. You believe me, don't you?'

The Queen nodded. The knife caught the light and glittered.

'In which case,' said Bedevere, 'you've just proposed me for the post of –' he chuckled '– director in charge of takeovers and mergers. Bloody, foul and unnatural mergers. All those in favour say yes. Say yes.'

'Yyy.'

'Great. Now then, I vote that Lyonesse (Holdings) plc be wound up forthwith. All those in favour . . .'

The Queen started to scream, but Bedevere curled his lip. It was a long time since he'd last had occasion to do anything so melodramatic – not, in fact, since he'd been the Second Roman Soldier in the sixth-form mystery play – and as a result, parts of his moustache went up his nose. He sneezed.

'Save your breath, please,' he said. 'Nobody can hear you, and even if they could, what good would it do? Nobody can get in here, remember? Nobody can even find it. It moves about. Unless you know the trick with the jar, the only way in here is by fax, and I've cut the bloody thing's flex. And once you're in here,' he added, 'magic, even Gold 337, doesn't work, because of your extremely clever insulation system. I'm sorry,' he continued, moving the knife, 'but this is a cut-throat business. All those in favour.'

The Queen's tongue darted round the circuit of her lips but could do little to moisten them. She tried to speak, but nothing came out except a small, creased whimper.

'Ready?'

'No!' The Queen could feel her shoulder-blades against the wall. 'You can't. You're a knight, re-member; knights can't kill damsels in distress. It's . . .'

'Unethical?' Bedevere smiled. 'Three points, briefly. One, you're not a damsel, you're a sorceress, and

510

they're fair game, all year round, with or without a permit. Two, we're inside the registered office of the Lyonesse Group, which is outside all recognised jurisdictions, so nobody will ever know. Three ...' He grinned. 'Three is, what the hell, rules were made to be broken.' He grinned savagely, and the Queen instinctively raised her arm in front of her face.

'There is, of course, an alternative ...'

'Excuse me,' said the assistant cashier, 'but you can't go in there.'

Von Weinacht turned and stared at him. 'Sorry?' he said.

There was a brief moment when their eyes met; and the cashier remembered that he had a son, and the son wanted a mountain-bike and a Teenage Mutant Accountants Playset more than anything in the world, and that if he didn't get one ...

'No problem,' the cashier mumbled hoarsely. 'Where to?'

'The Forbidden City, I think it's called.'

'Third on the left,' the cashier said. 'Follow your nose, you can't miss it.'

'Is there?'

Bedevere nodded. 'Absolutely,' he said. 'Just give me my money back and,' he added, as nonchalantly as he could, 'the Personal Organiser of Wisdom, and we'll say no more about it. All right?'

Don't you just know, immediately and instinctively, when you've said the wrong thing? Like asking someone how his girlfriend is, just as you notice out of the corner of your eye that half the furniture is missing, and the picture of a dog burying a bone which he'd always told you he hated has vanished from the wall? And all the magic of the Great Pentagram won't drag the words back into your mouth, or do anything to mitigate the joint-cracking embarrassment of it all.

'So that's what it's all about, is it?' the Queen replied.

'Um.' Bedevere bit his lip. 'That's beside the point,' he said, 'and the point is very sharp, very sharp indeed, so . . .'

'Very well, then,' said the Queen, folding her arms and sticking her chin out. 'Kill me then, see if I care.'

Bedevere frowned, and then turned the frown into a scowl. 'Don't push your luck,' he growled; but the growl came out about as menacing as the mewing of a kitten.

'Go on.'

'Look . . .'

'Scaredy-cat!'

'Don't you—'

'Cowardy cowardy custard!'

'Damn!'

With a grunt of pure rage, Bedevere swung the knife up and hurled it into the floor, where it quivered like a violin string. Then he sagged, like an ice-cream skeleton in a microwave.

'I thought so,' said the Queen. 'You never had the faintest intention, did you?'

Bedevere scowled at her. 'Don't sound so damned disappointed,' he said, and slumped into the corner. 'Anyway,' he added, 'I had you going there for a moment, didn't I?'

The Queen had her powder compact out again.

'Certainly not,' she said to the mirror. 'You knights are all mouth and vambraces. You'll be hearing from my legal advisers about this, by the way.'

But Bedevere had made up his mind. One moment he was in the corner, about as taut and poised as a bag of old shoes; the next moment he was on his feet and grabbing the Queen's organiser bag with both hands.

'Hey!' the Queen squealed. 'Get off, will you?'

The strap broke – it was a fiendishly expensive bag, with one of those flimsy gold chain straps, and Bedevere weighed close on thirteen stone without armour – and the bag flew open. One of the things that landed on the floor was a small, leather-covered thing like a book. Before the Queen could move, Bedevere was standing on it, with a smirk on his face you could have built a trading estate on.

'And sucks to you too,' he said.

'You've got no right . . .'

'Granted,' said Bedevere. Then he stuck his tongue out.

The Queen shrieked and grabbed the hilt of the dagger, but it was too firmly stuck in the floor. So she called Bedevere a rude name instead.

'Sticks and stones,' replied the knight, and he stooped quickly, picked up the book, and stowed it carefully away.

'Now then,' he said, 'about my money . . .'

Just then, a chimney appeared in the corner of the room; and in the mouth of the chimney, a pair of boots . . .

'What the hell's keeping him?' said Turquine irritably.

The hackers looked at each other.

'Ten to one he's got lost,' Turquine continued, picking at the sleeve of his coat, where a loose thread was beginning to unwind itself. 'No more sense of direction than a tree, that man. Got us lost on the way here, and that was just on the ring road.'

The hairy hacker coughed meaningfully. 'Look,' he said, 'I know this isn't going to be easy for you to accept, but people . . .'

'What?'

The hacker flushed under his superabundance of facial hair. 'When people go in . . . in *there*,' he said, 'well, coming out is the exception rather than the norm, if you see what I mean. Like, your friend is probably . . .'

'Balls,' Turquine replied. 'He's just got lost somewhere, that's all. Come on, you dozy lot, I suppose we'd better go and get him.'

The hacker shrugged; a what-the-hell, Light-Brigade, last-one-into-Sebastopol's-a-sissy shrug.

'All right,' he said. 'Wait for us.'

'Freeze,' said a voice from the fireplace.

Bedevere and the Queen turned and stared. The boots kicked, like the feet of a hanged man, and there was a vulgar expression from about where the mantelpiece should have been. Then a lot of soot and what looked rather like a dead bird fell into the grate, followed by a man in a somewhat grubby red cape.

'Hold it right there,' he said. 'Don't even think of moving, either of you.'

He extracted himself from the fireplace, brushed a good deal of soot off himself, and straightened his

514

back. He was very tall and broad, and he had eyes like little red traffic lights.

'Where you made your mistake,' he said to Bedevere, turning round and tugging at something still lodged in the chimney, 'was in assuming that there was no other way into this room. Well, you were wrong. I can get in *anywhere*.'

Bedevere turned to the Queen. 'Excuse me,' he said, 'but do you know this gentleman?'

The Queen mumbled something and nodded. Good Lord, Bedevere said to himself, she's terrified. Then a tumbler fell in the combination lock of his mind.

'Just a moment,' he said, 'aren't you . . .?'

Von Weinacht snarled at him. 'Don't say it,' he said. 'Don't make things worse for yourself than they already are.' He tugged, and a sack came down into the grate with a heavy crunch. From it, von Weinacht produced a transparent cellophane package with a brightly coloured piece of cardboard at the top. Bedevere recognised its contents as one of those plastic swords given to children by parents who don't value their neighbours' daffodils. The Queen gave a little shriek.

'Now,' said von Weinacht, 'to business.' He tore off the cardboard and took out the plastic sword. 'Two birds with one stone. You,' and he nodded his streaming white beard at Bedevere, 'are searching for the Holy Grail. You aren't going to find it. And you . . .' He gave the Queen a long and unfriendly look. 'You and I go way back. I'll deal with you later.'

'Excuse me,' Bedevere interrupted, 'But how did you know . . .?'

Von Weinacht laughed. 'I know everything,' he said,

with conviction. 'I know the ground-plan and floor layout of every house in the world. I can read the minds of every parent and every child ever born. Of course I know what you're up to, and you aren't going to get away with it. Now, give me that book before I take it from you.'

He pulled off the plastic scabbard and threw it on to the ground, revealing a horribly shiny steel-blue blade. If that's plastic, Bedevere realised, then I'm Sir Georg Solti.

'Sorry,' he said, 'no can do.'

Von Weinacht grinned repulsively, then roared like a bull and swung his sword. There was a disturbance in the air where Bedevere's head would have been if he hadn't moved it; and at the same moment, a patch of honey appeared on the wall, followed by a door, which opened to reveal Sir Turquine. He was slightly out of breath and holding a two-foot-long adjustable spanner.

'Oh good,' he said, 'fighting. That's more like it.'

Von Weinacht wheeled round and scowled at him. Turquine did a double-take.

'Just a tick,' he said, 'I know you. You're that burglar.'

There was a moment of perfect stillness while two memories rewound many hundreds of years . . .

. . . To the Yuletide Eve before Turquine's seventh birthday, when he'd been sleeping peacefully in the hall at Chastel Maldisen and this burglar had tried to break in through the smoke-hole in the roof. Ugly customer, dressed all in red for some reason, carrying a whopping great swag-bag on his shoulder. Luckily, Turquine's father had bought his son a crossbow for Yule, and hadn't hidden it very carefully . . .

516

... To that nightmare back in the Chastel Maldisen, when some horrible little child had kept him holed up in the roof for ten very long minutes by shooting arrows at him while he clung to a rafter and yelled frantically for reindeer support ...

Turquine was the first to recover. 'It's been a constant source of aggravation to me, that has,' he said, 'the one and only time I've ever had a burglar and I kept missing. Mind you,' he added, 'bloody thing wasn't properly shot in, kept pulling to the right ...'

'You didn't do so badly,' von Weinacht hissed, and he drew back the sleeve on his left arm to reveal a long, white scar. 'Three birds,' he added. Then the sword flashed in the air like a blue firework.

Turquine parried with the spanner, and there was a ringing sound like a fight in a belfry. The head of the spanner fell to the ground.

While von Weinacht was celebrating with a horrible gloating cry and whirling the sword round his head for a final devastating blow, Turquine very shrewdly kicked him in the nuts, belted him with what was left of the spanner, and ran for it.

Von Weinacht recovered quite remarkably quickly, screamed like a wounded elephant and followed.

Bedevere shrugged and turned to the Queen. 'Anyway,' he said, 'time I was going. Thanks for everything.'

The Queen tried to hit him with the register of shareholders but missed, and he darted out of the door just before it healed up and vanished. Bedevere stood in the corridor and caught his breath. A long way away, he could hear running feet and curses. That way, he decided.

He was running flat out, one hand clamped on the book, the other pumping rhythmically at his side, when the corridor turned back into a spiral staircase.

Of course, he came the most terrific purler. First he banged his head on the ceiling, then he bounced several times off the walls, and then the steps got him. As if that wasn't enough to put up with, he had just managed to arrest his rapid progress by sticking his legs out when a stunned PA came down on top of him, landing a sharp elbow in his midriff before rolling away into the darkness.

Come on, Bedders, pull yourself together, this isn't getting you anywhere.

He hauled himself on to a step, rubbed his head to make sure he wasn't bleeding, and breathed in a couple of times. Nothing broken, as far as he could tell. Splendid.

Down below, there was the most appalling racket, rather as if a lot of people were falling down on top of each other and swearing a lot. Grinning ruefully, Sir Bedevere got up and began walking carefully down the staircase.

The Queen had emptied her bag out on the floor. It must be here somewhere. She always had one, for just such emergencies as these.

Lipsticks. No. Nail varnish. No. Purse, credit cards, tissues, calculator, notebook, diary. No.

Ah . . .

She took the small jar of cold cream, drew back her arm, and let fly . . .

Von Weinacht had, apparently, knocked himself out

cold on the stone pillar at the foot of the staircase. Under him, squashed flat and moaning slightly, was a PA. Various semi-conscious hackers lay about untidily. Bedevere smiled, feeling ever so slightly superior, and stepped over them.

'Turkey?' he called. 'You there, Turkey?'

'Over here,' came the reply, and Bedevere followed the sound of the voice under a low doorway. There was Sir Turquine, sitting astride a large oak chest, trying to lever off the lid with von Weinacht's sword.

'Not now, Turkey,' said Bedevere. 'I think it's time we left, don't you?'

Turquine shook his head. 'Haven't got it yet, have we?' he replied. The sword broke.

'What makes you think it's in there?'

'What makes you think it isn't?' Turquine replied, hammering at the padlock with the sword-hilt. 'I'm just being thorough, that's all.' The padlock broke.

'Well,' said Bedevere, 'is this what you're looking for?' He produced the notebook and held it up. If Michelangelo had ever wanted to do an allegorical statue of Smugness, he couldn't have found a better model.

Turquine looked up and grinned. 'That's it, is it?' he said.

'Reckon so.'

'Good lad.' He got up off the chest and threw back the lid. 'Might as well have a look in here anyway, while I'm here,' he said. 'Good Lord, it's full of diamonds and things. There's a turn-up.'

Bedevere shook his head affectionately. 'Hurry up, then,' he said, 'and then we'd better be off. And don't take any gold.'

Turquine nodded. 'Because of buggering up the earth's axis, I know,' he replied. 'Load of old socks if you ask me. Just the sort of thing you'd expect from a lot of bankers. Want some?'

Bedevere thought of twenty thousand gold-mine shares and nodded. 'Why not?' he said. 'Just to show willing, you understand.'

'Exactly,' Turquine agreed. He scooped out a double handful of emeralds and handed them to his friend, who stowed them away in his pockets.

'Ready?'

'Almost,' Turquine replied, scrabbling about in the chest. 'I think this one's rather nice, don't you?' He held up an enormous ruby, then kicked the lid shut.

'It's not stealing,' he added, 'because in return, they can have *this* back.'

He threw down a piece of paper and stamped on it. Bedevere recognised it, and smiled.

'Lyonesse Goldfields?' he asked.

'Worse,' Turquine replied. 'Lyonesse Capital Growth Trust Income Units. When I told my dad what I'd done he nearly flayed me alive.'

The knights grinned at each other.

'Time we weren't here,' said Turquine. 'Now then, this way.'

Bedevere shook his head. 'Not unless you want to see the boiler room,' he replied. 'Follow me.'

'But I think there's a short-cut—'

'Follow me.'

As they walked, Bedevere asked Turquine what had kept him.

'I like that,' Turquine replied. 'Honestly, Bedders, you've got a nerve. If it hadn't been for . . .'

Bedevere shrugged. 'I knew I could rely on you, Turkey. You just cut it a bit fine, that's all.'

Turquine nodded. 'I know,' he said. 'As soon as you didn't follow, I guessed something was up. No, finding the spanner was easy, it was just finding a jar . . .'

'You tried the kitchens?'

'Yes, and . . .'

'You stopped for a sandwich.'

Turquine blushed. 'I was *starving*, Bedders. It wasn't like this in the old days. There were always pages and squires and things you could send down to the baker's while you waited for the dragon to come out. I don't hold with progress, personally.'

'It's a bit overrated, certainly,' Bedevere replied. 'Now then, left here, and we should be . . .'

They stopped. The Queen was standing in the doorway, and behind her were about seventy heavily armed clerks.

'Hello, boys,' she said.

Bedevere blinked. 'How the hell did you get here?' he said.

'Simple,' the Queen replied, 'I used the lift. Grab them, somebody.'

'Well,' said Turquine, 'this is extremely jolly, isn't it? Right, who's going to be first?'

There was something about his tone of voice which the clerks seemed to find quite remarkably eloquent. They just stood there, in fact, listening to him, as if he were Maria Callas.

The Queen made a little clicking noise with her teeth, rather like someone loading a rifle. 'Come on, boys,' she purred. 'Let's not be all tentative about this. Grab them.'

That was even more eloquent; as if Maria Callas had been elbowed out of the way by Elizabeth Schwartzkopf and Joan Sutherland. The clerks shuffled forward in an unhurried but determined phalanx, while Turquine reached behind him and, as if by magic,* wrapped his hand round thirty inches of scaffolding pipe. It made a soft, heavy sound as he patted it against the palm of his left hand.

'Excuse me,' said Bedevere.

Nobody was paying the slightest attention. One does one's best to take the heat out of the situation, and one might as well have stayed in bed. He frowned, and then pulled something out of his pocket.

'Excuse me,' he repeated, and this time everyone stopped what they were doing and looked at him. It was so quiet you could hear a pin drop. And, shortly afterwards, they did.

'It's all right,' Bedevere went on, displaying a grenade prominently in his left hand. A rather superior example, admittedly; if Fabergé had ever made grenades, they would have looked like this one. 'So long as I don't let go of this lever thing,' he said, trying to sound extremely reasonable, 'it won't go off. Now...'

Turquine nudged him so hard that he nearly drop-

---

*As if? Who are we trying to fool?

By a quirk of magic and genetics, all the first-born males in Turquine's family had the knack of being able to put their hands on heavy blunt objects suitable for use as weapons whenever they needed to. Which probably explains why so many of them became warriors, and so few of them went into catering, stockbroking or graphic design.

ped the bomb, and whispered, 'Where in God's name did you get that from, Bedders?'

Bedevere turned to him and smiled gently. 'You gave it to me, Turkey. From that big chest you broke open, remember? Now then . . .'

Turquine's hand flew to his pockets, which clinked faintly. 'Mine aren't,' he said. 'Mine are all diamonds and sapphires and . . .'

'Really?' Bedevere clicked his tongue. 'You always did have rather a limited imagination, though.' He turned back to the clerks, just in time to stop them drifting away.

'Now then,' he said, 'playtime's over, so if you all pay attention we can get this all sorted out and then we can get on with what we're supposed to be doing instead of playing at cowboys and Indians. Happy?'

Happy probably wasn't the word Flaubert would have chosen, but at least he had the audience's attention. He held up his hand – his other hand – and cleared his throat.

'Gather round now, please,' he said. 'Thank you. Right, first things first. This is indeed a real hand grenade, which I made out of a diamond about ten minutes ago, with the help of . . .' he dipped his right hand in his inside pocket and pulled out the leather-bound book. 'This. The Personal Organiser of Wisdom. Note the tiny gold clasp; made, of course, from Gold 337; hence the transformation from a decorative but useless form of carbon to a highly practical firework. Neat, yes?'

The clerks shuffled their feet. If it's possible to be scared out of your wits and ever so slightly bored at the same time, they were.

'Second,' Bedevere went on, 'we mean you no harm, honestly. All we want is this little notebook thing. It's not for us, it's for a friend. I know it'll mean removing a minute quantity of Gold 337 from Atlantis, and yes, that'll mean a slight wobble in the earth's axis. So what? By my calculations, it'll mean a small contraction in the orbit pattern, and we won't have to bother with leap-year any more, and that'll—'

'Hey,' Turquine interrupted, 'it so happens I was born in a leap-year.'

Bedevere turned to him irritably. 'So what?' he said.

'So I'm still four hundred and sixteen,' Turquine replied. 'Just thought you might be interested, that's all.'

Bedevere nodded, and turned round again. 'Be that,' he said, 'as it may. If we leave, it'll be no skin off your noses and you can get back to fleecing the greedy and making money, we can press on with our job, nobody gets hurt, big anticlimax but really the best solution in the circumstances. If you try and stop us leaving, we'll throw this bomb at you. Anybody here feeling lucky?'

Nobody, apparently. Bedevere nodded, and pointed to the Queen. 'Right,' he said. 'To make things easy, you lead the way.'

The Queen gave him a look you could have put on dandelions and started to walk. She didn't get very far.

With a roar like the sound of a dinosaur having a filling done, the Graf von Weinacht appeared in the corridor behind them.

'Oh drat,' Bedevere sighed. He released the handle of the grenade, counted to three, shouted 'Catch!', and tossed the grenade at the Graf, who caught it one-handed and popped it in his sack. A moment later there was a soft, distant thump.

Followed, shortly afterwards, by a louder, nearer thump as Turquine wiped the smile off his face with the scaffolding pipe and bolted, followed closely by Bedevere, the Queen and the clerks.

For the record, Klaus von Weinacht woke up about ten minutes later, looked at the footprints all over his cape and the scorched hole in the side of his sack, and decided to call it a day. He produced a fireplace, climbed up it and vanished. When, many hours later, the Queen went to bed, she found on her bedside chair a large stocking filled with scorpions and a card with 'Happy' crossed out and replaced with 'Really miserable'; both of which she placed in the waste-disposal system.

'I liked him,' Turquine said as they ran. 'No mucking about, straight to the point. If he had better reflexes he'd be quite handy.'

Bedevere had no breath with which to reply, which was probably just as well. They were in another corridor; but this one was carpeted and there were doors with frosted glass windows in them leading off it at regular intervals. In other words, they were back Topside again.

'Let's try this one,' Turquine suggested.

Bedevere, who could run no further in any case, nodded, and they leant heavily on the door and fell into a small office.

If they'd had time they would have seen the writing on the window, which said:

COMPLAINTS

The Atlantean financial services industry prides itself on the fact that it has never yet received a complaint from one of its clients. There are three reasons for this:

1. All Lyonesse Group financial packages are tailored to meet your exact requirements by a team of dedicated experts with more than two thousand years of experience in all forms of monetary planning behind them.

2. The Lyonesse Group investment management team continually monitors all investment and insurance portfolios on behalf of their clients and advise immediately when a change in investment strategy is desirable.

3. Under the doormat in the Complaints Department there's this trapdoor thing that leads to a soundproof dungeon.

'Turkey.'

'Yes?'

'It was you who said Let's try this one, wasn't it?'

'Yes.'

'Fine. I was worried there for a moment that I was losing my grip.'

'No, it was me.'

'Fine.'

A rat hesitated in the doorway of its hole, lifted itself on to its back paws, and sniffed. Something didn't smell right.

With a flick of his tail he retreated, demonstrating that animals are far more sensitive to atmosphere than human beings. If he had been so foolish as to go much further, there can be little doubt that Turquine would have caught him and eaten him.

'I'm famished, Bedders,' he said for the seven hundredth time. 'I mean, prison's one thing, you can't really squeal when you land up in a dungeon, it's all part of the game. They capture you, Dad comes up with the ransom, you go home, finish. But they're supposed to feed you while you're here. It's in some convention or other.'

Bedevere stirred uneasily. He had tried to keep his friend off the subject of why they were there, for fear it might upset him.

'Turkey,' he said quietly, 'I don't think you quite realise what's going on. I don't think this is the sort of dungeon you're meant to get out of.'

Turquine laughed. 'Don't be an ass, Bedders,' he replied. 'There's no such thing as a dungeon you're *meant* to get out of. That's the whole point about dungeons. They're containers for the thing contained, like shoe boxes.'

'Up to a point,' Bedevere replied, staring up at where the roof should be but seeing only darkness. 'Only, with your ... your conventional dungeon, you're only kept there for a limited time – you know, till the ransom's paid or until you've served your time or whatever. Somehow I don't think this is one of those.'

'Why not?'

'No door,' Bedevere replied. 'The only way in is through that trapdoor thing we fell through. I think you more, sort of, stay here.'

Turquine shuffled about on the straw. 'Surely not,' he said. 'I mean, don't take any notice of there not being a door. They don't seem to hold with doors in this place. Reminds me of an office I delivered a couple

527

of pizzas to once, there was just this sort of partition thing and—'

'No, hold on a moment,' Bedevere interrupted. 'You see, I'm basing my theory on all the, er, skeletons.'

'Skeletons?'

By way of reply, Bedevere rattled together a couple of tibias. 'I don't think they were on diets, Turkey. I think nobody fed them. Not for ages and ages.'

'Oh.'

'In fact,' Bedevere went on (and as he spoke, he had the feeling that if he was trying not to alarm his friend unduly, he had probably gone about this the wrong way), 'not at all. Do you follow?'

'Sort of,' Turquine replied. 'Bit unsporting, that, don't you think?'

'Absolutely.'

'Not on, really.'

'Yes.'

Turquine found one of the skeletons, and amused himself by pretending to be a ventriloquist; something that Bedevere found somewhat irritating. Still, he said to himself, if it takes his mind off things it's all right by me. Turquine's mind, as he knew from long experience, was a bit like nuclear war; when he got an idea into it, things were often very noisy and unpleasant for a while, but it was soon over. He lay on his back and tried to think of something clever.

A human pyramid to reach the trapdoor? No, not enough manpower.

Magic, perhaps? He felt in his pocket for the Personal Organiser, but the gold clasp wasn't even warm. No magic down here that he could detect, or if there was, it wasn't compatible. Probably the place was insulated, like the registered office.

He was just weighing up the possibility of using some of the bones to build a makeshift ladder when Turquine's ventriloquist's dummy started to laugh hysterically. Better put a stop to that straight away, he thought, or else the poor chap'll be right off his trolley in no time, which won't help matters.

'All right, Turkey,' he said, as gently as he could, 'Pack that in, will you? It's starting to get on my—'

'Um.'

'Turkey?'

'Bedders.' There was a note in Turquine's voice that Bedevere had never heard before, in all the years they'd known each other. Fear. Say what you liked about old Turkey, he never seemed to get the wind up. If you asked him what the word fear meant, he'd probably think for a bit and say it was the German for four.

'Turkey?'

'Um, could you come over here and ask this, er, lady to stop talking? She won't listen to me, and . . .'

That's it, said Bedevere to himself, the poor idiot's finally flipped. My fault for letting him play with the thing in the first place.

'Now don't be silly, Turkey,' he said, edging over across the straw on his hands and knees. 'You know it's you doing the voice and not the skull at all, so just—'

There was another peal of laughter, and Bedevere winced. Laughter like that meant only one thing. And then something occurred to him.

Turquine was talking to the skull in his own voice, asking it – begging it, even – to shut up. And the skull was still laughing. Either Turkey was a damn sight better at ventriloquism than he thought (and he wasn't;

there's no 'g' in 'bottle') or else it actually was the skull talking . . .

'Turkey,' he shouted, 'pack it in, you hear me?'

'Leave him alone.'

Silence. The only sound in the echoing dungeon was that of the rat banging the rathole door and jamming a piece of coal against it.

'Sorry?'

'I said leave the poor boy alone, you big bully.'

'I . . .'

'Go and pick on someone your own size.'

Great, thought Bedevere, absolutely spiffing. Now I've gone round the bend too. If ever I get out of here, I'm going to kick young Snotty's arse all the way from here to Benwick.

'Excuse me,' he said.

'Yes?'

'Who am I talking to, please?'

There was more of the laughter, and Bedevere found that he was getting a bit tired of it. He coughed meaningfully.

'Don't you get on your high horse with me, young man. I'm old enough to be your grandmother.'

'Actually,' Bedevere couldn't resist saying, 'I doubt that, rather.'

'Don't you answer me back.'

'Sorry,' Bedevere said, 'but I do happen to be well over fifteen hundred years old.'

There was a click, like rolling dice or – but it didn't do to think too hard about it – a skull's jaw falling open.

'Don't you try being funny with me, young man, because—'

'Really,' Bedevere said. 'I used to be one of King Arthur's knights, you see, and I'm here on a—'

'King *Arthur*?'

'Yes.'

'Oh. Oh I see.'

'Good.'

'No disrespect intended, I'm sure.'

'Not at all.'

'My name's Mahaud, by the way.'

'Sir Bedevere de Haut Gales.'

'I've heard of you. Aren't you the knight who used to—'

But Bedevere interrupted. The name was familiar, and the voice – ye gods, how could he ever forget that voice? But no, surely not. It wasn't possible.

'Did you say Mahaud?' he said.

'That's right,' Mahaud replied. 'Mahaud de Ville-hardouin.'

Bedevere's voice quivered as he spoke. 'Matron?'

The skull laughed again, and this time Bedevere laughed too.

'You remember me, Matron,' Bedevere exclaimed. 'I was in the same year as Aguisant and Bors and Gaheris Minor.'

'Of course I remember! You kept beetles in a shoe box in the junior dormitory.'

'Look ...' It was Turquine, and there was just a hint of peevishness in his voice. 'I hate to interrupt, but aren't you going to introduce me?'

There was a puzzled silence and then Bedevere said, 'Sorry, Turkey, I forgot. Matron left the term before you arrived. Matron, this is Sir Turquine le Sable. He was at the old Coll too, but after your time.'

'Pleased to meet you.'

'Likewise. Look, Bedders, do you know what's going on here, because—'

'Shut *up*, Turkey, there's a good chap. Sorry, Matron. How are you keeping, anyway?'

There was a long silence. 'I'm dead.'

'Surely not?'

'I most certainly am.'

'I see. Oh I am sorry to hear that, Matron. I . . .'

Bedevere stopped in mid-sentence. Was it just him, or was something turning out a bit counter-intuitive here? 'Dead?' he repeated.

'As nail in door,' Matron replied. 'And I'm not at all pleased about it, let me tell you.'

'I'm not surprised.'

'I mean to say,' Matron went on, 'when I retired, the Coll was *extremely* generous – much more than I expected, really very moving – and so of course I wanted to invest my little nest-egg for my old age. And then I met this charming young lady, said she was the elder sister of one of the boys at the Coll . . .'

Bedevere felt a lump rise in his throat. 'Lyonesse Capital Growth Trust units?' he asked.

'Lyonesse Managed Income Bond, actually,' Matron replied. 'And not six months after I'd taken out the policy, I got this letter saying the whole thing had gone into liquidation and how sorry they were. It made my blood boil, I can tell you. So I came straight down here and . . . Well, here I am. And if ever I get my hands on that wicked little chit of a sales girl, I'll . . . Well, she'd better watch out, that's all.'

'That's awful, Matron,' Bedevere said. 'Cheating you like that and then murdering you as well. That's –

well, awful. They really shouldn't be allowed to get away with it.'

'Hear hear,' muttered Turquine, and added something about it needing no ghost come from the grave, which Bedevere thought was in rather poor taste. He shushed firmly, and then scratched his head.

'Excuse me asking,' he said after a moment's thought, 'but how come you can still, well, talk? I thought you needed to be . . .'

The skull clicked its teeth. 'Some people may let themselves run to seed when they retire,' Matron said. 'Not me. Like I always used to say to you boys at the Coll, the important thing is willpower, willpower and determination. I was *determined* not to let myself get out of shape, and it's worked.'

'I can see that,' Bedevere replied, and added, 'Good for you.' But he still felt there was something lacking. An explanation, for instance. Still, it was bad manners to keep on, and Matron had always been most particular about things like that. He changed the subject, and they chatted for a while about the other boys in Bedevere's class. This kept them entertained for a while; except that all of them were dead, and there was a risk of the whole thing getting a touch morbid; not to say repetitive. Very carefully, he reverted to the earlier topic.

'Matron,' he said, 'do please excuse me if this is a bit, well, personal, but I'd always understood . . .' Inspiration! 'When I was at the Coll, Sir Giraut taught us that when a person's sort of dead, that's it, you know . . .'

'Giraut!' snapped the skull, contemptuously. She has no lips to purse now, Bedevere reflected; otherwise . . . 'The man was a charlatan. Used to leave applecores behind the radiators.'

'I never liked him much.'

'Good for you,' Matron replied. 'What did he know about being dead? Just because he'd got a fancy degree from some university somewhere, that doesn't mean to say he's got the right to pick the middle out of the bread.'

Bedevere nodded, not that anyone could see him. 'So what's it really like, then?' he asked. 'Death, I mean. I've always wanted to know.'

'Well,' Matron said, after a moment's reflection, 'I can only speak as I find, you understand. You won't catch *me* pontificating about things I know nothing about, like some people we could mention. But personally, I find it's quite like being alive. Of course, the magic makes a difference.'

'I see,' Bedevere said. 'The magic.'

Matron laughed. 'I can tell *you* didn't pay much attention in class, young Master Bedevere. Too busy playing Hangman with that Ector de Maris, I'll be bound.'

Bedevere flushed, for nobody likes to be maligned; but he repressed his indignation and said, 'About the magic, Matron. What does it do?'

'Magic,' Matron said, in that slightly plonking voice of hers, 'is a by-product of the decay of the gold isotope Gold 337. It's a form of radiation. All radiation can make living things mutate; it influences molecular structures, you see. But magic radiation is extremely powerful. It can make living things mutate very quickly – turn you into a frog, for example – or it can affect inanimate objects, such as vases of flowers or the flags of all nations; make them pop out of top hats, that sort of thing. It can also, well, raise the dead.' Matron

534

hesitated for a moment. 'No, that's not strictly true. More a case of making death a bit more like life, you might say. No, that's still not quite right. More the other way round.'

'Make life seem like death, you mean?' Bedevere enquired. This was like GCC Philosophy with Dr Magus; and then he remembered, very faintly, that Matron and Dr Magus used to take long walks down by the archery butts. Under cover of the friendly darkness, he grinned.

'Exactly,' Matron was saying. 'If there's a lot of magic about – and there's plenty down here, I can tell you; if you don't believe me, ask the rat to show you his conjuring tricks – then a person can be dead and alive at the same time. That's to say, she's alive, but her body is dead. It's all a bit spooky, really,' she added, 'but you get used to it after a while.'

'I see.'

'Not,' Matron continued, 'that it's the slightest bit of use to me being alive if the rest of me is nothing but a lot of old bones. In fact it's the worst of both worlds, except that I don't get toothache any more. One must be grateful for small mercies, I always say.'

Bedevere sat in silence for a while. Turquine, for his part, was surreptitiously trying to fit together the bits of the skeleton that he'd started to use to make a set of stumps and a cricket bat with.

'How would it be,' Bedevere said at last, 'if we all got out of here? I mean what would happen, do you think? Would you – well, stop being half alive and be wholly dead, or would you stop being half dead and be . . .?'

'I really couldn't say,' Matron answered. 'Mind you, either would be an improvement. I never could be

535

doing with shilly-shallying, you know that.'

'Fine,' Bedevere said thoughtfully. 'So if we could get out of here . . .'

'If, young man. As we used to say when I was a girl, if ifs were horses, beggars would ride.'

'Quite,' Bedevere agreed. 'But you've been down here a long time. Haven't you, well, noticed anything?'

The skull mused for a moment. 'Not a great deal, no,' it said. 'From time to time, people drop in, they die, we talk for a while, then usually we fall out and they sulk, and they give up the power of speech. Some people can be so petty.'

'So you haven't got any suggestions about how we might . . .?'

'Well.' A long silence. 'There is something. I tried it with a young man who dropped in fifty years or so back, but I'm afraid he made rather a muff of it. No backbone, you see.'

'Ah.'

'Especially after he fell off the wall.'

'Right.' Bedevere scratched his ear thoughtfully. 'I'm game,' he said. 'What about you, Turkey?'

Turquine looked up. He was having difficulties. Beyond the basic principle that the leg bone connecka-to the thigh bone, he was no anatomist.

'You know me,' he said, 'I'll try anything once. Er, Bedders, do you know anything about knees?'

'This isn't going to work,' said Turquine. 'Don't ask me how I know, I just do.'

'Shut up, Turkey,' Bedevere grunted.

'All right, I'm just saying, that's all. Don't blame me if—'

536

'Boys!' said the skull sharply. 'No getting fractious, please.'

'Sorry,' said Turquine. 'It's just—'

'That'll do, Master Turquine,' the skull said. 'Oh, by the way, did you have a cousin called Breunis?'

Turquine raised an eyebrow. 'That's right,' he said. 'Breunis Saunce Pitie. Come to think of it, he was at the Coll, too.'

'I knew you reminded me of someone,' said the skull. 'He was a *horrid* little boy.'

Many years ago, Lyonesse Market Research discovered that market penetration for Lyonesse financial services among the Giants of South Permia was less than $18\frac{1}{2}$ per cent, and a major marketing drive was launched. It was quite successful, and, as a result, the Giants (who were basically personifications of glaciers and could trace their ancestry back to the Second Ice Age) were soon extinct.* One such Giant, Germadoc the Violent, had taken out an offshore roll-up sterling assets bond which went yellow on him about ten minutes after the ink was dry on the policy document, and he had come straight across to Atlantis City to complain. The customer service people had had to fire catapults at him just to stop him moving about. Then they tied him up and put him in the dungeon. In sections.

Being a Giant, his femurs were a touch over twelve feet long. The trapdoor was very slightly more than eighteen feet above floor level.

---

*Giants are nothing if not single-minded. If you tell a Giant that if he dies he stands to make thirty thousand marks, he doesn't hang about.

'I saw someone at a circus do this once,' Turquine was saying. 'Garcio the Magnificent, they called him, he was very good. Mind you,' he added, 'he had proper stilts, with little ledges you put your feet in and hand-grips and everything.'

Bedevere, clinging on to an enormous bone for dear life, nodded impatiently. 'Are you there yet?' he demanded.

'Not sure,' Turquine replied. 'It's so dark, you see ... Ah, what's this?'

The stilts swayed alarmingly, and Bedevere was nearly swept off his feet. He braced himself against the wall and hugged the bone to his chest. This had jolly well better work, he was saying to himself, otherwise ...

'Gotcha!'

And then a loud cry and an oath, and suddenly there wasn't any weight at the top of the stilts any more. Bedevere yelled 'Turkey!' and tried to peer upwards, but it was pointless. There were some grunting noises.

'Turkey!'

'It's all right,' came a strained voice from above. 'There's a handle or something, I'm hanging on to it. If I could just loosen this catch ...'

And then there was a flood of light.

And then things in the dungeon got a bit fraught.

Germadoc the Violent was very good about it all, considering. Once Bedevere and Matron had explained, and he'd understood that he was alive again and it really wasn't their fault at all, he'd helped them all up out of the cellar – Bedevere was amazed how many of them there had been – and then led his fellow-complainants away to find somebody to complain to. They could hear them doing it, far away in the distance.

'Well,' said Turquine, 'that's that. Piece of duff, really.'

Matron smiled. Once she got the flesh back on her bones, Bedevere saw that she hadn't changed a bit.

'Thank you, both,' she said graciously. 'Very much obliged, I'm sure. It was very perceptive of you, young Bedevere, to realise that we weren't dead at all, and it was just the magic in the dungeon all along.'

Under normal circumstances, Bedevere would have explained that Sir Giraut at the dear old Coll had explained to him that since death is final, anything that permits the patient to carry on talking must be something else. But he remembered the apple-cores behind the radiators and contented himself with a bashful smile. 'That's all right,' he said.

'And you, Master Turquine,' Matron continued, 'that was very brave of you. Well done.'

Turquine, unused to compliments, blushed. Usually when he was brave, the only witnesses were the people he was being brave against, and they tended to be hyper-critical.

In the distance there was a crash which made the floor shake, followed by a lot of cheering. That was probably Germadoc, complaining. By the sound of it, he had decided against putting it in writing.

'Well,' Bedevere said, 'we've got the Personal Organiser, the Atlanteans don't seem to be about, I think it's time we were on our way. Can we drop you off anywhere, Matron?'

Mahaud de Villehardouin smiled. 'Thank you,' she

said, 'that would be most kind. Would Glastonbury be out of your way?'

Glastonbury ... Bedevere knew the name from somewhere, but although the bell rang in his mind, nobody came to answer it. He assured her that that would be fine, and together they went in search of the fax machine.

It was hard to find. Although under normal circumstances Atlantis City is crawling with faxes, just then none of them seemed to be working. In fact, most of the office equipment was out of order, one way or another, which only goes to show that a good concerted complaint can make itself felt.

Eventually they tracked one down in a snug little room with comfortable chairs and a calendar with pictures of kittens on it. Something told Bedevere that this was probably the Queen's office.

'Here we are,' Turquine said, thumbing through the directory. 'Any number of places in Glastonbury are on the fax. Any preference?'

Mahaud shook her head. 'I expect it's changed rather a lot since my day,' she said. 'And besides, I won't be stopping.'

Glastonbury. The town of the Glass Mountain.

Bedevere did his best not to stare; he managed to get by with just glancing out of the corner of his eye as he dialled in the number. If she was going into the Glass Mountain, that meant that she was . . .

She was smiling again. 'You are a sharp one, Master Bedevere,' she said. 'You're quite right. Not in my own right, though; just by marriage, so to speak.'

The last piece dropped into place in the jigsaw of Bedevere's memory. Dr Magus and Matron had, of course, both left in the same term. All those long walks.

'How is Dr Magus, by the way?' he asked, as nonchalantly as he could.

'Simon?' Matron beamed. 'Very well indeed, thank you, or at least he was when I last saw him. That was some time ago now, of course, but I don't imagine he'll have noticed. A brilliant man, of course, but something of a dreamer. I expect I'll find fifteen hundred years' worth of washing-up waiting for me in the sink when I get home. I'll tell him you were asking after him; he always said you were rather brighter than you looked.'

Bedevere was going to say something, but then it occurred to him that from what he had heard, time in the Glass Mountain is rather different, somehow.* Rather like life, he remembered someone telling him once; you only get out of it what you're prepared to put into it. Something like that, anyway.

'Here goes,' he said. 'Hold tight . . .'

Transmitting.

---

*The best way to describe Glass-Mountain time is to consider the analogy of first- and second-class post. Both get to exactly the same place eventually; but whereas one of them usually arrives within twenty-four hours, the other can take a great deal longer, is far more prone to get lost on the way, and somehow always arrives at its destination tatty, heavily stamped on and via Preston.

6

In the stables of the Schloss Wei-
nachts, the reindeer were restless.

Because the Graf has distinctly
idiosyncratic requirements in transport, the stables are twice the size of
the rest of the castle; and the rest
of the castle is rather larger than,
say, Tuscany.

There are sports reindeer, touring reindeer, four-
leg-drive reindeer, turbo-charged reindeer with six
stomachs and extremely antisocial digestive systems,
reindeer with red go-faster stripes down their flanks;
even a few with 'My other reindeer's a Lappland Red'
stickers on their rumps. And then there is Radulf.

Radulf and the Graf go way back; right back to when
he started out as a Finno-Ugrian storm-deity with
responsibility for punishing perjury and collecting the
souls of the dead. They have seen some high old times
together, howling through the midwinter skies with the
wind in their hair and the world splayed out below

them like a spilt breakfast. It wasn't Klaus and Radulf then, of course; it was Odin and Sleipnir – and there have been other names, too, which the race-memory has been only too glad to forget. All the stuff with the red dressing-gowns and the sleigh bells is comparatively recent, the result of one of the biggest balls-ups in theological history.

Radulf is virtually retired now, and only rides the winds once a year. He hates the Americanised form of his name, and the song and the greetings cards make him sick. The slight discolouration of his nose (he prefers to think of it as a snout, anyway) is an honourable wound, the red nose of courage; a lasting memento of a desperate ten minutes with the Great Frost-Bear, back when the world was young, violent and not nearly so damn soppy.

Retired from flying, anyway; there's plenty of work for him to do on the ground, what with all the various jobs that need to be done under the terms of the Great Curse. There are toy catalogues to be pored over, order forms to make out, deliveries to supervise, and mountains and mountains of requisition chits to be sorted through as the requests from every family in the world come cascading through. And last, but definitely not least, there are the preparations for each year's Ride; itineraries to plan, architects' plans to study, ingenious methods of breaking into chimneyless houses, converted windmills and blocks of flats to be worked out.

'Radulf!'

A girl's voice, echoing melodramatically in the vastness of the stables. The old reindeer lifted his snout, took off his reading glasses and mooed softly. He knew the Graf didn't hold with the Grafin coming down to the stables. Not safe for a young girl, he said, and he was right. Some of the reindeer were special thoroughbreds, wild and savage, with antlers like pneumatic drills and tempers to match; and the Grafin was young and silly. She carried sugar-lumps in the pocket of her dress. Not sensible.

'Radulf, the phone for you!' she was saying. It sounded like she was down among the drag-racers. Radulf flicked his left ear apprehensively. Give a sugar-lump to one of those high-octane monstrosities, you could have an explosion.

He mooed loudly to her to stay where she was and not feed anything, then sprang to his hooves and padded silently through the rows of stalls. He knew the layout of the stables as well as a taxi driver knows Bayswater. He should do, by now.

'There you are, Radulf,' said the Grafin, and handed over the portable phone. 'It's Father. He says it's urgent.'

Radulf nodded his head, and the dim light of the chandeliers high above under the rafters glinted on the tinsel wrapped round his horns. He put the receiver to his ear and mooed into it.

'Moo. Moo. Moo. Moo? *Moo*? Mo . . .' The antlers nodded a couple of times, and Radulf hung up. 'Moo,' he explained.

'Oh dear,' said the Grafin. 'I suppose we'd better get back to the house, then.'

'M.'

'I expect he'll need plenty of hot water and bandages.'

'M.'

They left the stables, switching out the lights as they

544

went. For a while, the enormous building was silent – except, of course, for the shuffling of innumerable hooves and the quiet whinnying of the reincalves.

Then a voice spoke in the Number 2 hayloft.

'Are you sure this is the right place?' it said.

There was a sharp intake of breath next to it, and a muffled click as a torch was switched on.

'Be quiet, Gally, I'm trying to think.'

'Please yourself.'

In the hayloft, Boamund was turning the situation over in his mind; or at least he was trying to. Something – he hadn't the faintest idea what – kept getting in the way. His companion, Galahaut the Haut Prince, had gladly abdicated any participation in the decision-making process at a very early stage, and was filing his fingernails. Toenail was cleaning the boots.

'Who was that?' Boamund asked suddenly. Galahaut shrugged, and so it was left to Toenail to reply.

'Looked like a bloody great big deer, boss,' he replied. 'Domesticated, too, by the looks of it.'

'Thank you,' said Boamund, with what he hoped was irony. 'Actually, I meant—'

'It's amazing the things you can train animals to do,' Toenail went on. 'Cousin of mine, worked in a circus, used to tell me how they trained the lions—'

'Toenail.'

'Sorry.'

Boamund leant his chin on his cupped hands. 'That girl,' he said. 'I don't remember there being anything about a girl . . .'

Toenail pointed out that they had heard her speak of somebody, presumably the Graf, as Father, and suggested that she might be his daughter.

545

'Don't be silly, Toenail,' Boamund replied. 'Whoever heard of the Graf von Weinacht having a daughter?'

'Whoever heard of the Graf von Weinacht?' Toenail answered.

Boamund clicked his tongue. 'Not under that name, maybe. But – well, surely you've twigged by now. It's *him*. You know . . .' Boamund rubbed his stomach and said 'Ho ho ho!' with a sort of manic jollity. Toenail smiled tactfully.

'Yes,' he said, 'I'd managed to get that far, sure. What I mean is, all this –' he waved his arms in an encircling gesture '– doesn't actually fit in with what you might call his public image. I mean,' he went on ruefully, 'the barbed wire. The dogs. The searchlights. The mines. The moat full of piranhas . . .'

He glanced down at his boots, which had nibble-marks where the toecaps had once been. Boamund nodded.

'I think I see what you're driving at,' he said. 'You mean, he isn't really like how he seems to us.'

'Exactly,' Toenail replied, relieved. 'The image and the man. It turns out that we don't know anything about the real Santa . . .'

Boamund put his hand over the dwarf's mouth and hissed. 'Not here, you clown. I don't think you should say that name here.'

'Why not?' asked Toenail through a gag of fingers.

'I don't know,' Boamund replied. 'I just have this feeling, all right?'

'About the real Graf von Weinacht, then,' Toenail said. 'I mean, the person with the sack and the sleigh doesn't have a daughter, admittedly, but then, I've never seen a Christmas card with claymore mines and attack dogs on it, have you?'

Galahaut yawned. 'You mean,' he said suddenly, 'we should abandon our preconceptions?'

The other two looked at him.

'Forget about stereotyped role-perceptions,' he continued. 'Look for the real persona behind the image. Fair enough.'

For the seventy-third time since they'd set out, Toenail gave his master that Why-did-we-have-to-bring-him look. Boamund shrugged and grimaced back. Galahaut, for his part, was completely engrossed in dealing with a potential whitlow.

'So,' Boamund said, 'you reckon that girl was his daughter, then?'

'Could be.'

'Right.'

Boamund lowered his chin back on to the palms of his hands and sat for a while, completely still. If this was a cartoon, Toenail said to himself, he'd have a big bubble with 'Thinks' in it coming out of his head.

'Anyway,' said Boamund at last, 'I reckon it's about time we got on with the job in hand. Right.' He nodded his head purposefully and punched the palm of his hand to register decisiveness. Boamund, Toenail decided, would have been a great success in the silent movies.

He waited.

'So,' Boamund said. 'First things first, eh? Let's . . .' He bit his lip thoughtfully. 'How'd it be if . . .?'

The dwarf looked at him expectantly. An X-ray of his head, he said to himself, would show up completely blank at this particular moment.

547

'Sorry to interrupt,' Toenail said, therefore, 'but if I could just break in here . . .'

Boamund registered the democratic attitude to supreme command and nodded. Toenail thanked him.

'What I was thinking was,' he said, 'we want to get inside the castle proper, don't we?'

'Correct.'

'Just off the top of my head, then,' Toenail went on, 'wouldn't you say our biggest problem was getting past the gates?'

The gates. They'd seen them already, of course. They made you feel vertiginous half a mile away. The two flanking towers were black needles of masonry soaring up into the sky, and the gates themselves were cliff faces in hobnailed black oak.

'Tricky, certainly,' Boamund replied. 'I thought we might actually give the gates a miss and try the wall instead.'

Toenail couldn't help shuddering. Eighty metres high at least, and built of polished black marble. Probably best, he decided, to try and divert the boss's mind away from that one.

'Good idea,' he said, 'I hadn't thought of that. Yes, that's much better than what I had in mind.'

Boamund raised his eyebrows, registering his willingness to listen to any suggestion, however puerile. 'What were you thinking, then?' he said.

'Oh, it was just . . . No, it was silly.'

'Out with it.'

'I thought,' Toenail said, 'we could pretend to be postmen.'

Boamund's face clouded over. 'Postmen,' he said.

'That's right,' said Toenail. He waited for what he

548

judged to be the right moment, psychologically speaking, and added, 'Didn't you notice the letterbox, then?'

'Letterbox?'

'In the gate,' Toenail said artlessly. 'Well, not in the big gate, of course. I meant the little side gate we passed when we were trying to find a place to cross the moat.'

'Ah,' Boamund said. 'The *side* gate.'

'That's it,' Toenail said brightly. 'You remember. I kept trying to point it out to you and you kept telling me to shut up, so I guessed you must have noticed it for yourself. Well, it had a letterbox in it, so it stands to reason . . .'

'Yes,' Boamund said, 'of course. I was wondering when you were going to . . .'

'Of course,' Toenail continued, 'to begin with, I was puzzled how the postman gets to the letterbox, what with the moat and the piranhas and everything. Had me thinking there, I can tell you.'

'I bet!'

'And then,' Toenail went on, 'I saw what you'd seen.'

'Oh good.'

'The little boat,' said Toenail, kindly, 'tied up under the weeping willow. Of course, you with your trained eye, you saw that like a shot.'

Boamund managed to register smugness.

'And then I wondered, Why did he make us paddle across the moat on that floating log when there was a perfectly good boat just sitting there? Pretty slow on the uptake, wasn't I?'

'Oh, I don't know,' said Boamund feebly. 'It takes a

549

special sort of mind, I always think.'

'Anyway,' Toenail said, 'it wasn't till after we were across the moat and in the potting shed and I was putting TCP on where the piranhas—'

'Um . . .'

'Then,' said the dwarf, 'I realised. Of course, I said, we couldn't have taken the boat, or else it wouldn't have been there for the milkman, and he'd have raised the alarm, and . . .'

'Ah,' said Boamund. 'Just out of interest, what was it put you on to there being a milkman?'

'Same as you, I expect,' said Toenail, maliciously.

'Good man.'

'The empty milk bottles outside the little gate, I mean.'

'Splendid,' said Boamund, and he laughed. 'Make a general of you yet, we will.'

'Thank you,' said Toenail. 'Must be marvellous to think of things the way you do.'

'It's a knack.'

'So,' Toenail said, 'my idea was that we wait until the postman comes along in the morning – that'll be after the milkman's been and gone, of course – and then one of us knocks on the door, as if there was a parcel . . .'

'Or a registered letter,' said Boamund, excitedly.

'Yes, even better,' said Toenail resignedly. 'And then, when somebody comes to answer the door, we thump him and get in.' He paused for a moment. 'Pretty silly idea, really.'

'Oh, I don't know,' said Boamund slowly. 'I mean, put like that . . .'

'I thought you said something about the wall.'

'Oh, just thinking aloud,' Boamund replied. 'Got to

consider every possibility, you know. Actually, I was coming round to the postman scenario myself. Neat, I thought.'

'One of your better ideas?'

Boamund registered modesty. 'Simple, anyway,' he said. 'What do you think?'

Toenail smiled. 'I don't know how you do it, boss,' he replied.

The sleigh howled through the night sky, the clanging of its bells drowned by the shrieking of the wind.

Klaus von Weinacht, head down over the console to reduce the coefficient of drag, stared out through the driving snow for the first glimpse of his battlements. On the instrument panel, the compass stopped its crazed spinning and jammed dead.

Nearly home. Good.

He ran back through the timings in his mind. If they had all left the Grail Castle at the same time then, allowing for pack ice in the Nares Straight and contrary winds over Permia, then it would still be two or three days before they were due to arrive. Plenty of time. He laughed cruelly.

The reindeer pounded the clouds with their hooves.

'Ready?'

Toenail, concealed behind a bush, nodded, while Galahaut yawned and picked bark off the branch they had found for a club. Boamund took a deep breath, and knocked on the gate.

'Let's just run through it once more,' he hissed. 'The porter opens the door, I distract his attention. Galahaut, you hit him. Toenail . . .'

There was the sound of heavy bolts being shot back, and the door opened.

'Hello.'

Galahaut gripped the club and started to move. Then he stopped.

'Er . . . hello,' Boamund was saying. He had gone a very pretty shade of pink.

'Was there something?' said the girl, nicely.

For four seconds, Boamund just stood there, irradiating pinkness. Then he smiled idiotically.

'Postman,' he said.

'Oh good,' said the girl. 'Something nice, I hope. Not more horrid old bills. Daddy gets so bad-tempered when it's bills.'

Toenail had covered his face with his hands. The worst part was not being able to do anything.

'Letter,' Boamund gurgled. 'Registered. Got to sign for—'

'How exciting!' said the girl. 'I wonder who it's from.'

There was a moment of perfect equilibrium; and then it dawned on Boamund that he didn't have about his person anything that looked like a registered letter.

Toenail had to admit that he coped as well as could be expected in the circumstances. After he had made a right pantomime of patting all his pockets and rummaging about in his knapsack, he said, 'Damn, I seem to have left it in the van.' It could have been worse, said the dwarf to himself, just conceivably.

'Never mind,' said the girl. 'I'll wait for you here.'

In retrospect, Toenail realised that there was a funny expression on her face, too. At the time, though, he put it down to a complete absence of brains.

'Right,' said Boamund, rooted to the spot. 'I'll just go back and, er, fetch it, then.'

'Right.'

They stood for a moment, gazing at each other. Then Boamund started to walk slowly backwards. Into the bush.

'Be careful!' the girl called out, too late. 'Oh dear, I hope you haven't hurt yourself.'

Toenail, who had broken Boamund's fall very neatly indeed, could certify that he hadn't. But the fool just sprawled there. It was only natural that the girl should come and look . . .

'Oh,' she said.

Boamund grinned feebly. Galahaut tried to hide the club behind his back, and waved.

'Actually,' said Boamund, breaking a silence that was threatening to become a permanent fixture, 'we aren't postmen at all.'

'Not . . . postmen?'

My God, thought the dwarf, and I thought *he* was a pillock. He tried to wriggle the small of his back away from the sharpest roots of the bush.

'No,' Boamund said. 'That was a ruse.'

'Oh!'

'Actually, we're—'

'Knights,' Galahaut interrupted. 'Knights of the Holy Grail. At your service,' he added.

Boamund gave him a filthy look.

'Knights!' the girl squeaked. 'Oh, how *exciting*!'

The hell with this, said the dwarf to himself, things can't get any worse, they just can't. With a tremendous wriggle, he extricated himself from under Boamund, shook himself free of leaves and bits of twig, and tugged at his master's sleeve.

'Boss,' he said.

Boamund looked round. 'What?'

'The plan, boss. You know.'

'Go away, Toenail.'

Dwarves cannot, of course, disobey a direct order. He shrugged his shoulders and drifted away to the shelter of a wind-blasted thorn tree, crossed his legs, and sulked.

The girl's eyes were shining. 'This is so thrilling,' she said. 'What are you doing here? Or is it a secret?'

'We're . . .' A tiny spark of common sense flared up in Boamund's brain. 'It's a secret,' he said. 'A quest,' he added.

'Gosh!'

'And you mustn't tell a soul.'

'I won't.'

'Promise?'

'Promise.'

A long silence followed, as the girl gazed at Boamund, Boamund and Galahaut gazed at the girl, and Toenail darned a sock. It could have gone on for ever if it hadn't been broken by the sound of a door slamming.

The girl gave a startled squeak and looked round. The gate had blown shut.

'Oh *dear!*' she wailed. 'And I've forgotten my key again.'

Toenail closed his eyes and counted under his breath. One, two . . .

'Never fear, fair damsel,' Boamund said. 'We'll have you back in there in two shakes, won't we, Gally?'

(Three, said Toenail, opened his eyes and returned to his darning.)

'Absolutely,' said Galahaut. 'No trouble at all.'

Wearily, Toenail picked himself up, put the sock carefully away, and walked over. He took his time. Why hurry? Where's the point?

'You'll be wanting the rope now, then,' he said.

Boamund's eyes were fixed on the girl. 'Rope?' he said.

'The rope I just happen to have with me in this holdall,' Toenail continued resignedly. 'And goodness me, what's this? Gosh, it's a grappling hook and some crampons. Talk about coincidence, eh?'

Boamund nodded, with all the animation of a hunting trophy. 'Right,' he said, 'this won't take a jiffy. We, er, take the hook like *so*, we pass the line *behind* the hook to make sure it doesn't tangle, then we swing the hook one, two, three and . . .'

The hook soared into the air, hung for a moment like a strange steel falcon, and came down again, precisely where the girl would have been standing if Galahaut hadn't moved her.

'You idiot!' Galahaut shouted. 'Give me that hook.'

'Shan't.'

There was a tussle. Both knights fell over and started pulling each other's hair. Toenail finished off the sock and started on another.

Eventually, Galahaut won control of the hook, stood up and dusted himself off. 'Like this,' he said. 'Watch.'

He threw the hook, and far above their heads there was a faint chink of steel on stone. Toenail stared in amazement.

'All *right*,' he said.

Not long afterwards, the gate opened and the four of them passed through. They didn't, however, pass unnoticed. On the main security monitor in Radulf's stall, a green light began to wink ominously. The old reindeer narrowed his brows, studied the screen and shook his head until the tinsel in his horns swayed.

Then he sounded the alarm.

'Pass the salt.'

'Sorry?'

'I said pass the salt, there's a good fellow.'

'There you are. Sorry. I was miles away.'

Aristotle shrugged, salted his kipper and turned to the sports pages. There is a difference, he always said, between not being one's best in the mornings (which was something he could respect) and being dozy. His mood wasn't improved when he read that Australia had gone down thirty-seven to three against the All Blacks.

'Typical!' he said.

On Aristotle's left, Simon Magus looked up from the letter he was reading and said, 'What is?'

'Huh?'

'You said something was typical.'

'Oh.' Aristotle closed the paper. 'The bloody Newzies have walked all over us again, that's all. We've been no good ever since they capped that idiot Westermann.'

Simon Magus looked at his neighbour over the tops of his spectacles. 'By us, I gather, you mean the Australians,' he said. 'I never knew you came from those parts, Ari.'

'Certainly not,' replied Aristotle severely. 'As a philosopher, I am above nationalism. On the other hand, I am logical. There is no point following rugby

556

football unless you support a particular team. On purely rational grounds, I selected the Australians.'

Simon Magus grinned. 'I did that once,' he said. 'At five to one on. Never again.'

Aristotle frowned at him down the great runway of his nose, and reached for his toast.

'Beats me why you want to follow sport anyway,' Simon Magus went on. 'Complete waste of time, if you ask me, a lot of idiots running about chasing things. When I used to be a teacher we had to take it in turns to be referee. I loathed it.'

'You,' Aristotle replied, 'are not a philosopher. If one has any pretensions to philosophy, one must cultivate understanding. I study humanity. Humanity is obsessed with sport. Therefore, if I want to understand humanity, I must study sport. It's purely scientific, you see.'

Simon Magus grinned. 'It wasn't entirely scientific a couple of months back,' he said, 'when you made us have the telly on all day in the Senior Common Room for Wimbledon. I distinctly remember you standing on the table waving a bloody great flag round your head and chanting *There's only one Boris Becker* every time the other one fell over. It was embarrassing.'

'Research,' Aristotle mumbled through a mouthful of toast. 'Just research, that's all.'

'Or what about that time after the World Cup when you made that big statue out of wax, and you called it Maradona and threw teacups at it? You can still see the marks on the wall.'

'One has to try and enter into the spirit ...'

'Spirit, maybe,' Simon Magus replied, 'but there was no need to throw a brick through Dante's study window just because he supports Italy.'

Little red spots appeared in the corners of Aristotle's cheeks. 'It *was* offside,' he snarled. 'I've got it on video, you can see if you like. And Dante had the ... the *infernal* nerve to suggest ...'

Simon Magus chuckled. 'I'll say this for you,' he said, 'I do believe you've got into the spirit of the thing. Have some more coffee?'

Aristotle, offended, waved the pot away and returned to his newspaper. Still chuckling, Simon Magus leant back in his chair and called to the small, wizened figure sitting on the other side of Aristotle.

'Merlin,' he said. 'More coffee?'

'Sorry?'

'Would you like some more coffee?'

'I do beg your pardon, I was miles away. No, no more coffee for me, thank you. Two cups are quite sufficient.'

Simon Magus nodded and turned back to his letter. He had read it seven times already, but he wasn't bored with it yet, not by a long way.

... Such a charming young man, though inclined to be a little bit hot-headed. Sir Bedevere also wishes to be remembered to you. You always did have a very high opinion of him.

And now I must close, dear heart, and trust that it will not be too much longer before we are together again. All my love, and do remember to wrap up warm!

Your very own,

Mahaud

P.S. I almost forgot. While I was talking to him, young Bedevere happened to mention that he had seen the Graf von Weinacht while he was in Atlantis! Such a coincidence, don't you think! I wonder how the poor dear Graf is these days. They say that they can do wonders with drugs and leeches and things nowadays, but perhaps he is beyond help.

As he read the final paragraph, Simon Magus's brows gathered in a slight frown. Perhaps it was indeed all a coincidence, but perhaps not.

He lifted his head and looked out of the window – easy enough, since all the walls, floors and ceilings of the Glass Mountain are windows of a sort. Far away, he could see the earth, twirling gracefully and apparently aimlessly on its axis like an enchanted and very stout ballerina. He looked at his watch. Only another two hours to go . . .

To keep himself from being impatient, Simon Magus turned his thoughts to the Graf von Weinacht. A sad case, certainly; understandable, too, very understandable. In his position, anyone would probably react the same way. And a brilliant man, too, before it happened, although even then people were saying some very strange things about him.

The hall steward removed his plate and he sat for a moment, letting his mind relax. Nice to know that young Bedevere had finally made something of himself. Always a lot of promise there, he had often thought, just waiting for an opportunity to get out. No, that's not quite right; waiting for a situation in which he would be forced to take charge and make sure the job got done. Without that extra little bit of pressure, he could never achieve anything. Well, then.

He pushed back his chair, nodded affably at Nostradamus and Dio Chysostom, and strolled through into the library in search of the latest issue of the *Philatelic Monthly*. Instead, he found himself stopping in the Astrotheology section and taking down a very big, extremely dusty book that nobody had moved for quite some time.

Simon Magus pulled up a chair, crossed his legs and began to read.

Klaus von Weinacht knelt in the snow and howled at the sky.

Five hundred and twenty miles north of Nordaustlandet, in the middle of the bleakest, wildest, most inhospitable of all the desert places of the earth, is no place to break down. The nearest telephone box is in Hammerfest, five hundred miles the other way, and it's usually out of order. Besides, the chances of getting a garage to come out this far on a Sunday are practically nil.

Having vented his rage on the howling winds, von Weinacht opened the toolbox, took out a cold chisel, a wrench and a very big hammer, and set to work on the broken runner.

'Bloody – cheapskate – Far – Eastern – gimcrack –' he snarled in time to the hammer-blows. 'Ouch,' he added. He paused, sucked his throbbing thumb and calmed himself down. Now then, Klaus, he could hear his mother saying, you'll only make things worse if you lose your temper.

He picked up the wrench and set to work. Last time

he allowed himself to be talked into buying a stinking Japanese sleigh. No idea of craftsmanship, just thrown together any old how, Friday afternoon job. Anger surged up inside him, and he stripped a thread.

'Sod!' he roared at the flat horizon. Then he hurled the wrench to the ground and jumped on it.

Permafrost may be thick, but there are limits. There was a cracking sound, like the earth's crust yawning, and the Graf jumped clear just in time to avoid going down a ravine. The wrench, however, was gone for good.

'Right,' said the Graf. 'Let's all keep absolutely icy calm, shall we?' He went back to the toolbox, found another wrench, and continued with the job.

He ached all over. If ever he caught up with that misbegotten bloody knight – what was the bastard's name? Something sounding like turquoise. Any bloody knight, come to that. They're all the same, knights. Scum, the lot of them. Without realising it, he picked up the hammer and started to beat the hell out of the oilcan.

An hour later, he had managed to destroy a complete set of tools, smash the sleigh quite beyond repair, and frighten fifteen heavy-duty Trials reindeer into a stupefied trance. He threw down the hammer, lay on the ground and beat the ice with his fists.

Then he got up and pulled the walkie-talkie out of the saddlebags.

'Radulf,' he shouted. 'Beam me up.'

'Gosh!'

'Yes, miss,' said Toenail automatically. His head

swivelled from side to side, looking for somewhere safe. Optimism is another dwarfish characteristic.

'What's that funny ringing noise?' asked Galahaut.

'That's the alarm,' the girl replied. 'Do you think somebody could have broken in?' She shivered a little.

Brill, said Toenail to himself. 'I'm already lumbered with two idiots, now it looks like I've got a third one to look after as well. Any more, while I'm at it? Bring out your idiots.

He nudged Boamund in the ribs.

'Boss,' he said, 'don't you think we ought to be, well, getting along? You know . . .'

Boamund looked at him blankly for a moment. 'What?' he said. 'Oh, I see what you mean. Yes, good idea.' He remained where he was. In fact, the dwarf noticed, the three of them together looked remarkably like the legs of a table.

It was, in fact, the girl who broke the spell.

'Do excuse me,' she said, 'I'm completely forgetting my manners. Would any of you care for some tea?'

The early history of the Grail is surrounded by legends, most of which were put about by the PR department of Lyonesse back in the tenth century to create artificial runs on Byzantine long-dated government stock.

When the emperors of Byzantium ran into financial difficulties, they raised money by hocking sacred relics – the Crown of Thorns, the True Cross, the shin-bone of St Athanasius, and so forth. The record of the Empire in those days is not so much history as pawnography.

The value of these relics was determined by the market, which in turn was influenced by supply and demand. So complete, however, was the Empire's collection of holy bits and bobs that it very nearly constituted a full set. There was only one worthwhile relic missing; but it was also the big one. So long as it was unaccounted for, the market could never crystallise, for fear of what might happen if it should ever reappear.

Clearly, as far as the market-makers were concerned, this was a situation that had to continue, if they were to have any hope at all of controlling the market. And in order that the Grail should stay missing, it stood to reason that they had to find it themselves, quickly. Then they could arrange for it to get permanently and definitively lost.

The result was the massive outburst of knightly energy which swept Christendom, playing a major part in the fall of Albion. In due course, Atlantis did indeed find the Grail, and re-lose it so thoroughly that it has stayed lost ever since. Just in case, however, the Chief Clerk made a secret note of its whereabouts, which he then put in a safe place; to be precise, in the library of Glastonbury Abbey.

After the Dissolution of the Monasteries, however, the library was dispersed; and a certain manuscript found its way into the hands of one Gabriel Townsend, bookseller of Stratford-upon-Avon. When Townsend fell into debt and was sold up by the bailiffs, a local man called John Shakespeare was attracted by the picture of naked angels illuminated on the flyleaf and bought it. To prevent his wife finding it, he wrapped it round the pendulum of his clock.

Where, of course, it has remained to this day.

It's all right for them, Toenail muttered to himself.

They can sit there stuffing themselves with Bakewell tart and digestive biscuits, because they've got no imagination. They can't see what's going to happen when we get caught.

He gritted his teeth and returned to the job in hand, which was sewing a button back on Galahaut's pyjama jacket.

'Are you sure you won't have another biscuit?' the girl was saying. 'Go on, there's plenty.'

Boamund, who had eaten seven biscuits, three slices of fruit cake and a scone, all washed down with four cups of tea, shook his head politely and subconsciously longed for a nice slab of cold roast ox. Galahaut, who had a digestion like a cement mixer, helped himself to a coconut pyramid.

The girl tried to think of something to say. In her dreams, of course, it had all been much simpler; it always is. All her life she had known that one day, a handsome young knight would call in on this gloomy old castle on his way somewhere, and Father would happen to be out, and she would offer the knight tea, and they would talk . . . She had insisted on having this room converted from a subsidiary boiling-oil store into a nice little sitting room with flowery pink curtains and frilly cushions. She had spent hours – thousands of hours – baking and icing, so that when the moment came there would be plenty of fresh, home-made things to eat to go with the tea. She had thought of everything; except, of course, what she was going to say. That, she had somehow assumed, would come naturally.

'It must be wonderfully exciting,' she said, 'being on a quest.'

'Oh, it's not as wonderful as all that,' Galahaut

drawled, leaning back in his chair and hoping the light through the arrow-slit would catch his profile. 'Most of it's just plain, hard slog. Hours in the saddle, out in all weathers, nights under canvas or just huddled under a blanket against the rain ...'

Toenail snorted, but nobody heard him. Had the girl chosen to ask him, he could have pointed out that the Haut Prince refused to spend the night anywhere that didn't have at least two stars and a southerly aspect, and insisted on his own private bathroom. And the fuss he made if the bed wasn't properly aired ...

The girl nodded eagerly. It was hard to decide which of them was the more romantic, really; the world-weary thin one with the pimple, or the strong, silent one with the pink face. On the whole, probably the pink one; but it was too early in the story to choose.

'This quest,' she said, 'I bet it's terribly dangerous.'

'Um,' said Boamund. 'Hope not.'

The girl laughed prettily. 'Oh, you're so modest,' she replied. 'I'm sure you're not the least bit scared.'

Boamund fidgeted with the tablecloth, while Gala-haut broke in and said that without fear you can't have courage. That did for the conversation what a damp towel does for a burning chip-pan, and the girl offered them another cake.

'That bell's still ringing,' the girl observed. 'I wonder what on earth it can be.'

The two knights glanced at each other. 'Probably just a loose connection in the wiring,' Galahaut said. 'Always going wrong, burglar alarms. We used to have one at the Castle, but next-door's cat was always setting it off so we took it down again. Nobody ever takes any notice of them, anyway.'

The girl looked surprised. 'Don't they?' she said.

Galahaut shook his head. 'Not usually. This is delicious angel cake, by the way. Did you make it yourself?'

Inside Boamund's heart, a great coiled spring of anger was being compressed, slowly and painfully, until he felt sure that he could stand it no longer. Damn Gally, he thought. I never liked him. Why did I bring him with me? Why couldn't it have been Lamorak or Turquine or one of the others? Old Turkey would have wandered off to look for the socks by now, and I could have . . .

'Actually,' he said – it was the first thing he'd said for ages – 'I think it's time we were going. Come on, Gally.'

Galahaut raised his eyebrows. 'What's the rush?' he said.

'You know perfectly well.'

'No I don't,' Galahaut replied. 'You must excuse my friend,' he said to the girl. 'So impatient.'

Boamund had gone bright red. 'Thank you, Sir Galahaut,' he said, as stiff as a newly laundered shirt. 'I don't need you to make my apologies for me.'

'Someone's got to do it,' Galahaut replied, grinning. 'Pretty nearly a full-time job it can be, sometimes.'

'What do you mean by that?'

'You understand plain Albionese, I take it.'

The girl's heart beat faster. They were going to fight! And because of her – yes, of course it was, knights only ever fight among themselves because of a lady. How marvellously, unspeakably thrilling!

Toenail edged across to the coal-scuttle, climbed in and shut the lid firmly.

'By God,' Boamund was saying, 'if there wasn't a lady present, I'd have a good mind to jolly well . . .'

'Jolly well what?'

'Jolly well ask you what you meant by that.'

'Well then, I'll save you the trouble of asking. I mean you're a liability, young Boamund. Can't take you anywhere, never could. Do excuse him,' he said to the girl. 'He always gets a bit over-excited if he eats too much chocolate. I remember once at school—'

'Sir Galahaut!'

'Sir Boamund. If only you could see how ridiculous you look.'

Boamund reached slowly into his pocket and drew out a glove. Actually, it was a woolly mitten with the fingers cut off, but it would have to do.

'My gage,' said Boamund. 'If you will do me the honour . . .'

'What do you want me to do with your glove, Bo? You lost the other one again, have you?'

'Sir Galahaut . . .'

'Always were a terror for losing gloves. At school Matron made you tie them round your neck with a bit of string.'

'Very well.' Boamund picked up the glove and slapped the Haut Prince across the cheek. 'Now, sir . . .'

'Don't do that, Bo, it tickles.'

Oh God, thought Toenail. I suppose I'd better do something, before they hammer each other into quick-fry steak. Carefully, he raised the lid of the scuttle and lifted himself out. Then he tiptoed across the room to the door, opened it, and left.

'Don't pretend you don't understand,' Boamund

was saying. 'That is unworthy of you.'

'Honestly, Bo, I haven't the faintest idea what you think you're talking about. Please stop drivelling, you're upsetting the lady.'

'I . . .' Boamund was lost for words. All he could think to do was to take out the other mitten and dash it in the cur's face.

'There,' Galahaut said, 'it was in your pocket all the time.'

'That does it. I demand satisfaction.'

The Haut Prince giggled. 'You what?' he said.

'You heard. You're a knave, a cad and a blackguard, and . . .' Boamund delved back into the archives of his mind, 'you cheated in falconry.'

A red curtain of rage swept unexpectedly across Galahaut's consciousness, obscuring everything else. 'What did you just say?' he gasped.

'You heard,' Boamund snarled. 'At the end of the summer term back in '08. You bought a cage of white mice from the pet shop, and you—'

'It's a lie!'

'It's not,' Boamund retorted. 'I found the receipt in your tuck box.'

'And what were you doing looking through my tuck box?'

'That's beside the point. You used those mice to—'

'So that's where my Aunt Ysoud's fruit cake got to!'

'You used those mice—'

'Greedy pig!'

'Cheat!'

The girl looked at them, puzzled. Well, at any rate, they were definitely going to fight.

★ ★ ★

Von Weinacht jumped down from the sleigh and called for his axe.

It had taken two hours – *two hours*! – for the pick-up sleigh to arrive, and then the tow-rope had broken, one of the reindeer had escaped, and they'd flown the wrong way over the Harris Ridge. The Graf took the axe from a trembling page and advanced towards the malfunctioning sleigh. He'd give it metal fatigue!

He noticed the alarm, and snapped his fingers imperiously.

'All right,' he yelled, 'I'm back now, you can turn that God-awful racket off!'

Radulf, who had come out to meet him, was trying to tell him something, but von Weinacht couldn't be bothered right now. All he wanted to do was give that worthless heap of Nipponese junk a service it would never forget.

'Excuse me.'

Something was tugging at his sleeve.

The Graf looked down and saw a dwarf. He frowned. Years since he'd seen a dwarf about the place. The last one, he remembered, had handed in his notice and gone south to work in the diamond mines. Funny.

'Excuse me,' the dwarf repeated, 'but could you possibly spare a moment? You see, two dangerous knights have broken in, and—'

'Knights?' Von Weinacht scooped the dwarf up in one enormous hand and held him about an inch from his nose. 'Knights?'

'Yes, sire, two knights. Boamund and Galahaut, sir. They're in your daughter's sitting room. Having tea.'

'Tea!' Von Weinacht roared, dropped the dwarf, and

broke into a run. Toenail picked himself up, rubbed his elbow vigorously, and followed.

He just hoped he was in time, that was all.

7

'Will these do?' the girl asked.

It was odd, she was saying to herself, I thought knights always had their own swords. In all the books she'd ever read, a knight didn't go anywhere without at least one sword, sometimes two. Still, there it was. Sometimes, she felt that she didn't really know an awful lot about real life.

'Thanks,' Boamund said gruffly. 'That'll do fine.'

'I found them,' the girl was saying, 'in Father's study. He's got lots of swords and things in there. I think he collects them or something. I brought swords, but there's axes and flails and maces and daggers too, if you want them.'

'Just swords will do fine,' Galahaut said. 'Unless, of course, Sir Boamund wants a shield or anything. He always insisted on having a shield at school.'

'I did *not*.'

'And if he couldn't have one, he used to burst into tears.'

'At least I didn't put an exercise book down my front when I was tilting.'

'What do you mean by that?'

'You heard.'

'There are some books in the library,' the girl put in helpfully, 'if anyone wants one.'

Boamund drew his sword from its scabbard. It was very cold. 'Shall we get on with it?' he asked. 'That is, if Sir Galahaut is ready.'

'Perfectly ready, thank you.'

'After you, then.'

Von Weinacht stood outside the sitting room and caught his breath.

'In there?'

Toenail nodded.

'Right.'

One kick from the Graf's enormous boot sent the door flying open. But the room was empty.

Oh God, Toenail thought, I was too late. They've gone off to fight it out; there'll be nothing left but torn clothes and a hundredweight of minced knight. Bugger.

'I thought you said . . .'

'They must have left, sir,' Toenail replied. 'Gone somewhere else, I mean.'

'Somewhere else?' There was an extra edge to the Graf's voice, which implied that it was bad enough their being there at all without them moving about like a lot of migratory wildfowl. 'Where?'

'Somewhere where there's plenty of room, I expect,'

Toenail replied. 'You see, they were wanting a fight . . .'

The Graf lifted his head and roared with laughter.

'A fight,' he repeated. 'Well, they've come to the right place, then, haven't they?'

'Yes, sir. Only we haven't.'

'Apparently not.' The Graf turned to his pages and shouted, 'You lot! Search the castle, understood. Two dangerous knights. Jump to it.'

Then something thudded into place in von Weinacht's brain, and he swung down a hand and grabbed the dwarf.

'You,' he growled. 'Who are you supposed to be, then?'

'Toenail, sir. I'm a dwarf.'

'I can see that.'

'Attendant on the knights, sir. I came with them from Albion.'

'I see.' Von Weinacht breathed out fiercely through his nose. 'And why are you betraying your masters to me?' he asked.

Toenail squirmed slightly. 'Oh, no reason,' he said. 'I just thought, blow this for a lark, all this mending things and cleaning things. I have nothing to lose but my chains, I thought, and—'

'What chains?'

'Figuratively speaking, sir.'

'Right,' said the Graf. 'I'll deal with you later. Follow me.'

He released the dwarf, smashed up a coffee table for good measure, and strode out of the door. Toenail didn't follow him at once; he darted back to his knapsack, retrieved something from it, and then

573

followed as fast as his legs could carry him.

'Will this do?' the girl asked.

They were standing in the main courtyard. Because the entire staff was occupied in searching for intruders, the place was empty except for an abandoned and rather beat-up looking sleigh.

'Yes, that's fine,' said Boamund. 'I suppose we'd better get on with it.'

Although he was still burning with pent-up fury and rage, he was doing it rather more sheepishly than he had been a few minutes before. True, Sir Galahaut had wronged him quite unforgivably, and the shame would have to be washed out in blood; nevertheless, when you thought about it, it was a dashed silly way to settle an argument, chopping the other fellow's head off. Or getting your own chopped off. And a fellow you'd been at the dear old Coll with, into the bargain. He couldn't help feeling, deep down, that there might be a better way of dealing with situations like this. A really aggressive, hard-fought game of squash, for example.

Galahaut had taken off his jacket and was doing flamboyant practice sweeps with his sword. The girl was sitting on the sleigh. She had picked up a box of chocolates from somewhere, and was eating them avidly.

'Ready?' Boamund asked.

'Just a tick,' Galahaut called back. 'Um – got a bit of cramp in the forearm, I think. You don't mind if I just loosen up a bit, do you?'

'Not at all.'

'Jolly decent of you, old man.'

'Not a bit of it, Gally. Have as long as you like.'

The Haut Prince did a few more practice sweeps, and then some arm-flinging exercises. Not, he assured himself, that he wasn't eager to get on with it and give young Snotty the hiding he'd been asking for ever since he could remember; but there wasn't any rush, was there? All the time in the world.

'Excuse me,' said the girl, 'but why haven't you started yet?'

The knights looked at her.

'We aren't ready yet.'

'Can't rush these things.'

'Wouldn't be sporting.'

'Oh.' The girl shrugged. 'I see. Sorry.'

The knights circled gingerly. Once or twice they tried a few very tentative lunges, but not without asking the other fellow whether he was ready first. The Grafin, meanwhile, finished her chocolates and started clapping. Slowly.

In desperation, Boamund attempted a double left-hand reverse *mandiritta*, a fiendishly complex and difficult manoeuvre which, as he remembered only too well once he'd started, he'd never quite managed to master. It involves a duplex feint to the right side of the head, a slow pass to the left body, and finally a long lunge, executed by the fencer on one knee with his left hand passing behind his back until it touches the inside of his right knee.

'Help,' he said. 'I'm stuck.'

'Oh, hard luck,' exclaimed Sir Galahaut, sheathing his sword and helping him up. 'Better?'

'I think I've sprained my wrist.'

'That does it, then,' said Galahaut quickly. 'No earthly good fighting if you're not feeling a hundred

575

per cent. Wouldn't be right.'

'Absolutely.'

'Pity,' Galahaut went on, 'but there it is. We'll have to call it a draw, I suppose.'

'Good thinking.' Boamund levered himself to his feet, winced, and put up his sword. 'Just when we were getting back into the swing of it, too.'

'Can't be helped,' said Galahaut sympathetically. 'Hey, where's that dratted girl gone?'

They both looked round. They were alone.

'Got bored, I expect,' said Boamund with contempt. 'That's girls for you, of course. I never did meet one who was really interested in Games.'

When the Graf came thundering down the main staircase into the Great Hall, he found his daughter sitting on the steps of the dais crying into a small lace handkerchief. He dropped his axe and hurried over to her.

'What's the matter, precious?' he said. 'Tell Daddy all about it.'

'It's those silly knights,' the Grafin sniffed. 'They won't fight. They're just standing there chatting.'

'There, there,' said the Graf. 'Don't upset yourself over a couple of silly knights. They're not worth it really.'

'And I thought they were both so brave,' the girl went on. There were little tears, like pearls, on her cheeks. She blew her nose loudly.

'Huh!' The Graf snorted contemptuously. 'Knights! They don't know the meaning of the word.'

'And they just left me sitting there,' the Grafin said, 'after I'd given them tea and everything.'

'Young blackguards,' said von Weinacht. 'I'll soon teach them a thing or two.'

The girl's eyes lit up and she smiled.

'I love you, Daddy,' she said.

'I love you too, Popsy,' muttered von Weinacht, gruffly. 'Right, where are those knights? Dwarf!'

Toenail, who had been standing on a chair and looking out of the window at the courtyard, jumped down and ran over to him.

'Yes, sir?'

'You got any idea where those knights are?'

'In the courtyard, sir. Not fighting,' he added, thoughtfully.

'Where's that dratted dwarf got to?' said Boamund. 'Always wandering off somewhere, I've noticed.'

'Typical,' Galahaut said, putting on his jacket. 'Especially when there's work to be done.'

'And he's got the luggage.'

The two knights looked around the huge courtyard.

'Could be anywhere,' Galahaut said at last. 'Big place, this.'

'Gloomy, though.'

They started to stroll towards the main hall.

'I vote,' said Galahaut, 'that we find this Graf von Weinacht, make him tell us where the Socks are, and buzz off. How does that sound to you?'

'Pretty shrewd,' Boamund replied. 'Where shall we start?'

'How about over there?'

'Good idea.'

They pushed open the doors of the main hall and walked in. They stared.

'Toenail?' they said, in unison.

In front of them, sprawled on the hearthrug like a pile of bright red bedclothes, was the Graf von Weinacht. An enormous Danish axe lay by his right hand. Standing over him, grinning and holding an aerosol can of chemical Mace, was the dwarf.

'I suppose,' the Graf said, 'I'd better begin at the beginning.'

It had been a long day. Acting on the information received, he had gone dashing off to Atlantis in search of Grail Knights, had been beaten up twice and rolled down a spiral staircase, crash-landed his sleigh in the middle of nowhere, arrived home to find the place knee-deep in knights, been Maced by a dwarf and tied up with his own dressing-gown cord. It was enough to make you spit.

'Is that necessary?' yawned Galahaut. 'Only . . .'

'Yes,' the Graf snapped. 'Absolutely essential. All right?'

'Fire away, then,' replied the Haut Prince. He leant back, put his feet up on a stuffed bear, and helped himself to a big, fat bunch of grapes.

Simon Magus turned the page and settled his reading-glasses comfortably on his nose.

The Pitiful History, he read, *of the Count of Christmas*. He reached for his notebook.

It was a hell of a story. If it wasn't quite the greatest story ever told, that was just because the Graf wasn't quite in the mood to give it the full treatment.

. . . About how, getting on for two thousand years

ago, he packed in his promising career as a weather-god to study astrology at the University of Damascus. About how he and three of his fellow students, looking through the University's electron astrolabe, discovered what at first they took to be a bit of dirt on the lens, and then realised was an entirely new star.

About how they set off to observe it from the University's hi-tech observatory near Jerusalem. About how there was the inevitable cock-up with the hotel bookings, which meant that they arrived in Galilee one cold, wet night to find that their rooms had been given to a party of insurance salesmen from Tarsus, and they were going to have to doss down in the stables.

And how, just as they were squelching across the courtyard and muttering about suing somebody, young Melchior happened to look up and notice that the star was slap-bang over their heads; and that the group of shepherds who'd just come out of the stables were looking very worried indeed . . .

'And another thing,' said the shepherd, grinning in-sanely. 'I don't know if you're superstitious or any-thing, but if you are, don't go in there. The place is knee-deep in angels, okay?'

'Angels?'

'I don't want to talk about it.'

The shepherds hurried away, leaving Caspar, Melchior, Balthazar and Klaus standing in the rain.

'Did that man just say the Angels were in there, someone?' Balthazar asked.

'I thought so.'

They groaned. As if they didn't have enough to put

579

up with without sharing their sleeping accommodation with a gang of greasy, leather-clad, foul-mouthed, camel-riding hooligans.

It was dark in the stable. The oil lamp flickered atmospherically in the slight draught. Suddenly, all four of them felt this very great urge to kneel down.

'Hello,' Balthazar called out. 'Anybody here? Hey, lads, I don't like this, it's kind of spooky in here . . .'

It grew lighter; there was a soft golden glow coming from the far manger.

'Hush,' said a woman's voice, 'he's asleep.'

It was Melchior who spoke first. Very gently, he crept forward towards the crib, peeped into it, and then rocked back as if he had been stunned. Then he knelt down and covered his head with the hem of his cloak.

'Lady,' he said.

The woman's face was in shadow. 'Welcome,' she said. 'Blessed may you be for ever, for you are the first to look on the face of the Son of Man.'

Melchior rocked backwards and forwards on his heels. 'Lady,' he said again, 'is it permitted that we might offer gifts to your son?'

The woman smiled, and nodded, whereupon Melchior searched in his satchel and produced a small, shiny box. The woman nodded, as if she had been expecting it.

'Gold,' Melchior explained. 'Gold is a fitting gift for a king.'

The woman took the box without looking at it and laid it down beside the crib. Caspar stepped forward, fell on his knees and offered the woman a little alabaster jar.

'Frankincense, lady,' he said shyly. 'To anoint Him who shall be crowned with thorns.'

The woman nodded, and put the jar down by the box. Balthazar, his knees trembling, now stepped forward, knelt, and held out a silver phial.

'Myrrh, lady,' he whispered. 'To embalm Him who shall never die.'

Again, a trace of a smile crossed the woman's lips. She took the phial from Balthazar's hands, looked at it for a moment, and put it with the other gifts.

Why didn't they tell me, Klaus muttered to himself. The bastards. Why didn't they *say* something?

There was a moment's pause, while the other three looked at him. He decided to improvise. He grabbed something out of his satchel, tore a page out of a book to wrap it in (the book was a treatise on ornithology, and the page he had selected had little pictures of robins on it) and stepped forward.

'Um,' he said, and thrust the parcel into the woman's hands.

She gave him a long look, then slowly unwrapped the parcel.

'Socks,' she said. 'Just what He always wanted.'

The expression on her face told a different story as she held up two knee-length stockings to the light. Klaus winced.

'They're probably a bit big for him right now,' he said, as lightly as he could, 'but never mind, he'll grow into them.'

The woman gave him another long, hard look; then she rolled the socks up into a ball and dropped them. 'You may go,' she said.

'Thank you,' Klaus mumbled, backing away. 'Oh

yes, and a happy ... happy. The compliments of the season, anyway.'

He banged his head on a rafter, reversed out of the door, and ran for his life.

'A fortnight later,' the Graf went on, breathing heavily, 'I got a parcel. It contained a pair of socks, and a letter. It was delivered by an angel.'

He hesitated, closed his eyes, and continued. 'The letter wasn't signed, but then, it didn't need to be. I won't bore you with the first three paragraphs, because they were mostly about me. What you might call the business part of the letter came in the last few lines.

'To cut a long story short, I was cursed. For the rest of Time, it said, until the Child comes again to judge the quick and the dead, it would be my job to deliver presents to all the children in the world, every year, on the anniversary of my ... on Christmas Eve. Presents as inappropriate, unwanted and futile as the present I had seen fit to choose for the King of Kings. And, just to drive the point that little bit further home, just in case I hadn't quite grasped it by now, on each ensuing Christmas Eve every child in the world would henceforth see fit to hang at the foot of its bed the longest, woolliest sock it could find, as a perpetual reminder.'

There was a long silence.

'Yes,' said Galahaut, pulling himself together, 'be that as it may, what about these Socks?'

'Socks?' Klaus von Weinacht looked up at him and laughed. 'Haven't you worked it out yet? The socks you and your friend here have been looking for are *the* Socks. Hence,' he added with a bitter chuckle, 'the

582

name. Do you seriously believe that I can hand them over to you, just like that?'

Boamund set his face in what he hoped was an impassive expression. 'You'd better had,' he said, 'or it'll jolly well be the worse for you.'

Von Weinacht turned his head and looked at him.

'Please?' Boamund added.

'No.' The Graf curled his lip. 'You don't think I wouldn't be delighted to see the back of them, do you? I hate the very sight of them. But they aren't mine to dispose of. Certainly not,' he added, 'to you.'

Boamund became aware of an urgent digging in his ribs and glanced down.

'What is it?' he said. 'Can't you see we're busy?'

'It won't take a moment,' Toenail replied. 'Just come over here, where he can't hear us.'

Boamund shrugged and got to his feet. They walked over to the fireplace.

'He's not telling you the whole story,' Toenail said, 'I'm sure of it.'

'Really?' Boamund raised an eyebrow. 'It must be a pretty long story, then, because . . .'

Toenail shook his head. 'It's true all right, about the Socks and that. But there's more to it. I know there is.'

'Do you?'

'Yes.'

Boamund considered. He had always known that everybody, even servants, knew much more about everything than he did, and that was the way it should be. A knight has far more important things to do than go around knowing things. The way he saw it, if your head's full of knowledge, it'll get too big to fit inside a helmet. Nevertheless, wasn't the whole thing supposed to be a secret?

'How do you know, exactly?' he asked.

Toenail looked round. 'I just do, that's all. Maybe it's because I'm a dwarf.'

'How does that come into it?'

'Race-memory,' Toenail replied. 'That and it's easier for dwarves to keep their ears to the ground. Look, just ask him about the Grail, see how he reacts. Go on.'

Boamund nodded. Great heroes, he knew, had faithful and wise counsellors, invariably of lower social rank, but dead clever nonetheless; and the good part of it was that *their* names tended to drop out of history at a relatively early stage.

He turned to the Graf, narrowed his brows to indicate thought, and walked slowly back across the hall.

'You're keeping something back, aren't you?' he said. 'Come on, out with it.'

'Drop dead.'

'Don't you take that tone with me,' Boamund replied. 'What about the Grail, then? You tell me that.'

By way of response, von Weinacht roared like a bull and struggled furiously with the dressing-gown cord that held him to the chair. Galahaut frowned and reached for the rolling pin he'd found in the kitchens.

'Now cut that out,' he said. 'Honestly, some people.'

'Knights!' Von Weinacht spat. 'Bloody knights! Always the same. If I ever get my hands on you two . . .'

Galahaut hit him with the rolling pin. It seemed to have a mild therapeutic effect, because he stopped roaring and confined himself to looking daggers. Boamund nodded.

'Thanks, Gally,' he said.

'Don't mention it, Bo. It was a pleasure.'

Boamund drew up a chair and sat down. 'Let's start again,' he said. 'Now then, about the Grail.'

Von Weinacht made a suggestion as to what Boamund might care to do with the Grail as and when he found it. The rolling pin moved through the air once more.

'The Grail,' Boamund repeated. 'What about it?'

This time von Weinacht remained resolutely silent, and the two knights looked at each other.

'Don't think you can hit him just for not saying anything,' Galahaut remarked. 'Probably. What do you think?'

'Probably not,' Boamund agreed. 'Pity, but there it is. What do we do now, then?'

Galahaut shrugged his shoulders. 'Find the Socks, I suppose. Hey, you,' he said, leaning down and placing the rolling pin under the Graf's nose. 'Socks. Where?'

Von Weinacht tried to bite the rolling pin and Galahaut removed it quickly. 'I wonder what he's got against knights,' he mused. 'Is it just us, or knights *per se*, or what?'

'Don't think he likes anyone very much,' Boamund replied. 'Odd, that, given the line of work he's in. You'd think somebody who spends his whole time delivering Christmas . . .'

Von Weinacht howled like a wolf. The knights exchanged glances.

'Seems like he doesn't like you to mention a certain word,' Galahaut remarked.

'It does, rather, doesn't it?' said Boamund. 'Christ-

585

mas!' he hissed in the Graf's ear, and then jumped back, startled. He wouldn't have believed a human being could make such an extraordinary noise.

'Well now,' said Galahaut, with a malicious grin on his face, 'that changes things rather, doesn't it? Doesn't it?' he shouted in the Graf's ear.

'Get knotted.'

'I think,' Galahaut said, 'it's time for a sing-song, don't you?'

It was a scene that Toenail would never be able to forget until the day he died. The Graf, twisting and squirming in his chair and roaring until you thought his voice would crack; and on either side of him, the two knights, singing *The Holly and the Ivy*, *Silent Night*, *Away in a Manger*, *God Rest Ye Merry Gentlemen* and *Rudolf the Red-Nosed Reindeer*. It was the last of these that finally did the trick.

'All right,' the Graf sobbed. 'You swine, you inhuman swine. I'll talk.'

Radulf grabbed the walkie-talkie impatiently.

'Moo,' he grunted into it; then he slammed the aerial down and nodded his horns. Three pages armed with halberds at once set off down the stairs.

They must be somewhere. Two knights and a supernatural being can't just vanish off the face of the earth . . .

Use your brains, Radulf. What are the knights here for? Suppose – just suppose – they've managed to overpower him somehow and forced him to show them the secret hiding place. Of course! That must be it.

The only problem being that the secret hiding place is – well, secret . . .

'In here?'

Von Weinacht nodded. 'And the very best of luck,' he added.

Boamund didn't quite follow that, but following things wasn't his forte, unless they happened to be hounds. He was quite good at that, provided there weren't too many gates and things in the way.

He grabbed the handles of the drawer and pulled.

Socks. The drawer was *full* of socks . . .

'My God,' said Galahaut, in an awed voice, 'there must be several hundred pairs in there.'

Von Weinacht chuckled dryly. 'One thousand and forty-one,' he said. 'A good idea, no?'

'I don't suppose,' Galahaut said, 'that you care to tell us which pair is the right one?'

'Correct.'

Galahaut grinned. 'Did you ever hear the one about Good King Wenceslas?' he enquired. But the Graf was ready for him. With a sudden movement, he broke away from Galahaut's grip and dashed his head against the frame of the door, knocking himself out cold.

'Hey,' exclaimed the Haut Prince, 'that's cheating!'

Boamund lifted a heaped handful of socks and let them fall again. 'Just look at them all,' he said. 'I've never seen so many socks in all my born days.'

'Nor me.'

'Oh well,' Boamund sighed. 'I suppose we'll just have to take the lot, and try and sort them out later. Toenail, get us a very large sack.'

The dwarf made a resigned gesture with his shoulders and wandered off. Between them, Boamund and

Galahaut pulled out the drawer and emptied its contents on to the floor.

'I expect we can discount the ones with St Michael written on the label,' Galahaut said. 'Although he might have had a false label sewn in as camouflage. He's a clever devil, I'll say that for him.'

Boamund nodded. 'We'd better take all of them, Gally,' he repeated. 'Gosh, though. Who'd have thought socks could be so heavy?'

'So's sand,' Galahaut replied, 'in bulk. Did you follow all that stuff about Atlantis and offshore banking?'

'Not really,' Boamund admitted, 'all that sort of thing goes right over my head. But I sort of gathered that he'd had the Grail at one time, and then this Joseph person—'

'Joseph of Arimathea.'

'You know,' Boamund said, 'I've heard that name before somewhere. Anyway, this Joseph took the Grail himself and disappeared with it, so we're not much further forward in any event. Not that it matters, really. Once we've got the Apron and the Personal Organiser, and we've sorted out these socks, it won't really matter very much, will it?'

'Hope not,' Galahaut said. 'I prefer things to be as simple as possible. Where's that wretched dwarf got to?'

They looked round.

'Wandered off somewhere, I expect,' Boamund said. 'They do that.'

'Shouldn't be any problem finding a sack in this place,' Galahaut said. 'One thing you'd expect to find, a sack. Probably full of presents. I remember one year,

I was resting, I got a job as a Father Christmas in one of those big department stores. Of course, there was nothing in the sack except old newspapers and bits of cardboard.'

Boamund looked across at the stunned figure on the floor. 'We could try waking him up, I suppose. Sing some more, that sort of thing.'

'We could try,' Galahaut agreed, but with just a touch of hesitation. It wasn't that Boamund's voice was *flat* exactly – it was certainly no worse than a pneumatic drill – but there was no guarantee of results, and he didn't want to get another one of his headaches.

'Or,' he suggested, therefore, 'we could find someone else who's in on the secret. Must be someone,' he added.

'Such as?'

'Well,' replied Galahaut diffidently, 'there's that awful bloodthirsty girl, for a start.'

'The one who doesn't appreciate Games?'

'The impatient one, that's right. Bet you anything you like she knows which pair of socks it is.'

Boamund nodded fervently. 'Brilliant,' he said. 'Where is she?'

Galahaut was just about to say that he hadn't the faintest idea, when the door opened and the girl herself came in.

She was simply but attractively dressed in an organdie-print blouse with pin-tucks and a Peter Pan collar and a Liberty cotton skirt in pale lilac, and she was holding an assault rifle.

Aristotle was losing his temper with the pinball machine.

'It's rigged,' he muttered, fumbling in his pocket for change. 'Every time you get beyond three hundred thousand, a little gate opens down there and the ball sort of trickles down into it.' He gave the side of the machine a hard blow with the heel of his hand.

'You aren't using your upper flippers properly,' Simon Magus observed quietly.

'What the hell do you know about anything?'

'Sorry,' Simon Magus replied, 'just trying to be helpful. You haven't seen my wife anywhere, have you?'

'No.' Aristotle pulled back the handle and put the first ball into play. There was a short, tense interval while he pressed both buttons about a hundred times in the space of ten seconds, and the ball ran unerringly down the table and into the jaws of the machine.

'She's wandered off somewhere again,' Simon Magus said. 'Funny creatures, women.'

Aristotle glowered at him. 'Exactly,' he replied. 'Not really appropriate on campus, either, if you ask me.'

'Then I'll make sure I don't,' Simon Magus replied. 'Thanks for the warning.'

Aristotle grunted and launched into the second game, while Simon Magus wandered through into the coffee room. Nobody in there had seen Mahaud, either.

Eventually he ran her to ground on the balcony. She had a big pair of binoculars and was looking out in the general direction of the North Pole.

'Something,' she said, 'is going on.'

'Yes,' her husband replied. 'I know.'

She looked round at him. 'You do?' she said. 'What? Is it anything to do with that quest young Bedevere was on?'

'You might say that, yes. Lend me those glasses a moment, would you?'

He focused them, and stood for a while; then he lowered them and bit his lip thoughtfully. 'Oh well,' he said. 'Too late to do anything about it now, I suppose.'

'What do you mean?'

'It looks rather like I chose the wrong man for the job,' he replied. 'Do you remember a boy called Boamund? One of the Northgales kids, tall, gangling, unfortunate manner.'

'Of course I do,' Mahaud said. 'Snotty, the other boys called him. Not a very agreeable name, but apt.'

'Well,' Simon Magus said, 'he was one of my Sleepers. This spot of business that's going on now, I put him in charge of it. He was doing all right, too, until . . . Oh well.'

Mahaud took the glasses back. 'What's happened?' she said.

'Girl trouble.'

'Oh dear. I never thought he was the type, really.'

'They're the worst sort, usually,' Simon Magus replied. 'Anyway, it's not that sort of trouble. Oh *damn*,' he added peevishly.

'Never mind,' said Mahaud briskly. 'Can't be successful every time.'

'Suppose not,' replied the magician, philosophically. 'A great pity, though. I'd rather set my heart on this one coming off.'

'Put a lot of work into it?'

'Rather a lot, yes,' Simon Magus said. 'And I thought I'd made sure it was fairly idiot-proof. Still, there are idiots and idiots.'

Mahaud thought for a moment. 'It's never too late

to – well, give him a helping hand, you know.'

Simon Magus looked at her. 'But that's unethical,' he said. 'Once they've started and everything. Most improper.'

'Nobody would ever know.'

'I would.'

'Oh.' She stood for a moment, playing with the binoculars. 'Fair enough,' she said. 'Fancy a quick game of Scrabble?'

Simon Magus studied his wife for a moment.

'Mahaud,' he said, 'you're up to something.'

'Nonsense.'

'Come on, I know that expression. You're not to interfere.'

'I wouldn't dream of it,' replied his wife innocently. 'You know that.'

'Well, then.' He glanced at his watch. 'Blast,' he said, 'I must dash. I said I'd give Merlin a game of dominoes.'

'You run along then,' Mahaud said. 'See you later.'

It was an awkward moment.

'Hello again,' Galahaut said. 'We were just going to come and look for you.'

'Oh yes?'

'We were just,' Galahaut went on, 'helping your father have a really good sort-out of his sock drawer.'

'Really.'

'And then,' Galahaut persevered, 'he said he felt a bit tired and went to sleep, and so we thought we'd come and find you. But here you are anyway.'

The girl gave him a look. 'I don't believe you,' she said.

'You don't?'

'No, I don't'.

'Oh.'

'I think,' the girl said, 'that you're trying to steal Daddy's special Socks. I think you're *burglars*.'

'What makes you think that?'

'You are, aren't you?' the girl said. 'I think you tricked your way in here pretending to be knights, but really you're just sock-thieves. Probably,' she added, remembering a phrase from a book she'd been reading, 'an international gang.'

'Oh, we're knights all right,' Boamund interrupted. 'There's no question of that.'

The girl sniffed. 'Knights fight fair,' she said. 'Knights don't tie people up and go emptying drawers out on the floor. Burglars do that.'

'Knights do too, sometimes. It's all a matter of what's right in the particular circumstances.'

The girl shook her head. 'Daddy told me to be specially on the look-out for burglars,' she said. 'And he told me that if ever I saw any, I was to get this gun from his study and shoot them.'

'Gosh,' Boamund said. Galahaut smiled.

'And you always do what Daddy says?' he enquired.

'Always.'

'What a terribly dreary life you must lead.'

The girl frowned. 'What do you mean?' she asked.

Galahaut raised an eyebrow. 'I mean,' he said, 'I don't suppose you get out much, do you? No going to parties or anything like that.'

'Certainly not.' The girl looked pensive as she fidgeted with the safety catch of the rifle. Pensive but extremely dangerous.

'Can't be many people of your own age around here,' Galahaut went on. The girl nodded.

'None,' she said. 'Except for some of the pages, of course. Some of them are quite nice, or at least one of them . . .' She hesitated for a moment. 'But Daddy says I'm not to talk to the pages. He says . . .'

Galahaut raised his eyebrow a little bit more. It was very eloquent. But the girl suddenly shook her head.

'What's that got to do with burglars?' she said.

'Um . . .'

'You're just trying to confuse me,' the girl went on. 'That's a typical burglar trick, trying to confuse people. Knights wouldn't do that. They'd think it wasn't chivalrous.'

Slowly, she raised the rifle towards her shoulder, and Boamund shut his eyes. This didn't fit in with his preconceptions about damsels in distress at all.

A moment later he heard a hissing noise and a thump. At first he guessed the thump must be his own dead body collapsing to the floor; but after a few seconds he revised this opinion and opened his eyes again.

The girl was lying on the floor, snoring gently, and Toenail was putting an aerosol can back in his satchel.

'Knew it'd come in handy,' said the dwarf. 'Marvellous stuff, Mace. Works wonders with large dogs, too. I couldn't find a sack, by the way, but I thought a couple of pillow cases might do instead. Is that all right?'

Galahaut, who had gone a very funny colour, extricated himself from the corner of the room, into which he had backed, and grinned.

'Jolly good timing, that,' he said shakily. 'Nice work.'

594

'Thank you,' Toenail replied, rather taken aback. He tried to remember if anyone had ever thanked him before; good question. 'I met this woman out in the laundry room who said I was needed back here, so I came in.'

'What woman?' Boamund asked.

'Dunno,' Toenail replied. 'Just a woman. Appeared out of nowhere holding a pair of binoculars, gave me a message about you two being in the ... you two wanting me for something, and vanished again. Might have been a hologram, even.' He opened a pillow case and began filling it with socks.

'We still don't know which pair is which, though,' Boamund observed. 'You know, I do think it'd be a good idea if we found out. Otherwise ...'

The other two looked at him.

'Bo,' Galahaut said, 'I don't want to seem slapdash or anything, but if it's all the same to you, I'd rather we escaped with our lives first and saved the underwear-sorting part of it till later. If that's all right with you, I mean.'

'I wonder who that woman was. She might have known.'

'Who?' Toenail asked, looking up from the pillow case. 'The hologram, you mean?'

'That's if it really was a hologram,' Boamund said. 'What is a hologram, anyway?'

Toenail was about to explain when a sound outside the door checked him. The sound, if he wasn't very much mistaken, of hooves. Feet, too. Lots of them.

'Oh God,' he said, 'more of them.' He reached for the aerosol, shook it and made a face. 'Not much left in there,' he muttered. 'May I suggest that you hide?'

'Where?'

Toenail nodded towards the fireplace. 'You could try the chimney,' he said.

'Good Lord,' Simon Magus said. 'How on earth did they manage that?'

Mahaud looked up from her Scrabble pieces. 'Manage what, dear?' she said.

'That young Snotty and the other one,' said the magician, putting the binoculars down. 'They've got away from that lunatic girl after all. There's more to Boamund than I thought, apparently.'

Mahaud smiled. 'That's nice, dear,' she said. 'Now, what can I make with this lot?'

She studied her hand carefully. There was a C, an H, an E, an A and a T.

'Is there such a word as theac?' she asked.

It was windy up on the roof.

'Hand me up that other pillow case,' Boamund called down the chimney. 'Careful now, don't drop it. That's the way.'

A moment later Galahaut emerged. He was very sooty, and he'd broken a fingernail.

'Pity we had to leave the dwarf,' he said. 'Still, never mind.'

'We'll just have to wait till we get home,' Boamund said. 'Still, it is a shame. I hate polishing shoes and sewing on buttons. It's so fiddly.'

A sleigh was floating in the air a few feet from their heads, tethered to a ring on the side of the chimney-stack. There was a full team of reindeer in the shafts.

'That's handy,' Boamund said. 'I was wondering

how we were going to escape.'

'Something always turns up,' Galahaut replied. 'Do you know how you drive one of these things?'

'Not really,' said Boamund. 'Still, I expect it's not too difficult once you've got the hang of it. Probably an ordinary flying spell will do.'

'I forgot,' Galahaut said, 'you know all that magic stuff for getting about and things. I could never be doing with it, personally.'

Boamund hauled himself up into the sleigh, took the pillow cases from Galahaut and gave him a hand up into the cockpit. 'Now then,' he said, 'we just say the magic words, and then we're away.'

He said them. Nothing.

'What's wrong?'

'It isn't working, that's what.'

Galahaut, the actor, sniffed. 'Try putting a bit more *feeling* into it. Motivation, that's what you need. Come on, let me try. What's the spell again?'

Boamund told him, and he sat for a moment, thinking himself into the part. Then he said the spell.

'Gosh,' Boamund said. 'That was very good.'

'Thanks.'

'We still aren't moving, though, are we?'

'Probably a bit too melodramatic,' Galahaut admitted. 'A bit too Olivier, maybe. I'll make it a bit more Marlon Brando this time, shall I?'

'Who's Marlon Brando?'

Galahaut said the words again. The sleigh continued to bob gently in the breeze.

'That's a bit tiresome,' he said. 'Are you sure you've got the right words?'

'I think so.' Boamund muttered them over to himself

under his breath. They sounded all right.

'Perhaps magic doesn't work here,' he suggested. 'I've heard that there are places like that.'

Just then, Galahaut noticed that an arm had appeared over the edge of the chimney-pot. He drew his sword, and then stopped.

'It's all right,' he said, 'it's only the dwarf.'

Sure enough, Toenail's head appeared a moment later. They helped him up on to the sleigh.

'Sorry you got left behind,' Galahaut said, 'only, well, it was you or the socks. Couldn't carry both, you understand.'

Toenail understood all too well. Still, it had been all right, just about. He had a nasty antler-gouge in his leg, and his neck ached where a page had thrown a teapot at him, but otherwise he was all right. All the Mace had gone, though.

'Would it be a good idea if we left now, please?' he suggested. 'Only, they were saying something about following us, and . . .'

'Easier said than done,' Boamund replied. 'We can't get this thing to budge. We've tried the magic spell, and it won't work.'

Toenail looked down at the console.

'It might help,' he said, 'if you took the handbrake off.'

'Running away,' Boamund said, 'is just not *done*.'

'I've done it,' Toenail interrupted, 'lots of times. It's quite easy once you get the hang of it.'

'But it's not right,' Boamund protested. 'Sir Lancelot never ran away from people.'

'Maybe not,' Galahaut retorted, as they skittered

over a patch of turbulence. 'Maybe the fact that everyone was shit-scared of him had something to do with it. I don't think that lot are terribly frightened of us, do you?'

He waved an arm behind them. Boamund looked over his shoulder. In the distance he could just make out the figure of von Weinacht in the leading pursuit sleigh – there were ten of them – standing up in the box and wielding his big Danish axe. He certainly didn't *look* frightened.

'That's beside the point,' Boamund objected, ducking to avoid a passing skua. 'I mean,' he added, 'they'll never be scared of us if we keep running away, will they?'

'I don't think they'll be all that scared if we suddenly decide to keep still,' Galahaut replied. 'Just rather surprised and very pleased.'

The sleigh rocked as a thermal hit it, and Boamund grabbed the rail. 'I still don't think . . .' he started to say, and then caught sight of the world, a very long way below. 'Gosh,' he said.

The pursuers were gaining on them. In the shafts of von Weinacht's sleigh, there was a very big reindeer with a red nose and grey hairs round its muzzle, the tinsel on its antlers cracking in the wind. It looked rather unfriendly.

Toenail, who had been exploring the glove compartment, tugged Galahaut's sleeve. 'Look at this,' he said, 'I think it's some sort of instruction manual.'

Galahaut took the booklet and glanced at it. 'Hey,' he said, 'that's not bad, is it? Here, Bo, how about a compromise? How'd it be if we ran away and fought them at the same time?'

599

'Talk sense, Gally,' Boamund replied, resolutely not looking down. 'How can we do that?'

'Look,' Galahaut said. 'Apparently this sleigh's got, like, built-in optional extras. I wondered what it was doing tethered up there. It must be the old Graf's escape sleigh. According to this, it can do some pretty antisocial things if you want it to.'

Boamund looked at him. 'Such as?'

'Well,' Galahaut said, 'apparently, this button here . . .'

There was a whooshing noise directly under them, and two vapour trails appeared behind the sleigh. A moment later there was a loud explosion in the sky to their rear.

'Heat-seeking rockets,' Galahaut said, 'disguised as gift-wrapped golf umbrellas. And this . . .'

He got no further with his sentence; the air was filled with thick, rolling black clouds which billowed away into their slipstream. Toenail finished the sentence for him.

'Smoke screen,' he said. 'Now, which of these is the machine-guns, and which is the rear wash-wipe?' He shrugged and pressed both.

When the smoke cleared, there were only seven sleighs following them. Boamund grabbed the instruction manual and started flicking through it.

'Jet boost,' he said. 'Hey, Gally, what does that . . .?'

Before Galahaut could answer, the sleigh was hurled across the sky like a fast leg-break. Boamund only managed to stay in it by clinging on to the strap of a sleigh-bell.

'Nice one,' Galahaut said, as he hauled him back into the cockpit. 'Won't be long before they've closed in, though. They're pretty nippy, those sleighs.' He looked at the dwarf thoughtfully. 'We're carrying too much weight,' he said. 'We could do with lightening this thing up a bit, really.'

Toenail didn't speak; he put his arms round one of the bags of socks and set his face into a grim expression. Galahaut shrugged, said that it was just a suggestion, and looked over Boamund's shoulder at the manual.

'Anti-aircraft mines,' he read. 'Don't see that myself, do you?'

'Does no harm to try.'

'All right.'

They pressed the button together, and at once the rear cargo-door of the sleigh flew open, scattering hundreds of little brightly wrapped parcels which hung in the air on tiny individual parachutes. A few minutes later, as the lead pursuit sleigh passed through the floating cloud, they found out how that one worked.

'That's about it,' Galahaut said wistfully. 'And there's still five of them following us.'

'There's still this button here.'

'I'd leave that alone if I were you.'

'Ejector seat,' Boamund read aloud. 'I wonder what that does?'

Toenail hit the surface of the ice, and bounced.

The sackful of socks burst under him, scattering its contents, and he slid for a while on his stomach until he came to rest in a snowdrift. He picked himself up slowly and examined the punctured sack. There was just one pair of socks left in it.

Then he lifted his head and looked up at the sky.

Without the dwarf's weight, the knights' sleigh was moving faster, drawing rapidly away from its pursuers. He stood and watched as the chase screamed away over the skyline.

Oddly enough, in the middle of the ice floe there was a signpost.

Hammerfest 1200 km, it said, and pointed.

The dwarf put his hand down into the pillow case and drew out the remaining pair of socks. Slowly he unravelled them, found the label and read it. The lettering was faint, worn away by incessant laundry, but after a while he was able to make out the words.

MADE IN SYRIA. 100% COTTON. HAND-WASH ONLY.

He grinned, stuffed the socks into his satchel, and began to walk.

Von Weinacht reined in his sleigh, leant forward and shook his fist at the tiny speck on the horizon.

'Next time, you bastards!' he yelled. 'Next time!'

8

Exit Ken Barlow, pursued by a bear.

The ghost looked at the page in front of him, wrinkled his broad, insubstantial forehead, and crossed out what he'd just written. No good; start again.

The Rovers Return. Alf Roberts and Percy Sugden are leaning against the bar.

Alf: The way I see it, Percy, there's a tide in the affairs of men which, taken at the flood, you understand, well – you could be on to a good thing there.

Percy: I'm with you all the way there, Councillor. I was saying to Mrs Bishop just the other day, if you don't grab hold of your opportunities in this life, you're bound in shallows and in miseries, like.

No. Something lacking there. Not punchy enough.

The ghost drew a line through it and noticed that the sheet of paper was completely full. He scowled irritably; a perfectly good sheet of A4 down the plughole, and nothing to show for it.

603

In the hall, the old clock whirred, hesitated for a moment and struck thirteen times.

Funny, the ghost reflected, how it did that. It always had, ever since he could remember, and it had always aggravated him beyond measure. Ironic, really, that the only piece of original furniture in the whole place should be that knackered old clock. Why they couldn't get one of those smart new digital affairs was beyond him.

He wrenched his mind back to work, bit the end of his pen, spat out a fragment of quill, and wrote:

The Rovers Return. Vera, Ivy and Gail sharing a table.

Vera: Well, here we all are again, like. Raining cats and dogs outside, an' all.

Another thing which had always annoyed him was the way his concentration tended to waver when he came to a sticky bit. Instead of pulling himself together and getting down to it, he had this tendency to let his mind wander away from the job in hand to quite irrelevant and unimportant things, like why that bloody clock had never worked, not since the day . . .

He strolled into the hall, trying to hear Vera's voice in his head. What would the confounded woman be likely to say? She's come home after a hard day, gone down the pub, run into her best friend and her best friend's daughter-in-law . . .

Maybe it was the pendulum. It wasn't the escapement; he'd had that out and in pieces all over the kitchen table that time he'd had a block with *Titus Andronicus*. But the pendulum was something he hadn't considered. If the poxy thing was out of true – the weight not balanced right, or whatever – that might well account for it.

Maybe he shouldn't start the scene with Vera at all. Maybe two courtiers . . .

First Courtier: They say Jack Duckworth's been off his feed lately.

Second Courtier: Perhaps he hasn't heard that their Terry's in trouble with the police over that vanload of stolen eiderdowns that was found round the back of Rosamund Street . . .

Nah.

He opened the door of the clock and looked inside.

There were his initials, where he'd scratched them on the case when he was twelve. There was the stain where he'd hidden the rabbits he'd had off the Squire's back orchard, the night Sir John Falstaff's men had got a warrant to raid the place. Happy days.

He reached in and located the pendulum. Seemed all right, not loose or anything. Maybe it's the . . .

The ghost raised an immaterial eyebrow. There was something wrapped very tightly round the pendulum and tied on with a bit of binder cord. It had plainly been there some time. Maybe Dad had tried to adjust the timing by packing the pendulum. That could account for it; a good sort, Dad, but not mechanically minded. Didn't hold with machines of any sort, which was why he'd refused to fork out when there was that chance of being prenticed to the instrument-maker. The ghost shook his head sadly; still, it didn't do to dwell too much on lost opportunities. Things hadn't worked out too badly in the end.

The something tied round the pendulum turned out to be a sheet of old-fashioned parchment. Swept away by nostalgia, the ghost removed it carefully, smoothed it out, and studied it. Marvellous stuff, parchment;

605

miles better than this squashed-tree rubbish you got these days. Once you'd finished with it, all you had to do was get a pumice-stone and you could wipe off all the old writing and there you were.

He closed the door of the clock and wandered slowly back to his desk, squinting at the writing on the parchment. Pretty old-fashioned writing, even by his standards. Pictures, too; *naughty* pictures. A piece fell into place in his mind, and he remembered Dad coming home from the Fair one night, when he was quite young ... saying something about – that was right, about fixing the clock. But it didn't need fixing, Mum had said. I'll be the judge of that. Soon have it right. And the blessed thing had been up the pictures ever since. Hardly surprising, really.

Fancy that, the ghost muttered to himself. After all these years, and it was a bit of porn round the pendulum all the time.

The words, he realised, were in Latin, which was a closed book as far as he was concerned; and the pictures weren't as naughty as all that. Good piece of parchment, though, keep you going for weeks if you were careful and didn't rub too hard. He smiled and nodded his head, then put the parchment down and went off to the bathroom to look for a piece of pumice.

'Great,' said Sir Turquine. 'Now what do we do?'

They had cleared the table in the Common Room of shirts, empty pizza boxes and Lamorak's angling magazines, and had mounted a sort of trophy.

An apron, a small leather-covered book and a pair of socks. The silence in the Common Room was tainted with just the tiniest degree – one part in a hundred thousand – of embarrassment.

'Maybe I'm just being more than usually obtuse here,' Turquine went on, 'but speaking purely for myself, I don't see that we're *that* much closer to finding the Grail. Do you?'

Pertelope had taken a biro from his top pocket and used it to poke the socks experimentally.

'They don't *look* old,' he said. 'You sure that ruddy dwarf got the right pair?'

'Positive,' Boamund replied.

'Why?'

'Because.' The other knights looked at him, and in a disused compartment of his mind Boamund began to speculate as to why 'Because' wasn't as convincing a reason as it had been when he was a boy.

'Maybe it's an acrostic or something,' Lamorak suggested.

There was a brief moment of silence, as six knights tried to make sense out of the initial letters of the items before them.

'No,' said Bedevere, 'I think there's more to it than that. I mean, if it was that we wouldn't actually need the things themselves. I think there must be, well, clues in there somewhere.'

'Clues,' Turquine repeated.

'Like,' Galahaut suggested, 'some common factor, maybe?'

Six pairs of eyes rested on the exhibits; an apron, a leather book and a pair of socks.

'Animal, vegetable or mineral?'

'Shut up, Turkey, I'm thinking.' Bedevere rubbed his nose with the heel of his hand and picked up the apron. 'I'm asking myself,' he said, 'what does an apron say to me?'

'Not a lot,' Turquine replied. 'Not unless you've been out in the sun again.'

Bedevere ignored him. 'Apron,' he said. 'That suggests housework, cleanliness, tidiness, cookery . . .'

'Kitchen floors,' said Lamorak, whose turn it was to clean it. 'Fruit cake. Rubber gloves. Persil. I don't think we can be on the right lines here, somehow.'

'Maybe we're missing the point,' Galahaut interrupted. 'It's not just aprons, it's this apron in particular. Has anyone examined it? In detail, I mean?'

'Well, not as such,' Boamund said. 'I mean, an apron is an apron, surely.'

'Not necessarily,' Galahaut replied. 'Give it here, someone, and let's take a closer look.'

He took the apron in his hands and stared at it for a while. 'It's just an apron, that's all,' he said.

'Brill,' Turquine said. 'The fundamental things apply, and so on. If you ask me, someone with a very odd sense of humour's had us for a bunch of mugs.'

'We're approaching this from the wrong angle,' Pertelope interrupted. 'There you all go, trying to understand things. That's not what we're for; if they wanted things understood, they'd have given the job to a bunch of professors instead of us. As it is, we're doing it; and what are we good at? Being brave and socking people. Therefore . . .'

Bedevere held up his hand for silence. 'Per's right,' he said. 'That's got to be it, hasn't it? I mean, the thing about knights is, they're fundamentally – well, stupid, aren't they? I mean we. Obviously, what we're meant to do is take these things, ride forth for a year and a day and have adventures, and then it'll just happen. Stands to reason, really.'

'What's *it*, Bedders?' Lamorak asked.

'It,' Bedevere replied. 'Thing. Finding the Grail. I mean,' he said, waving his hands about, 'th^t's the way it's always been done. You set forth, you meet a wise old crone by the wayside, she gives you a scrotty old tin lamp or a bit of carpet or a magic goldfish, and next thing you know you're in business. You've just got to have a bit of patience, that's all. Leave it to them.'

'Them,' Turquine muttered, 'we, they, it. You're nothing but a pronoun-fetishist, Bedders.'

'What's a pronoun?'

'And who are you calling stupid, anyway?'

Galahaut, frowning, banged the table with his fist.

'I vote we give it a shot,' he said. 'I mean, can't do any harm, can it? And if all that happens is that we wander around for a year and a day having a good time, then so what? We can start again from scratch, no skin off our noses.'

'He's right,' Bedevere said. 'Whoever heard of knights having to organise things? It's just a matter of getting on with it.'

Boamund nodded suddenly. 'Bedevere is right,' he said decisively. 'Put all that stuff in a bag, somebody, we're going questing.'

Toenail, who had been curled up in a cardboard box under the table polishing the sugar-tongs, jumped up, loaded the three treasures into a plastic carrier, and stowed them in his knapsack. He had come to this conclusion half an hour ago.

'Ready?' he asked.

'I'll just do my packing,' said Lamorak. Toenail pointed out that he'd done everyone's packing that morning, while they were all having breakfast. The cases were in the hall, he said.

'Right,' said Boamund happily, 'that's settled. Let's get on with it, shall we?'

Thus it was that three minibuses set off from three very different places at precisely the same moment.

The first – an ex-British Telecom Bedford, property of the Knights of the Holy Grail – headed off down the Birmingham ring road towards London, with Sir Pertelope driving and Sir Turquine doing the map-reading. Perhaps because of the human chemistry involved, it missed all the relevant turnings and ended up on the A45 to Coventry.

The second – an Avis eight-seater Renault nominally on hire to the Faculty of Experimental Mythology skittles team – left Glastonbury, joined the M5 north-bound to Bristol and the Midlands, made good time and stopped at the Michael Wood service station for a cup of tea and a go on the Space Invader machines in the front lobby.

The third – a brand new, jet-black Dodge with tinted windows, fat tyres, diplomatic number plates and a sticker in the window saying 'Tax Disc Applied For' – materialised on the M40 at its junction with the M25 and drove like a bat out of hell northwards, staying in the fast lane all the way and flashing the cars in front with its lights until they pulled over and let it pass.

'No,' said Aristotle, '*I* had the iced bun, *Dio* had the Black Forest gateau, *Merlin* had the toasted teacake, *you* had the croissant and the black coffee, so *you* owe *me* thirty pee.'

The soi-disant skittles team glowered at each other. Nostradamus, who had the bill, took a pencil from behind his ear and began to do sums.

'Actually,' Merlin said, 'I just had a cup of tea. It was, er, Mrs Magus who had the . . .'

Simon Magus glanced at his watch. 'All right,' he said, 'I'll treat you. I'll pay. Can we go now, please?'

The magi looked at him.

'There's no need to take that tone,' Aristotle growled. 'It's perfectly simple. I gave Nostradamus a fiver—'

'We haven't got time, Ari,' Simon Magus growled. 'Let's sort it out in the van, all right? Mahaud – oh God, where's she got to now?'

'I think she went to the shop to buy some peppermints,' Merlin said. 'She said that sucking a peppermint stops her feeling travel-sick.'

'Oh for crying out loud,' Simon Magus exclaimed. 'Dio, be a good chap, go and tell her . . .' But Dio Chrysostom, who was adamant that he'd had nothing but a hot chocolate and a digestive biscuit, folded his arms and pretended not to hear. Things were starting to get just a little bit out of hand.

Simon Magus frowned. On the one hand, here were eight of the finest minds in the whole of the Glass Mountain, the final repository of the wisdom of the world, the fountain of magic, the shield and pillar of mankind. On the other hand, they made the Lower Shell back at the Coll seem positively rational by comparison. He cleared his throat meaningfully.

'Right,' he said. 'The bus leaves in three minutes.

Anybody not back by then gets left behind. Clear?'

He jingled the keys and stalked off across the car park.

'Oh bother,' said the Queen of Atlantis, frowning slightly. 'That *is* a nuisance. Get out and change it, somebody.'

There was a certain degree of shuffling in the body of the bus, but otherwise nobody moved.

'Don't tell me,' the Queen said. 'There isn't a spare wheel in this thing.' She smiled glacially. 'Am I right?'

'There, um, wasn't room,' said a foolhardy young PA. 'You see, we had to strip out everything that wasn't absolutely essential so's we could fit the surveillance devices and the mobile fax transceiver in, and . . .'

'And somebody decided that a spare wheel wasn't essential.' The Queen pursed her exquisite lips. 'More a sort of luxury, I suppose, like a built-in cocktail cabinet. I *see*. Well then, did we also discard the puncture repair kit as the last word in Sybaritic self-indulgence, or have we still got that somewhere?'

'Oh yes, we've . . .'

The searchlight eyes homed in. The wire-guided smile locked on target.

'How simply splendid,' the Queen said. 'Out you get, then.'

Reluctantly, like a toreador going out to meet a bull with nothing but a bunch of flowers and a toothpick, the foolhardy young PA stood up, banged his head on the roof of the bus, and shuffled across to the door.

'Now then.' The Queen turned her head and turned the smile up to saturation level. 'While we're waiting, let's just see what else we've forgotten, shall we?'

Fortunately, the phone rang.

'Turkey.'

Sir Turquine looked up from his map. By his calculations they should be in Hertfordshire by now, which meant that some damn fool had moved Coventry a hundred miles to the south. 'What?' he snapped.

'Are you *sure* this is the right way?'

'Look . . .'

Boamund, who had been fast asleep ever since Perry Bar, woke up with a jolt and said, 'Stop the van!'

'Sorry?'

'I said,' Boamund repeated, 'stop the van.'

Turquine looked at him and shook his head. 'You can't,' he said, 'it's a main road. You'll have to wait till we pass a Little Chef or something.'

'Not that, you fool,' Boamund snapped. 'We're here. This is it.'

Pertelope shrugged. 'You're the boss, Snotty,' he said. 'There's a lay-by just ahead. Will that do?'

'Yes,' Boamund said impatiently, 'that's fine, just pull over.' He was frowning – a bad case of concentration, by the looks of it, as if he was struggling to keep something large and slippery in his mind.

'You all right, Bo?' Bedevere asked. 'You look all funny.'

'Actually,' Boamund replied, 'I had a dream.'

'Hello,' Turquine said, 'here we go. Young Snotty's been at the glue again.'

Boamund waved his hand angrily. 'Shut *up*, Turkey,' he said. 'This dream was important, and I'm trying to remember it. It's not easy, you know.'

The van stopped, and the knights jumped out. It was cold, and a fine shower of rain was falling. Beyond the post-and-wire fence, mist was blurring the edges of a large pine wood.

'That's it,' Boamund said, pointing. 'That forest over there. The other side of those trees, there's a lake. That's where we've got to go.'

Bedevere had managed to get hold of the map, and was examining it carefully. 'He's right, you know,' he said. 'At least, there's flooded gravel pits all round here. At least,' he added, lowering the map and nodding northwards, 'if that's Meriden over there, then there's gravel pits behind those trees. Otherwise, we could be anywhere.'

He stopped and looked down. Toenail was tugging at his sleeve.

'Did you say Meriden?' the dwarf demanded excitedly.

'Yes,' Bedevere replied, 'that's right. Why?'

'Meriden,' the dwarf repeated. 'Where the bikes come from.'

Bedevere raised an eyebrow. 'What's he going on about bikes for, anybody?' he said. Galahaut nodded.

'The old Triumph factory was at Meriden,' he said. 'What of it?'

The dwarf grinned. 'Nothing,' he said. 'Only, Meriden happens to be the exact geographical centre of Albion, that's all.'

Galahaut frowned. 'How extremely interesting,' he said. 'Now puddle off, there's a good little chap, because . . .'

'Say that again,' Bedevere interrupted.

'Meriden,' the dwarf repeated, 'is the exact centre of

Albion, geographically speaking.' He winked at Bedevere. 'Just thought I'd mention it,' he added.

'Thanks.' Bedevere twitched his nose a few times and looked at the map. 'You know,' he said, 'that's rather interesting, if you think about it.'

Lamorak looked at him quizzically. 'Is it?' he said. 'Personally, I could never get the hang of geography. What's the capital of Northgales, all that stuff. I mean, who wants to know?'

'In the exact centre,' Bedevere said, as much to himself as to anyone else. 'Well, I'll be blowed.'

'Your Majesty.'

'Mmmm?'

'I think you'd better pull over, Your Majesty.'

The Queen glanced in her rear-view mirror, sighed, and slowed down, while the PAs looked at each other and grinned. They were going to enjoy this.

The policeman who walked over and tapped on the window was young, tall and red-haired. In fact, the Queen said to herself, it's funny how young they all look these days. She wound down the window and smiled.

'Good afternoon, officer,' she said pleasantly.

The policeman didn't react to the smile; or if he did, he didn't show it.

'Do you realise,' he said, 'you were doing over a hundred and ten miles per hour back there, madam?'

'Gosh!' the Queen replied. 'How frightfully exciting! It didn't feel like that at all.'

'Please get out of the van, madam.'

'But it's raining.'

The policeman's face remained impassive. 'Out of

the van, please,' he said. 'Now I'm going to ask you to blow into—'

'Sorry?'

'I'm going to ask you rivet rivet rivet rivet,' said the small green frog; and then it seemed to notice that something was different. It hopped up and down on the spot once or twice and then it just sat there with its mouth open. The Queen shook her head sadly and beckoned to the other policeman.

'Officer,' said the Queen, 'I'm going to turn you into a frog, too.'

The policeman stared at her.

'Please don't take it personally,' the Queen went on, 'because I know you're just doing your job, and really it's not your fault, it's just the way things are. It won't hurt, I promise you.'

She smiled, and a second frog appeared at her feet. Very carefully, so as not to damage the little creatures' fragile legs, the Queen picked the two amphibians up and put them on the palm of her hand.

'Now then,' she said. 'One day, a princess will come along this road. Probably,' she added, 'doing a hundred and twenty and towing a horsebox. If you're terribly nice to her and don't ask to see her driving licence, she may kiss you and then you'll be back to being policemen. If not, try mayflies. I'm told they're a bit of an acquired taste, but well worth persevering with. Ciao!'

She put her index finger gently behind the frogs' back legs to encourage them to jump off her hand, smiled once more and got back into the van.

'Right,' she said.

★ ★ ★

'Where?'

Boamund scowled. It had been such a vivid dream, the sort you know you're going to remember, and now all there was in his mind was a sort of sticky silver trail where it had once been.

'It's about here somewhere,' he said. 'A lake. All misty. You know the sort of thing.'

Turquine shook his head. 'No sign of a lake here, Snotters,' he said. 'I mean, a thing like a lake, it's not easily overlooked. You must just have imagined it.'

'I did *not* imagine it,' Boamund shouted. 'It was a lake, and it was *here*.'

'Isn't here now,' said Turquine, and he smirked. 'Just a lot of trees, and this.'

He waved his arm at the small, exclusive, half-finished development of executive starter homes and shrugged. The other knights, unusually sensitive to their leader's embarrassment, said nothing.

'We could try over there,' Boamund suggested; and Bedevere was reminded of a cat he'd once known who had the habit of going to each door and window in turn every time it rained, presumably on the off-chance of finding one where it was sunny. 'It must just be hidden by the mist. I'm sure if we looked *properly* . . .'

'Come on, now,' Turquine was saying, in that unbearably aggravating let's-be-reasonable tone of his. 'We've given it a jolly good go, there's no lake here, so let's say no more about it and—'

There was a splash. Turquine had found a lake all right.

The ghost read back what he'd written and knew that

it was good. You get that feeling sometimes, when you're a ghost.

He looked at the clock, which was now keeping perfect time, and saw that it was just on half past nine. Just time to fax it through before everyone at the Manchester studios went home.

As the ghost strolled through the abandoned house, he wondered to himself what he'd found so difficult. As soon as he'd cottoned on to the idea of having Mike Baldwin start off the scene, it had just come; as if someone somewhere had been feeding it directly into his head. He'd just sat down, grabbed the paper, never blotted a line.

For the first time, he noticed what he'd been writing on; it was that funny piece of parchment he'd found in the clock. Without thinking he'd pumiced away the pictures and the initial capitals, but he hadn't touched all that silly Latin writing. Still, too late to do anything about it now.

A brief spasm of curiosity took hold of him, and he sat down on the lid of a chest and squinted at the manuscript. Years now since he'd tried to read any Latin, thank God – bloody silly language, anyway, with half the words ending in -us and the rest ending -o. The handwriting was small and cramped, too, which didn't help.

Historia Verissima de Calice Sancto, quae Latine vortit monachus Glastonburiensis Simon Magus ex libello vetere Gallico, res gestas equitum magorumque opprobria argentariorumque continens . . .

. . . A very true history of the holy something or other, which Simon the Magician, a *monachus*, that's monk, yes, monk of Glastonbury something-ed to

618

Latin; the verb's at the end of the line; containing, containing, oh yes, containing the things done of horsemen and magicians and the *opprobria*, opprobrious things of somethings, *argentariorum*, people who have something to do with money . . .

Load of old cod. As soon as I've faxed my copy in, the ghost promised himself, I'll take the pumice to this lot, and then maybe I can write something worth reading on it. Opprobrious things of people who have to do with money indeed! Who on earth would want to read about that?

He went into the office, dialled the number into the fax machine and fed the sheet of parchment into the automatic feed. There were the usual strangled-duck noises, and the parchment started to twitch spasmodically into the little plastic jaws. When it had finished transmitting, he pulled it out, carefully removed the little record slip, and went in search of pumice.

'Boamund.'

'Yes?'

'I don't want to appear personal, but you know that leather book thing, you know, the one we got back from Atlantis?'

'Yes?'

'There's a ruddy great piece of paper coming out of it.'

Danny Bennett yawned, reached for his coffee cup, found it empty, and swore.

Nine thirty. It had been a long day. Still, the new documentary was coming along, the ideas were flowing, the adrenaline was starting to move. Now, if only he could find some way to connect the Highland and Islands Development Board in with the Massacre of Glencoe, he'd really have something here.

He pulled the diagram towards him and gave it a good long stare. Like all his conspiracy charts, it was drawn out in at least seven different colours – blue for the CIA, green for the FBI, red for MI6, purple for the English National Opera, and so on. There was a pleasingly kaleidoscopic nexus round the escape of Bonnie Prince Charlie, and a straight orange line linking that with the North Sea oil franchises; all it needed now was some frilly pink bits up in the top right-hand corner. What was pink? Oh yes, the Public Lending Rights people. There was definitely something going on there. But what?

Down the corridor, in the part of the building where the soap opera people lived, he could hear a fax quietly chuntering away. Soaps! The scum of the earth. Opium of the masses. Why didn't *he* ever get any faxes, anyway?

Still, you had to say this for commercial television, they had a better class of felt-tip pen than he'd been used to at the BBC. If you inadvertently bit into the stem of one of these little babies during the throes of composition, you didn't go around for the next three days with a bright green tongue.

Something was disturbing his concentration. He tried to block it out of his mind, but it wouldn't go away; a persistent whining noise, like a machine in pain. It was that fax down the corridor, he realised; jammed, probably, and all those lazy sods in Soap Opera had gone home long since. Reluctantly – for he had seen a way to get the pink to join up with the yellow

620

without crossing the blue – he got up and went down the corridor to sort the blasted thing out.

Predictably enough, the paper feed had jammed. A few sharp blows with the side of his hand soon put the thing out of its misery, and he pulled the paper out, dumped it down on the desk and turned to leave. Then he frowned and turned back.

What in God's name were the soap people doing getting faxes in Latin?

Sure, it started off in English – and whoever had written it was truly awful at spelling – some sort of rubbishy drama script about people called Alf and Deirdre. But then, where the handwriting finished, there were ten or so paragraphs of tiny handwriting in what Danny was sure was Latin, if only he could make it out. Odd, to say the least. Very odd.

It was – oh, fifteen years, twenty even, since they'd stopped trying to teach him Latin at school; but Danny's mind was like the boot of the family car. Things that nobody wanted and which they were certain they'd chucked out ages ago tended to congregate there, hiding, waiting to pop out when nobody expected them. To his surprise, he found he could just about make it out . . .

Without realising what he was doing, he sat down on the desk and began to read.

'What's it doing, Bedders?' Boamund demanded.

'Printing out,' Bedevere replied, startled. 'Gosh, Bo, it looks like that thing's got a built-in miniature fax in it, Clever!'

'What's a . . .?'

Bedevere was examining the narrow strip of paper

emerging steadily from the side of the Personal Organiser of Wisdom. 'It's a magic thing,' he said. 'It means you can send letters and documents and things right across the world in a matter of seconds.'

'Oh, one of *those*,' Boamund said, relieved. 'Only, where's its wings?'

Bedevere raised an eyebrow. 'What do you mean, wings?' he asked.

'In my day,' Boamund replied, 'when you wanted to send a letter from one end of the world to another in a matter of seconds, you used a magic raven. Where's its wings?'

'They've improved it,' Bedevere said, his attention on the paper in his hands. 'All done with electricity now. That's why they call it wingless telegraphy. You know, this could be interesting. We've got a crossed line here, and . . .'

In spite of themselves, the knights gathered round and peered over his shoulder; all except Turquine, who was too busy wringing out his shirt and shivering. The small group fell silent.

'Well well,' said Lamorak at last. 'Interesting's putting it mildly, I should say. Fancy that, Ken Barlow and Liz McDonald . . .'

'Not that bit,' Bedevere said. 'The bit after that. My God . . .'

'But it's in Latin, Bedders. I was always useless at Latin.'

Bedevere was a quick reader, and his finger had already arrived at the foot of the page.

'Hell,' he said, 'The rest of it's missing. Still, it's a start. How the devil did that come to be passing across the airwaves, I wonder?'

Boamund interrupted him impatiently. 'What does it say, Bedders?' he demanded. 'And if it hasn't got wings, then how come . . .?'

Bedevere, however, wasn't listening. Instead, he was smiling.

'I see,' he said, slowly. 'Oh, very clever, very clever indeed. So that's what this thing was for all along.' Then he seemed to notice the rest of the knights, and turned to face them. 'What we've got here,' he said, 'is the first part of a contemporary account – well, near as dammit contemporary – of the losing of the Holy Grail.' His face melted suddenly into an enormous grin. 'And you're never going to guess,' he added, 'who it's written by.'

They were going to be absolutely livid, Simon Magus told himself, especially Mahaud. Still, he had warned them, and one can't make an omelette, et cetera. He'd probably be better off on his own, anyway.

He glanced down at the map on the seat beside him, but it was too dark to see. He'd have to rely on memory, and it must be at least eight hundred years since he'd been this way last. Luckily, he had a good sense of direction.

'Coventry,' he said aloud. Good idea, these new-fangled road signs; saved you all that stopping and asking the way from gnarled old rustics. He leant forward and switched on the radio. *Round Britain Quiz*; oh good. He liked that. Mildly entertaining, didn't have Robert Robinson in it.

Quite understandable that he was feeling slightly nervous. This job had been a long time coming to fruition, and a lot of work had gone into it. He glanced at the speedometer and eased his foot off the accelerator. No need to rush, and it would be stupid to be stopped for speeding.

('Rivet rivet rivet,' croaked a frog on the hard shoulder as the van swished by.)

As he drove, he went over in his mind the various things that still remained to be done. There was plenty that could still go wrong, but that was always the way. There came a time when you just had to sit back and let them get on with it. They were a pretty sound bunch of lads, if you didn't expect too much out of them, and they had the dwarf to make sure they didn't get themselves into too much trouble.

After *Round Britain Quiz* came the weather forecast – remarkably accurate, Simon Magus noted with approval; they do a good job, considering how abysmally primitive their technology is – followed by a repeat of a gardening programme. Simon Magus yawned and switched the thing off. Should be nearly there by now, anyway.

The shape of the country was definitely familiar, and Simon Magus turned off the motorway on to the A45. He could almost hear it, calling to him ...

'Magus!'

He looked up, and saw Aristotle's face in the rearview mirror. Blast! He'd forgotten to switch the damn thing off.

'Hello, Ari,' he replied. 'I warned you. Three minutes, I said.'

'How could you?' Aristotle said, white with rage. 'Just leave us here, I mean, in the middle of nowhere ...'

'I'll pick you up on my way back,' Simon Magus

replied. 'Look, why don't you just go and have a cup of tea and a go on the electronic games, there's a good lad. And, er, tell Mrs Magus I was called away suddenly or something, will you? Thanks.'

He reached up and flicked a little switch behind the mirror. Aristotle disappeared, and was replaced by the distant prospect of a Daf truck.

Well. If he'd forgotten anything, it was too late now.

The knights were getting wet.

'So,' Bedevere was saying, 'it's all very straightforward, really. Albion isn't Albion at all, it's a sort of . . .' He racked his brains for the right term. 'It's what you might call a financial institution,' he said, lamely. He knew it was all wrong, but never mind. There was no point in trying to understand; all they had to do was get on with it, and everything would be fine.

'I see,' Boamund lied. 'So what do we do now, then?'

'I've got a travelling backgammon set,' said Lamorak.

Boamund considered that. 'All right,' he said. 'And then what?'

'Well, by then someone will have turned up and we'll know what we're meant to do, I suppose. You heard what Bedders said, Bo. We've got to be patient.'

It turned out, rather inevitably, that Lamorak had mislaid the dice, so in the end they sat down under the intermittent shelter of a tree and played Twenty Questions. It was pitch dark by now, and the mist was starting to swirl round them in clouds.

'Your turn, Bo. Think of something.'

Boamund knitted his brows for a moment. When he

625

said 'Ready,' there was something in his voice which made Bedevere wonder; but he kept his thoughts to himself.

'Two words,' said Boamund. 'And it's mineral.'

'Mineral,' Galahaut repeated. 'Is it something you'd expect to find about the house?'

Boamund considered for a moment; it was almost as if he was listening to a voice telling him the answer. 'Yes,' he said, and he sounded rather surprised. 'That's one.'

'Bigger or smaller than a football?' Turquine asked.

'Bigger,' Boamund replied. 'Gosh,' he added. 'Two.'

'Is it made of metal?'

'Yes,' Boamund said, and then frowned. 'No,' he corrected. 'No, it's not, actually. Three.'

'A household object, not made of metal, bigger than a football,' Pertelope mused. 'Is it mechanical?'

'No. Four.'

'Not mechanical, right. Would you expect to find it in the kitchen?'

Boamund waited for the answer. When it came, it seemed to amaze him. 'Yes,' he said. 'Five.'

'Right,' Galahaut said. 'Mineral, not metal, bigger than a football, not mechanical, you'd find it in the kitchen. Dustbin?'

'No. Six.'

'Vegetable rack?'

'No. Seven.'

'Is it,' asked Lamorak, 'made of plastic?'

Boamund listened, and his mouth opened for a moment in wonder. 'Yes,' he said. 'Eight.'

'Pasta jar?'

'That's not bigger than a football, idiot.'

'Some of them are,' Turquine replied. 'I went into this shop once . . .'

'It's not a pasta jar,' Boamund said quietly. 'Nine.'

'Kitchen scales,' Pertelope suggested. 'No, that's mechanical, I take that back. I know, it's a large tupperware cake box.'

'No. Ten.'

'Mixing bowl?'

'No. Eleven.'

'God, we're so *close*,' Lamorak said. 'Let's see, it's a large plastic kitchen utensil, not mechanical. Plate rack?'

'No. Twelve.'

'Tricky one,' said Galahaut. 'Can't be a flour jar, 'cos that'd be pottery, not plastic. Lammo, what do we keep in the cupboard under the sink, just behind the blender?'

There was a tense silence. Bedevere looked up, and saw that it had stopped raining.

'How about a sink tidy?' Pertelope suggested. 'We haven't had that yet, have we?'

'It's not a sink tidy, and that's thirteen,' Boamund said. 'What's a sink tidy, anyway?'

'How about a bucket?' suggested Galahaut. 'You know, for doing the floor with?'

'Fourteen.'

'Let's recap,' Turquine suggested, and while they were doing it, Boamund stared (so to speak) at the sharp, clear picture in his mind. It couldn't be . . .

'Dustpan and brush,' said Galahaut, the spokesman. 'I mean, you could keep it in the kitchen if you didn't have a cupboard under the stairs.'

'Fifteen,' replied Boamund, absently. The image in his mind refused to fade; if anything, it grew brighter.

'I'm trying to think,' Turquine was saying, 'what they've got in the kitchen at Pizza To Go.' He shook his head. 'But it's not mechanical. I dunno, it's a good one, this.'

'Lampshade,' Lamorak broke in, and there was a hint of desperation in his voice. But Boamund simply shook his head and said, 'Sixteen.'

'I know,' Pertelope said. 'Silly of me not to have guessed. It's a plastic colander.'

'Seventeen.'

'Salad shaker.'

'Eighteen.'

'In the *kitchen*, for God's sake.'

'Cutlery drawer.'

Boamund shook his head again. 'Nineteen,' he murmured.

The knights looked at each other; and then Bedevere, who had been looking up at the sky and noticing that the clouds were breaking up and the stars were coming out, cleared his throat.

'I think,' he said, 'it's the Holy Grail.'

'That's right,' Boamund said. 'Twenty.'

9

Before anyone had a chance to speak, there was a soft cough behind them, and a man stepped forward.

'Good evening, gentlemen,' he said.

A thousand-year-old instinct brought the knights smartly to their feet.

'Good evening, Mr Magus, sir,' they chorused.

Simon Magus looked down at his clothes and sighed. He had done his best to disguise himself as an aged woodcutter, but fancy dress had never been his cup of tea.

'Ready?'

The knights looked at each other. 'Yes, sir,' said Boamund. 'All ready.'

'Splendid,' Simon Magus replied. 'In that case, Boamund, if you'd care to follow me? The rest of you, stay here till I call.'

There was a faint rumble of murmuring from the

knights – something mutinous about it not being fair, and a certain person being the teacher's pet. When Simon Magus turned round and looked at them, it died away completely.

'Be good,' Simon Magus said. Then he walked away.

'You'll need this.'

Boamund had been wondering what was in the canvas bag. It could have been fishing rods, or drain rods even, or a small collapsible easel, or possibly a photographer's tripod. But it wasn't.

'Mind out,' the magician warned, 'it's sharp.'

Boamund, who had already discovered this, sucked his finger. Very sharp and remarkably light, and it seemed to shine of its own accord in the pale moonlight.

'Excalibur,' said Simon Magus casually. 'Been up on the top of my wardrobe for years now, so I said to myself, I'm never going to get any use out of it, might as well pass it on to somebody who will.' He looked at it wistfully.

Excalibur! Someone or something with just a little more imagination than Boamund – a rock, say, or the root of a tree – might have imagined that the dim flame of light dancing on the blade of the sword flickered at the sound of the name. Boamund bit his lip.

'Um,' he said, 'are you sure, sir? I mean, I always thought that the King sort of chucked it in the lake.'

Simon Magus grinned. 'He did,' he replied. 'That's how I got it. Look.'

He pointed to a small group of letters engraved in gold on the ricasso of the sword; and as he did, one could have been forgiven for thinking that they glowed brightly for a fraction of a second.

SHEFFIELD, they said.

'Anyway,' Simon Magus went on, rather self-consciously, 'put it away for now and let's hope we won't need it. Should all be perfectly straightforward . . .'

'Halt!'

Out of the darkness, a figure loomed. Moonlight glinted on blued steel.

'All right,' said Simon Magus patiently, after a relatively long pause. 'We've halted. What can we do for you?'

'Um.' The silhouette turned its head and whispered something urgently into the bush from which it had emerged. A couple of other silhouettes emerged rather reluctantly and stood behind it. 'You may not pass,' it said.

'Why not?'

'You can't. Go away.'

Simon Magus and Boamund exchanged glances.

'Can I?' said Boamund hopefully.

'Go on, then,' Simon Magus replied. 'But don't get carried away.'

With a whoop of delight, Boamund drew the sword from the canvas bag, swung it round his head so fast that Simon Magus nearly lost an ear, and lunged into the darkness. There were a few loud but very musical clangs, and Boamund came back.

'They ran away,' he said. It was almost a whimper.

'Never mind,' the magician replied. 'There'll be others, I expect.'

Boamund nodded stoically and sheathed the sword.

'Perhaps,' he said eagerly, 'they'll ambush us.'

Simon Magus shrugged. 'Actually,' he said, 'I rather think that was meant to be an ambush just then. I don't think they've had an awful lot of practice at this sort of thing.'

'Oh.' Boamund sounded surprised. 'You know who they are, then?'

'I've got a pretty good idea,' Simon Magus replied. 'I think they're independent financial advisers. That or portfolio managers. Come on.'

They walked on round the edge of the lake. In a tree above their heads, an owl hooted. Boamund got something in his eye and paused to get it out again.

'Excuse me asking,' he said tentatively, 'but was it you who was that hermit I saw when I woke up, the one who said I should go and do this quest?'

Simon Magus nodded. 'That's right,' he said.

'Oh. I didn't recognise you.'

'I was in disguise. It wouldn't have done for you to know, you see. Actually, it was a pretty terrible disguise. I'm surprised you didn't see through it.'

Boamund considered this revelation for a moment. 'So you've been behind the whole thing, then? Me going to sleep and all that.'

'That's right.' He hesitated, and then added, 'You didn't mind, did you? I mean, you weren't about to do something else, or anything like that?'

'No, not at all,' Boamund replied.

'Good. I was a bit worried, you know, that I'd messed you about rather.'

A shadowy figure with a knife in its mouth dropped from a tree. Unfortunately, it had mistimed its descent. There was a thump; and when the shadowy figure came round, there were two men standing over it solicitously.

'Are you all right?' asked Simon Magus.

'I'th cut my mouf on this thucking dagger,' the assailant replied. 'Thod it.'

'You should be more careful, then, shouldn't you?' Simon Magus replied. 'Here.' He gave the assailant a handkerchief.

'Thankth.' He wiped his face, spat out a tooth and crawled away into the bushes.

Simon Magus shrugged. 'Something tells me we're up against the B-team tonight,' he said. 'Never mind. Bit of an anticlimax, though.'

They walked on in silence for a while, and then Boamund asked:

'I know about the personal organiser, but what about the socks and the apron? I mean, are they *for* anything, or . . .?'

Simon Magus made a clicking noise with his tongue. 'Me and my memory,' he said. 'Good job you reminded me. Have you got them with you?'

'They're in my satchel.'

'Good lad. Now,' said Simon Magus, lowering his voice, 'let's just duck under this tree where it's nice and—'

'Ouch,' said a masked assassin tetchily.

'Sorry.'

'Why the hell don't you look where you're going?'

'Sorry,' Boamund replied, 'it's dark. Have at you?' he suggested hopefully.

The masked assassin scowled at him. 'Not bloody likely,' he said, getting to his feet and hopping a few paces. 'You've done enough damage as it is.'

Muttering to himself, he limped away into the gloom.

'Right,' said Simon Magus. 'Put on the socks and the apron, there's a good lad.'

Boamund frowned. 'Have I got to?' he said.

Simon Magus looked at him. 'Of course you've got to,' he said.

'Oh,' Boamund replied. 'Only I'll feel such a twit wandering about the place in a pinny with flowers on it.'

'You can put it on under your coat if you like,' said the magician tolerantly. 'Just hurry up, that's all.'

Boamund knelt down and unlaced his shoes. 'They're important, are they?' he asked.

'Vital, absolutely vital. Get a move on, will you? We haven't got all night.'

'They're tickling my feet.'

'Look...'

There was a bloodcurdling cry just behind him, and Simon Magus spun round.

'Sorry,' he said, 'but can you just hang on a tick? We aren't quite ready yet.'

The hooded thug froze in mid-swing. 'What?' he said.

'Won't keep you a moment,' Simon Magus replied. 'The lad's just changing his socks.'

'His *socks*? Now just a minute...'

'It's all right, I'm ready now,' Boamund said, and there was a sudden flash of blue light as Excalibur swished out of the canvas bag. 'Lay on!' he cried happily, and he darted forward. There was a metallic note, approximately D sharp, followed by the sound of someone in armour tripping over his feet and falling into a bush.

'That's not fair,' said a voice from the undergrowth. 'I wasn't ready.'

'Tough,' said Simon Magus. 'We ambushed you.'

'No, you've got it all wrong, *I* ambushed *you*.'

Simon Magus grinned. 'Didn't make a very good job of it, then, did you? Come on, Boamund, we'd better not be late.'

They walked on a few paces. 'That wasn't very fair, was it?' Boamund said. 'I mean, if he waited for us, then surely . . .'

'Nonsense,' replied the magician firmly. 'An ambush is an ambush. If he doesn't know that, then he's not fit to be out on his own.'

'*I* didn't know that—'

'Ah,' replied Simon Magus, 'but you're not on your own, are you?'

'Oh, I see.'

They had come to a sort of jetty or landing-stage, and Simon Magus stopped and looked about him.

'I think we're here,' he said. 'Well, best of luck and all that. Don't forget what I told you.'

Boamund's face fell. 'You're not leaving me, are you?' he said. 'Only I thought . . .'

''Fraid so,' the magician replied. 'Any further intervention on my part would be most irregular, and I don't want the whole quest set aside on a technicality.'

'Oh,' Boamund said. A light breeze began to blow, rippling the surface of the lake. 'What do I do now, then?'

'You'll find out,' said the magician through a curtain of blue fire. 'Cheerio.'

'Cheerio, then,' Boamund replied. He turned and looked at the lake. 'Oh, sir.'

'Yes?'

'What was it you told me that I'm supposed to remember?'

'I've forgotten,' Simon Magus replied, and his voice was hollow and indistinct. His immortal half was already thousands of miles and hundreds of years away. 'It probably wasn't important. Keep your guard up, remember to roll your wrists, something like that. Good luck, Boamund.'

The blue pyramid flared up briefly and faded, leaving only a few lingering sparkles and an empty crisp packet. The wind started to blow harder, rustling the leaves of the trees round the lake. The moon came out. It was getting colder.

'Good evening.'

Boamund spun round. Standing beside him – he hadn't been there a moment ago, unless he'd been very heavily disguised as a small ornamental cherry tree – was what Boamund took to be a hermit.

'Hello,' Boamund replied. 'Are you a hermit?'

'Yes,' said the hermit. 'How did you guess?'

'I just sort of did,' Boamund replied. 'Excuse me, but what do hermits actually do?'

The hermit scratched the lobe of his ear. 'It depends, really,' he said. 'In the old days, we used to meditate, pray, fast and converse with spirits. These days, though, most of us sit in lay-bys on main roads with a big painted board saying "Strawberries". You've probably seen us.'

'Well, no, actually,' Boamund replied. 'You see, I've been asleep for rather a long time, and—'

'So you have,' the hermit replied. 'I forgot. Well now, young Boamund, I expect you're rather excited.'

'Um,' said Boamund, 'yes. Quite. Are you going to tell me what happens next?'

The hermit shook his head. 'I'm afraid not,' he said. 'My role is what you might call a nice little cameo. Very cameo,' he added, with a touch of bitterness. 'All I'm supposed to do is tell you something true but misleading. You don't mind if we spin it out a bit, do you? Only I've been waiting fifteen hundred years for this, and I'd hate to rush things. I mean,' he added, 'it's not as if I've got a great deal to look forward to, is it?'

'Is it? I mean, haven't you?'

'Not really, no,' the hermit said. 'I'm booked in at that terribly dreary Glass Mountain place. Have you ever been there?'

'No.'

'You haven't missed much,' replied the hermit. 'That's why I volunteered for this job, actually, just to have an excuse to put it off for a while. It wasn't exactly a riot of fun sitting beside the A45 in the rain with twenty pounds of squishy strawberries for all those years, but anything's better than where I'm going next.' The hermit sighed deeply and brushed a fly off the tip of his nose.

'Oh,' Boamund said. He felt rather awkward. 'I'm sorry,' he said.

'Not your fault,' the hermit replied. 'That's where we go, you see, when we finally leave the world. They'll all be there, all the great magicians and sorcerers and hermits and anchorites, all sitting about yammering away or falling asleep in big leather armchairs. I expect I'll get used to it.' The hermit shook his head sadly. 'They all do, apparently, after a while. That's the really awful part of it, in my opinion.'

'I'm sorry,' Boamund replied. It was hard to know what to say.

'Thank you,' the hermit said. 'Now, the message is this. Only the true King of Albion will recover the Holy Grail. Good luck.'

A blue pyramid, smaller than the one Simon Magus had vanished into and somehow indefinably but perceptibly second class, formed over him, gave a few perfunctory twinkles and vanished. Boamund looked at where it had been and chewed his lip for a moment.

'Oh,' he said.

He turned to look at the lake; and then in the corner of his eye he caught sight of a stealthy shadow creeping furtively towards him. He whipped out the sword and sprang.

'Hold it,' said the figure. 'Have you just been talking to the hermit?'

'Yes,' Boamund said. 'Why?'

'Oh nuts,' said the figure. 'I'm late. Forget it.'

'But . . .'

'I'm sorry,' the figure said, 'my fault, I blew it. What I'm going to say to the bloody woman when I come back without a scratch on me I really don't know. Probably I'll be back behind the counter Monday morning doing car insurance. Still, there it is.'

Boamund frowned. 'You *want* me to thump you?' he said. The figure nodded.

'Still,' he said, 'no use crying over spilt milk. Thanks anyway. Be seeing you.'

Boamund moved to strike, but the figure had gone. He shrugged, and returned to his seat on the landing-stage.

'Gosh,' he said.

Where he'd been, there was now an enormous blue car – a Volvo – with a strange yellow object fastened to its wheel. Under one of its windscreen wipers was a scrap of paper. Boamund lifted it out, unfolded it and read:

WHOSO EXTRICATES THIS CAR FROM THIS CLAMP SHALL BE THE RIGHTFUL KING OF ALBION.

He scratched his head, and looked down at the yellow thing. It looked like some sort of trap or snare, and he wondered if the car was in pain. Perhaps it was dead; it certainly wasn't moving.

Rightful King of Albion . . .

'Well,' he said, 'here goes.'

Excalibur whistled in the air, and he struck with all his might. Because of a slight miscalculation – the blade was some six inches longer than he'd imagined – the net effect was that a tree immediately behind him lost the tip of one of its branches. He steadied himself, rubbed his wrist where he'd jarred it, and tried again. There was a clang, and the yellow thing broke in two and fell to the ground.

'Nice,' said a voice behind him. 'Very neat.'

It was a girl, wearing a blue and yellow uniform and holding a notebook. For some reason Boamund felt slightly apprehensive.

'It's all right,' the girl assured him, 'I'm purely allegorical, I'm not going to give you a ticket. You're supposed to get in and turn the key.'

'Oh,' Boamund said, 'right. Which key?'

The girl gave him a puzzled look, and then laughed.

'Sorry,' she said, 'I forgot, you've been asleep. Inside the car, there's a big wheel thing. Behind that on your right-hand side you'll find a small key. Give it a gentle turn clockwise and that'll start the engine. Clockwise is this way.' She demonstrated. 'Got that?'

'Thanks.'

'You're welcome,' said the girl and, rather to Boamund's disappointment, vanished. He climbed in, located the ignition and turned the key.

The car vanished.

Boamund sat up and felt the top of his head. There was something on it. A crown.

'Good Lord,' he said, and took it off. It was quite light and thin, and he had the feeling it was probably silver gilt; but it had little points like a saw-blade and a few rather small jewels set into it. He put it back on and tried to imagine being a king.

He looked up, conscious of a noise in the middle distance. It wasn't the sort of noise he had expected to hear beside a lake, somehow. It was, in fact, a telephone.

He looked round, and saw a hand breaking the surface of the lake, about a hundred and fifty yards from the bank. It was white, clothed in samite and holding a telephone.

Suddenly, Boamund wondered if the whole thing was a practical joke.

You know how it is with telephones. Whatever you're doing, however busy or preoccupied you are, sooner or later you give in and pick up the receiver. Boamund sighed and got to his feet. At the side of the jetty was a small boat – hadn't been there a moment ago; big deal, nothing surprised him about this caper any more – and

640

sitting in it was a hooded figure holding the oars.

'Come on, will you?' said the hooded figure. 'I'm catching my death in here.'

Boamund scrambled down into the boat, sat down and began to sulk. The hooded figure dipped the oars in the water and began to row. The boat made no sound as it moved, and the water was as smooth as glass.

'Is it Thursday today?' the ferryman demanded suddenly.

Boamund looked up. 'Sorry?' he said.

'I said, is it Thursday?' the ferryman said. 'You lose track of what day it is when you're on nights.'

'I think so,' Boamund replied. 'Does it matter?'

'Because if it's Thursday,' the figure went on, 'then I've forgotten to set the video. *She* won't bother, of course, the dozy cow. Probably got her feet up, watching the news. You married?'

'No.'

'Very wise,' the ferryman said, and Boamund noticed that there was no face under the hood. 'Go on, then, answer it.'

Boamund hesitated. 'If I do,' he said cautiously, 'this boat isn't going to disappear, is it? I mean, the car did.'

'Get on with it.'

'All right, then.' He leant over and took the receiver. 'You're sure the boat won't disappear? Only . . .'

The hooded figure gave him a scornful, eyeless look, and he put the receiver to his ear.

'Hello?' he said.

The boat vanished.

Danny Bennett reached the bottom of the page and sighed.

A thousand-year-old, ecologically significant international insurance, tax and financial services scam, protected by offshore trusts, conspiracies in high places, corruption, intrigue, cover-ups and graft, implicating virtually every well-known figure in history from Julius Caesar to Spiro Agnew, the implications of which would cast entirely new light on the Princes in the Tower, the Turin Shroud, Easter Island, the Loch Ness Monster, the Fall of Constantinople, Alexander Nevski, the *Mary Rose*, Christopher Marlowe, the *Flying Dutchman*, Cortés and Montezuma, the Gunpowder Plot, the Man in the Iron Mask, the Salem witches, the escape of Bonnie Prince Charlie, the death of Mozart, the War of Jenkins' Ear, the *Marie Celeste*, Jack the Ripper, Darwin, the Hound of the Baskervilles, Ned Kelly, Rorke's Drift, Anastasia, Piltdown Man, the Wall Street Crash, the Lindbergh kidnapping, the Bermuda Triangle, the Reichstag fire, fifty tons of Nazi gold going missing near Lake Geneva in 1945, McCarthy, Suez, Watergate, decimalisation, the death of Pope John Paul I, Three Mile Island, the sinking of the *Belgrano* and the disappearance of Shergar.

'Load of old rubbish,' he said.

He screwed the pages into a ball and threw them in the bin. Then he went back to his desk and got on with his work.

'Well, hello there,' said a voice. 'Your *Majesty*,' it added, and giggled.

Boamund opened his eyes. It was true that his entire life had flashed before him in that terrible few seconds in the water; since he'd slept through most of his life, however, it hadn't been terribly interesting. He'd seen himself lying there, snoring, while his clothes gradually rusted.

'Where am I?' he asked.

The voice (female) giggled again. 'That's a very good question,' it said. 'Shall we start with something a bit easier, like the square root of two?'

Boamund tried to move but couldn't. From where he was lying, all he could see was ceiling. It was a sort of dark green and it moved about, and there was a fish where the lampshade should have been.

'Water pressure,' the voice explained. 'You've got tons and tons and tons of water on top of you, you see, and since you aren't used to it, it's squashing you flat.'

'Oh,' said Boamund. 'Did I drown?'

'Certainly not,' the voice replied. 'If you'd drowned, you'd be dead, silly. You're at the bottom of the lake.'

'Oh,' Boamund repeated. There was something sharp digging into the small of his back.

'Well,' the voice said, 'you got here, then.'

'Yes,' Boamund said. 'Um, am I on the right lines, or did I go wrong somewhere? I mean, am I *meant* to be here?'

The voice laughed. 'Absolutely,' it said. 'You've succeeded. Well done.'

Boamund reviewed his position, and decided that success was probably over-rated. 'What happens now?" he asked. 'And who are you, anyway?'

Suddenly he could feel the weight sliding off him, and he sat up with a jerk. He found himself looking at a woman; tall, slim, graceful, with golden hair and a portable telephone. She was sitting in a tubular steel chair wearing a silky cream blouse and lemon Bermuda shorts. A pike swam past her with a saucer in its jaws, and on the saucer was balanced a tiny coffee cup, which the woman lifted off and held between thumb and forefinger.

'Can I get you anything?' she asked. 'Coffee? A doughnut, perhaps? You strike me as the sort of person who likes doughnuts.'

Boamund blushed. 'No, thank you,' he said stiffly. 'You seem to be a person of importance, please explain what's going on.'

'Business before pleasure, you mean?' the woman said. 'Fair enough. My name is Kundry.'

Boamund looked behind him and saw what it was that he'd been lying on. He picked up the crown, which had been flattened, and tried to bend it back into shape. He felt extremely depressed, but wasn't sure why.

'Don't worry about that,' said Kundry. 'It isn't a real crown, actually; just something to be going on with. Allegorical.'

The word made a connection in Boamund's mind. 'I recognise you,' he said. 'You were that girl with the car.'

Kundry smiled. 'The traffic-warden, that's right. Also the hand with the telephone.' She lifted the portable handset off the smoked-glass table beside her. 'Also the hermit, the unpunctual assassin and the owl. Cast of thousands, in fact.'

'You're a sorceress,' Boamund said.

'Quite right,' Kundry replied. 'Actually, it's not illegal any more. Hasn't been, since Nineteen Fifty-Something. In my position, one has to be very careful.'

'Um,' Boamund said. 'What is your position, then?'

'I'm the Queen of Atlantis,' Kundry replied.

'Among other things, of course. I'm also the high priestess of New Kettering and the Grafin von Weinacht. Actually,' she added, 'that's not strictly true; I'm not supposed to use the title since the divorce, so my daughter Katya's the Grafin now. She's a horrid little girl, my daughter. Let's say, shall we, that I'm the Dowager Grafin von Weinacht. I'm not absolutely sure what Dowager means, but I think that after being married to the Graf for six hundred years I deserve some sort of title. A medal, even,' she added. 'Anyway,' she went on, 'none of that really matters as far as you're concerned. What you should be in interested in is me being Kundry.'

'Ah,' Boamund said. He beat about furiously in his mind and stumbled across a phrase which seemed to fit. 'You have the advantage of me there, I'm afraid.'

Kundry raised a beautifully pencilled eyebrow. 'You've never heard of Kundry?' she said.

'Um . . .'

'Good Lord. What *did* they teach you at school, I wonder?'

'Falconry,' Boamund replied. 'Also fencing, tilting, heraldry – actually it was the New Heraldry, you do it all with little diagrams – courtesy, magic with divinity and dalliance to Grade 3. And the flute,' he added, 'but I never got the hang of it properly. I can play *Edi Bi Thu* and *San'c Fuy Belha ni Prezada* if I go slowly.'

'It was a rhetorical question,' Kundry replied. 'You're not the least bit what I expected, you know.'

'Aren't I?'

'No.' Kundry drank some coffee and dropped the cup. A tiny roach darted up, caught the handle of the cup in its mouth and disappeared with a flick of its tail, while a perch retrieved the saucer. 'A moment ago you asked me where you were.'

'That's right,' Boamund said.

'Well,' Kundry continued, 'this is the registered office of Lyonesse (UK) plc, and we're in the exact geographical centre of Albion. You're sitting on it, in fact.'

Boamund shifted rather uncomfortably.

'Here,' Kundry went on, 'you're exactly half way between Atlantis and the North Pole. Does that mean anything to you?'

'Well, no, not really.'

'Doesn't it? Well, never mind. I expect you want to know where the Holy Grail is.'

'I would rather, yes.'

Kundry smiled. 'In that case,' she said, 'I think I'd better begin at the beginning. It all started a very long time ago . . .'

In the narrow street outside, a Roman legionary was leaning on his shield, looking out over the city of Jerusalem and doing his best to ignore the smells of cooking coming from the upper room of the house behind him.

He could smell garlic. He could smell lamb, basting in its own juices. He could smell coriander, and freshly baked bread, and thyme, and sea-bass being steamed with dill and fenugreek. It was sheer torture.

In the kitchen above his head, Bartholomew's girl-friend was stirring the sauce for the roast peacock with one hand, and turning the pages of a cookery book with the other.

'Cream the yeast with a little of the milk,' she said

aloud, 'and leave until frothy.'

She hadn't tried the recipe before, but it sounded wonderful – spicy buns with cinnamon and currants! Yum.

Bartholomew's girlfriend liked cooking, and so when someone had suggested that they have a slap-up meal to celebrate Simon Peter's birthday, she had volunteered like a shot. And when they'd told her that the Master would be coming – well, she'd been in a right tizzy for days. Just imagine it, her cooking for the Master!

After a lot of soul-searching and internal debate, she'd decided on the lamb. You couldn't go wrong with lamb, not at this time of year; and anyway, the marinade would cover a multitude of sins. Then Simon Peter had caught those really nice bass – say what you like about Si, his fish was always properly fresh, which was more than you could say for some – and Philip had been given a peacock by the nice Roman lady whose garden he did twice a week, so that had been all right. The little cinnamon cakes had been her own idea, though.

'Turn on a floured surface,' she read, and 'knead for eight minutes until smooth and elastic.'

It would have been nice, she reflected, if once, just once, one of them had the good manners to say thank you; but that was men for you. She smiled indulgently, thinking of the time when they'd brought all those people back, and nothing in the house except a couple of loaves and a few tiddly little mackerel.

Bartholomew was nice, she said to herself; a nice, steady young man, not likely to go dashing off and joining the army or disappearing for months on end with a caravan. She didn't mind waiting while he went through this religious phase of his – long engagements were a good thing, really, you got to know each other's little ways, so it didn't come as a great big shock when you finally did get married. Besides, it gave her plenty of time to make her dress.

As she made the glaze for the buns, she turned over in her mind the rather peculiar rumours that she'd heard in the Market that morning. Not that there could possibly be anything *wrong* with the Master; he was a holy man, they said, one of these prophets or something like that. But it was true that the Romans didn't really hold with prophets, and really, no good ever came out of antagonising the Romans. She'd have to be firm, she decided. Once they were married, she'd have to stop Bartholomew going to all these prayer meetings and things. If he was really serious about having his own little sandalmaker's shop one of these days, there wouldn't be time for hobbies, anyway.

'There,' she said, and closed the oven door. She wiped her floury hands on a towel, nodded with satisfaction, and started to arrange the flowers on the table. Thirteen to supper would have panicked a lot of girls her age, but she'd managed.

The first to arrive was James the son of Alphaeus. A shy boy, always knocking over ornaments. He helped her lay the table, but didn't say a word. Preoccupied, she thought.

Andrew, James and John all came at once.

'John,' she said bitterly, 'I do wish you'd learn to wipe your feet. Just *look* at my nice clean floor.' She scurried away for the mop; but as soon as she'd cleaned up, in came Simon Peter and Thomas, in their work-clothes too, and she had to do the whole thing again. Nobody noticed the flowers, although it had taken her half an hour to get them just right.

Matthew and Simon the Zealot left their muddy cloaks on the worktop and Judas the brother of James picked the decoration off one of the buns. She was quite rude to him.

Just when she was starting to fret about the meat spoiling, Philip, the other Judas and Bartholomew came in; but she couldn't scold them for being late because they had the Master with them, and Bartholomew got so upset and difficult if she said anything to him in front of the Master. Judas wiped his hands on one of her lovely Damascus napkins, and Philip's dog knocked over the hat-stand, but she didn't say anything. Her mother had always said that she had the patience of a saint.

She hadn't enjoyed the meal. Although the lamb had turned out just right, the peacock was delicious and the sea-bass just the way it should have been, nobody seemed to be hungry. They just sat there, picking at it; and the Master ate nothing but a few pieces of bread all evening. The conversation had been very gloomy and depressing, all about theology, and she'd got the impression that they were all rather on edge. Mind you, what with bringing in the food and clearing away the dishes – and nobody raised a finger to help, of course, although she should have expected that – she hadn't been in her seat for more than a couple of minutes together. And, of course, Judas Iscariot had to go and upset the gravy-boat, all over her mother's best table-cloth. Finally, to put the tin lid on it, nobody had so much as tasted the clever little cinnamon buns with the pretty decoration on them. For some reason, she got the impression that everybody thought they were in rather poor taste, but she couldn't for the life of her think why.

Eventually, Simon Peter looked at the water-clock and said something about it being time they were going, and they all stood up to leave. That was rather more than Bartholomew's girlfriend could take.

'Excuse me,' she said, 'but aren't you forgetting something?'

Andrew and Thomas gave her a filthy look but she ignored them. She'd had enough; and if Bartholomew cared for her even a little bit then he'd say something, surely.

'The washing-up,' she said. 'You aren't just going to walk out of here and *leave* it, are you?'

There was an embarrassed silence; then Simon Peter mumbled something about them having to dash or they'd be late.

'It won't take a moment,' said Bartholomew's girlfriend. 'Not if six of you wash and the rest of you dry.' And she went and stood in front of the door with her arms folded.

'Oh for Chri – for crying out loud,' said Matthew. 'Get out of the way, woman, we're in a hurry.'

'You're not leaving this room until you've done the washing-up,' said Bartholomew's girlfriend. 'I'm *fed up* with you lot trooping in and out at all hours of the day and night in your muddy shoes, expecting to be fed and cleaned up after and have your silly cloaks darned, and knocking things over, and bringing your horrid dogs and nets full of fish, and leaving saws and drills and things all over the place. It's too bad, it really is.'

And then she'd burst into floods of tears.

'Look,' said James, 'we'll make it up to you later, right? Only, really, it is kind of important that we split now, okay?' He'd tried to edge past her to the door but she stuck out an elbow. There was a highly embarrassing silence.

The Master, who hadn't said a word, then looked at her and beckoned. She stayed where she was.

'And as for you . . .' she started to say. But he wasn't listening. Instead, he turned on his heel, marched over to the sink and grabbed the little mop. When Simon Peter tried to take it from him, he gave him a very fierce look.

'*Whether is greater*,' he said in that voice of his, '*he that sitteth at meat or he that serveth?*' And he gave the drying-up cloth to Judas the brother of James. '*Is it not he that sitteth at meat?*' he went on, scrubbing vigorously at one of the roasting dishes. '*But I am among you as he that serveth.*'

Judas the brother of James dropped a dish, which broke.

It was typical, of course; the rest of them just stood there, gawping and putting the dried-up things away in the wrong places, while Philip's dog jumped up on the table and started to lick the gravy off the plates. It was, all in all, one of those evenings you'd like to forget.

When they'd finished, she stood aside from the door and they all trooped through, thoroughly sullen and bad-tempered. Bartholomew didn't even speak to her, which was just as well, because she was damned if she was ever going to speak to him ever again.

'I just hope you're satisfied, that's all,' Simon Peter said. 'Honestly! Women!'

When they'd all gone, she went to the sink and put the things away properly. It was then that she noticed that the old brown terracotta washing-up bowl was

651

different. Something had happened to it. Instead of being brown and heavy it was light and a sort of pale blue colour. In her amazement, she dropped it; but instead of breaking, it bounced, spun round on its side for a moment and rolled behind the vegetable rack.

It was a miracle. Another one, just like that dreadful scene at cousin Judith's wedding at Cana, when everyone had got completely drunk and she'd had to call the watch out to them. As if she didn't have enough to put up with.

Kundry was silent for a moment, her face suddenly old.

'And?' Boamund asked. 'What happened then?'

'You can imagine how I felt the next day,' Kundry said, 'when I heard He'd been arrested, I mean. It was awful, really. I mean, none of our family had ever been in any sort of trouble with the police. I was just thankful my mother wasn't alive to hear about it. She'd have been horrified.'

'But . . .' Boamund stammered, 'you stupid woman, don't you know who that *was*?'

Kundry frowned at him. 'Of course I know,' she snapped. 'I found that out soon enough. An angel told me. I was *livid*.'

'Livid?'

'Absolutely furious,' Kundry said, tight-lipped. 'The unfairness of it all. Do you know what they did to me? They cursed me, that's what. They said that until the Son of Man should come again, and I was permitted – *permitted*, would you believe – to wash up for Him and all His fine friends as I should have done then, until then I was doomed to wander the earth for ever, lugging that horrid little plastic bowl around with me. Well, I told them—'

'That bowl,' Boamund interrupted, 'that's it, isn't it? The Holy Grail, I mean.'

'Of course it is,' replied Kundry, and the knuckles of her hands were white with fury. 'What did you think it was, you silly? *I* told them. I said that hanging around waiting was one thing, I was used to that, but lugging a cheap plastic bowl about with me was something else. Oh yes, I put my foot down there all right.'

Boamund stared at her. It was, he was saying to himself, rather a lot to take in, all in one go. After a moment, Kundry seemed to recover her composure, for she smiled and accepted an After Eight mint from a passing gudgeon.

'It wasn't long after that,' she said, 'that I met Klaus. He was still at the University in Damascus finishing his thesis, though he'd completely lost interest in it by then, and as soon as we discovered what we'd both suffered at the hands of that . . . that Person, we felt that we really had something in common, and so we got married. It was a mistake, of course, but neither of us was prepared to admit it. Instead, we just did our best to put up with each other.'

'That's Klaus von Weinacht, is it?' Boamund asked. 'I think I . . .'

'Yes,' Kundry said, with a hint of distaste, 'that was Klaus von Weinacht. Anyway, where was I? We'd been married about a year or so when Klaus decided he was going to leave the University and go back to Atlantis, where he'd originally come from. I went with him – I wasn't going to give up that easily, not without a proper settlement, at least – and so we both went to Atlantis.

He told me all about the magic gold and the moon and the rotation of the earth and so on, and I realised that there was a simply marvellous opportunity there for someone with a good head for business. I took charge of that side of it – I didn't tell Klaus what I was doing till much later, and he didn't find out, what with having to deliver all those presents and everything – and it wasn't long before the whole operation was well and truly under way. I expect you know all about that.'

'That's all this insurance stuff, isn't it?' Boamund said. 'I don't think I've quite got the hang of how insurance actually works yet, but never mind. You carry on with what you were saying.'

'It was about twenty years later,' Kundry said, 'that my Uncle Joe came to see me, all the way from Arimathea. He'd brought the washing-up bowl with him, and I was a bit taken aback when I saw it again, as you can imagine. But then he explained about all the marvellous things it could do, about tax and so forth – basic rate tax was three deniers in the sol tournois in those days, we didn't know we were born – and so I put it to good use right away. Uncle Joe stayed on and we gave him a seat on the board, and everything was fine for quite some time. Well, not fine, exactly; I mean, Klaus and I only spoke to each other during board meetings, and even then we quarrelled a lot. I had an idea that he was up to something, you see. There were a lot of rumours going around about him wanting to have me thrown off the board so that he and Uncle Joe could take the whole thing over between them. Of course, I wasn't having that. The very idea!

'I found out what they were up to, eventually. They'd worked out that this place – Albion, I mean –

had been built by the ancient Atlanteans to separate the two magnetic fields, years before my time, and that they could use it for a sort of tax fiddle. By the time I found out, actually, the whole thing was rather too far advanced for me to be able to nip it in the bud, but I got there in the end and plugged the loophole. They were sick as parrots about my spoiling their little plan, but there wasn't much they could do about it. The tiresome thing was that Uncle Joe had managed to get hold of the Grail – we might as well call it that, although personally I think it's a *silly* name for it, don't you? – and smuggled it out to Albion and hidden it. He knew where it was, and so did Klaus, and there was a monk or somebody like that in Glastonbury who was in on the secret too, but that was all. They couldn't use the Grail without me knowing, of course, but I couldn't use it either. It was a great shame and very silly, but that's men for you. Spiteful.

'Anyway, things came to a head and I divorced Klaus. He got custody of our daughter and took her away to the North Pole, where he built a whopping great big castle right on top of the magnetic iron ore deposit. I think he had some idea about using that to upset the balance between the two magnetic fields, purely and simply to get back at me, but he's never actually got around to *doing* anything about it yet. I think he's always too busy getting ready to do his delivery round. The population explosion in the last two hundred years has affected him very badly, you know. Serves him right.

'Uncle Joe just packed his bags and left, too. The last I heard of him was in this Glastonbury place; apparently, he just sort of vanished in a puff of blue smoke, if you can believe that. I heard rumours some time later that he'd taken a job teaching at a boy's school somewhere, but I don't know if it's true or not. Anyway, the long and the short of it is, he took the Grail with him, and that's all I know about it. So I can't help you any more. Sorry.'

Boamund sat for a while, his eyes as round as the full moon.

'Thank you,' he said. 'You've been most helpful. I think I know what's going on now.'

Kundry raised both eyebrows. 'Do you?' she said. 'I don't. *Something's* going on, I know that, or else why did Klaus suddenly turn up the other day chasing your friends? I hadn't seen him for years. Good job, too.'

'I think I know why,' Boamund said. 'He knew that Mr – that your Uncle Joe was helping us to find the Grail, and he wanted to find out what we knew.'

'Uncle Joe?' Kundry stared at him. 'What's Uncle Joe got to do with it? Like I said, I haven't seen or heard anything of him for simply ages. In fact, I rather thought he was dead or something.'

Boamund shook his head. 'No,' he said, 'not as such.'

'Have you seen him?' Kundry asked eagerly. 'Do you know where he is?'

'Yes,' Boamund said slowly. 'I know where he is. But I don't know where to find him. If you see what I mean.'

Kundry sighed. 'Not really,' she said. 'Oh, by the way, your friends took something of mine the other day. Would you be very sweet and let me have it back when you've finished with it?'

Boamund nodded. 'Thanks again,' he said, and

added, 'I think it was a swizzle, too. About the washing-up and everything. But, well, sometimes you've got to put up with people – *important* people, if you know what I mean. It's like knights and dwarves, really. I mean, knights aren't particularly clever and dwarves help them out a lot with the thinking. And dwarves do all the housework and the cleaning and tidying up, and we do sometimes forget to say thank you. But that's because that's the way things are. They understand, and we do, too. Sort of.'

Kundry frowned at him. 'That's men for you,' she said. 'Typical.'

Boamund stood up. 'I'd better be getting back,' he said. 'Um, how do I get out of here?'

'I'll see to that,' Kundry replied. 'Give my regards to your friend Bedevere. I quite liked him.'

'Thanks.'

'Goodbye then,' Kundry said. 'Your Majesty.'

Toenail was sitting in the boat when Boamund finally surfaced. He held out a boathook and Boamund pulled himself aboard.

'Lucky I brought a change of clothes and some towels,' said the dwarf. 'When I heard we were going to a lake, I said to myself, someone's bound to fall in, so I'd better . . .'

Boamund wiped the water out of his eyes. 'I didn't say we were going to a lake,' he said.

'*You* didn't, no,' Toenail replied. 'You wouldn't have known, would you?'

Boamund shrugged and towelled his hair for a moment. The dwarf picked up the oars and started to row for the shore.

'Toenail,' said Boamund suddenly, 'whose side are you on?'

'Yours, of course,' said the dwarf. 'Why d'you ask?'

'Nothing,' Boamund replied. 'I was just puzzled, that's all.'

The dwarf veered the boat towards the jetty with the left-hand oar. 'We've always been dwarves in our family,' he said, 'it's a tradition. I told you, remember?'

'Did you?' Boamund noticed that he'd lost Excalibur; that's if it really had been Excalibur. 'Sorry,' he said. 'I probably wasn't listening.'

'Don't suppose you were,' said the dwarf. 'You've found out, then.'

Boamund looked up. 'Found out?' he repeated.

'About the Grail, and Mr Simon,' Toenail replied. 'Or didn't she tell you?'

'You mean you knew all along?' Boamund said.

'Sort of,' Toenail replied. 'It's called race-memory, you see. Like, all dwarves can remember everything that's ever happened to all the other dwarves who've ever lived. Just not all at once. Bits of it come back to you, when it's necessary.'

'Right,' Boamund said. 'I think I follow. Yes, she told me. Came as a bit of a surprise, actually.'

'Everything comes as a surprise to me, sir,' replied the dwarf. 'I prefer it that way. Here we are.'

The boat nudged gently against the jetty, and Boamund jumped off.

'Can you manage?' he asked.

'Course I can,' Toenail replied cheerfully. 'Why do you ask?'

'Oh, no reason,' Boamund replied thoughtfully. 'Now then . . .'

'This way,' Toenail said.

'Bet you ten to one he's got lost,' Turquine was saying. 'Never did have a sense of direction, young Snotty. He could get lost in a lift.'

'Or else something's happened to him,' Galahaut replied. 'Not exactly practical, our Boamund. Accident-prone, too. I think we should go and look for him, don't you?'

Turquine yawned. 'Why bother?' he said. 'To be honest with you, I've had just about as much as I can take of being ordered about by him, the jumped-up little tyke. Worst thing Mr Magus ever did, making him a prefect. Gave him ideas. He's never been the same since.'

'You know,' Pertelope broke in. 'I always wondered why he did that. Anyone less suited to being a prefect than Bo you couldn't imagine.'

They had lit a fire, and Lamorak had somehow managed to hit a rabbit with an improvised catapult. They were having a late supper.

'I expect he thought it would be character-forming,' Pertelope replied as he turned the spit. 'Make something of him, you know. Bring him out of his shell. Didn't work, mind. Just made him insufferable.'

'More insufferable, anyway,' Turquine replied. 'He always was a pompous little git, even at the best of times. I reckon Mr Magus has got a lot to answer for.'

'Someone taking my name in vain?' said a voice from the darkness. At once, the five knights jumped to their feet and looked guilty. Pavlovian reflex.

'Hello again, sir,' Turquine mumbled. 'Just wondering where Boamund's got to, sir. Have you seen him?'

'He'll be all right,' Simon Magus replied. 'Well now, young Turquine, what have we here? Roast rabbit?'

'Yes, sir.'

Simon Magus sat down and warmed his hands in front of the fire. 'Quite like the old days, really. I remember you were always breaking out of the Dorm in summer, young Turkey, poaching rabbits and having – let's say, having unofficial barbecues behind the stables. The farmers used to complain quite dreadfully.'

Turquine went a deep shade of mauve and said nothing.

'Was I right in thinking,' Simon Magus continued as he poked the rabbit with a stick, 'that you were discussing why I chose to make young Boamund a prefect at the end of the Third year? Or were my old ears deceiving me?'

There was an awkward silence, which Bedevere broke.

'We were a bit puzzled, sir, yes,' he said carefully. 'It did seem rather an odd choice, if you don't mind us saying so. He wasn't really very good at it, was he?'

'I think the rabbit's about ready now,' Simon Magus replied, and Bedevere noticed that he was staring into the fire, as if he could see something there, in the blue part of the flame. 'It was an unconventional choice, certainly, but I had my reasons. In fact, if you're patient, you can hear them for yourselves in a minute or two. Have you got your famous penknife handy, Turquine? Or is it still confiscated? I can't remember.'

Very slowly, Turquine took an old and extremely worn penknife out of his pocket and handed it over. It wasn't the first time, either.

'Ah yes,' said Simon Magus. 'Old Faithful.' He

began to carve the rabbit.

'Actually, sir,' Bedevere said tentatively. 'I was meaning to ask you. About this whole quest business, sir . . .'

But before he could finish his sentence there was a rustling in the bushes and Boamund emerged, with Toenail trotting behind him carrying a bundle of wet clothes. Simon Magus got up slowly, put down the rabbit and smiled affectionately. Then he knelt down on one knee and said:

'All hail King Boamund the First, rightful King of Albion.'

There was a silence you could have built a house on, and then Turquine made a sort of choking noise.

'Oh, for God's sake,' he said. 'He isn't, is he? Tell me it isn't true, somebody.'

Simon Magus stood up. 'It's all right,' he said, 'the office is purely honorary. There isn't a kingdom of Albion any more.'

'God, I'm relieved to hear you say that,' said Turquine. 'Just imagine what it'd be like, having that horrible face peering up at your from postage stamps.'

Boamund was standing quite still. He looked pale, although perhaps it was just a trick of the light, and he was looking at the old magician. He made no attempt to speak.

'Well now,' Simon Magus said, 'did you manage all right?'

Boamund nodded. 'Yes, thank you,' he said. 'I managed.'

'And do you know where it is?'

'No,' Boamund replied. There was a disdainful

661

noise from Sir Turquine, but Simon Magus held up his hand for silence.

'I don't know where it is,' Boamund went on, 'but I do know who does know, if you follow me, sir. That's right, isn't it?'

Simon Magus smiled; or at least, the corner of his lip lifted about a quarter of an inch. 'Splendid,' he said. 'Very well done. Come and have some rabbit.'

10

'He's asleep,' Bedevere said quietly. 'He was absolutely exhausted.'

'I'm not surprised,' Simon Magus replied. 'Any chance of a cup of tea, by the way? I'm parched.'

They went into the kitchen. Unusually it was fairly presentable. Bedevere took down the jar where the tea-bags lived, and sighed.

'Empty,' he said. 'That'll be Lamorak. He's always using the last one and not telling anybody. We have a big shop once a month, you see; we go round the supermarket with a couple of those big trolleys and get everything we need. But we never seem to get enough tea-bags, or enough sugar, come to that. Will coffee do instead?'

'Coffee will be fine,' Simon Magus replied. 'Where are the others?'

'In the Common Room,' Bedevere replied, 'playing pontoon. Galahaut cheats.'

When the kettle had boiled they sat down on either side of the kitchen table and looked at each other thoughtfully.

'Biscuit?'

'No, thanks,' Simon Magus replied. 'When you went in and looked, did he still have it with him?'

'Yes,' Bedevere replied. 'He was holding it, like it was a teddy bear or something.' He laughed, but without much humour. 'Fancy it being in the garage all the time, in that big cardboard box full of junk. We all thought it was one of those crates of tins without labels that Lamorak's always buying in the market.'

Simon Magus had the grace to look slightly abashed. 'It was the best place I could think of,' he said. 'The one place nobody would ever dream of looking. I was right, too,' he added.

'It was a bit thick, though, wasn't it, sir?' Bedevere burst out. 'I mean, you've made us all look complete chumps. Honestly, here we are, the Grail Knights, and all the time the wretched thing's in our garage, hidden in an old cardboard box. We'll be the laughing stock of chivalry if anyone ever finds out.'

Simon Magus grinned sheepishly. 'You must admit, though,' he said, 'it was a good hiding place.'

'Exactly,' Bedevere said. 'So *why*? I mean, why this quest and so on? If you wanted it to stay hidden, why did you make us go and find it? It doesn't make sense.'

Simon Magus stirred his coffee and smiled. 'You always were bright, Bedevere,' he said. 'Unusually bright, but singularly lacking in energy. A pity, really, but there it is. I don't believe in forcing people to do things if they don't want to, and I don't think you ever wanted to be anything but ordinary. Am I right?'

'Absolutely,' Bedevere replied. 'But that's rather beside the point, isn't it? I mean, why hide the Grail so carefully and then send us out to look for it? And why did you make it take so long?'

'Ah.' Simon Magus nodded approvingly. 'You're asking the right questions, as usual. You remember what I taught you about the right question?'

'The right question,' Bedevere recited, 'is a question that can have only one possible answer. But I don't see—'

'Then think,' Simon Magus replied sharply. 'Why did I hide it, why did I make you – or rather, Boamund – find it, and why did it all have to take so long? Come on, you're nearly there.'

Bedevere thought for a long time.

'Well,' he said slowly, 'you hid it because you didn't want it found.'

'Quite right, yes.'

'You sent Boamund to find it because you wanted Boamund to find it.'

'Right again.'

'And,' Bedevere said, lifting his head, 'it took so long because it had to be found at the right time. Yes, I think I'm beginning to see daylight.'

Simon Magus leant back in his chair and sipped his coffee. 'Go on,' he said.

'You hid it,' Bedevere said, 'because you didn't want the Atlantis people to find it; not, what's her name . . .'

'Kundry,' Simon Magus said. 'She's my niece, actually, but we were never very close.'

'You didn't want her to have it,' Bedevere went on, 'and you didn't want old Father Christmas getting hold of it either.'

'Quite right,' said the magician. 'Dreadful people, both of them. I knew them quite well back in the old days, and they were a bit unbalanced even then. Now they're both quite mad, of course; but immortal, the pair of them, because of the curses they're both under. It wasn't just a case of waiting till they went away, you see. On the other hand, it was a holy relic, the holiest true relic that existed, so I couldn't just destroy it. Somehow or other, it had to be hidden.'

'Right,' Bedevere said. 'So you took the Grail and you hid it where nobody would ever find it. And you set up the Order of the Grail Knights deliberately so that we *wouldn't* find it, and that way everybody would know for sure that it was lost. Because the one place nobody would ever dream of looking would be in the Grail Knights' own garage.'

'Very good,' Simon Magus said. 'Carry on.'

'But . . .' Bedevere put his head between his hands and thought for a moment. 'Right,' he said. 'And then you took a knight, a particularly dopey but idealistic and upright knight, and you trained him from a boy to be *really* dopey and *really* idealistic and upright, so that he'd be the sort of person who you could be certain the Grail would be safe with . . .'

'The Holy Fool,' Simon Magus agreed. 'Biddable, virtuous, stupid, extremely pompous; the sort of person who would never be afflicted by greed, megalomania or anything like that. The perfect Grail Knight, in fact.'

'I should have guessed,' Bedevere said, 'when I remembered that you and he arrived at the Coll in the same term, and you left the term after he did.'

'Perhaps.' He smiled. 'It would have been very

inconvenient if you had, you know.'

'Anyway,' Bedevere went on, 'you trained this knight to be exactly the way you wanted him to be; but that wasn't enough. To be absolutely safe, you put him to sleep for hundreds and hundreds of years, so that when he woke up, he'd be completely disorientated. He'd have no family, no ties, no place in society or anything like that; but instead, he'd have this really enormous sense of his own destiny, because that's the only way he could account for what had happened to him.' Bedevere paused for a moment. 'That was a bit – well, ruthless of you, wasn't it? I mean, not exactly fair on the poor chap. He's a bit of a duffer, I know, but there are limits.'

Simon Magus shrugged. 'Boamund was – and is – the perfect knight,' he said. 'Brave, honest and stupid. Chivalry is what he was born to, and this is the ultimate in knightly adventures. I honestly don't think he's been all that hard done by, do you?'

Bedevere considered. 'Maybe not,' he said. 'Anyway, when you reckoned that the right time had come, you woke Boamund up and guided him unerringly to where the Grail was. Actually,' Bedevere added, 'I'm a bit puzzled about the three quests. What were they in aid of? Were the actual things, the socks and so forth, necessary? Or was it all sort of incidental?'

'Purely incidental,' Simon Magus replied. 'Really, the whole point of those exercises was to notify Klaus and Kundry, as loudly and clearly as possible, that the Grail still existed and that someone was looking for it. It's essential that they know, you see; I'm going to put a stop to all this Atlantis nonsense once and for all, before they do a great deal of harm. You heard about that task force which was sent to deal with them, I suppose, and what happened to it. They've been a menace for some time now, and that's why I acted when I did. Besides, that dratted woman Kundry had found out about that manuscript from Glastonbury which told the whole story. That was careless of me, leaving that lying about; but I honestly thought it had been destroyed back in the sixteenth century. Then, when I heard about the Lyonesse Group hiring the back rooms of all those ancient monuments, I realised that she was on the track of the wretched thing and might very well find it if I didn't act quickly. It was a close-run thing, actually.' And he told Bedevere about the fax from Shakespeare's birthplace.

'I see,' Bedevere said. 'Anyway, now Boamund's got the Grail and everything's going to be fine. It *is* going to be fine, isn't it?'

'Oh yes,' Simon Magus said, 'or at least it should be. Fingers crossed, anyway.'

'There's just one thing,' Bedevere said. 'What did you need us for? I mean, why did we have to wait around all this time? Couldn't Boamund have managed on his own?'

They looked at each other.

'No,' Bedevere said after a while. 'No, I suppose not. He's a good sort, Bo, but . . .'

'Exactly,' said Simon Magus. 'Thanks for the coffee.'

'I still think,' Boamund said, 'that he might have waited and said goodbye.'

It was cold on the hillside, and Bedevere shivered slightly. 'He had to rush,' he replied. 'An urgent meeting or something like that. But he sent you his very best wishes.'

Boamund nodded. 'Well,' he said, 'I'll see you back at the house later on. I've just got to, er, bury something in that cave up there, and . . .'

Bedevere started to say something; but he didn't manage it. Instead, he turned and walked briskly away down the hill. Boamund wrinkled his brow, then shrugged and looked down for the dwarf.

'Well,' Toenail said, 'here we are again. I've brought the spade like you said.'

Boamund nodded, tucked the black plastic sack that contained the Holy Grail (but only he knew it was that, of course) under his arm and set off uphill as fast as his long legs would carry him.

In the cave, everything was as it had been, not so long ago now, when he had woken up. There were still bits of rusty armour lying about, and a strong smell of must and penetrating oil.

'Clever of you to think of this place, Toenail,' he said. The dwarf avoided looking at him and muttered something about getting the cave tidied up.

'All right, then,' Boamund said. 'You do that while I just dig a hole.'

Ten minutes or so later, Boamund laid aside his spade, wiped his forehead and knelt down. The Grail fitted very nicely in its last resting place. He nodded respectfully at it, and then shovelled back the earth and patted it down.

'Gosh,' said Toenail, in a rather strained voice. 'I expect you're hot after all that digging.'

'I am, rather,' Boamund replied. 'I'd give a lot for a nice cool drink of milk right now.'

Toenail blushed scarlet and fumbled in his satchel. 'Just as well I remembered to bring one, then,' he tried to say, but his tongue seemed to get in the way.

'You're a marvel, Toenail, the way you think of everything,' Boamund said, after he'd swallowed a large mouthful of milk. 'Don't know what I'd do without you, really. I know I sometimes forget to say thank you, but ... Hey, now, there's no call to start bursting into tears, you know.'

'Hay fever,' snuffled the dwarf. 'Don't mind me.'

'Sorry,' Boamund said, and he drank the rest of the milk. 'You know something,' he said, 'all of a sudden I feel terribly, terribly ...'

He lay back, and a moment later he was fast asleep. Toenail took the milk bottle from his hands and put it on one side; then he unslung the large canvas bag he'd been carrying over his shoulder. It was as tall as he was and very heavy.

'Fall for it every time, that old milk routine,' the dwarf said softly. He opened the sack and gingerly took from it a sword and a golden crown.

'Cheerio, then,' said the dwarf. He placed the crown on Boamund's head and the sword under his hands, and tiptoed quietly out of the cave. Then he stopped, took out the scrap of paper which Mr Magus had given him, and read out the words written on it in a loud, self-conscious voice. There was a great flicker of blue fire, and the cave vanished, as if it had never been.

Toenail stood for a while, not thinking of anything in particular; then he remembered that the rest of the knights would be wanting their tea before they set off. They had a long way to go, too; all the way across the sea to the Isle of Avalon, where there is neither autumn nor winter, where men do not grow old, and where (according to Simon Magus, at any rate) if you wanted a pizza, you had to go and collect it yourself. Turquine could hardly wait.

'They'll be needing a dwarf,' Toenail said to himself. He glanced back once more at the hillside where the mouth of the cave had been, stooped instinctively to pick up an empty crisp packet, and ran swiftly away down the hill.

TALL STORIES

Tom Holt

Two fantastic comic fantasies available for the
first time in one volume

EXPECTING SOMEONE TALLER

All he did was run over a badger – sad, but hardly
catastrophic. But it wasn't Malcolm Fisher's day, for the
badger turned out to be none other than Ingolf, last of the
Giants. With his dying breath, he reluctantly handed to
Malcolm two Gifts of Power, and made him ruler of the
world. But can Malcolm cope with the responsibility?

YE GODS!

Being a Hero bothers Jason Derry. It's easy to get
maladjusted when your mum's a suburban housewife
and your dad's the Supreme Being. It can be a real drag
slaying fabulous monsters and retrieving golden fleeces
from fire-spitting dragons, and then having to tidy your
room before your mum'll let you watch Star Trek.

But it's not the relentless tedium of imperishable glory
that finally brings Jason to the end of his rope; it's
something so funny that it's got to be taken seriously.
Deadly seriously . . .

SAINTS AND SINNERS

Tom Holt

PAINT YOUR DRAGON

The cosmic battle between Good and Evil . . . But suppose Evil threw the fight? And suppose Good cheated? Sculptress Bianca Wilson is a living legend. St George is also a legend, but not quite so living. However, when Bianca's sculpture of the patron saint and his scaly chum gets a bit too life-like it opens up a whole new can of wyrms . . . The dragon knows that Evil got a raw deal and is looking to set the record straight. And George (who cheated) thinks the record's just fine as it is.

OPEN SESAME

Something was wrong! Just as the boiling water was about to be poured on his head and the man with the red book appeared and his life flashed before his eyes, Akram the Terrible, the most feared thief in Baghdad, knew that this had happened before. Many times. And he was damned if he was going to let it happen again, just because he was a fictional character didn't mean it always had to end this way.

Meanwhile, back in Southampton, Michelle gets a bit of a shock when she puts on her Aunt Fatima's ring and the computer and the telephone start to bitch at her. But that's nothing compared to what the kitchen appliances have to say . . .

FISHY WISHES

Tom Holt

WISH YOU WERE HERE

It was a busy day on Lake Chicopee. But it was a mixed bunch of sightseers and tourists that had the strange local residents rubbing their hands with delight. Most promising of all, there was Wesley Higgins, the young man from Birmingham, England. All he thought he had to do was immerse himself in the waters of the lake and he would find his heart's desire. Well, it seemed like a good idea at the time.

DJINN RUMMY

In an aspirin bottle, nobody can hear you scream. Outside an aspirin bottle, however, things are somewhat different. And when Kayaguchiya Integrated Circuits III (Kiss, to his friends), a Force Twelve genie with an attitude, is released after fourteen years of living with two dozen white tablets, there's bound to be trouble . . .

All Jane wanted to do was end her life in peace, in the privacy of a British Rail waiting room, but now she's got herself a genie for company. Lucky old Jane. Lucky, that is, until the apocalypse rears its ugly head.

LITTLE PEOPLE

Tom Holt

'I was eight years old when I saw my first elf'

... And for unlikely hero Michael it wasn't his last. Michael's unfortunately (but accurately) named girlfriend Cruella doesn't approve of his obsession with the little people, but the problem is that they won't leave him alone. And who can blame them when it is his own stepfather who is responsible for causing them so much misery. Oh yes. Daddy George knows that elves can do so much more than the gardening.

FALLING SIDEWAYS

Tom Holt

From the moment Homo Sapiens descended from the trees, possibly onto their heads, humanity has striven towards civilisation. Fire. The Wheel. Running Away from furry things with more teeth than one might reasonably expect – all are testament to man's ultimate supremacy.

It is a noble story and so, of course, complete and utter fiction.

For one man has discovered the hideous truth: that humanity's ascent to civilisation has been ruthlessly guided by a small gang of devious frogs.

Frogs that rule the Universe.

The man's name is David Perkins and his theory is not, on the whole, widely admired, particularly not by the frogs themselves who had, frankly, invested a great deal of time and effort in keeping the whole thing quiet.

Happily for humanity, however, very little of the above is actually true either.

Unhappily, things are a lot, lot worse.

THE PORTABLE DOOR

Tom Holt

Starting a new job can be extremely stressful. You meet your colleagues and forget their names. You meet your boss and forget his name. Then, after breaking the photocopier, you forget your own name.

And the next day you get to do it all again.

But what if your new employer is not the pen-pushing, paper-shuffling outfit you supposed it to be? What if it is an elaborate front for something far more sinister?

Not that Paul Carpenter; new recruit at J. W. Wells & Co. would even notice. He's become obsessed with wooing the enigmatic Sophie, a bizarre angular woman with all the sexual appeal of a hole-punch.

IN YOUR DREAMS

Tom Holt

The hilarious sequel to *The Portable Door*

Ever been offered a promotion that seems too good to be true? You know – the sort they'd be insane to be offering to someone like you. The kind where you snap their arm off to accept, then wonder why all you long-serving colleagues look secretly relieved, as if they're off some strange and unpleasant hook . . .

It's the kind of trick that deeply sinister companies like J. W. Wells & Co. pull all the time. Especially with employees who are too busy mooning over the office intern to think about what they're getting into.

And it's why, right about now, Paul Carpenter is wishing he'd paid much less attention to the gorgeous Melze, and rather more to a little bit of job description small-print referring to 'pest' control . . .